ALICE OSEMAN

HEARTSTOPPER

VOLUME 3

HODDER CHILDREN'S BOOKS

First published in 2020 by Hodder and Stoughton

28

Please be advised this book contains depictions of an eating disorder and one mention of self-harm.

This comic is drawn digitally using a Wacom Intuos Pro tablet directly into Photoshop CC.

A CIP catalogue record for this book is available from the British Library.

ISBN 978 1 444 95277 3

Printed and bound in Great Britain by
Clays Ltd, Elcograf S.p.A

The paper and board used in this book are made from wood from responsible sources.

MIX
Paper from responsible sources
FSC® C104740

Hodder Children's Books
An imprint of
Hachette Children's Group
Part of Hodder and Stoughton
Carmelite House
50 Victoria Embankment
London EC4Y 0DZ

An Hachette UK Company
www.hachette.co.uk

www.hachettechildrens.co.uk

www.aliceoseman.com

CONTENTS

✱ Not caught up with the story so far?
Read chapters 1 & 2 in **VOLUME 1**
and chapter 3 in **VOLUME 2!**

Sunday 23rd May

So... I came out as bisexual to my mum.

It feels like it's all happened so fast... but so much has happened. It's less than two months since me and Charlie kissed for the first (and second) time,

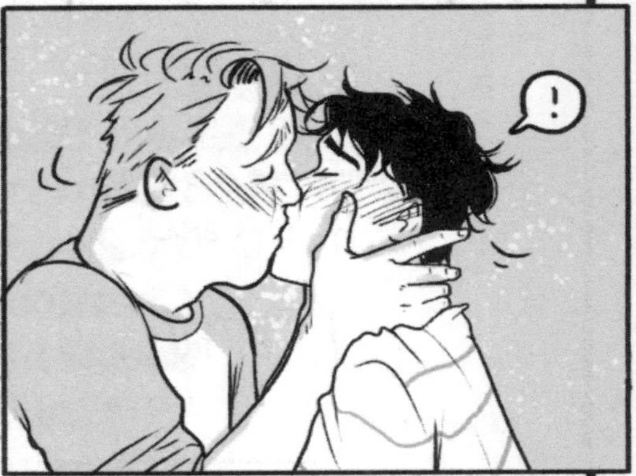
!

then started sort of going out (aka LOTS. MORE. KISSING.)

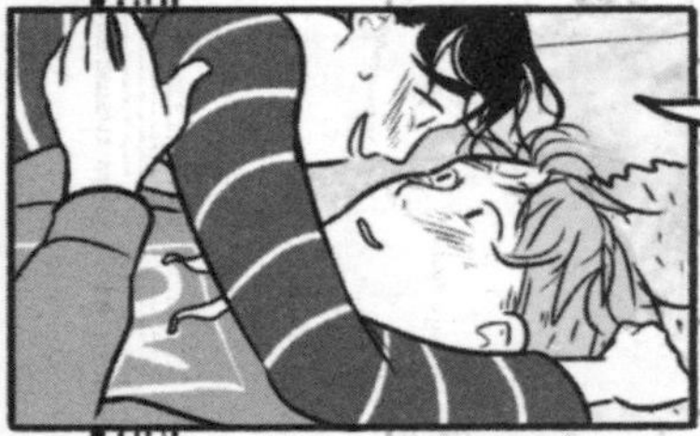
You're amazing

and then I spent some time trying to figure out my sexuality... which still feels kinda confusing sometimes!! Sexuality is COMPLICATED. But 'bisexual' feels right. :)

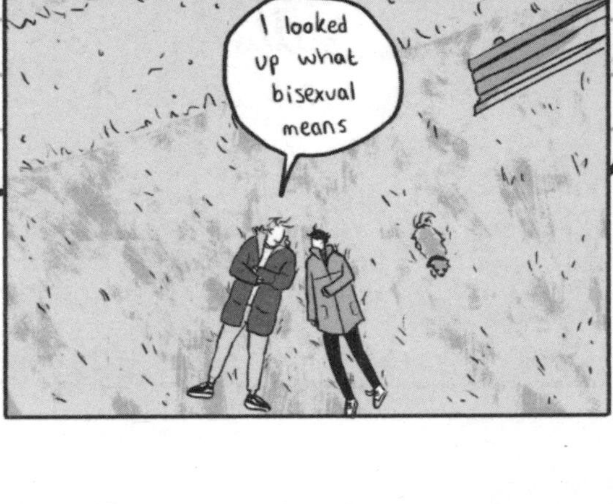
I looked up what bisexual means

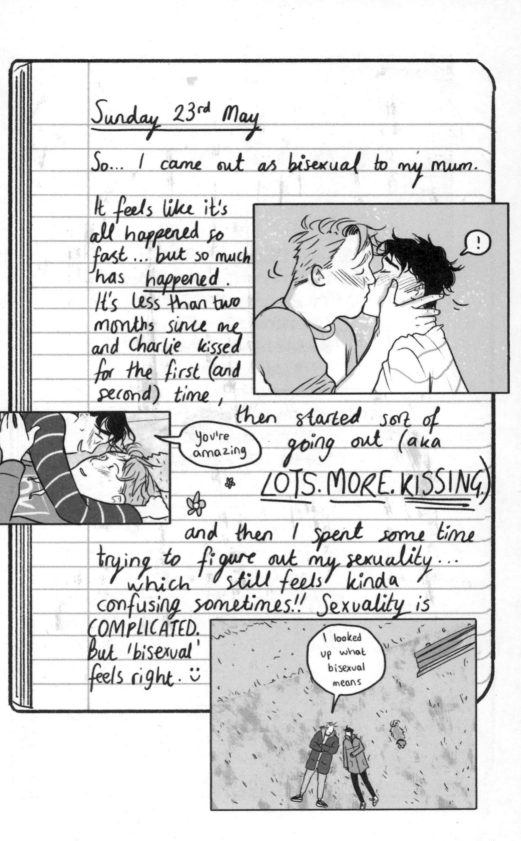

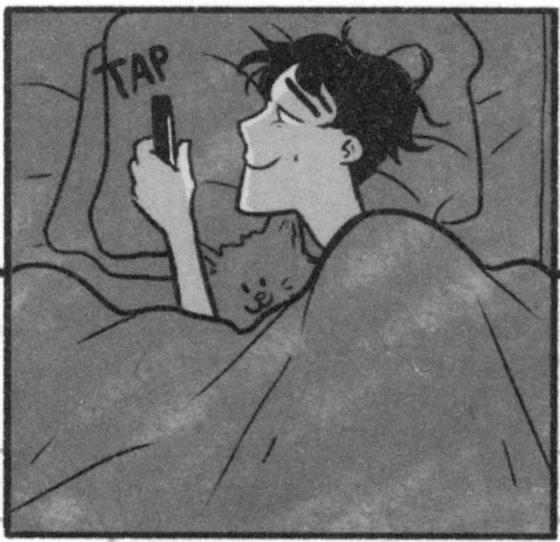
TAP

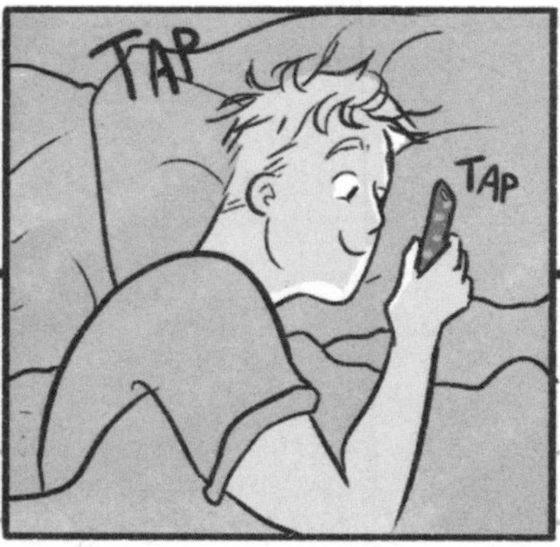
TAP
TAP

And now we're <u>officially</u> <u>boyfriends</u>.
That feels so awesome to say.

I HAVE A BOYFRIEND!!!!
(and he's amazing ♥)

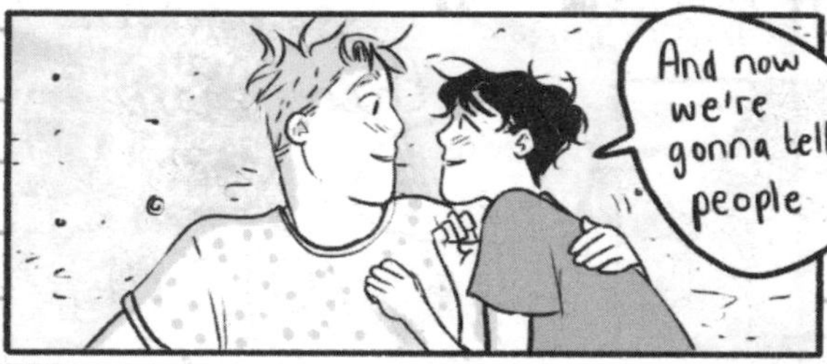
And now we're gonna tell people

We said we might start telling our friends and people at school, but... how would we do that?? No one even knows I like guys. And Charlie got bullied pretty badly when he was outed last year.

Maybe it'd be better to keep it a secret for a bit longer...

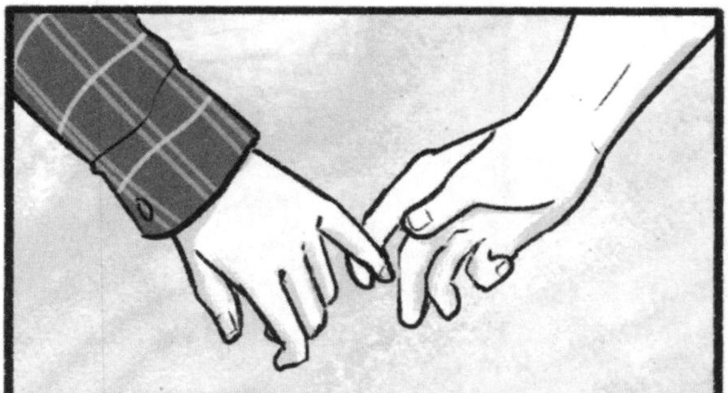

4. OUT

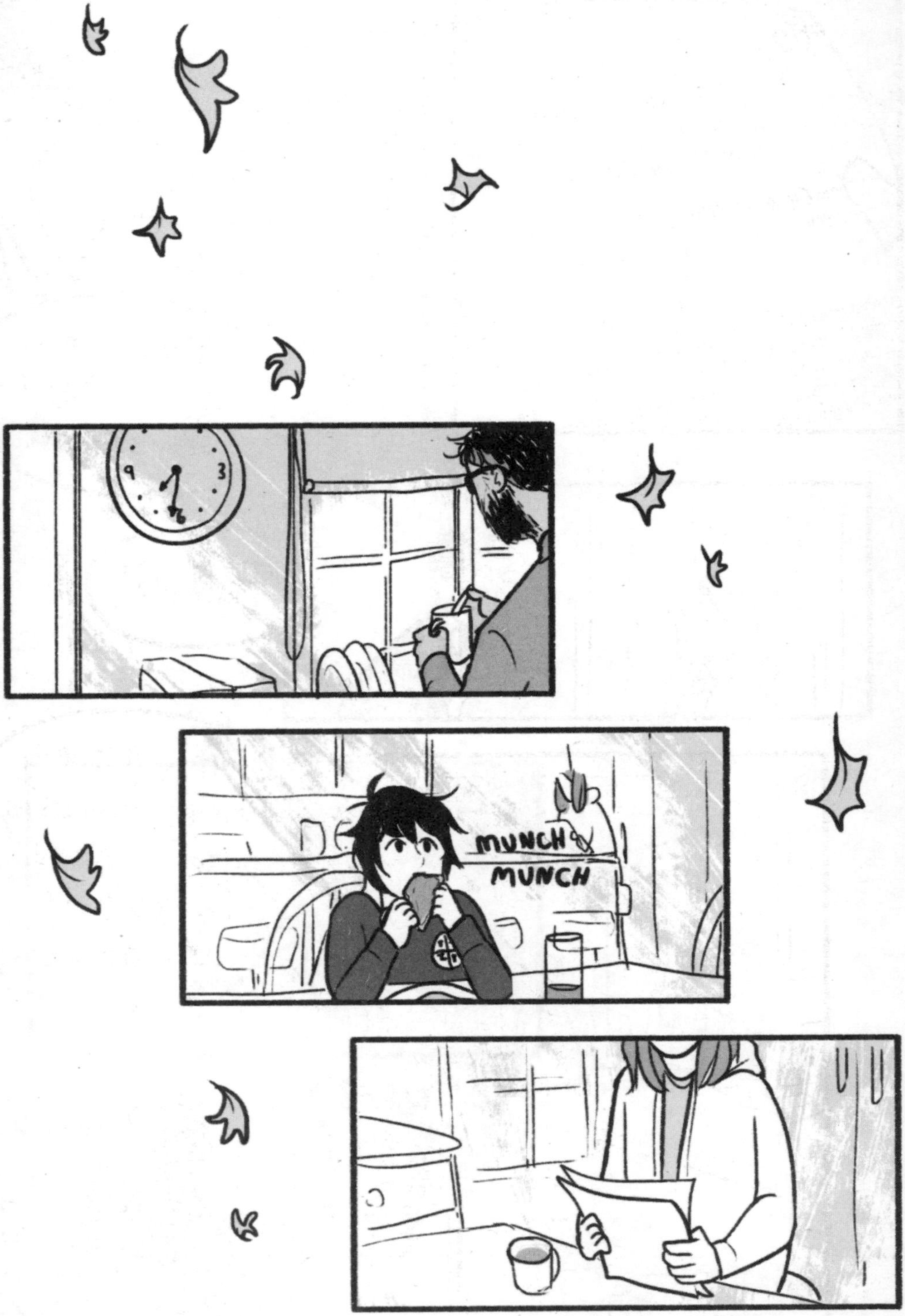
MUNCH
MUNCH

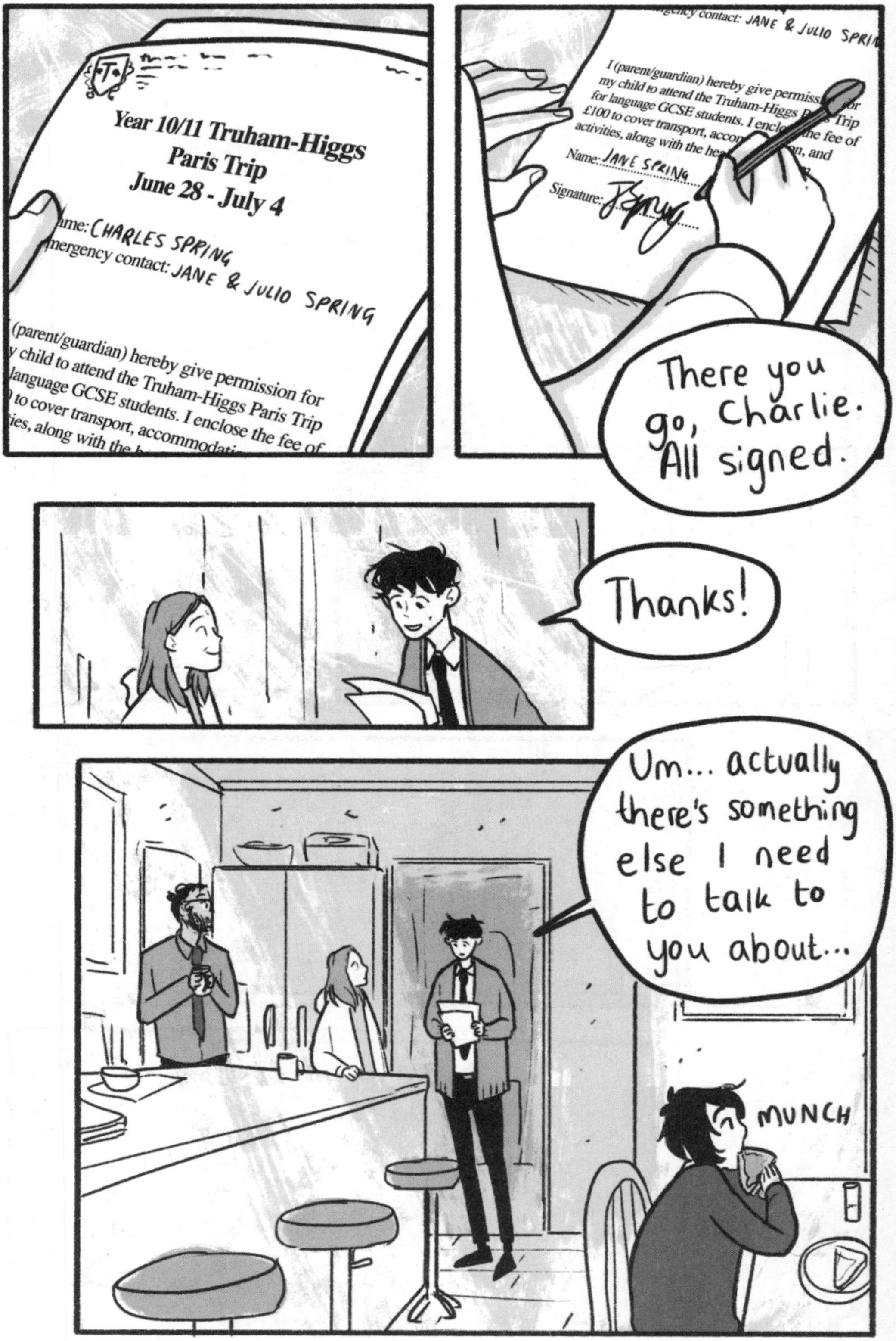

Year 10/11 Truham-Higgs Paris Trip June 28 - July 4
ame: CHARLES SPRING
mergency contact: JANE & JULIO SPRING
I (parent/guardian) hereby give permission for my child to attend the Truham-Higgs Paris Trip for language GCSE students. I enclose the fee of £100 to cover transport, accommodation,
Name: JANE SPRING
Signature:
There you go, Charlie. All signed.
Thanks!
Um... actually there's something else I need to talk to you about...
MUNCH

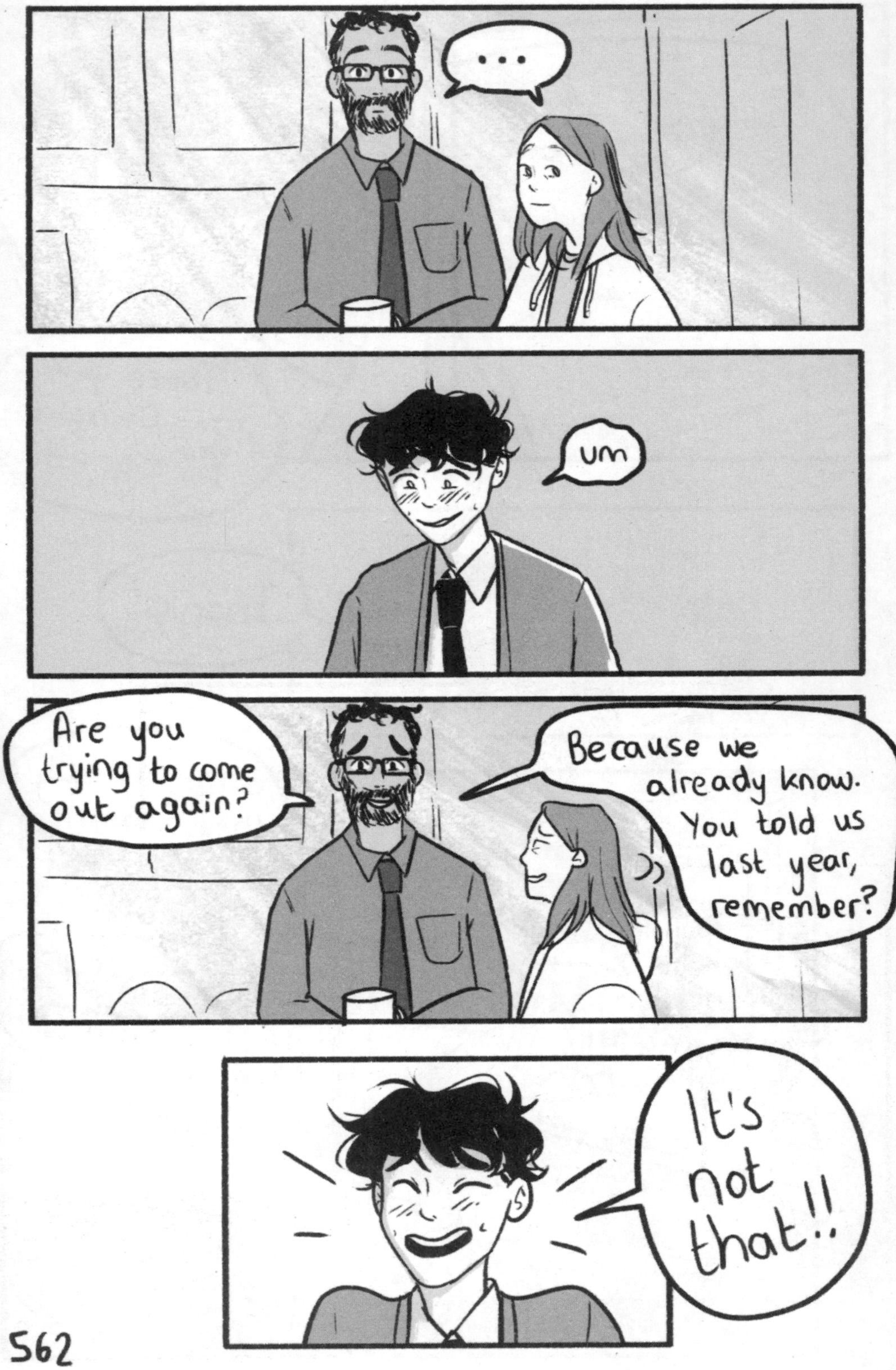
...
um
Are you trying to come out again?
Because we already know. You told us last year, remember?
It's not that!!

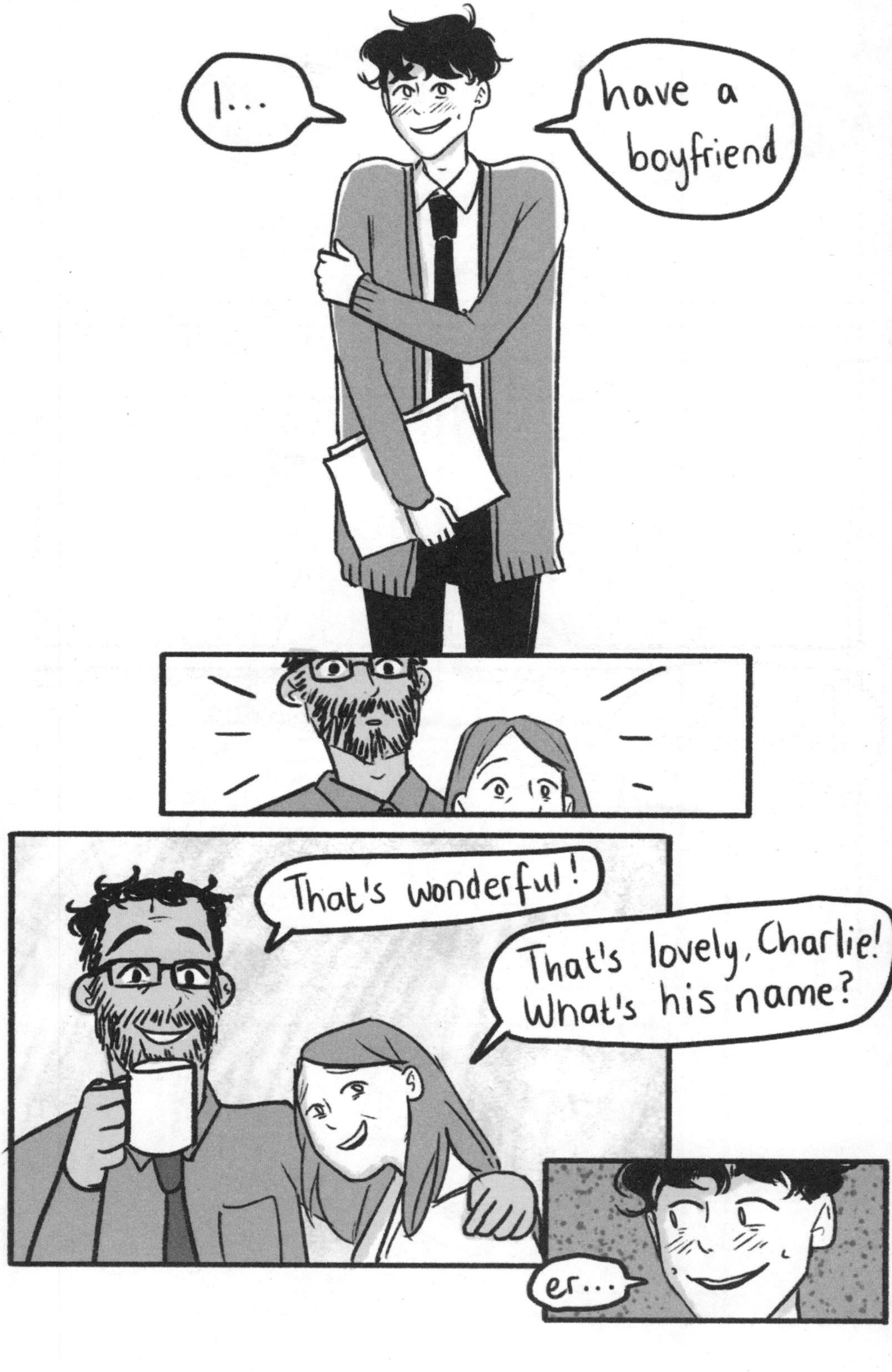
I...
have a boyfriend
That's wonderful!
That's lovely, Charlie! What's his name?
er...

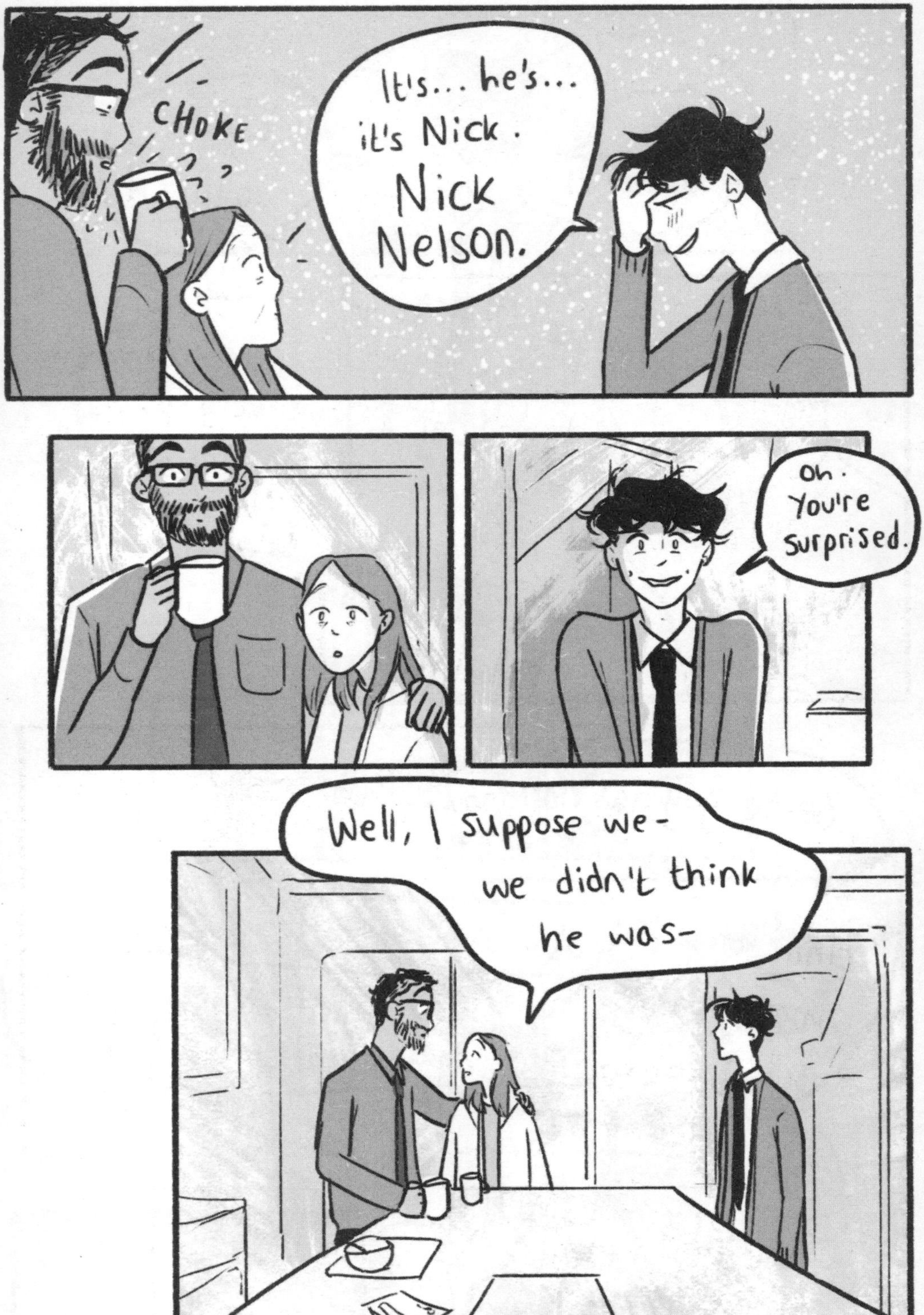
CHOKE
It's... he's...
it's Nick.
Nick
Nelson.
Oh.
You're
surprised.
Well, I suppose we-
we didn't think
he was-

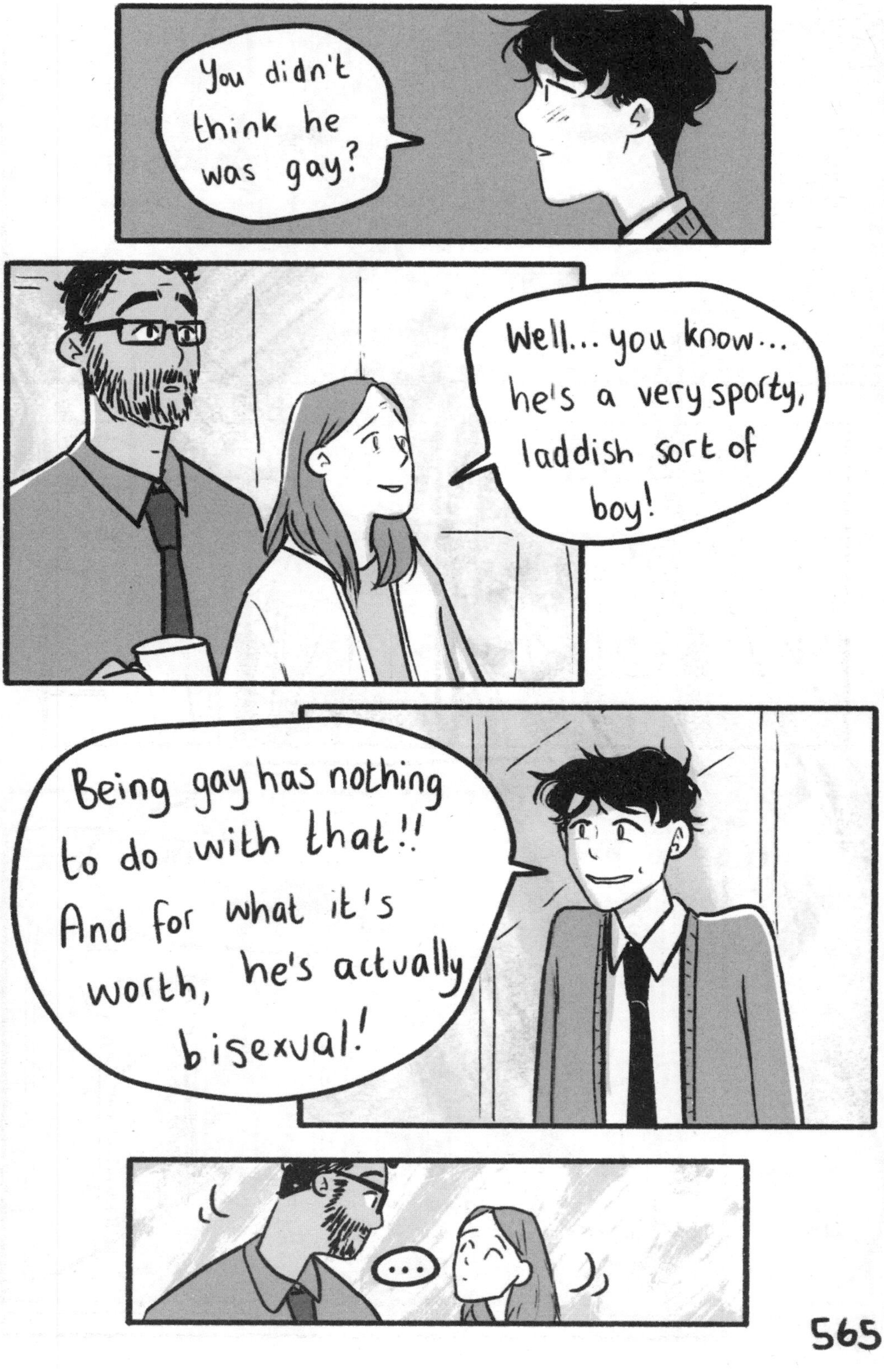
You didn't think he was gay?
Well... you know... he's a very sporty, laddish sort of boy!
Being gay has nothing to do with that!! And for what it's worth, he's actually bisexual!
...

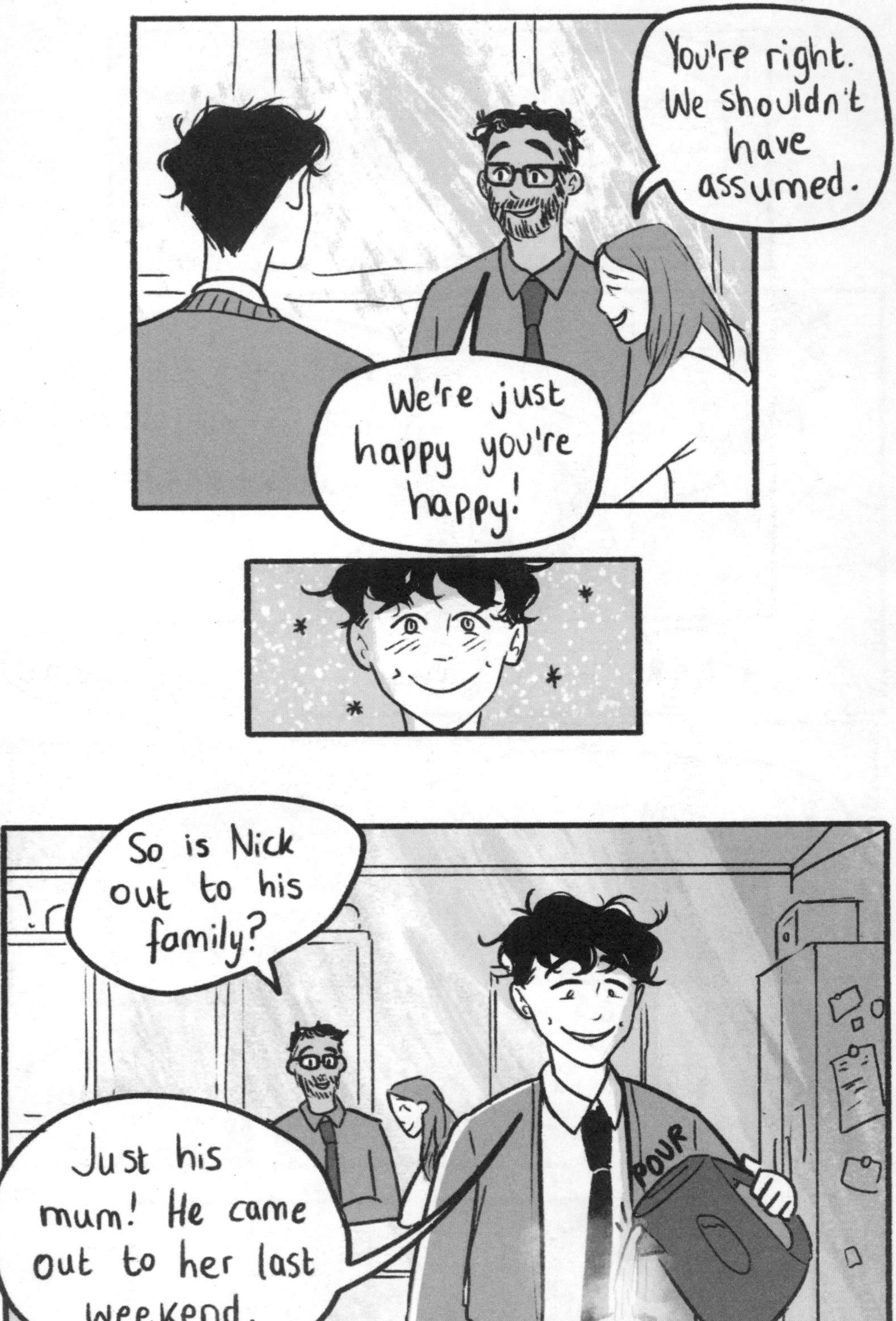
You're right. We shouldn't have assumed.
We're just happy you're happy!
So is Nick out to his family?
Just his mum! He came out to her last weekend.
POUR

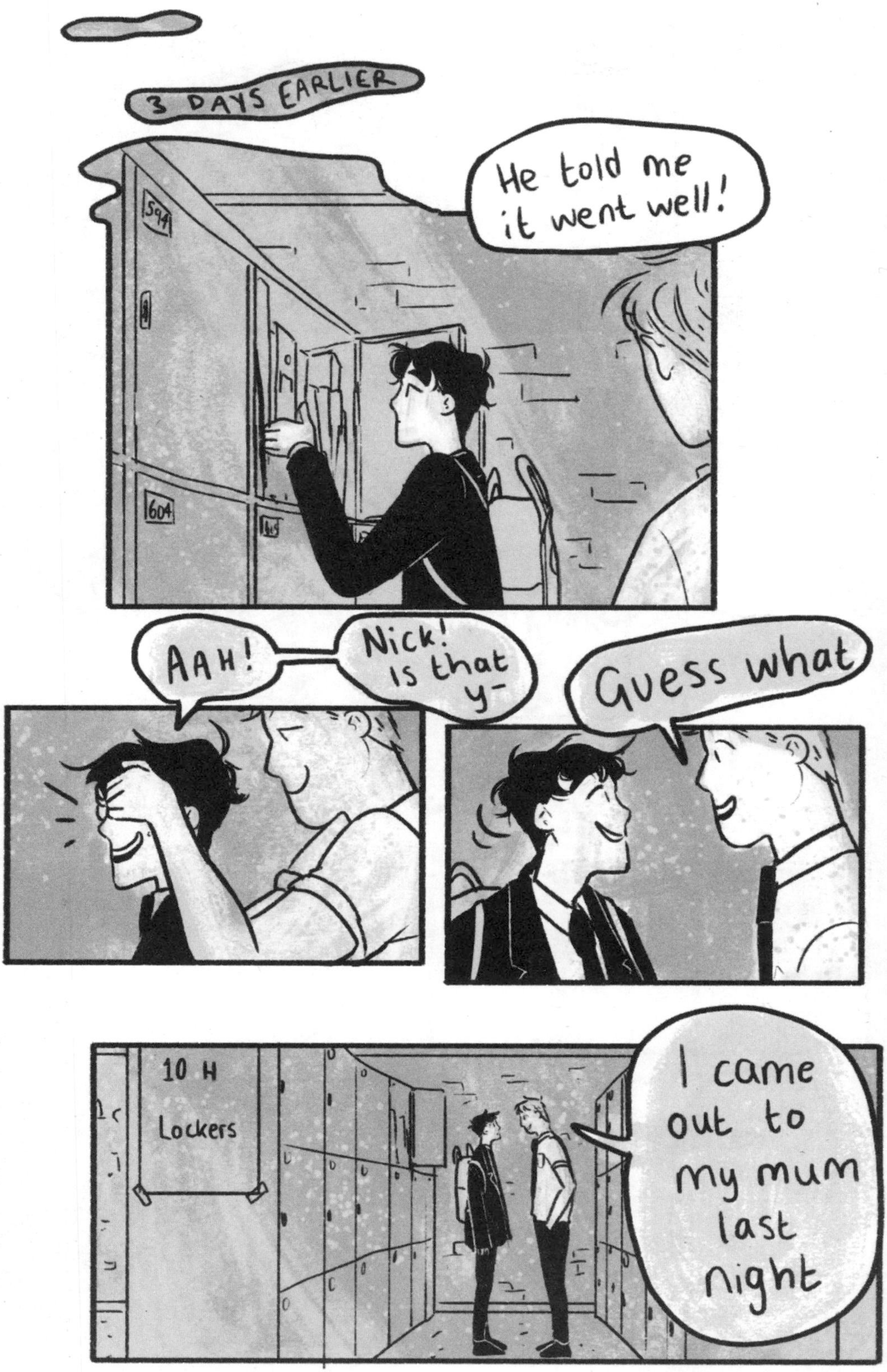
3 DAYS EARLIER
He told me it went well!
594
604
AAH!
Nick! Is that y-
Guess what
10 H Lockers
I came out to my mum last night

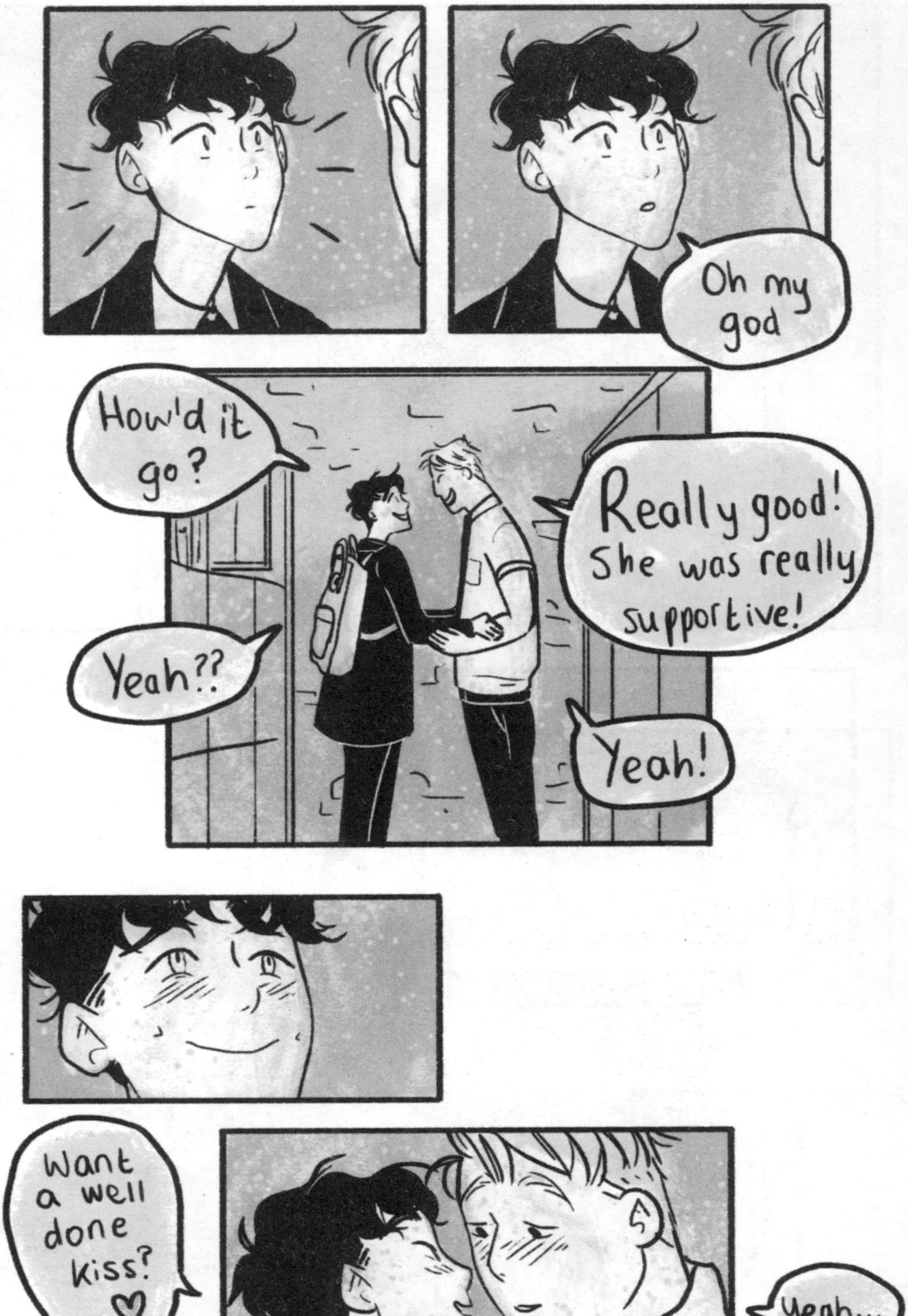
Oh my god
How'd it go?
Really good! She was really supportive!
Yeah??
Yeah!
Want a well done kiss? ♡
Yeah...

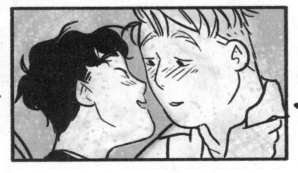

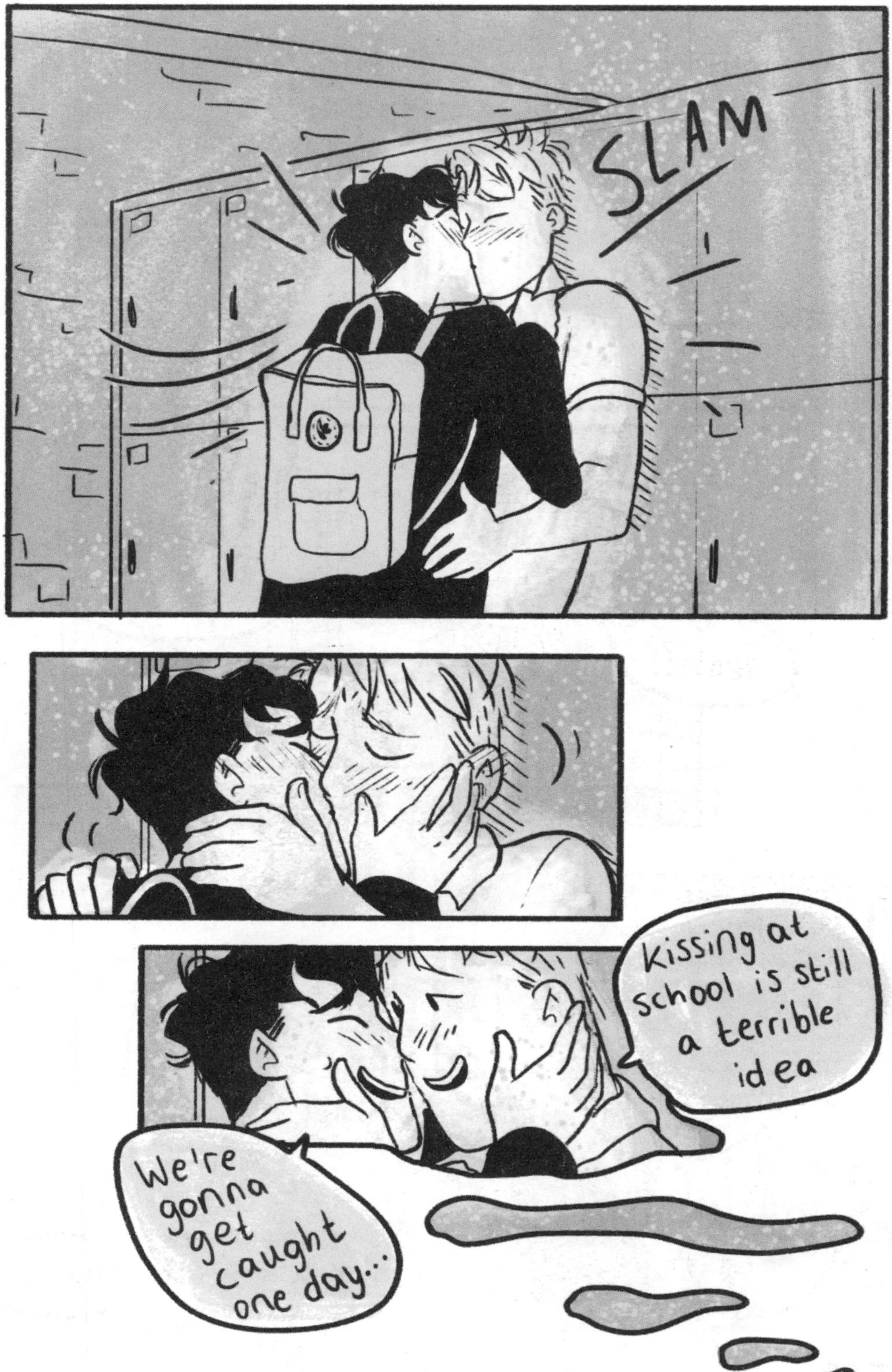
SLAM
Kissing at school is still a terrible idea
We're gonna get caught one day...

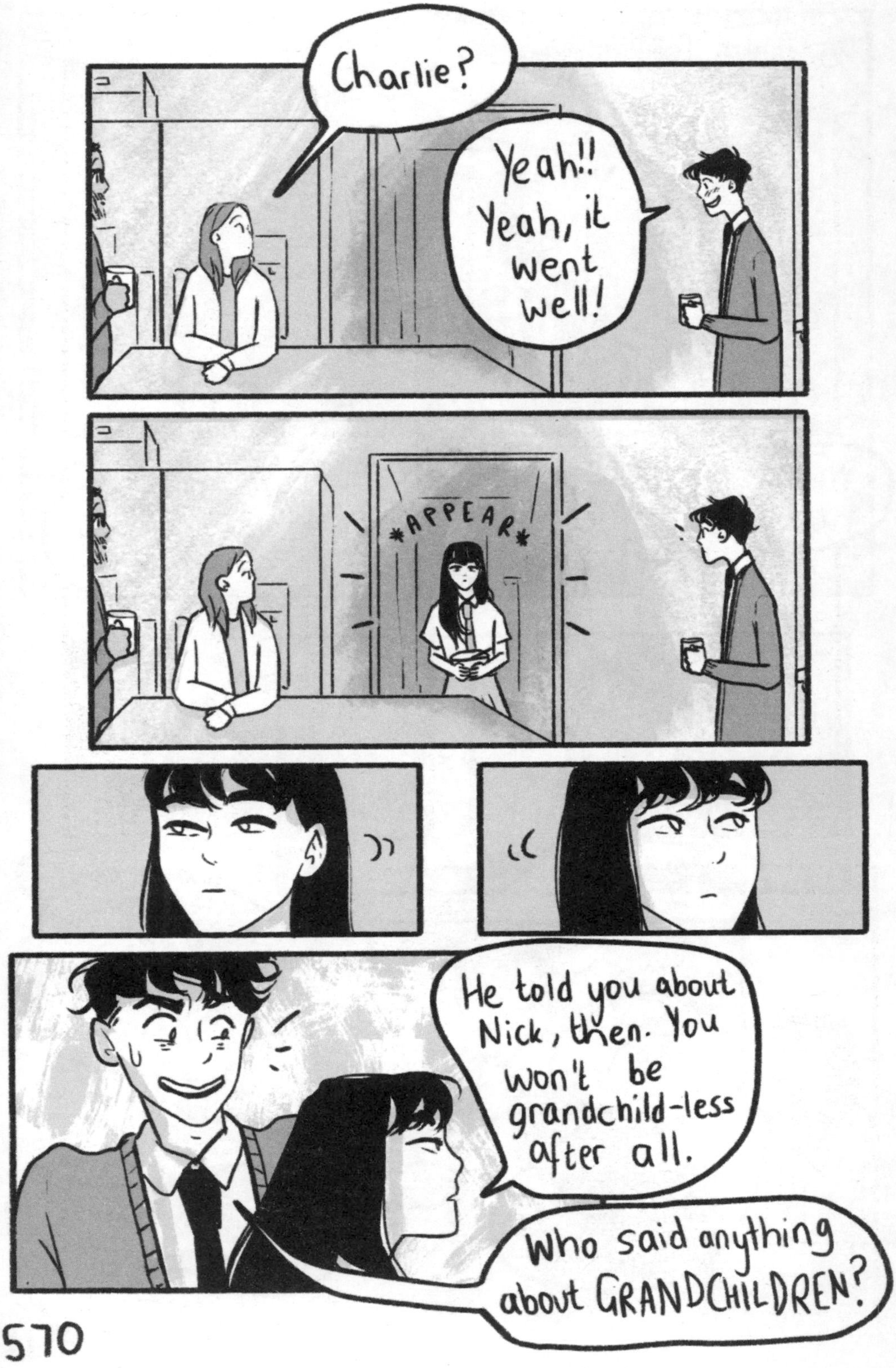
Charlie?
Yeah!! Yeah, it went well!
APPEAR
He told you about Nick, then. You won't be grandchild-less after all.
Who said anything about GRANDCHILDREN?

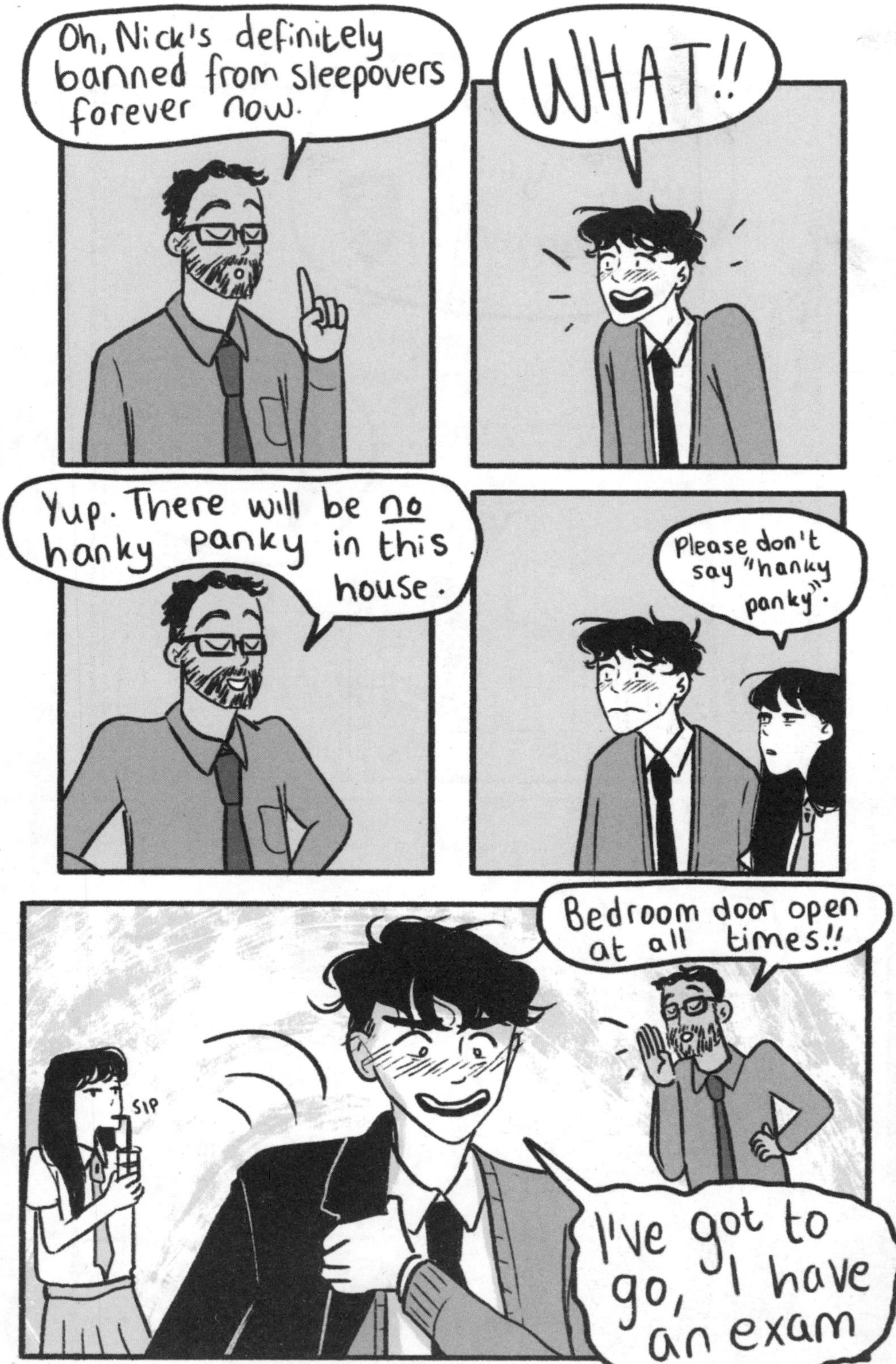
Oh, Nick's definitely banned from sleepovers forever now.
WHAT!!
Yup. There will be no hanky panky in this house.
Please don't say "hanky panky".
Bedroom door open at all times!!
SIP
I've got to go, I have an exam

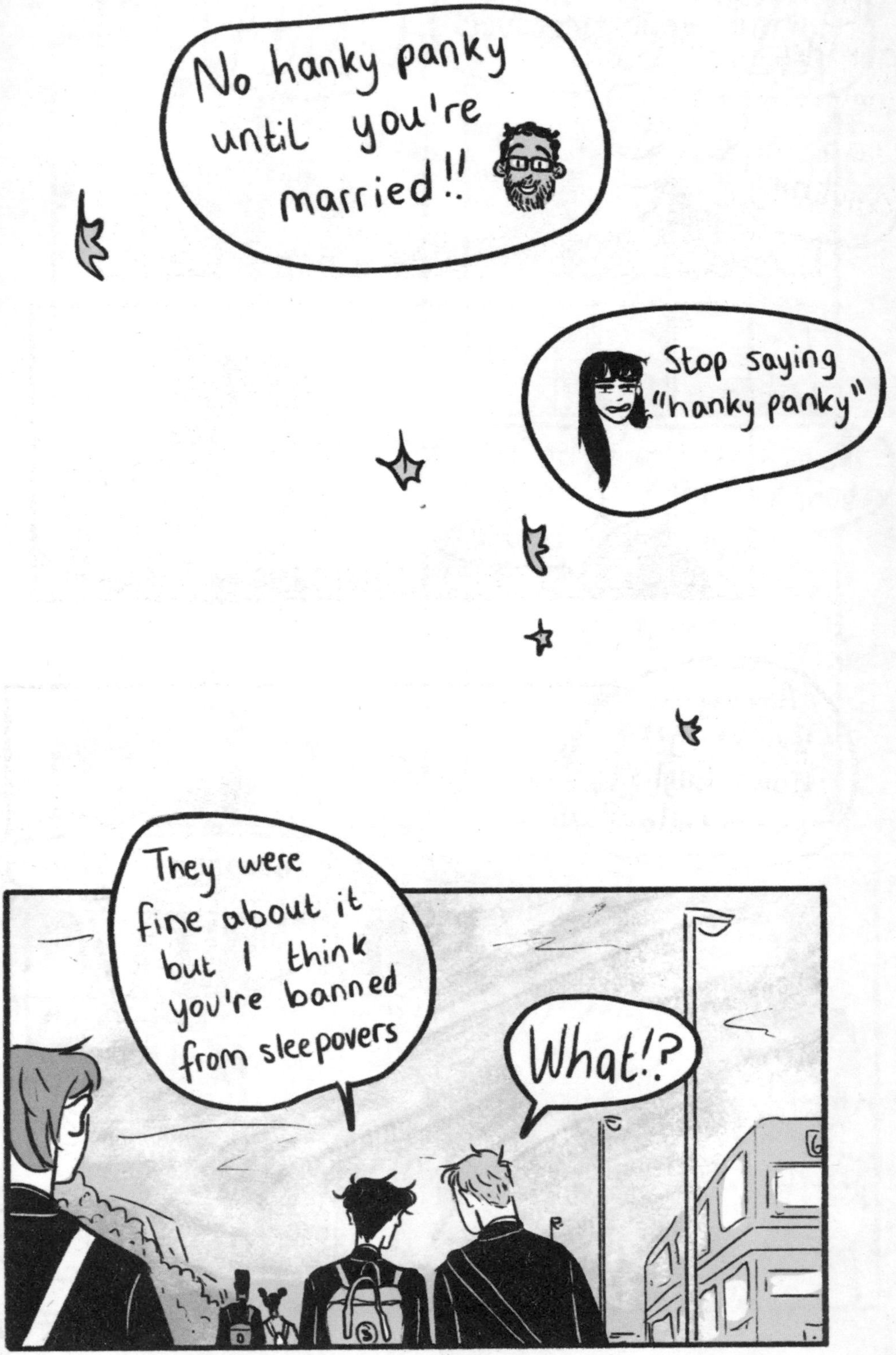
No hanky panky until you're married!!
Stop saying "hanky panky"
They were fine about it but I think you're banned from sleepovers
What!?

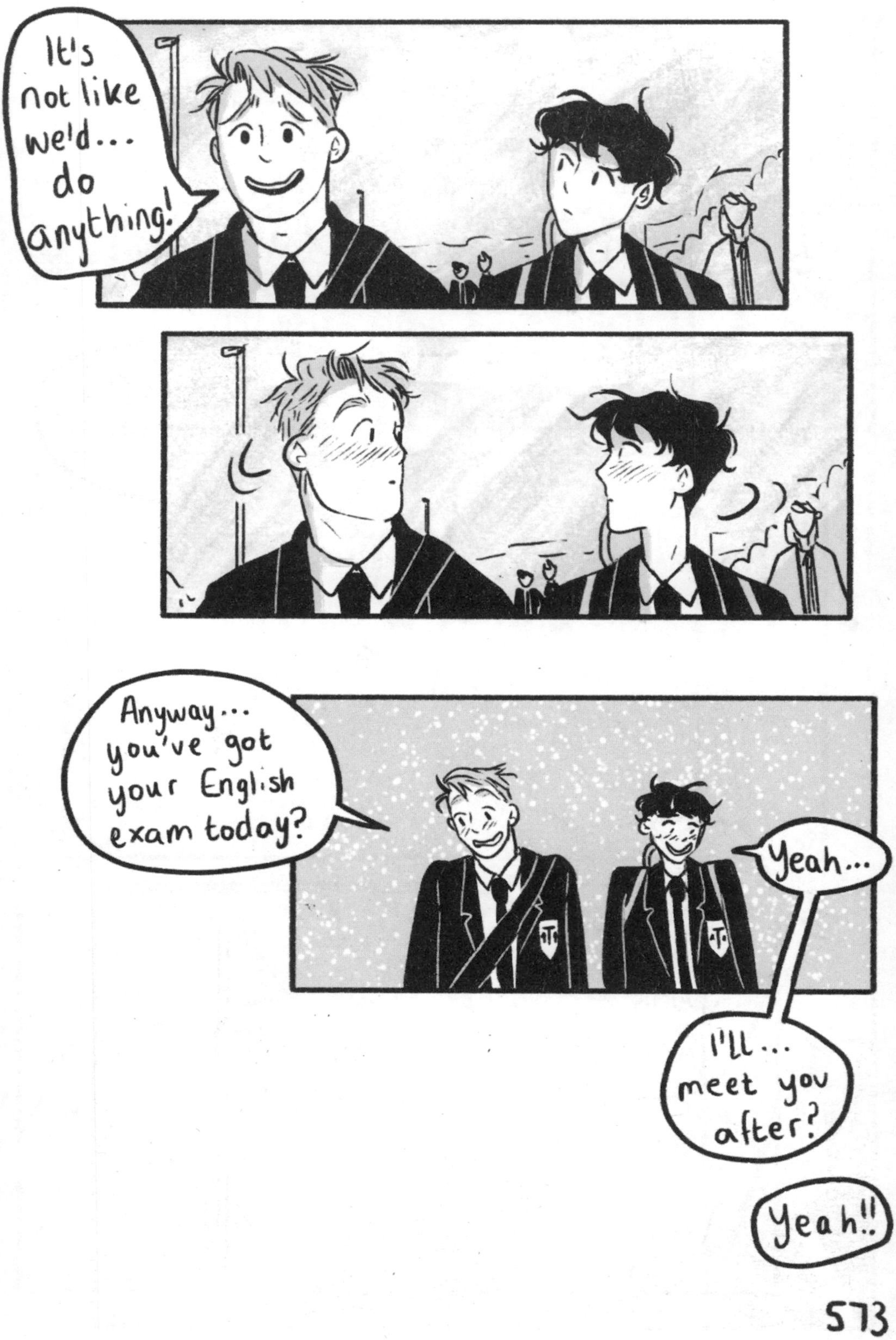
It's not like we'd... do anything!
Anyway... you've got your English exam today?
Yeah...
I'll... meet you after?
Yeah!!

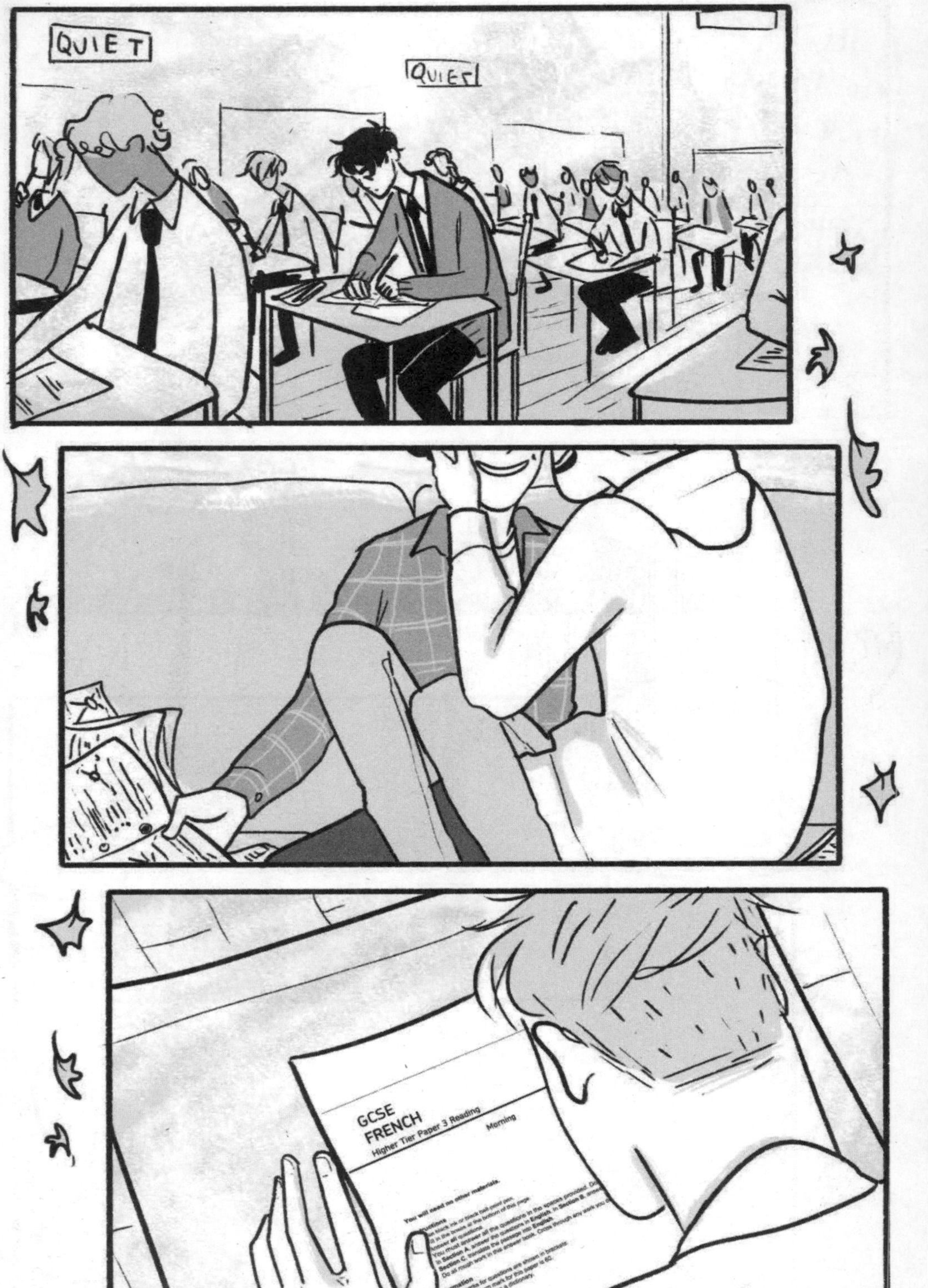
QUIET
QUIET
GCSE
FRENCH
Higher Tier Paper 3 Reading
Morning
You will need no other materials.

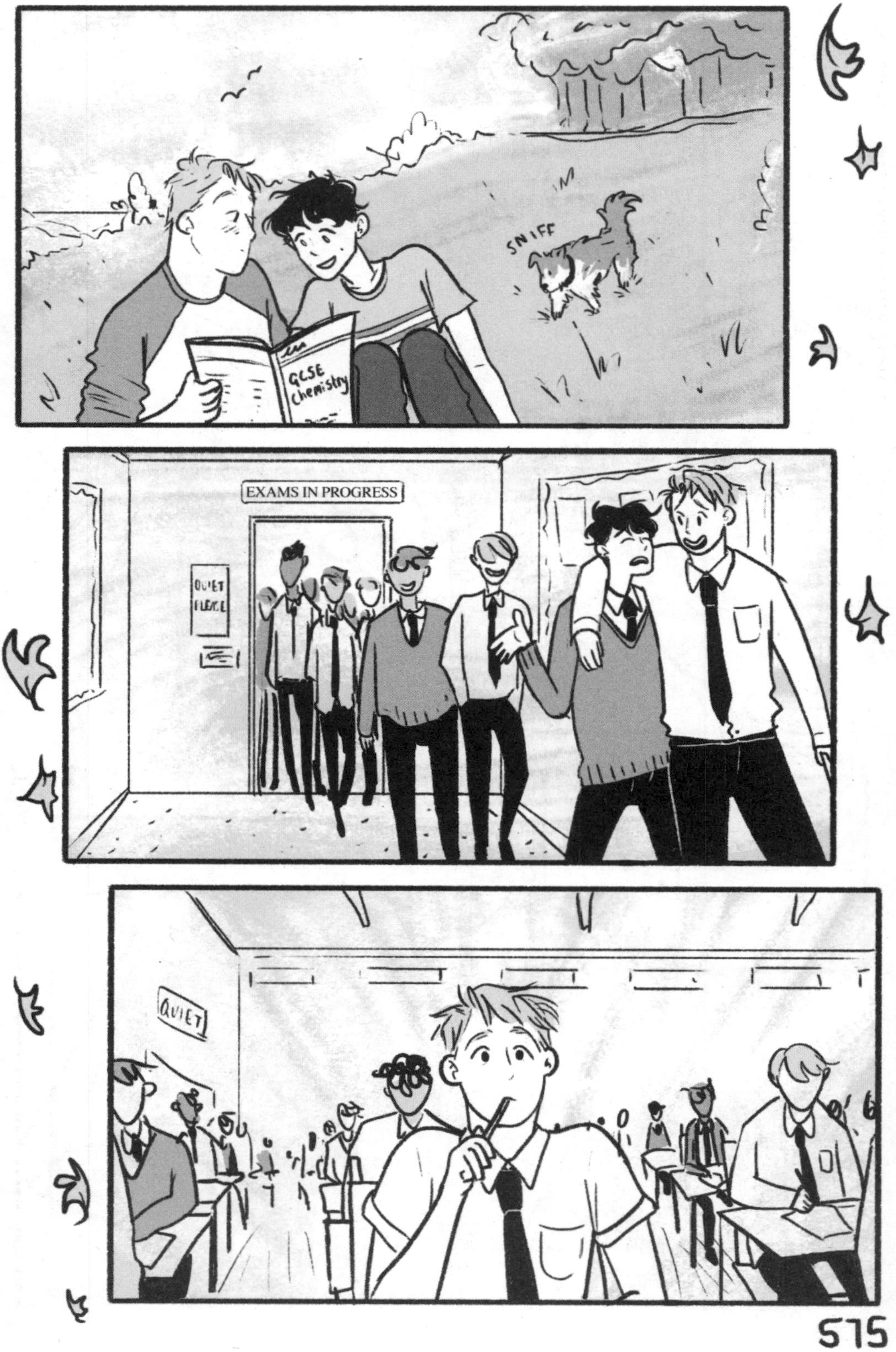
GCSE Chemistry
SNIFF
EXAMS IN PROGRESS
QUIET PLEASE
QUIET

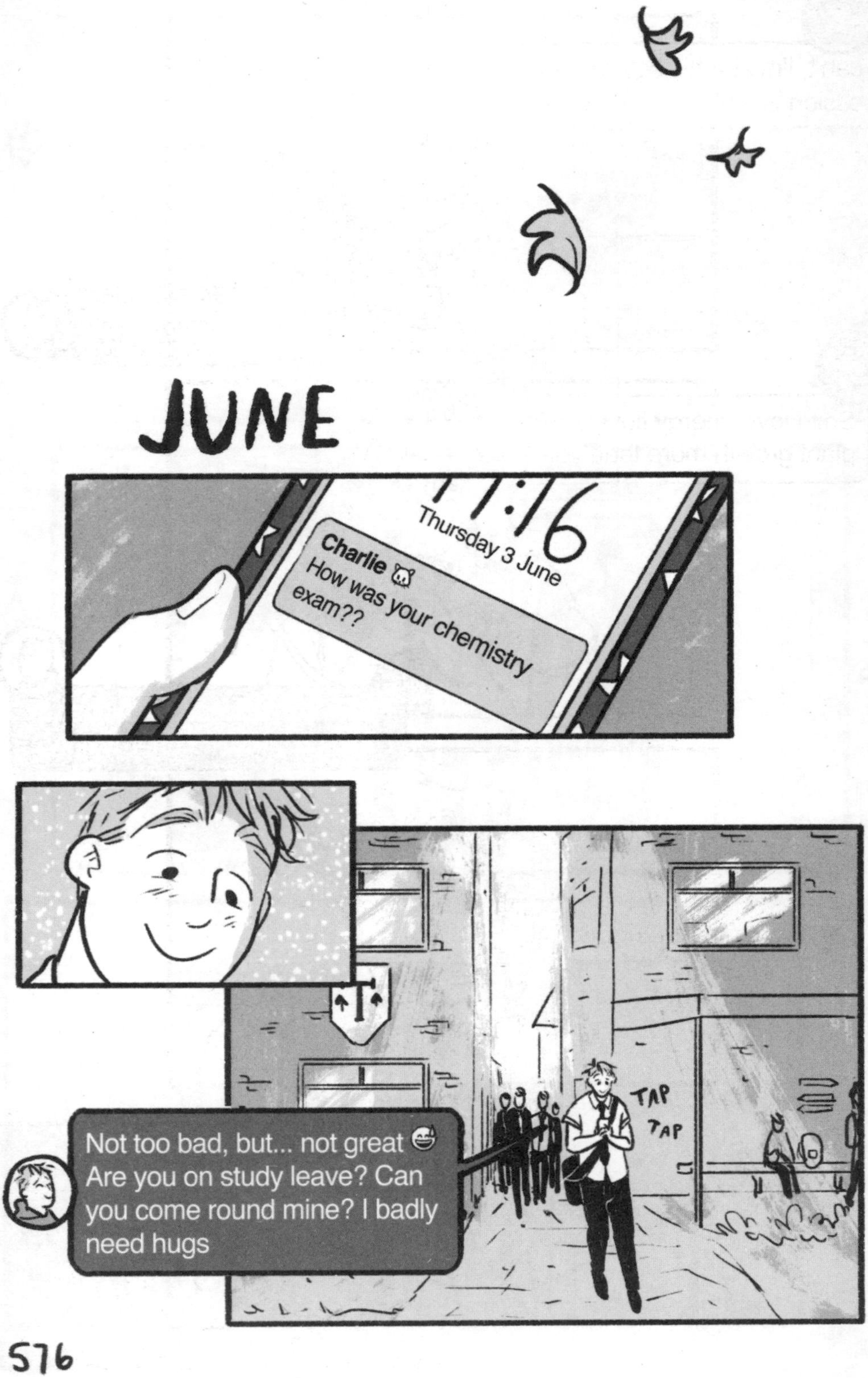
JUNE
11:16
Thursday 3 June
Charlie
How was your chemistry exam??
TAP
TAP
Not too bad, but... not great
Are you on study leave? Can you come round mine? I badly need hugs

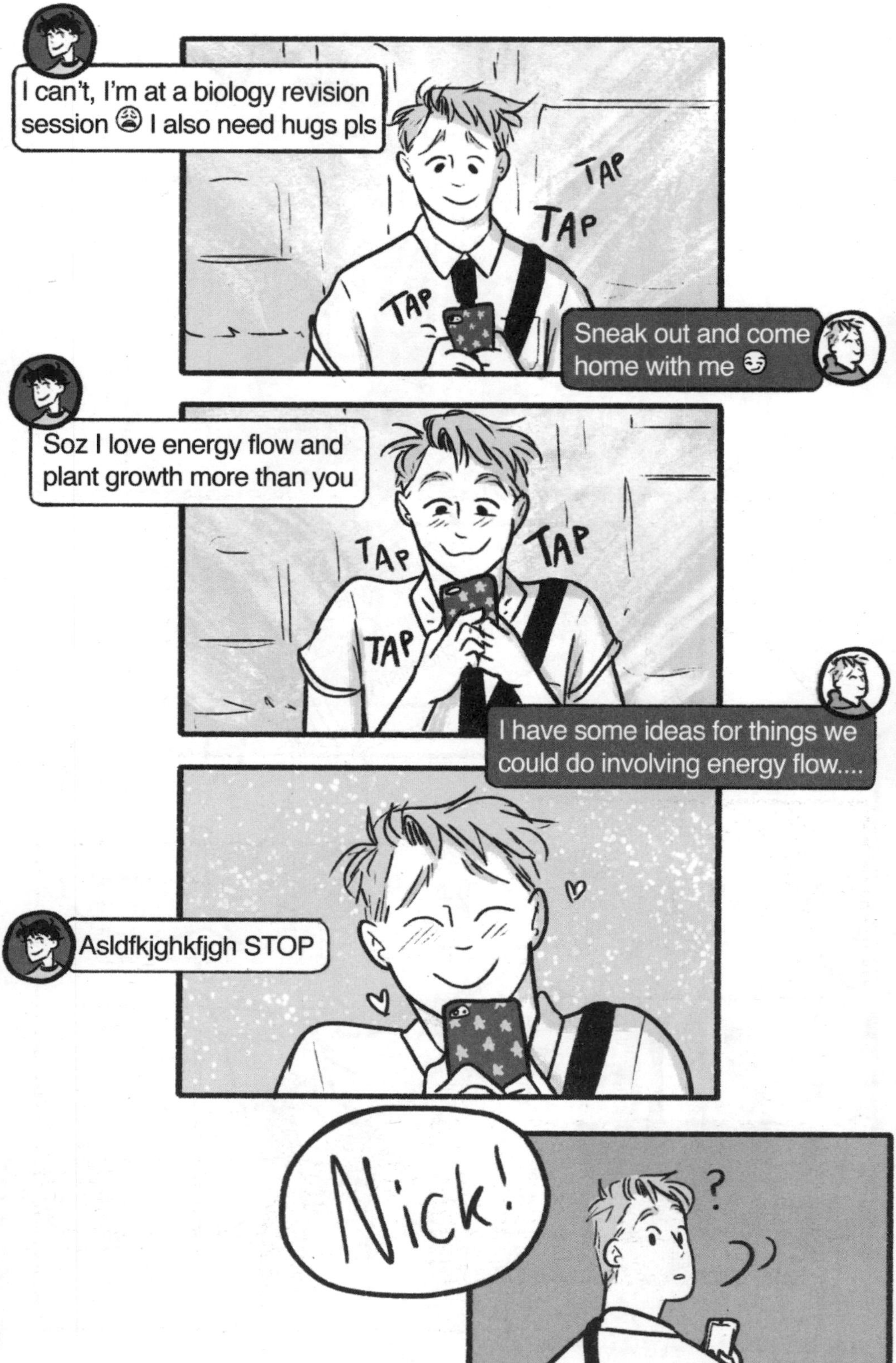
I can't, I'm at a biology revision session 😩 I also need hugs pls
TAP
TAP
TAP
Sneak out and come home with me 😏
Soz I love energy flow and plant growth more than you
TAP
TAP
TAP
I have some ideas for things we could do involving energy flow....
Asldfkjghkfjgh STOP
Nick!
?

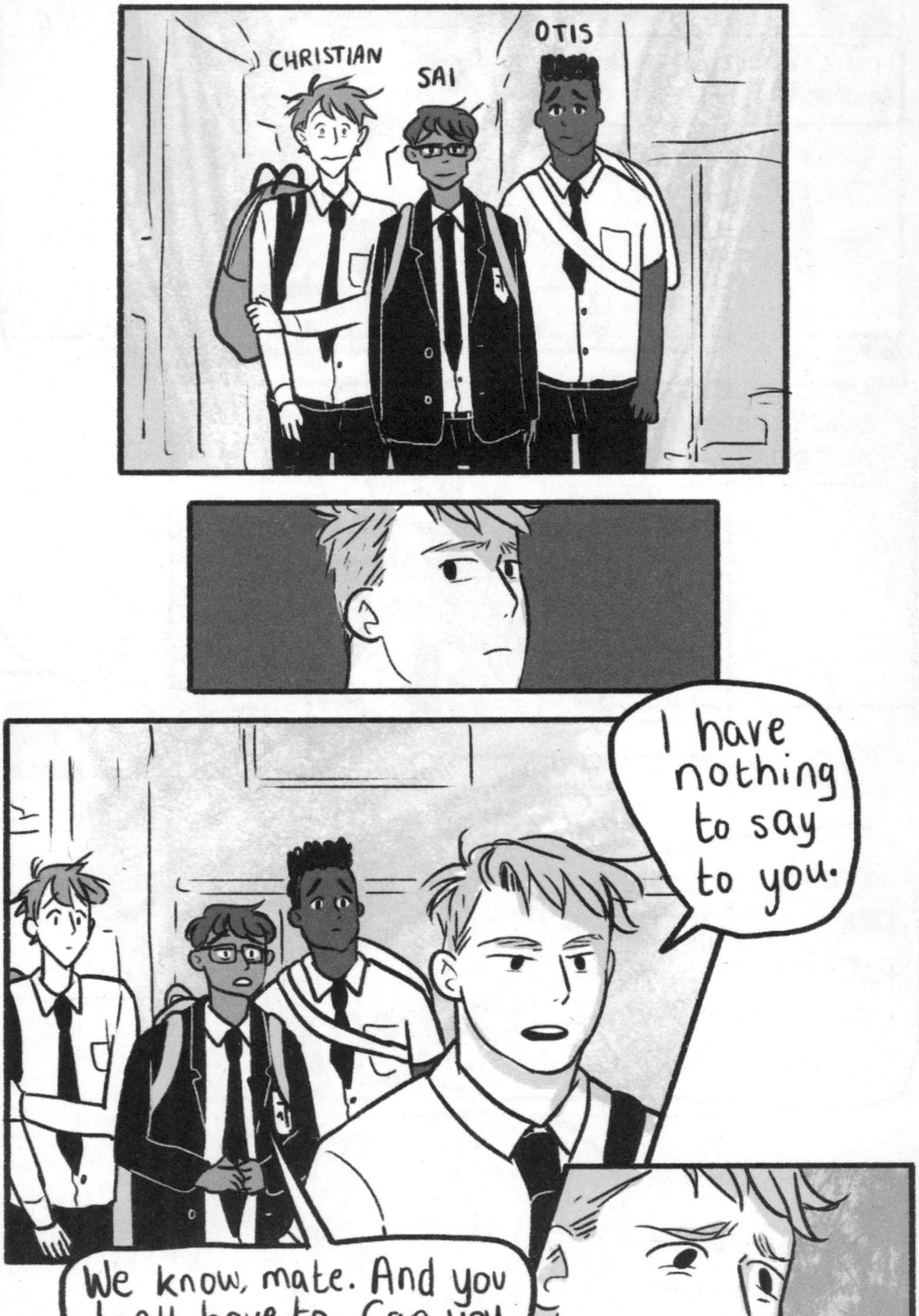
CHRISTIAN
SAI
OTIS
I have nothing to say to you.
We know, mate. And you don't have to. Can you just hear us out?

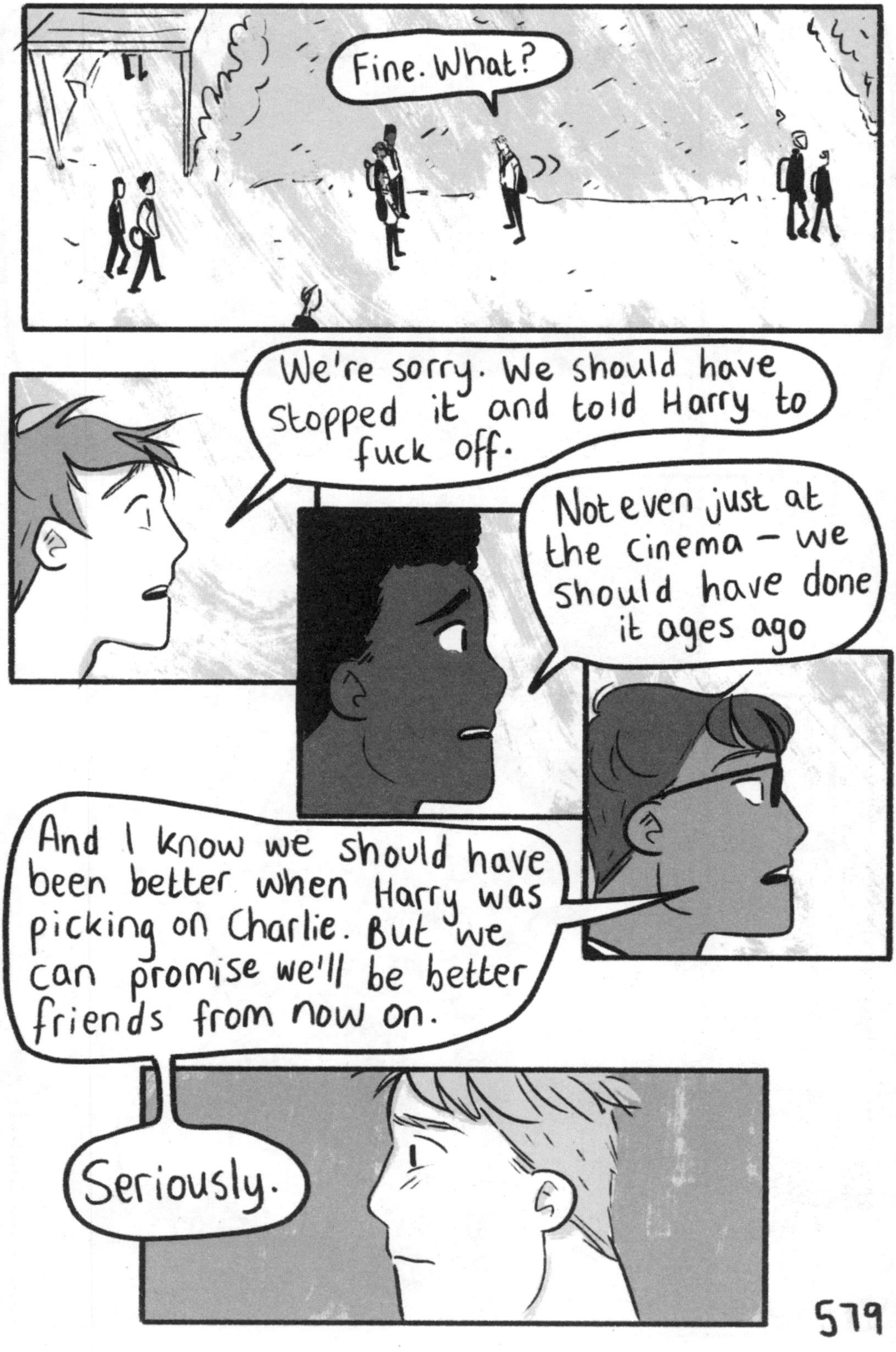
Fine. What?
We're sorry. We should have stopped it and told Harry to fuck off.
Not even just at the cinema - we should have done it ages ago
And I know we should have been better when Harry was picking on Charlie. But we can promise we'll be better friends from now on.
Seriously.

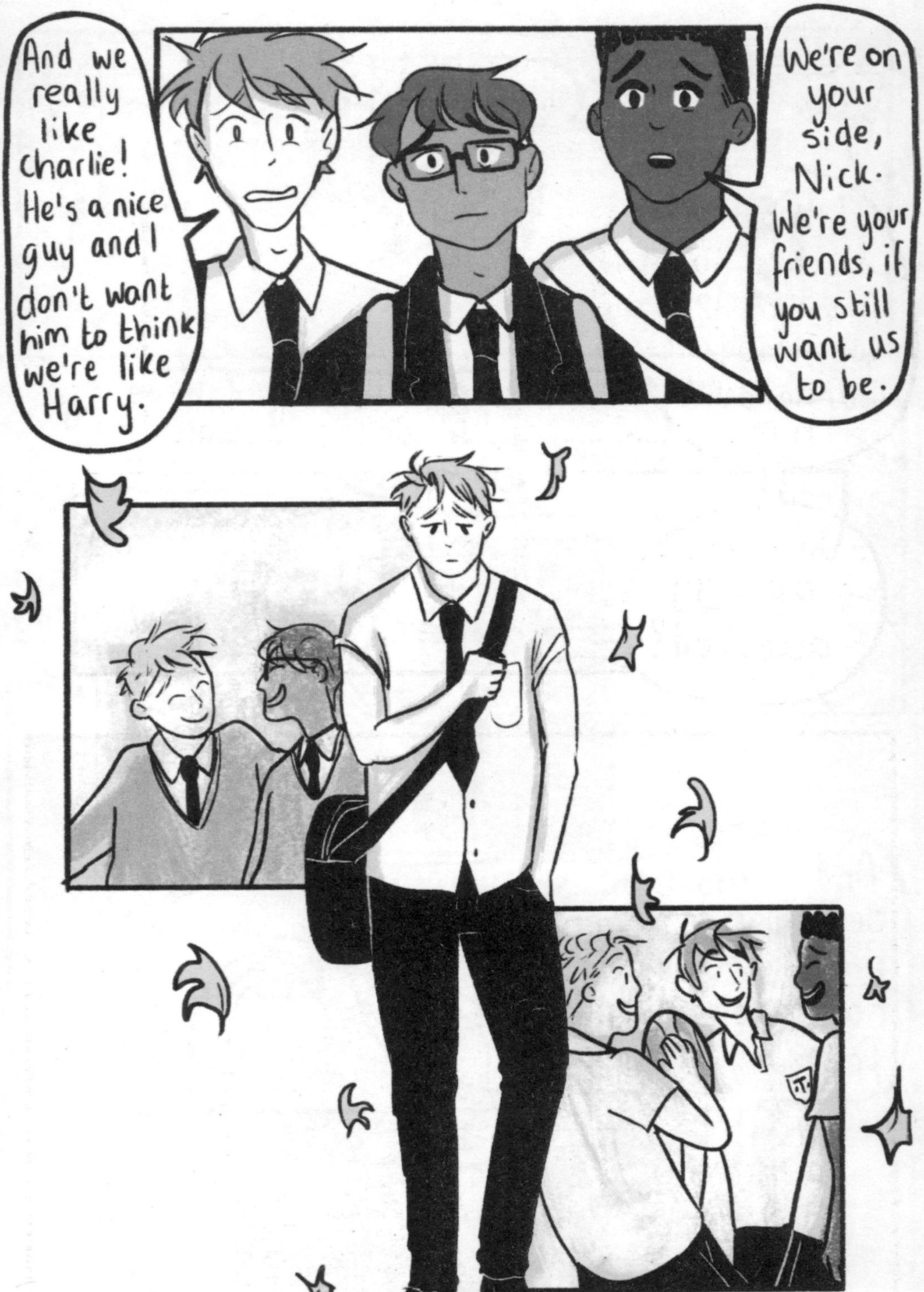
And we really like Charlie! He's a nice guy and I don't want him to think we're like Harry.
We're on your side, Nick. We're your friends, if you still want us to be.

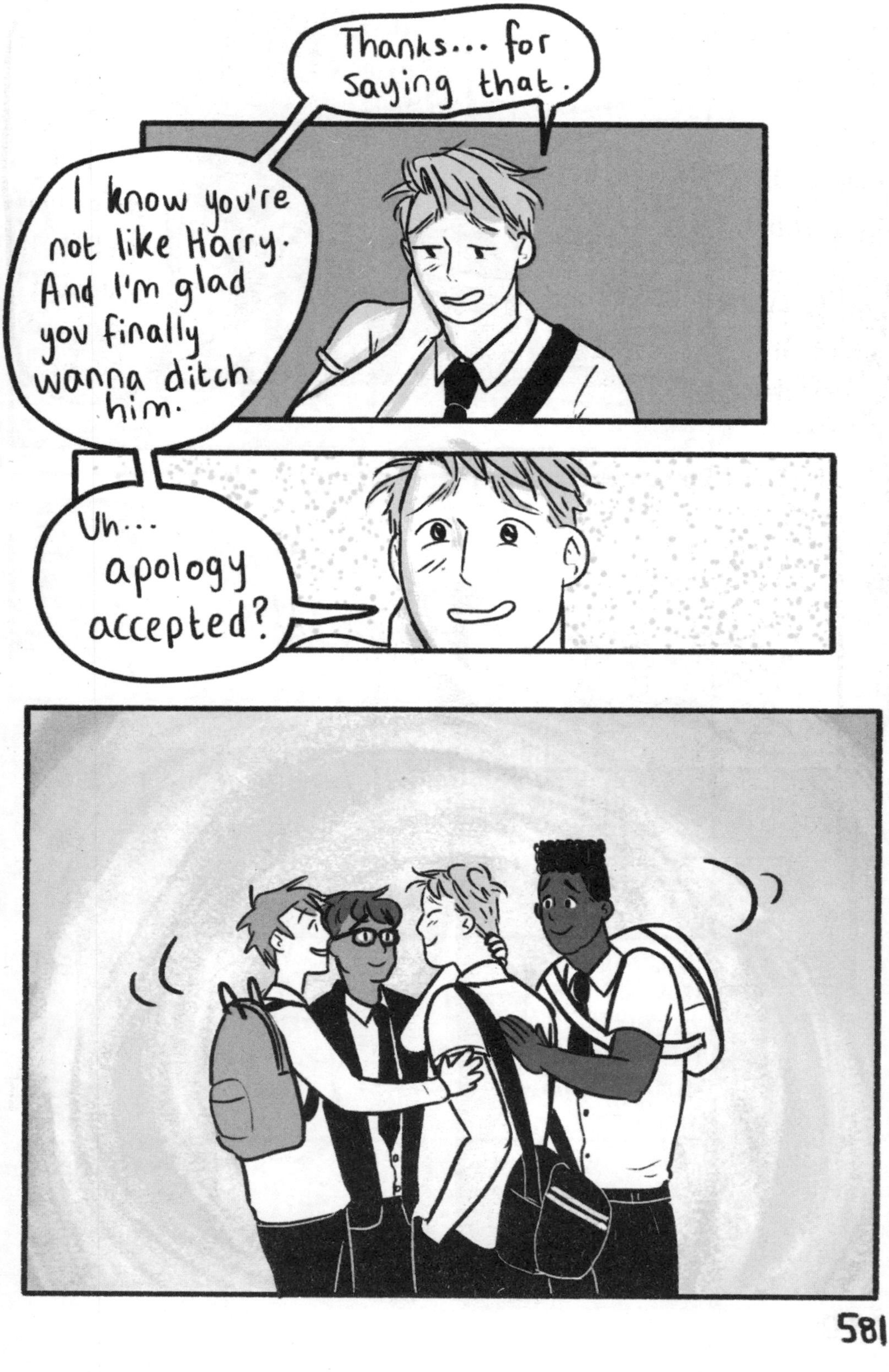
I know you're not like Harry. And I'm glad you finally wanna ditch him.
Thanks... for saying that.
Uh... apology accepted?

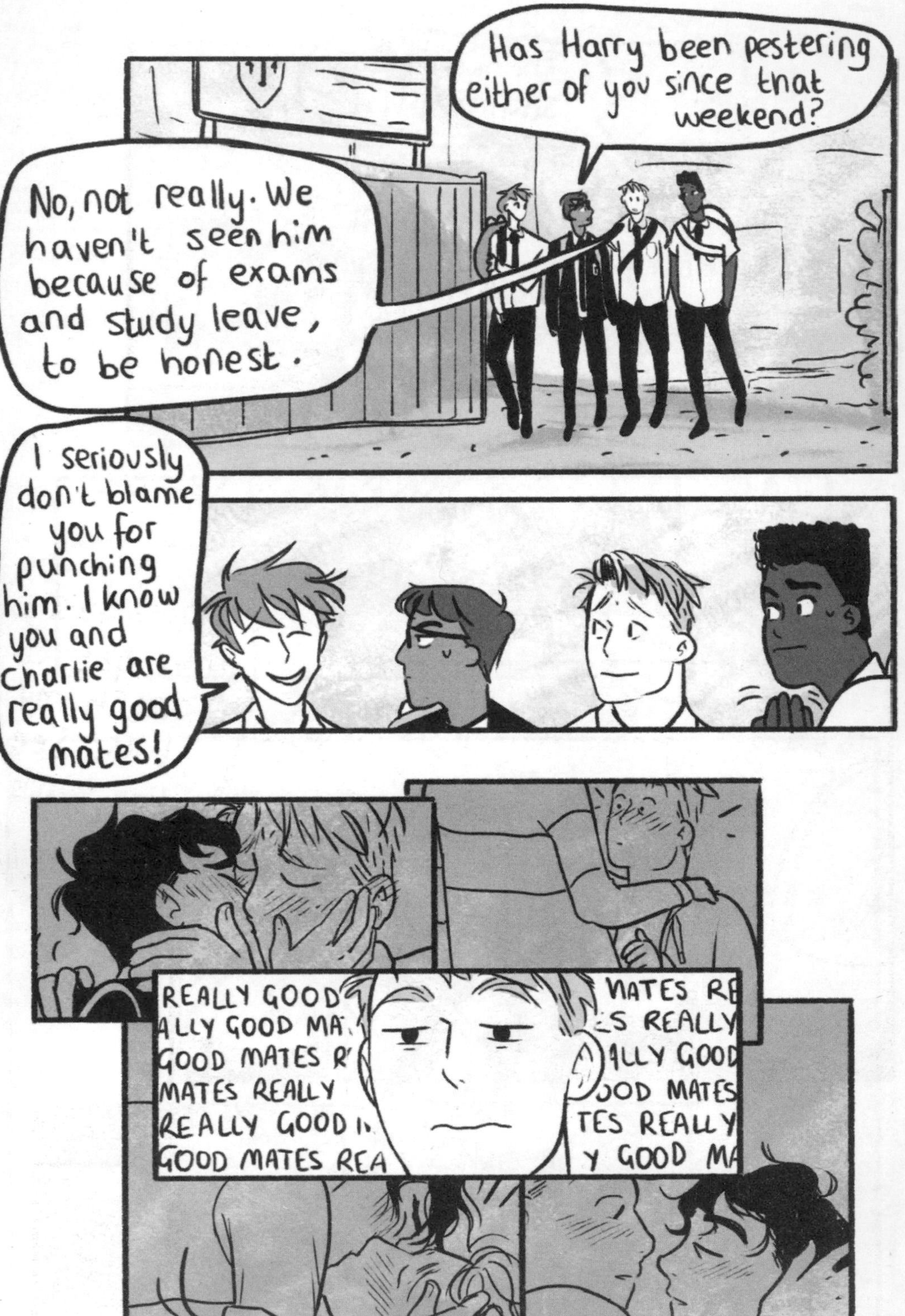
Has Harry been pestering either of you since that weekend?
No, not really. We haven't seen him because of exams and study leave, to be honest.
I seriously don't blame you for punching him. I know you and Charlie are really good mates!
REALLY GOOD
ALLY GOOD MA
GOOD MATES R
MATES REALLY
REALLY GOOD
GOOD MATES REA
MATES RE
S REALLY
ALLY GOOD
OD MATES
TES REALLY
Y GOOD M

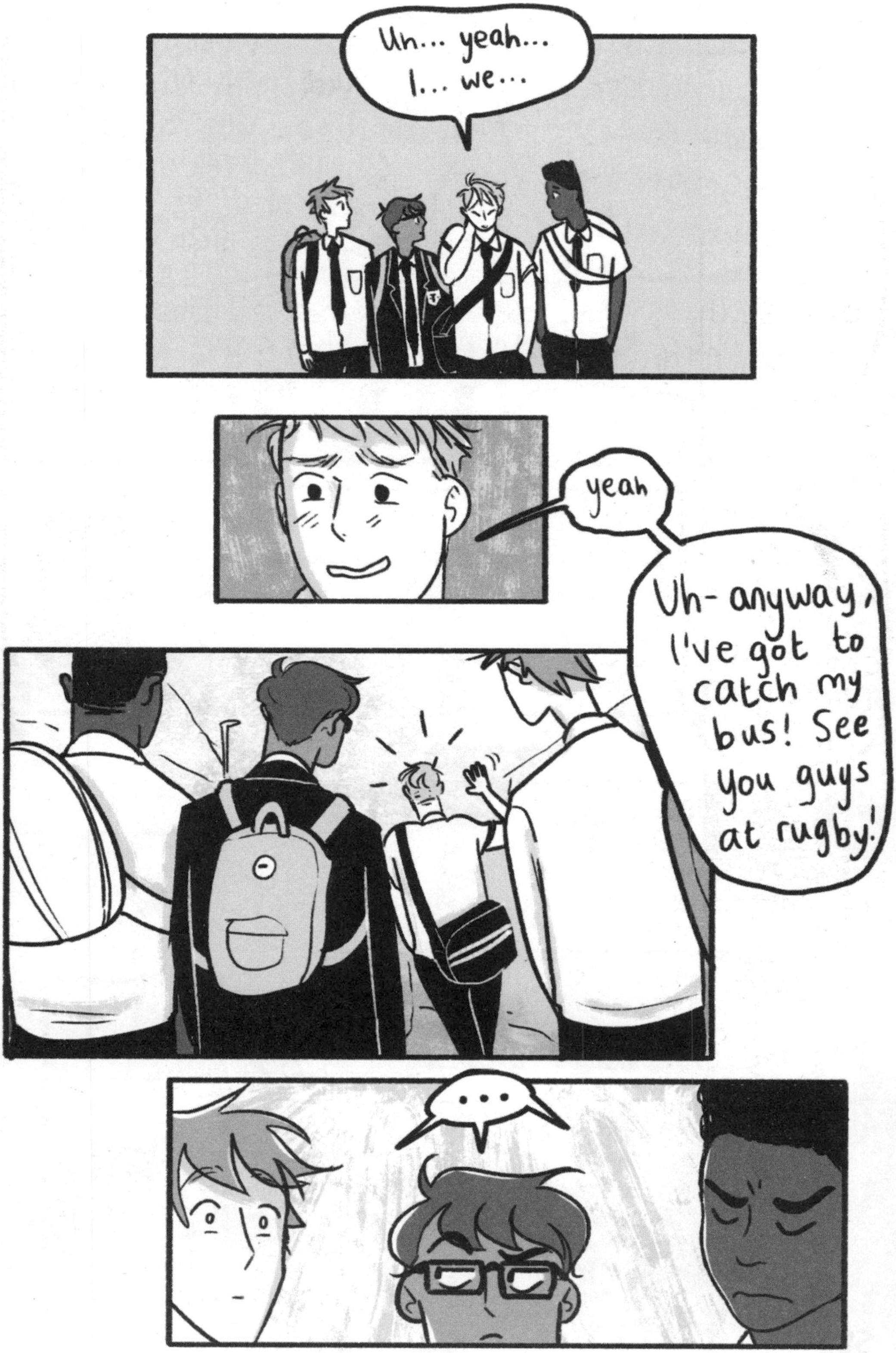
Uh... yeah... I... we...
yeah
Uh- anyway, I've got to catch my bus! See you guys at rugby!
...

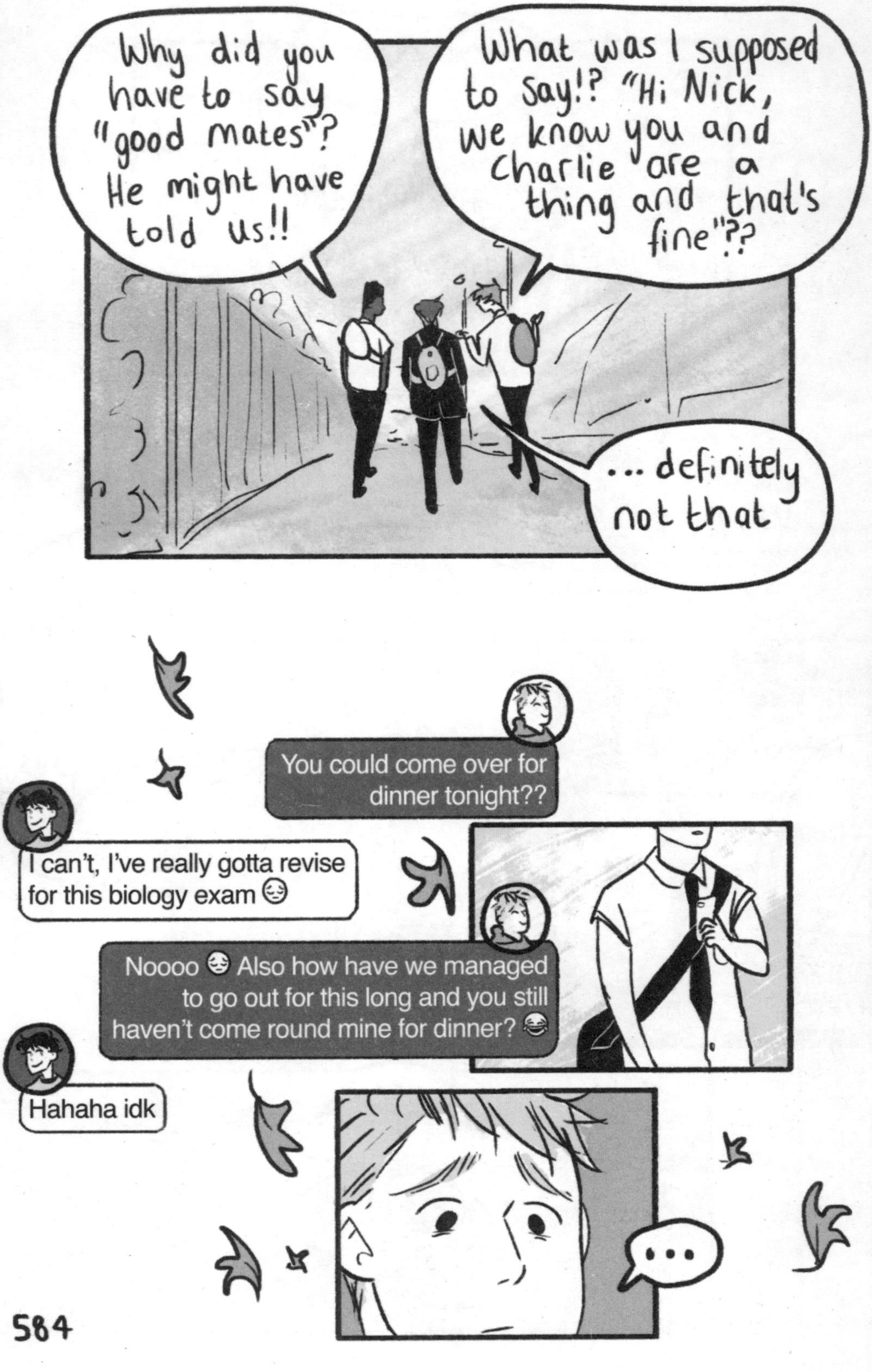
Why did you have to say "good mates"? He might have told us!!
What was I supposed to say!? "Hi Nick, we know you and Charlie are a thing and that's fine"??
... definitely not that
You could come over for dinner tonight??
I can't, I've really gotta revise for this biology exam 😔
Noooo 😔 Also how have we managed to go out for this long and you still haven't come round mine for dinner? 😂
Hahaha idk
...

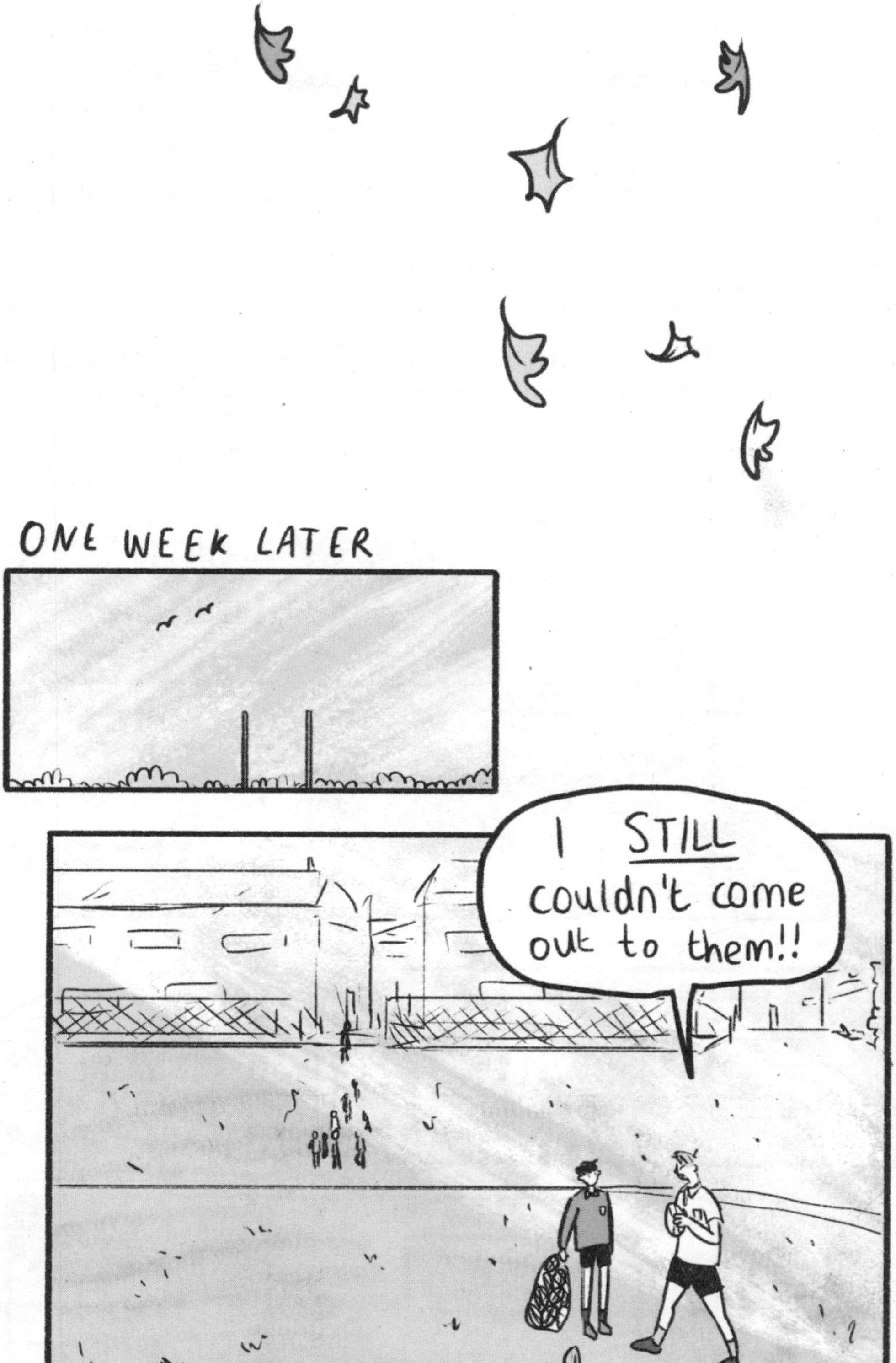
ONE WEEK LATER
I STILL couldn't come out to them!!

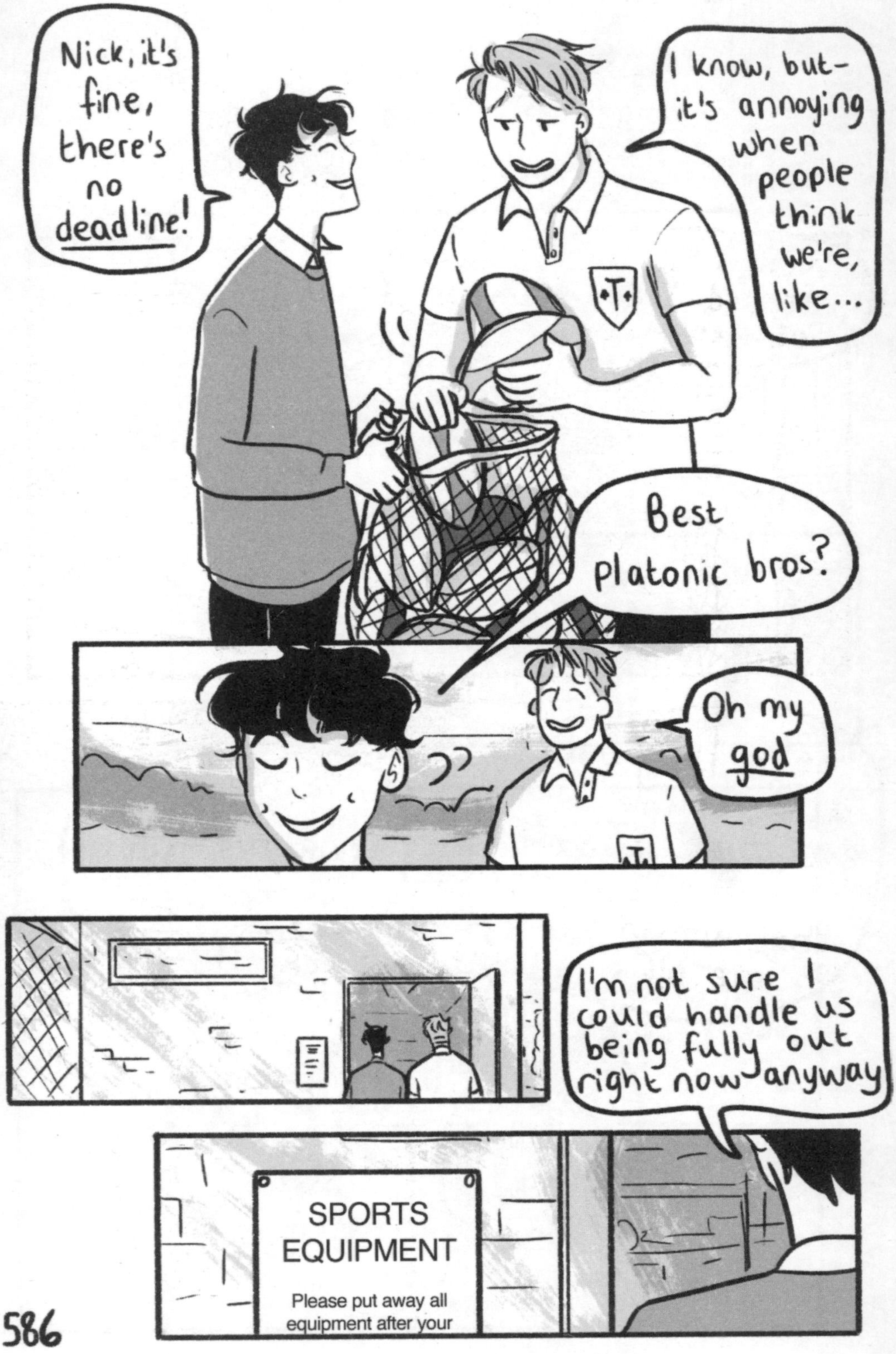
Nick, it's fine, there's no deadline!
I know, but- it's annoying when people think we're, like...
Best platonic bros?
Oh my god
I'm not sure I could handle us being fully out right now anyway
SPORTS EQUIPMENT
Please put away all equipment after your

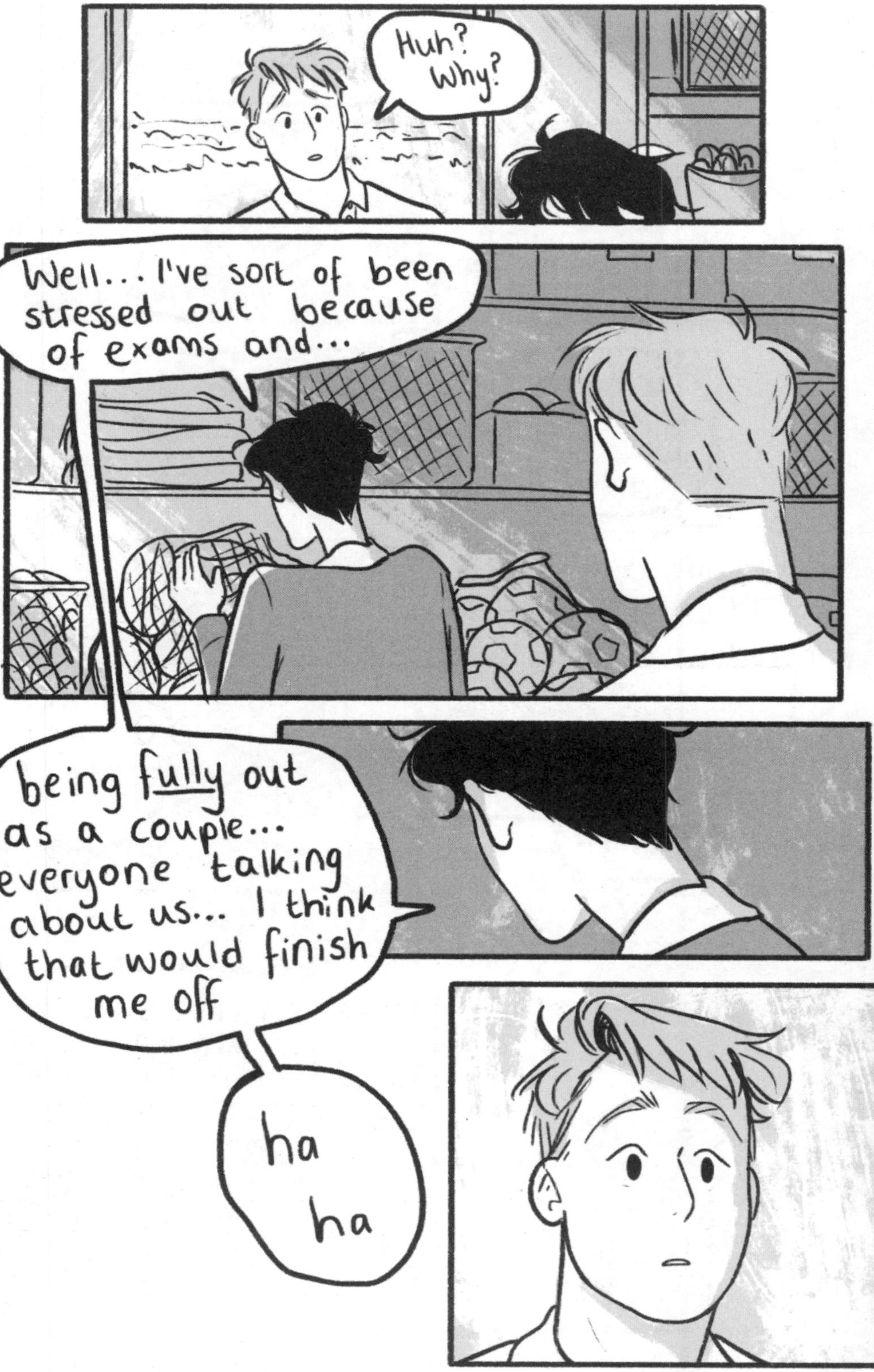
Huh? Why?
Well... I've sort of been stressed out because of exams and...
being fully out as a couple... everyone talking about us... I think that would finish me off
ha ha

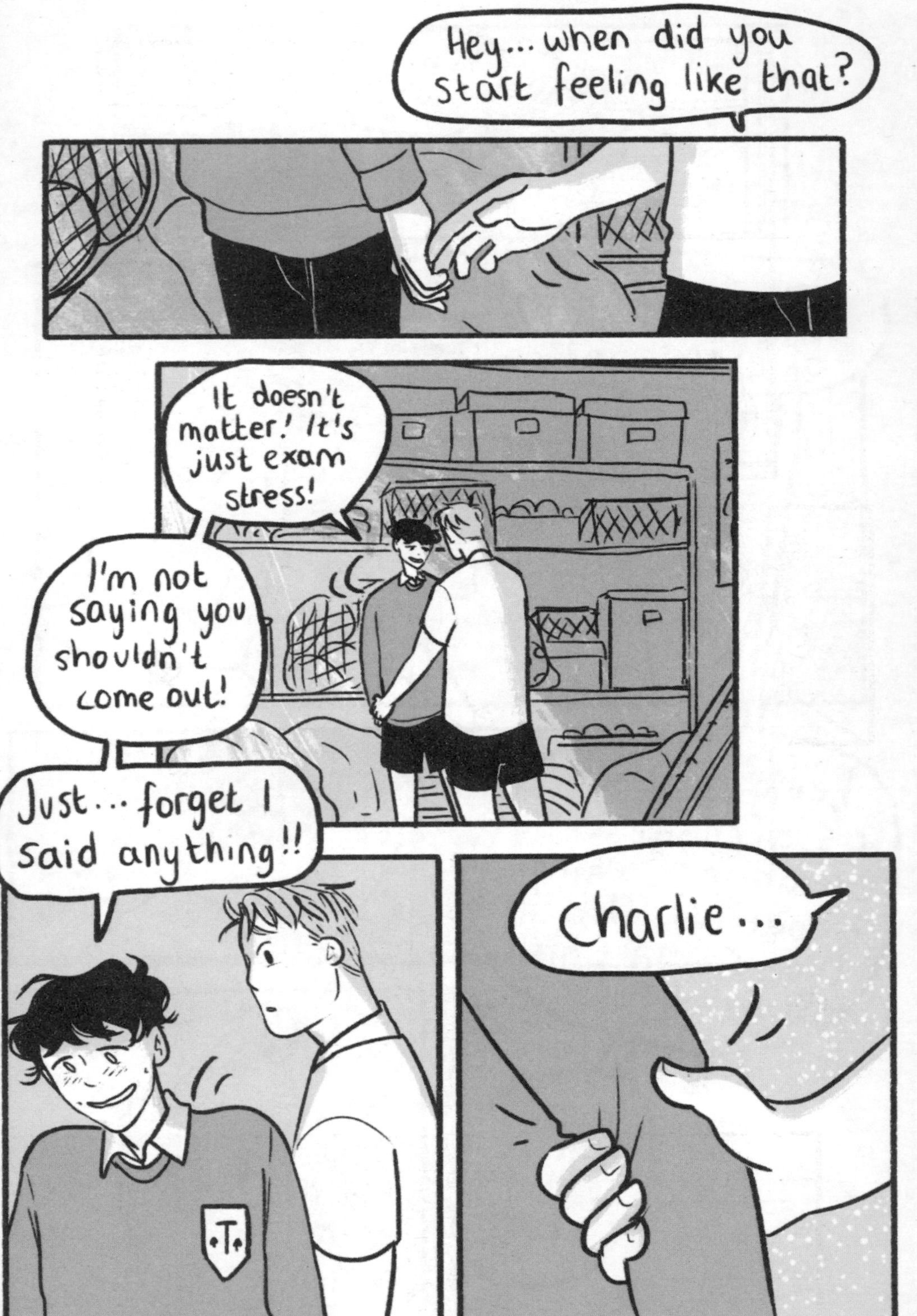
Hey... when did you start feeling like that?
It doesn't matter! It's just exam stress!
I'm not saying you shouldn't come out!
Just... forget I said anything!!
Charlie...

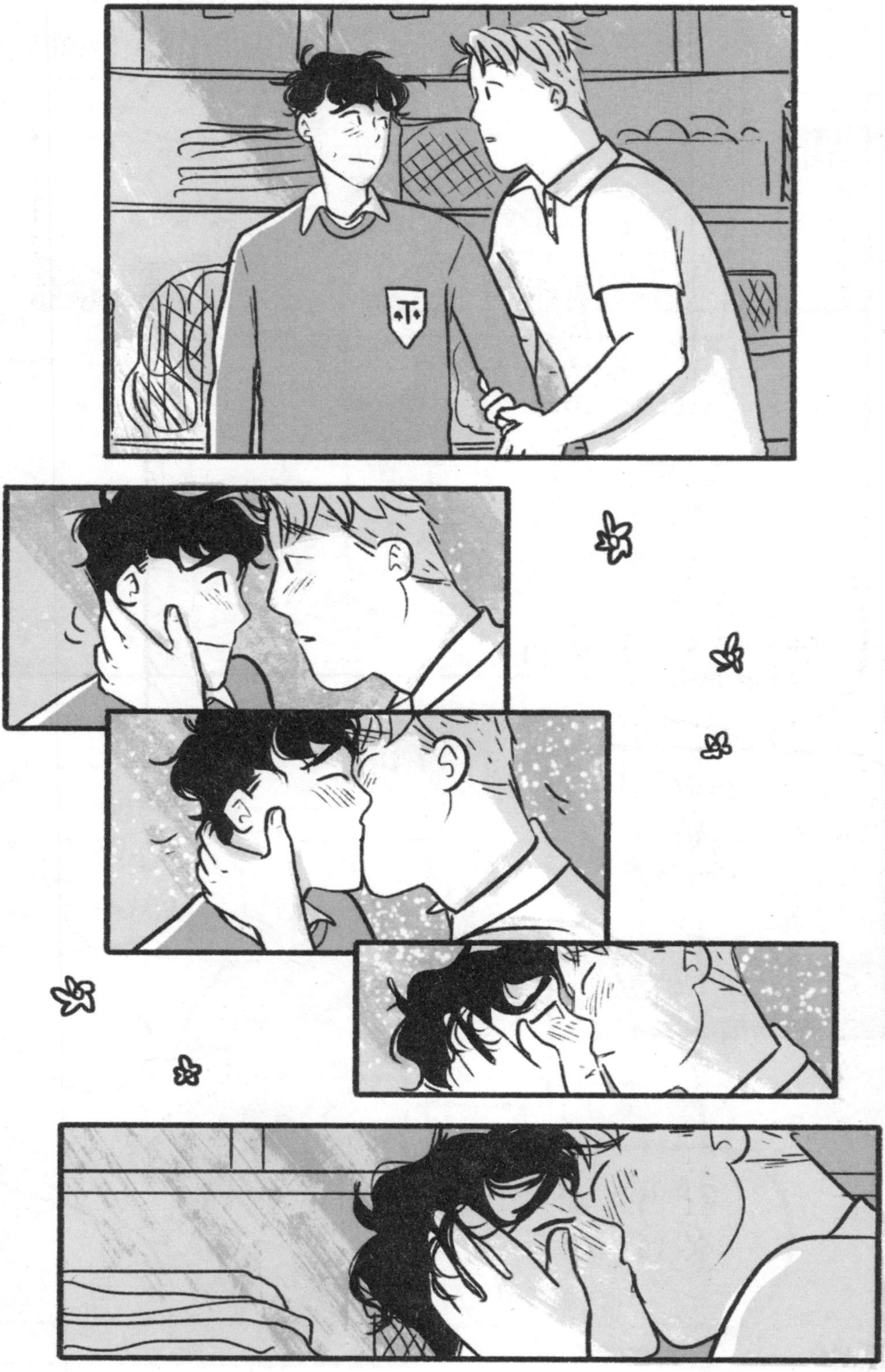

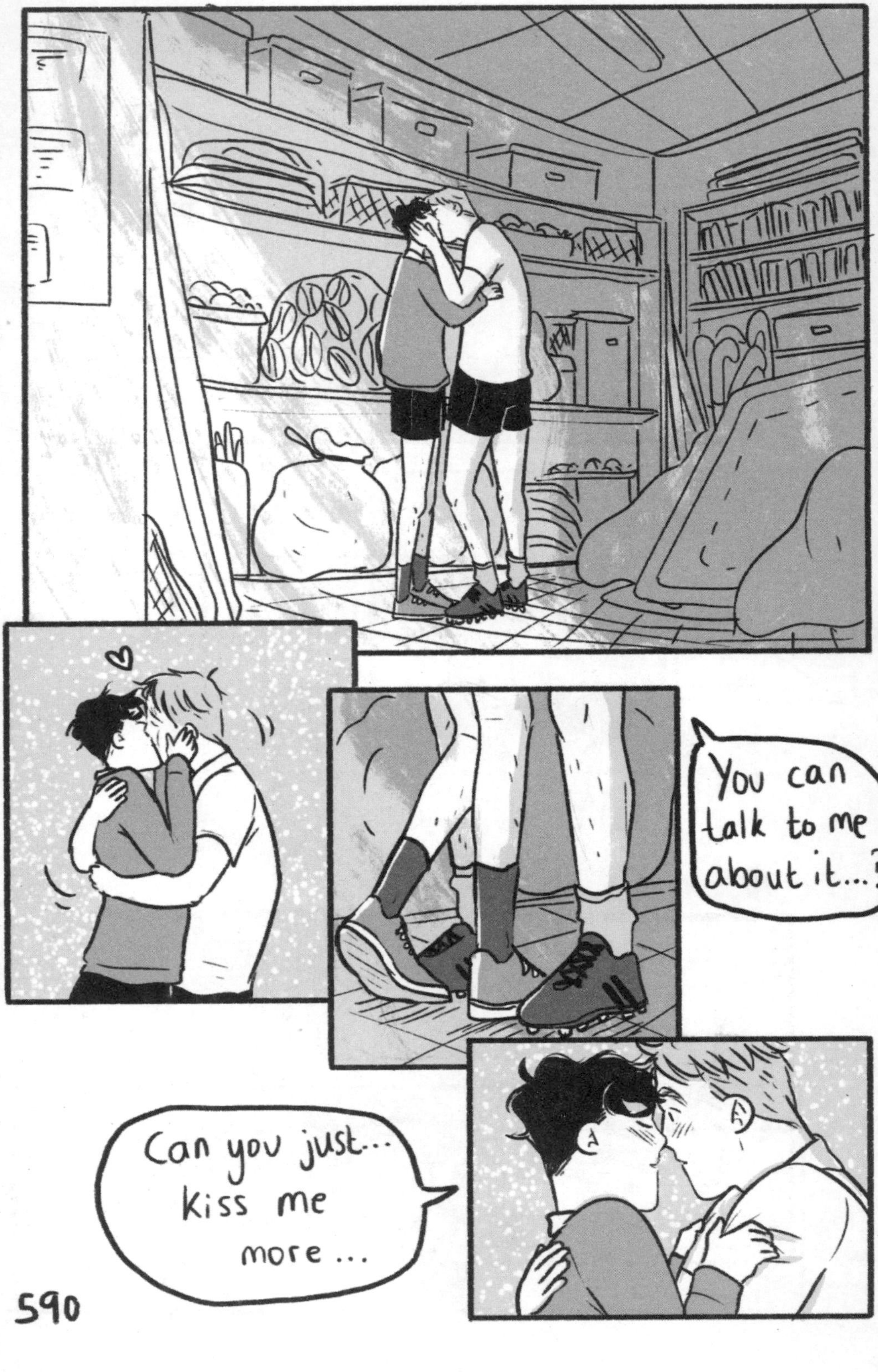
You can talk to me about it...?
Can you just... kiss me more...

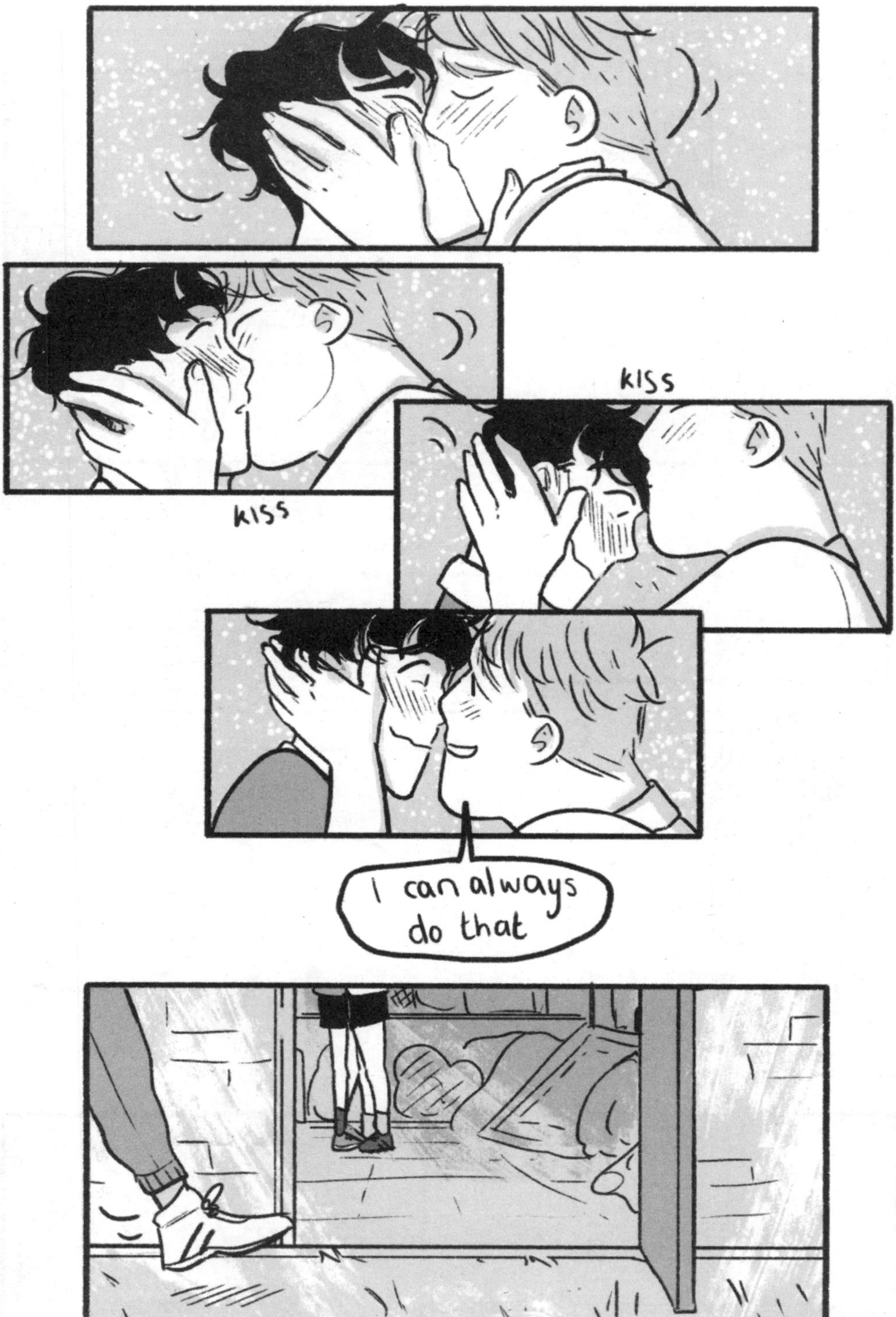
KISS
KISS
I can always do that

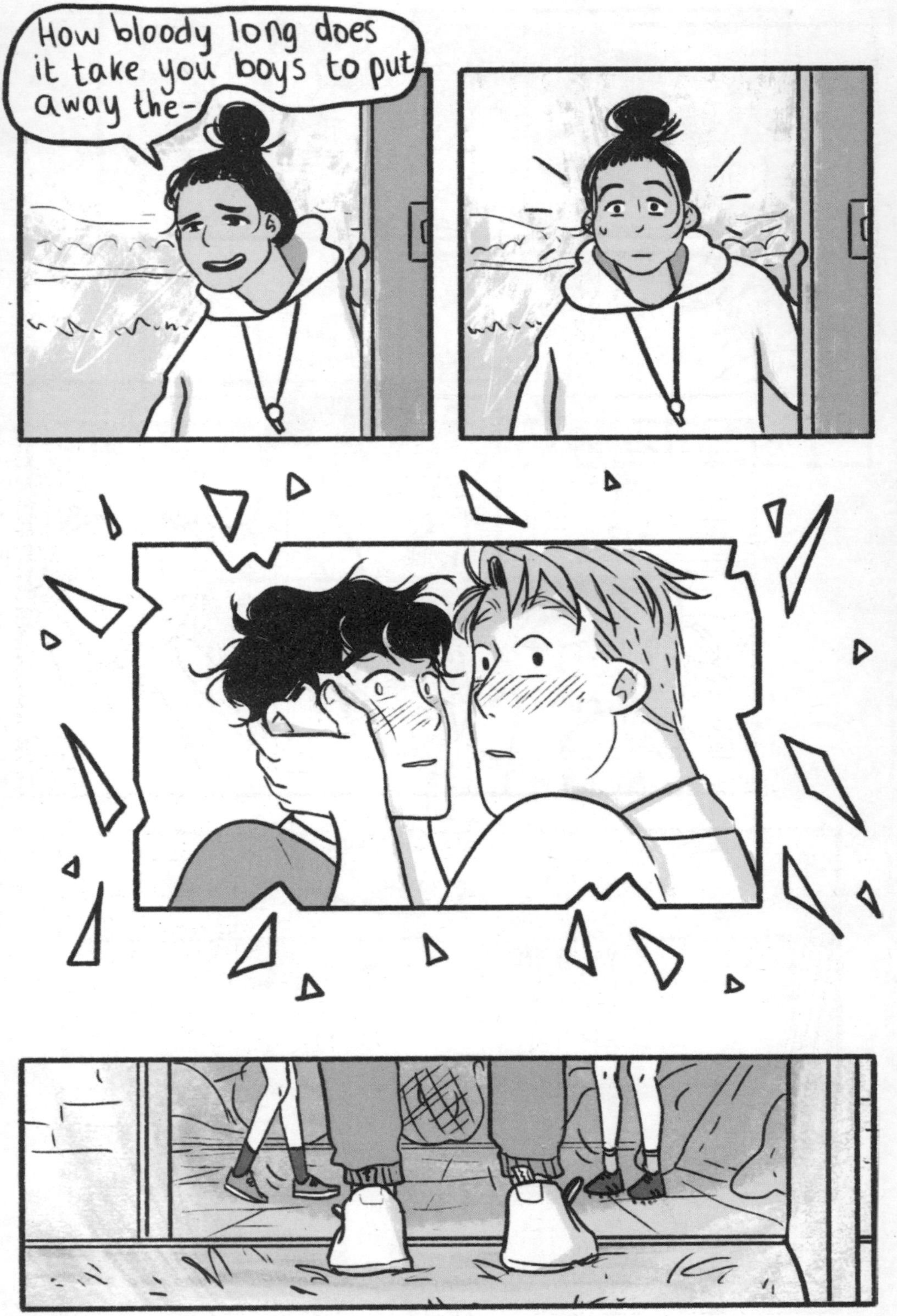
How bloody long does it take you boys to put away the-

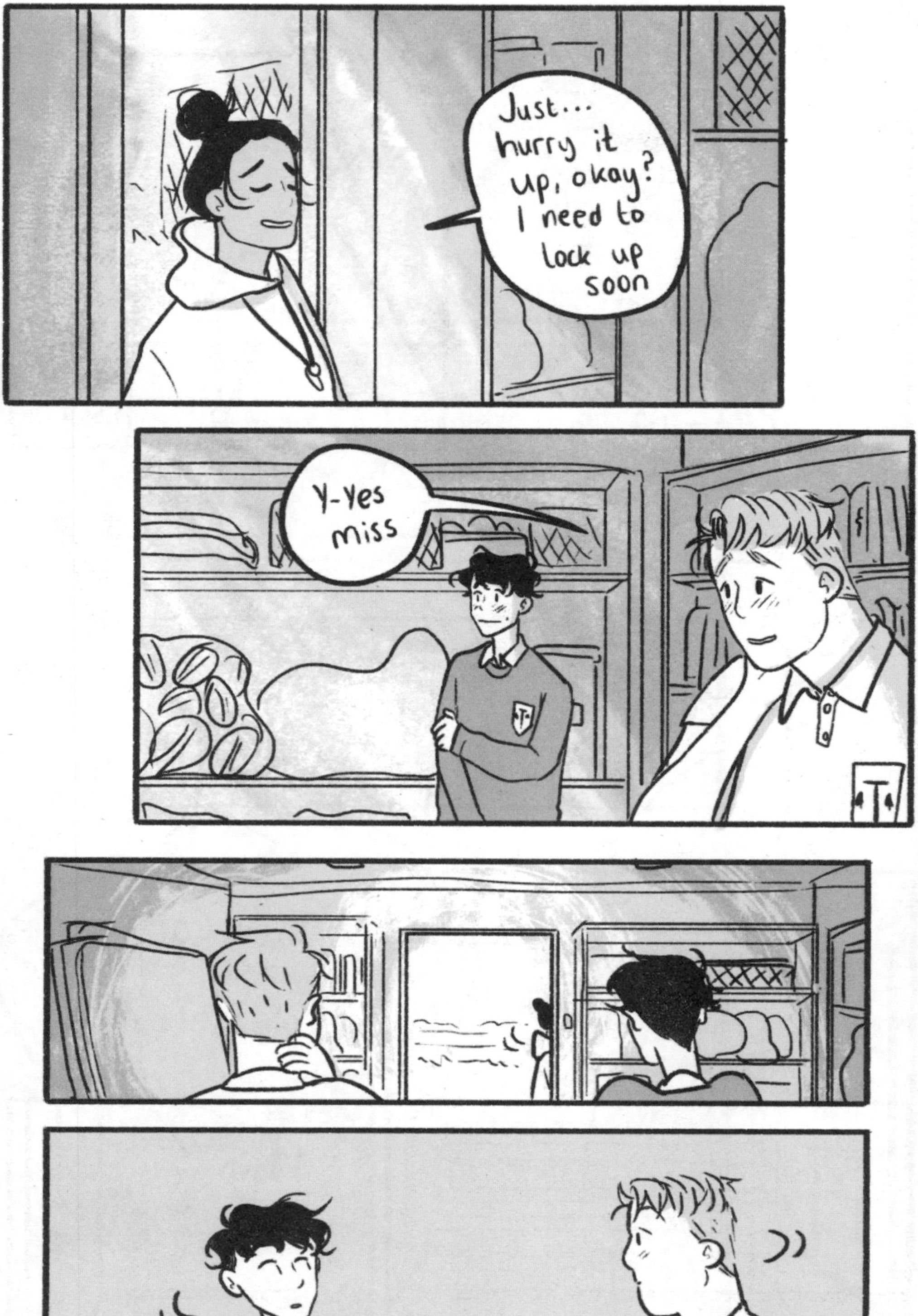
Just... hurry it up, okay? I need to lock up soon
Y-yes miss

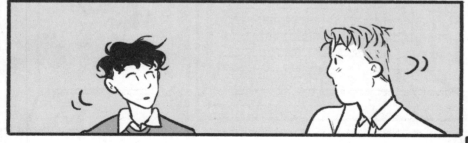

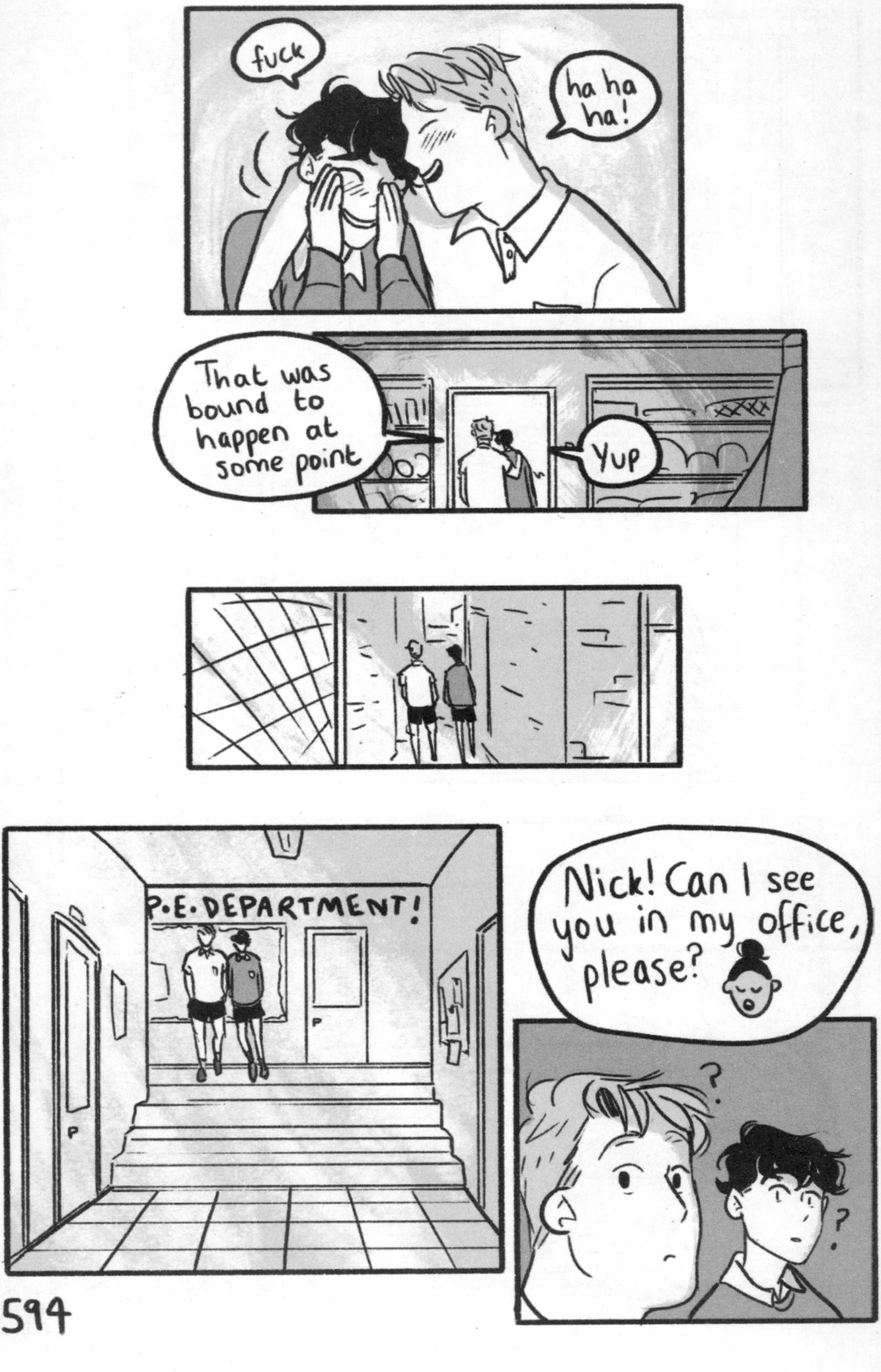
fuck
ha ha ha!
That was bound to happen at some point
Yup
P.E. DEPARTMENT!
Nick! Can I see you in my office, please?
?
?

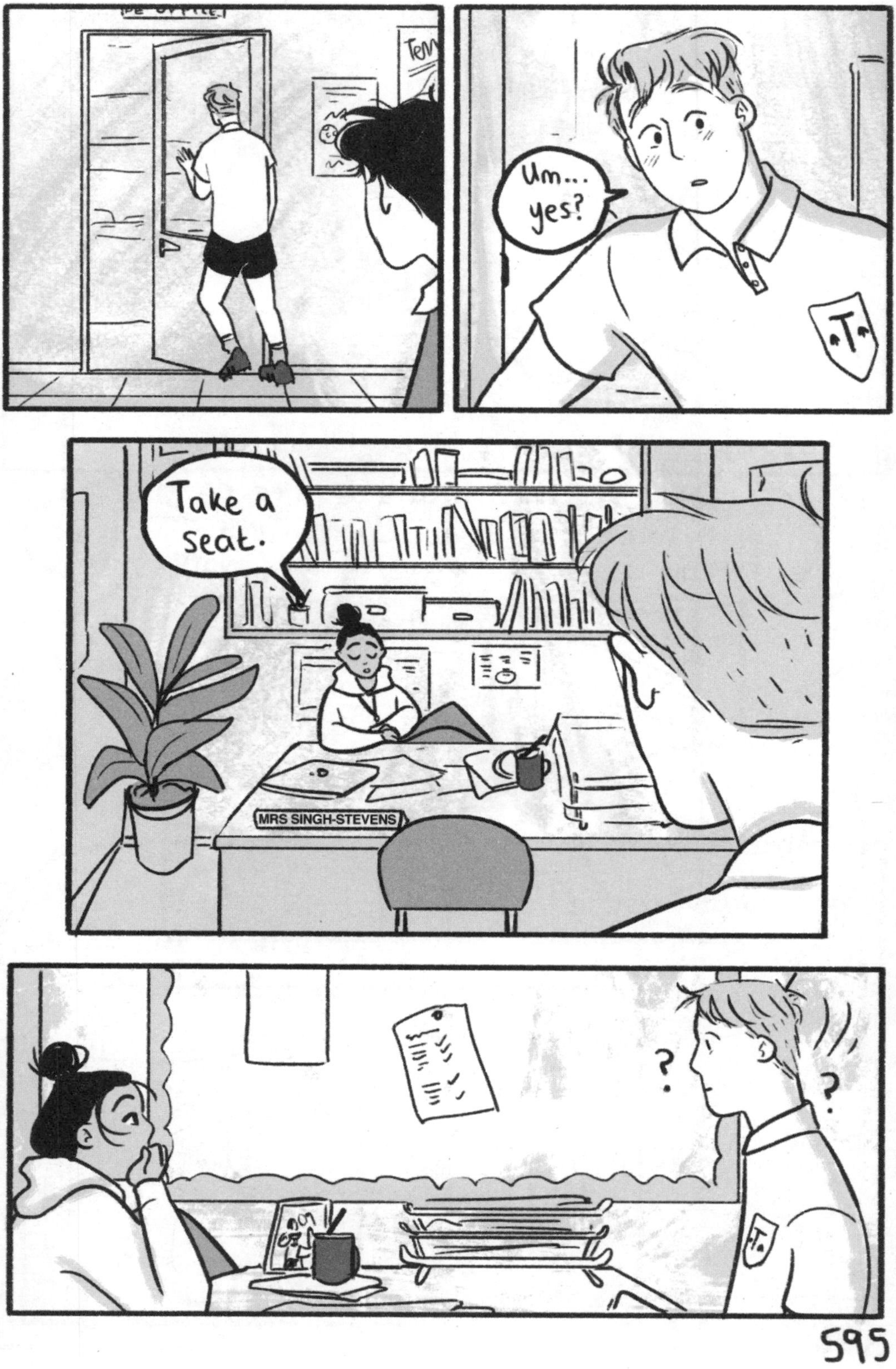
Um... yes?
Take a seat.
MRS SINGH-STEVENS
?
?

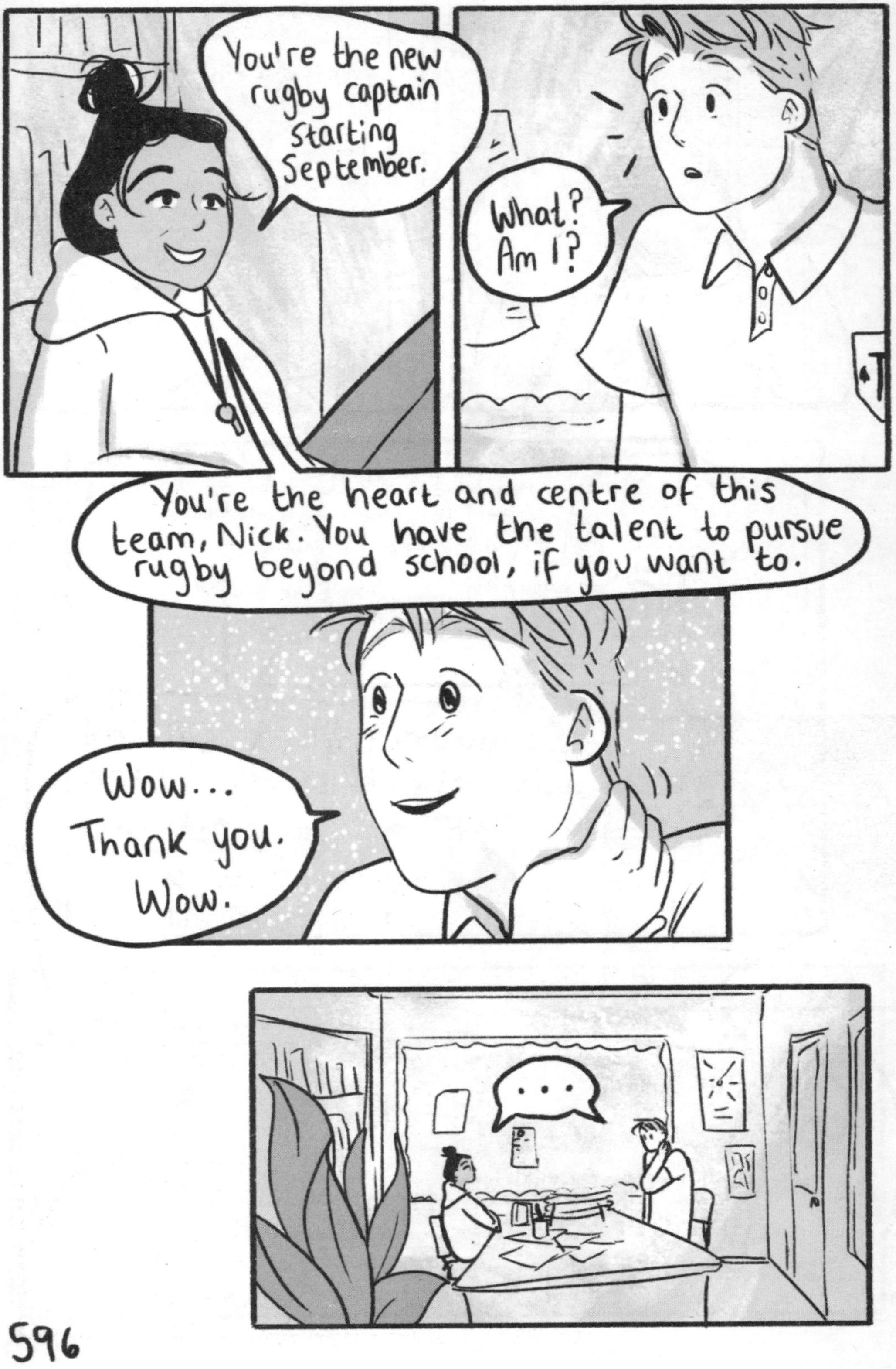
You're the new rugby captain starting September.
What? Am I?
You're the heart and centre of this team, Nick. You have the talent to pursue rugby beyond school, if you want to.
Wow... Thank you. Wow.
...

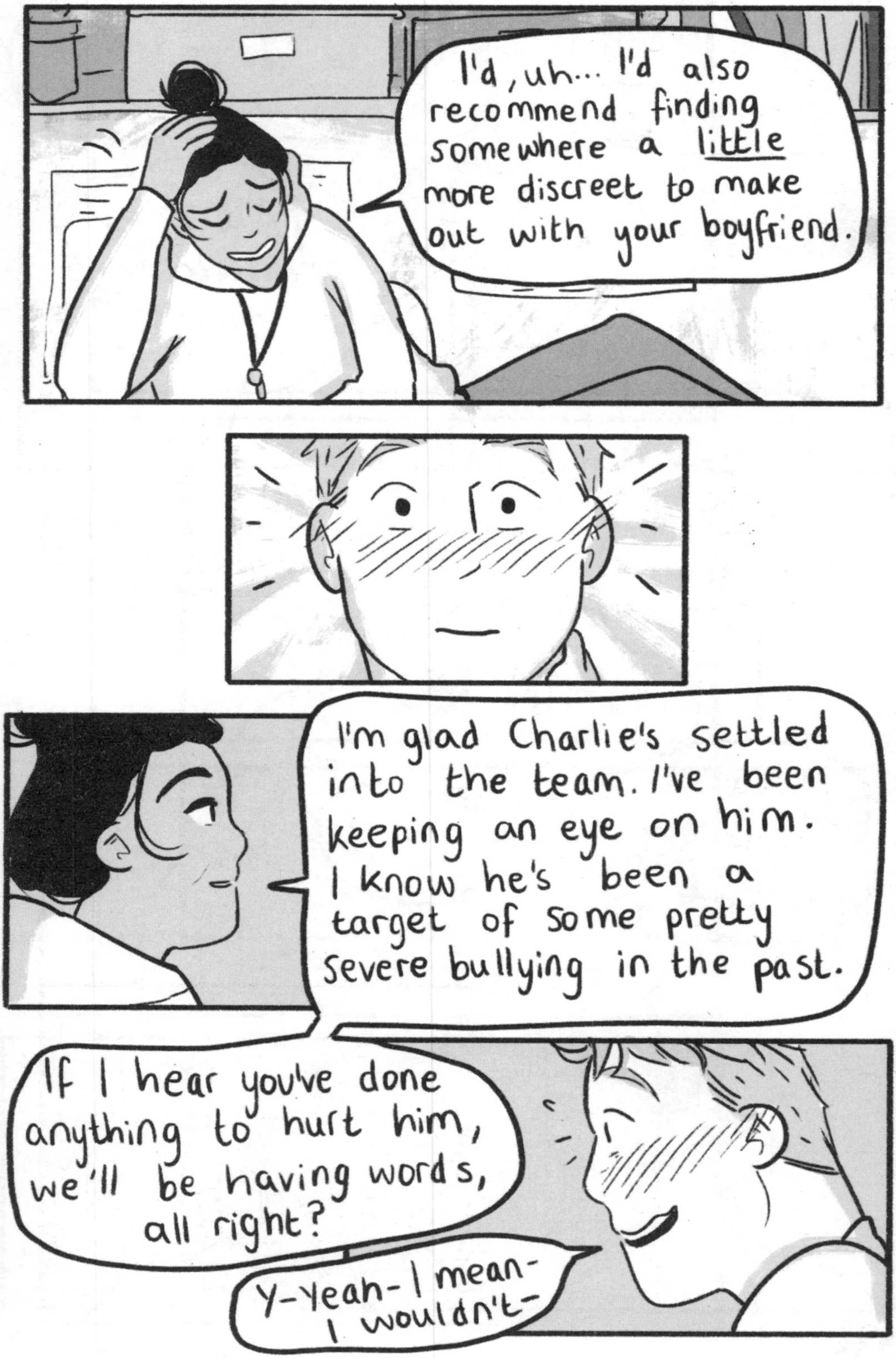
I'd, uh... I'd also recommend finding somewhere a little more discreet to make out with your boyfriend.
I'm glad Charlie's settled into the team. I've been keeping an eye on him. I know he's been a target of some pretty severe bullying in the past.
If I hear you've done anything to hurt him, we'll be having words, all right?
Y-Yeah- I mean- I wouldn't-

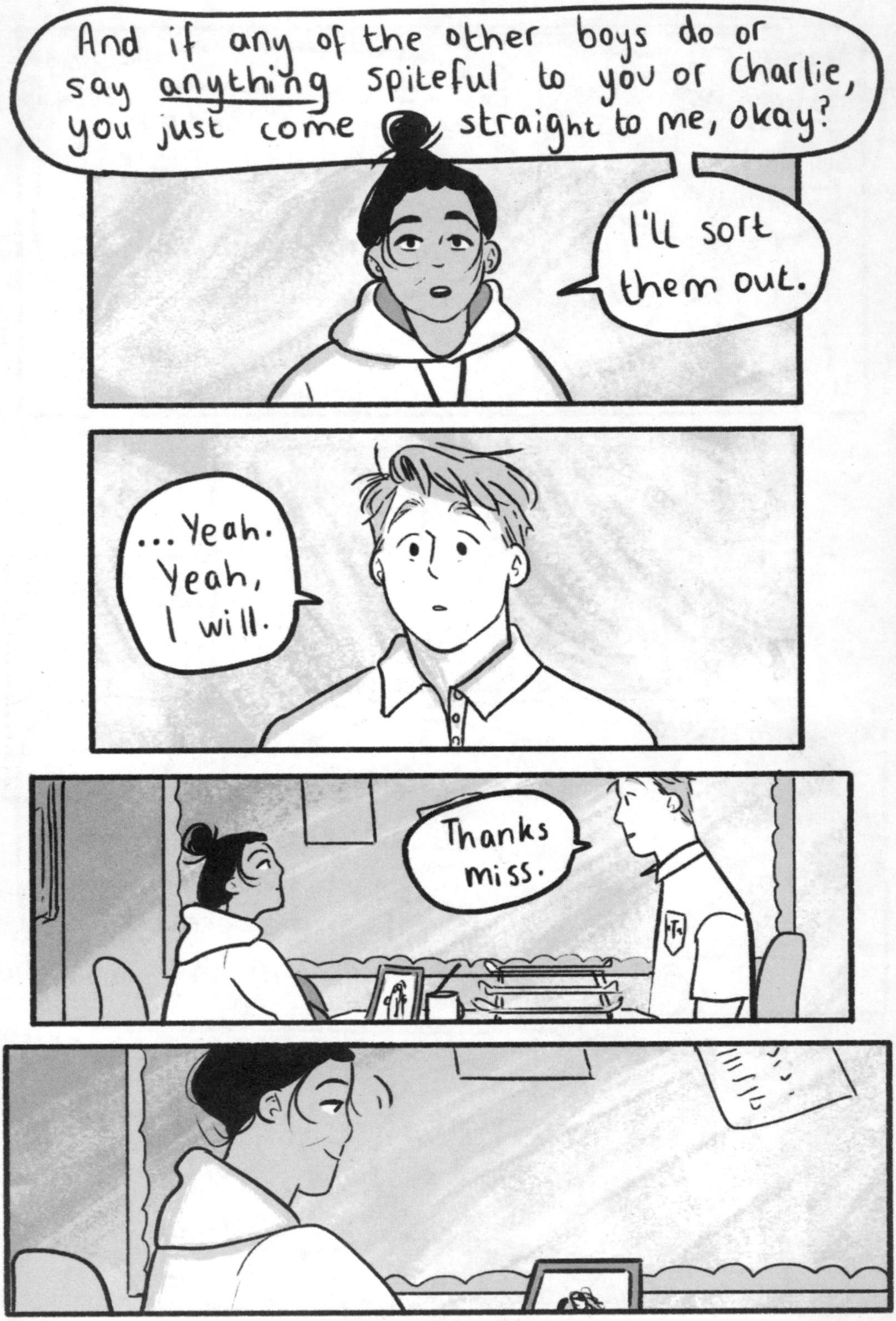
And if any of the other boys do or say anything spiteful to you or Charlie, you just come straight to me, okay?
I'll sort them out.
...Yeah. Yeah, I will.
Thanks miss.

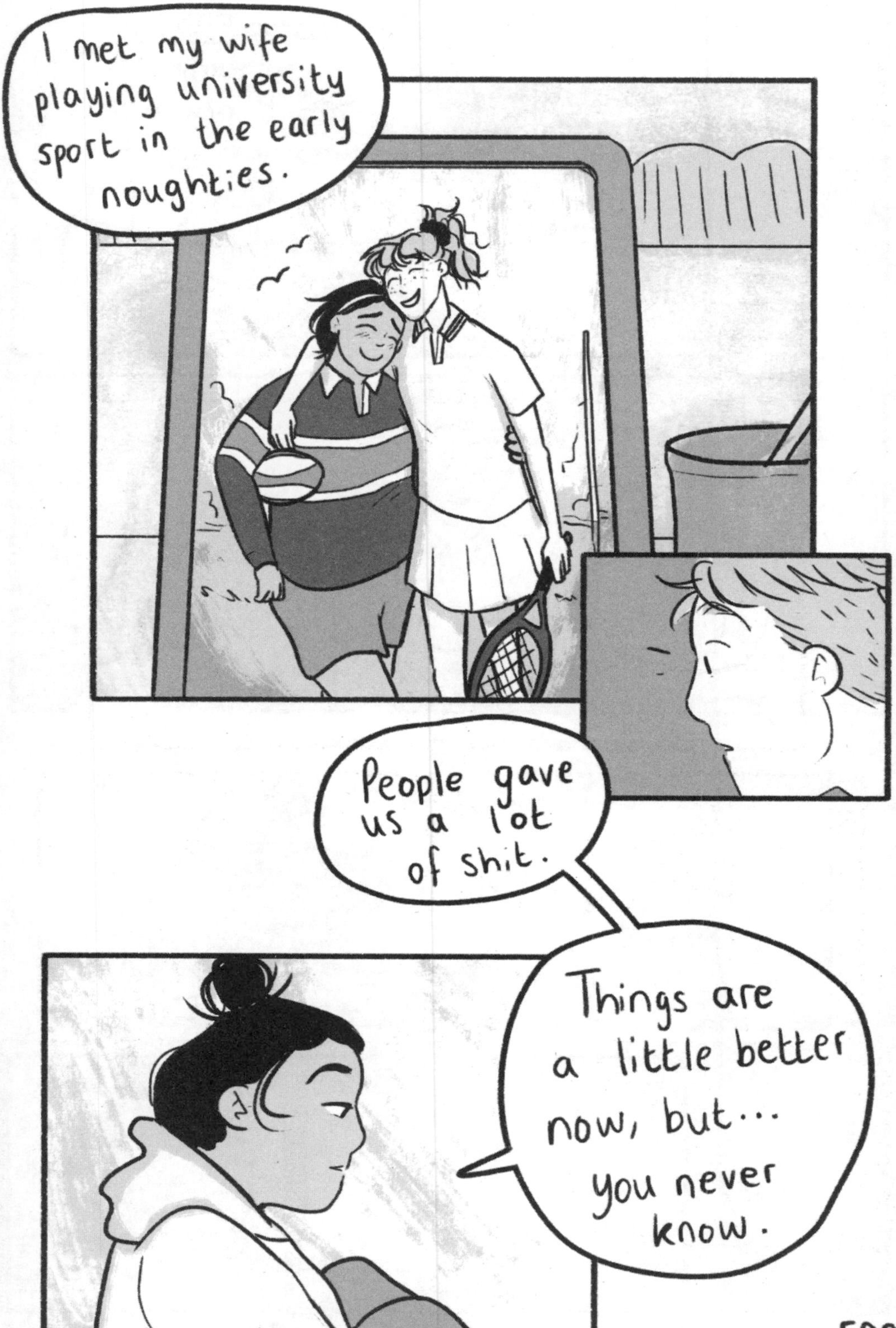
I met my wife playing university sport in the early noughties.
People gave us a lot of shit.
Things are a little better now, but... you never know.

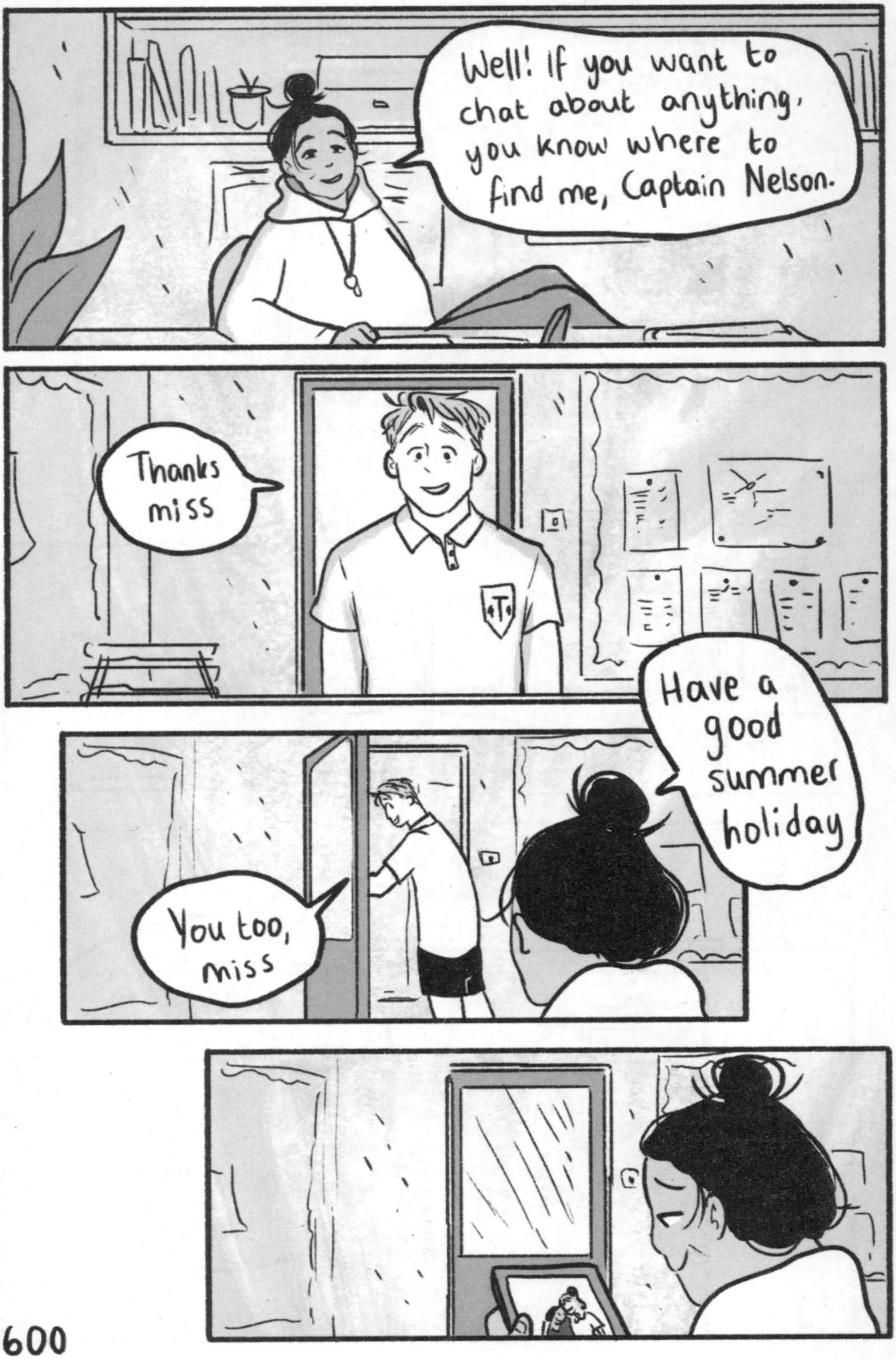
Well! If you want to chat about anything, you know where to find me, Captain Nelson.
Thanks miss
Have a good summer holiday
You too, miss

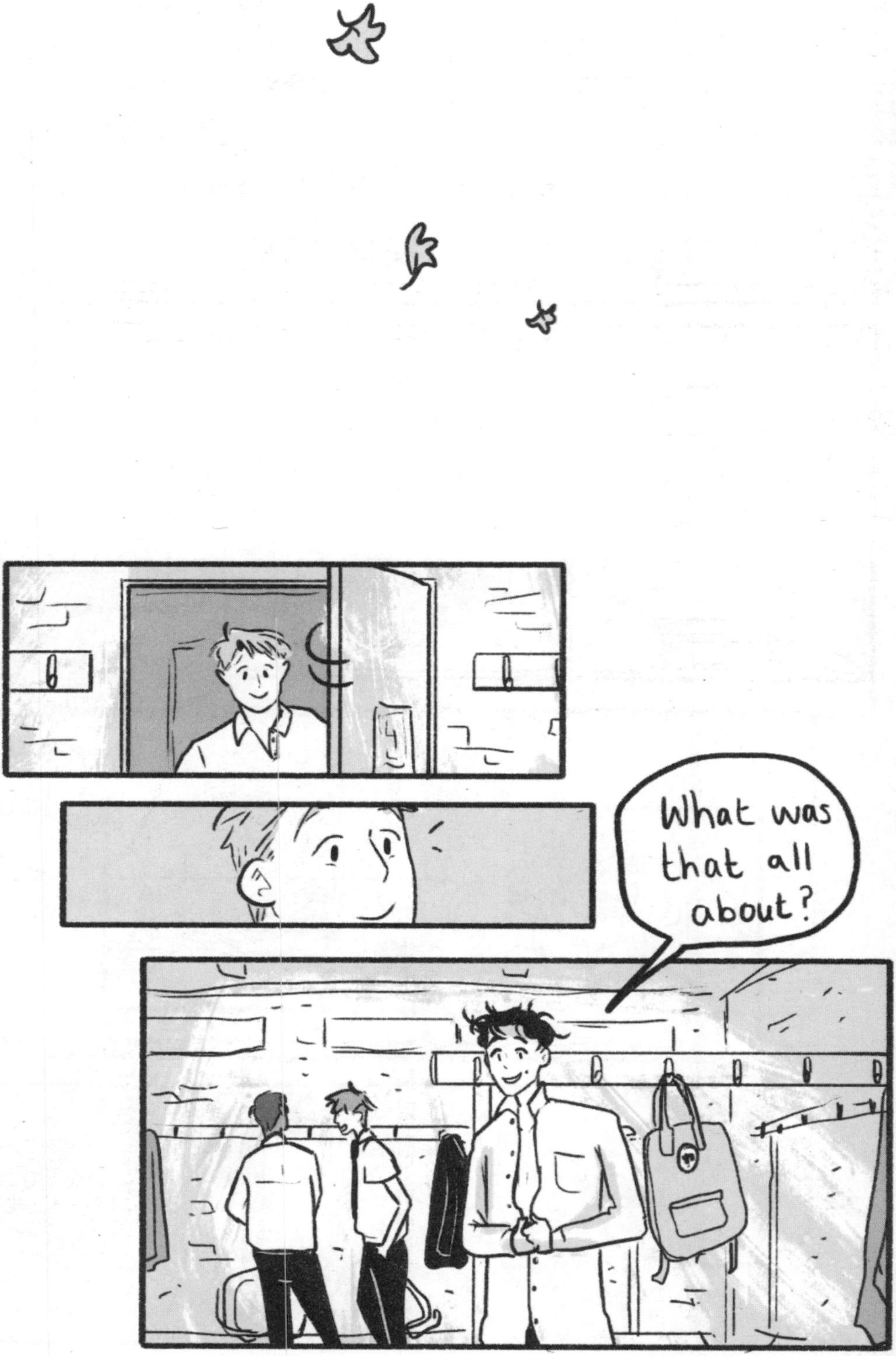
What was that all about?

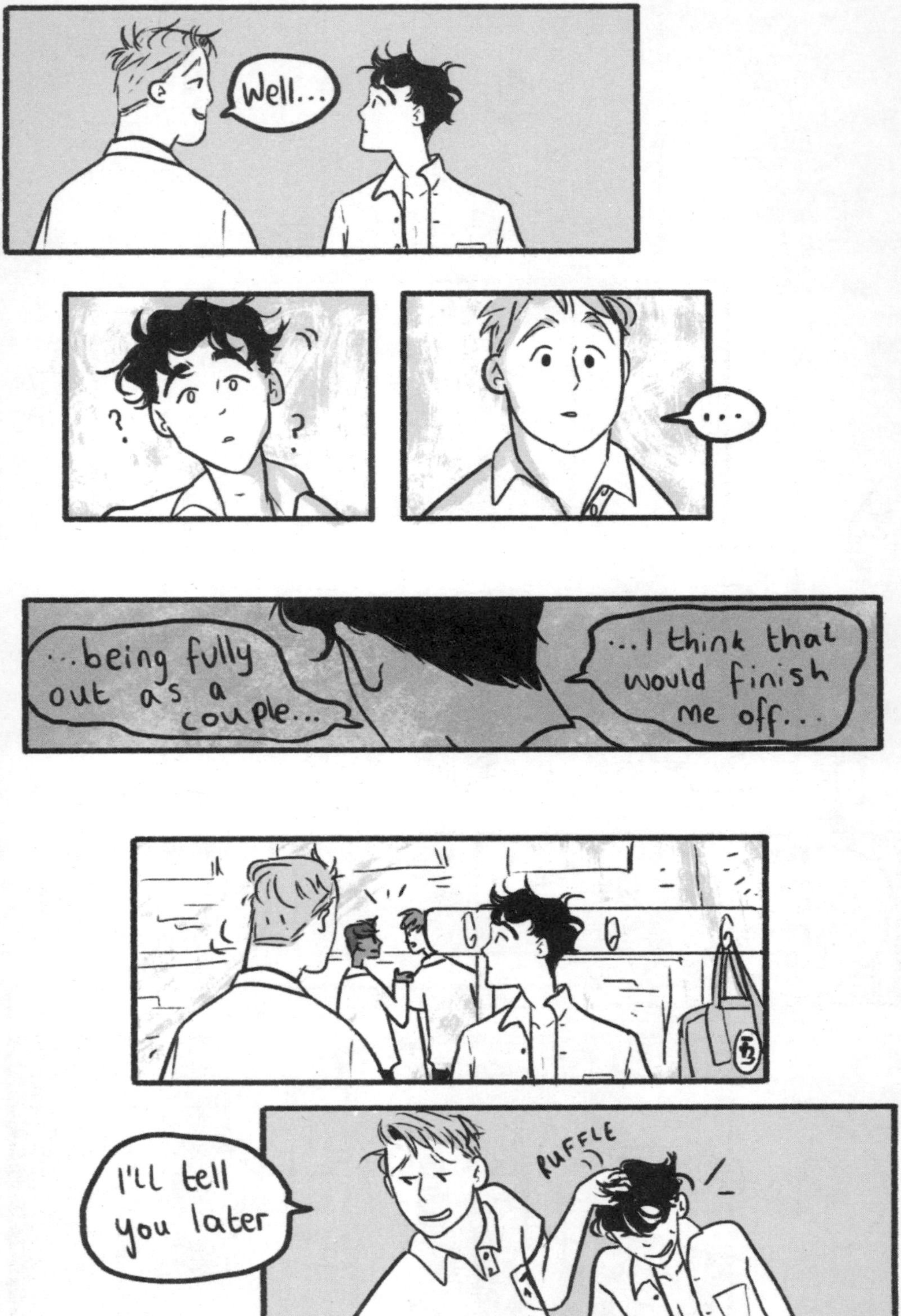
Well...
...
...being fully out as a couple...
...I think that would finish me off...
I'll tell you later
RUFFLE

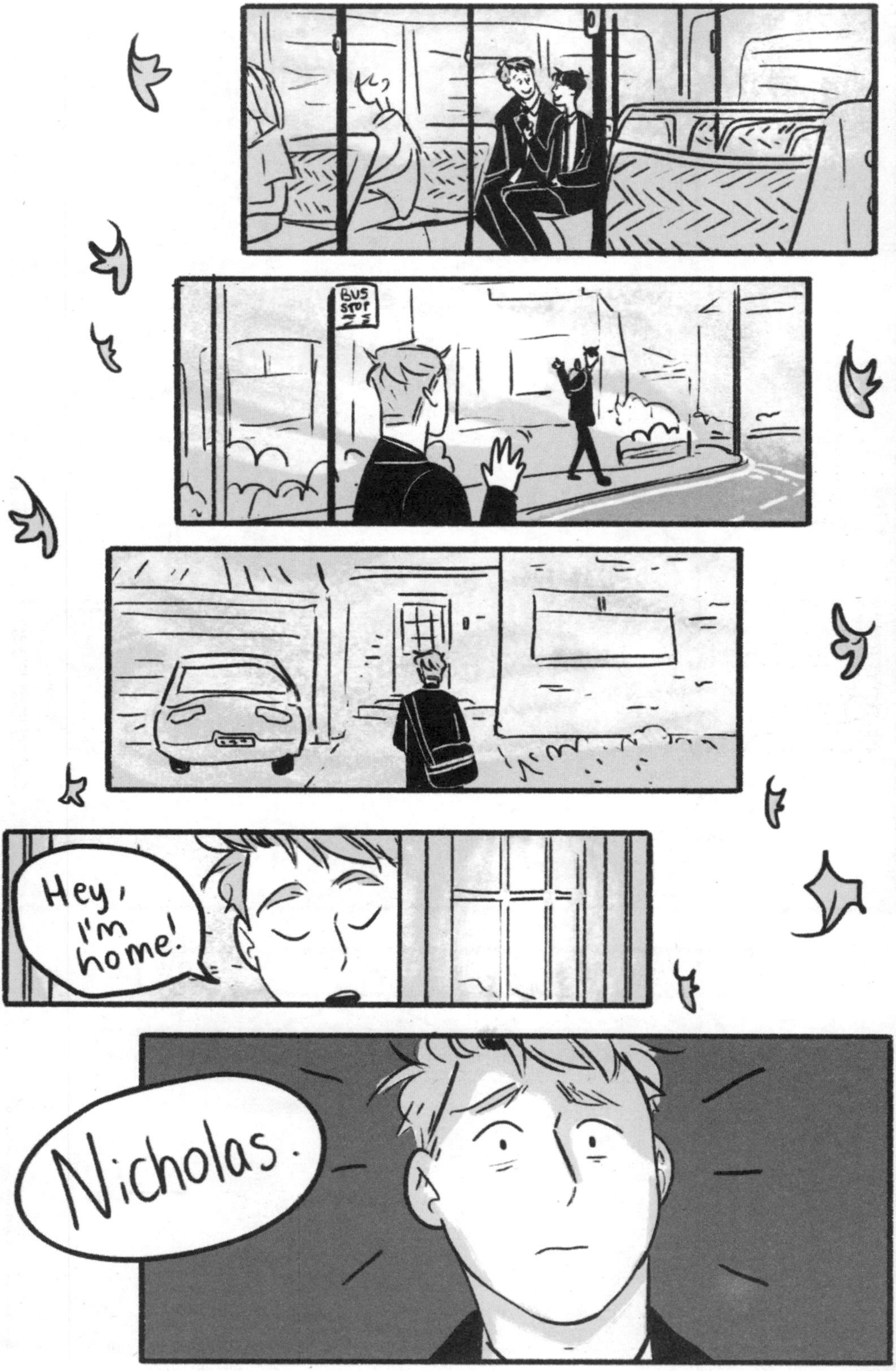
BUS STOP
Hey, I'm home!
Nicholas.

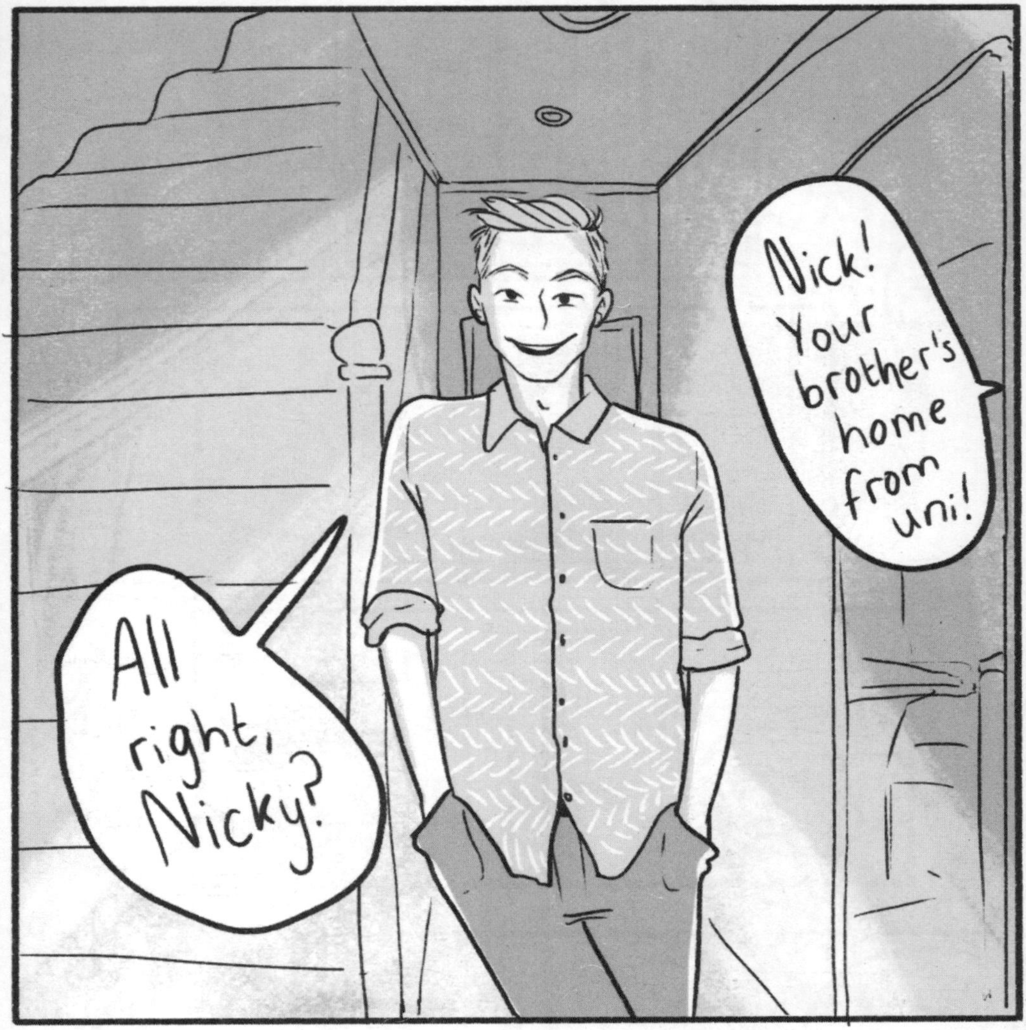
Nick! Your brother's home from uni!
All right, Nicky?

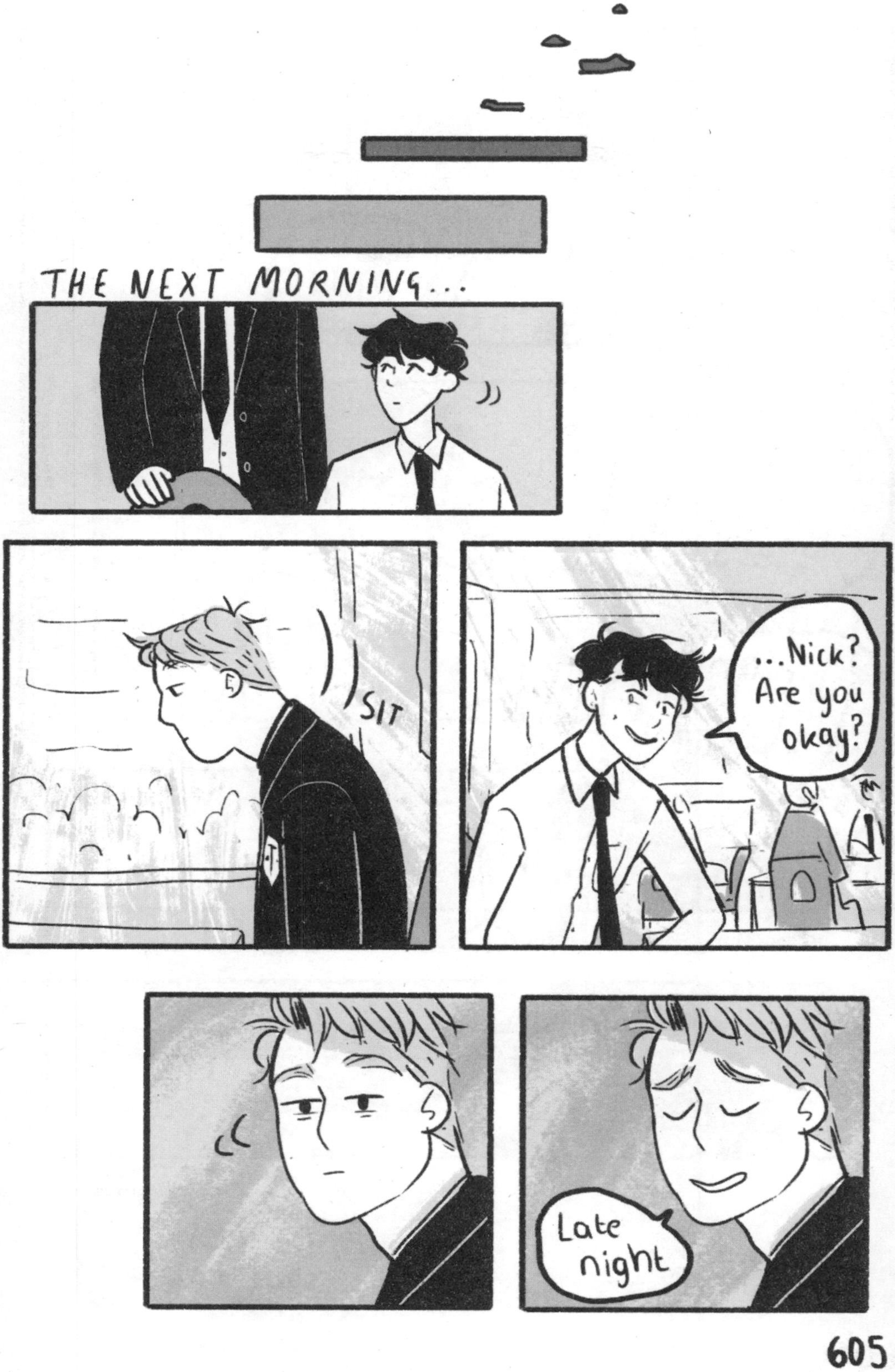
THE NEXT MORNING...
SIT
...Nick? Are you okay?
Late night

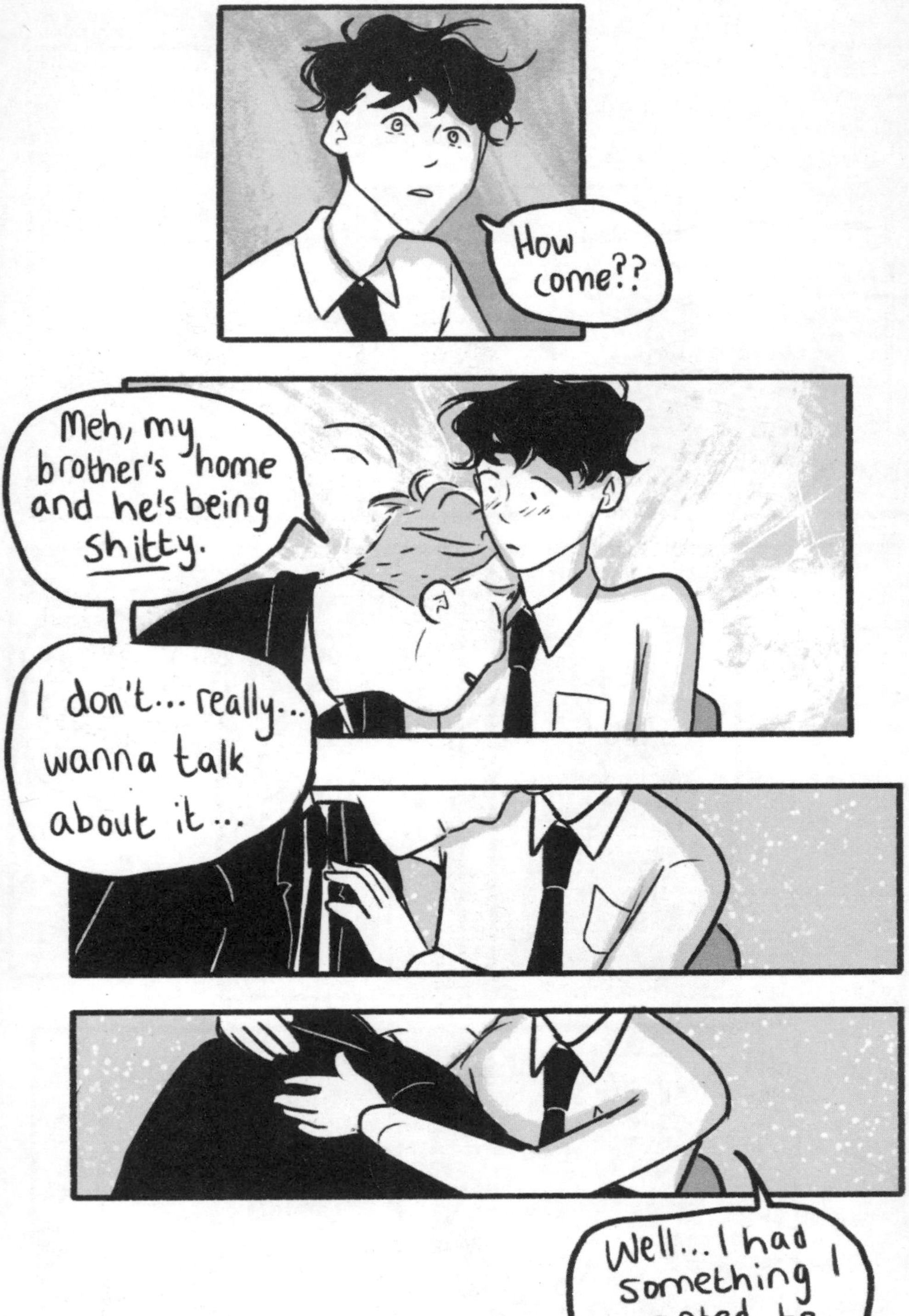
How come??
Meh, my brother's home and he's being shitty.
I don't... really... wanna talk about it...
Well... I had something I wanted to ask you...

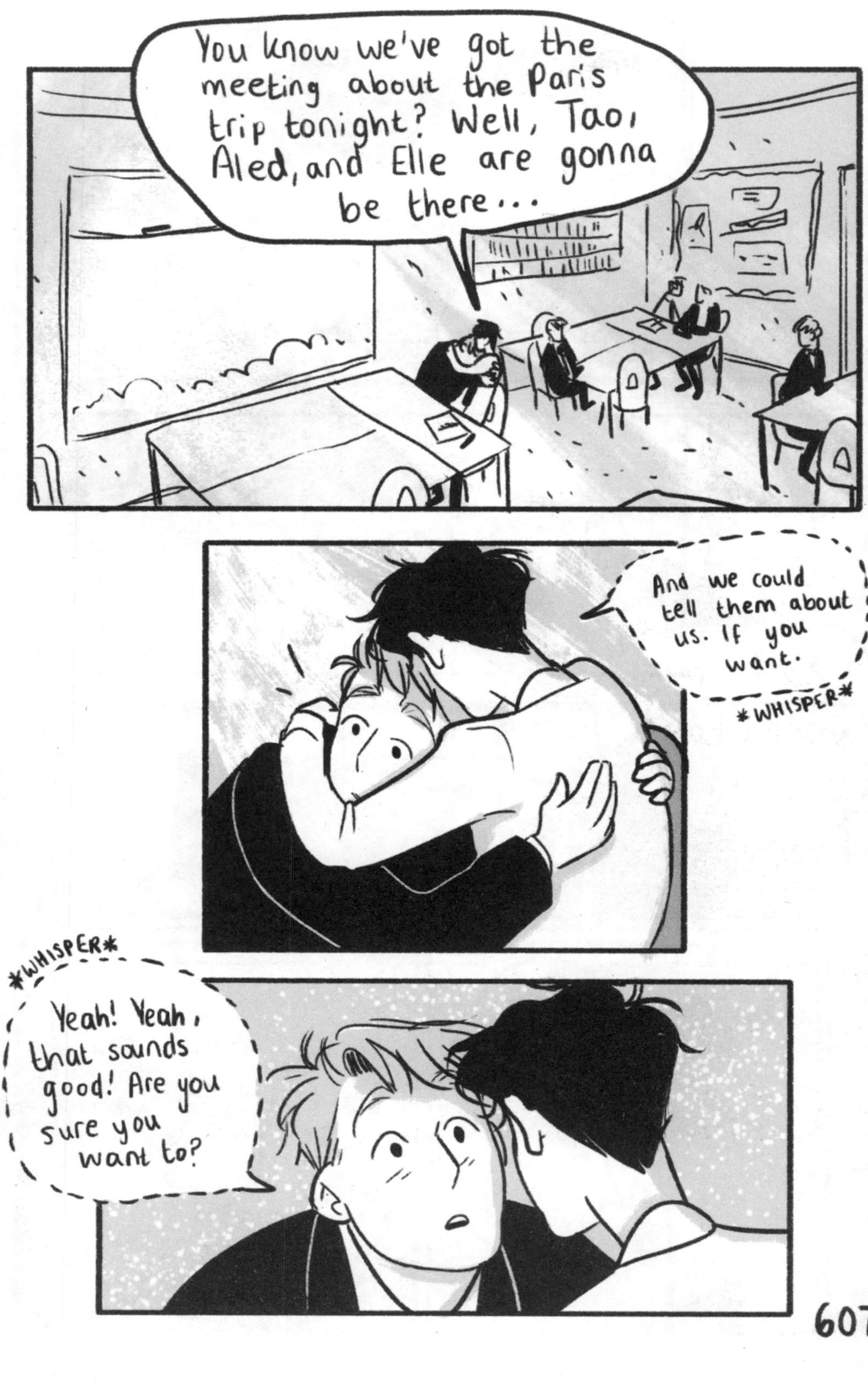
You know we've got the meeting about the Paris trip tonight? Well, Tao, Aled, and Elle are gonna be there...
And we could tell them about us. If you want.
WHISPER
WHISPER
Yeah! Yeah, that sounds good! Are you sure you want to?

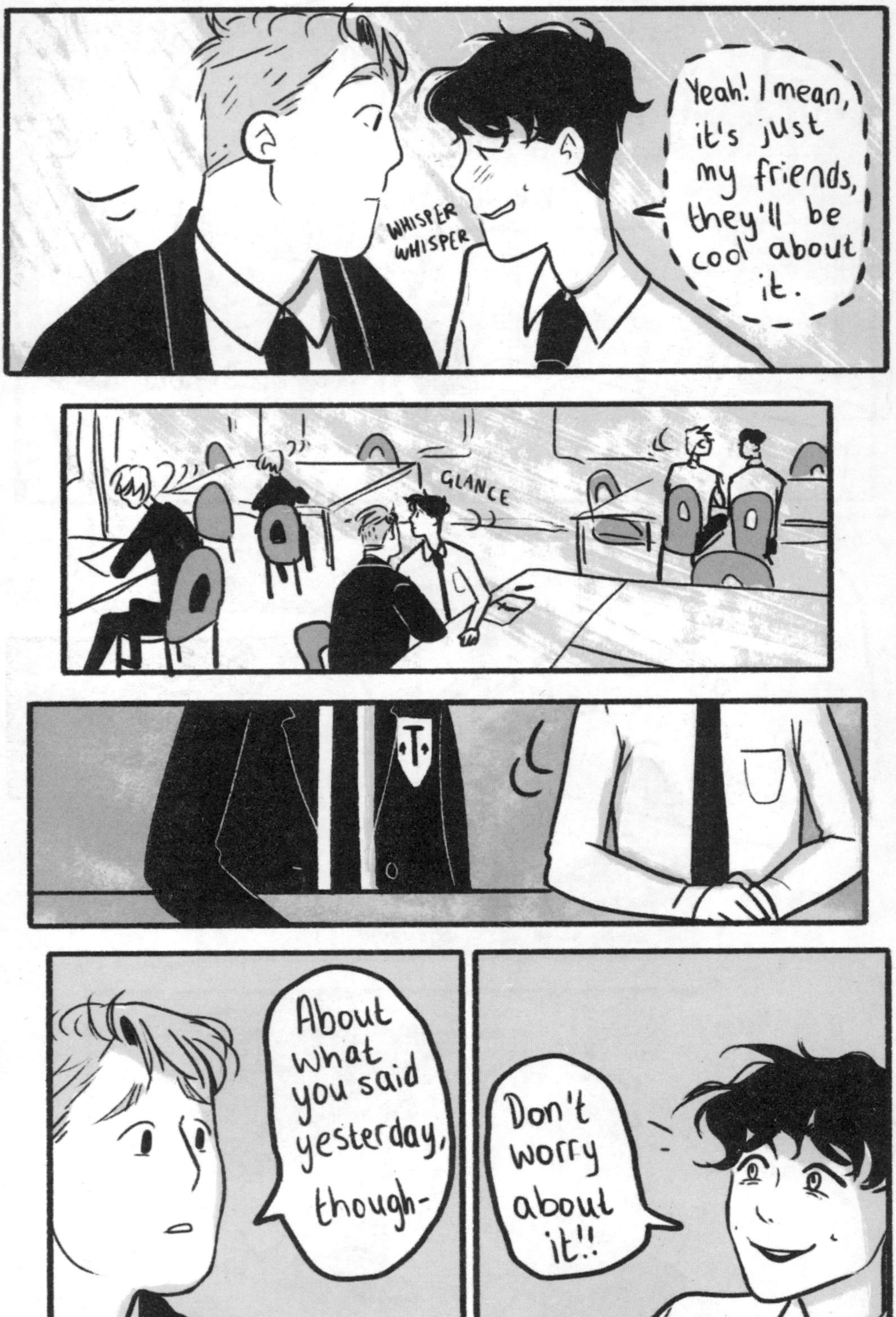
WHISPER WHISPER
Yeah! I mean, it's just my friends, they'll be cool about it.
GLANCE
About what you said yesterday, though-
Don't worry about it!!

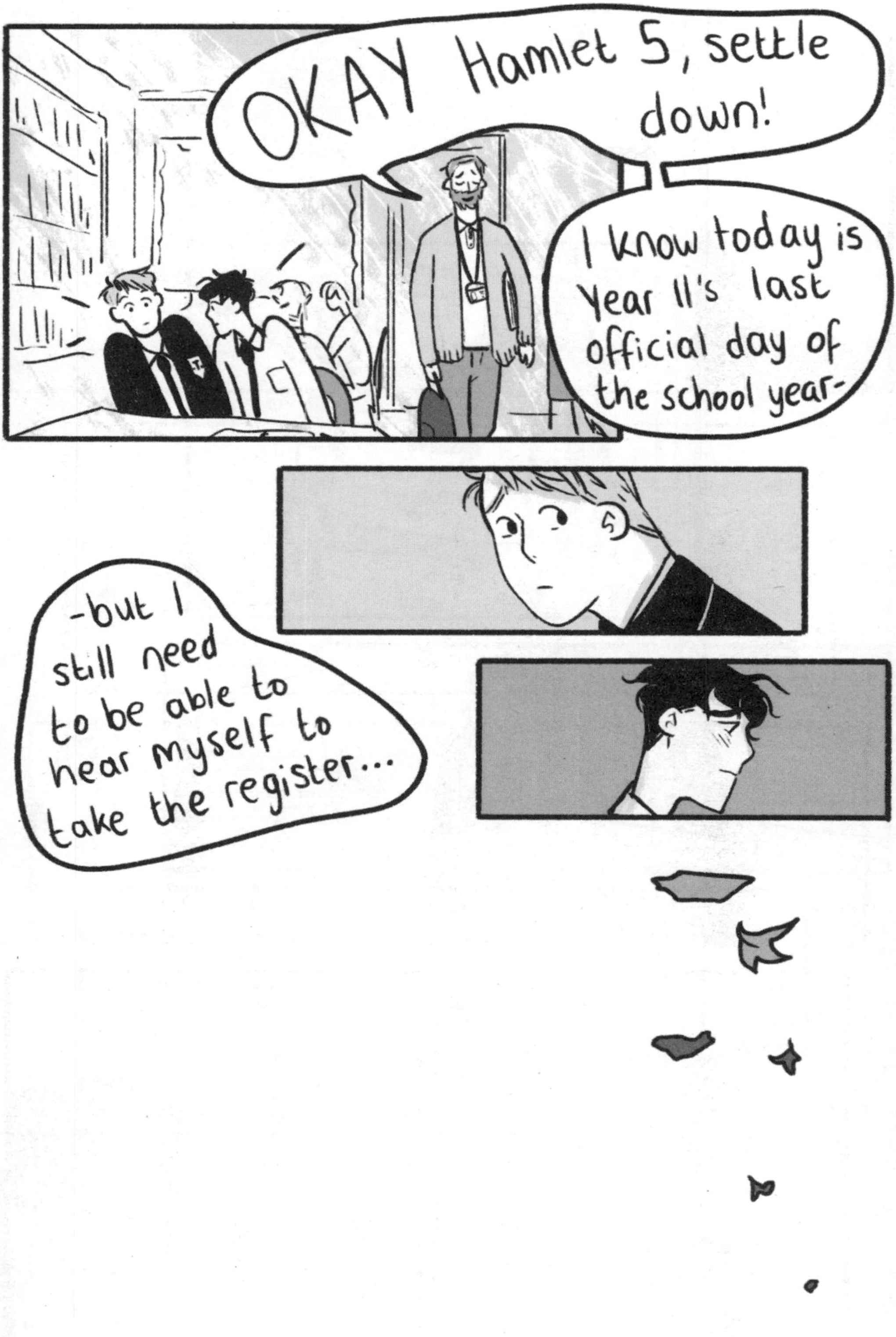
OKAY Hamlet 5, settle down!
I know today is Year 11's last official day of the school year-
-but I still need to be able to hear myself to take the register...

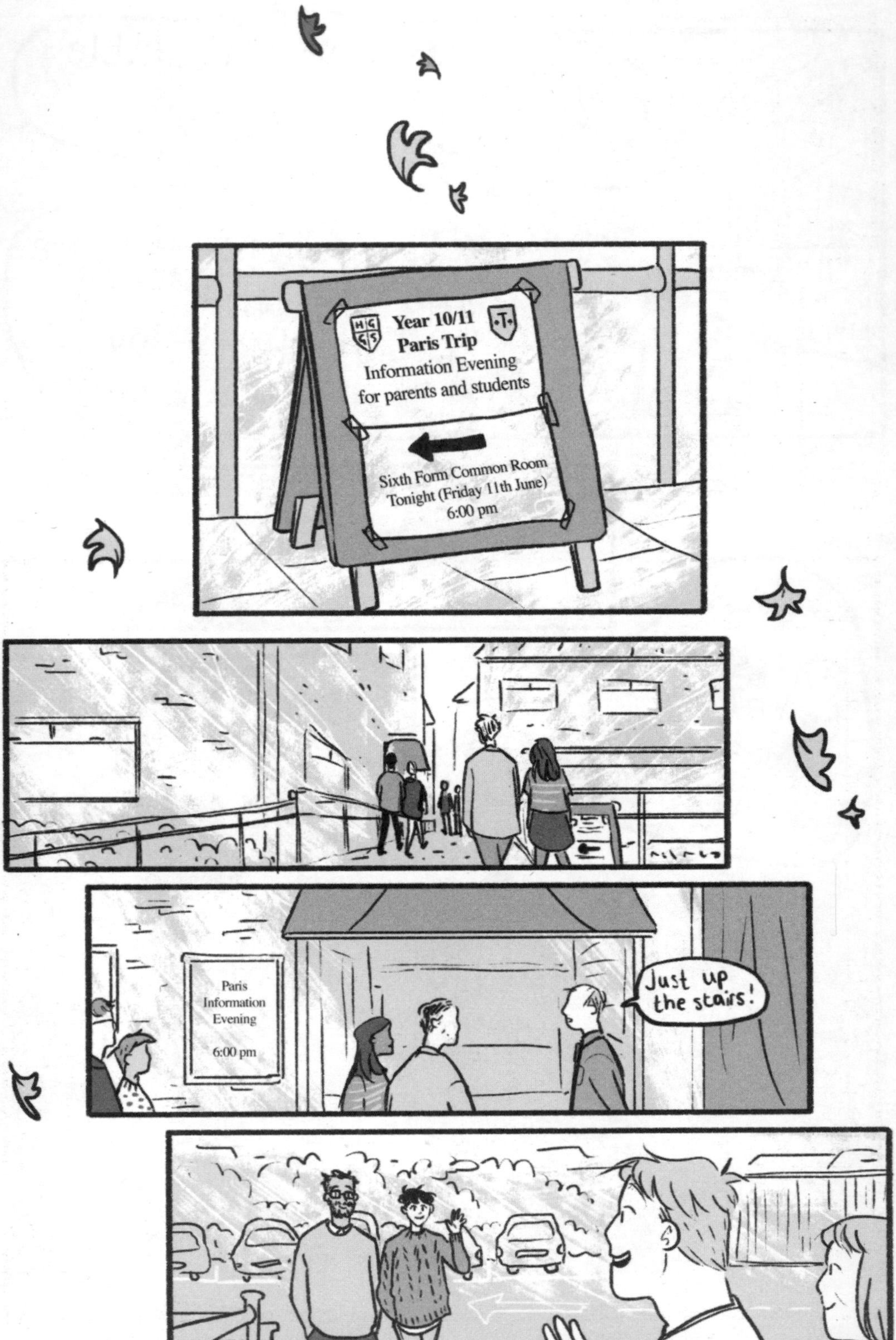
Year 10/11
Paris Trip
Information Evening
for parents and students
Sixth Form Common Room
Tonight (Friday 11th June)
6:00 pm
Paris
Information
Evening
6:00 pm
Just up the stairs!

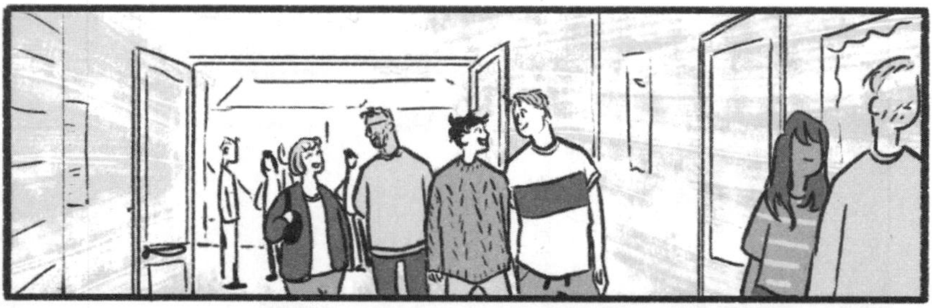

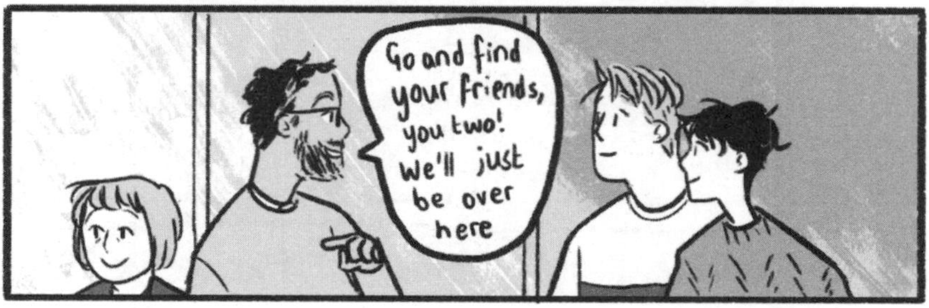
Go and find your friends, you two! We'll just be over here

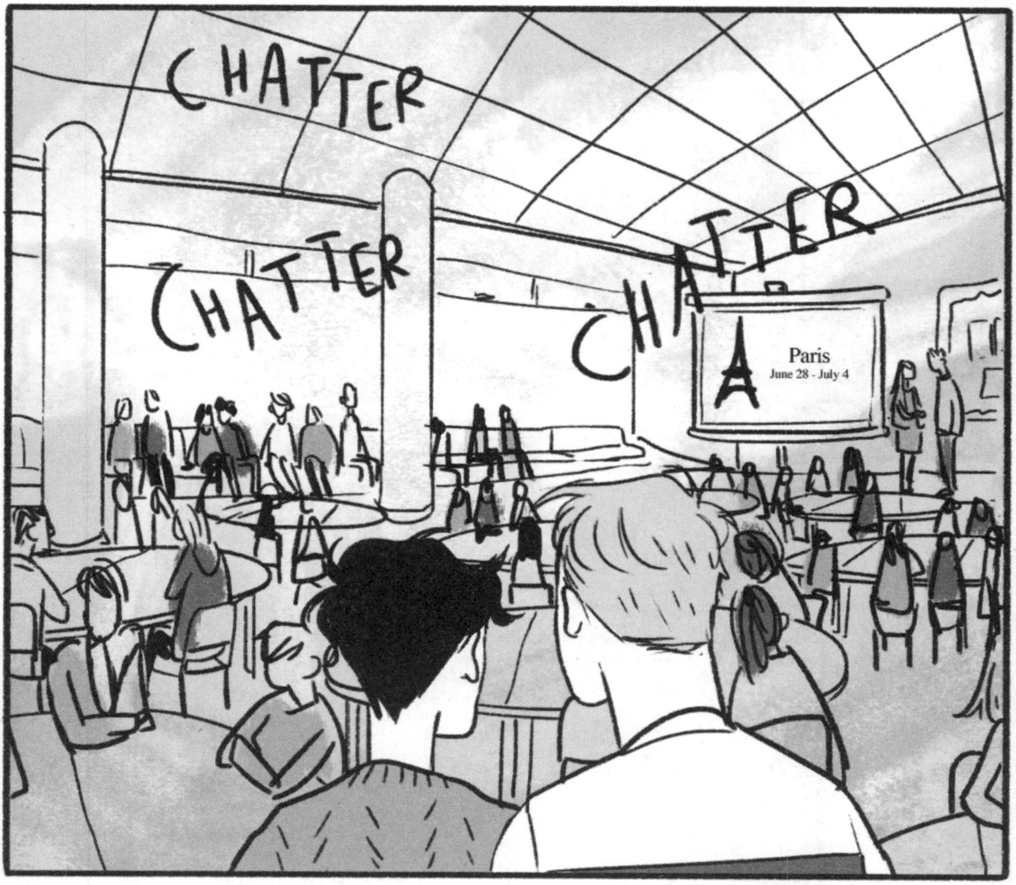
CHATTER
CHATTER
CHATTER
Paris
June 28 - July 4

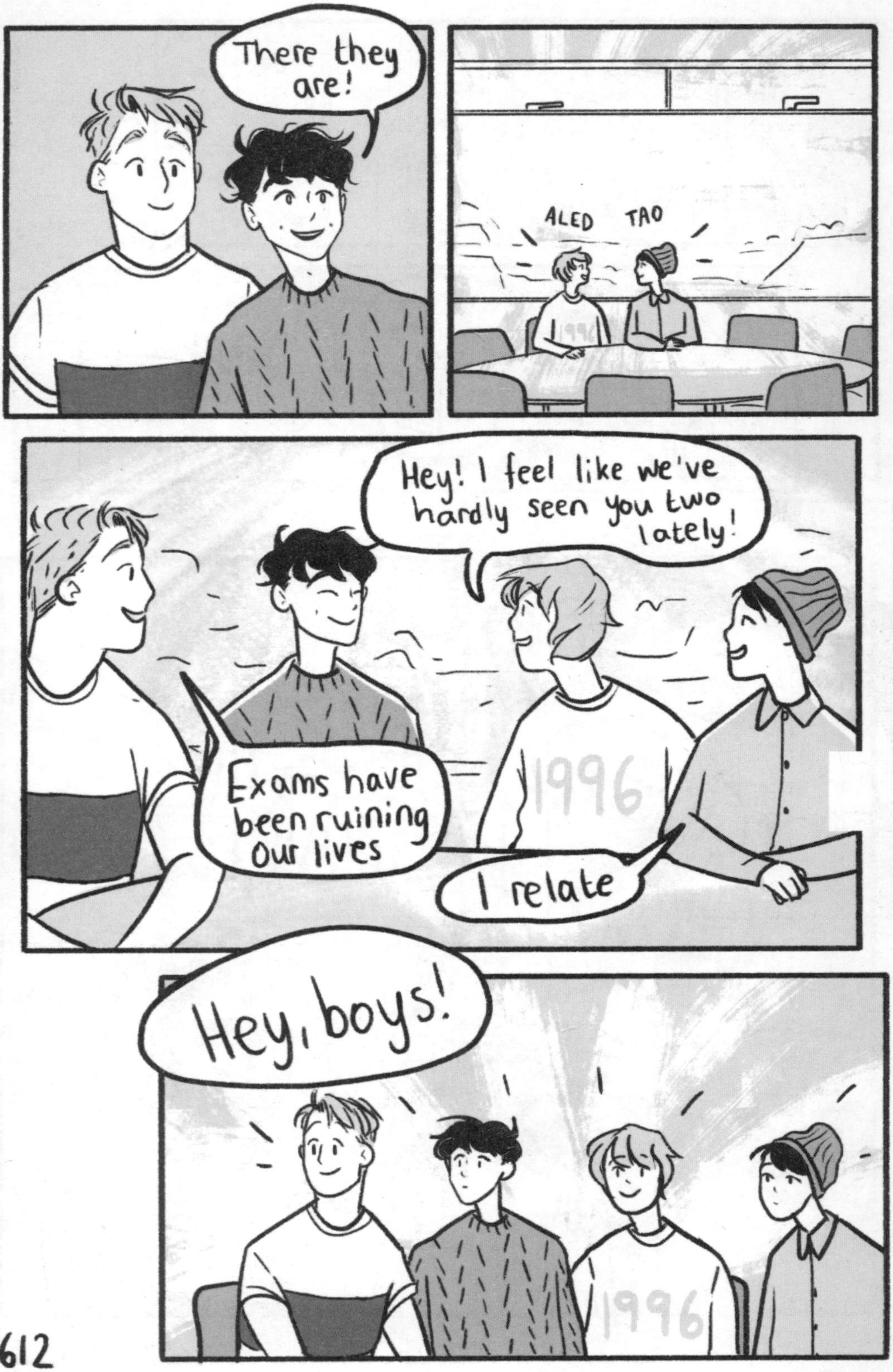
There they are!
ALED
TAO
Hey! I feel like we've hardly seen you two lately!
Exams have been ruining our lives
I relate
Hey, boys!
1996

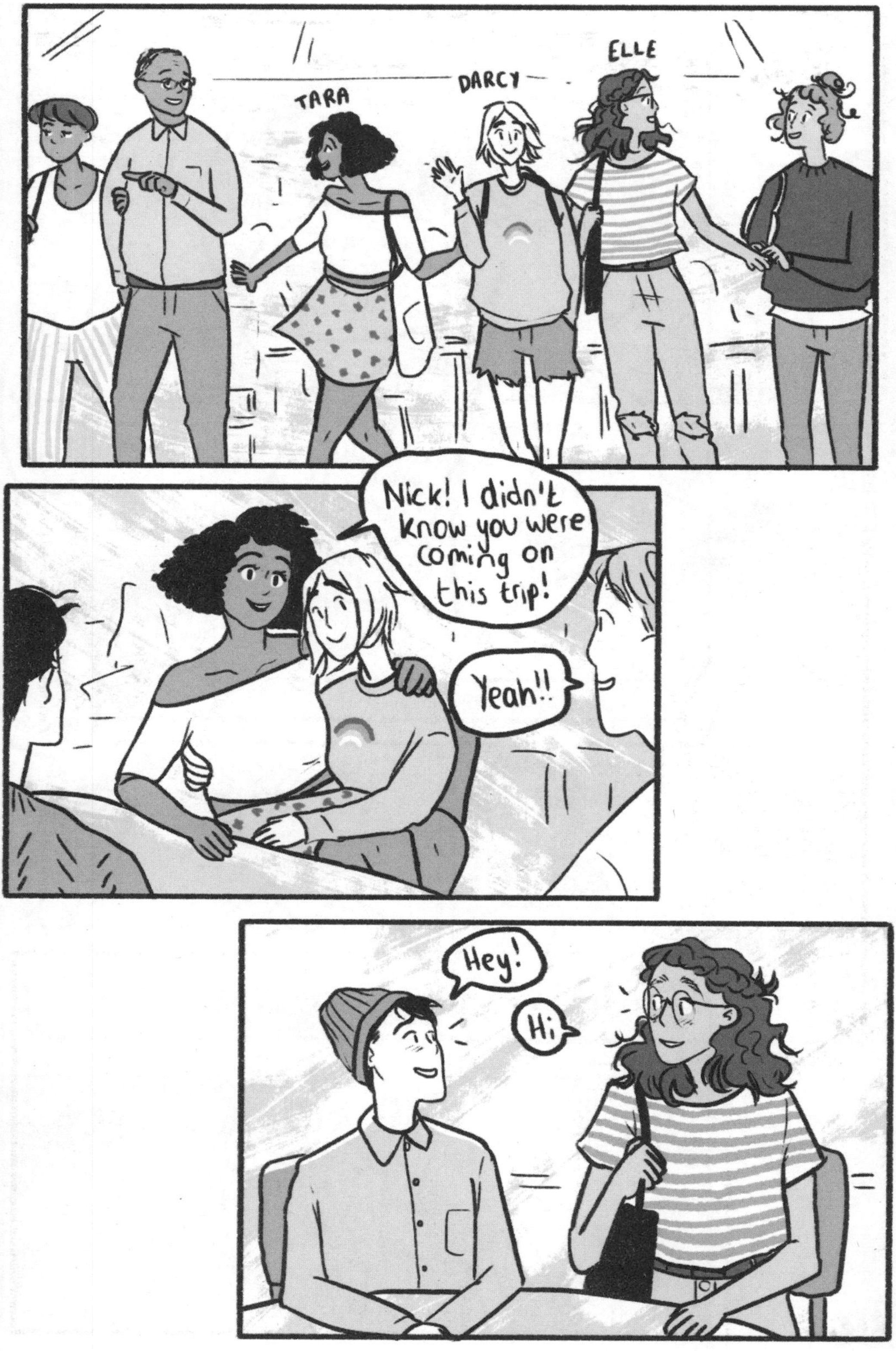

TARA
DARCY
ELLE
Nick! I didn't know you were coming on this trip!
Yeah!!
Hey!
Hi

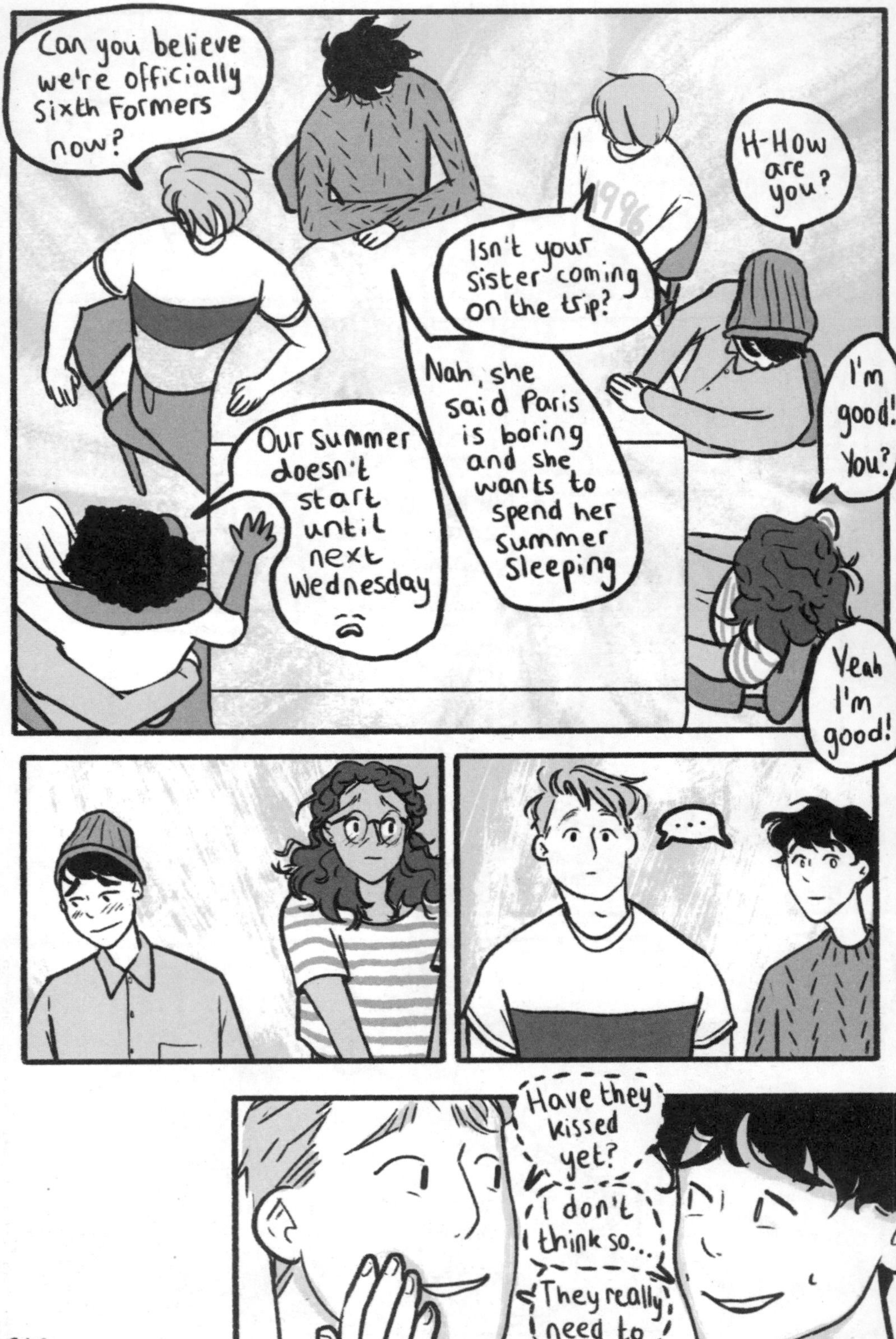
Can you believe we're officially Sixth Formers now?
Isn't your sister coming on the trip?
H-How are you?
Nah, she said Paris is boring and she wants to spend her summer sleeping
Our summer doesn't start until next Wednesday
I'm good! You?
Yeah I'm good!
...
Have they kissed yet?
I don't think so...
They really need to

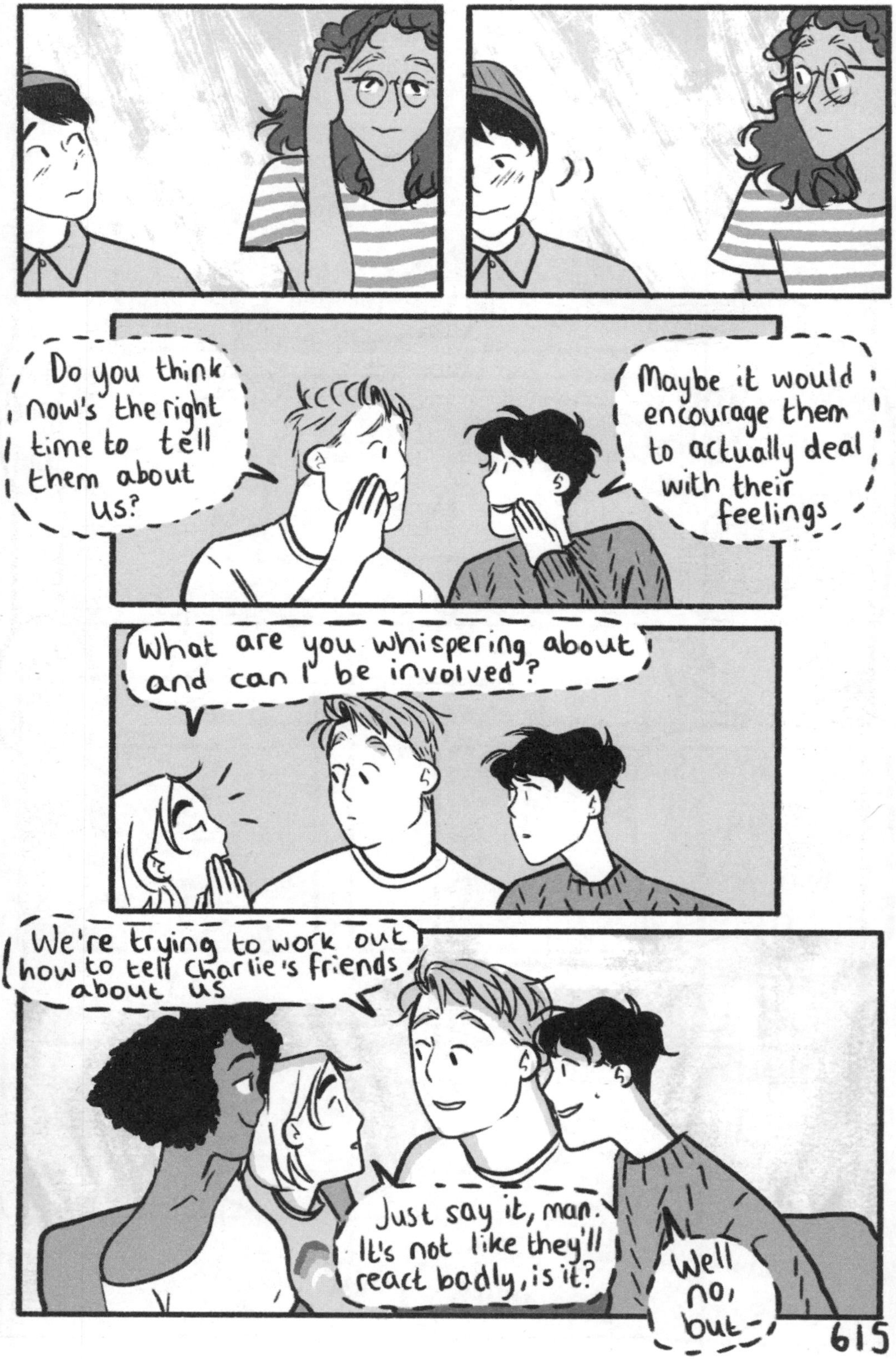
Do you think now's the right time to tell them about us?
Maybe it would encourage them to actually deal with their feelings
What are you whispering about and can I be involved?
We're trying to work out how to tell Charlie's friends about us
Just say it, man. It's not like they'll react badly, is it?
Well no, but-

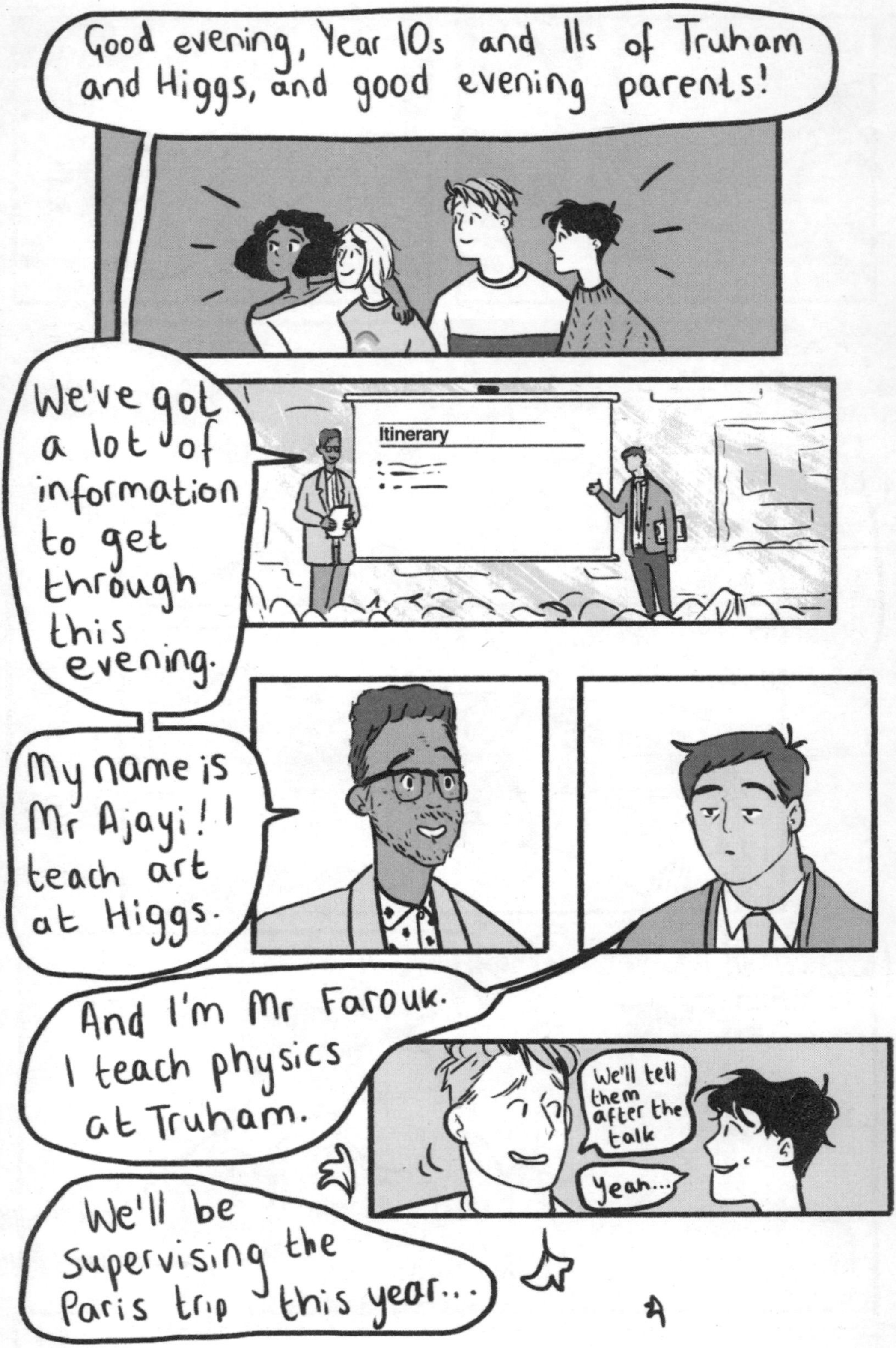
Good evening, Year 10s and 11s of Truham and Higgs, and good evening parents!
Itinerary
We've got a lot of information to get through this evening.
My name is Mr Ajayi! I teach art at Higgs.
And I'm Mr Farouk. I teach physics at Truham.
We'll tell them after the talk
Yeah...
We'll be supervising the Paris trip this year...

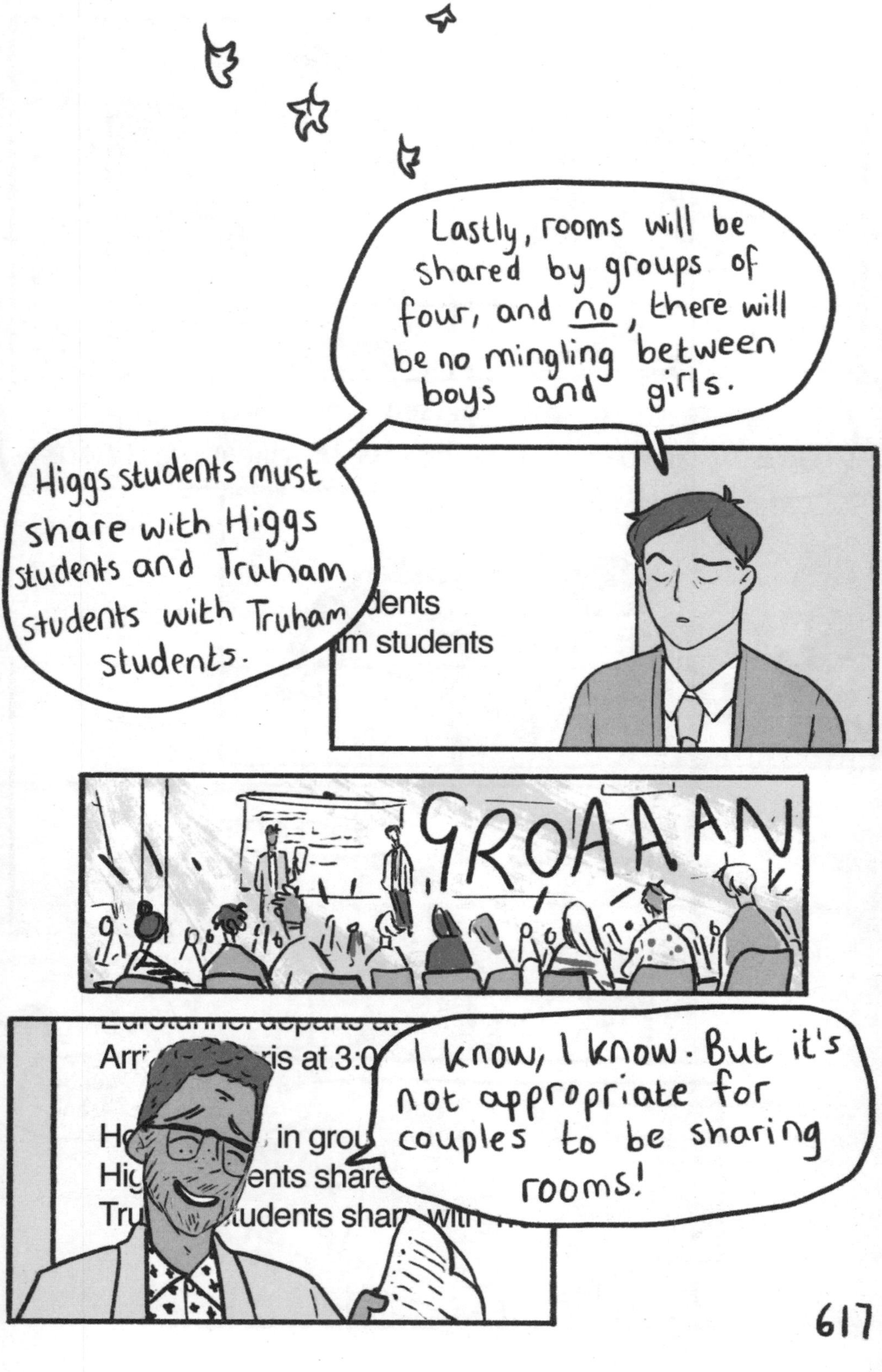
Lastly, rooms will be shared by groups of four, and no, there will be no mingling between boys and girls.
Higgs students must share with Higgs students and Truham students with Truham students.
GROAAAN
I know, I know. But it's not appropriate for couples to be sharing rooms!

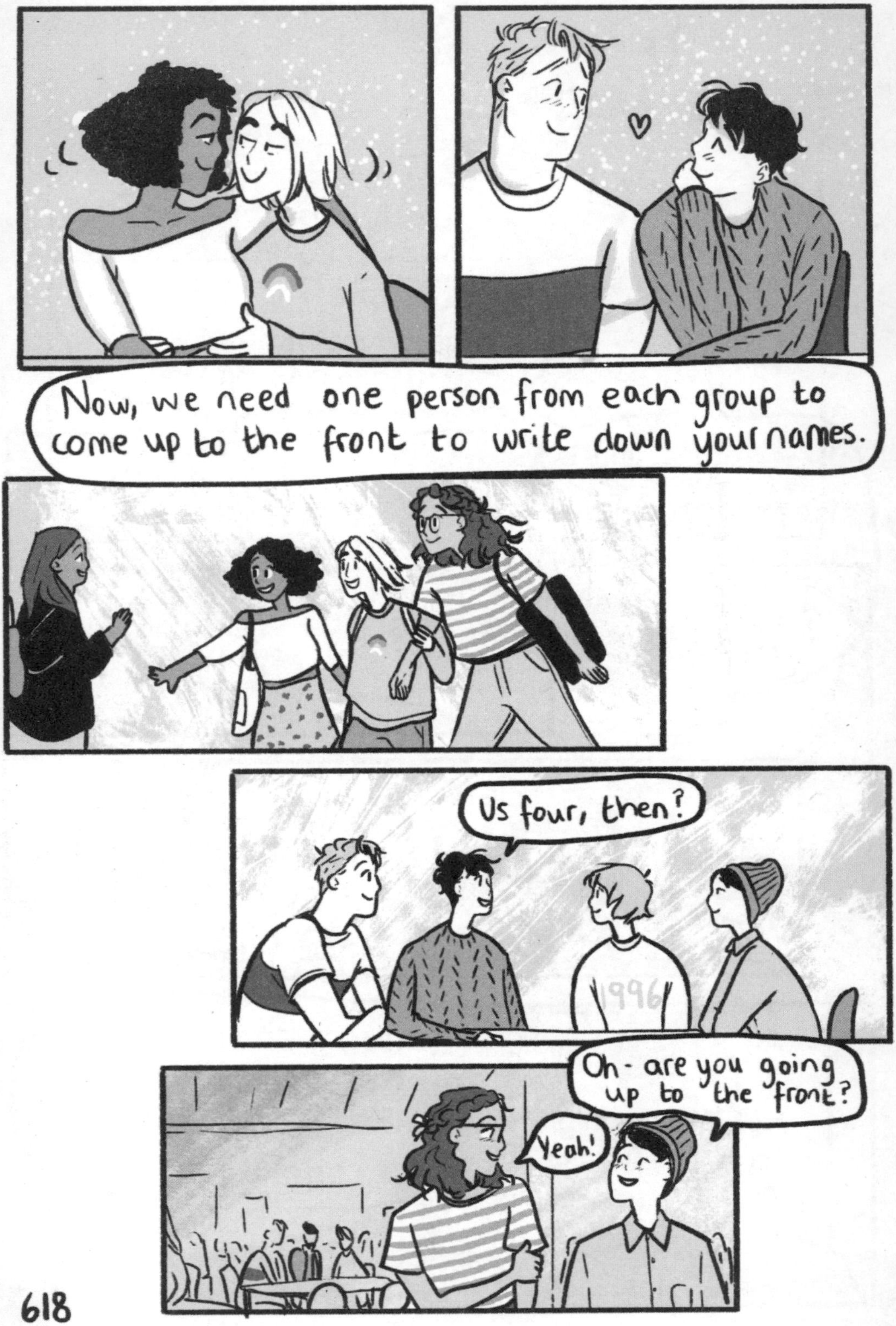
Now, we need one person from each group to come up to the front to write down your names.
Us four, then?
1996
Oh - are you going up to the front?
Yeah!

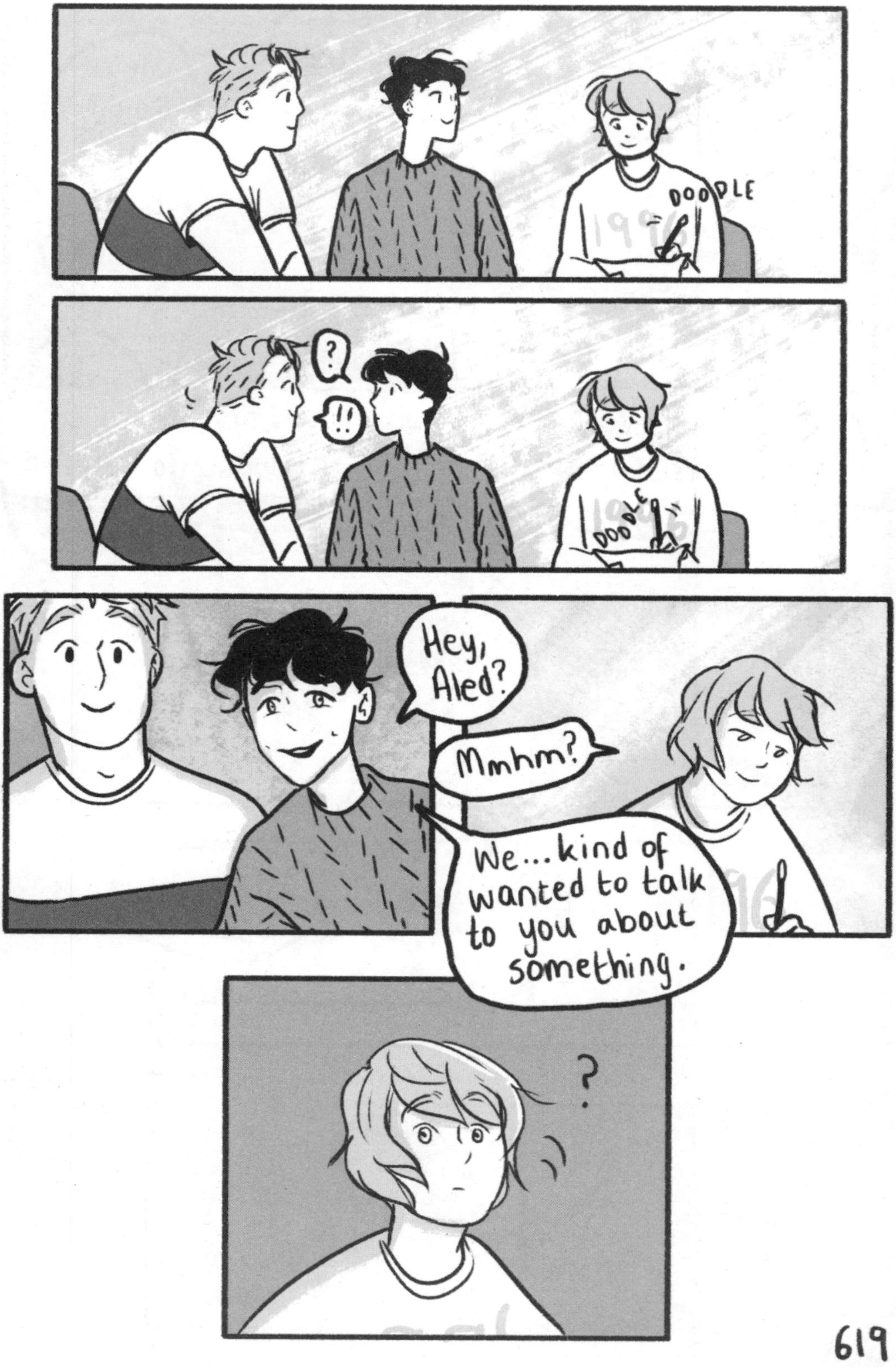
DOODLE
?
!!
DOODLE
Hey, Aled?
Mmhm?
We... kind of wanted to talk to you about something.
?

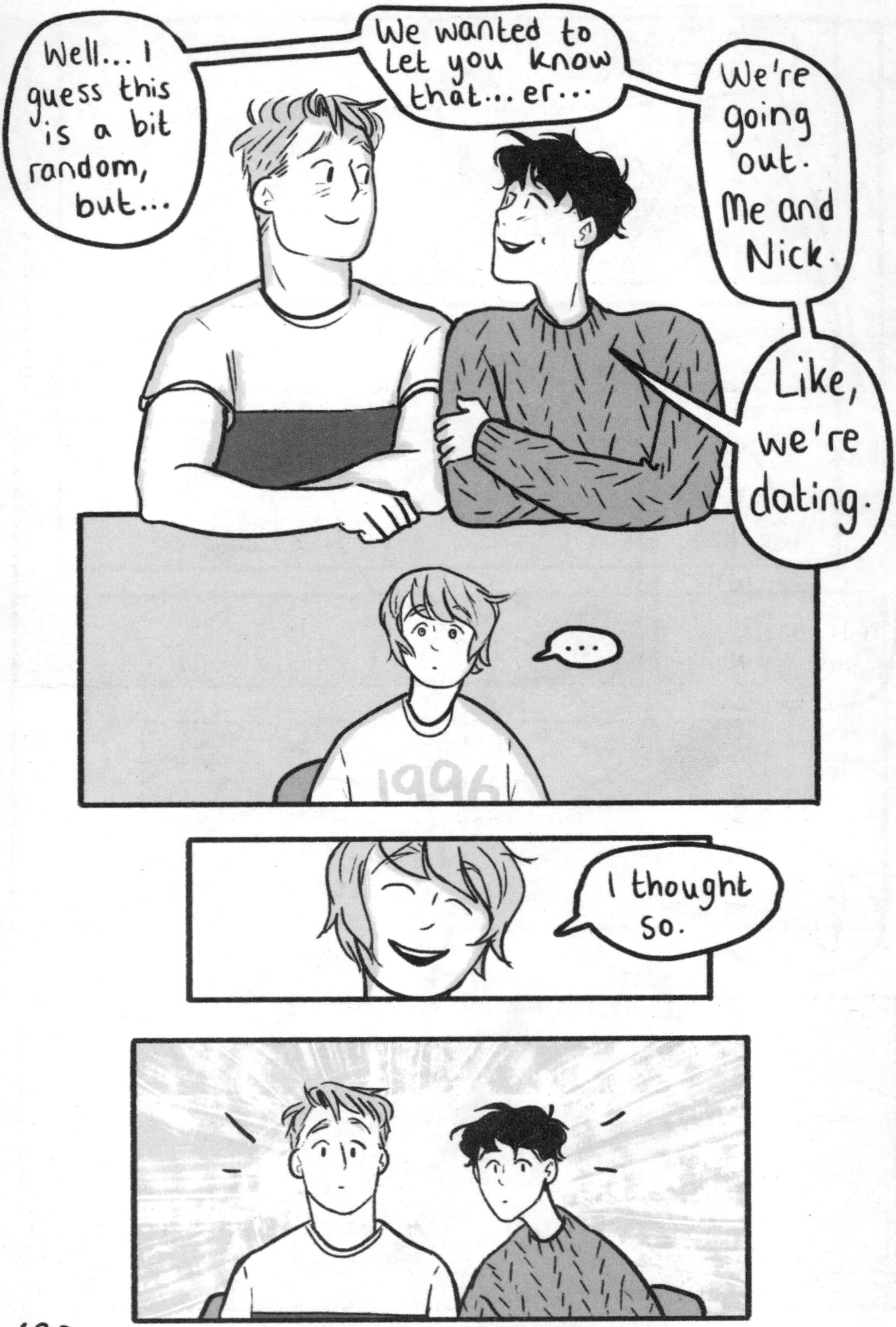
Well... I guess this is a bit random, but...
We wanted to let you know that... er...
We're going out. Me and Nick.
Like, we're dating.
...
I thought so.

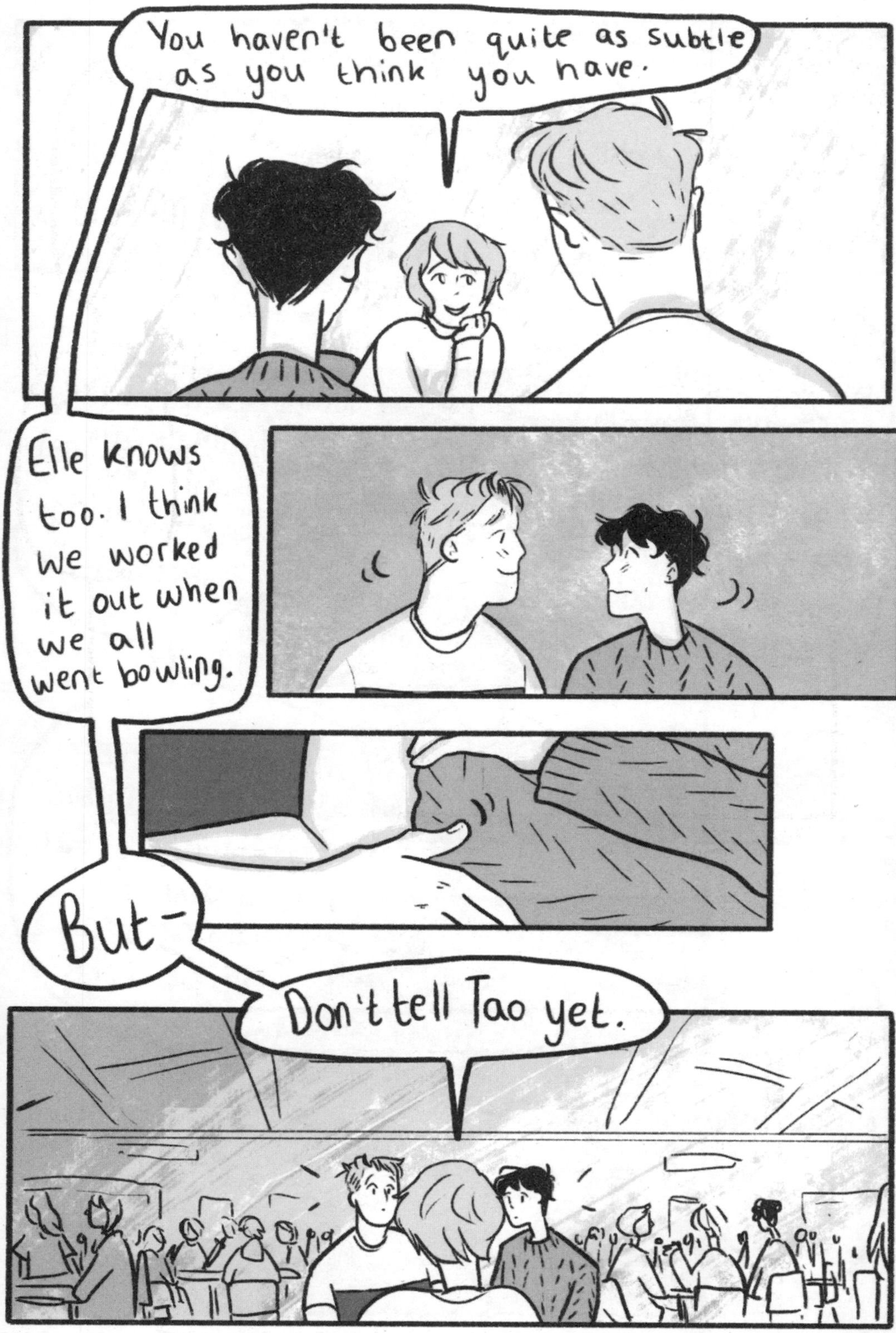
You haven't been quite as subtle as you think you have.
Elle knows too. I think we worked it out when we all went bowling.
But-
Don't tell Tao yet.

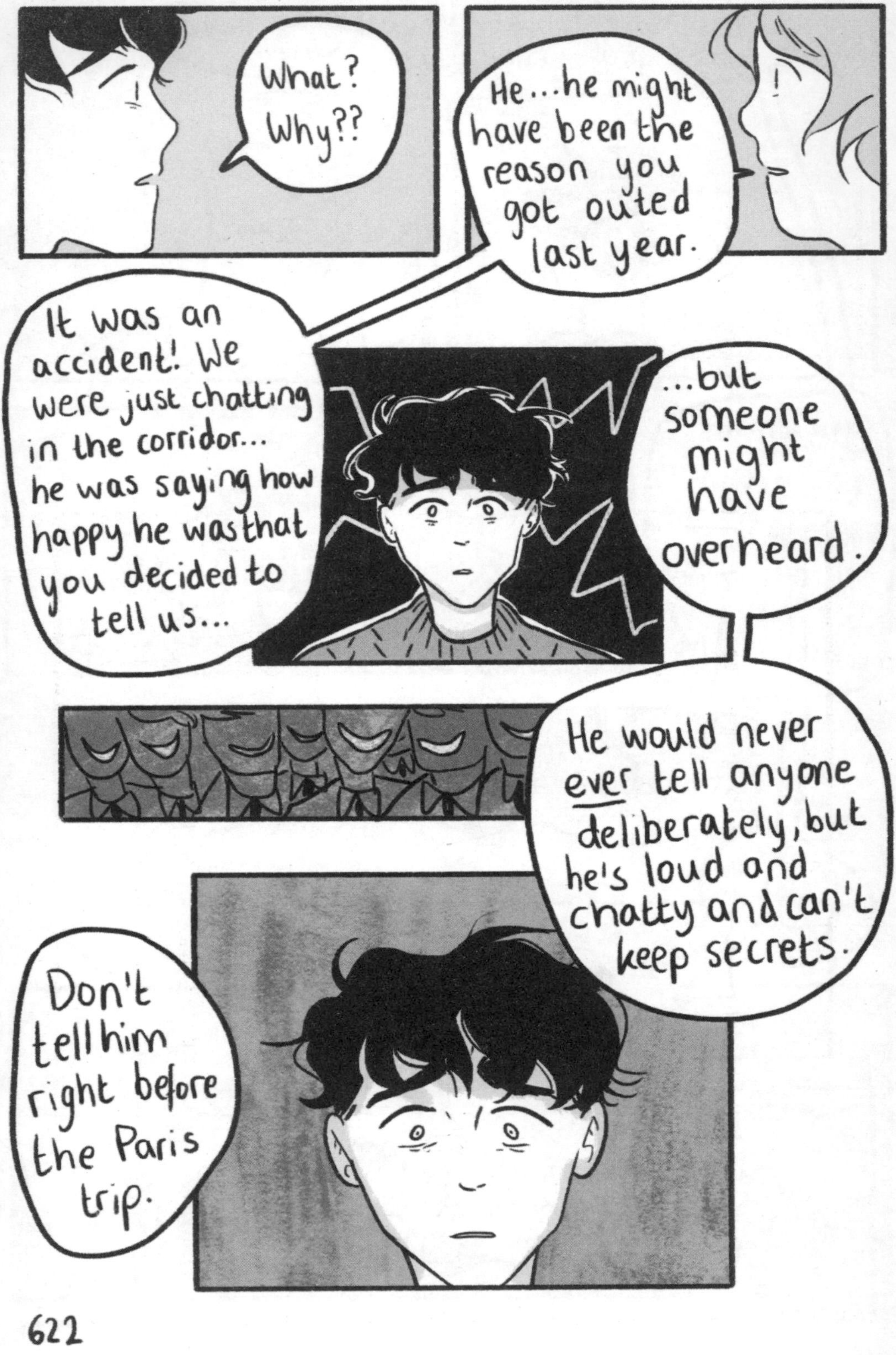

What? Why??
He...he might have been the reason you got outed last year.
It was an accident! We were just chatting in the corridor... he was saying how happy he was that you decided to tell us...
...but someone might have overheard.
He would never ever tell anyone deliberately, but he's loud and chatty and can't keep secrets.
Don't tell him right before the Paris trip.

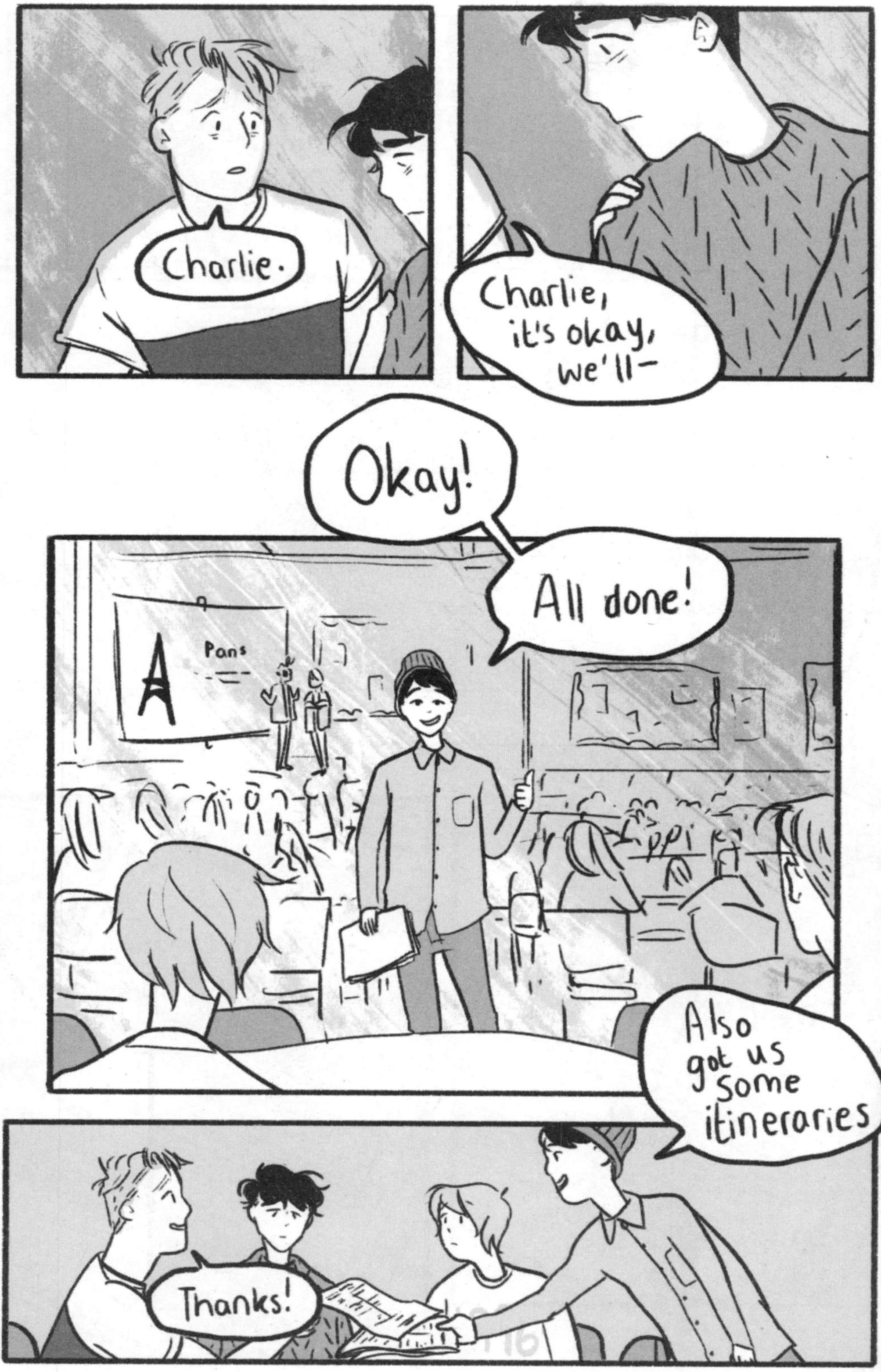
Charlie.
Charlie, it's okay, we'll–
Okay!
All done!
Paris
Also got us some itineraries
Thanks!

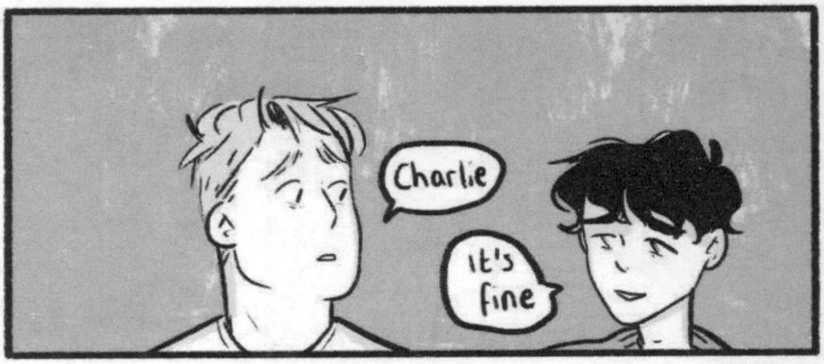
Charlie
it's fine

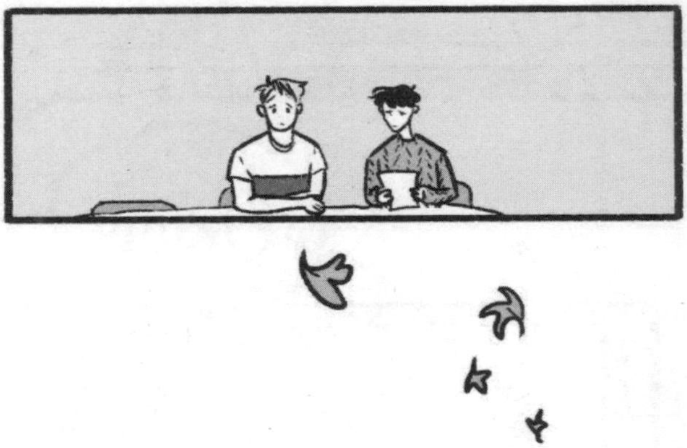

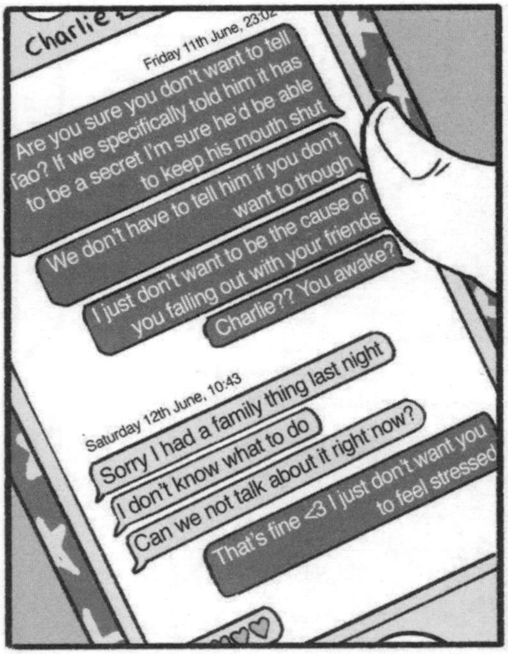
Charlie
Friday 11th June, 23:02
Are you sure you don't want to tell Tao? If we specifically told him it has to be a secret I'm sure he'd be able to keep his mouth shut
We don't have to tell him if you don't want to though
I just don't want to be the cause of you falling out with your friends
Charlie?? You awake?
Saturday 12th June, 10:43
Sorry I had a family thing last night
I don't know what to do
Can we not talk about it right now?
That's fine <3 I just don't want you to feel stressed

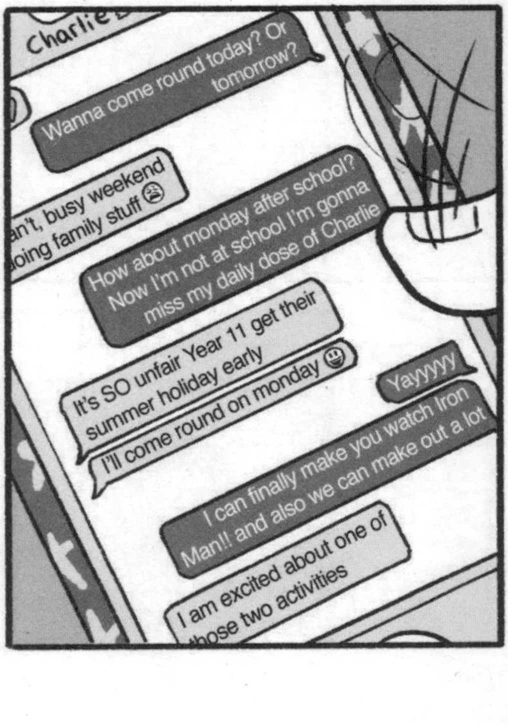
Charlie
Wanna come round today? Or tomorrow?
an't, busy weekend oing family stuff
How about monday after school? Now I'm not at school I'm gonna miss my daily dose of Charlie
It's SO unfair Year 11 get their summer holiday early
I'll come round on monday
Yayyyy
I can finally make you watch fron Man!! and also we can make out a lot
I am excited about one of those two activities

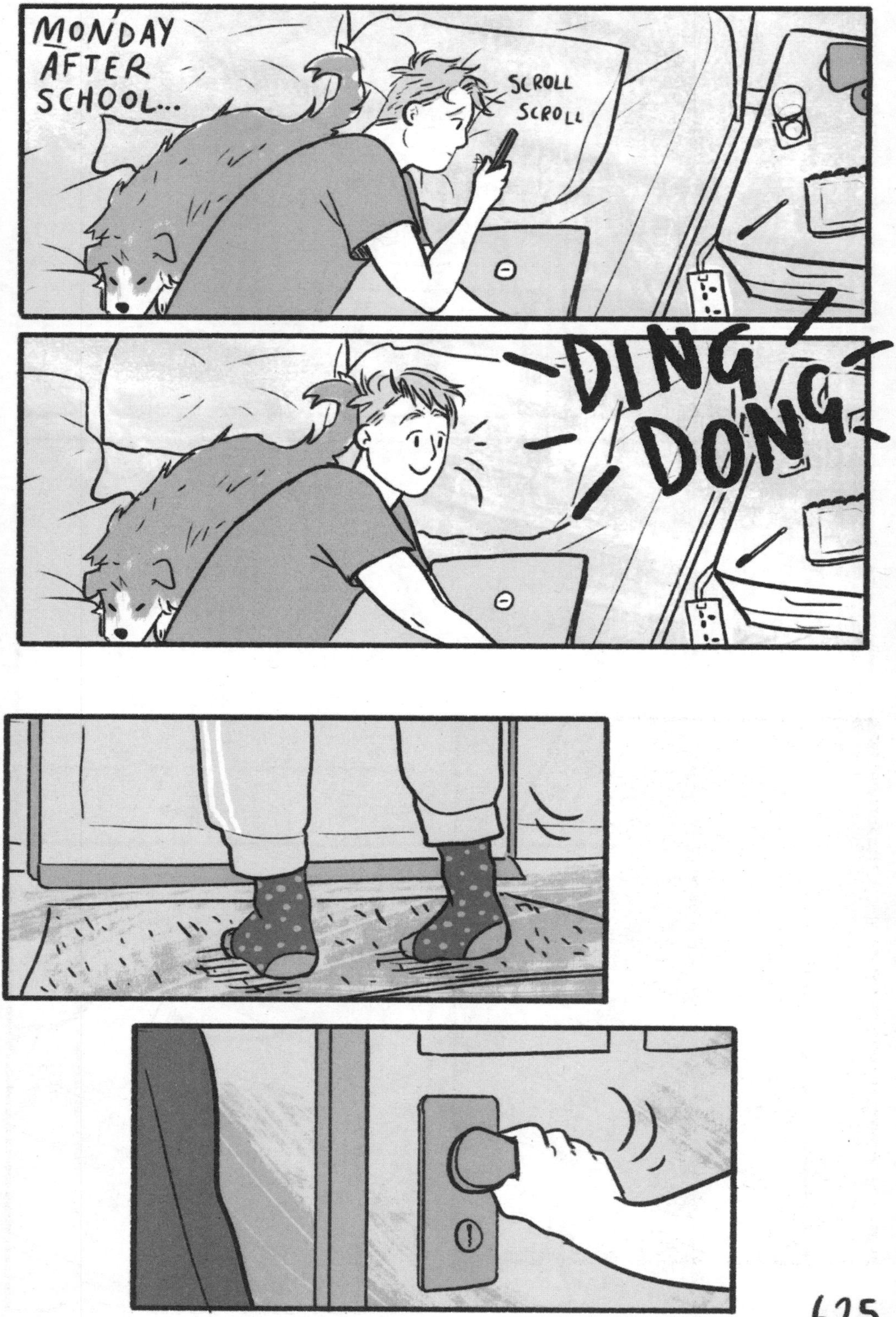
MONDAY AFTER SCHOOL...
SCROLL
SCROLL
DING
DONG

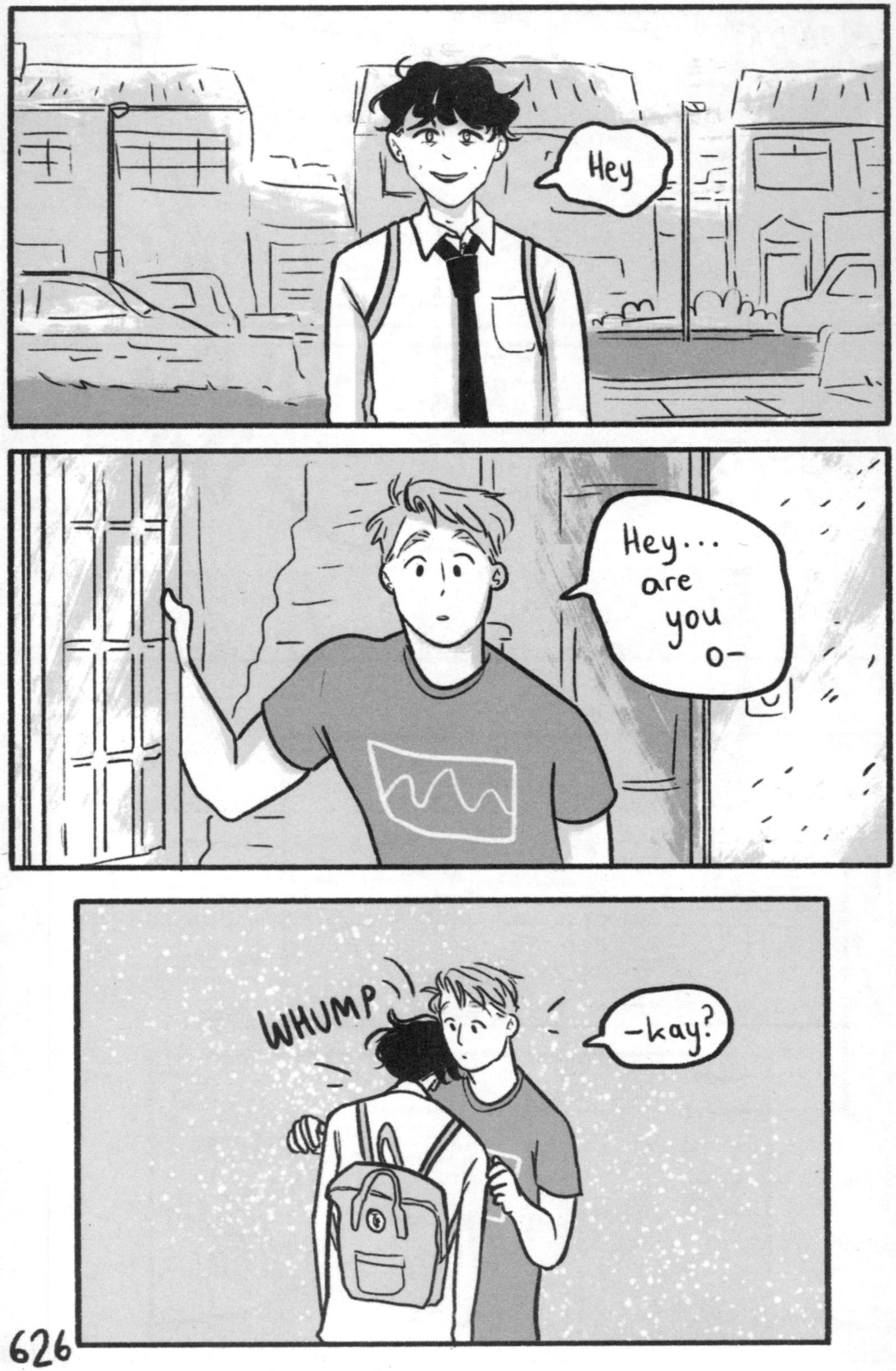
Hey
Hey... are you o-
WHUMP
-kay?

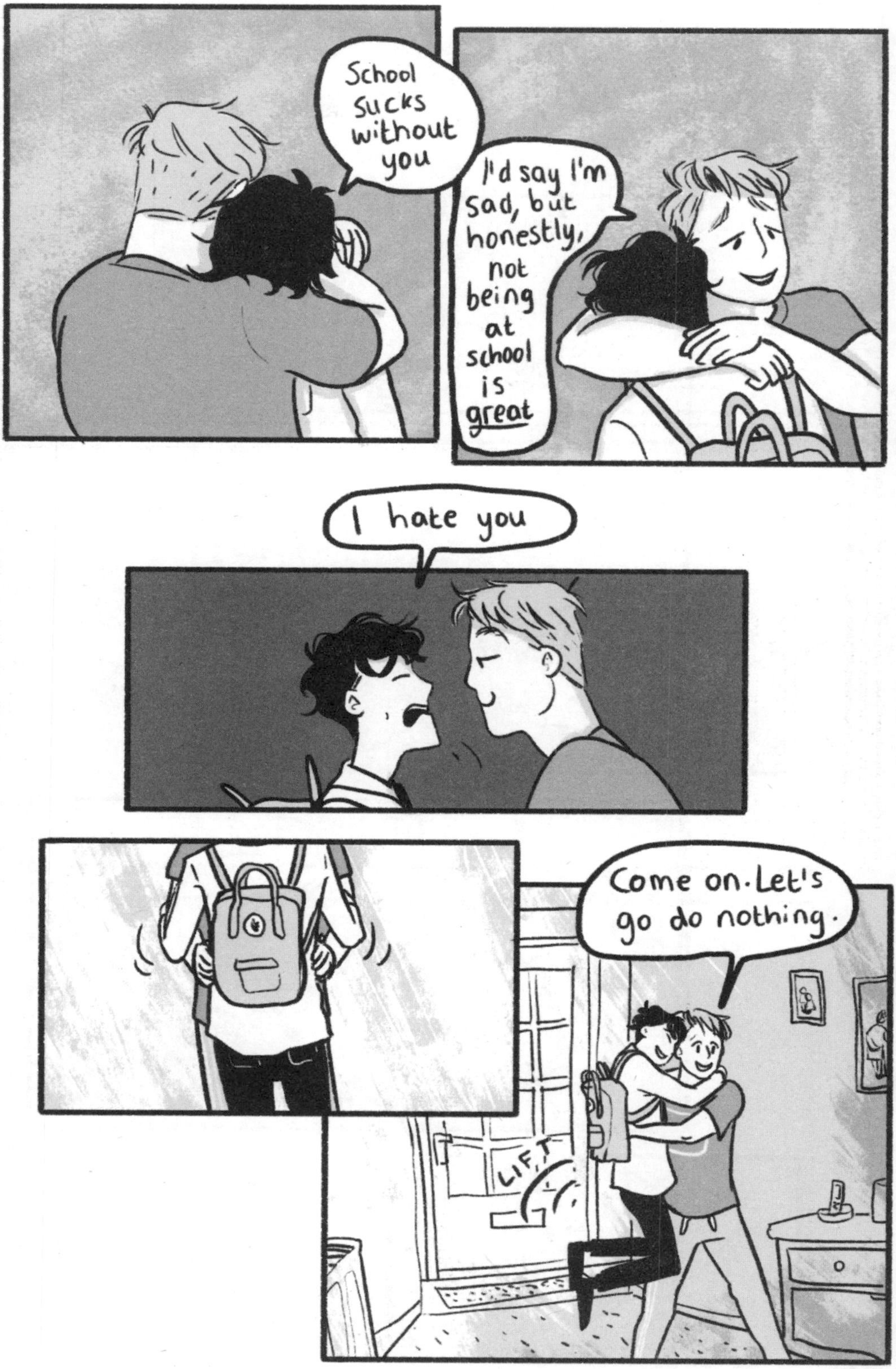
School sucks without you
I'd say I'm sad, but honestly, not being at school is great
I hate you
Come on. Let's go do nothing.
LIFT

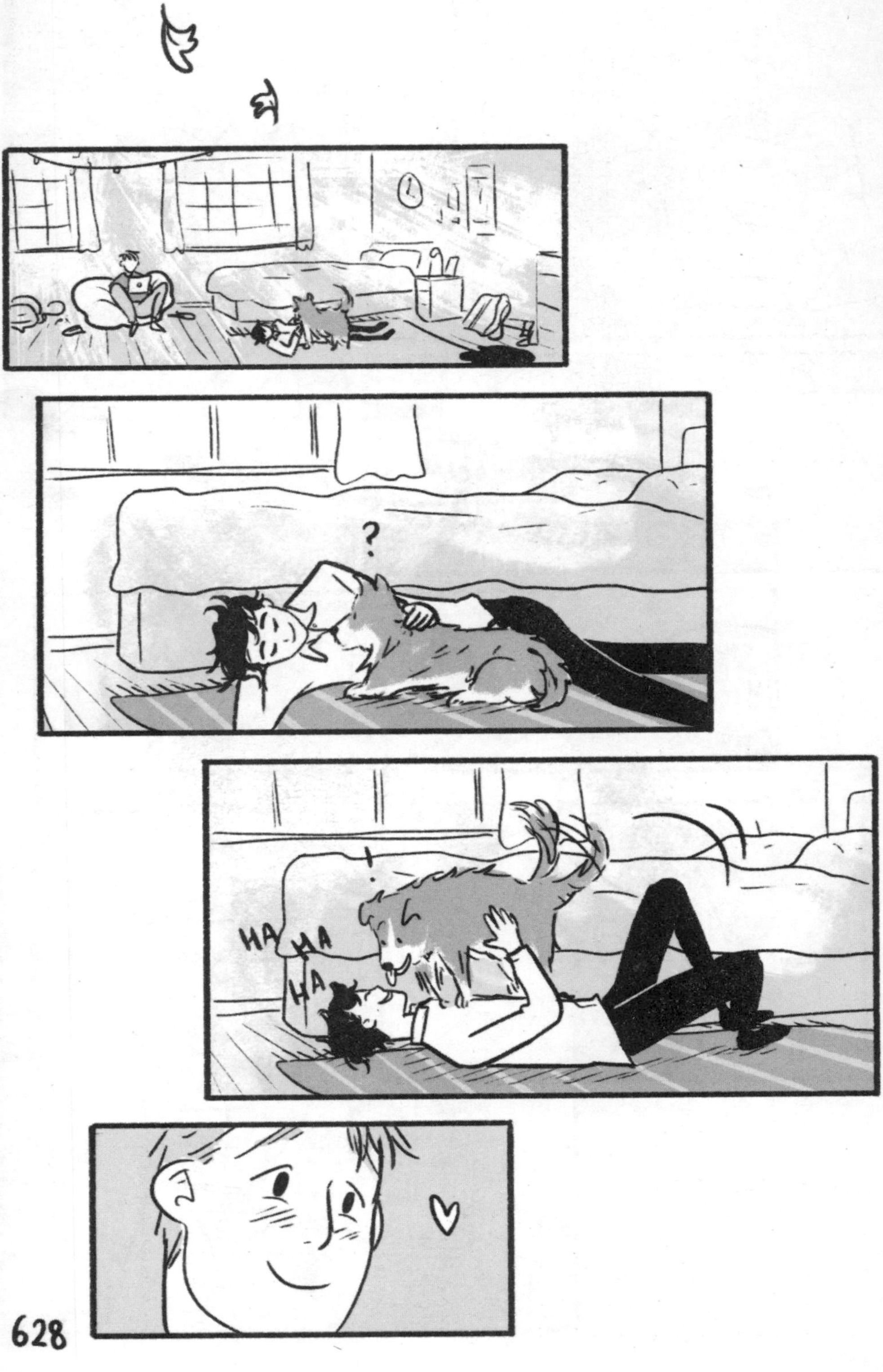
?
!
HA HA
HA

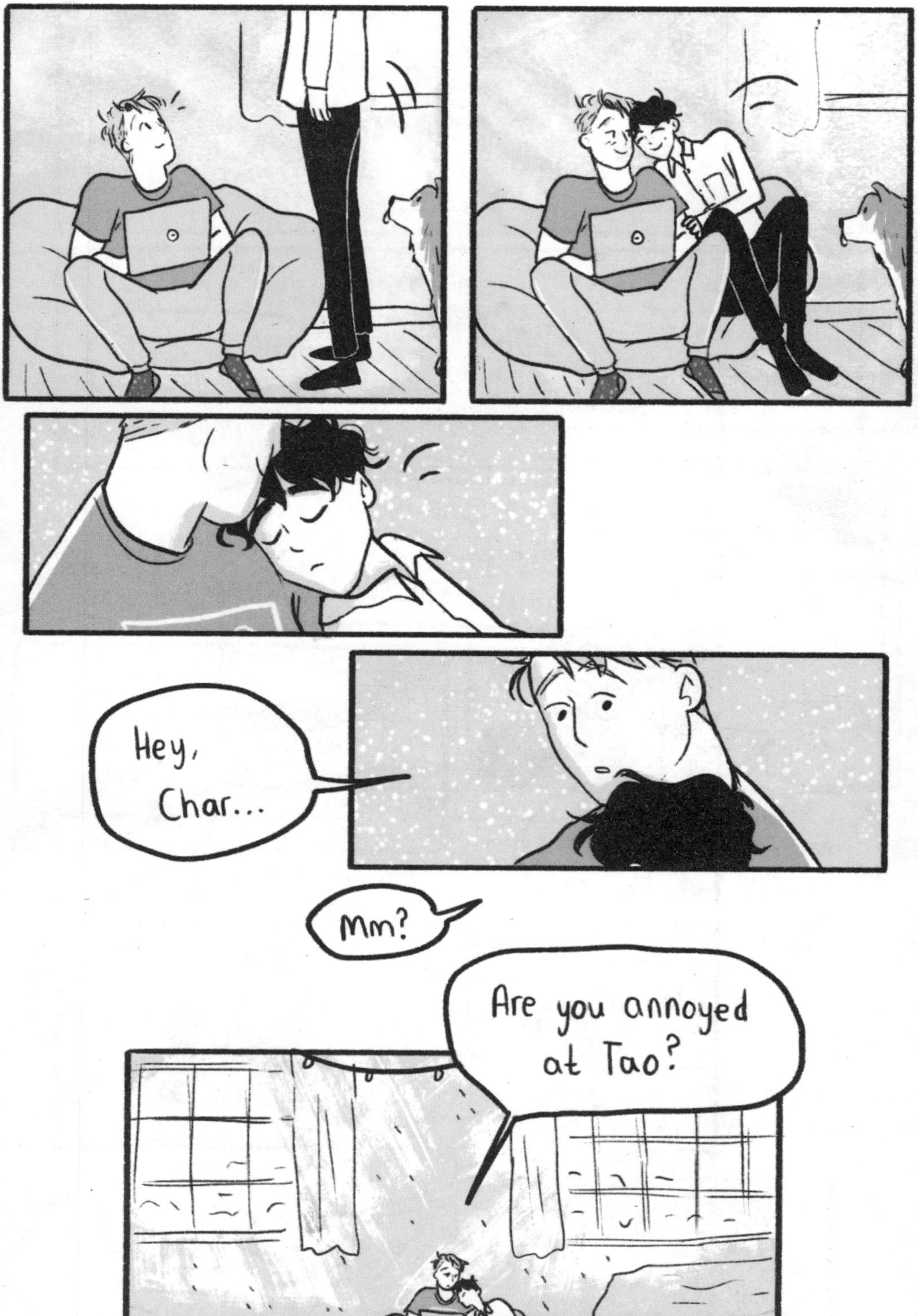
Hey,
Char...
Mm?
Are you annoyed at Tao?

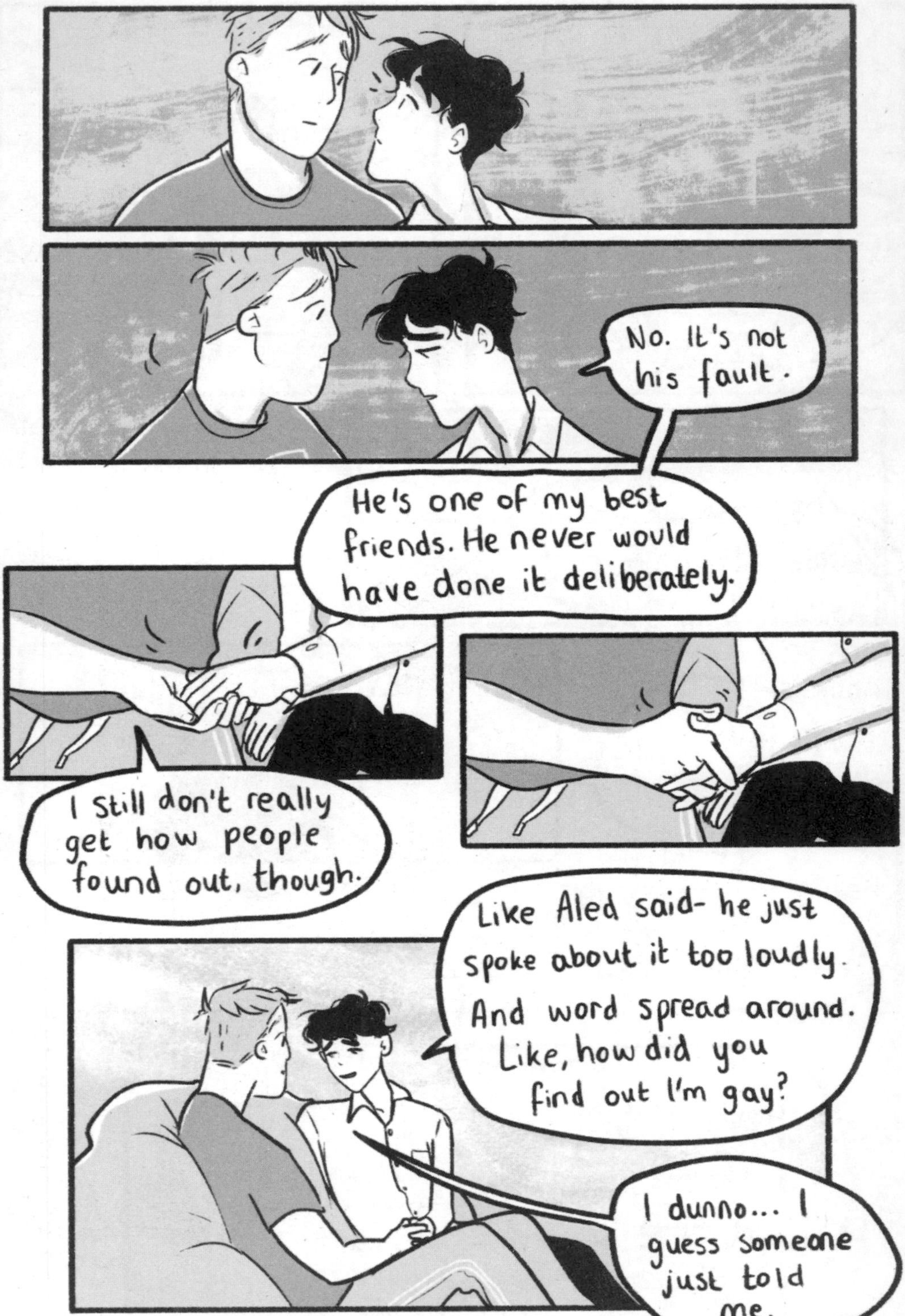
No. It's not his fault.
He's one of my best friends. He never would have done it deliberately.
I still don't really get how people found out, though.
Like Aled said- he just spoke about it too loudly. And word spread around. Like, how did you find out I'm gay?
I dunno... I guess someone just told me.

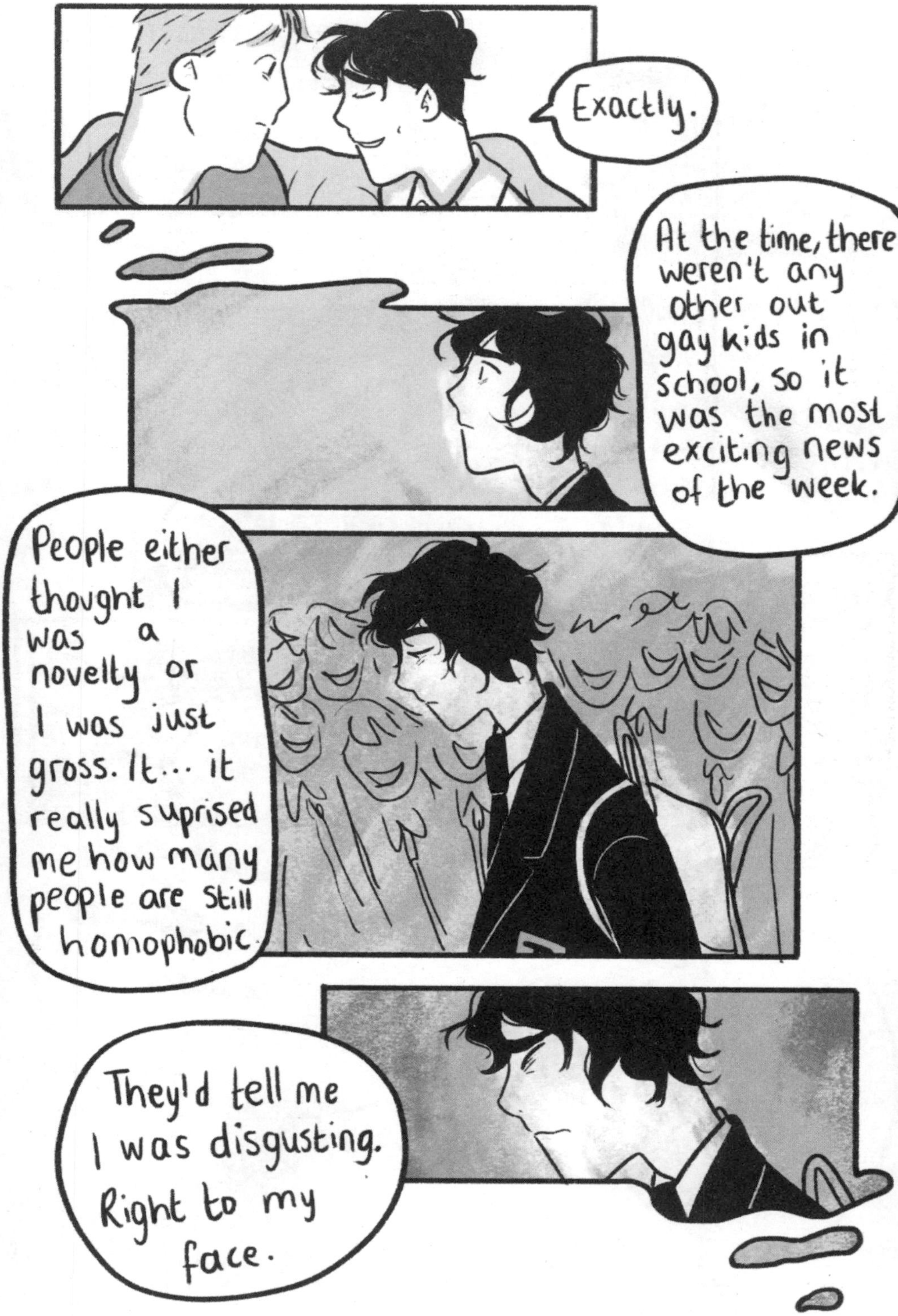
Exactly.
At the time, there weren't any other out gay kids in school, so it was the most exciting news of the week.
People either thought I was a novelty or I was just gross. It... it really suprised me how many people are still homophobic.
They'd tell me I was disgusting. Right to my face.

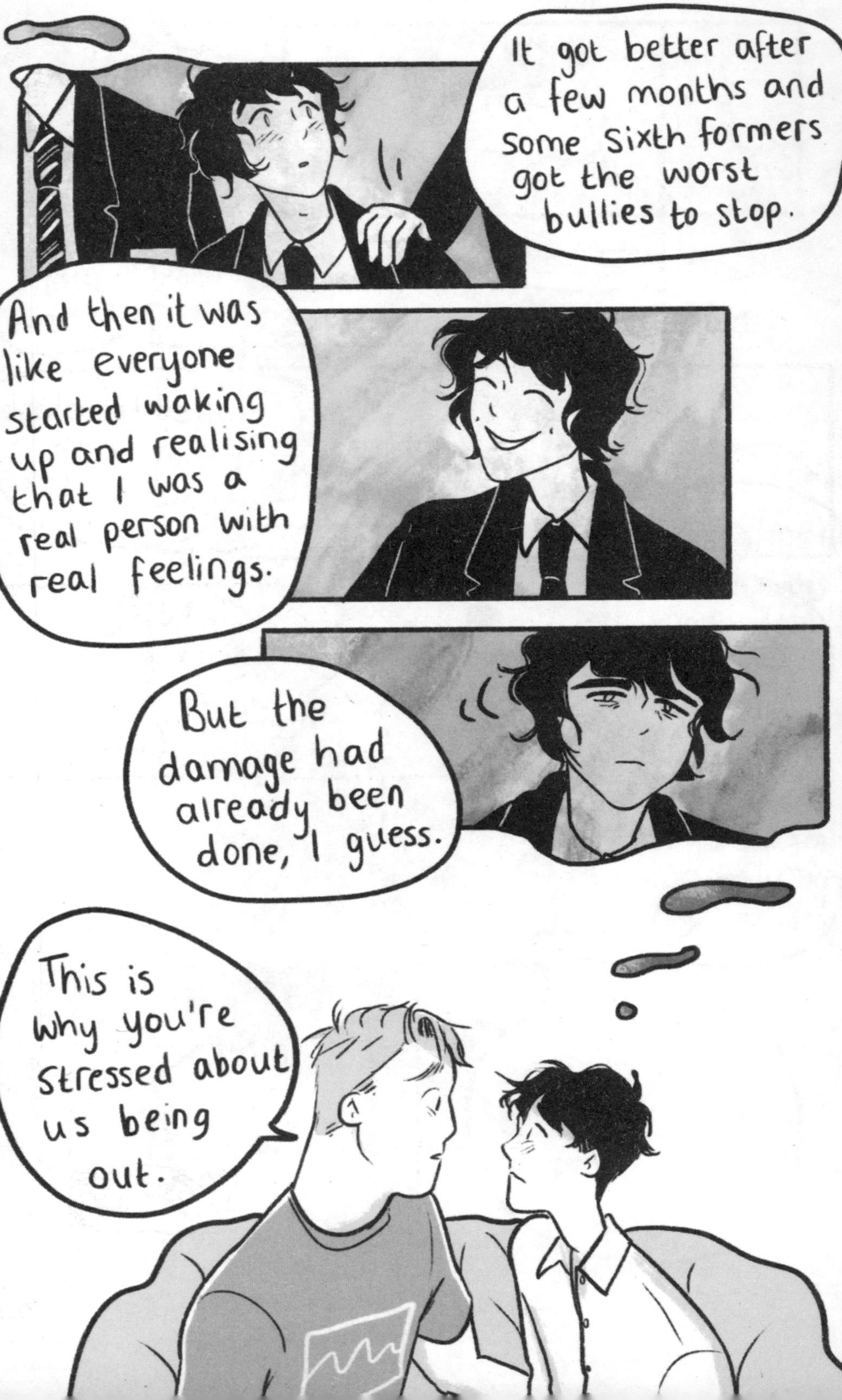
It got better after a few months and some Sixth formers got the worst bullies to stop.
And then it was like everyone started waking up and realising that I was a real person with real feelings.
But the damage had already been done, I guess.
This is why you're stressed about us being out.

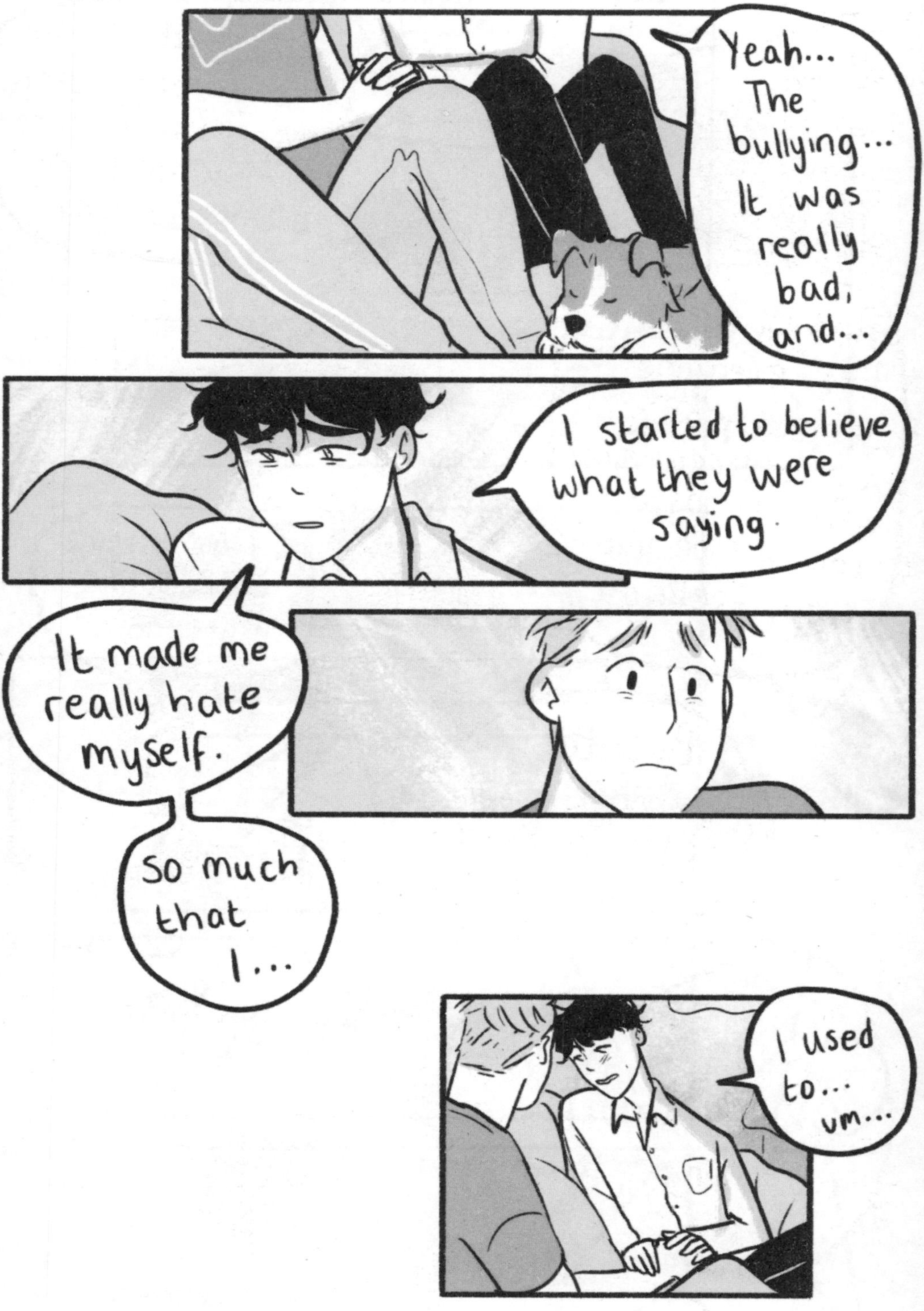
Yeah... The bullying... It was really bad, and...
I started to believe what they were saying.
It made me really hate myself.
So much that I...
I used to... um...

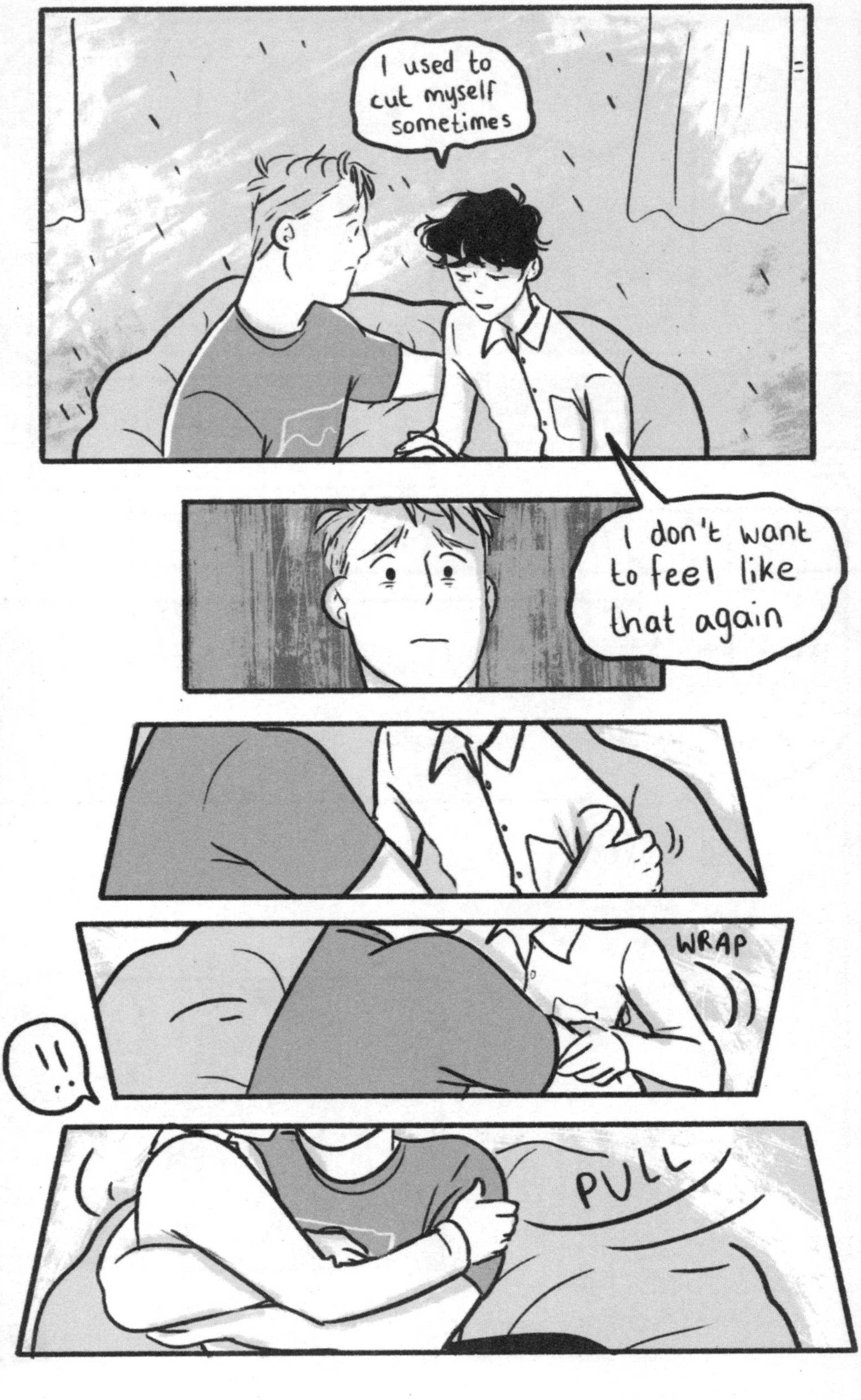
I used to cut myself sometimes
I don't want to feel like that again
WRAP
!!
PULL

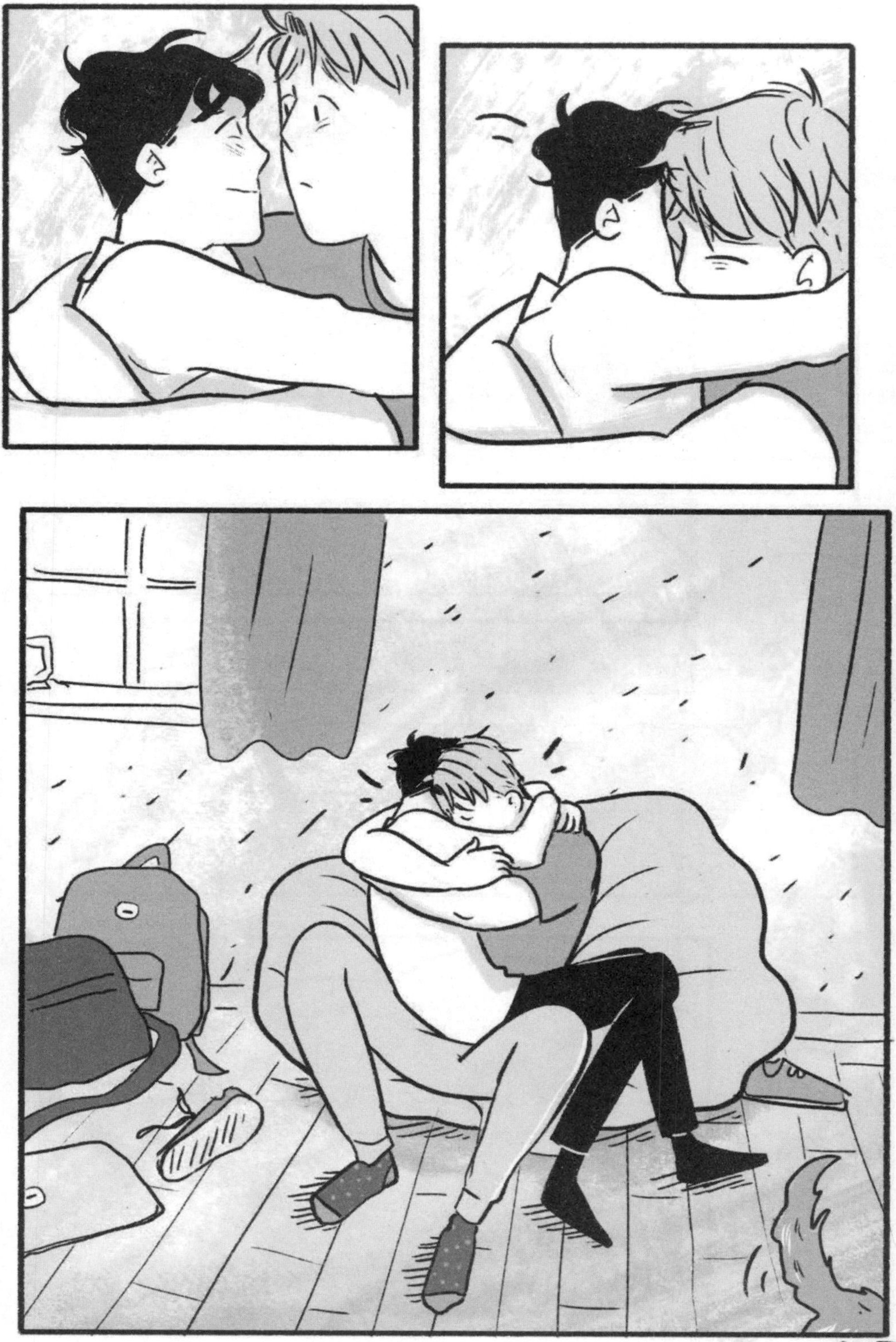

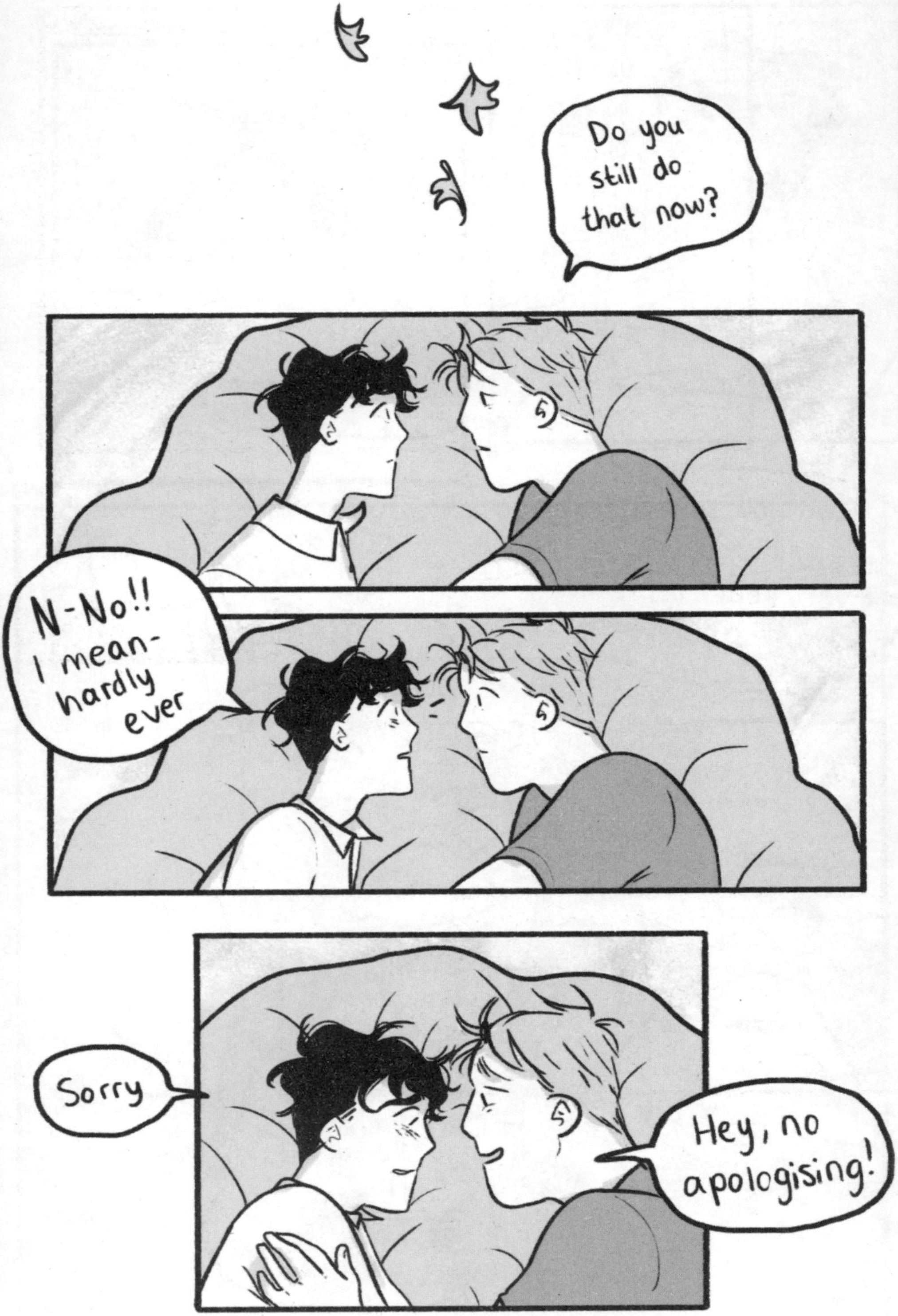
Do you still do that now?
N-No!! I mean- hardly ever
Sorry
Hey, no apologising!

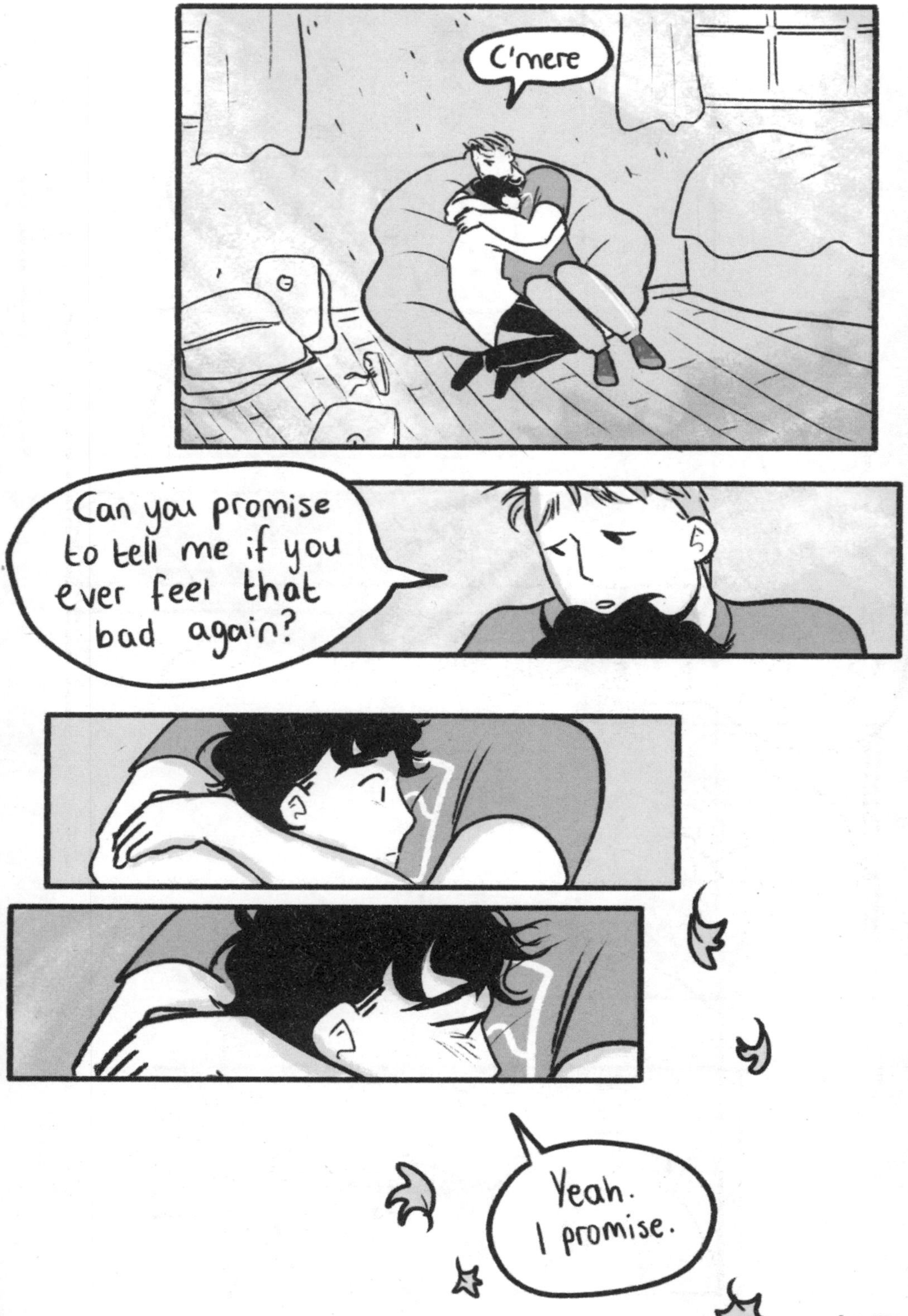
C'mere
Can you promise to tell me if you ever feel that bad again?
Yeah. I promise.

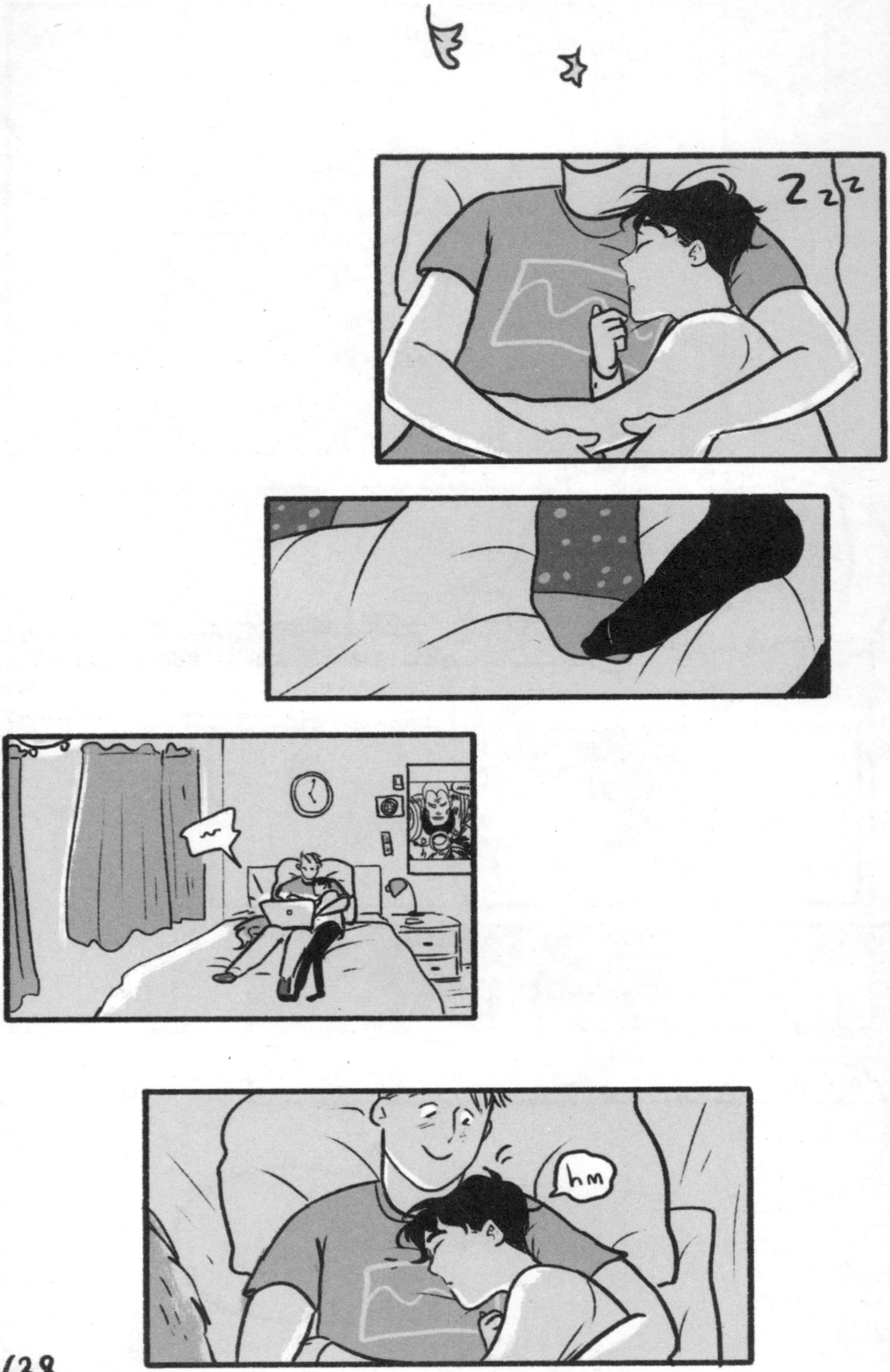
Z z z
hm

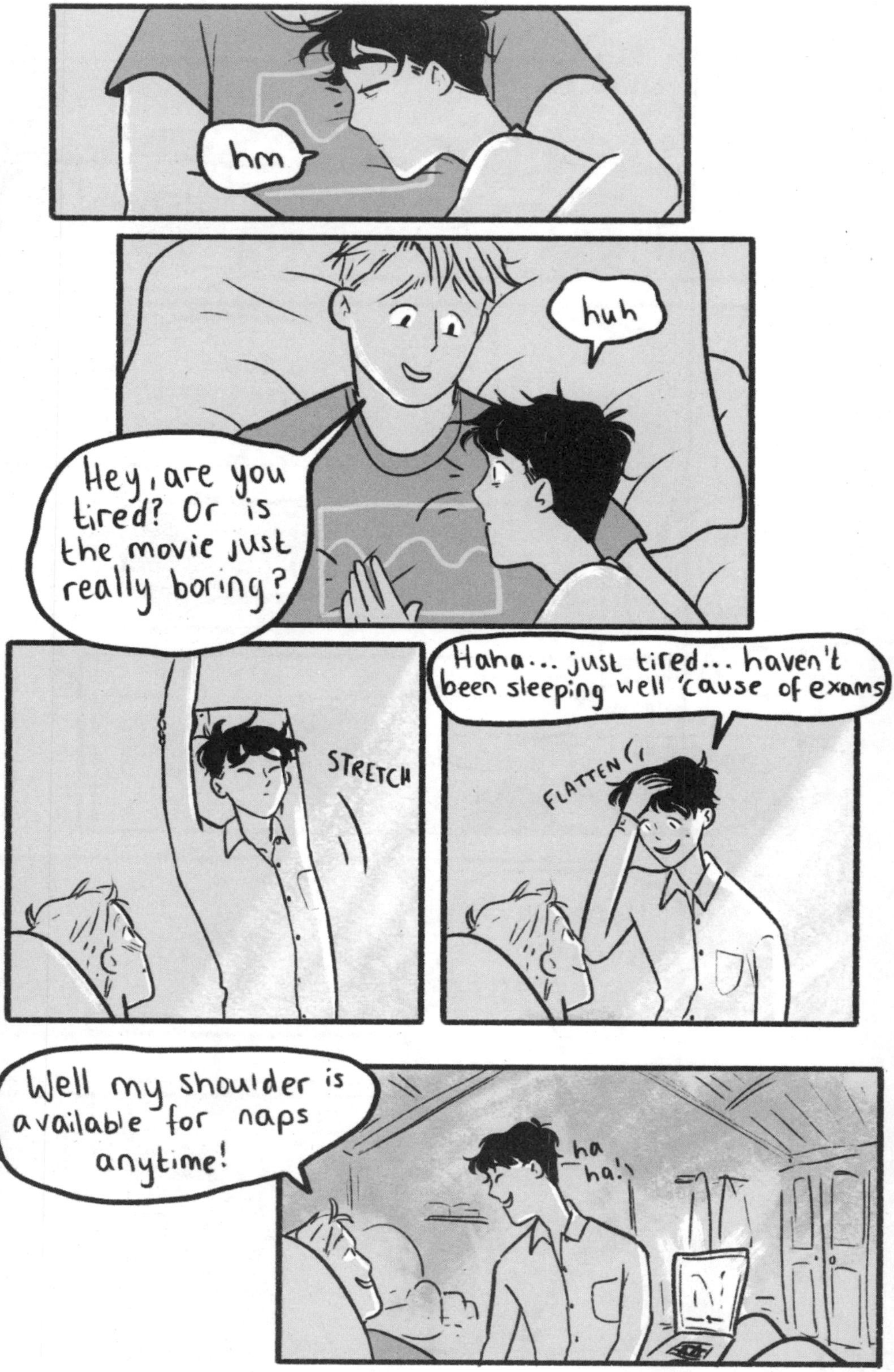
hm
huh
Hey, are you tired? Or is the movie just really boring?
STRETCH
Haha... just tired... haven't been sleeping well 'cause of exams
FLATTEN
Well my shoulder is available for naps anytime!
ha ha!

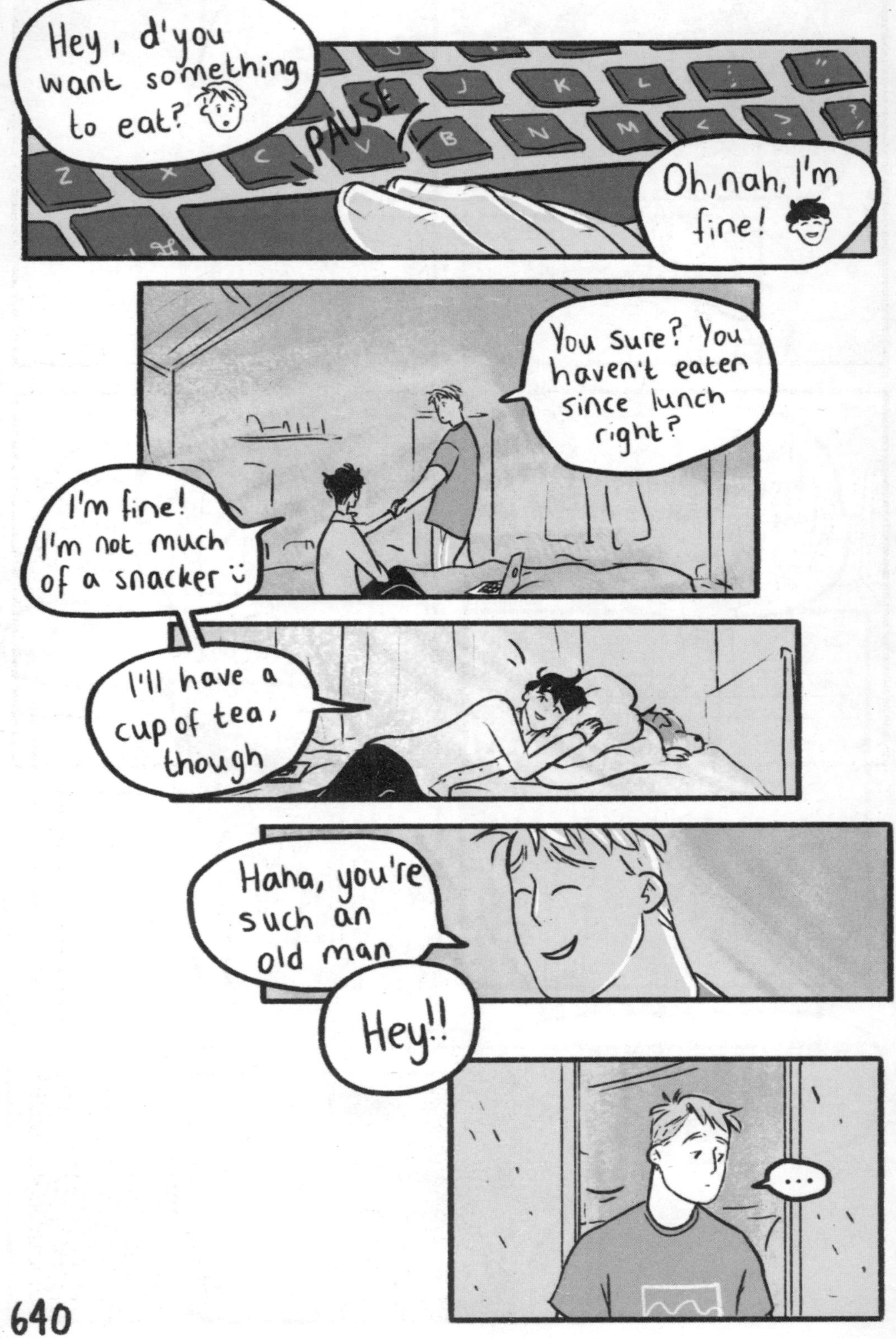
Hey, d'you want something to eat?
PAUSE
Oh, nah, I'm fine!
You sure? You haven't eaten since lunch right?
I'm fine! I'm not much of a snacker :)
I'll have a cup of tea, though
Haha, you're such an old man
Hey!!
...

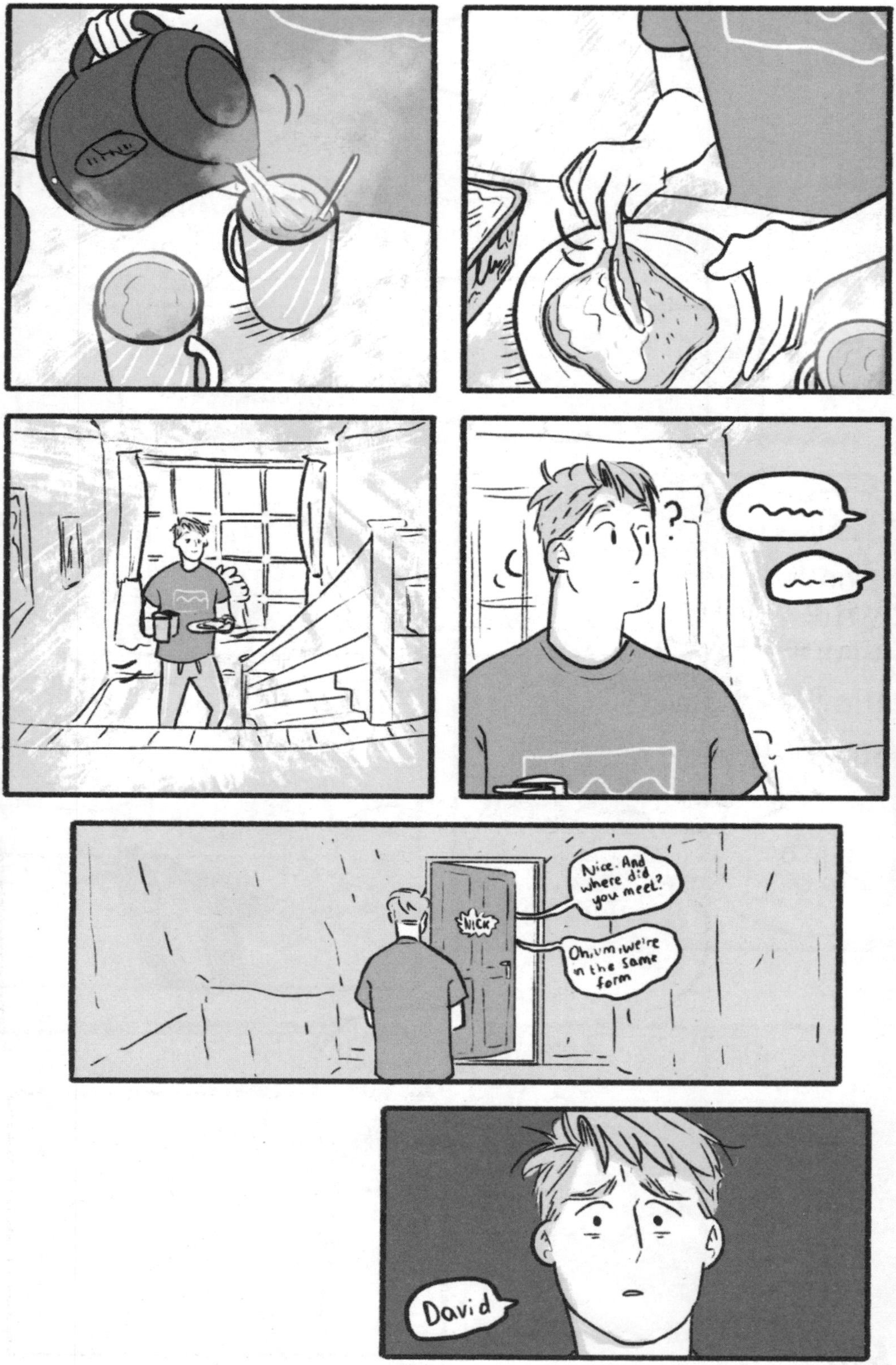
Nice. And where did you meet?
Oh, um, we're in the same form
NICK
David

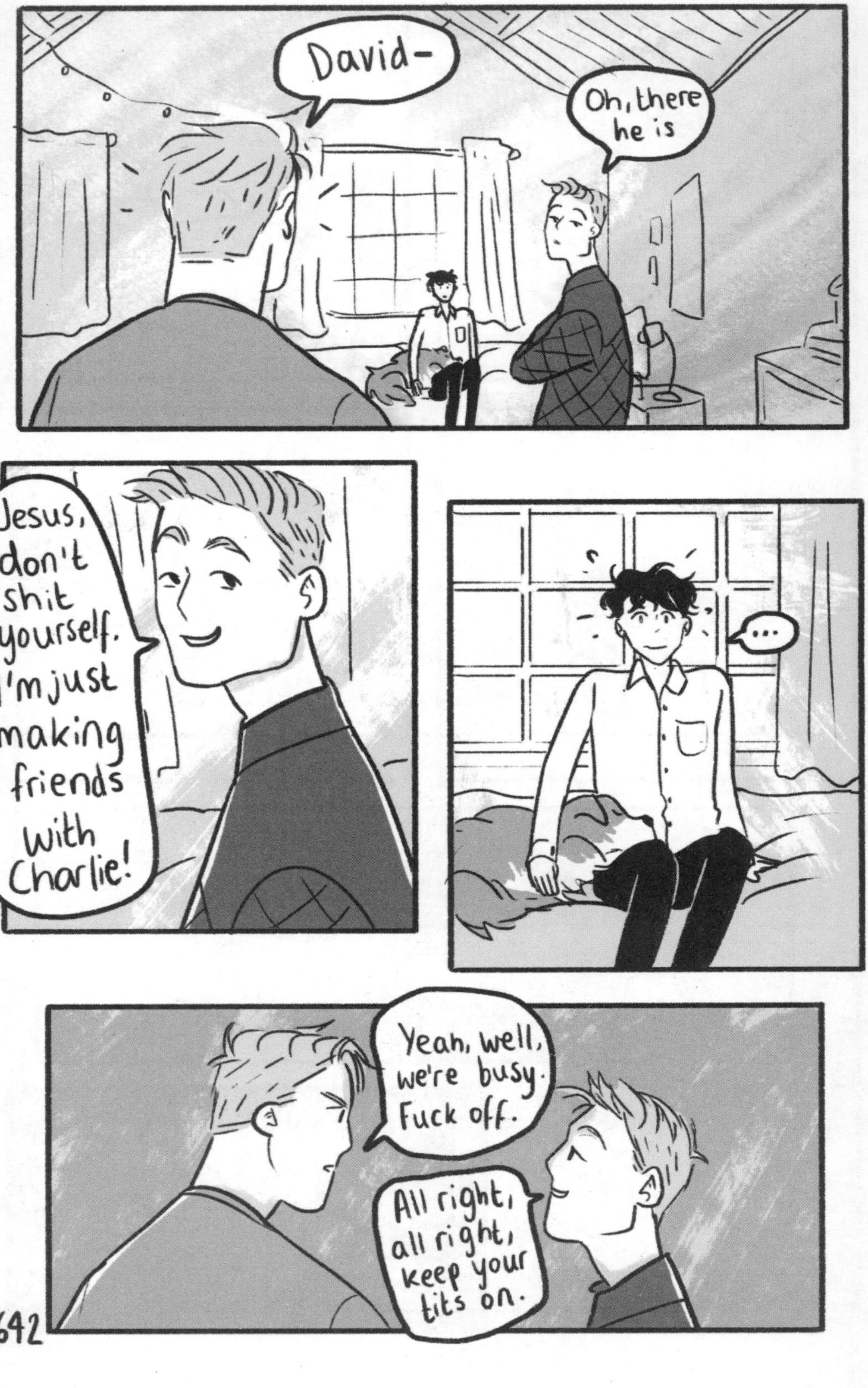
David-
Oh, there he is
Jesus, don't shit yourself. I'm just making friends with Charlie!
...
Yeah, well, we're busy. Fuck off.
All right, all right, keep your tits on.

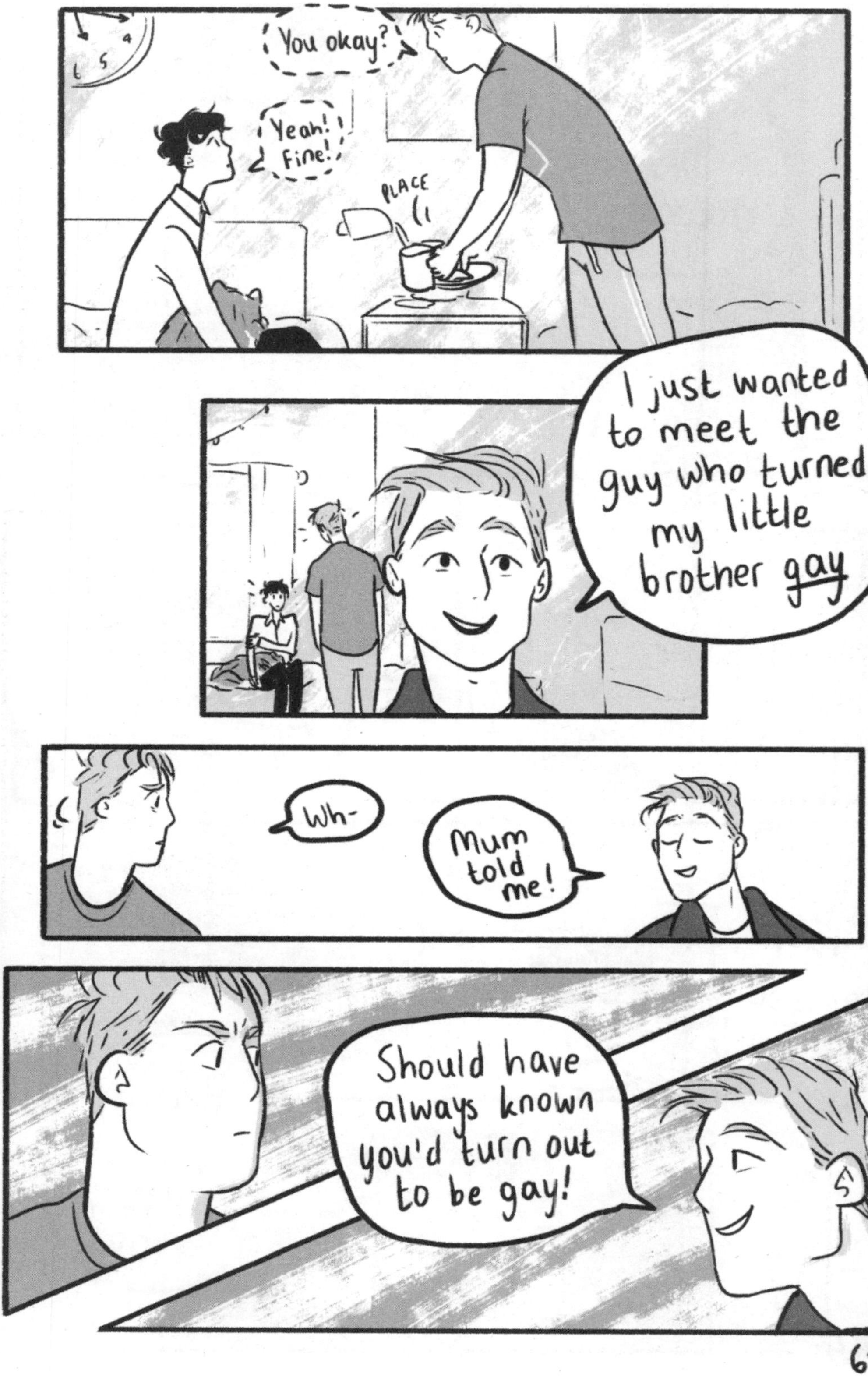
You okay?
Yeah! Fine!
PLACE
I just wanted to meet the guy who turned my little brother gay
Wh-
Mum told me!
Should have always known you'd turn out to be gay!

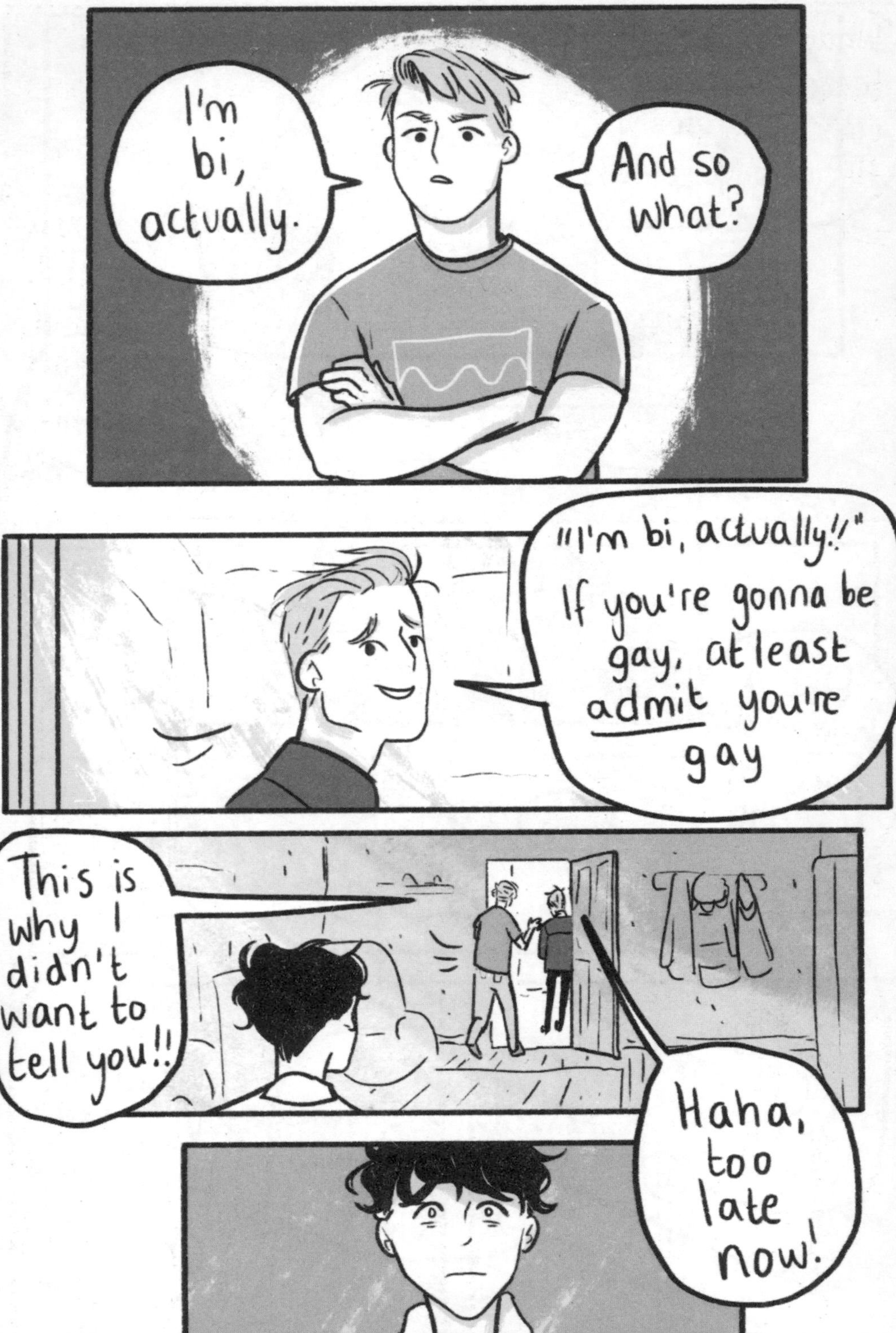
I'm bi, actually.
And so what?
"I'm bi, actually!!"
If you're gonna be gay, at least admit you're gay
This is why I didn't want to tell you!!
Haha, too late now!

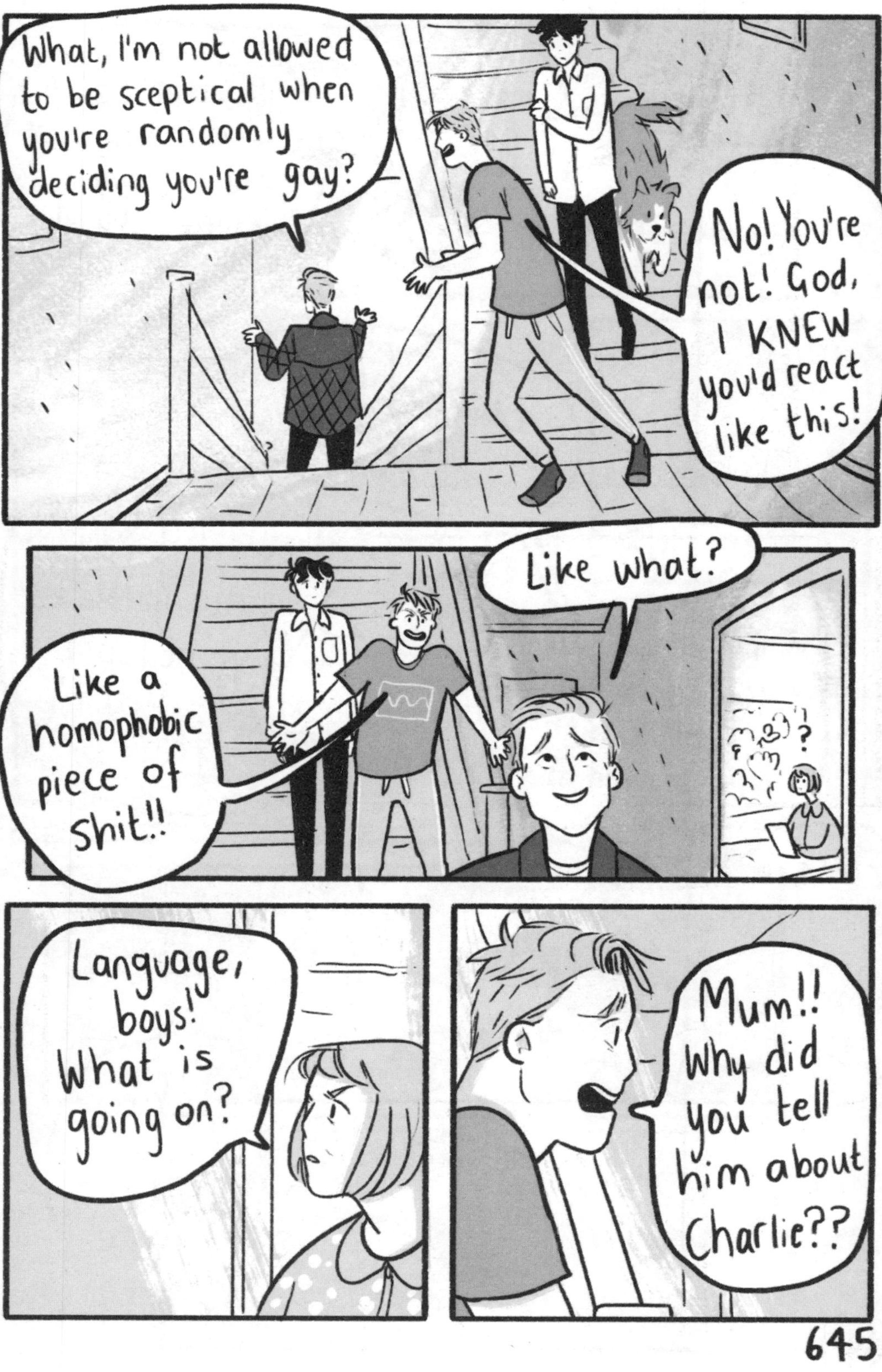
What, I'm not allowed to be sceptical when you're randomly deciding you're gay?
No! You're not! God, I KNEW you'd react like this!
Like what?
Like a homophobic piece of shit!!
Language, boys! What is going on?
Mum!! Why did you tell him about Charlie??

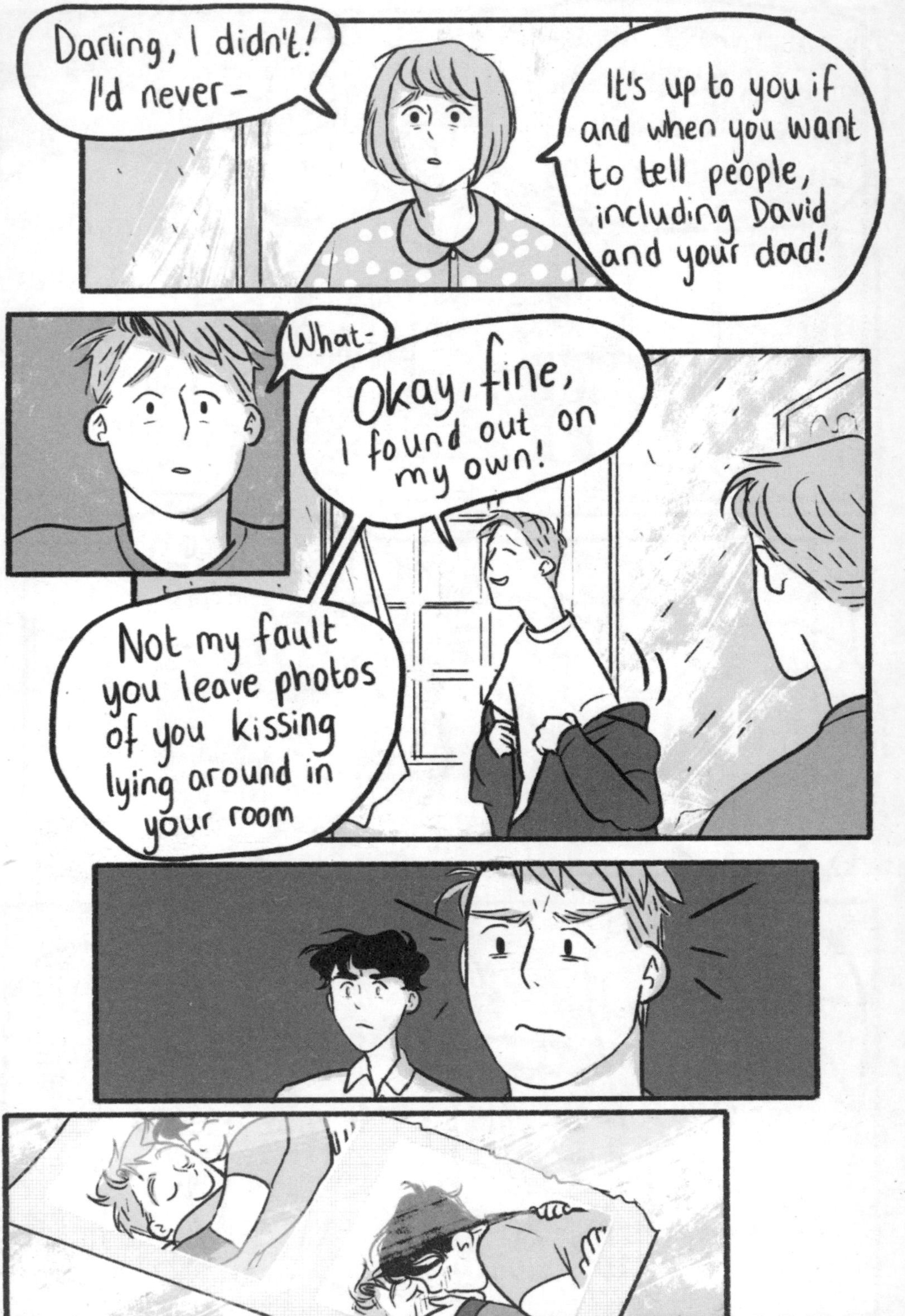
Darling, I didn't! I'd never-
It's up to you if and when you want to tell people, including David and your dad!
What-
Okay, fine, I found out on my own!
Not my fault you leave photos of you kissing lying around in your room

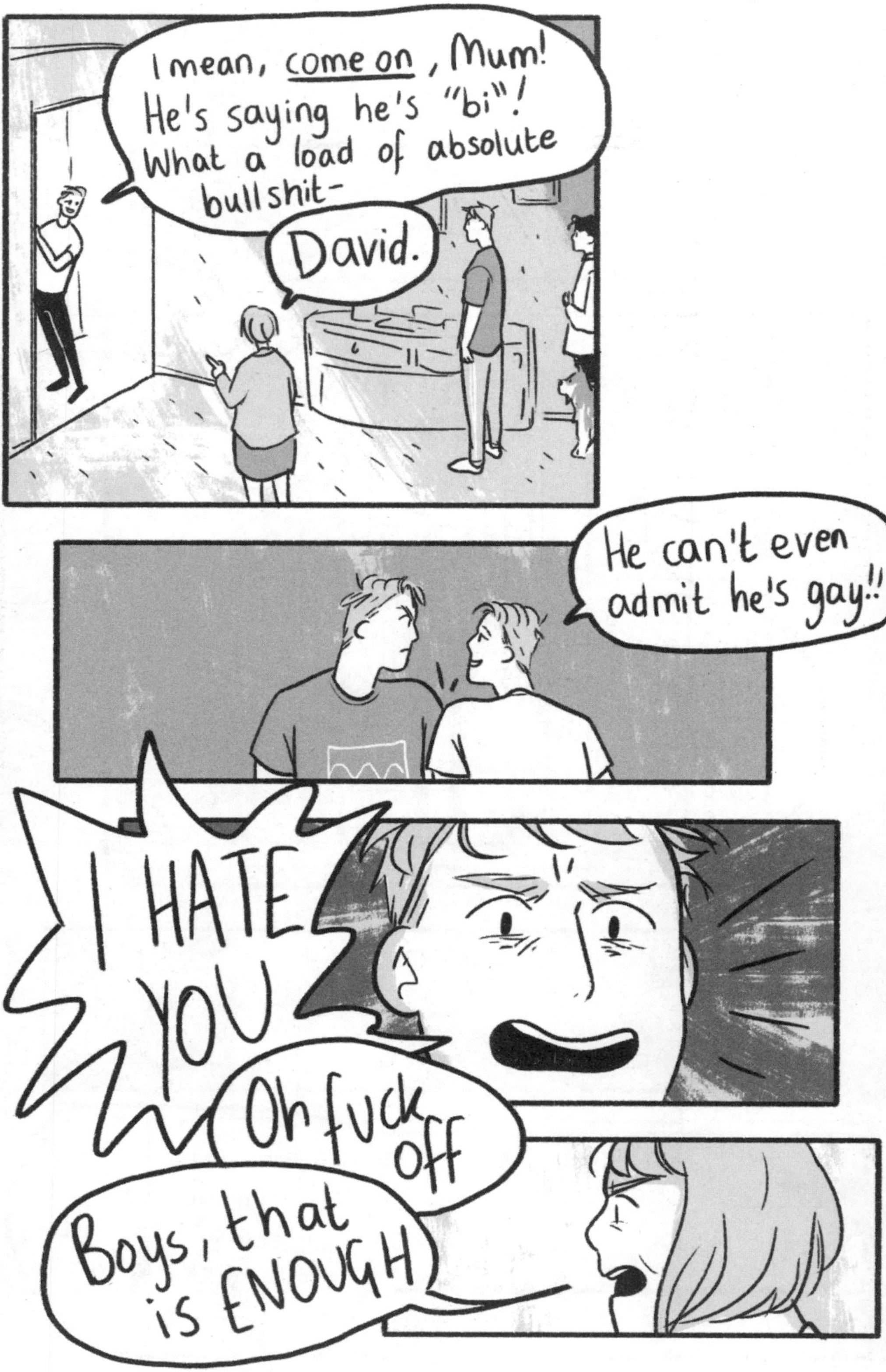
I mean, come on, Mum! He's saying he's "bi"! What a load of absolute bullshit-
David.
He can't even admit he's gay!!
I HATE YOU
Oh fuck off
Boys, that is ENOUGH

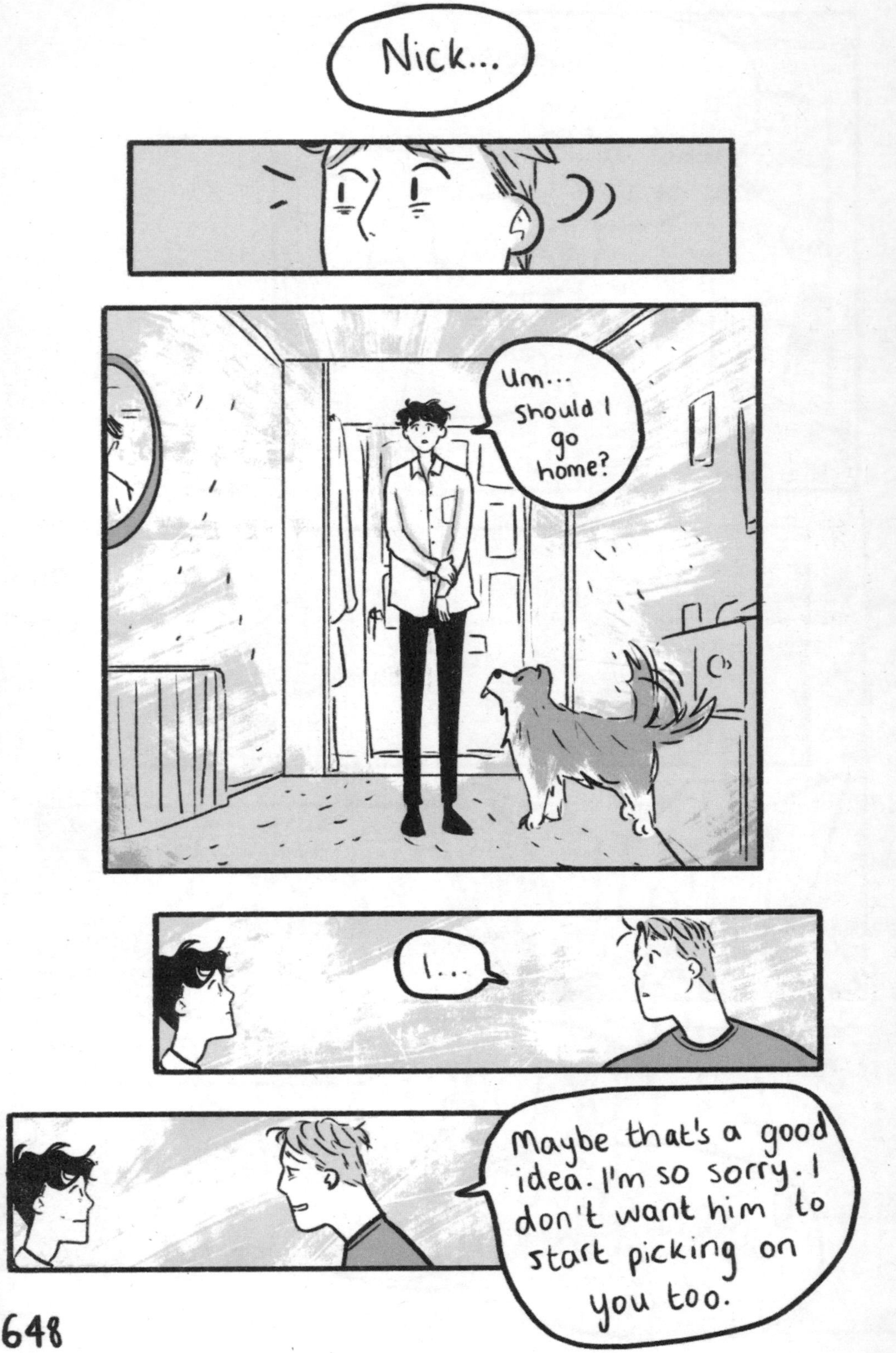
Nick...
Um... should I go home?
I...
Maybe that's a good idea. I'm so sorry. I don't want him to start picking on you too.

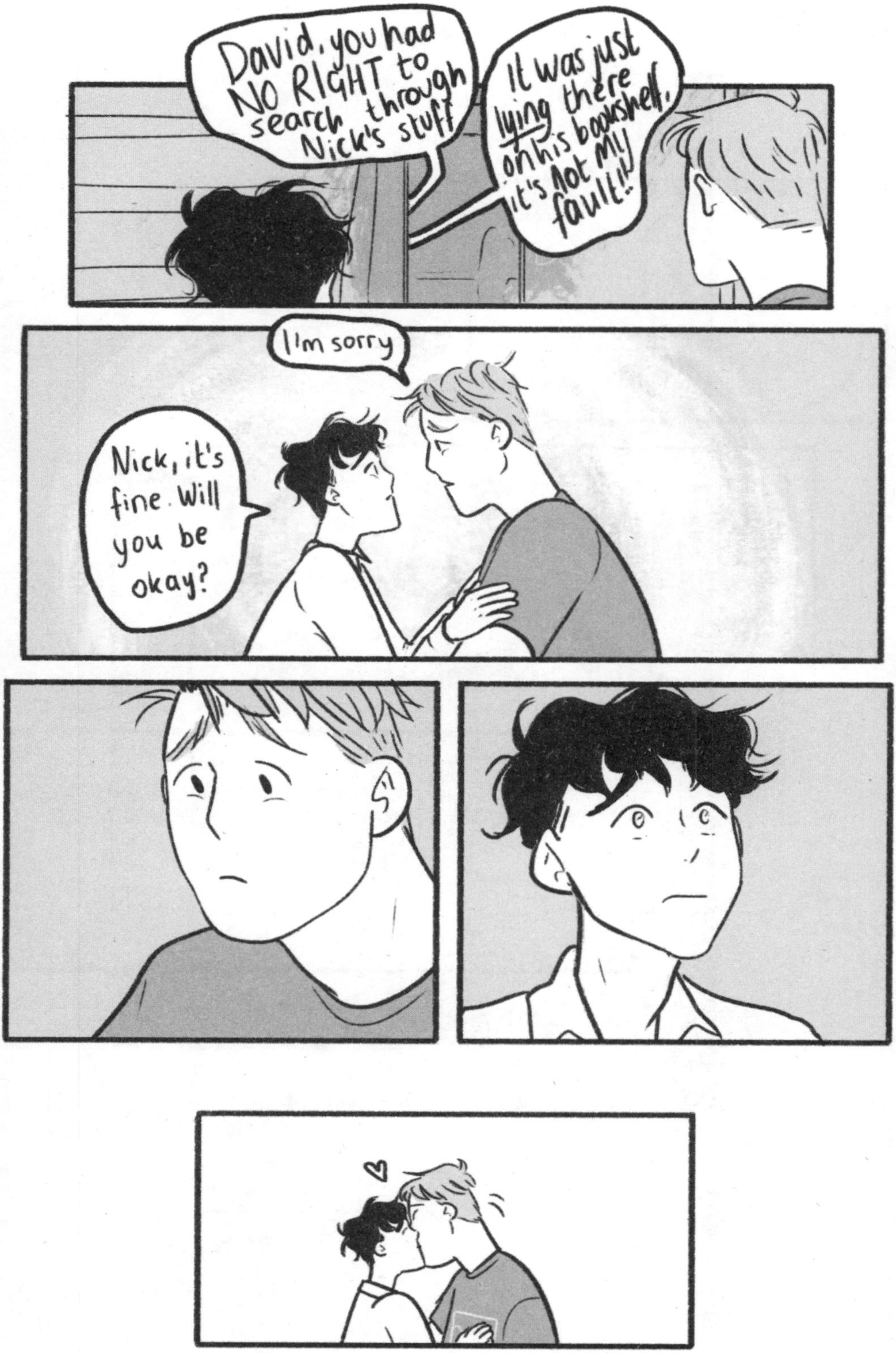
David, you had NO RIGHT to search through Nick's stuff
It was just lying there on his bookshelf, it's not my fault!!
I'm sorry
Nick, it's fine. Will you be okay?

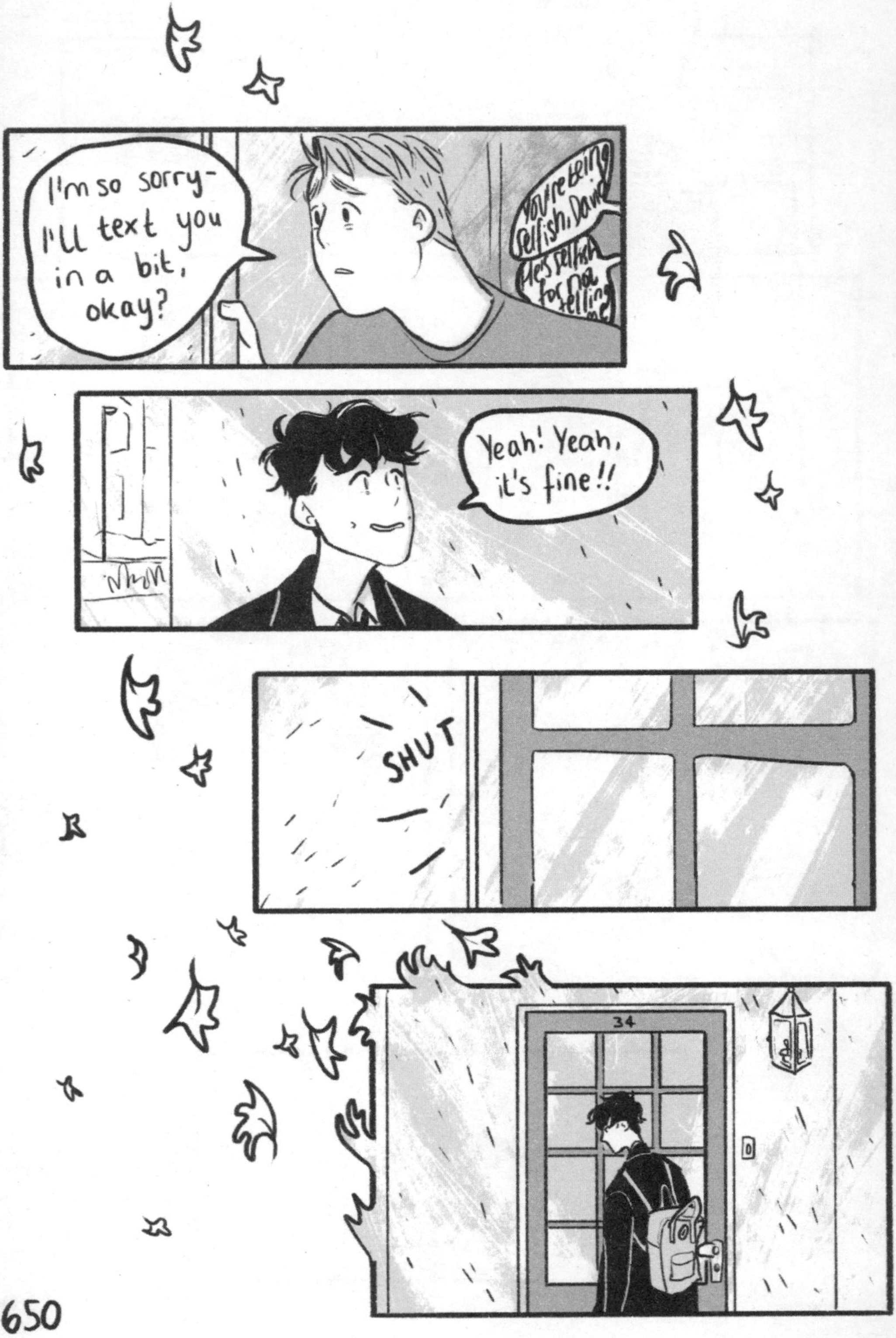
I'm so sorry- I'll text you in a bit, okay?
You're being selfish, Davi
He's selfish for not telling me
Yeah! Yeah, it's fine!!
SHUT
34

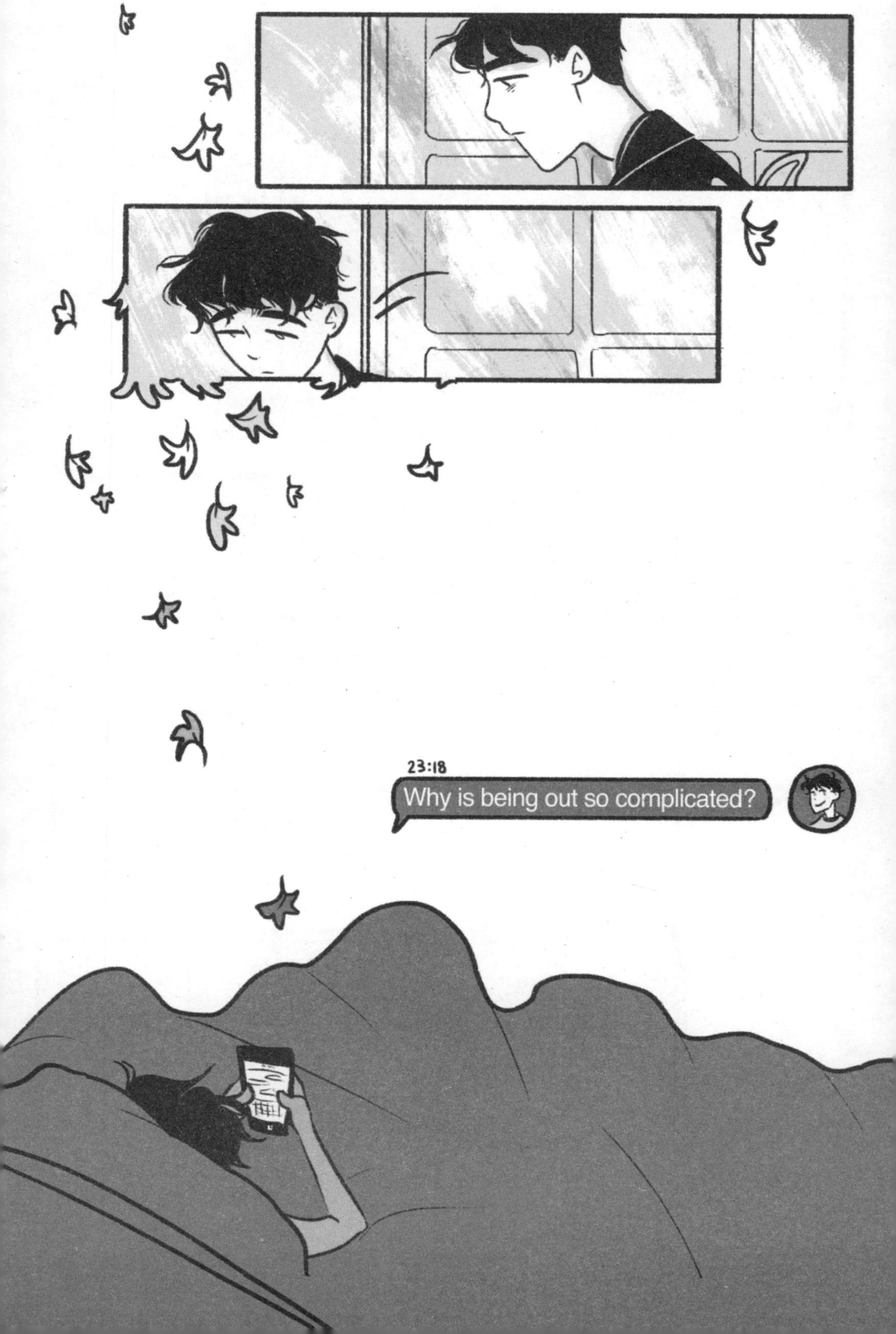
23:18
Why is being out so complicated?

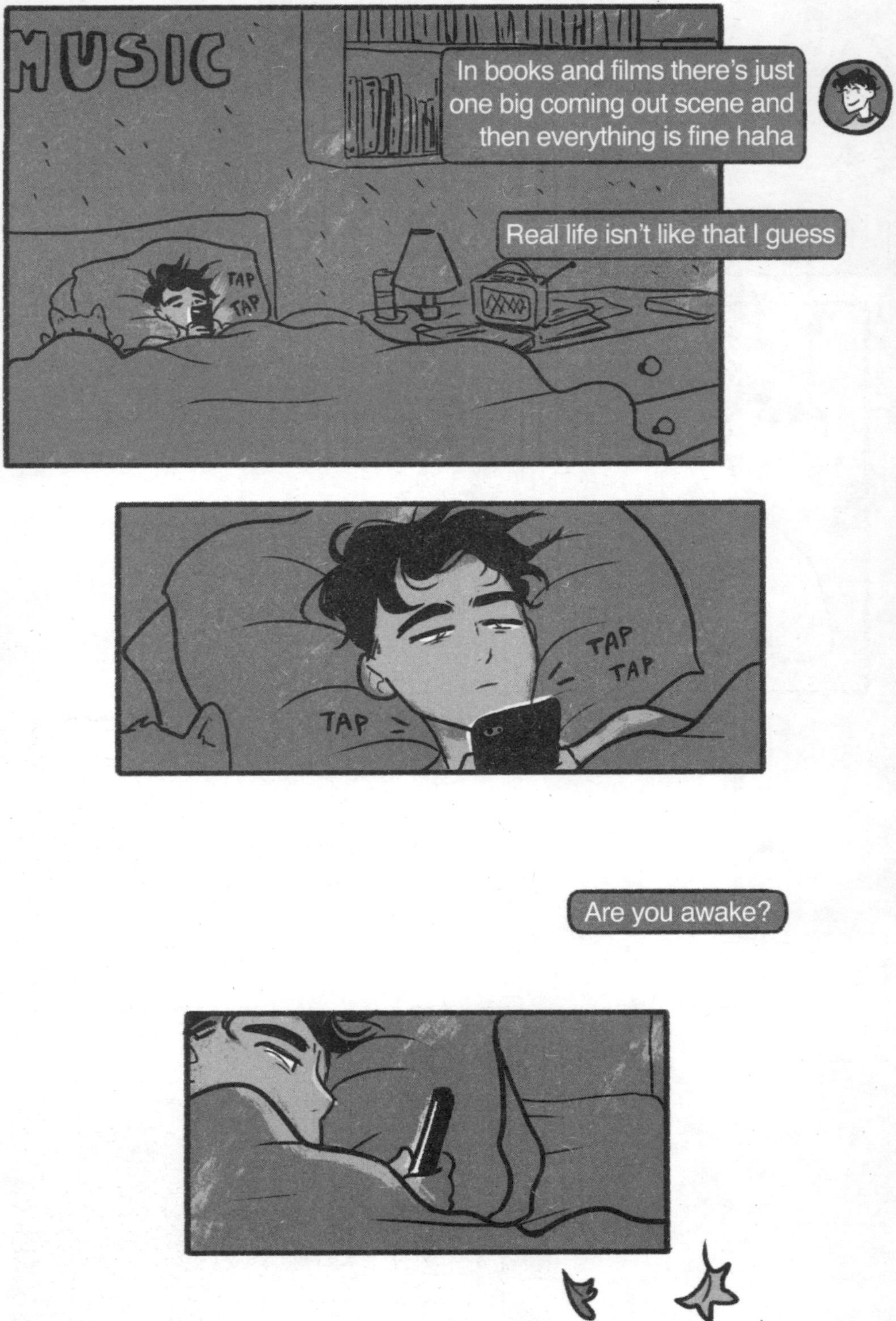
MUSIC
In books and films there's just one big coming out scene and then everything is fine haha
Real life isn't like that I guess
TAP TAP
TAP TAP
TAP
Are you awake?

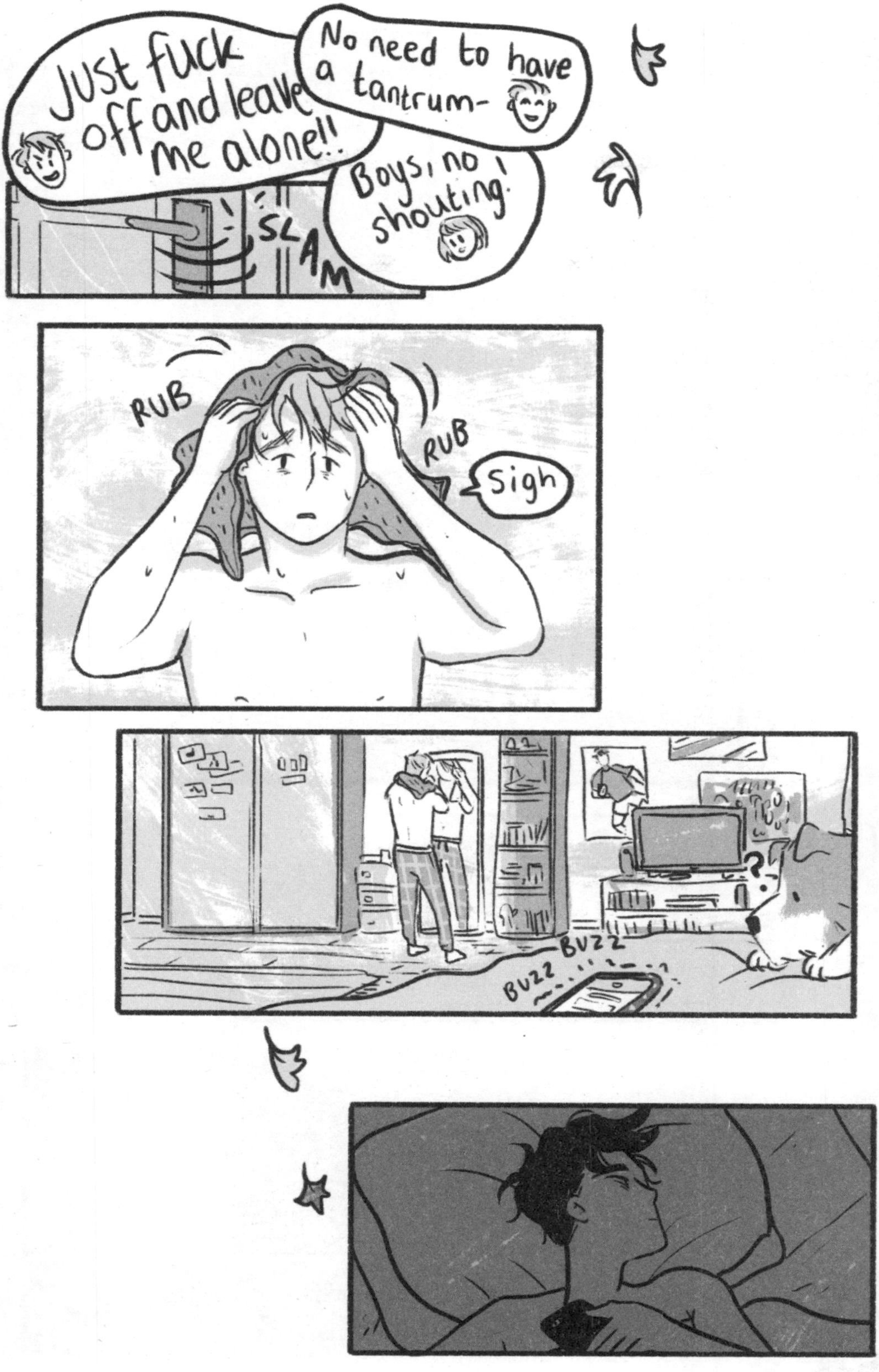
Just fuck off and leave me alone!!
No need to have a tantrum-
Boys, no shouting!
SLAM
RUB
RUB
Sigh
BUZZ
BUZZ

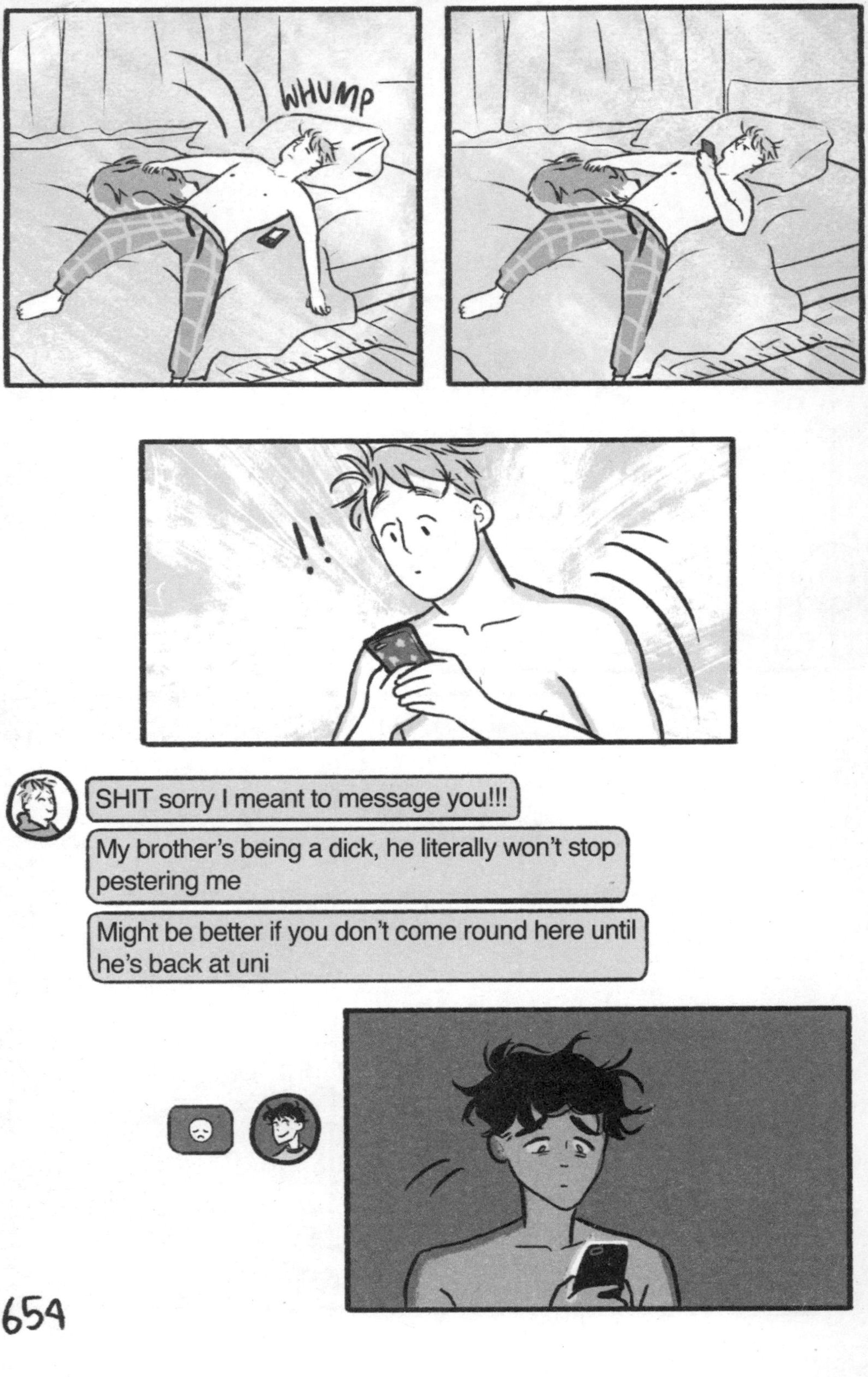
WHUMP
!!
SHIT sorry I meant to message you!!!
My brother's being a dick, he literally won't stop pestering me
Might be better if you don't come round here until he's back at uni

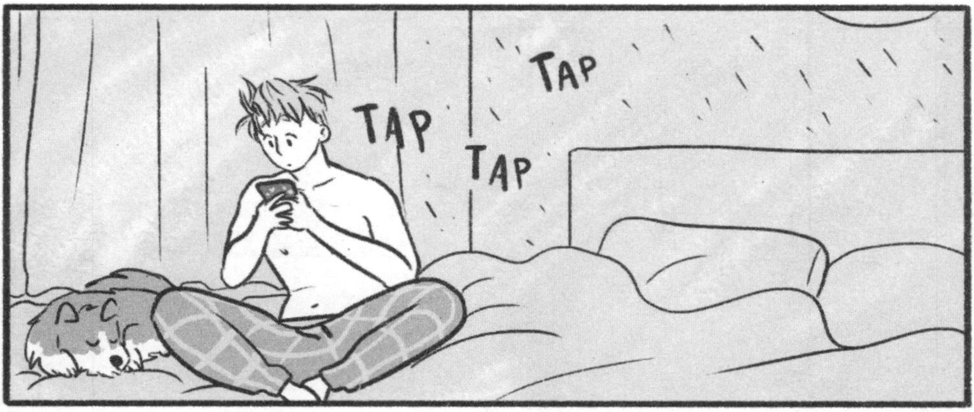
TAP
TAP
TAP

It was my fault for not telling him sooner tbh

No! You shouldn't have to tell him if you didn't want to

I guess he would have found out eventually one way or another. I should probably call my dad soon and tell him too

You don't have to! you can take your time!

I want him to know about you!! Plus I want to be the one to tell him, not David

😞😞😞

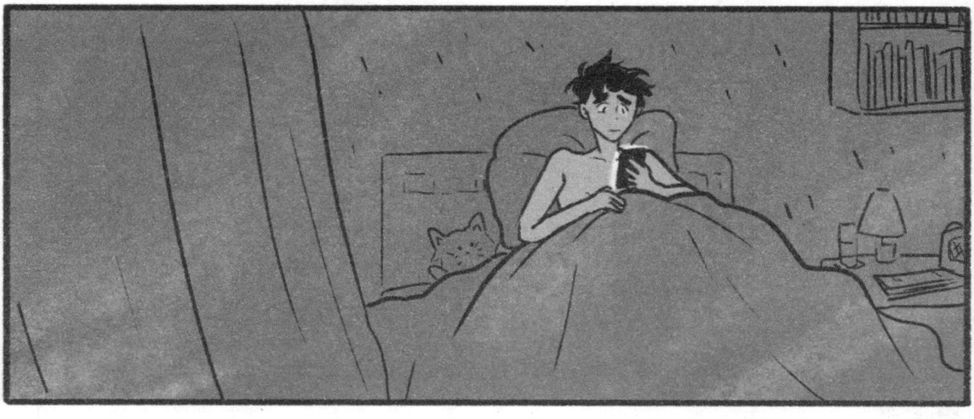

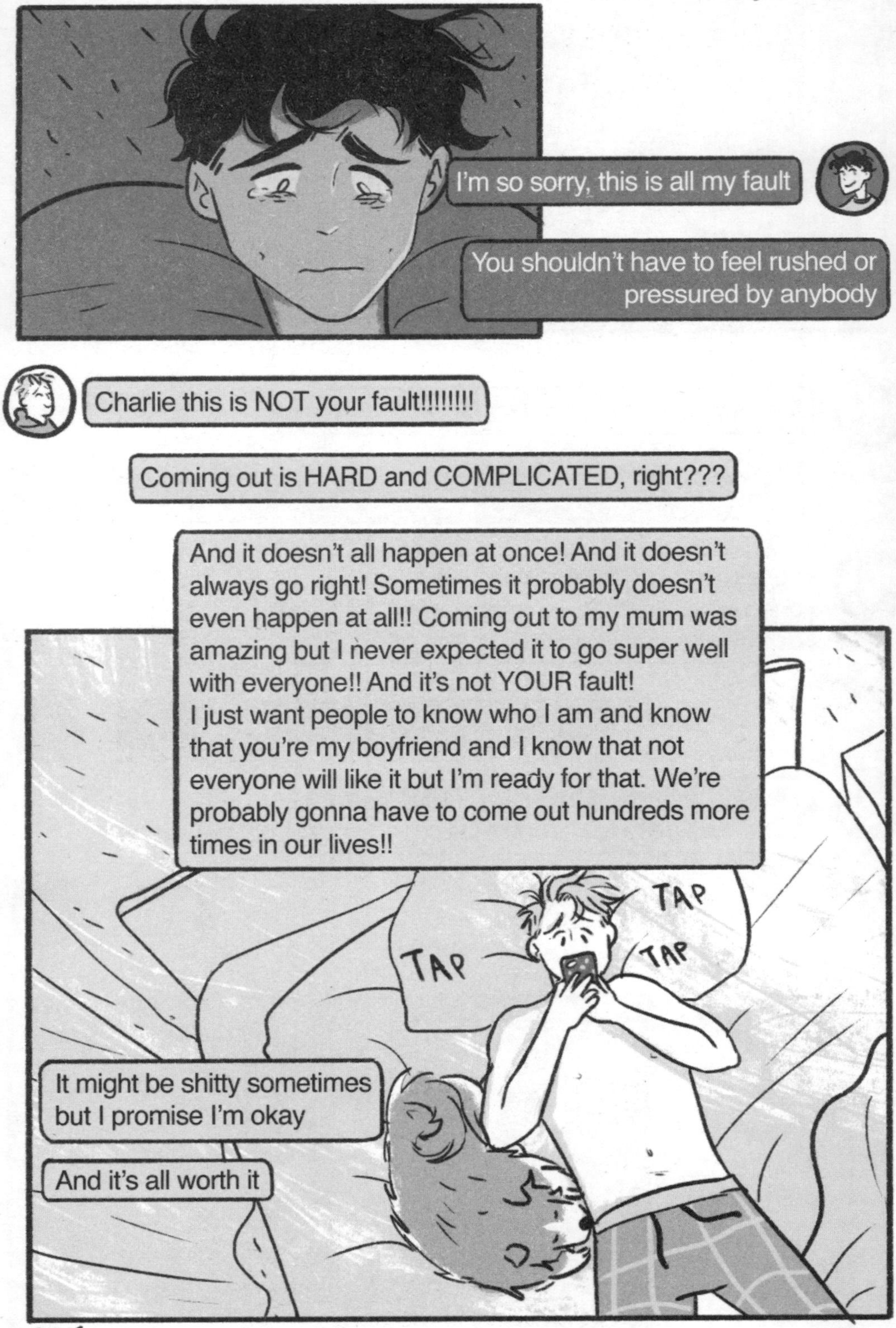
I'm so sorry, this is all my fault
You shouldn't have to feel rushed or pressured by anybody
Charlie this is NOT your fault!!!!!!!!
Coming out is HARD and COMPLICATED, right???
And it doesn't all happen at once! And it doesn't always go right! Sometimes it probably doesn't even happen at all!! Coming out to my mum was amazing but I never expected it to go super well with everyone!! And it's not YOUR fault!
I just want people to know who I am and know that you're my boyfriend and I know that not everyone will like it but I'm ready for that. We're probably gonna have to come out hundreds more times in our lives!!
TAP
TAP
TAP
It might be shitty sometimes but I promise I'm okay
And it's all worth it

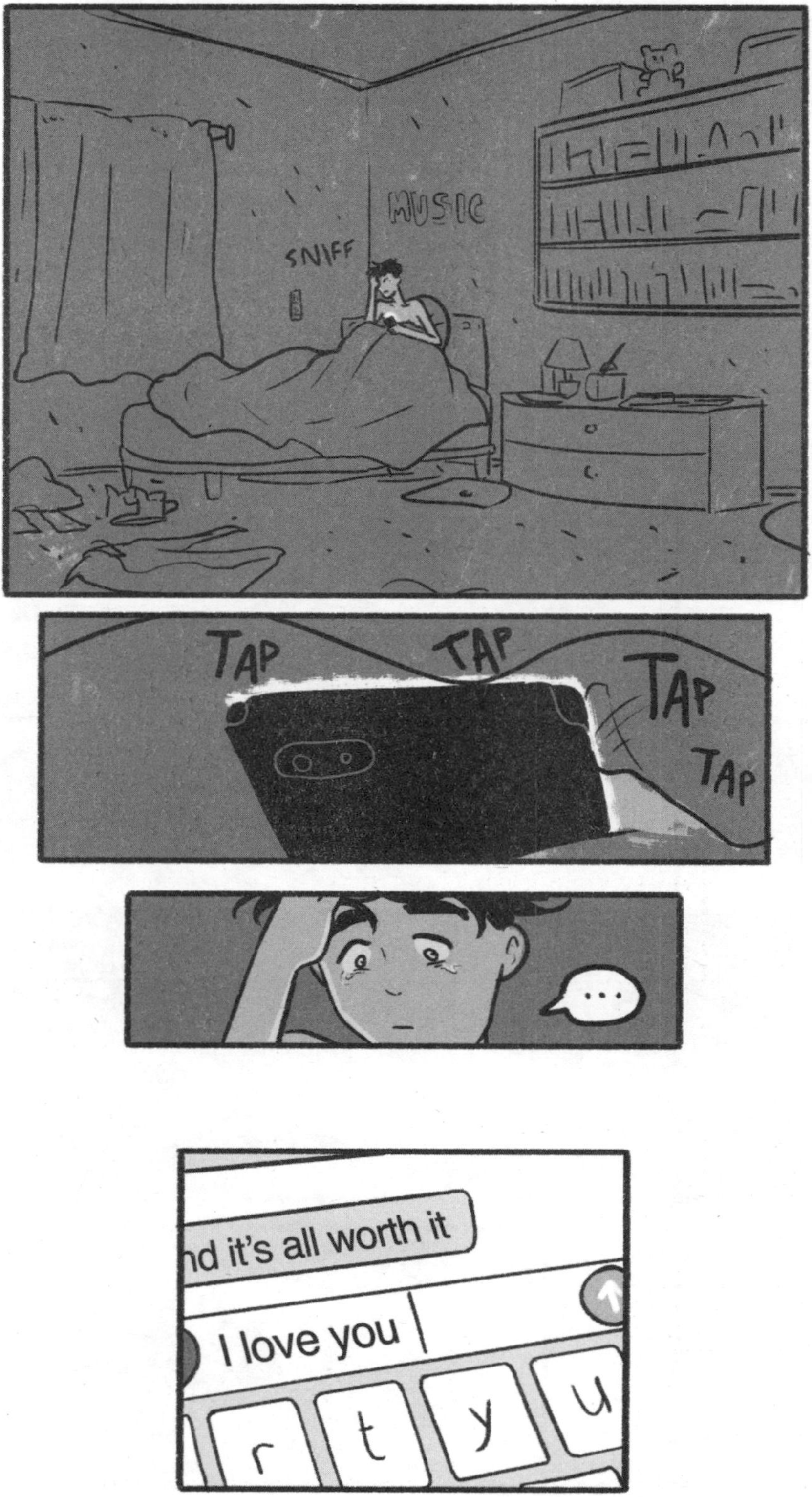
MUSIC
SNIFF
TAP
TAP
TAP
TAP
...
nd it's all worth it
I love you
r t y u

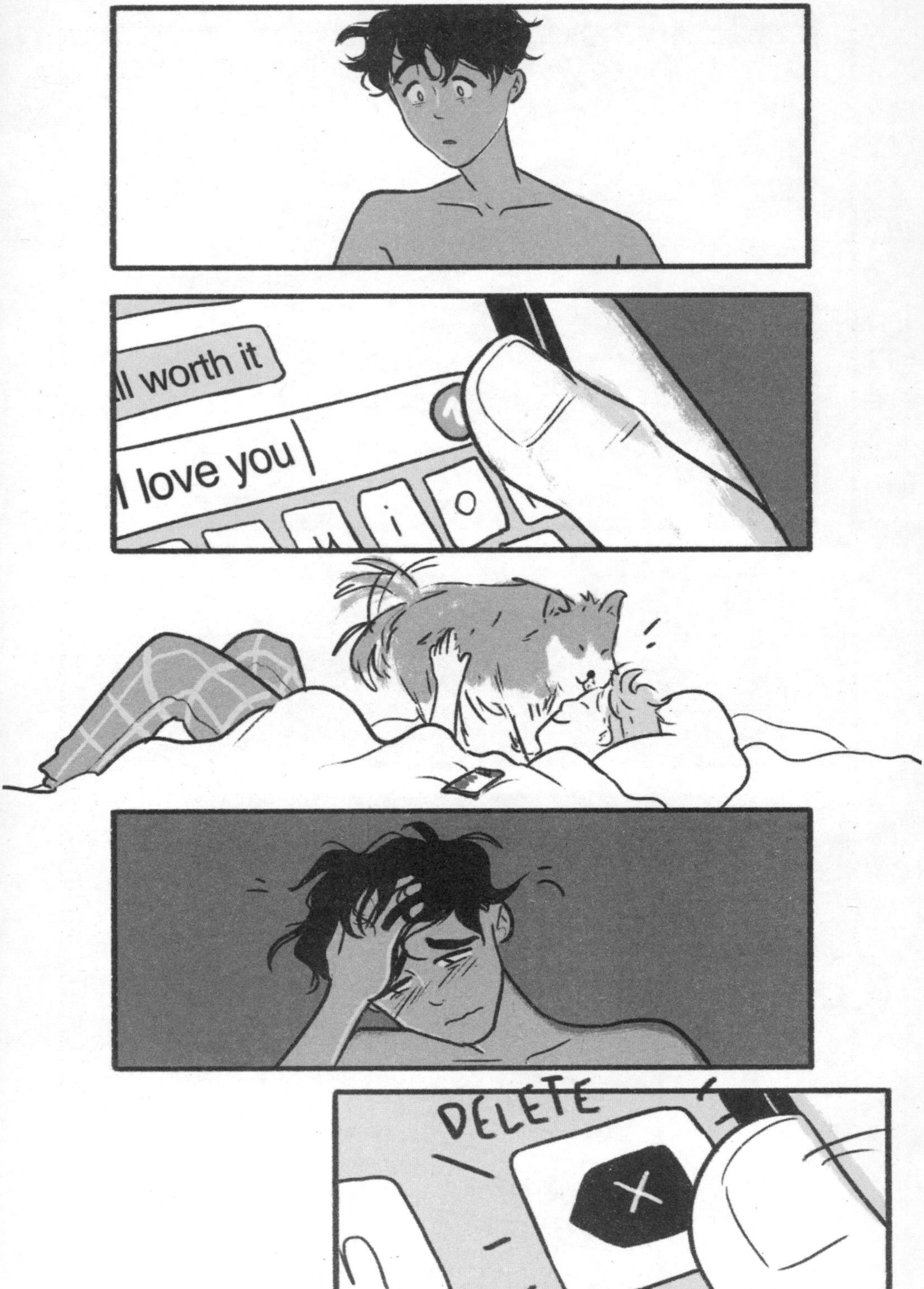
ll worth it
I love you
DELETE

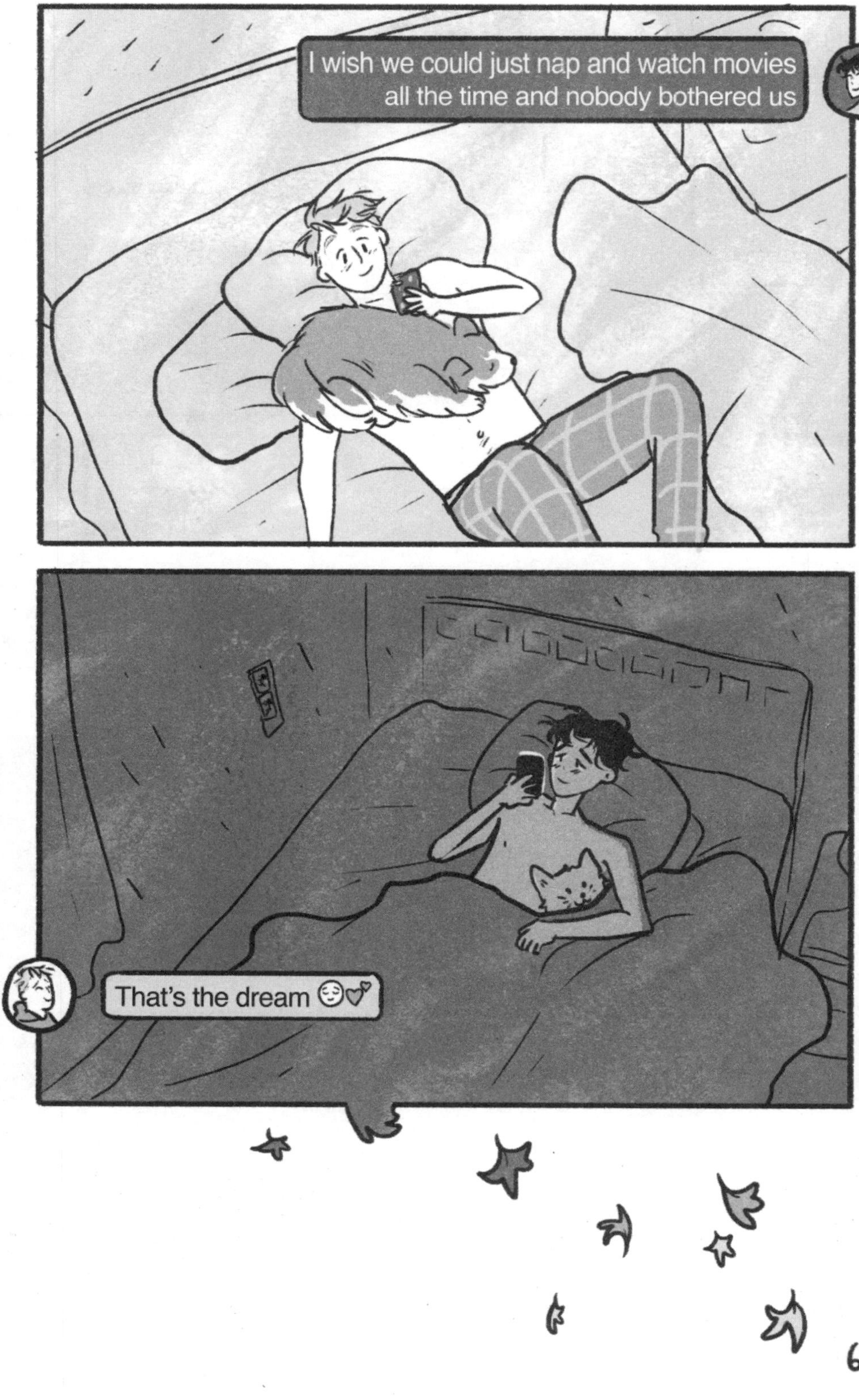
I wish we could just nap and watch movies all the time and nobody bothered us
That's the dream 😌💕

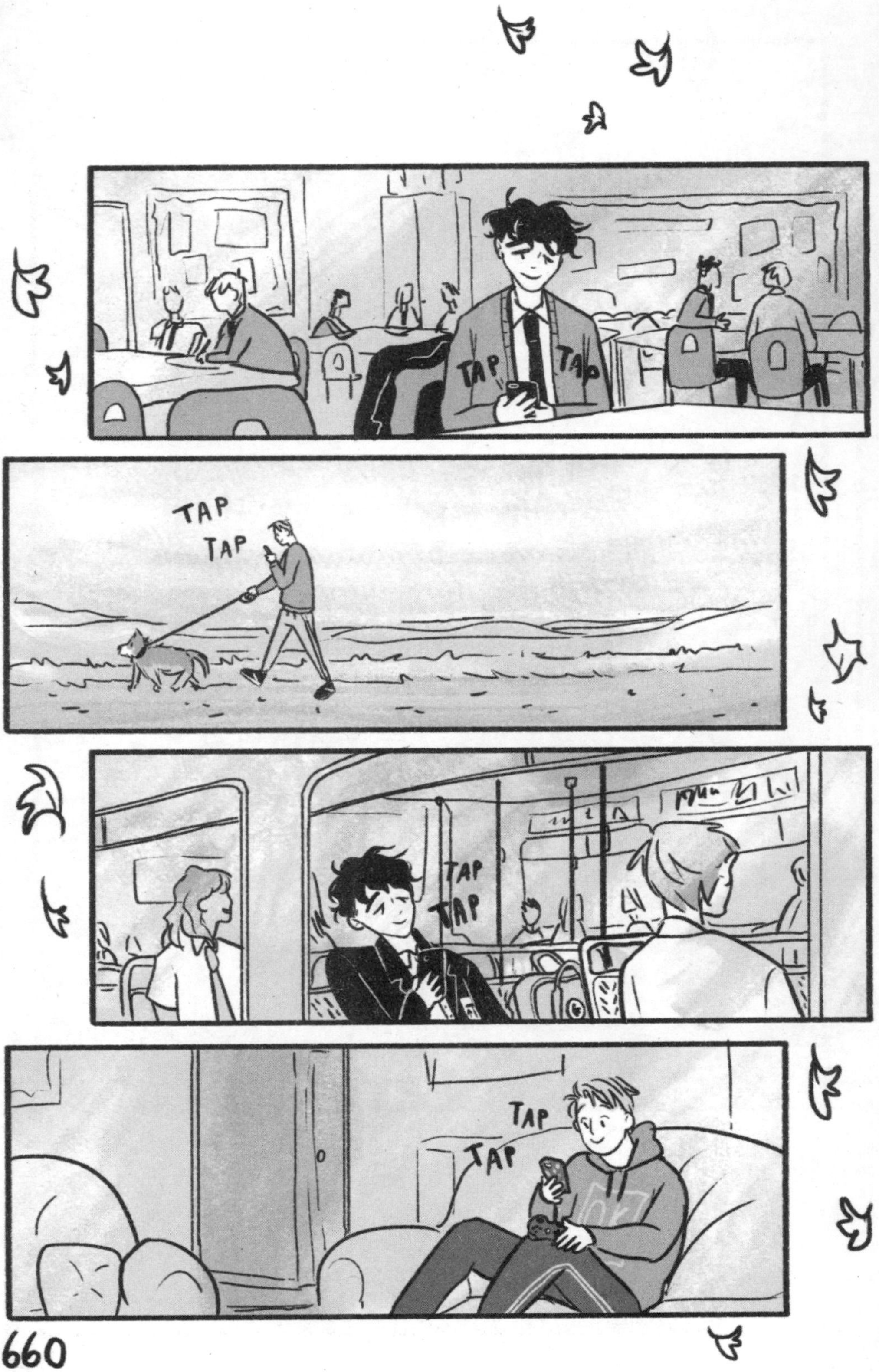
TAP
TAP
TAP
TAP
TAP
TAP
TAP
TAP

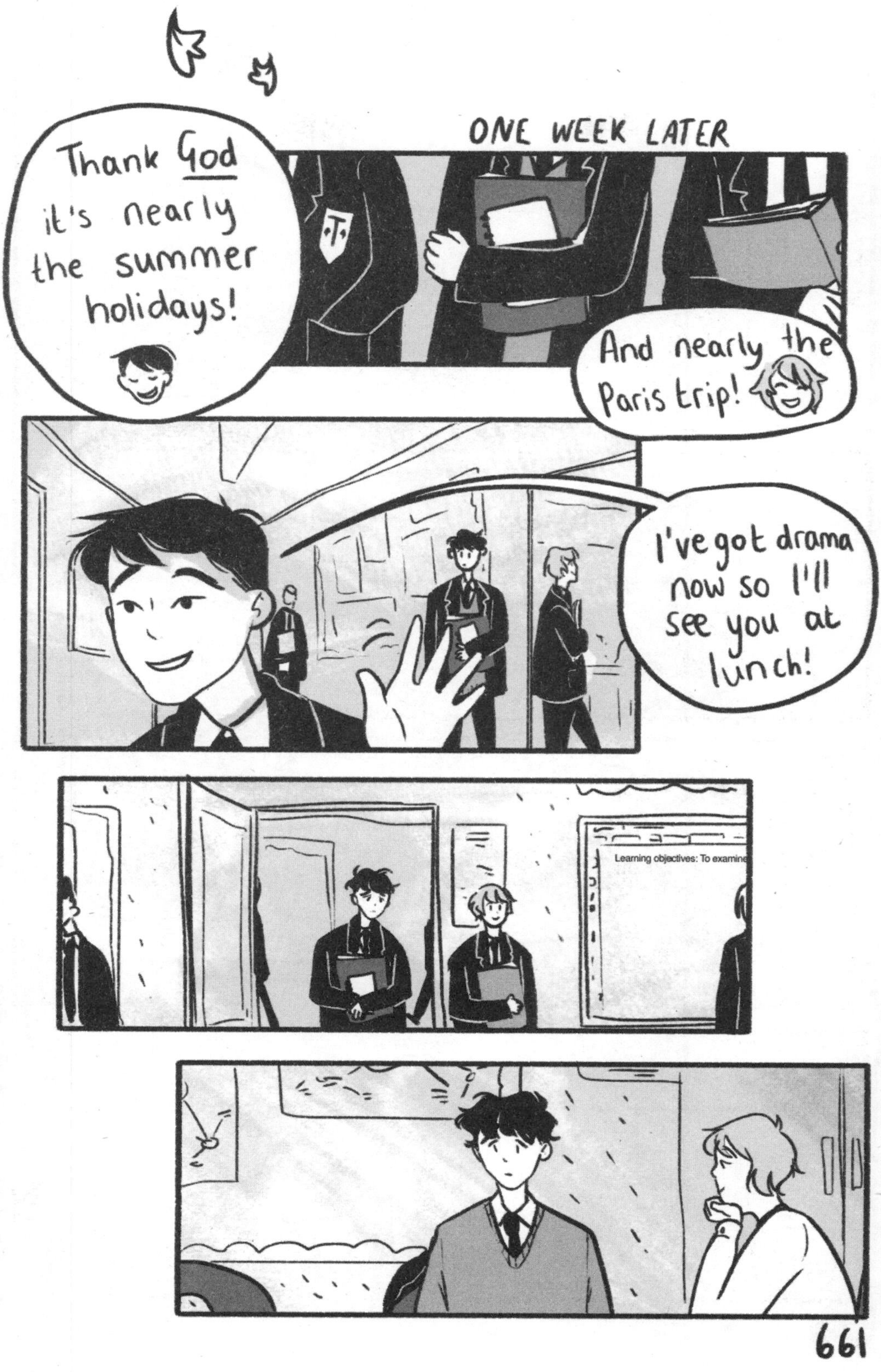
ONE WEEK LATER
Thank God it's nearly the summer holidays!
And nearly the Paris trip!
I've got drama now so I'll see you at lunch!
Learning objectives: To examine

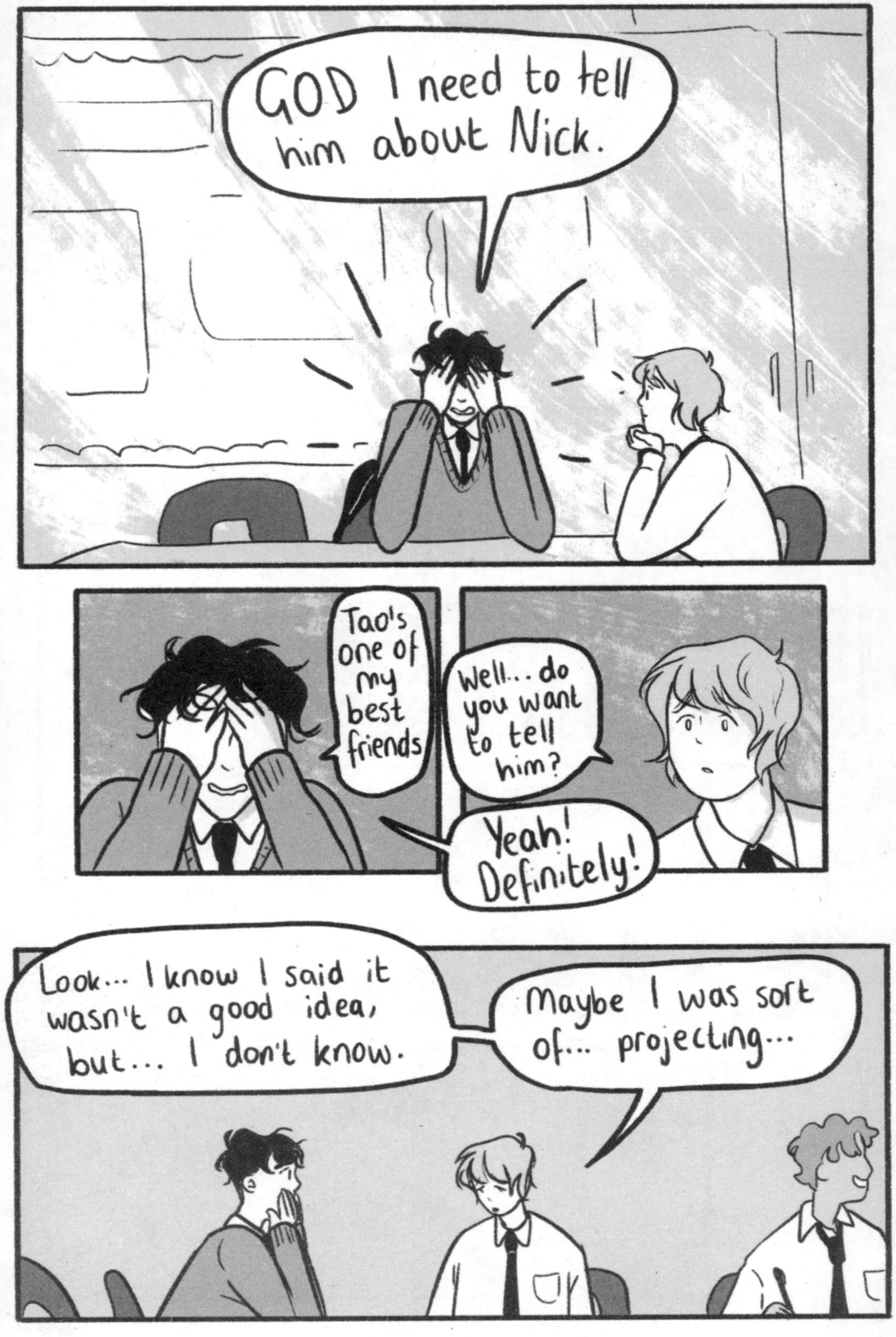
GOD I need to tell him about Nick.
Tao's one of my best friends
Well... do you want to tell him?
Yeah! Definitely!
Look... I know I said it wasn't a good idea, but... I don't know.
Maybe I was sort of... projecting...

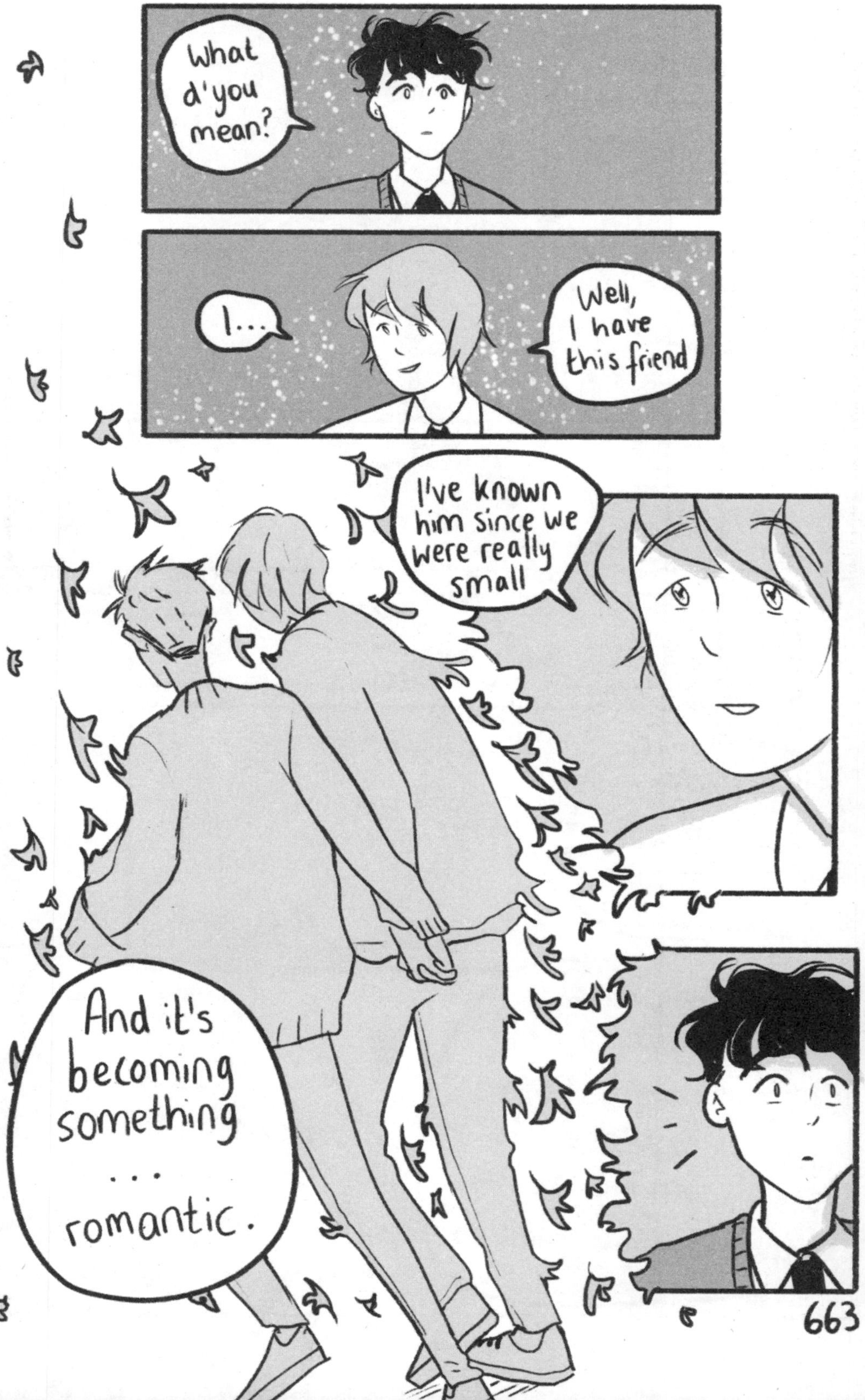
What d'you mean?
I...
Well, I have this friend
I've known him since we were really small
And it's becoming something ... romantic.

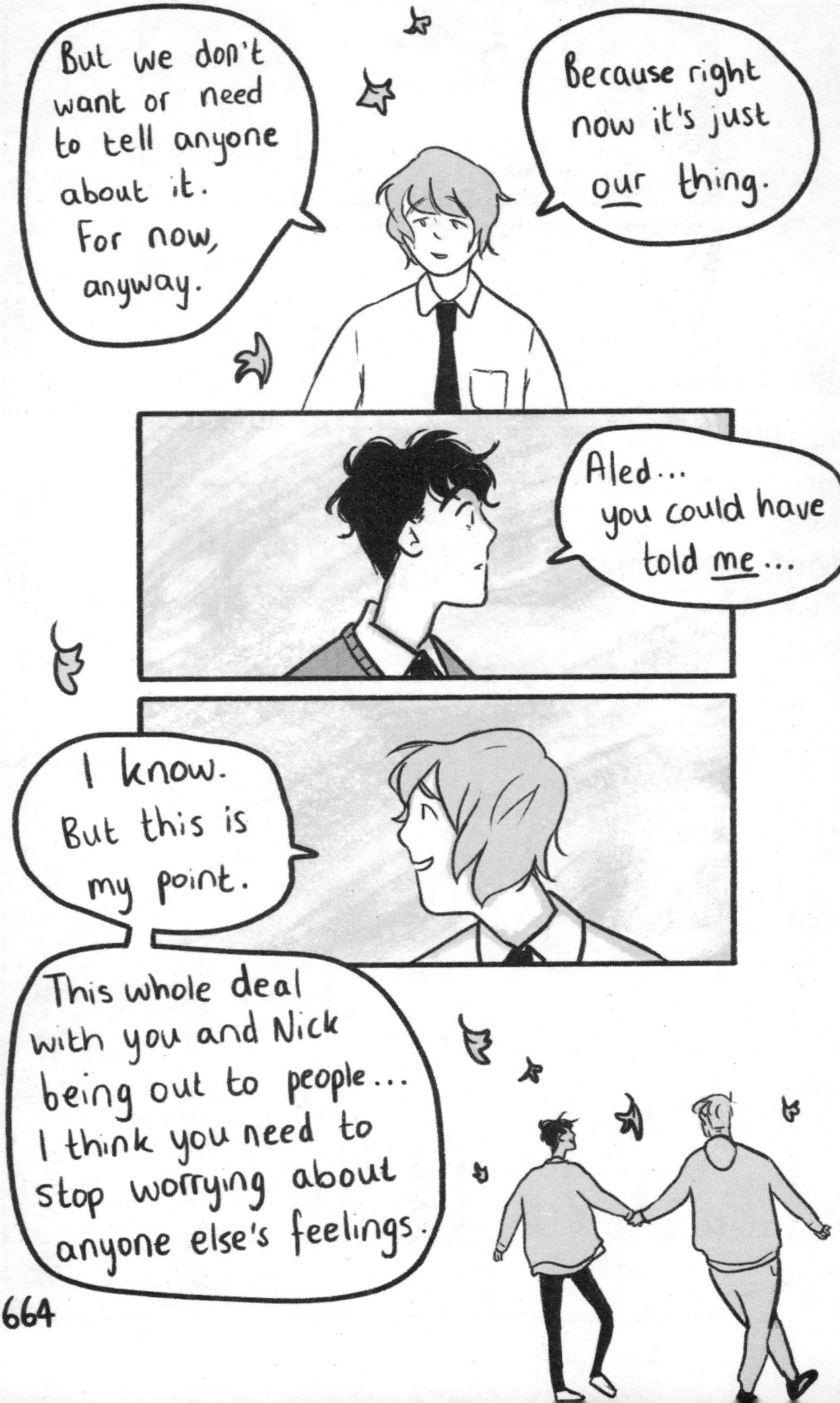
But we don't want or need to tell anyone about it. For now, anyway.
Because right now it's just our thing.
Aled... you could have told me...
I know. But this is my point.
This whole deal with you and Nick being out to people... I think you need to stop worrying about anyone else's feelings.

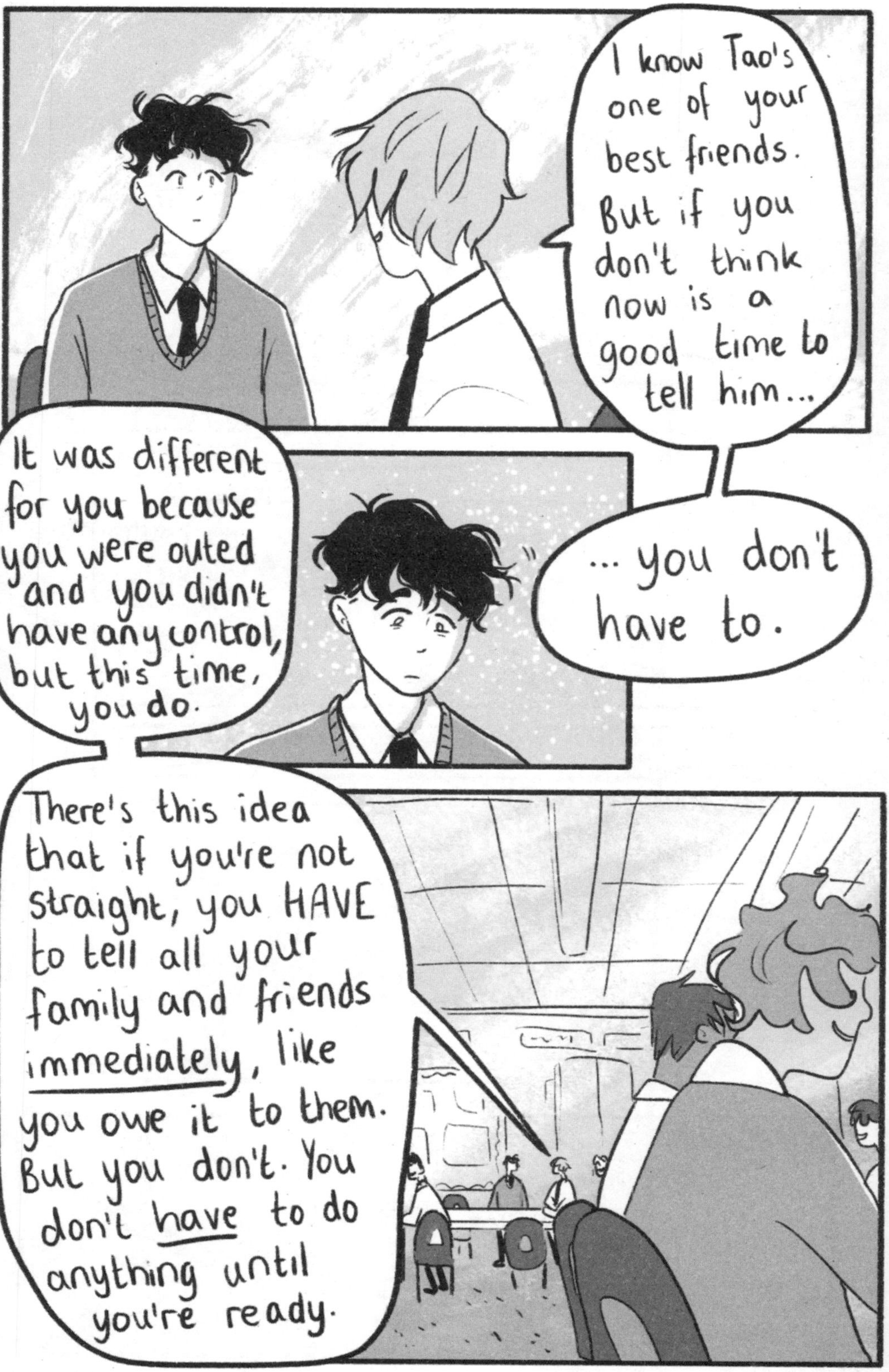

I know Tao's one of your best friends. But if you don't think now is a good time to tell him...
... you don't have to.
It was different for you because you were outed and you didn't have any control, but this time, you do.
There's this idea that if you're not straight, you HAVE to tell all your family and friends immediately, like you owe it to them. But you don't. You don't have to do anything until you're ready.

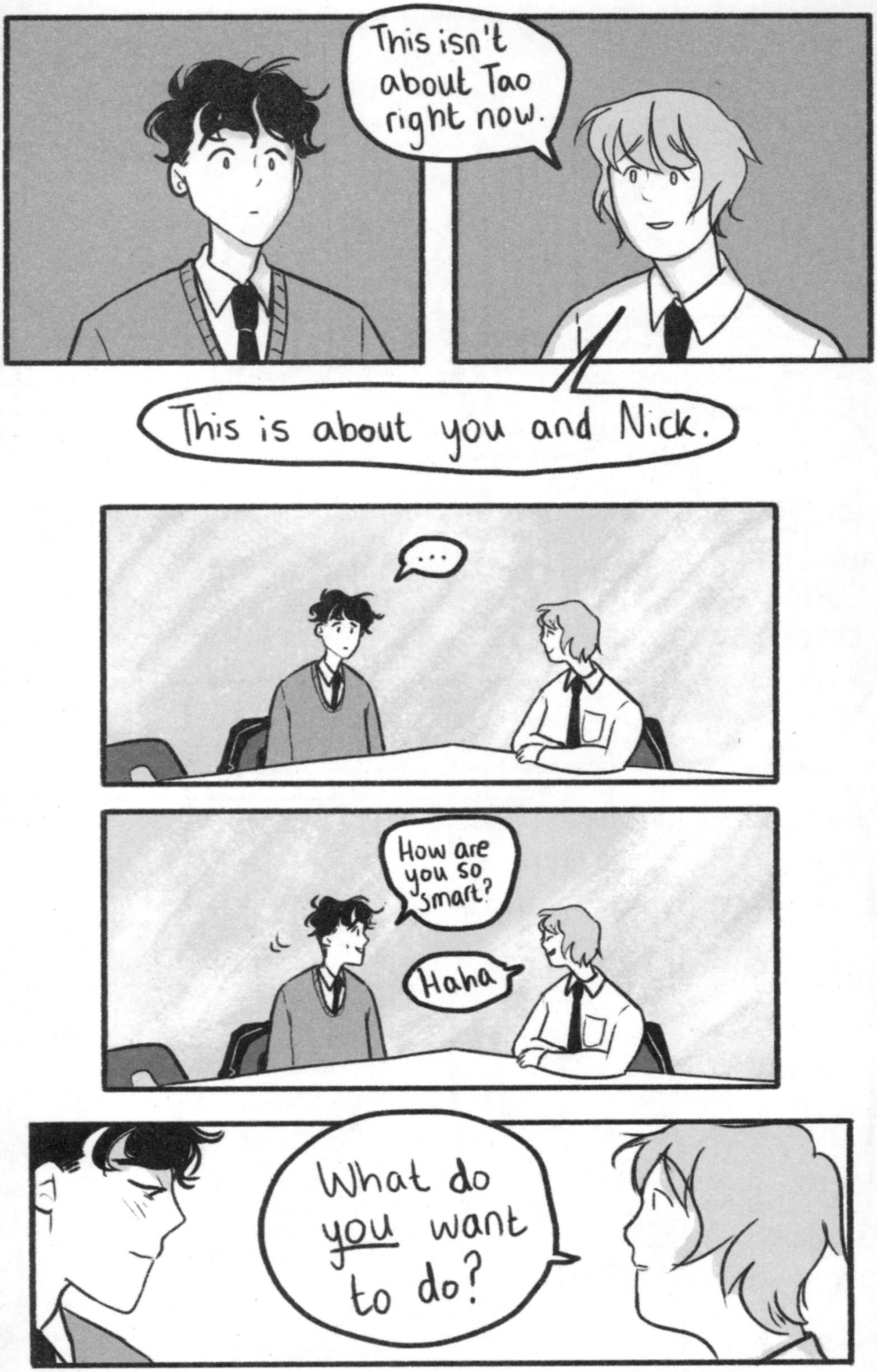
This isn't about Tao right now.
This is about you and Nick.
...
How are you so smart?
Haha
What do you want to do?

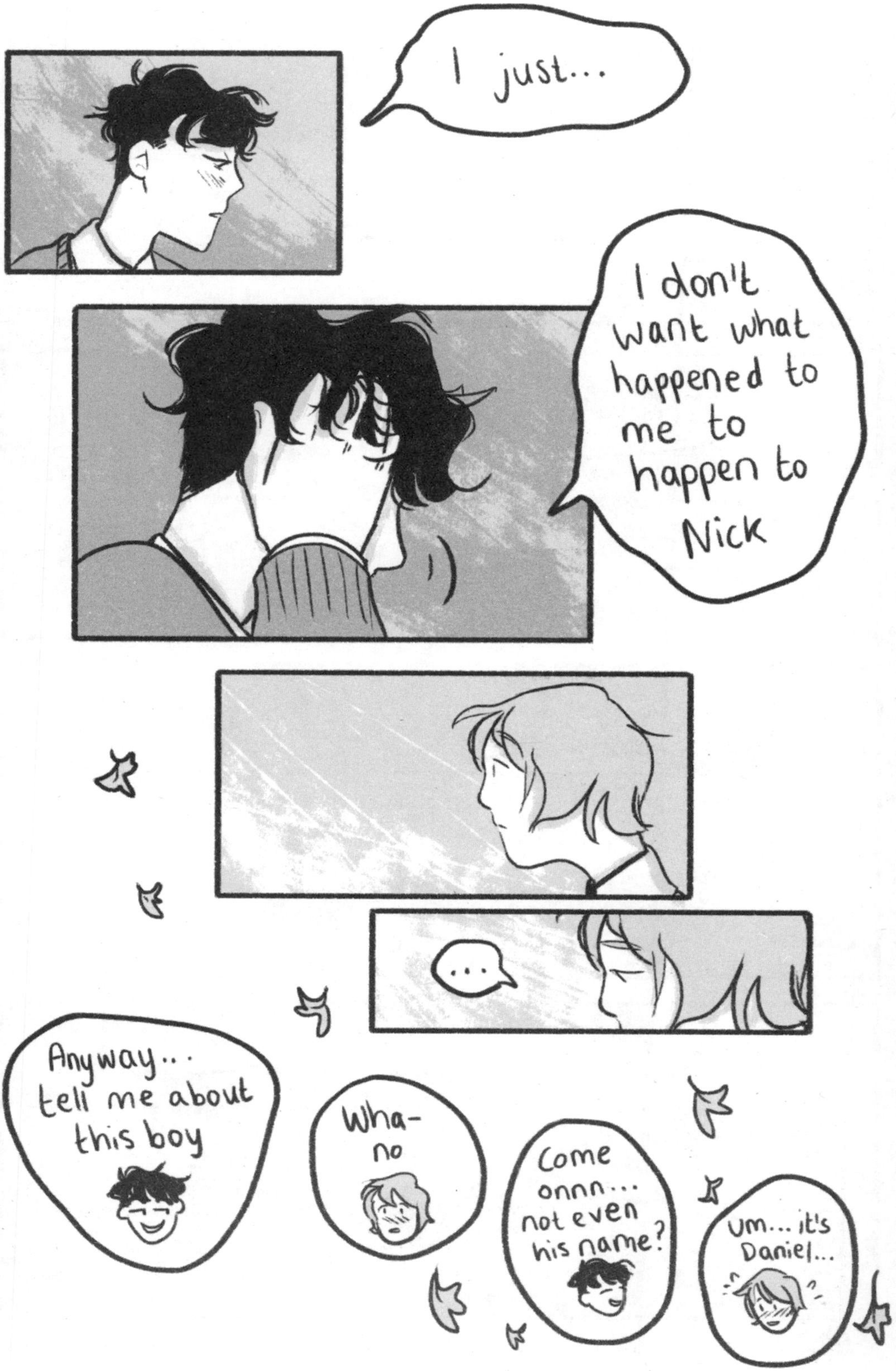
I just...
I don't want what happened to me to happen to Nick
...
Anyway... tell me about this boy
Wha- no
Come onnn... not even his name?
Um... it's Daniel...

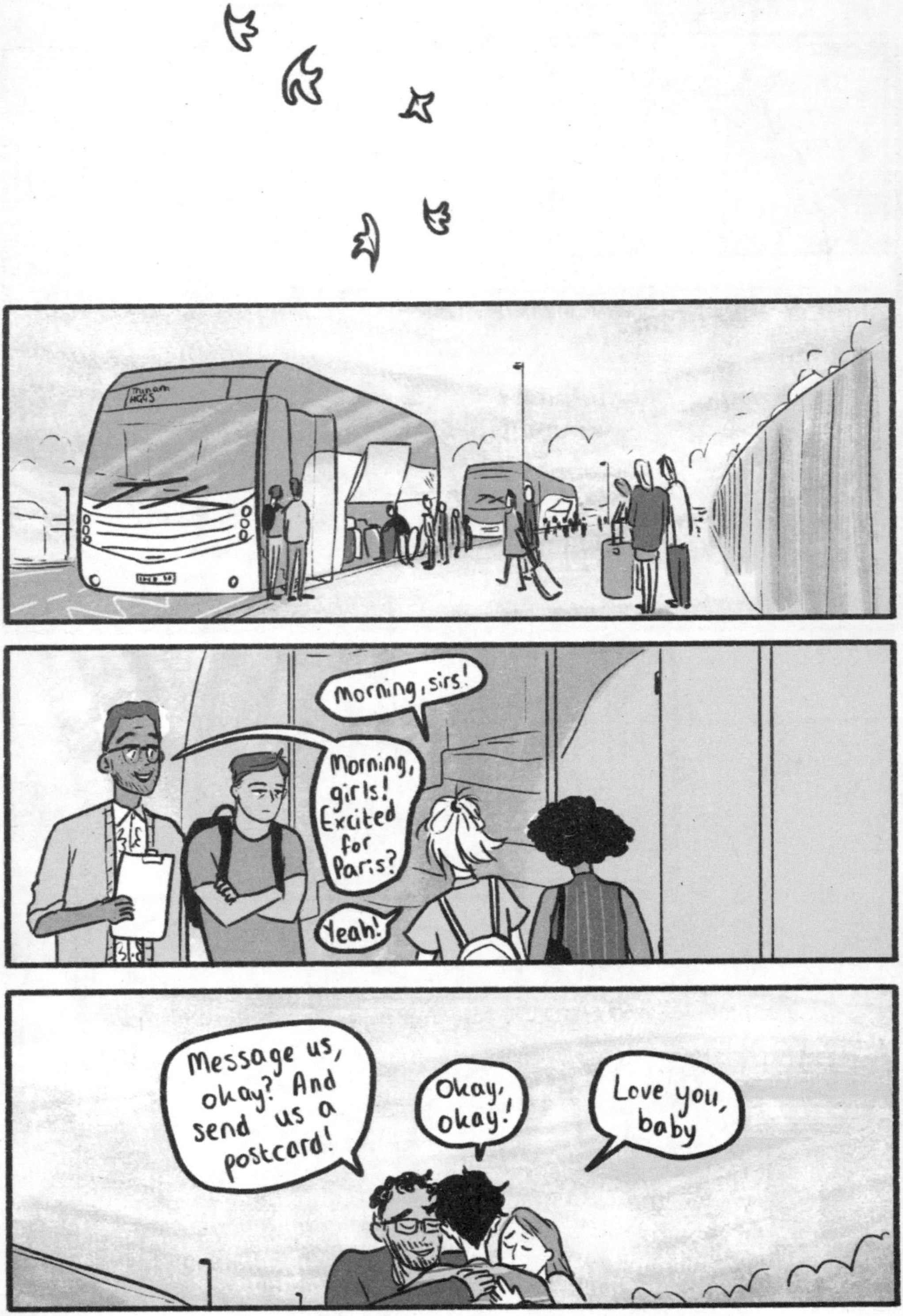
Morning, sirs!
Morning, girls! Excited for Paris?
Yeah!
Message us, okay? And send us a postcard!
Okay, okay!
Love you, baby

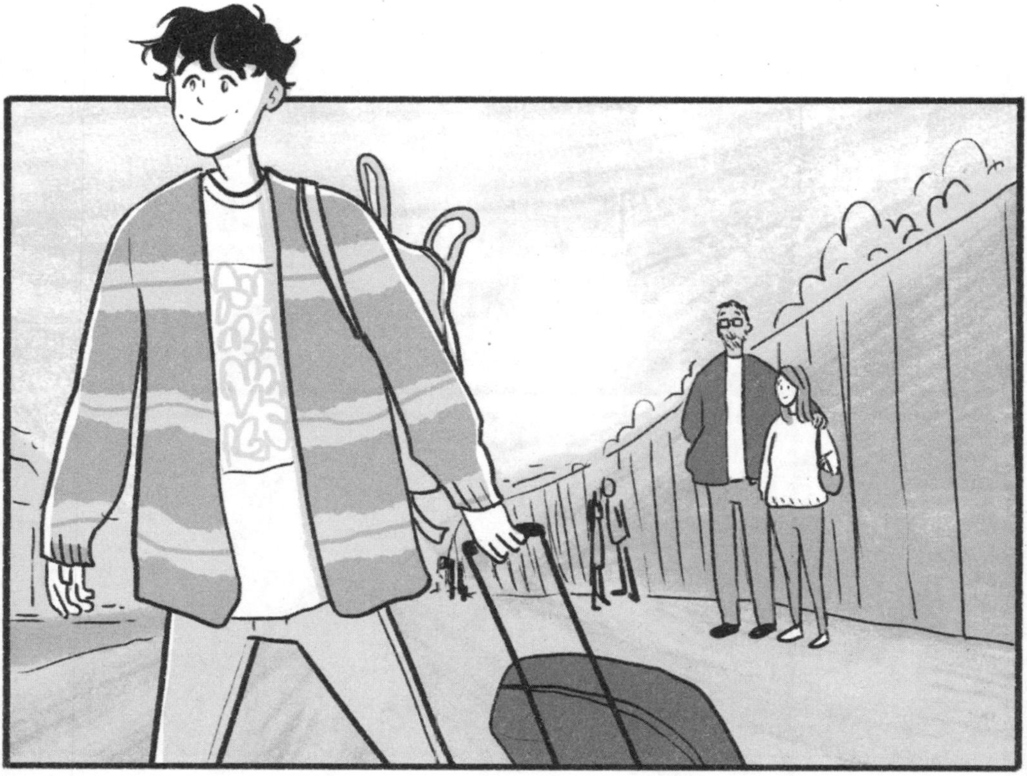

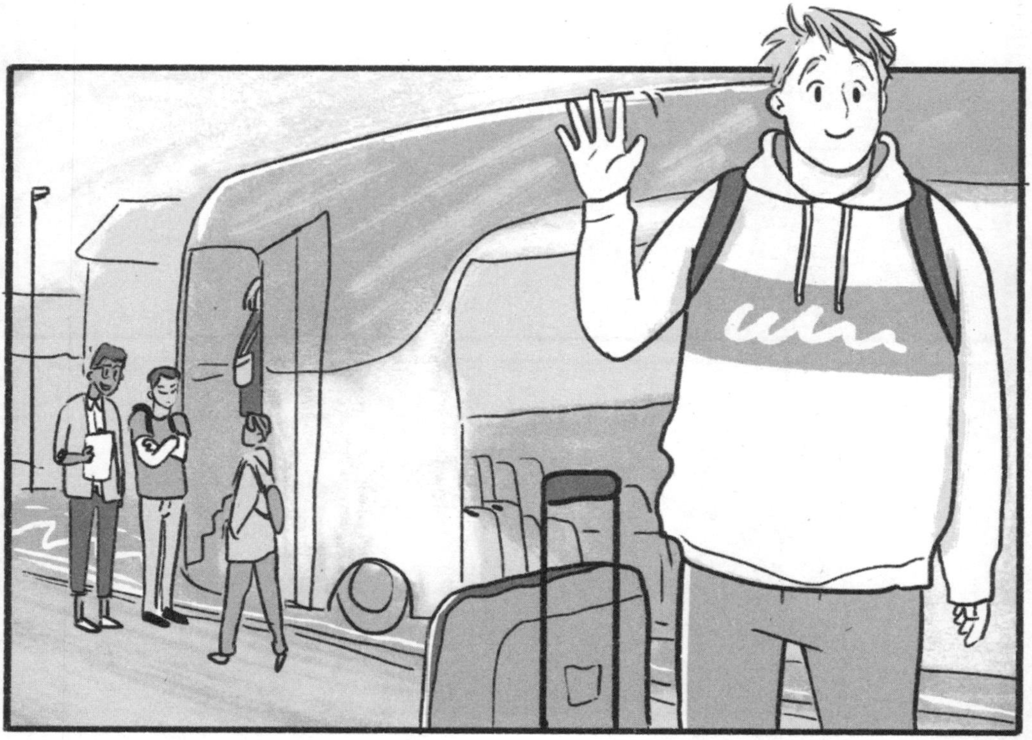

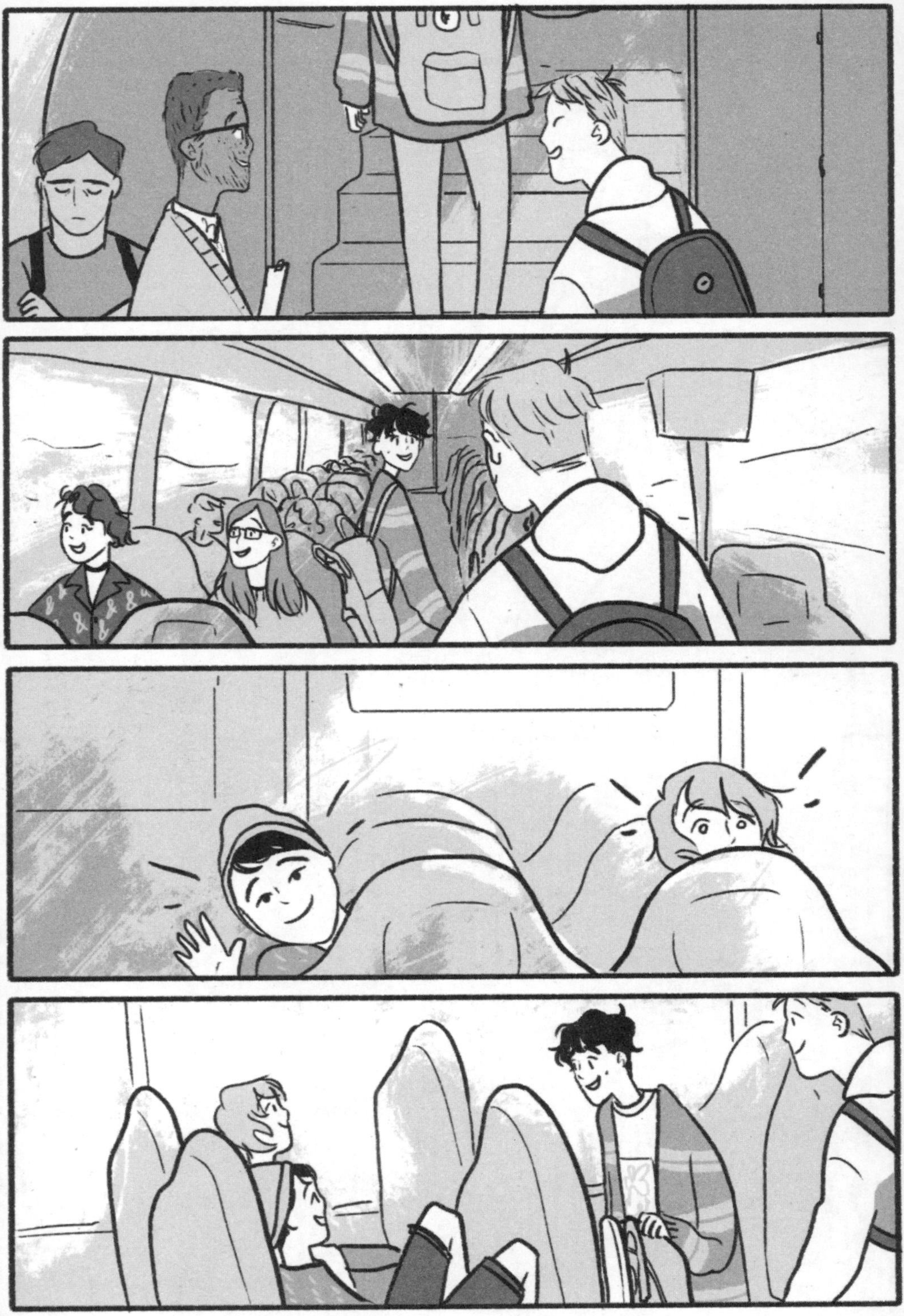

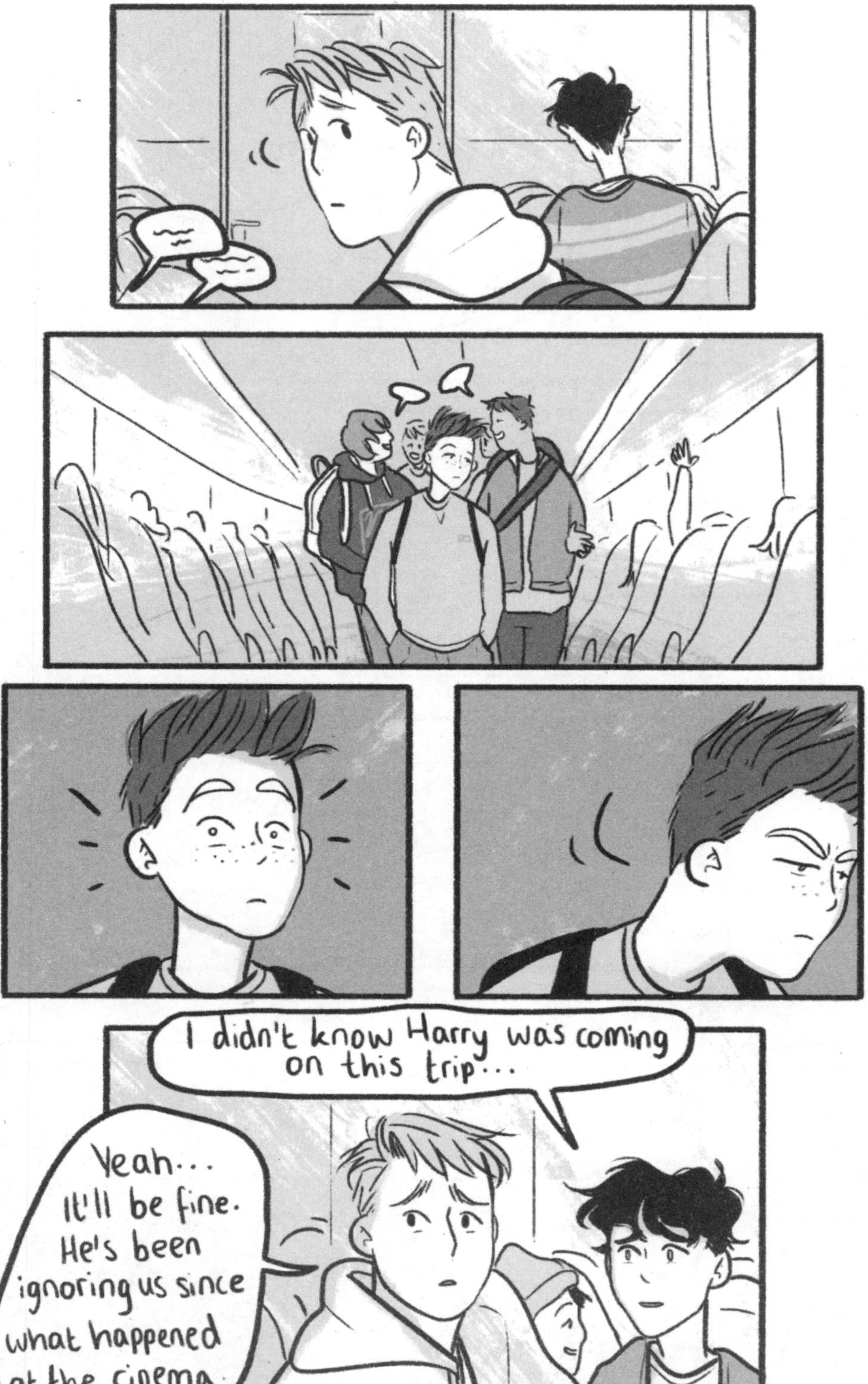
I didn't know Harry was coming on this trip...
Yeah... It'll be fine. He's been ignoring us since what happened at the cinema

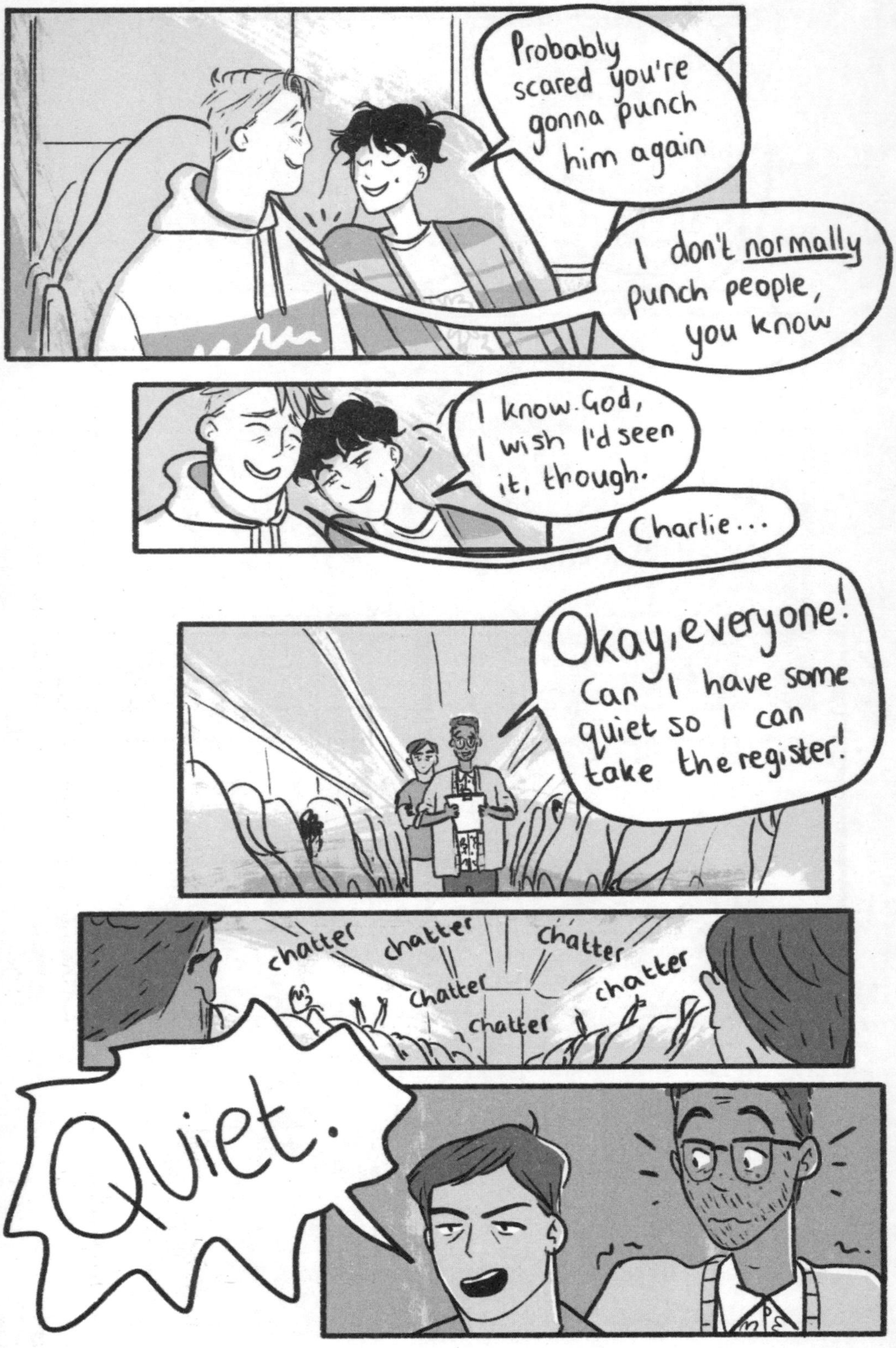
Probably scared you're gonna punch him again
I don't normally punch people, you know
I know. God, I wish I'd seen it, though.
Charlie...
Okay, everyone! Can I have some quiet so I can take the register!
chatter
chatter
chatter
chatter
chatter
chatter
Quiet.

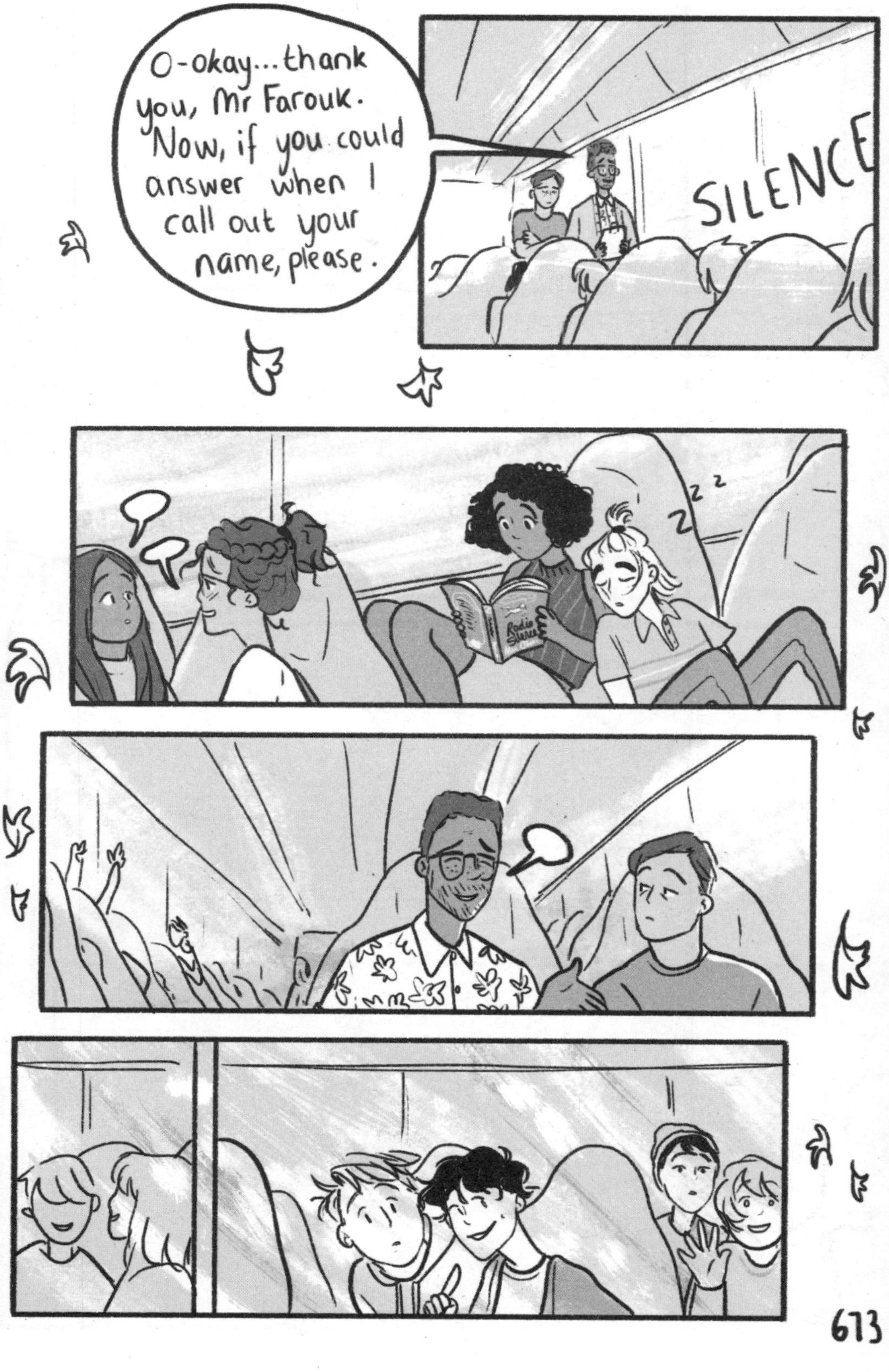

O-okay...thank you, Mr Farouk. Now, if you could answer when I call out your name, please.
SILENCE

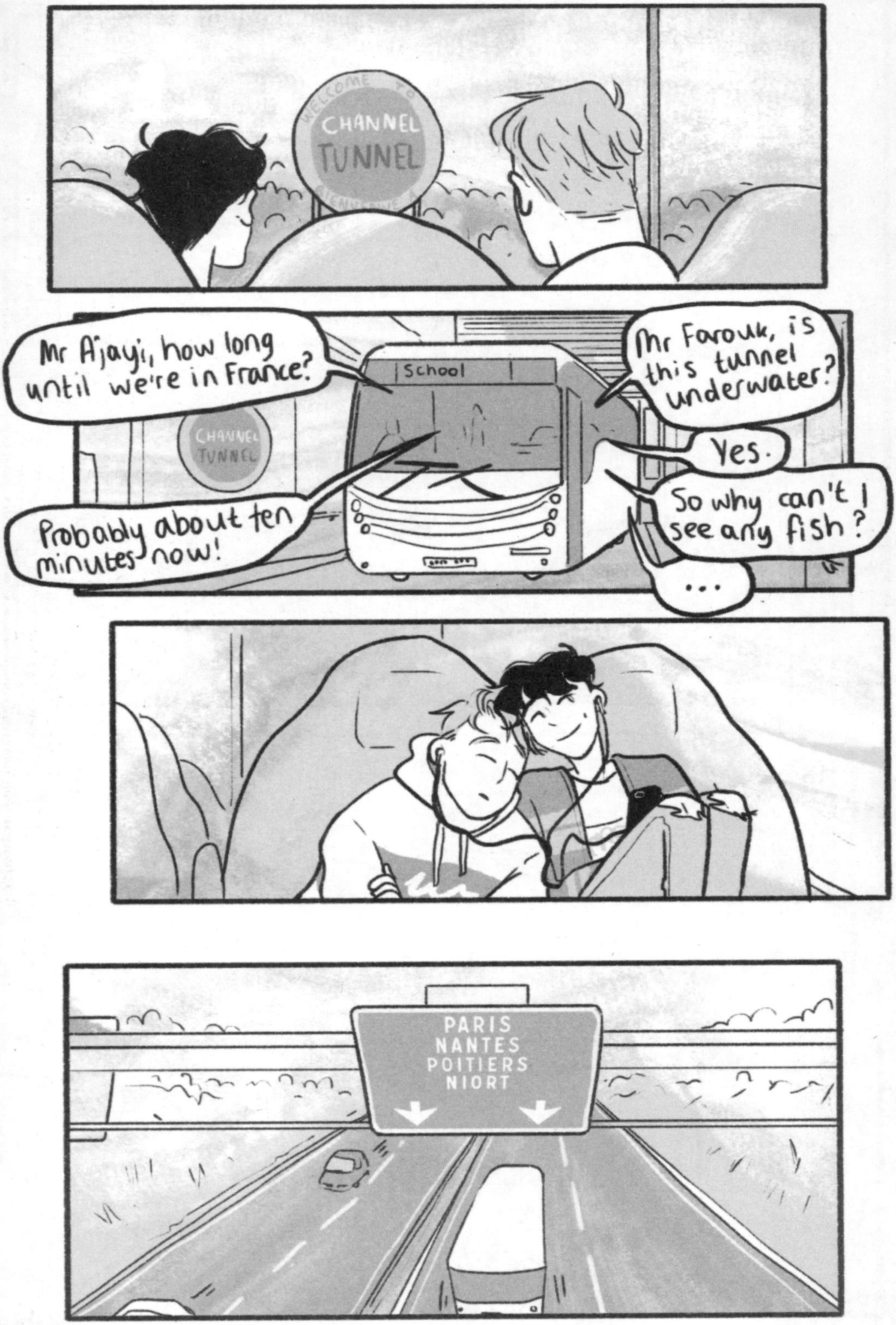
WELCOME TO
CHANNEL TUNNEL
Mr Ajayi, how long until we're in France?
School
CHANNEL TUNNEL
Mr Farouk, is this tunnel underwater?
Yes.
So why can't I see any fish?
Probably about ten minutes now!
...
PARIS
NANTES
POITIERS
NIORT

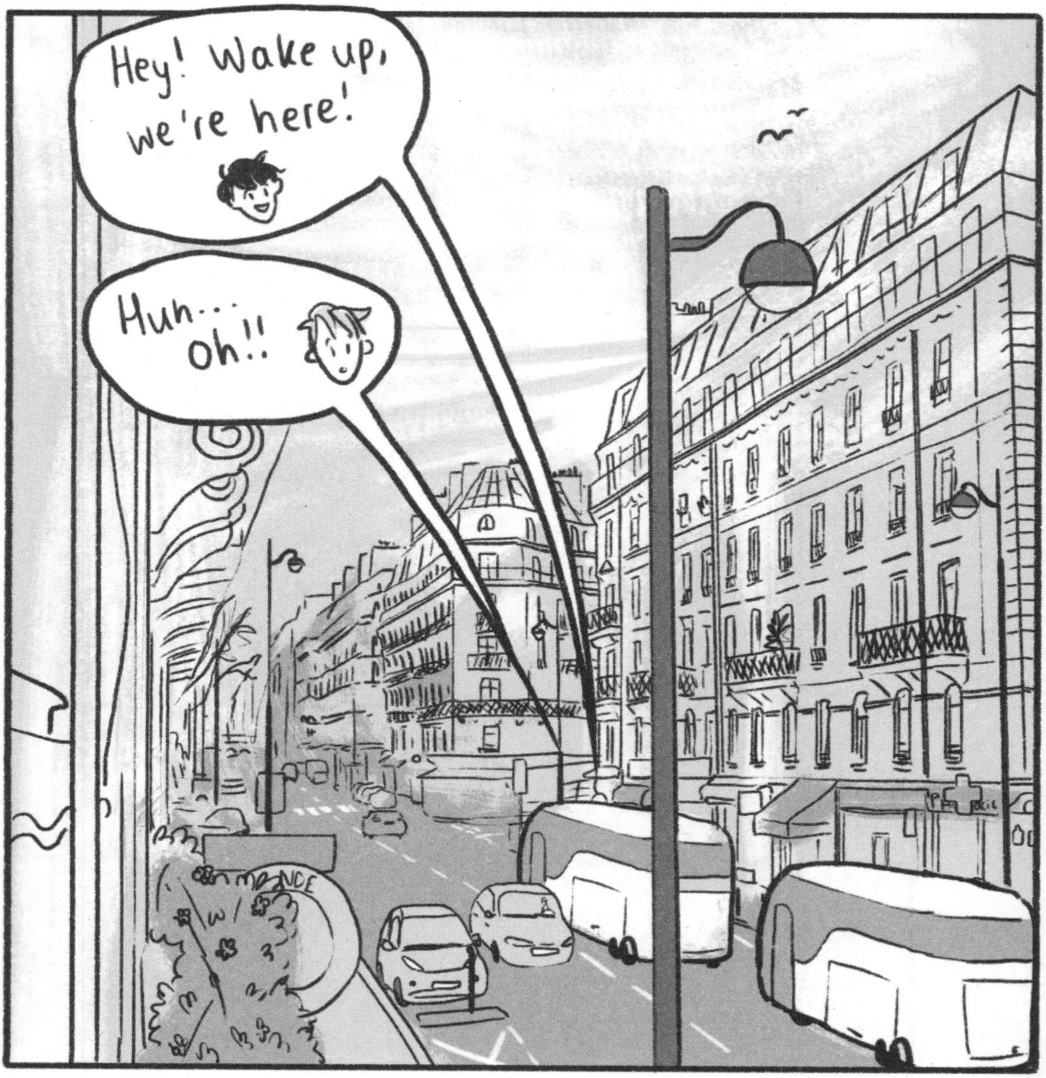
Hey! Wake up, we're here!
Hun... oh!!

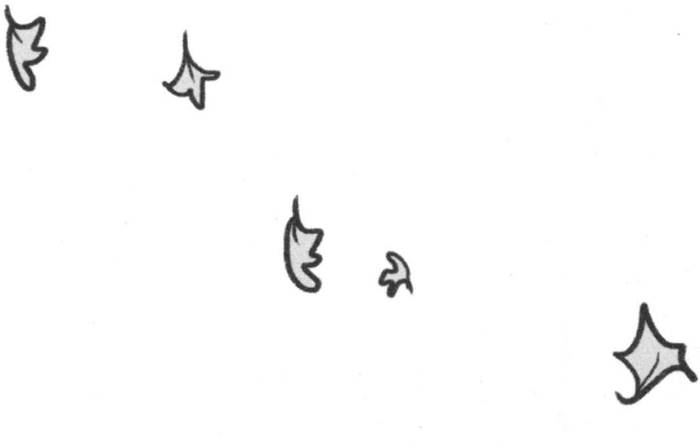

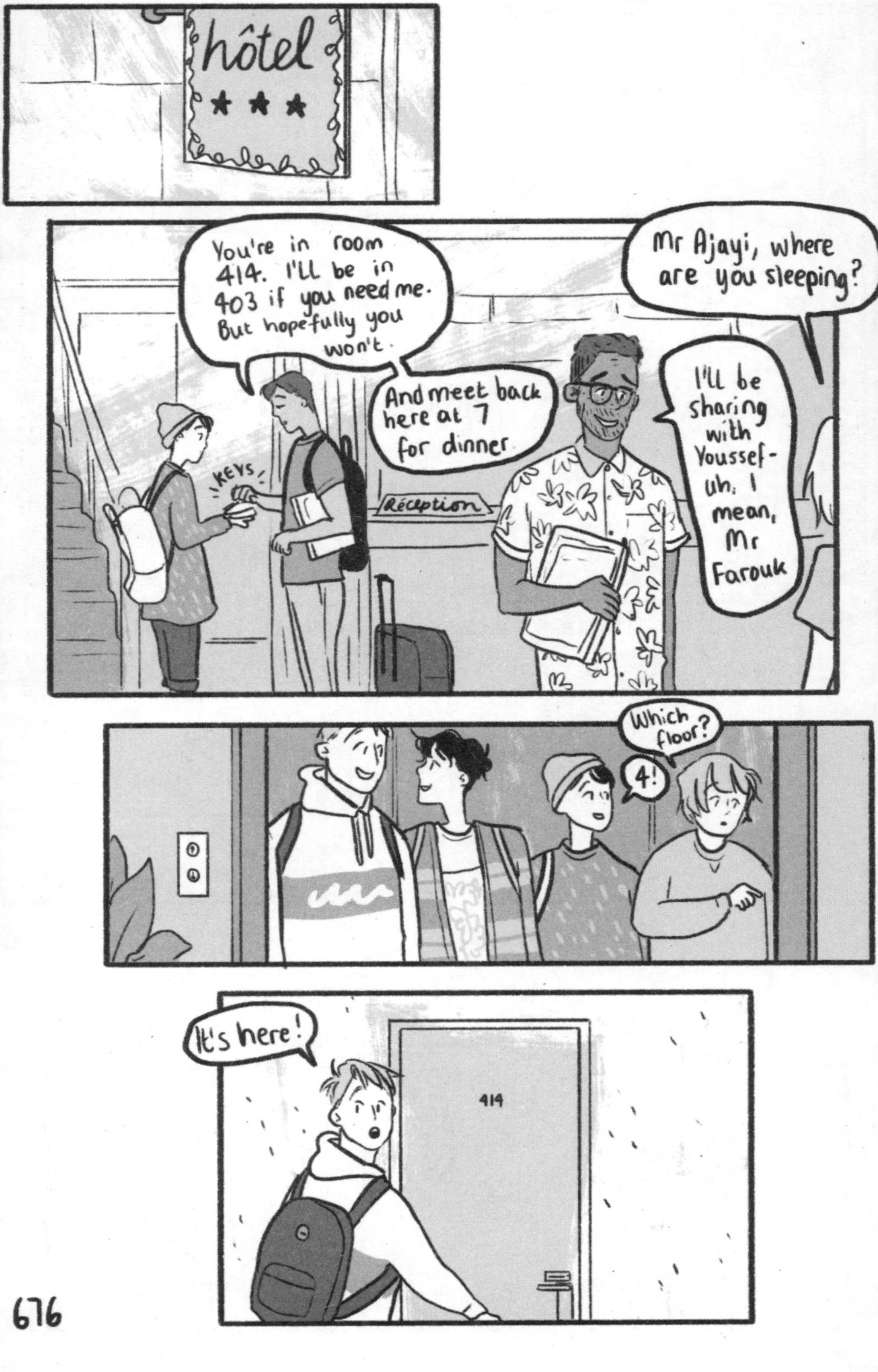
hôtel
You're in room 414. I'll be in 403 if you need me. But hopefully you won't.
And meet back here at 7 for dinner.
KEYS
Réception
Mr Ajayi, where are you sleeping?
I'll be sharing with Youssef- uh, I mean, Mr Farouk
Which floor?
4!
It's here!
414

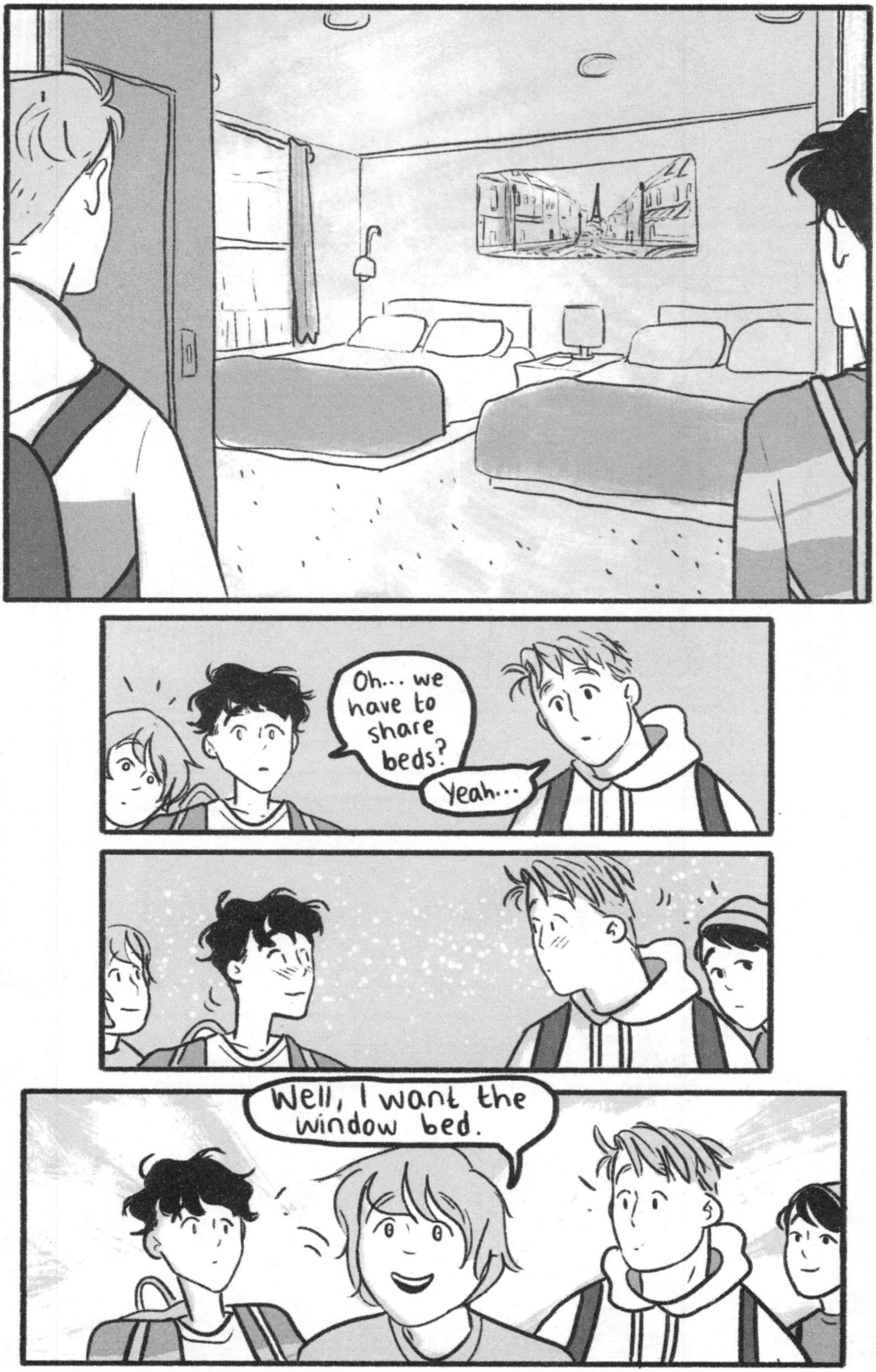
Oh... we have to share beds?
Yeah...
Well, I want the window bed.

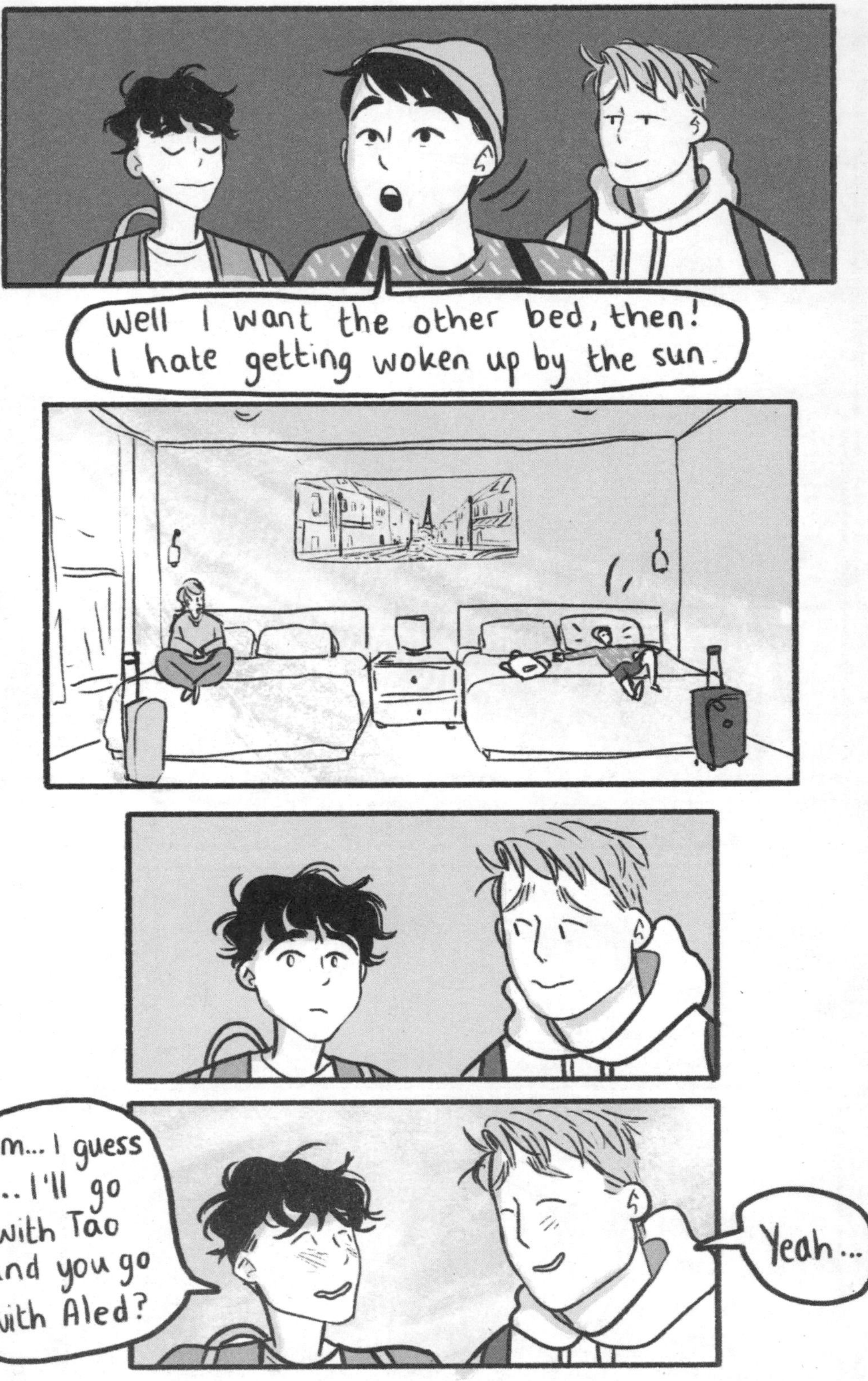
Well I want the other bed, then! I hate getting woken up by the sun.
Um... I guess ... I'll go with Tao and you go with Aled?
Yeah...

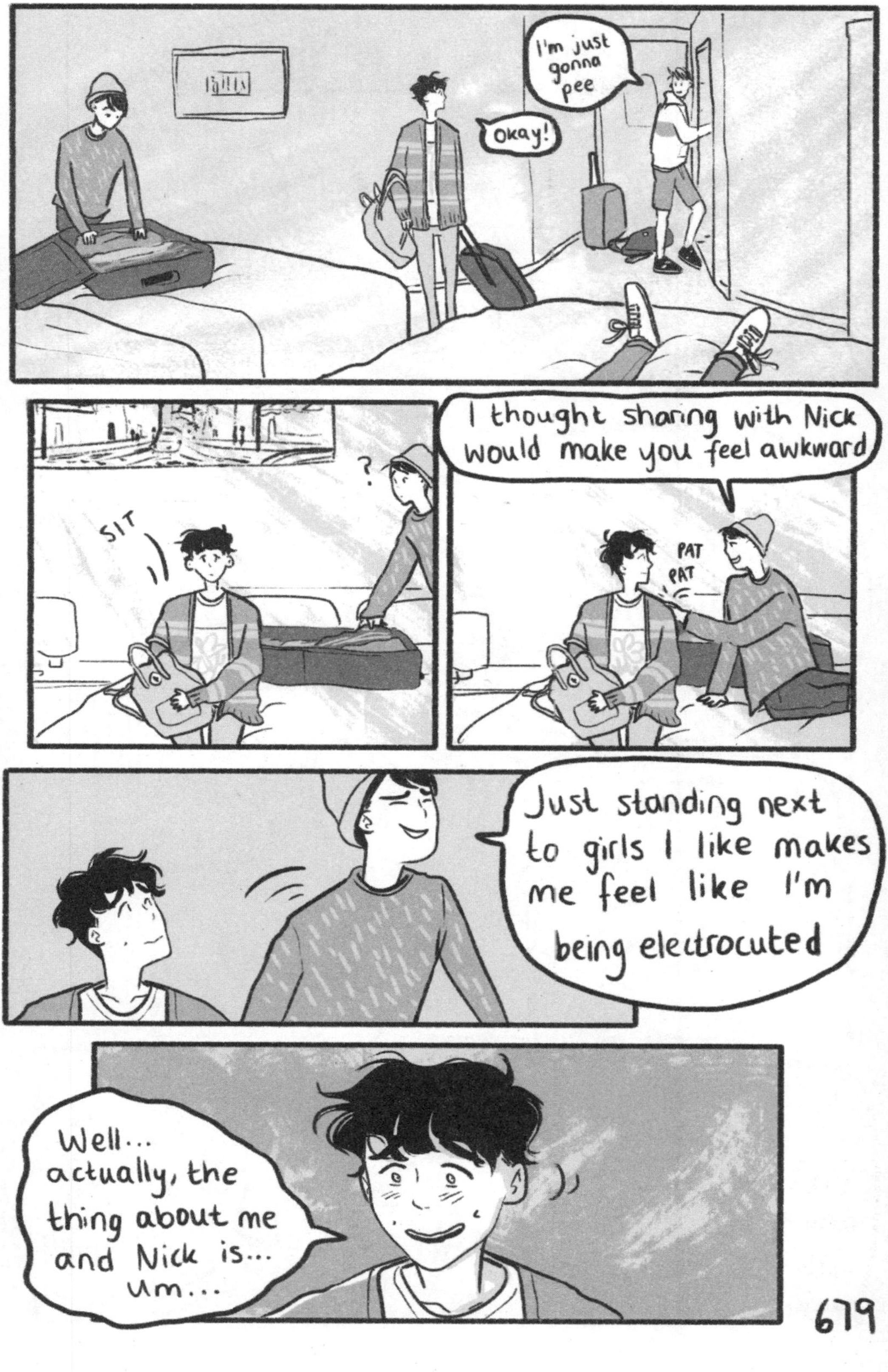
I'm just gonna pee
Okay!
SIT
?
I thought sharing with Nick would make you feel awkward
PAT PAT
Just standing next to girls I like makes me feel like I'm being electrocuted
Well... actually, the thing about me and Nick is... um...

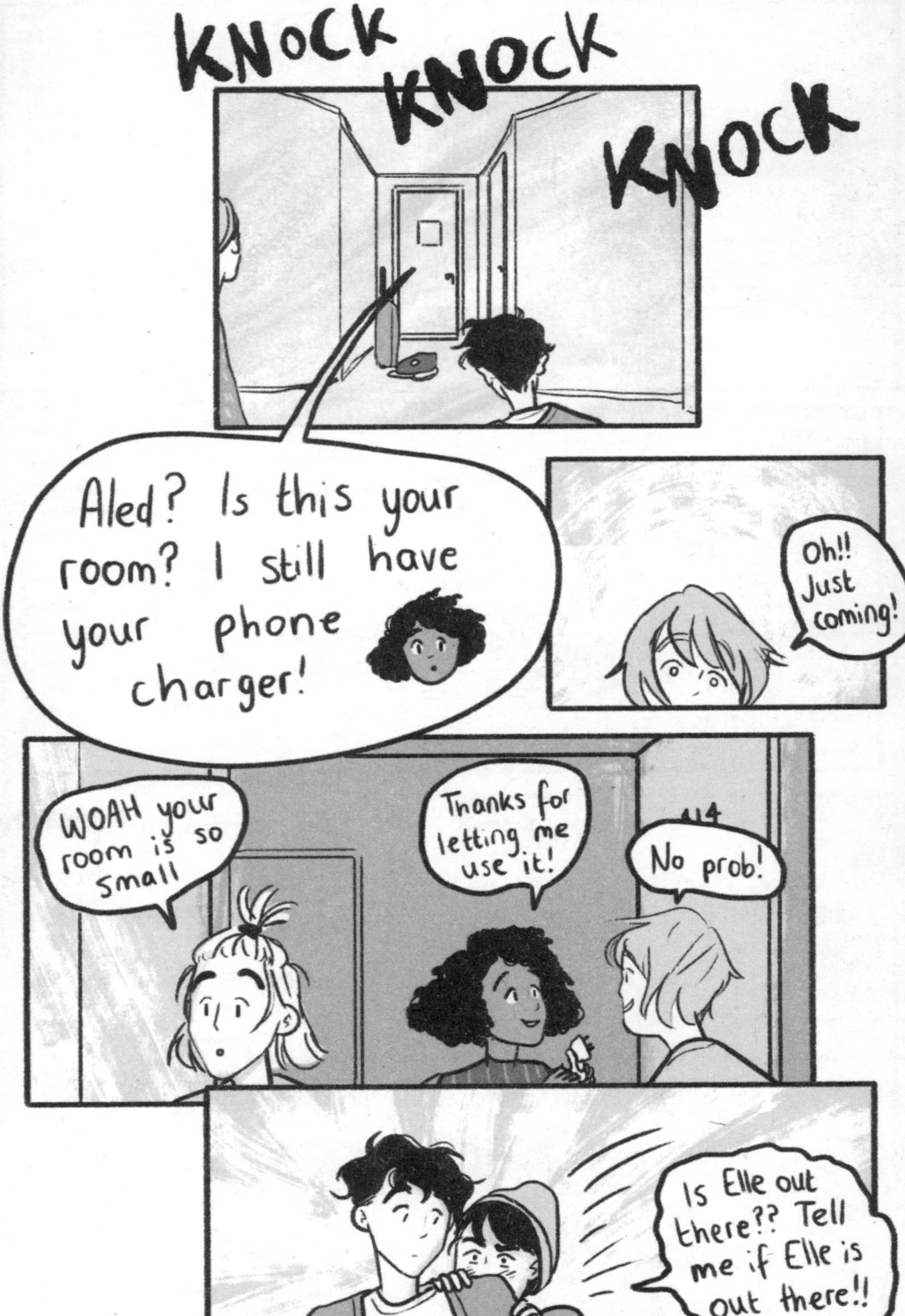
KNOCK
KNOCK
KNOCK
Aled? Is this your room? I still have your phone charger!
Oh!! Just coming!
WOAH your room is so small
Thanks for letting me use it!
No prob!
Is Elle out there?? Tell me if Elle is out there!!

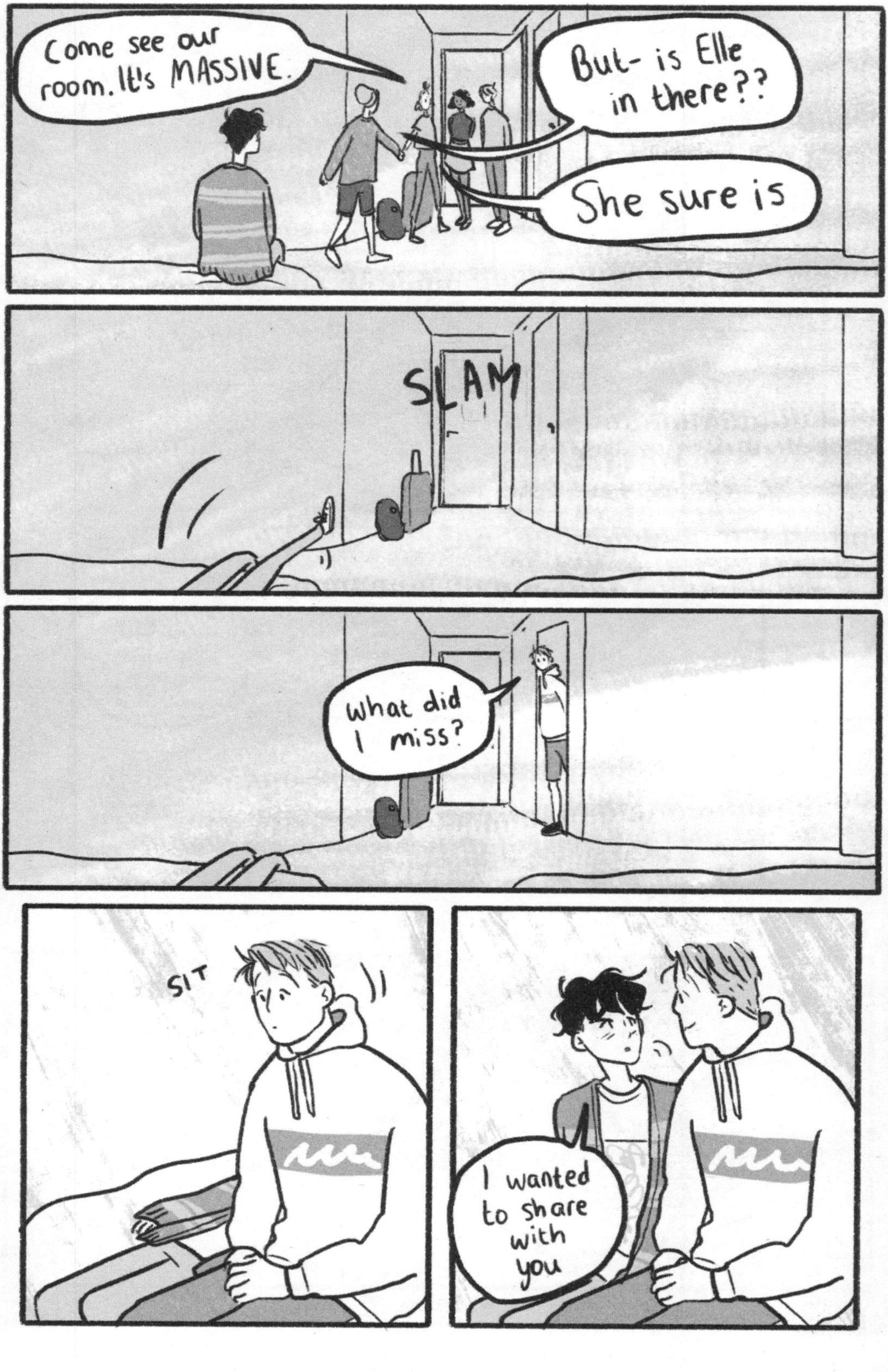
Come see our room. It's MASSIVE.
But- is Elle in there??
She sure is
SLAM
What did I miss?
SIT
I wanted to share with you

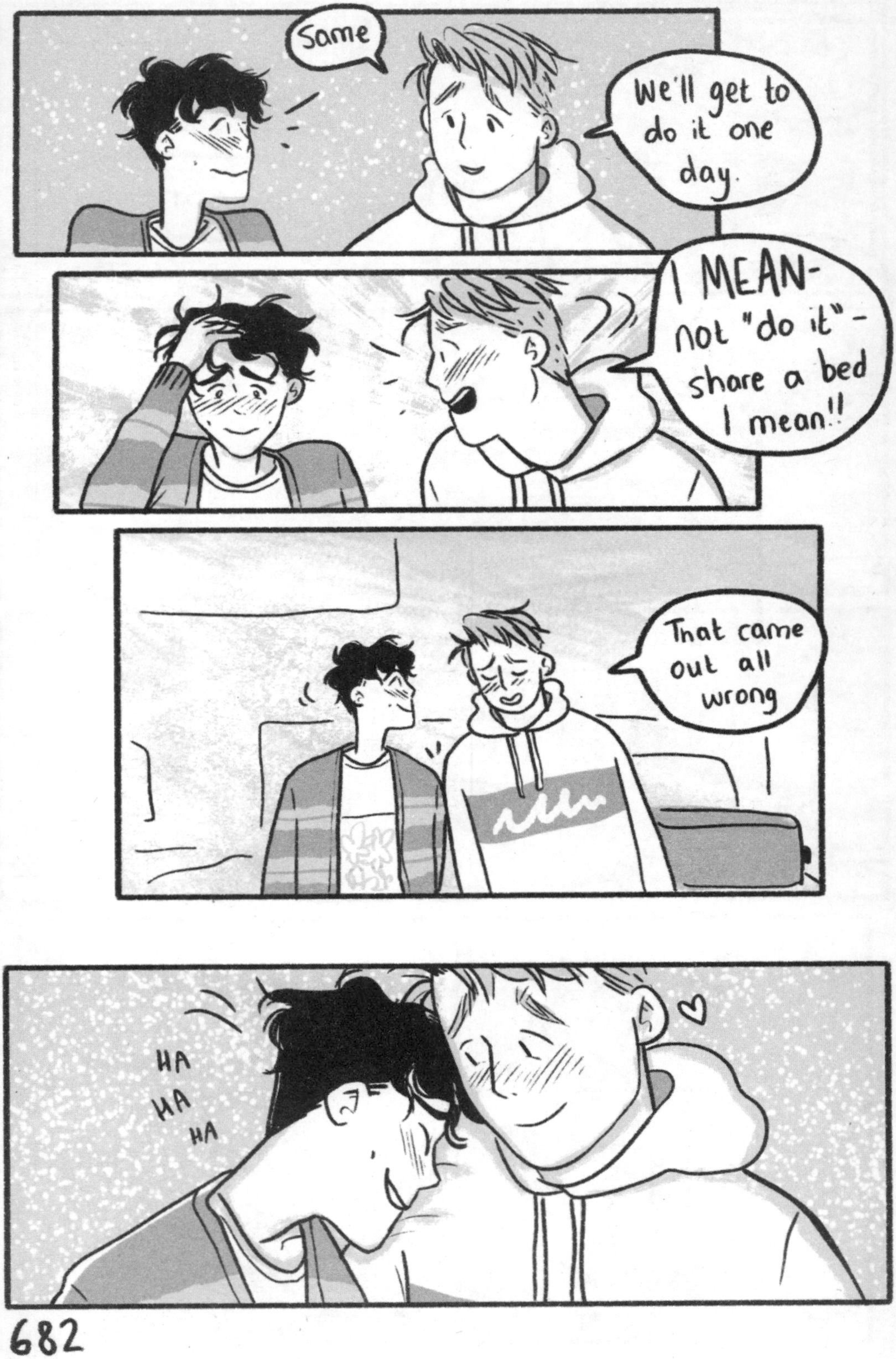

Same
We'll get to do it one day.
I MEAN- not "do it" - share a bed I mean!!
That came out all wrong
HA HA HA

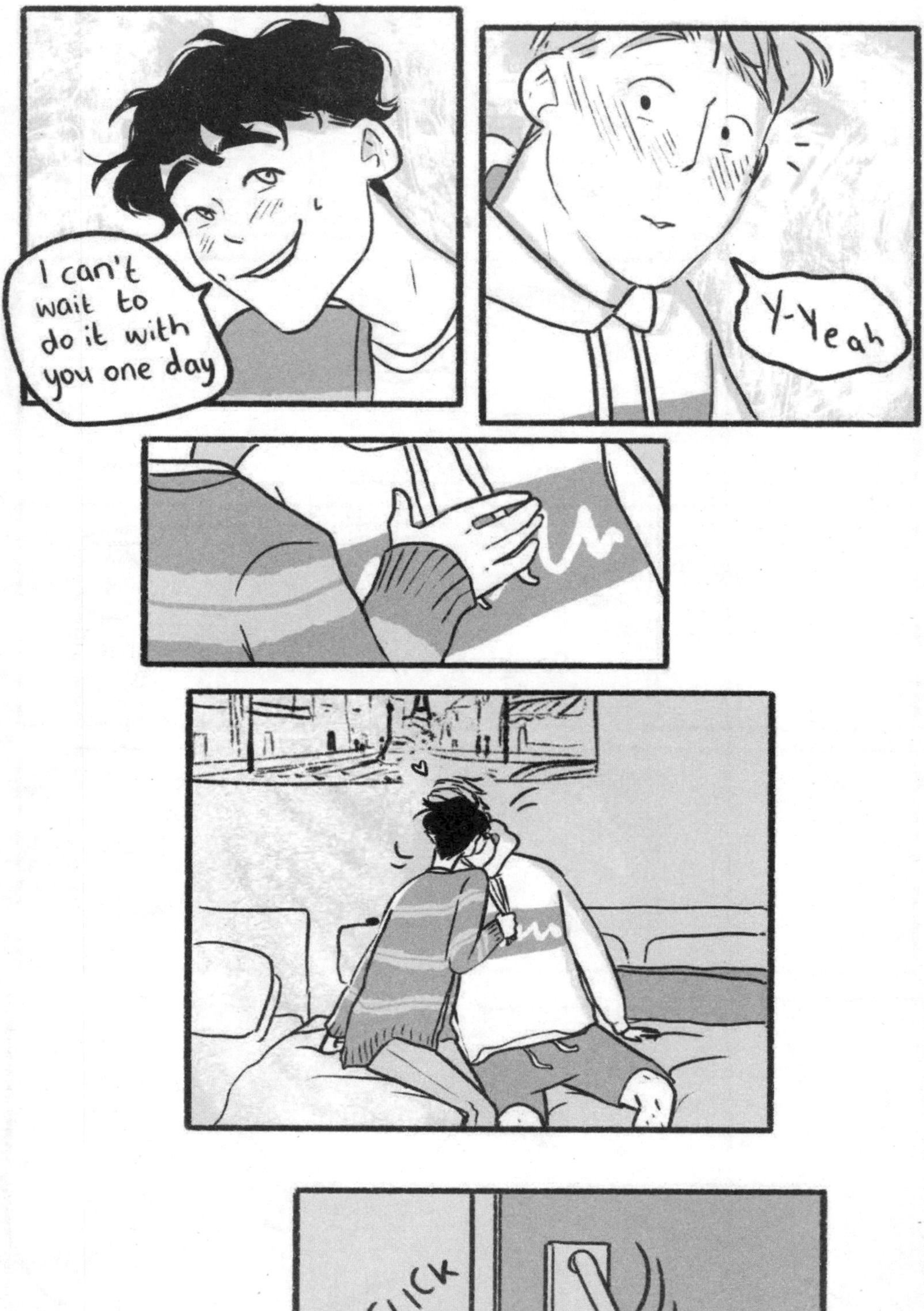
I can't wait to do it with you one day
Y-Yeah
CLICK

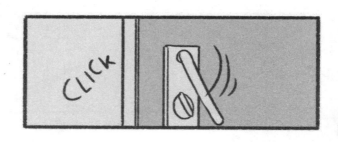

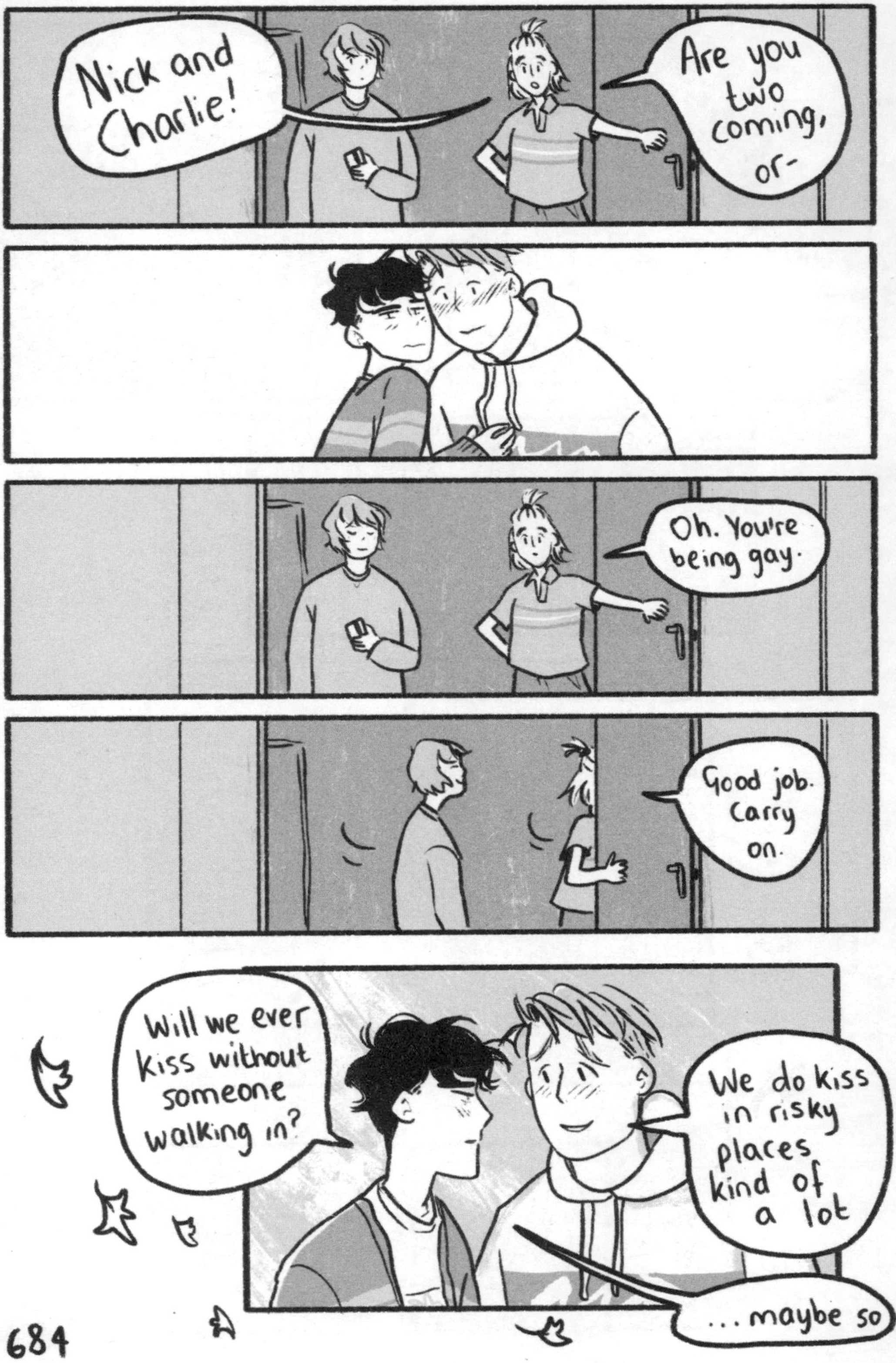
Nick and Charlie!
Are you two coming, or-
Oh. You're being gay.
Good job. Carry on.
Will we ever kiss without someone walking in?
We do kiss in risky places kind of a lot
...maybe so

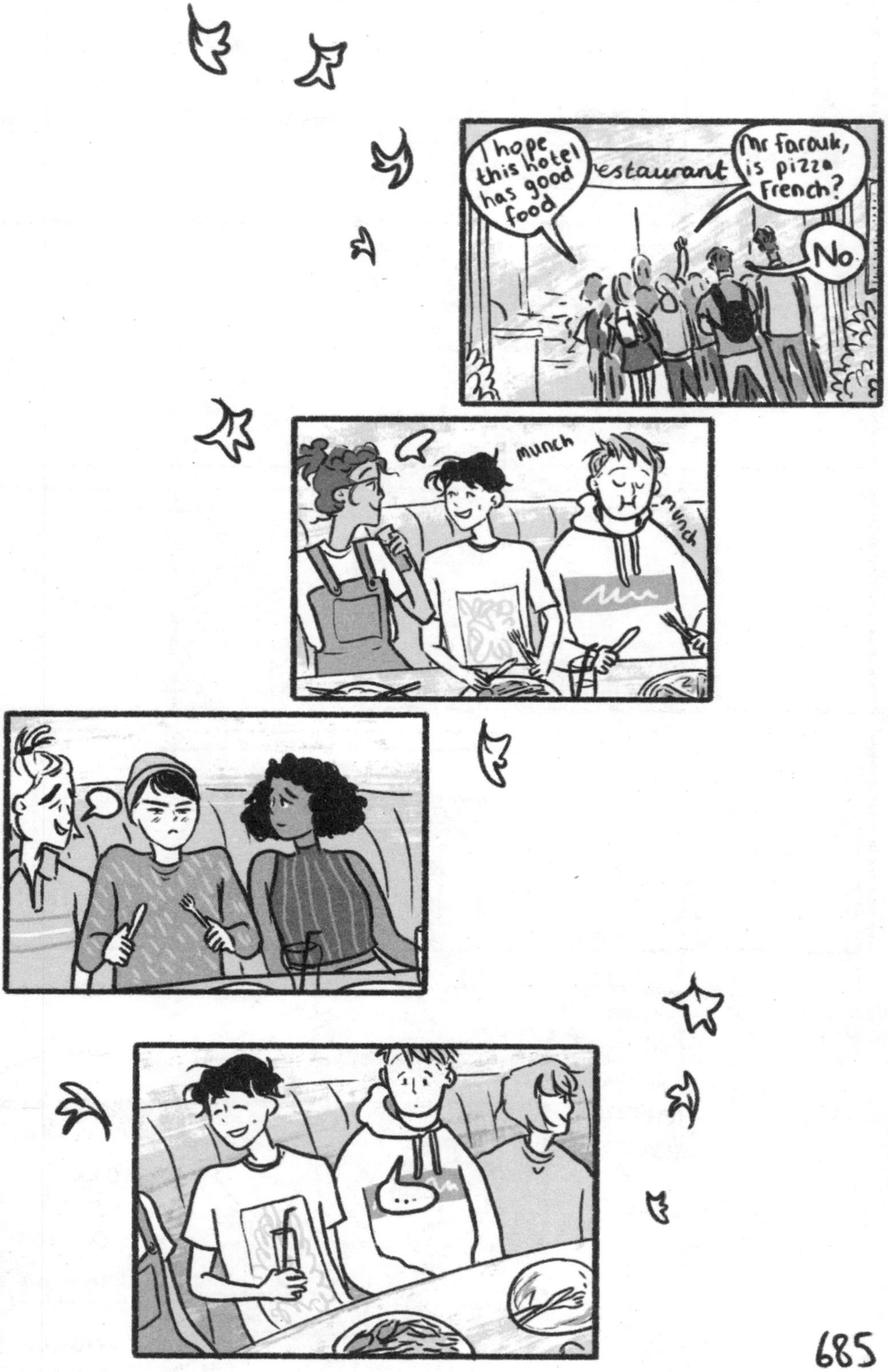
I hope this hotel has good food
restaurant
Mr Farouk, is pizza French?
No.
munch
munch

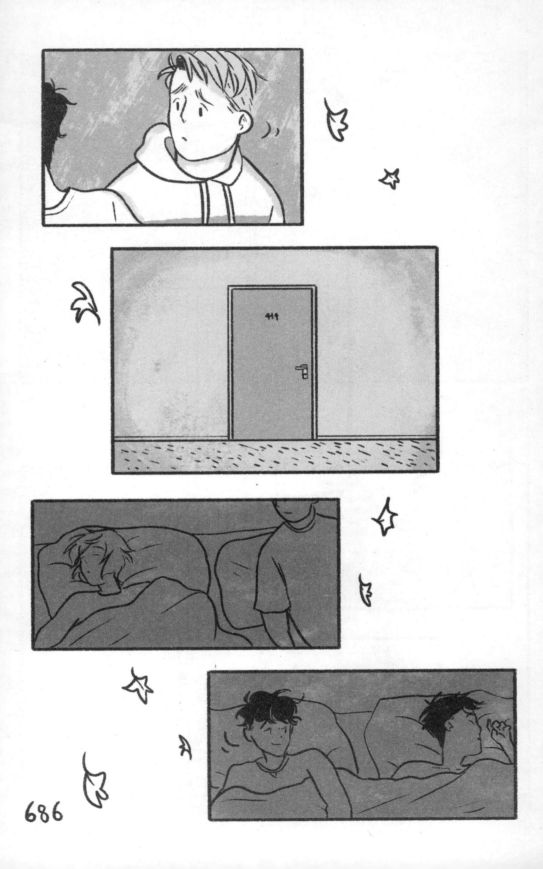

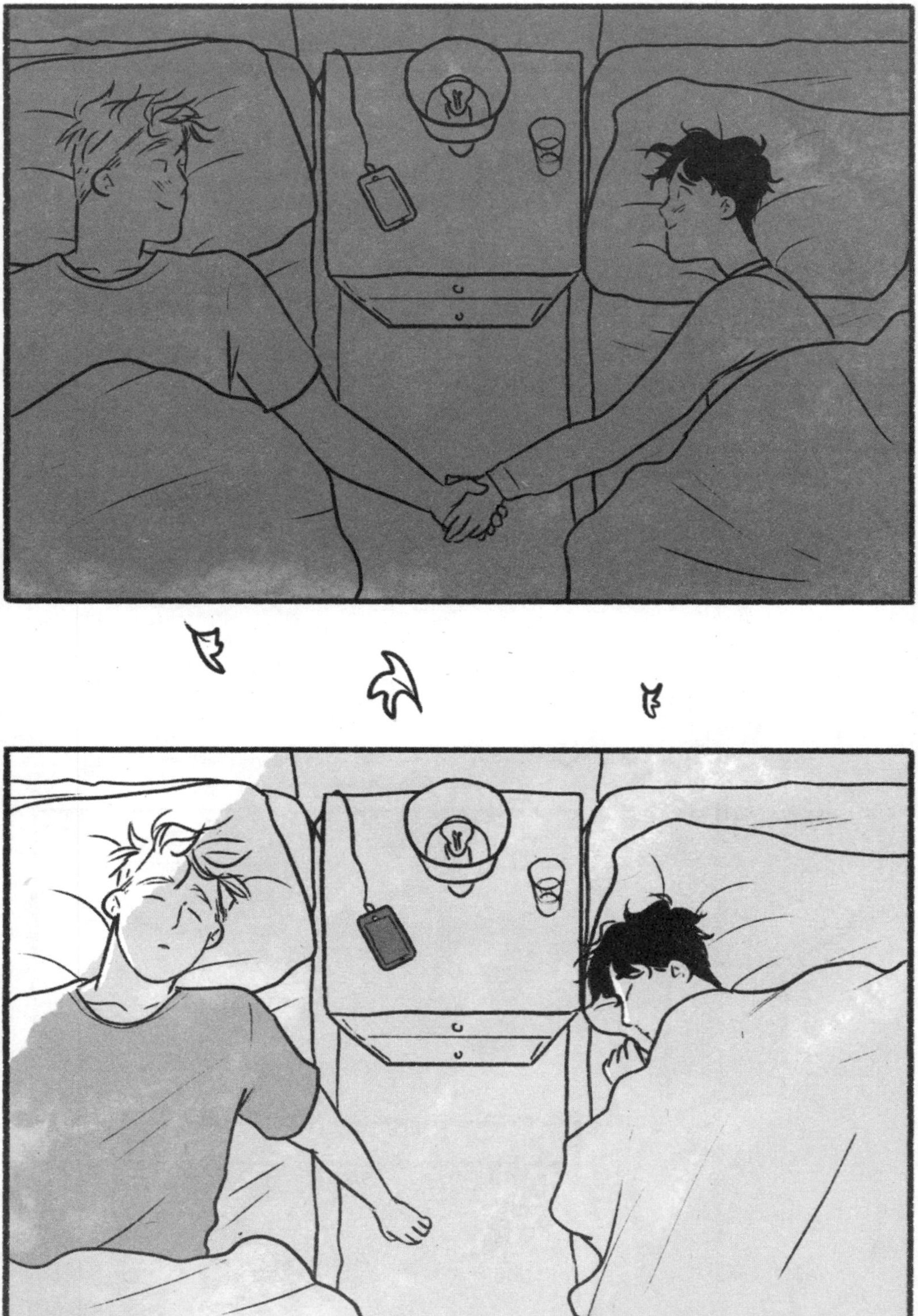

Paris - Day 2

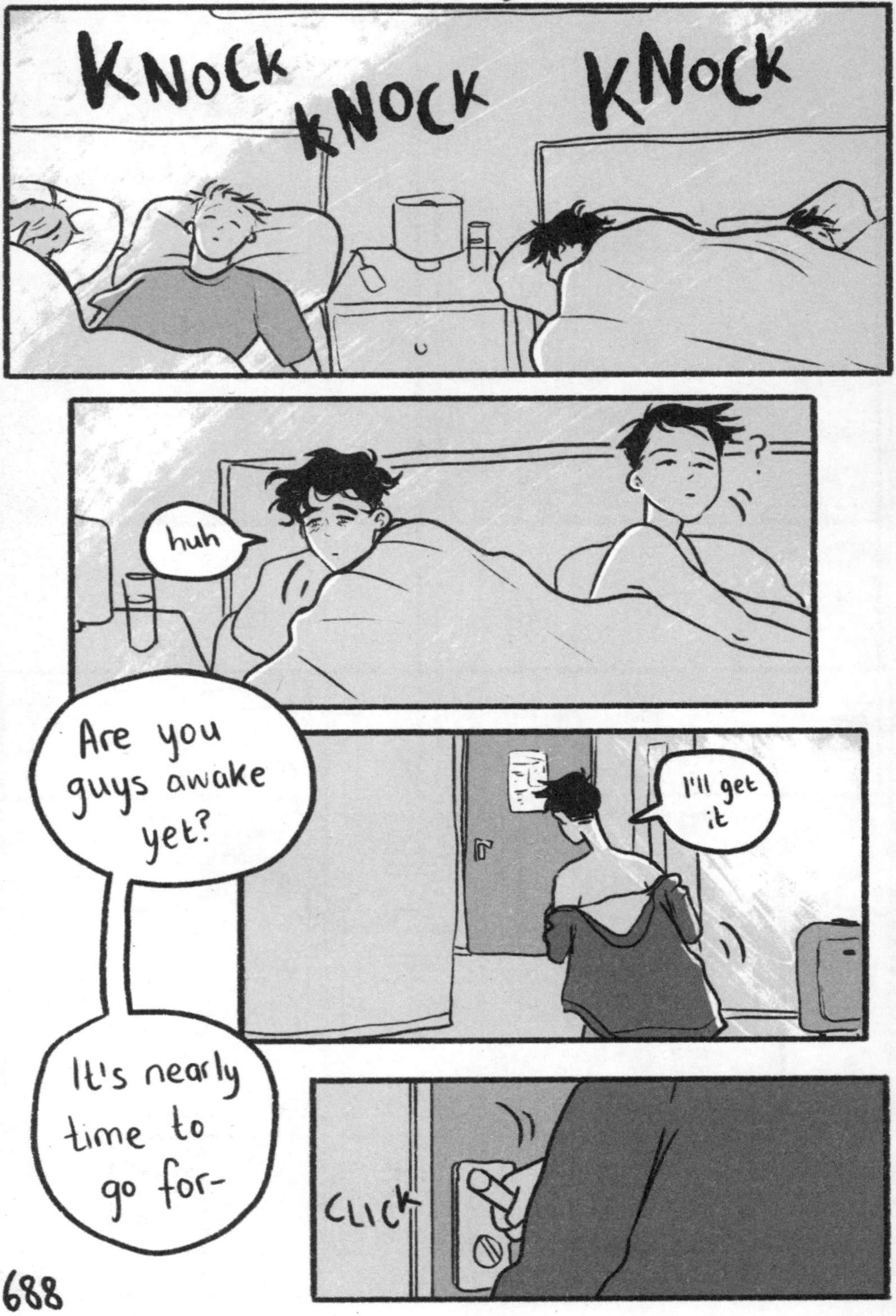
KNOCK
KNOCK
KNOCK
huh
?
Are you guys awake yet?
I'll get it
It's nearly time to go for-
CLICK

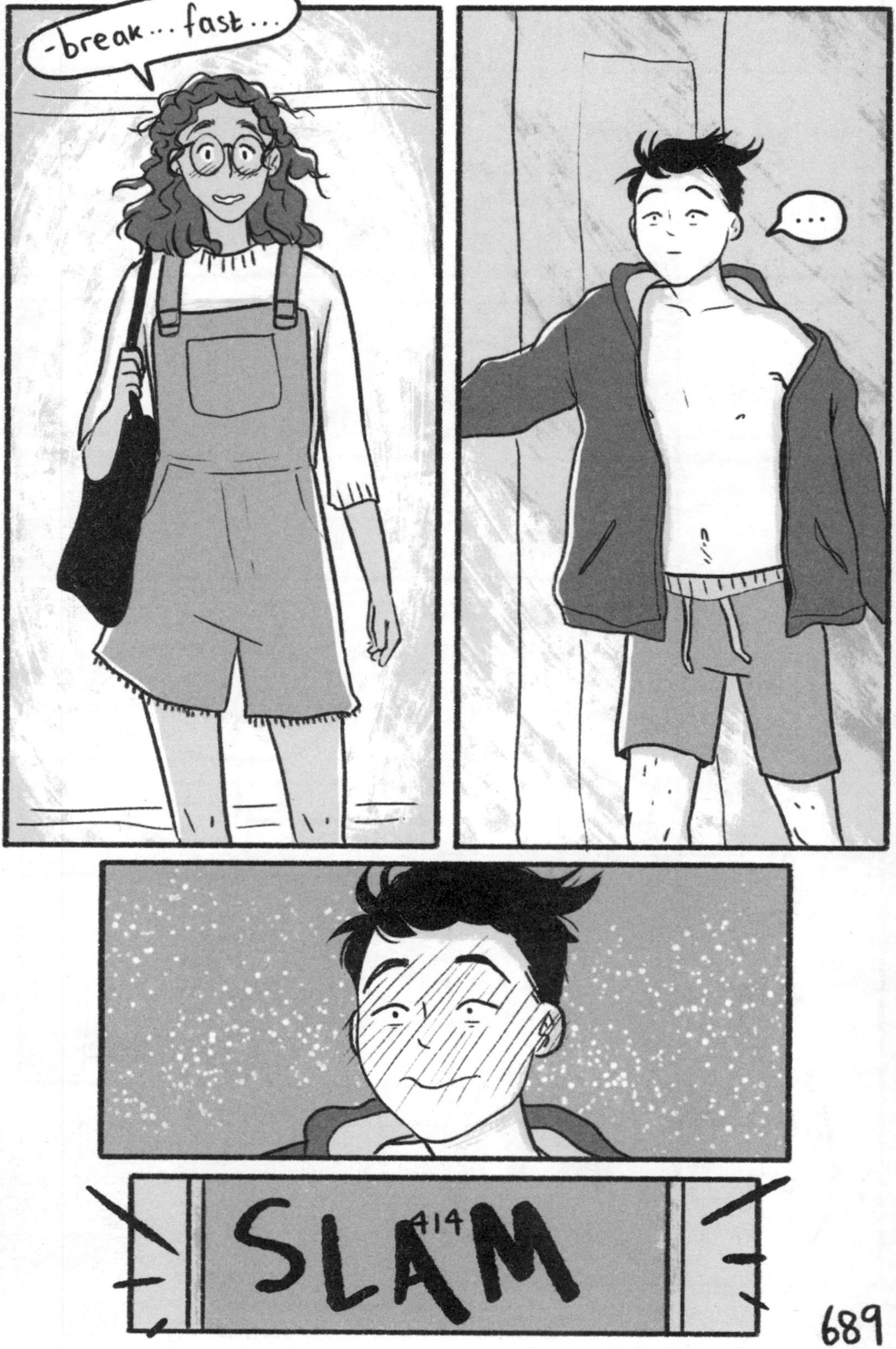
-break... fast...
...
414
SLAM

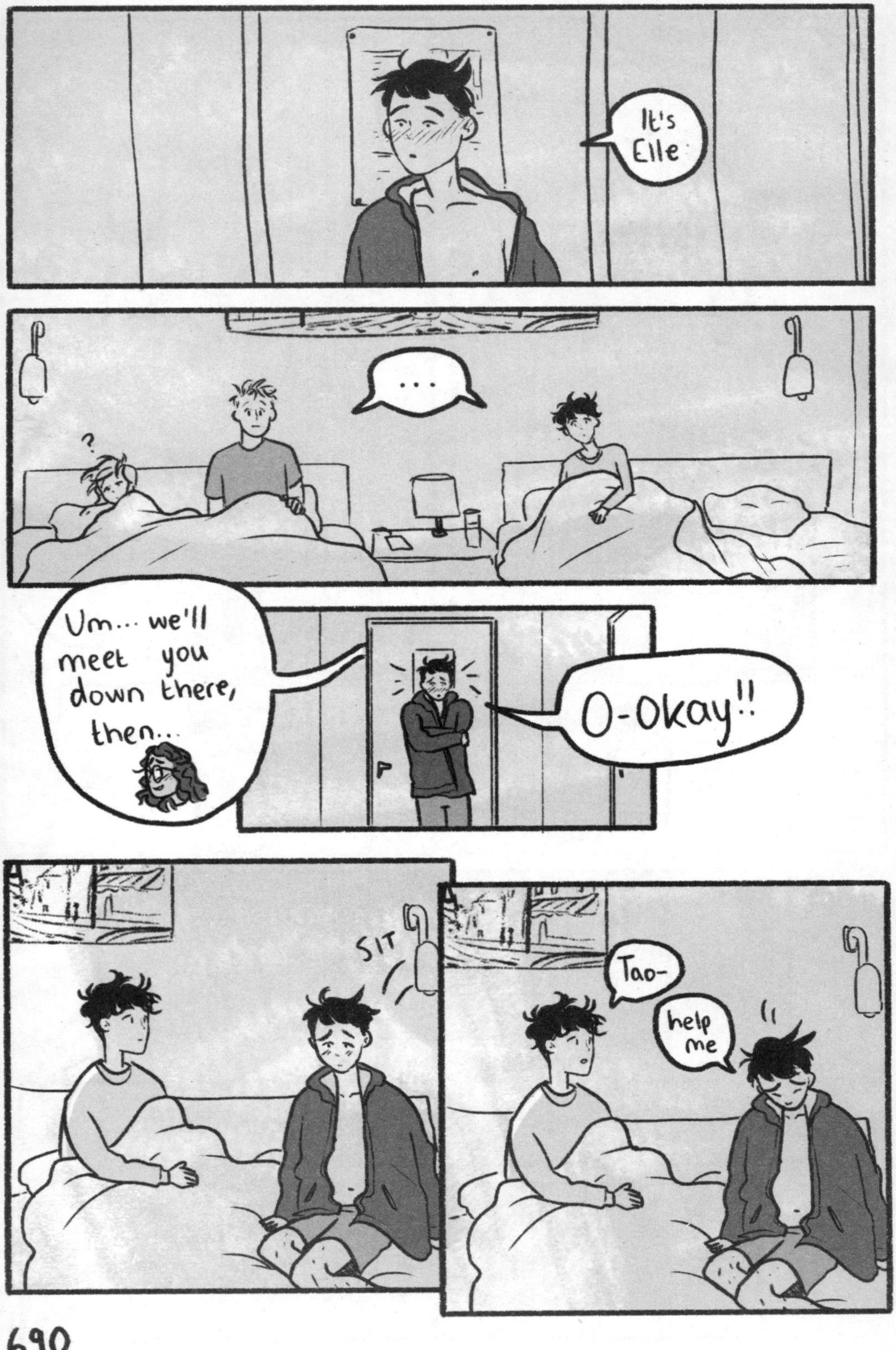
It's Elle
...
?
Um... we'll meet you down there, then...
O-Okay!!
SIT
Tao-
help me

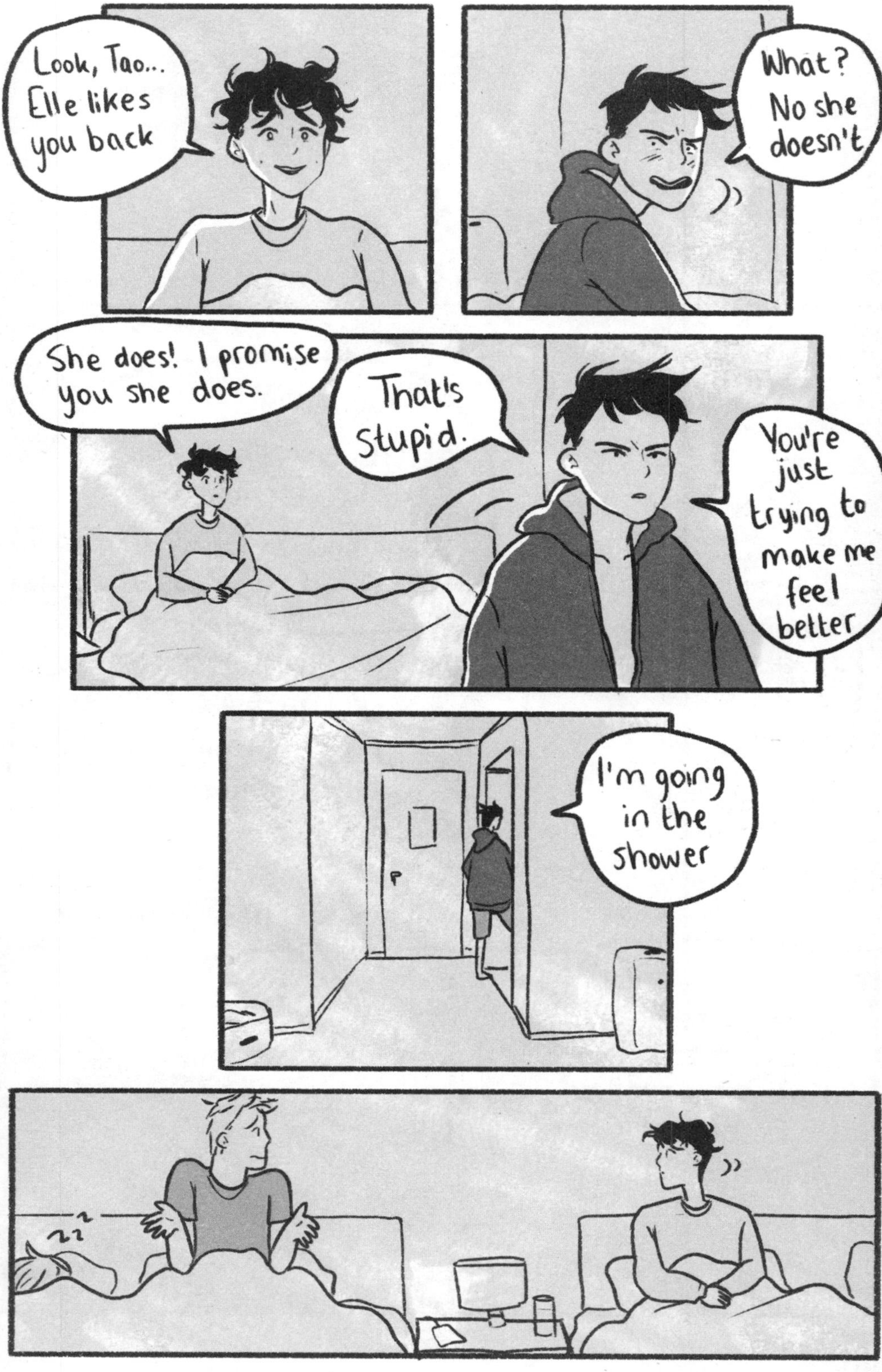
Look, Tao... Elle likes you back
What? No she doesn't
She does! I promise you she does.
That's stupid.
You're just trying to make me feel better
I'm going in the shower
zz

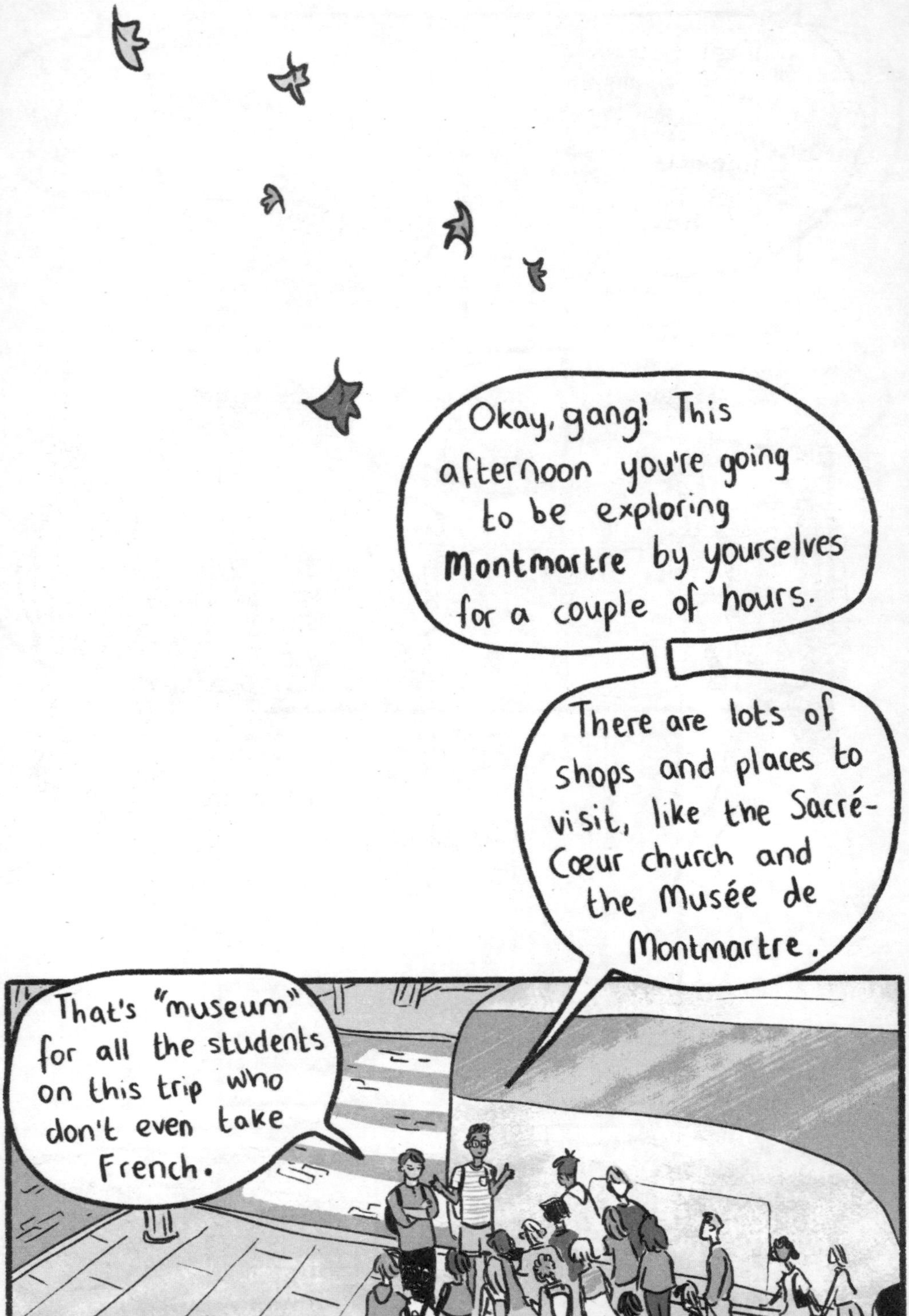
Okay, gang! This afternoon you're going to be exploring Montmartre by yourselves for a couple of hours.
There are lots of shops and places to visit, like the Sacré-Cœur church and the Musée de Montmartre.
That's "museum" for all the students on this trip who don't even take French.

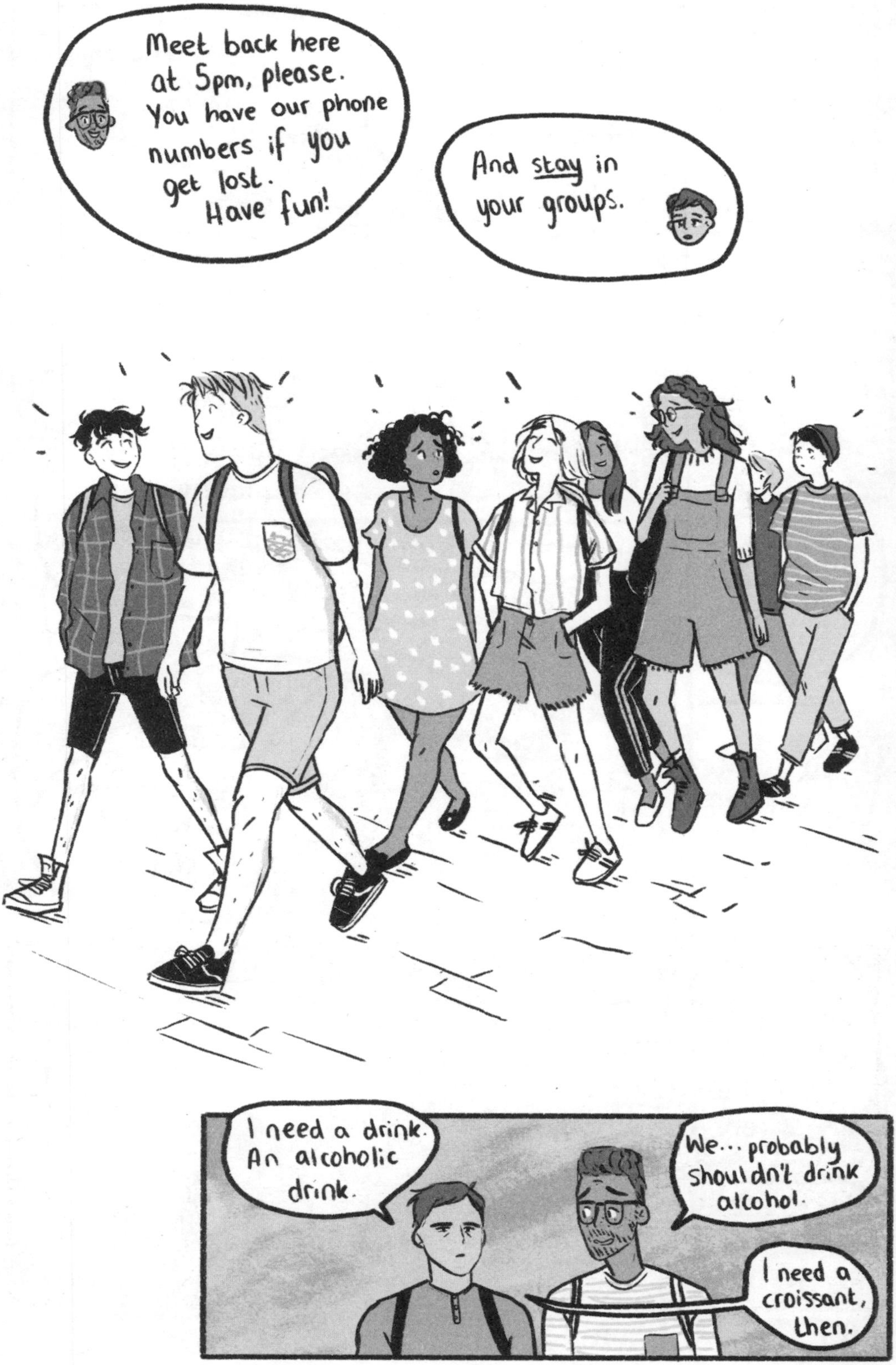
Meet back here at 5pm, please. You have our phone numbers if you get lost. Have fun!
And stay in your groups.
I need a drink. An alcoholic drink.
We... probably shouldn't drink alcohol.
I need a croissant, then.

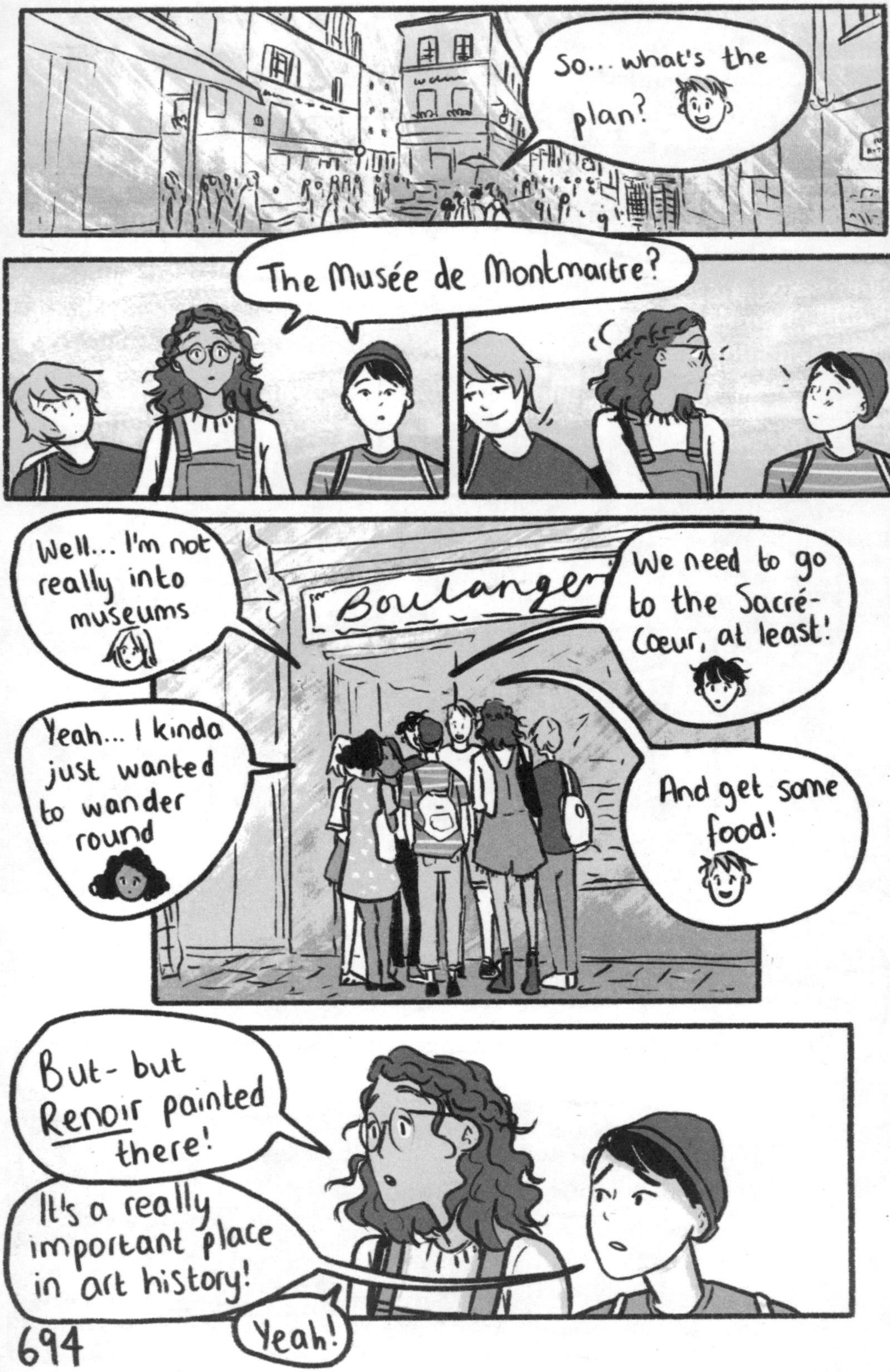
So... what's the plan?
The Musée de Montmartre?
Boulanger
Well... I'm not really into museums
We need to go to the Sacré-Cœur, at least!
Yeah... I kinda just wanted to wander round
And get some food!
But- but Renoir painted there!
It's a really important place in art history!
Yeah!

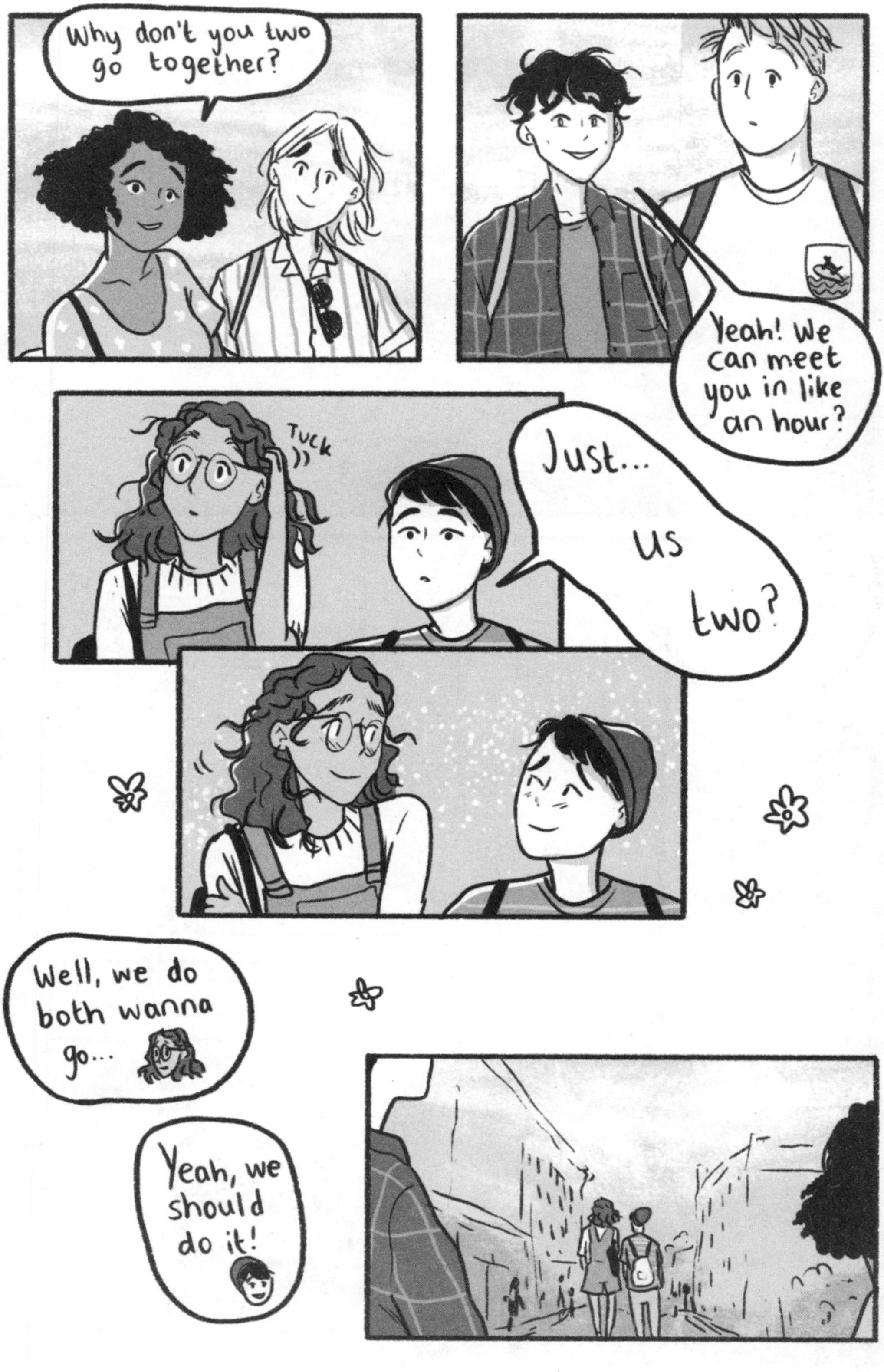
Why don't you two go together?
Yeah! We can meet you in like an hour?
TUCK
Just... us two?
Well, we do both wanna go...
Yeah, we should do it!

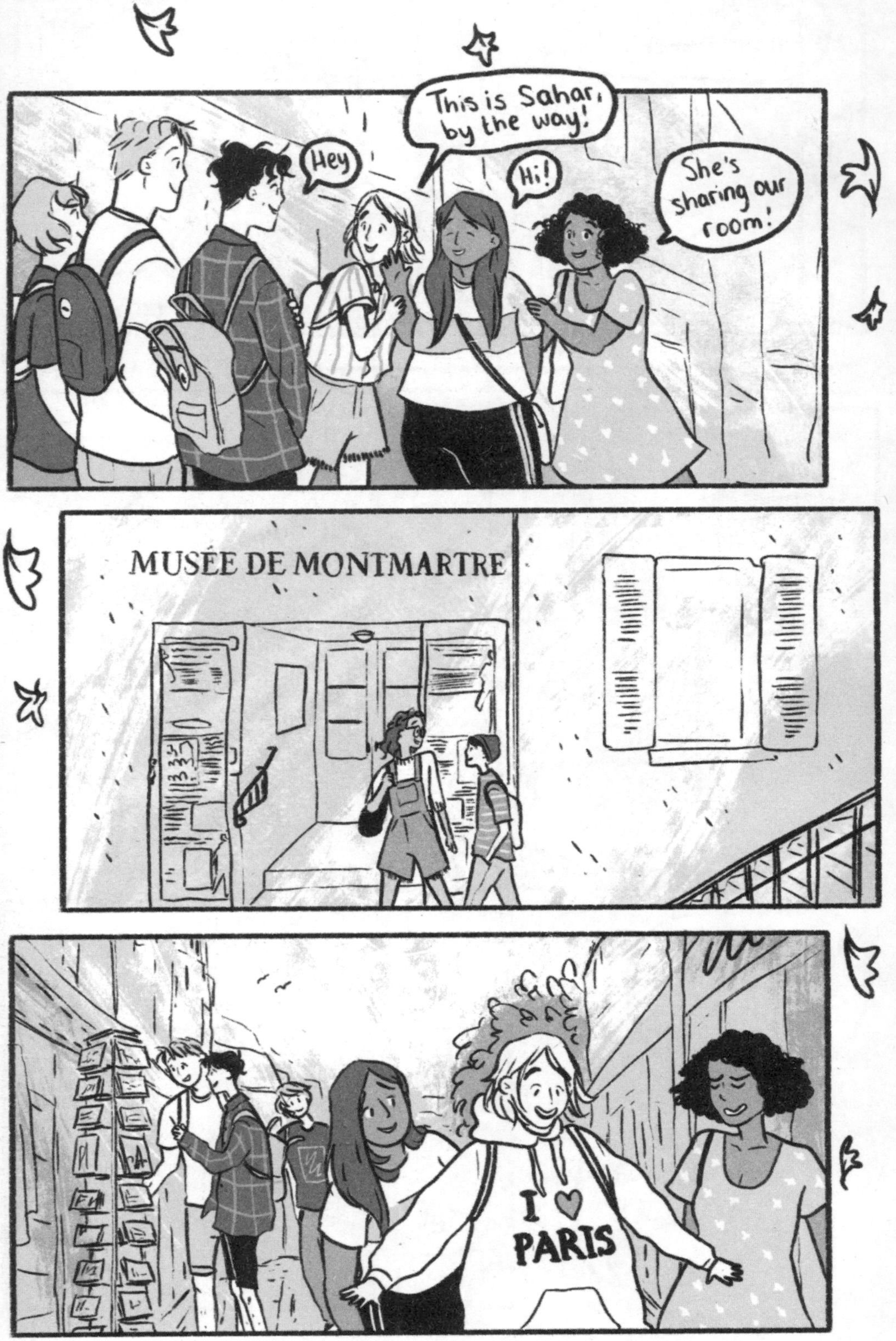
Hey
This is Sahar, by the way!
Hi!
She's sharing our room!
MUSÉE DE MONTMARTRE
I ♥ PARIS

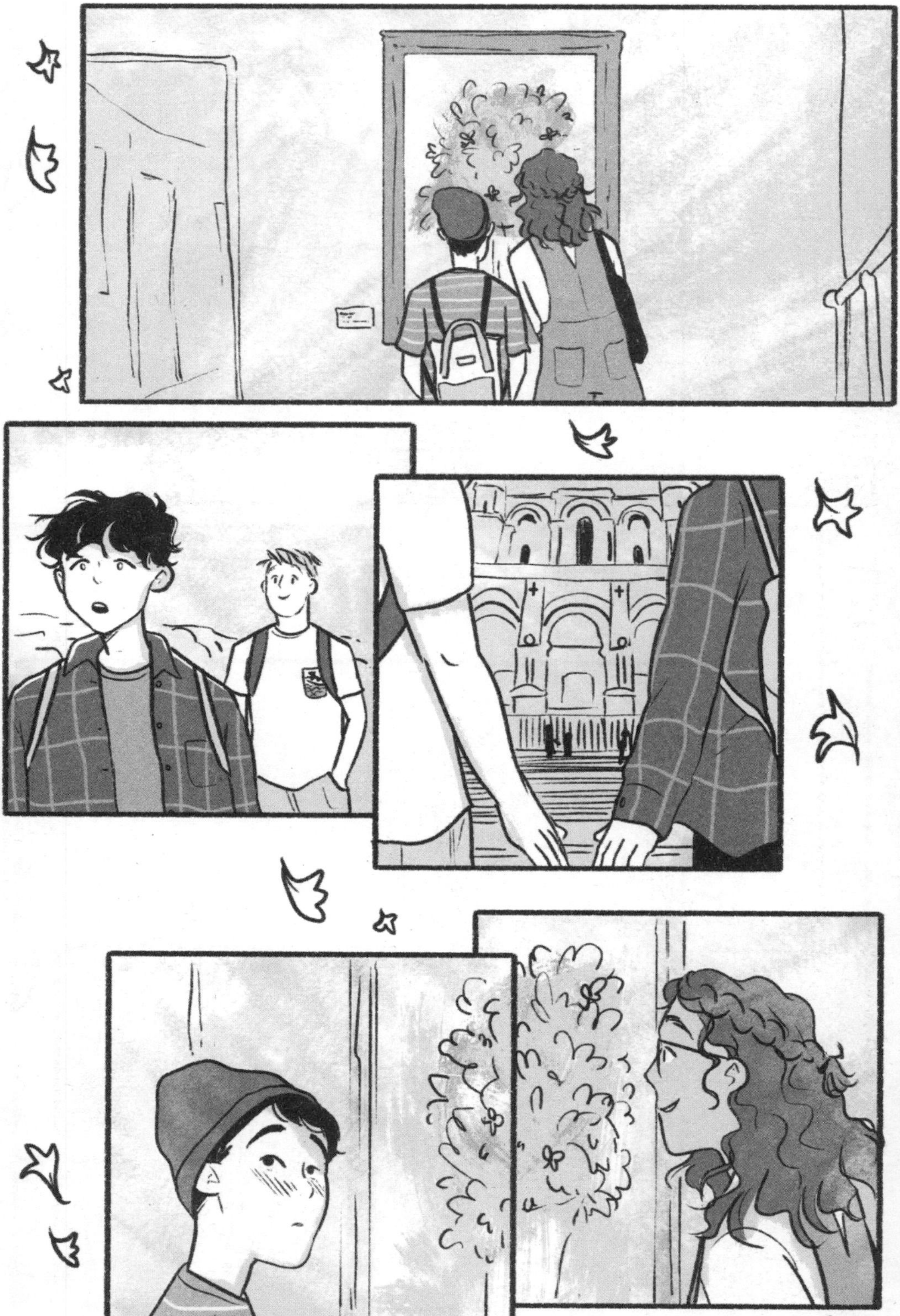

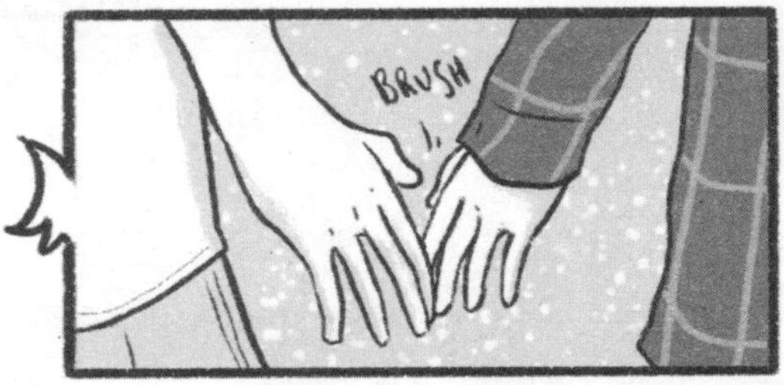
BRUSH

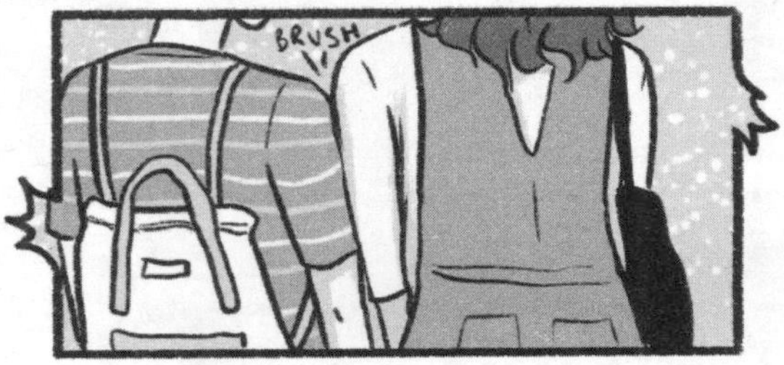
BRUSH

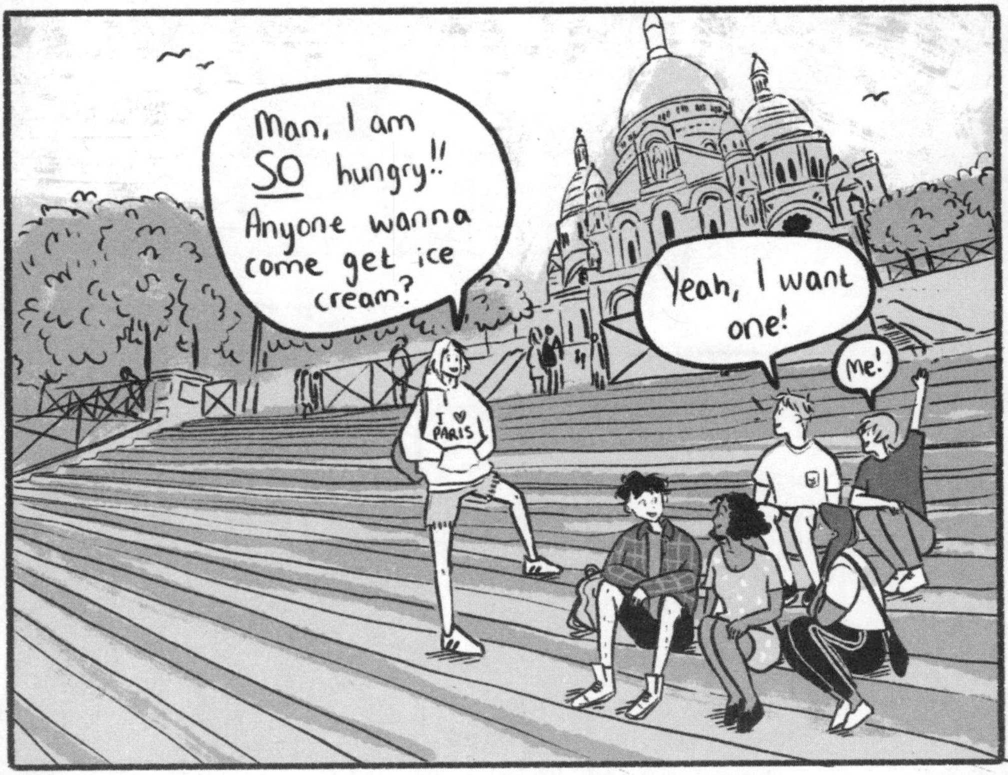
Man, I am SO hungry!!
Anyone wanna come get ice cream?
Yeah, I want one!
Me!
I ♥ PARIS

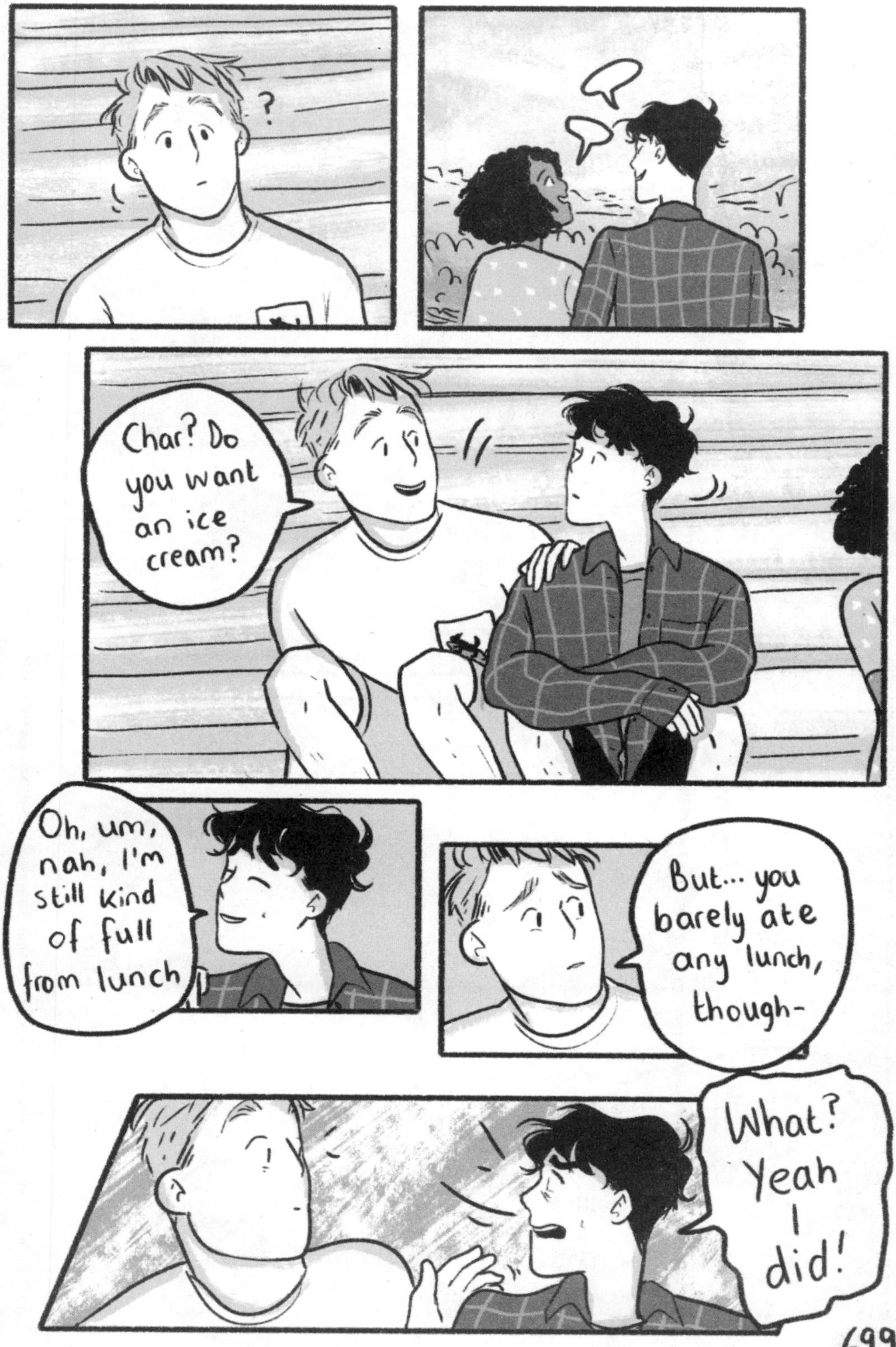
?
Char? Do you want an ice cream?
Oh, um, nah, I'm still kind of full from lunch
But... you barely ate any lunch, though-
What? Yeah I did!

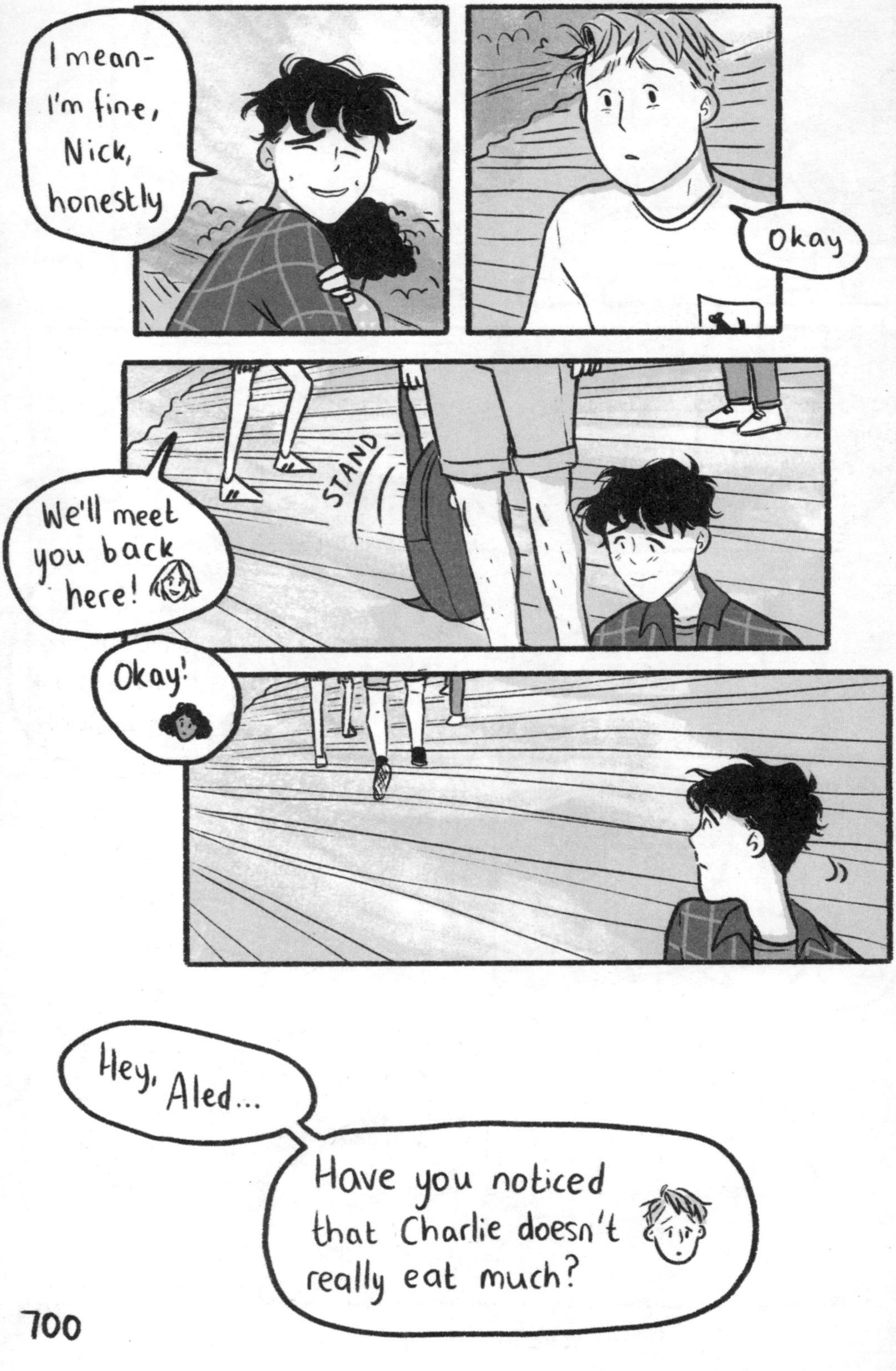
I mean- I'm fine, Nick, honestly
Okay
We'll meet you back here!
STAND
Okay!
Hey, Aled...
Have you noticed that Charlie doesn't really eat much?

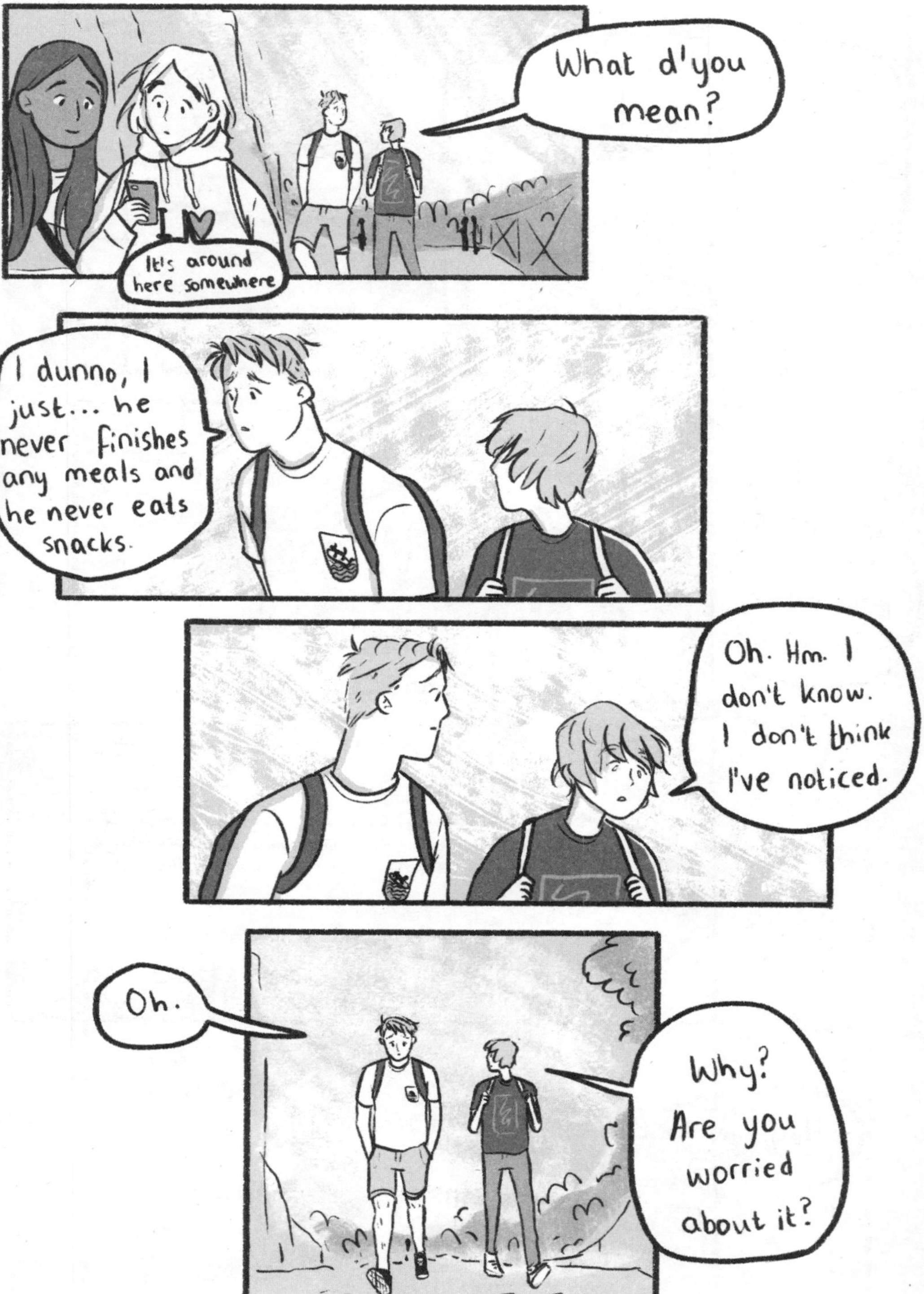
It's around here somewhere
What d'you mean?
I dunno, I just... he never finishes any meals and he never eats snacks.
Oh. Hm. I don't know. I don't think I've noticed.
Oh.
Why? Are you worried about it?

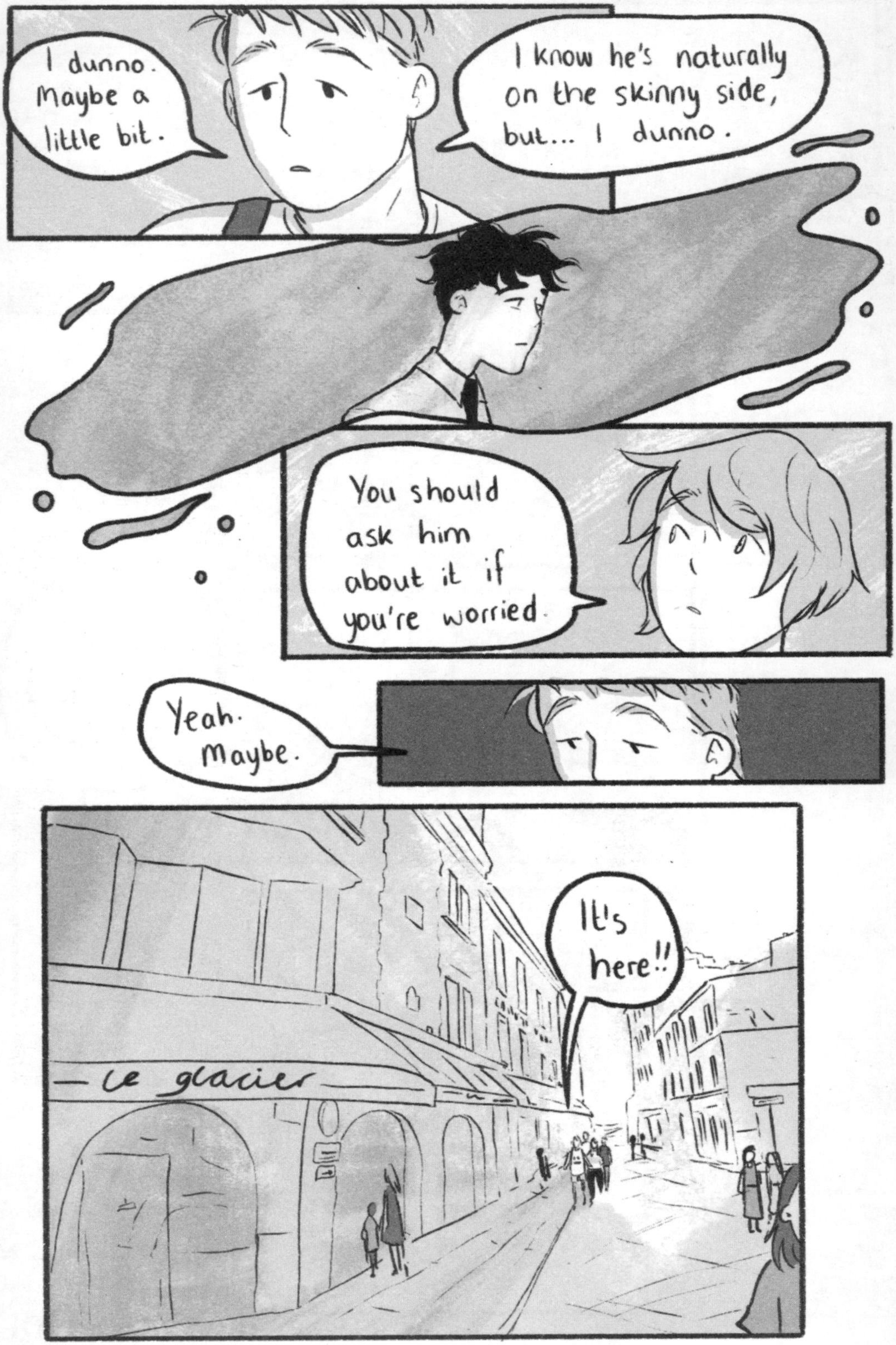
I dunno. Maybe a little bit.
I know he's naturally on the skinny side, but... I dunno.
You should ask him about it if you're worried.
Yeah. Maybe.
le glacier
It's here!!

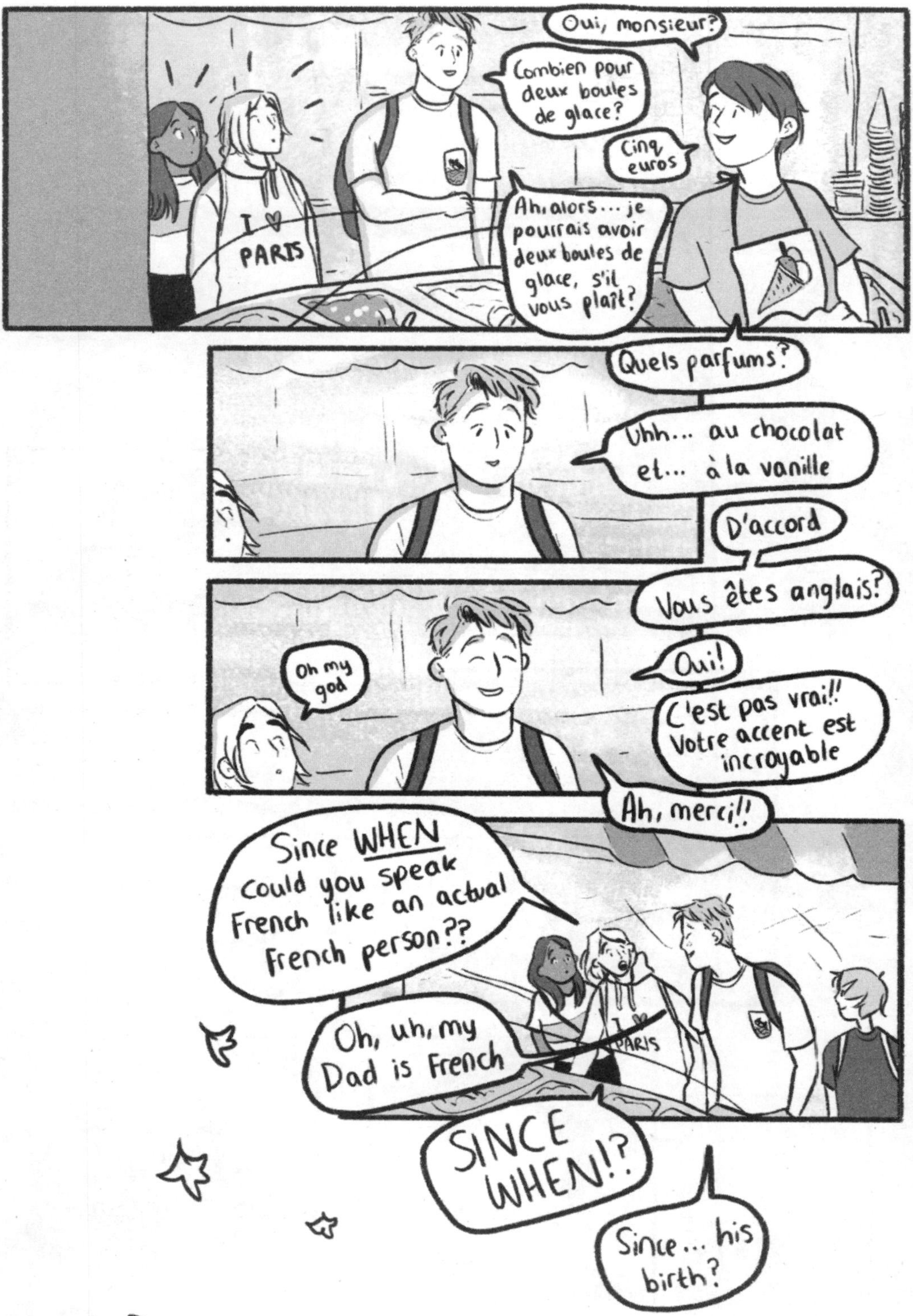
Oui, monsieur?
Combien pour deux boules de glace?
Cinq euros
Ah, alors... je pourrais avoir deux boules de glace, s'il vous plaît?
I ♥ PARIS
Quels parfums?
Uhh... au chocolat et... à la vanille
D'accord
Vous êtes anglais?
Oui!
Oh my god
C'est pas vrai!! Votre accent est incroyable
Ah, merci!!
Since WHEN could you speak French like an actual French person??
Oh, uh, my Dad is French
SINCE WHEN!?
Since... his birth?

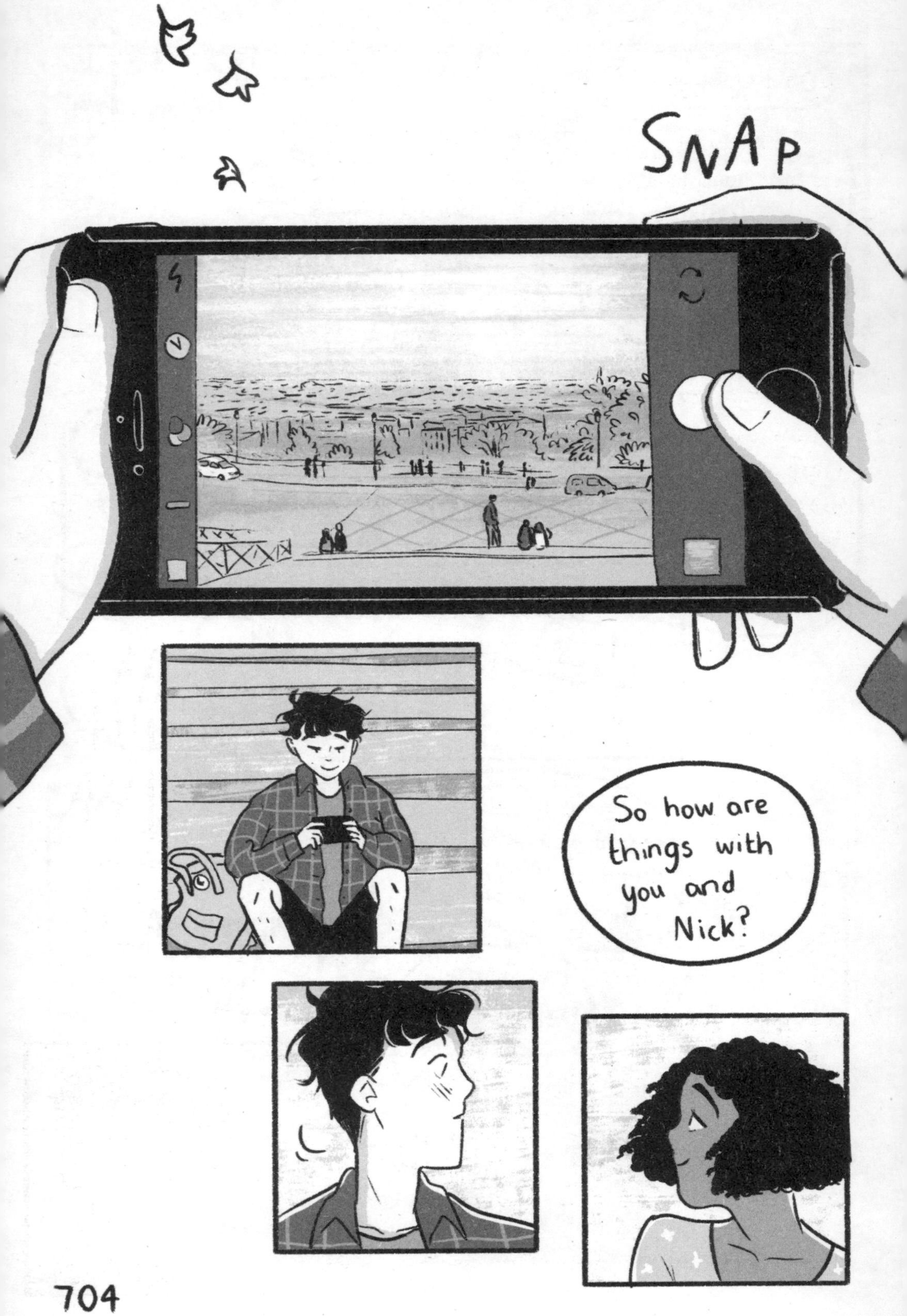
SNAP
So how are things with you and Nick?

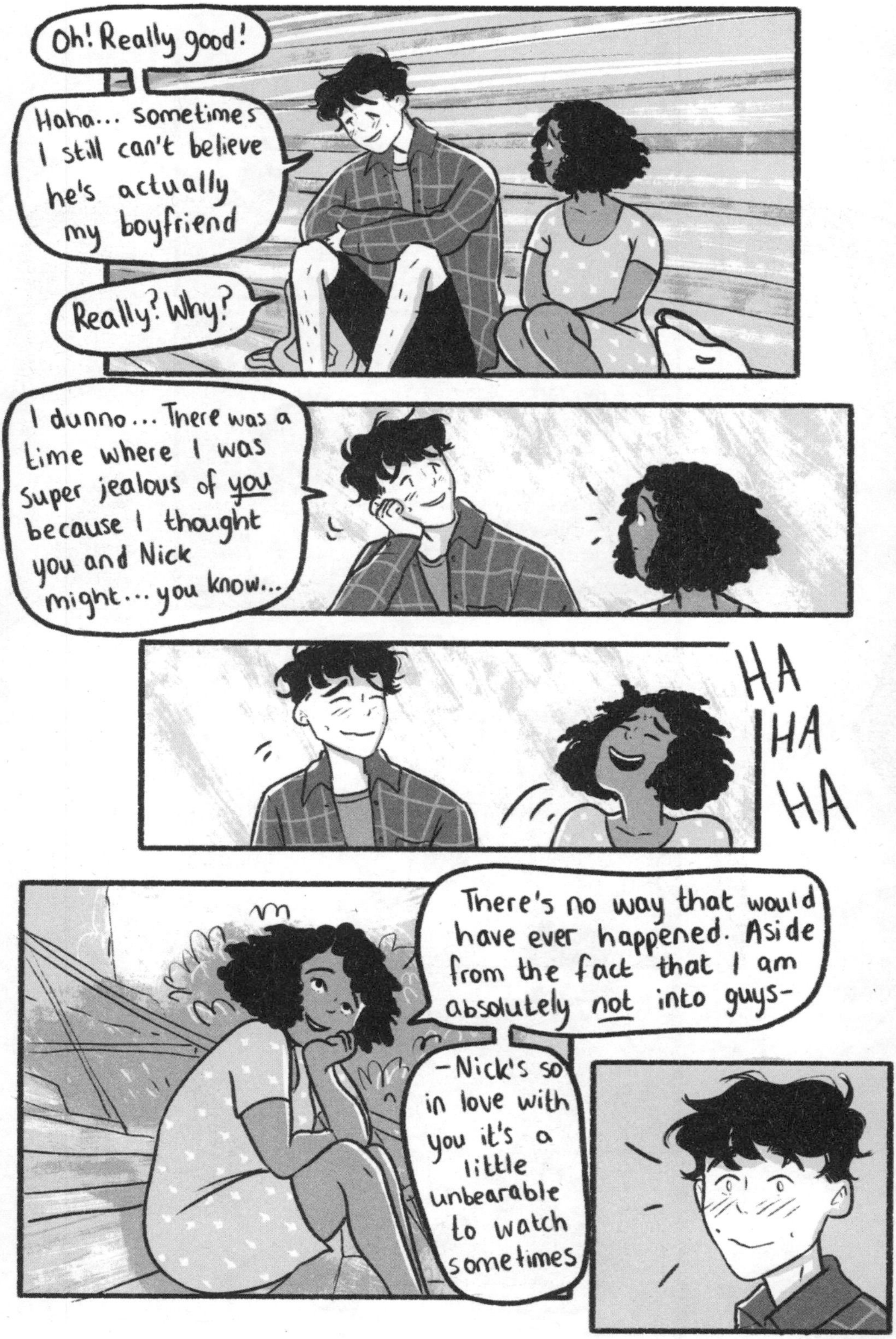
Oh! Really good!
Haha... sometimes I still can't believe he's actually my boyfriend
Really? Why?
I dunno... There was a time where I was super jealous of you because I thought you and Nick might... you know...
HA HA HA
There's no way that would have ever happened. Aside from the fact that I am absolutely not into guys-
-Nick's so in love with you it's a little unbearable to watch sometimes

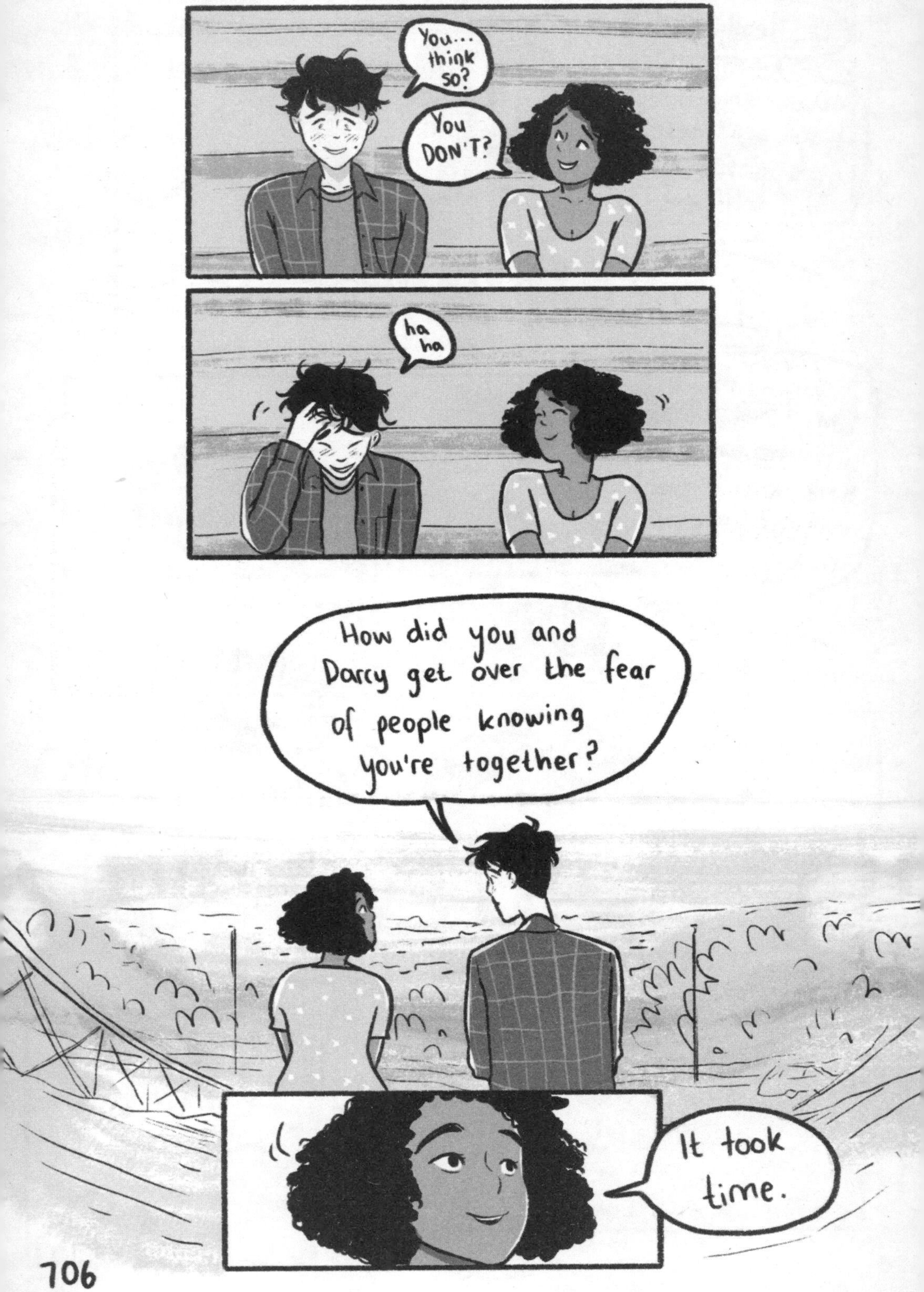
You... think so?
You DON'T?
ha ha
How did you and Darcy get over the fear of people knowing you're together?
It took time.

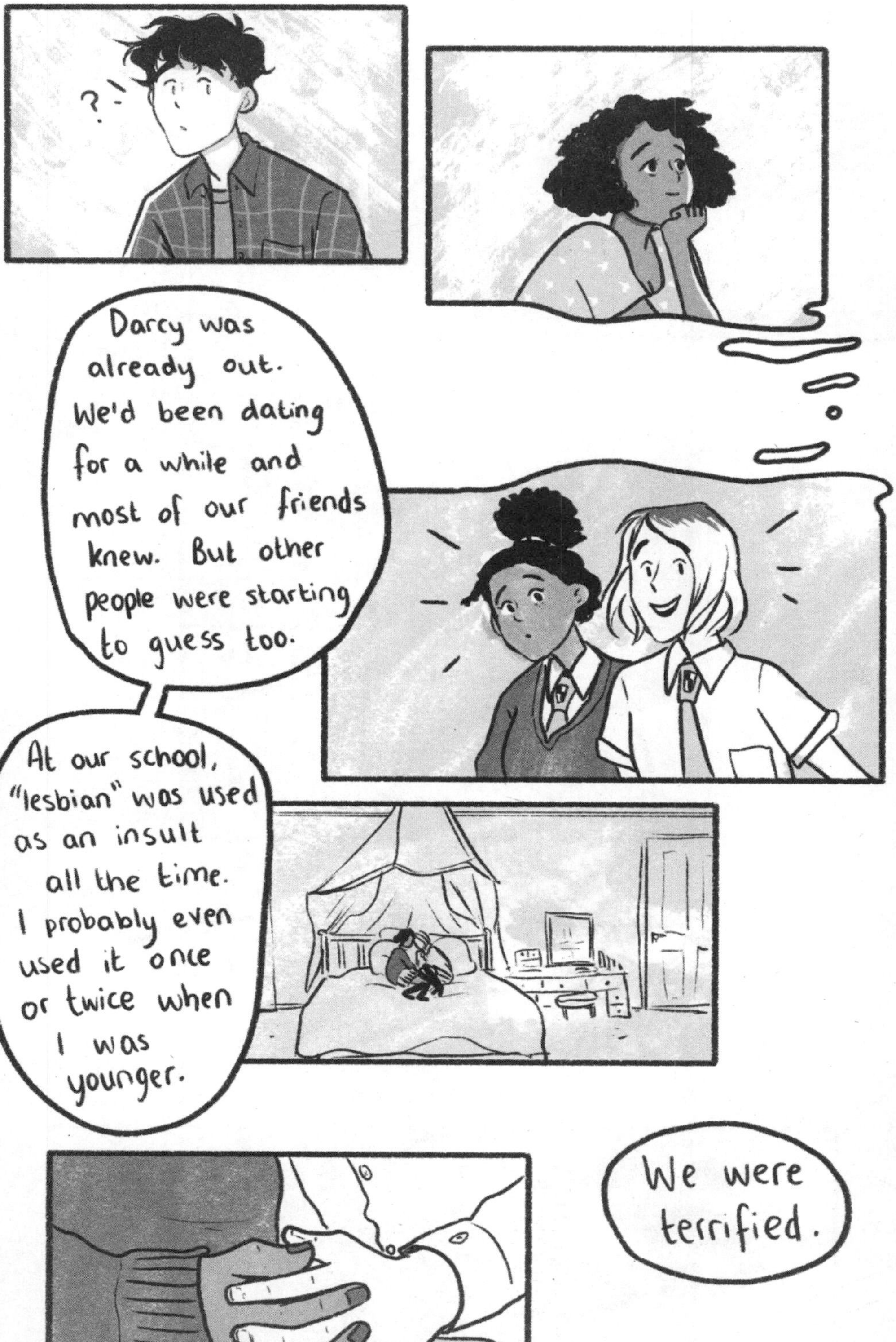
?!
Darcy was already out. We'd been dating for a while and most of our friends knew. But other people were starting to guess too.
At our school, "lesbian" was used as an insult all the time. I probably even used it once or twice when I was younger.
We were terrified.

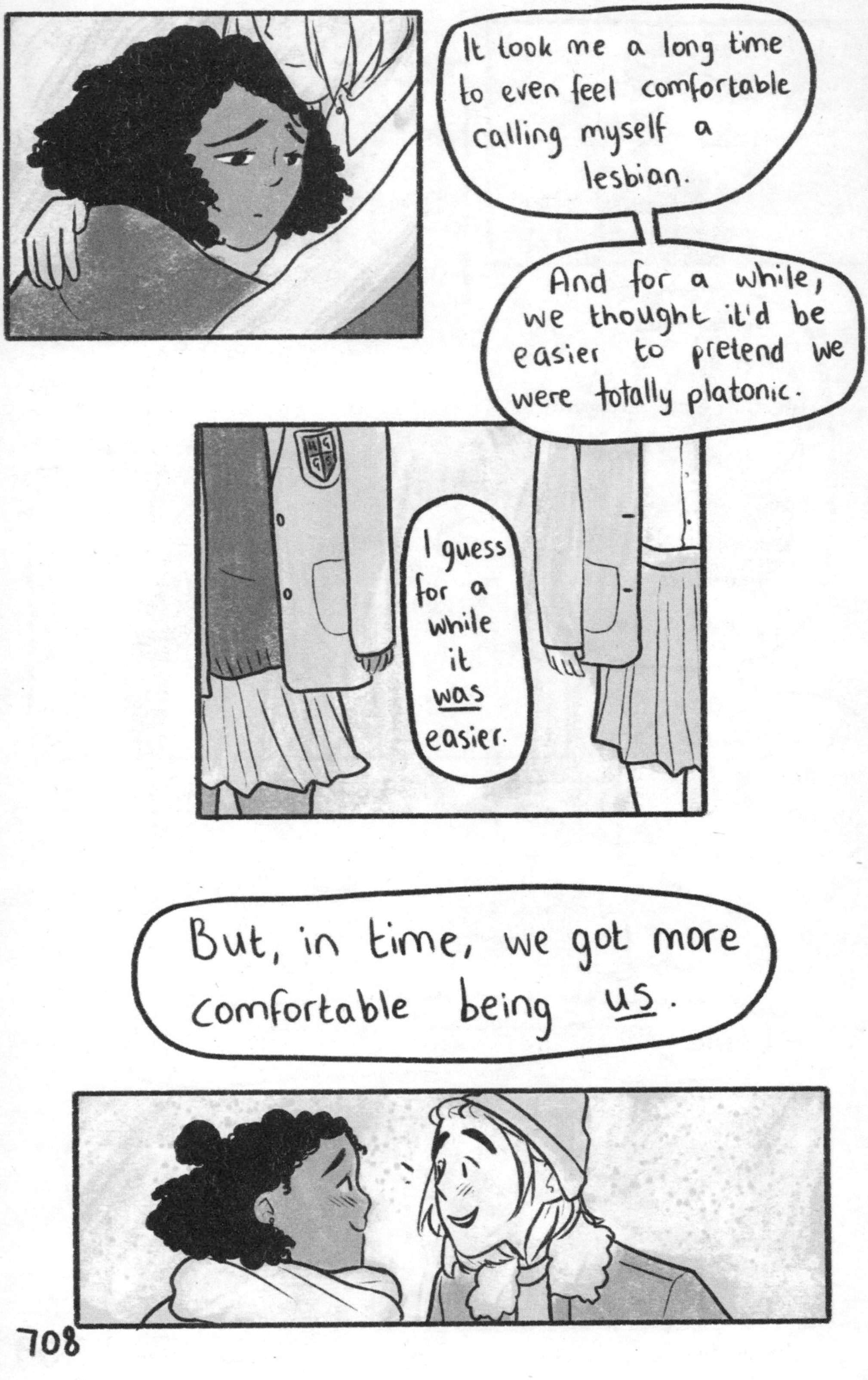
It took me a long time to even feel comfortable calling myself a lesbian.
And for a while, we thought it'd be easier to pretend we were totally platonic.
I guess for a while it was easier.
But, in time, we got more comfortable being us.

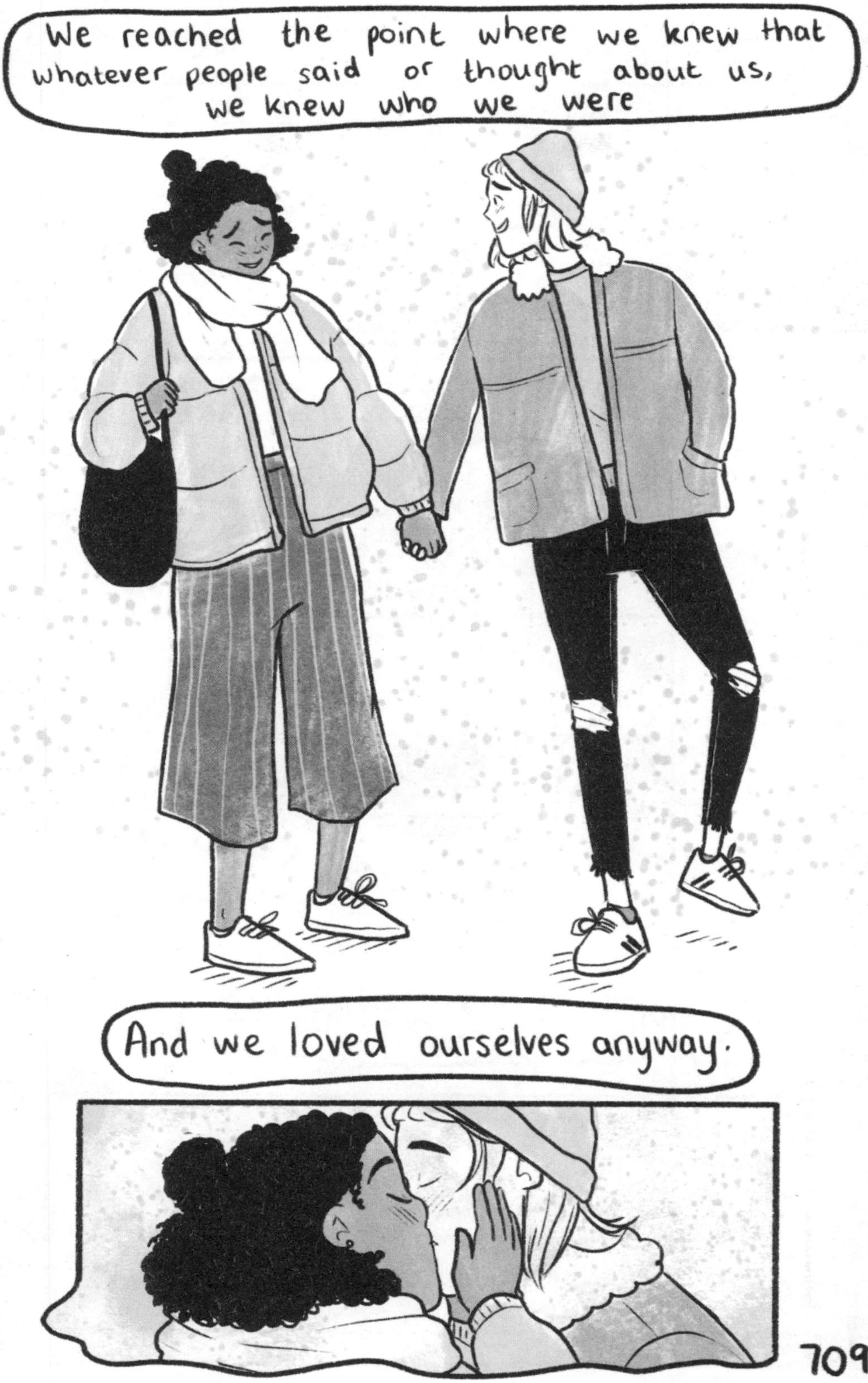
We reached the point where we knew that whatever people said or thought about us, we knew who we were
And we loved ourselves anyway.

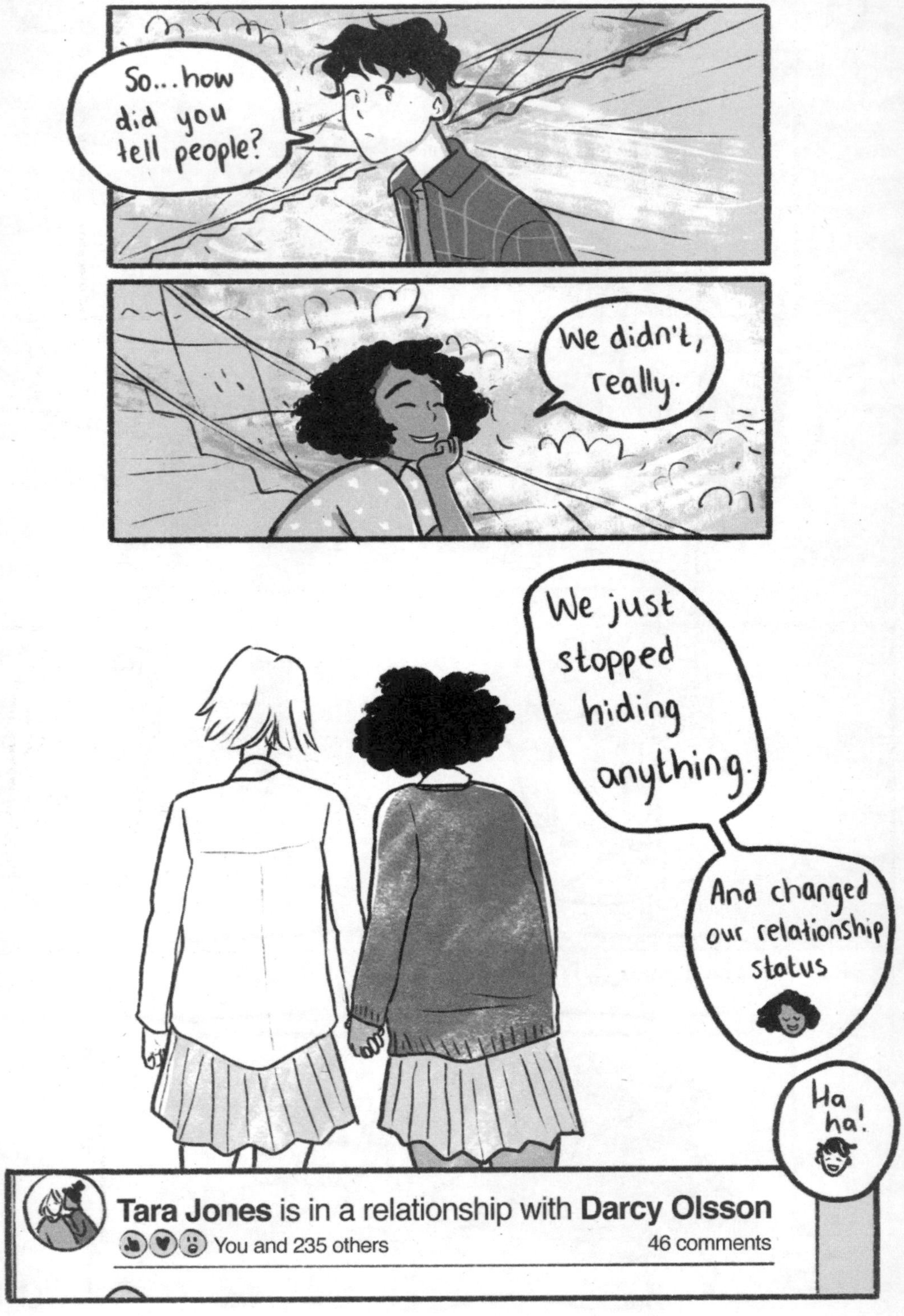
So... how did you tell people?
We didn't, really.
We just stopped hiding anything.
And changed our relationship status
Ha ha!
Tara Jones is in a relationship with Darcy Olsson
You and 235 others
46 comments

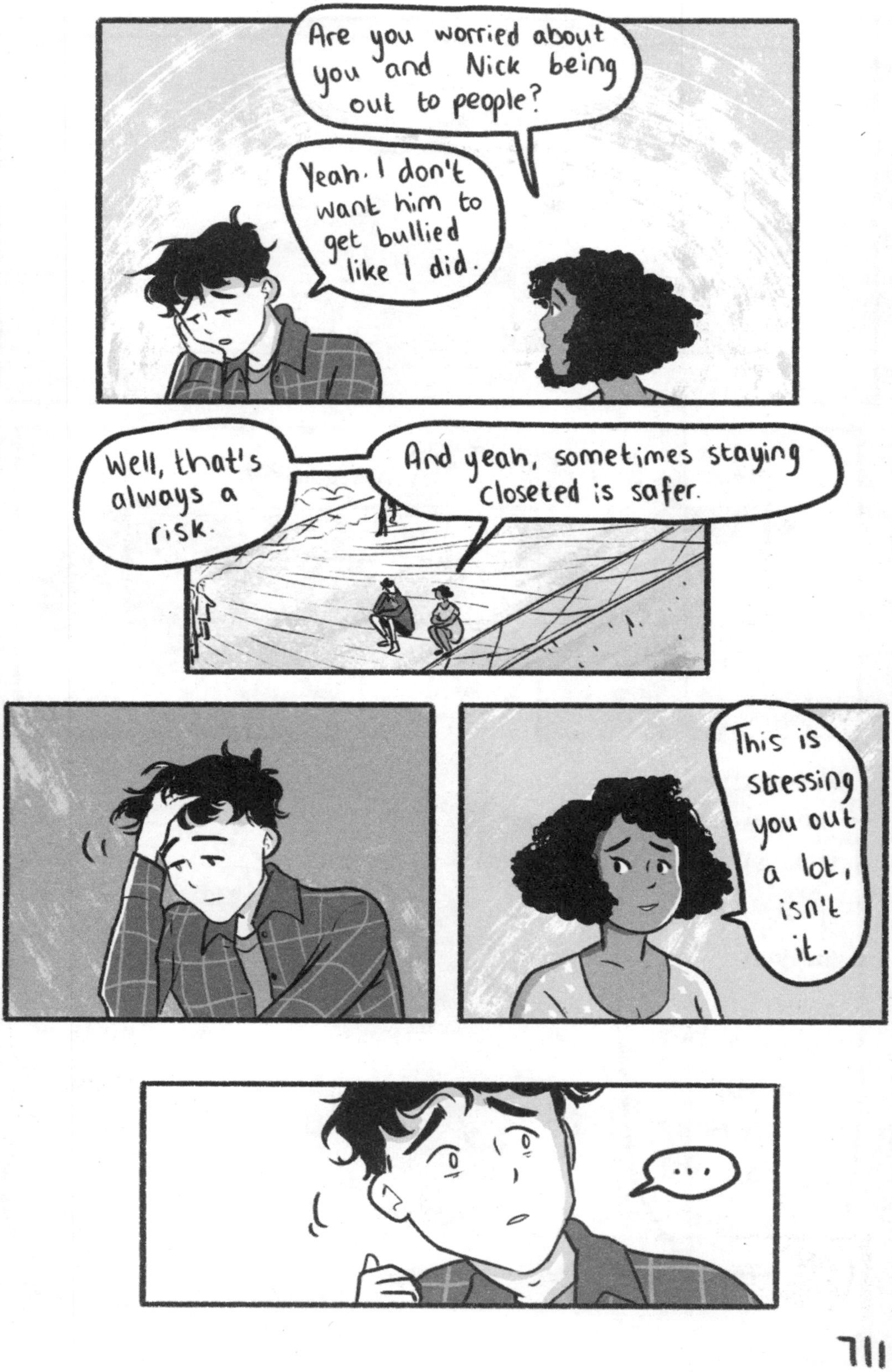
Are you worried about you and Nick being out to people?
Yeah. I don't want him to get bullied like I did.
Well, that's always a risk.
And yeah, sometimes staying closeted is safer.
This is stressing you out a lot, isn't it.
...

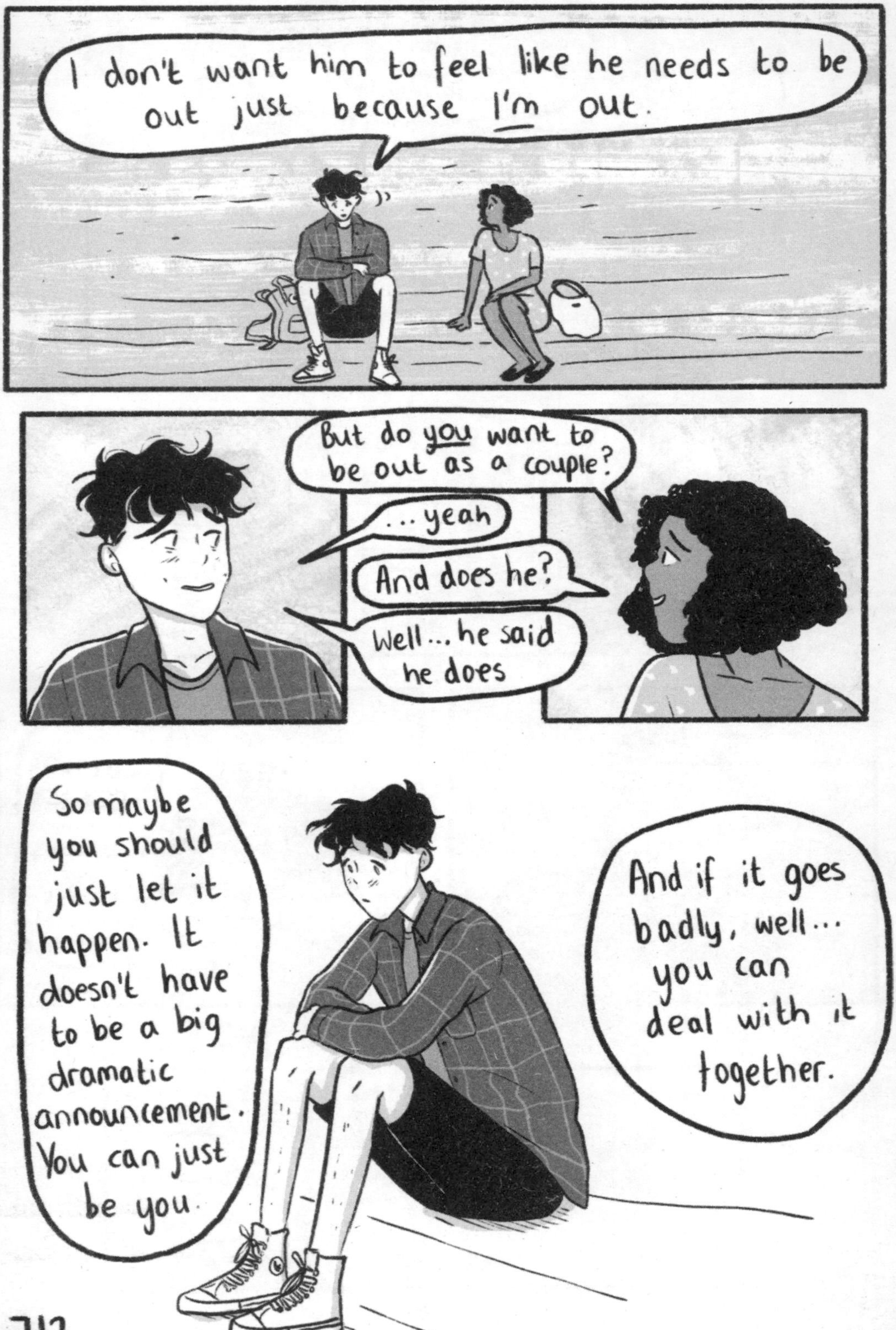

I don't want him to feel like he needs to be out just because I'm out.
But do you want to be out as a couple?
...yeah
And does he?
Well... he said he does
So maybe you should just let it happen. It doesn't have to be a big dramatic announcement. You can just be you.
And if it goes badly, well... you can deal with it together.

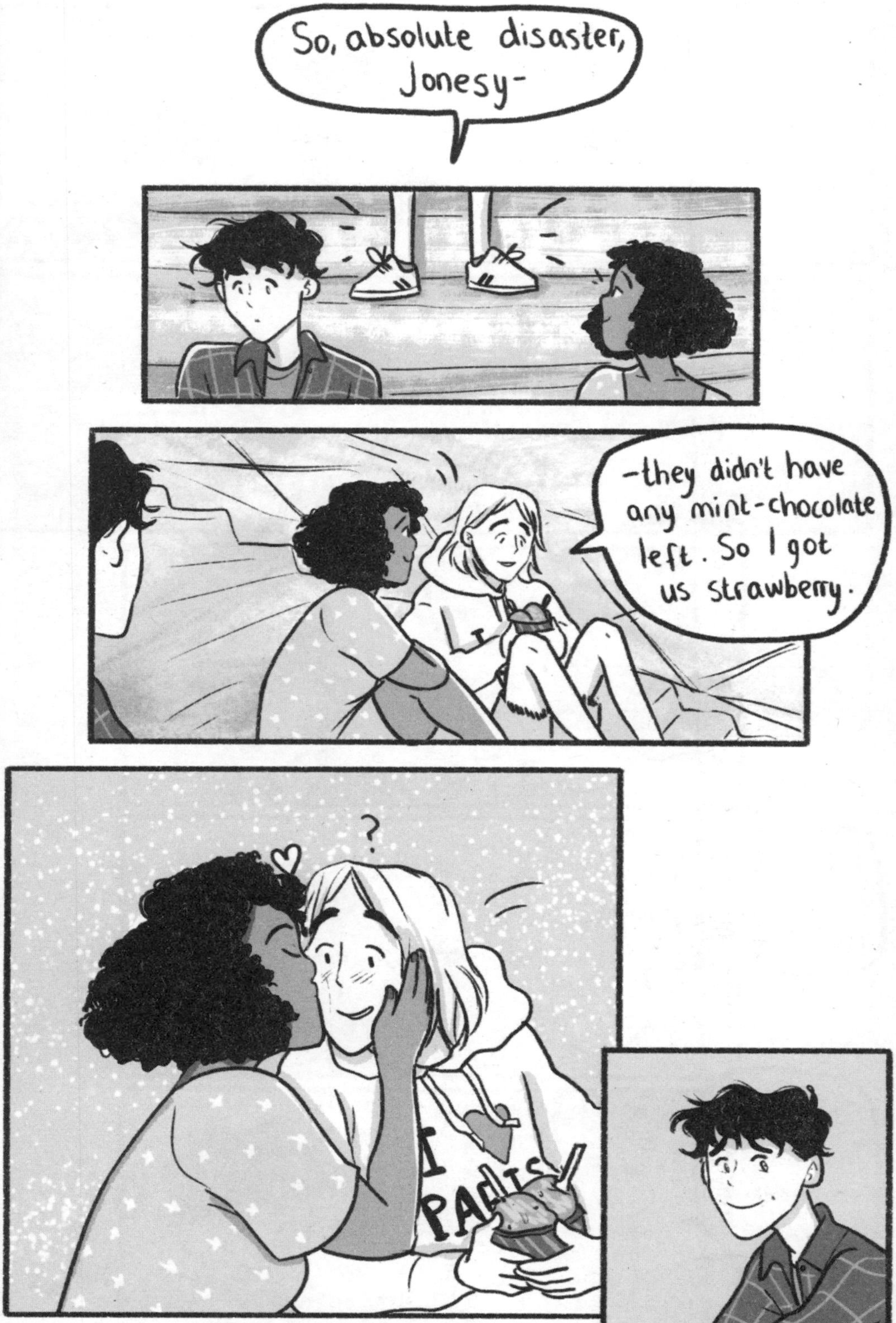
So, absolute disaster, Jonesy-
-they didn't have any mint-chocolate left. So I got us strawberry.
?

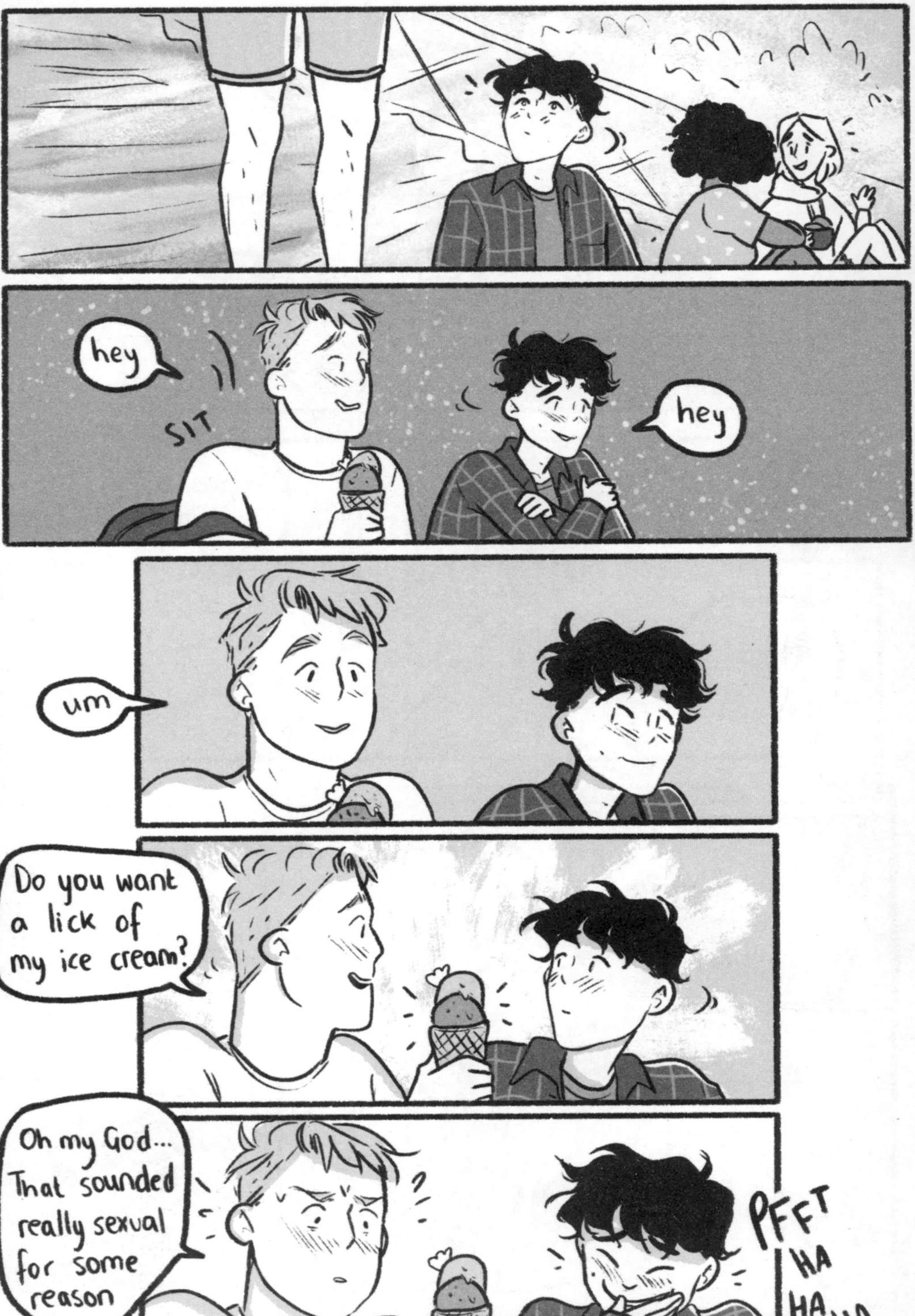
hey
SIT
hey
um
Do you want a lick of my ice cream?
Oh my God... That sounded really sexual for some reason
PFFT
HA
HA
HA

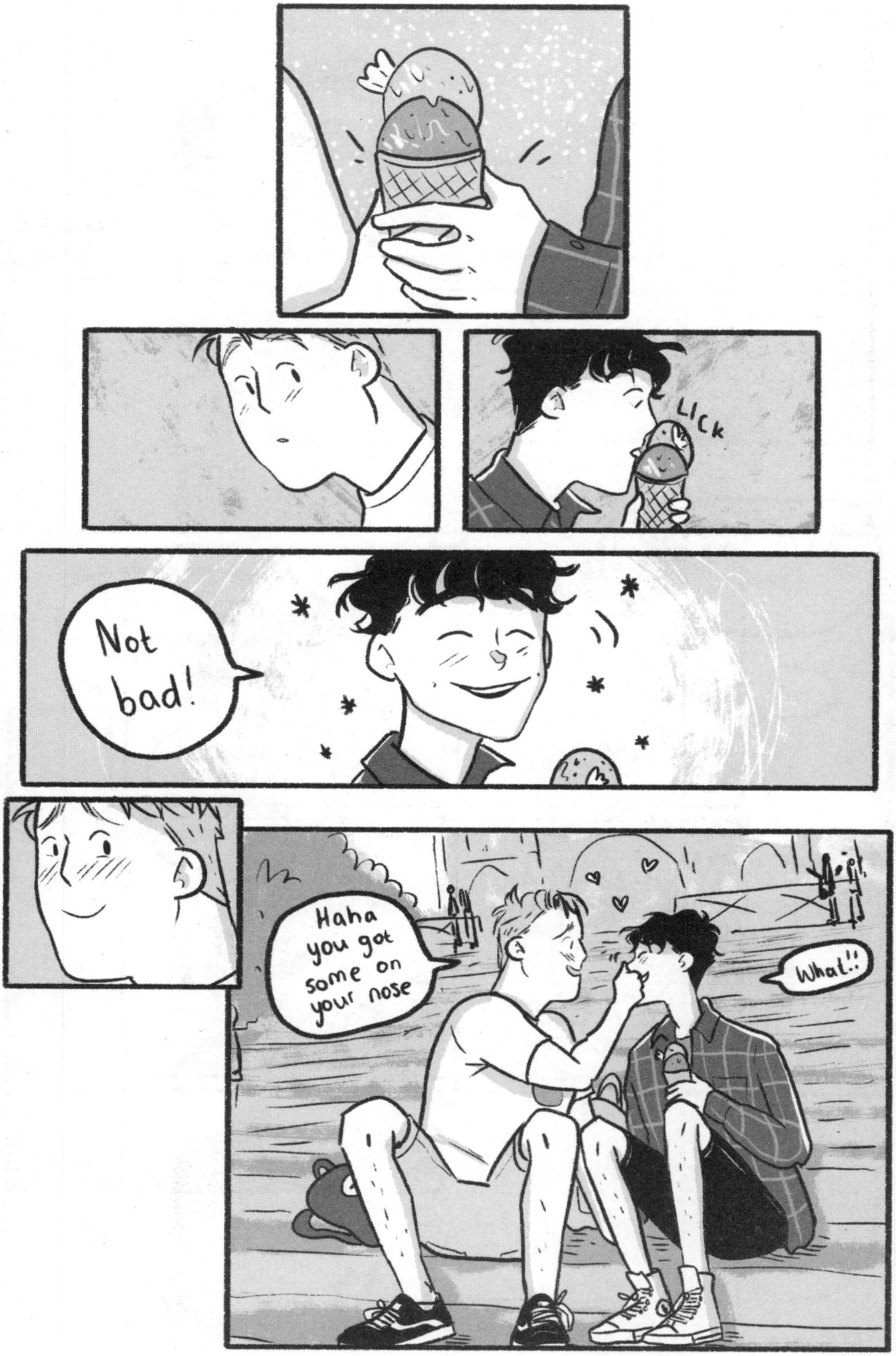
LICK
Not bad!
Haha you got some on your nose
What!!

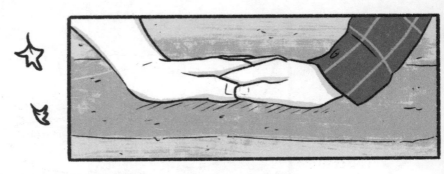

There they are!

Oh my God, d'you think anything happened?

I hope so, or Tao is gonna pine to death

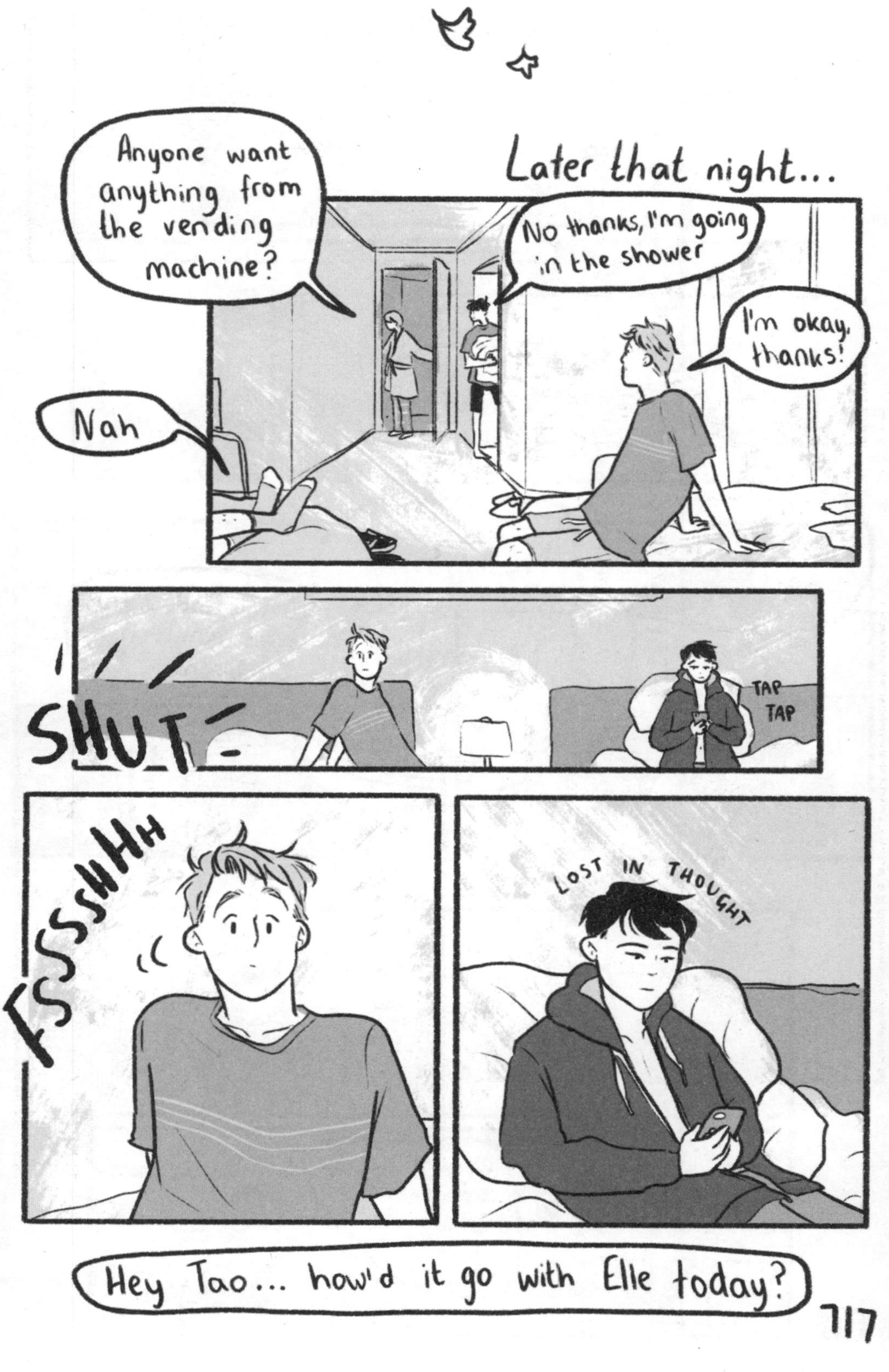

Later that night...
Anyone want anything from the vending machine?
No thanks, I'm going in the shower
I'm okay, thanks!
Nah
SHUT
TAP TAP
FSSSHHH
LOST IN THOUGHT
Hey Tao... how'd it go with Elle today?

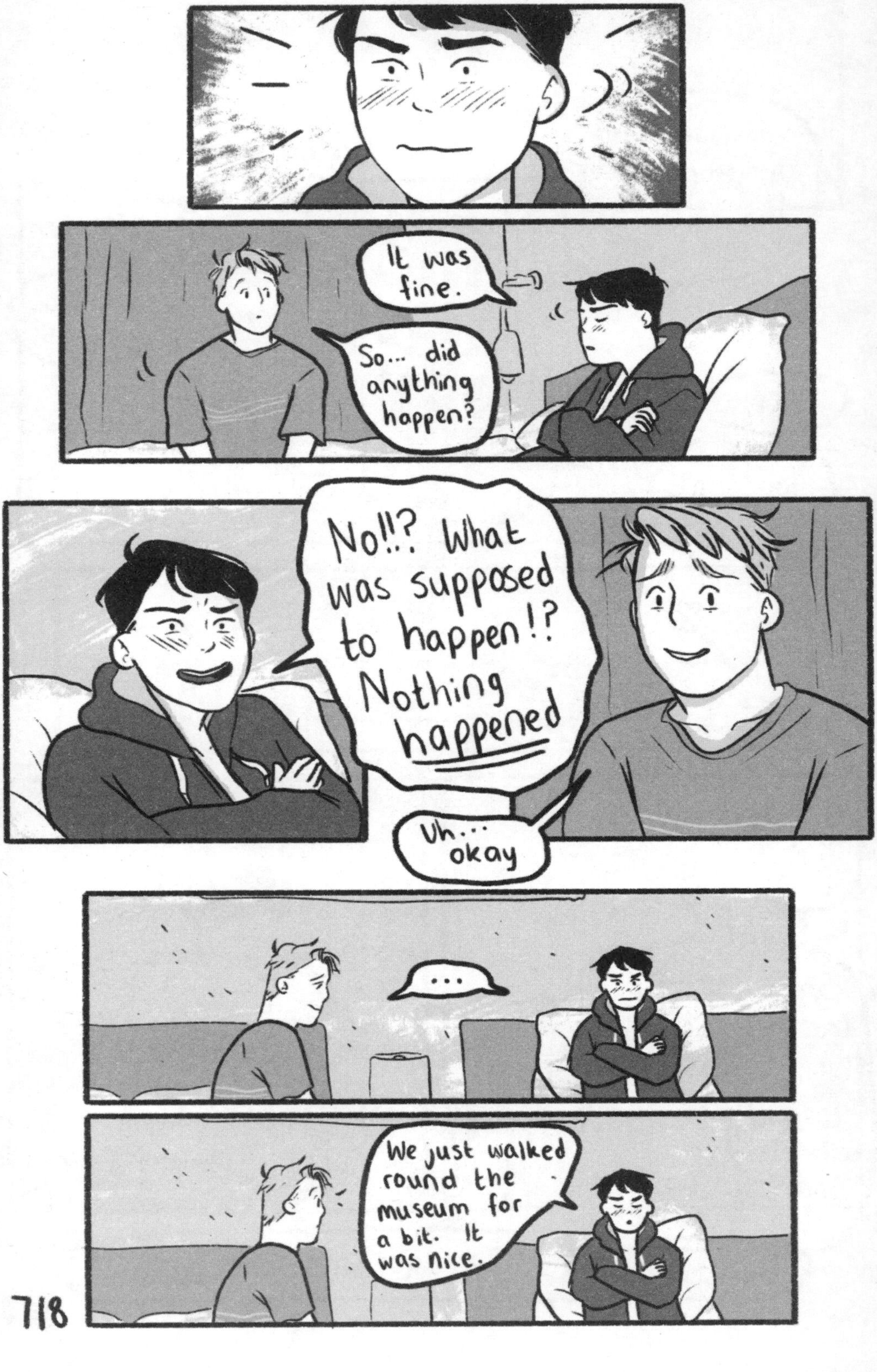
It was fine.
So... did anything happen?
No!!? What was supposed to happen!? Nothing happened
Uh... okay
...
We just walked round the museum for a bit. It was nice.

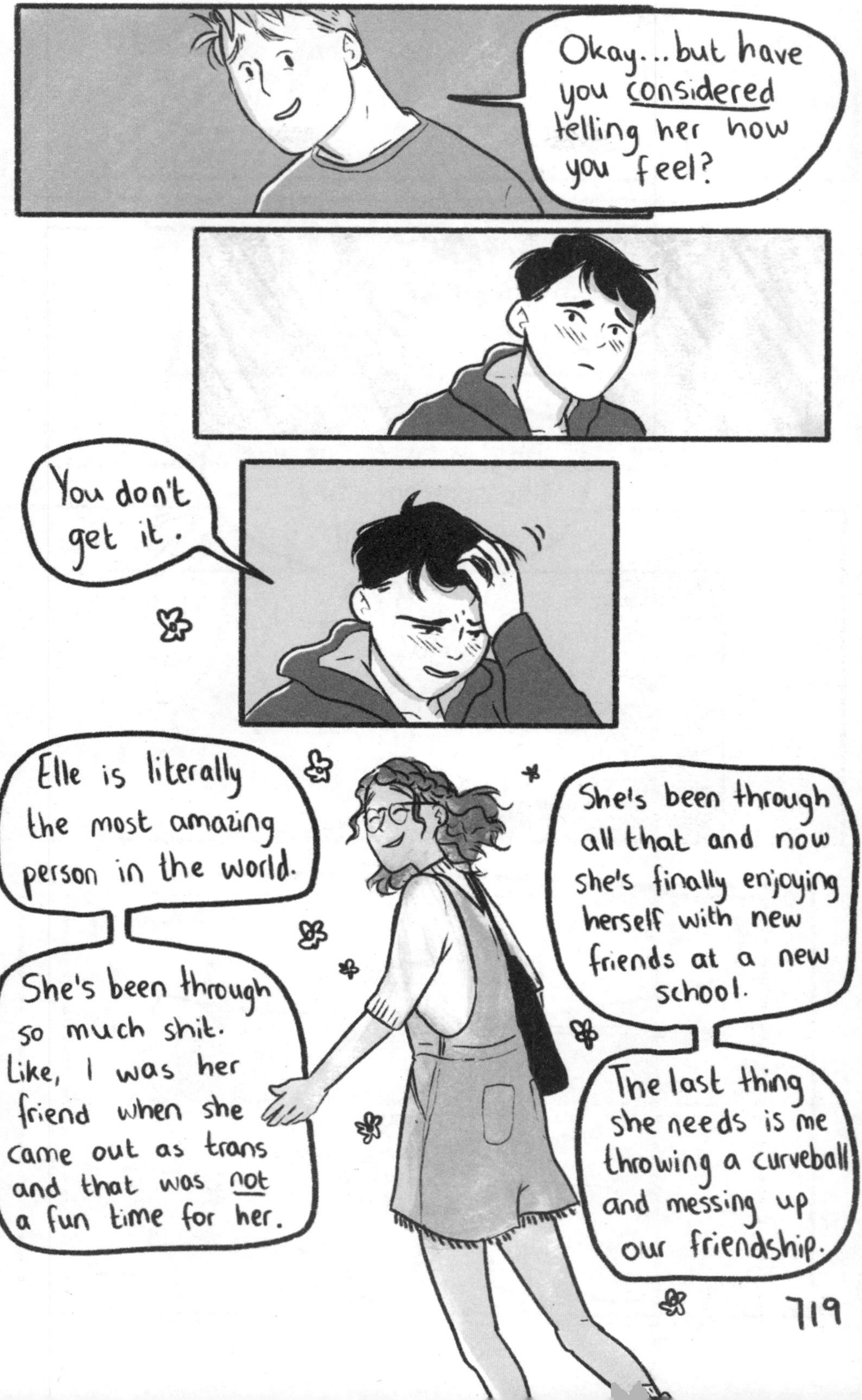
Okay... but have you considered telling her how you feel?
You don't get it.
Elle is literally the most amazing person in the world.
She's been through so much shit. Like, I was her friend when she came out as trans and that was not a fun time for her.
She's been through all that and now she's finally enjoying herself with new friends at a new school.
The last thing she needs is me throwing a curveball and messing up our friendship.

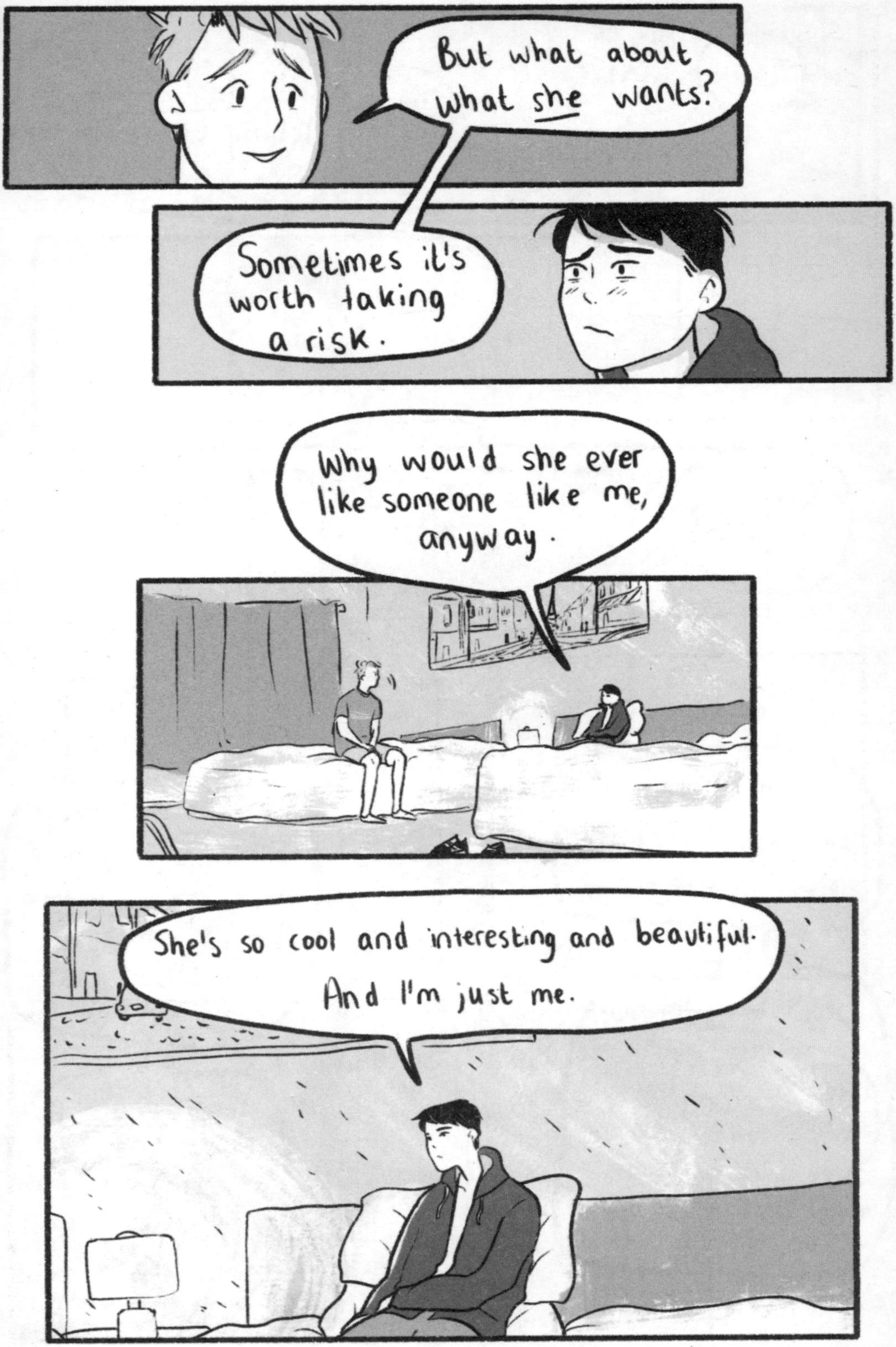
But what about what she wants?
Sometimes it's worth taking a risk.
Why would she ever like someone like me, anyway.
She's so cool and interesting and beautiful.
And I'm just me.

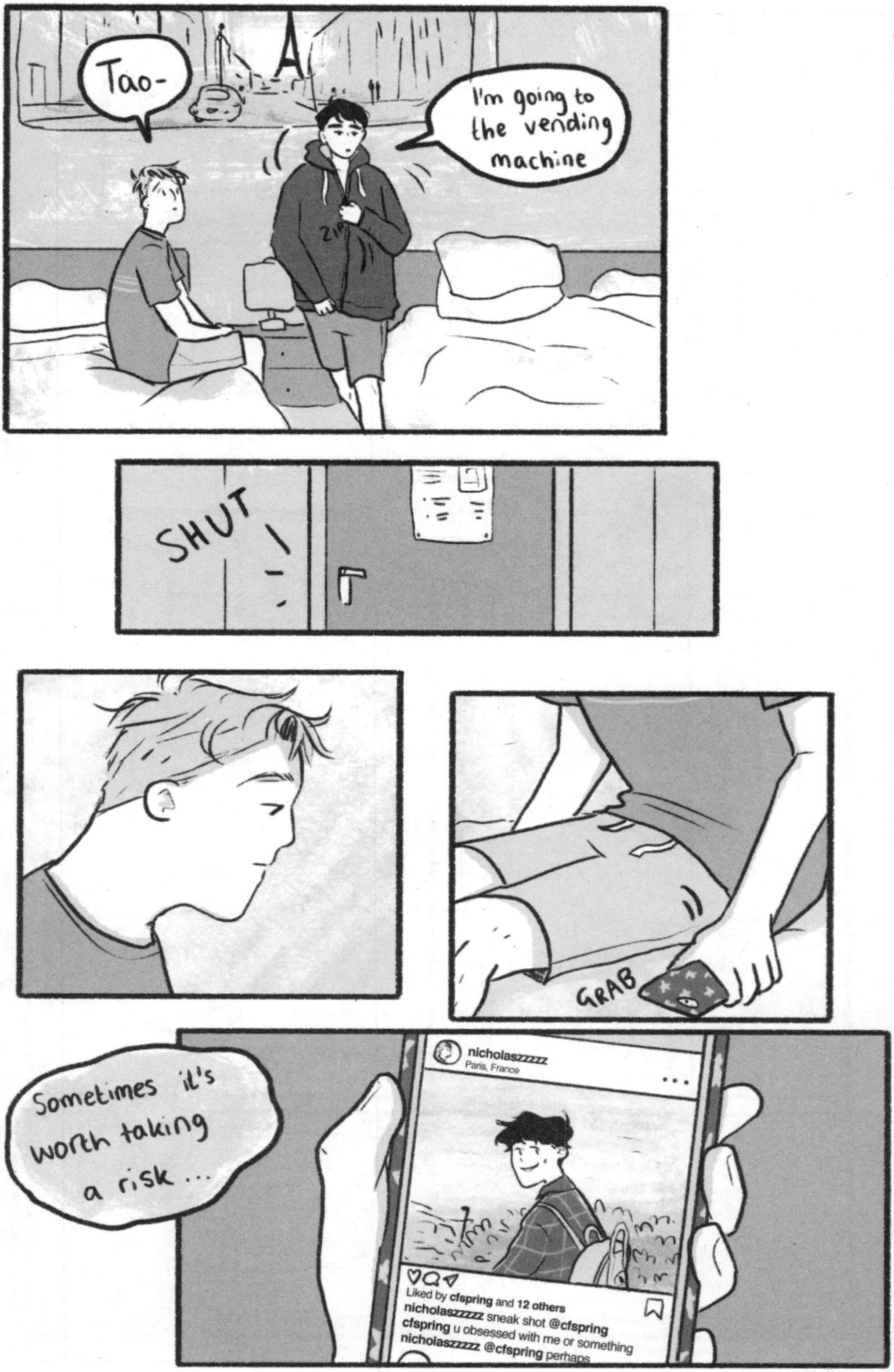
Tao-
I'm going to the vending machine
ZIP
SHUT
GRAB
Sometimes it's worth taking a risk ...
nicholaszzzzz
Paris, France
Liked by cfspring and 12 others
nicholaszzzzz sneak shot @cfspring
cfspring u obsessed with me or something
nicholaszzzzz @cfspring perhaps

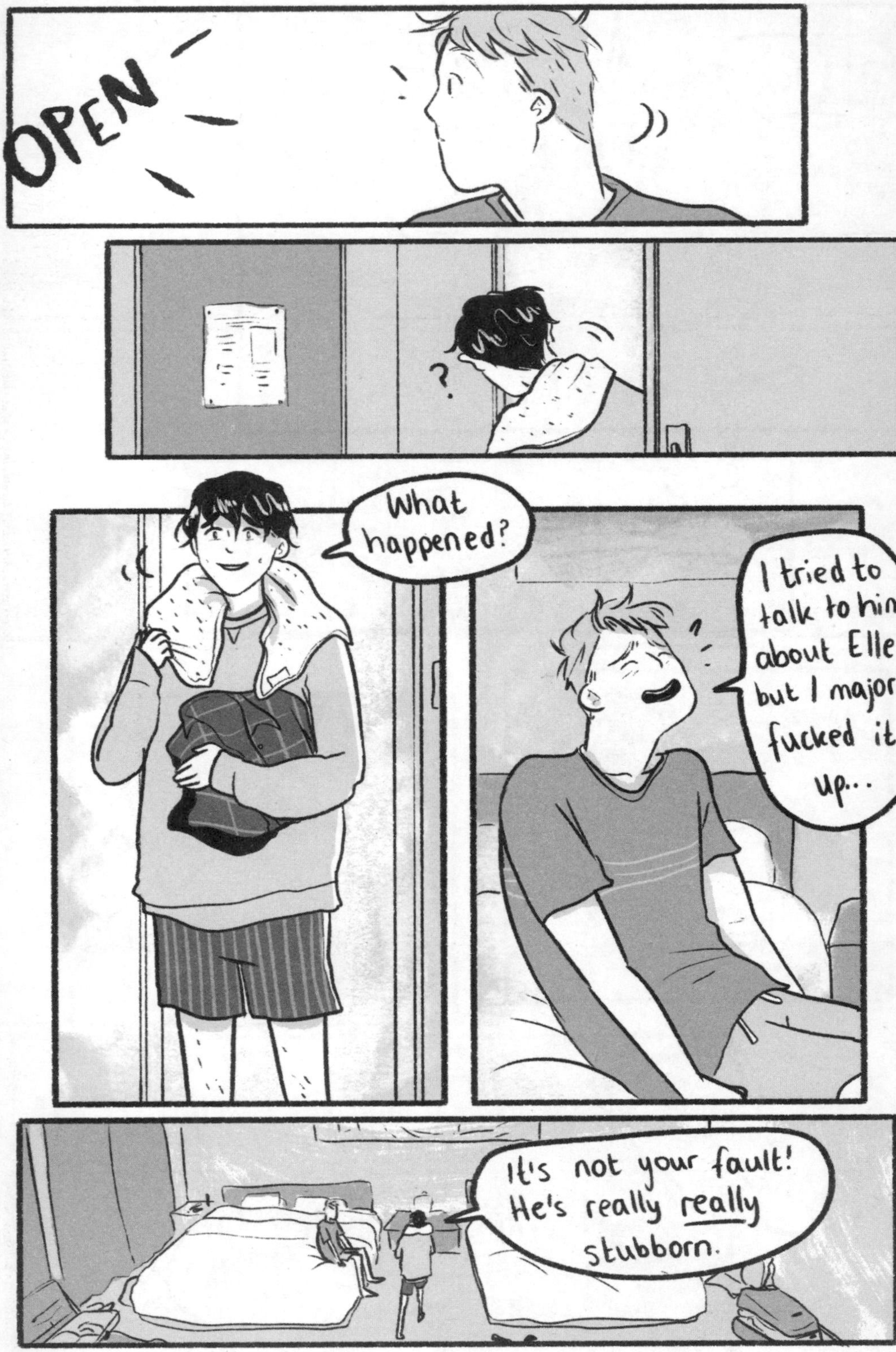
OPEN
What happened?
I tried to talk to him about Elle but I majorly fucked it up...
It's not your fault! He's really really stubborn.

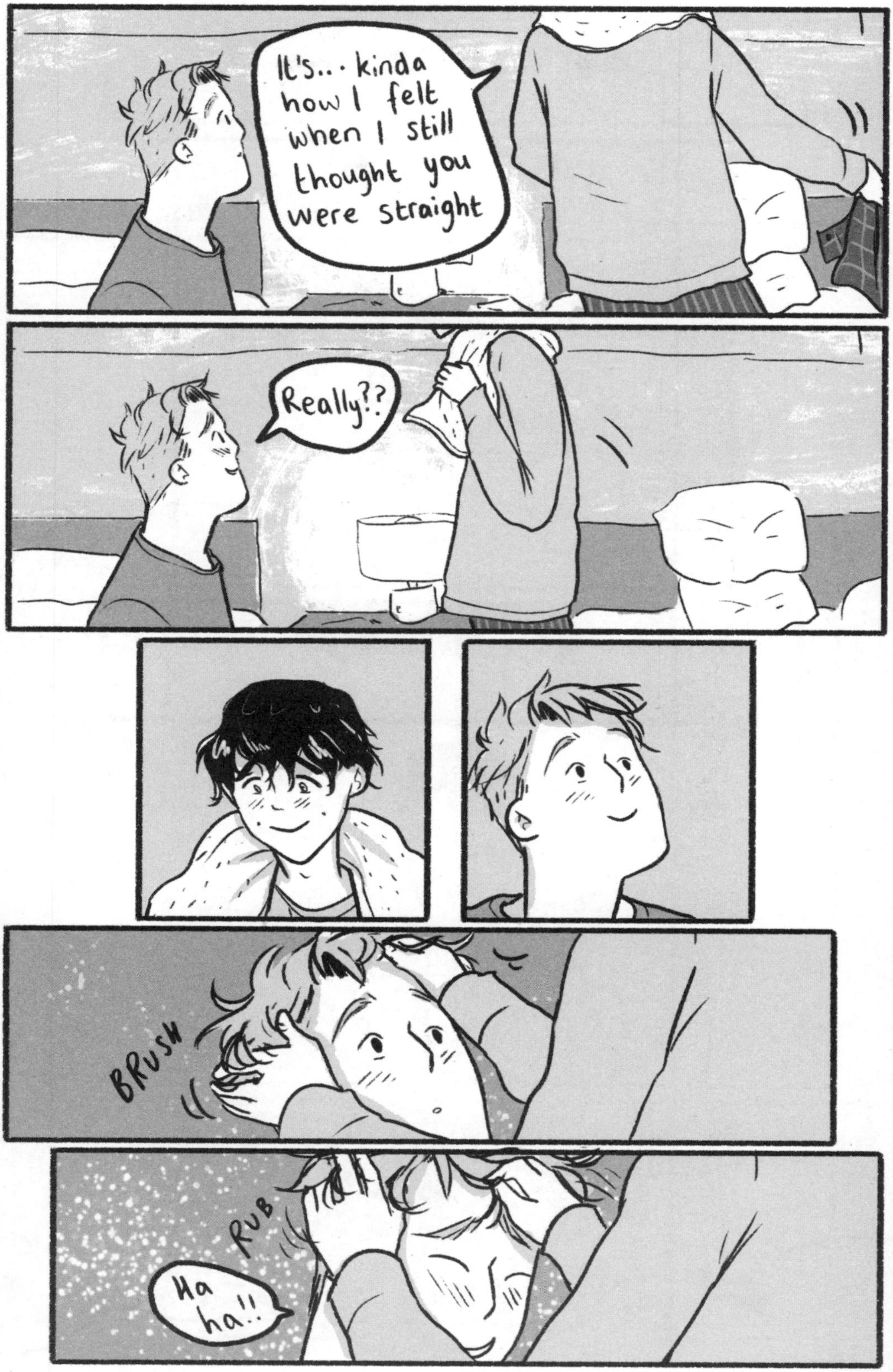
It's... kinda how I felt when I still thought you were straight
Really??
BRUSH
RUB
Ha ha!!

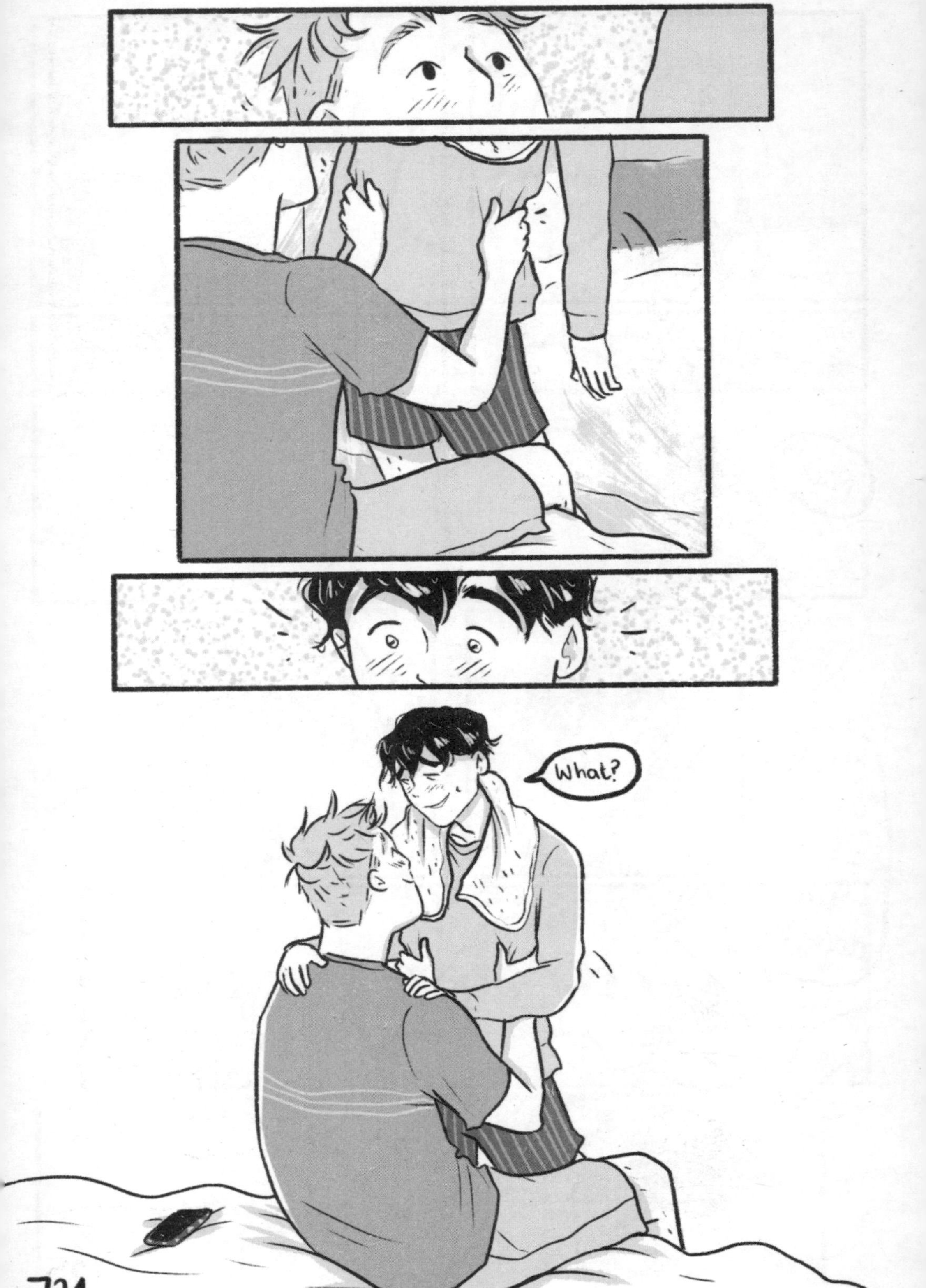
What?

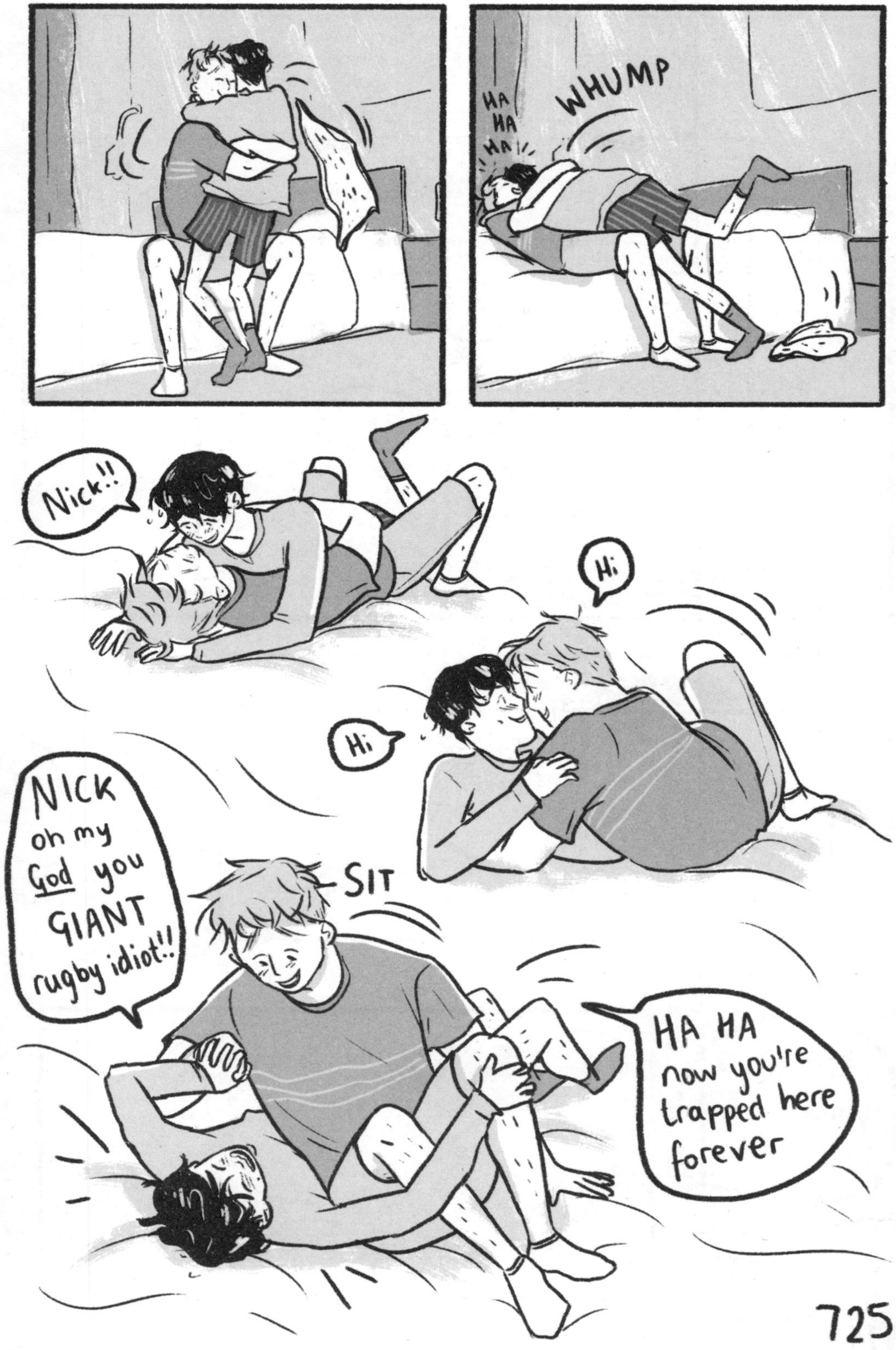
HA
HA
HA
WHUMP
Nick!!
Hi
Hi
NICK oh my God you GIANT rugby idiot!!
SIT
HA HA now you're trapped here forever

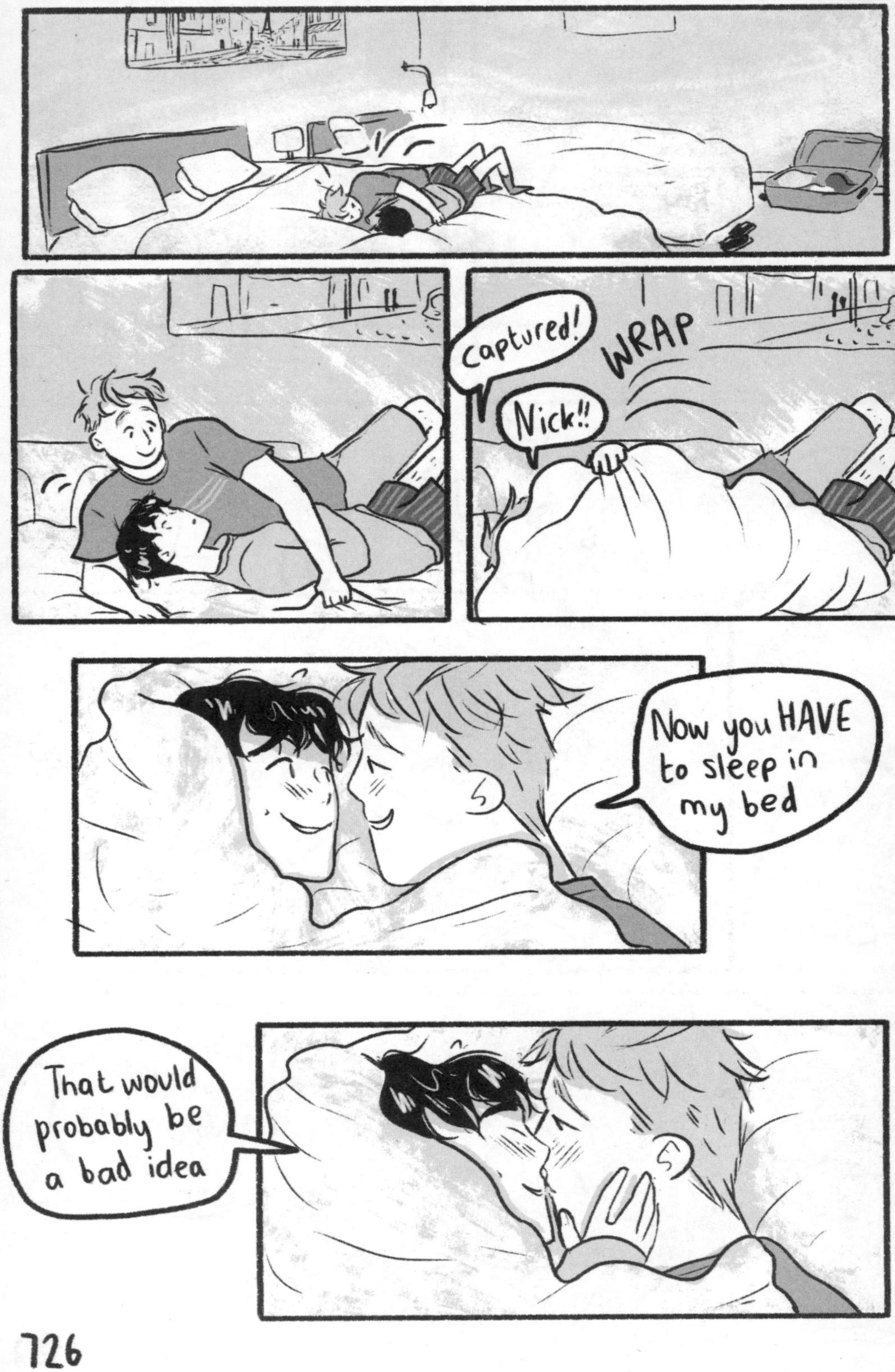
Captured!
WRAP
Nick!!
Now you HAVE to sleep in my bed
That would probably be a bad idea

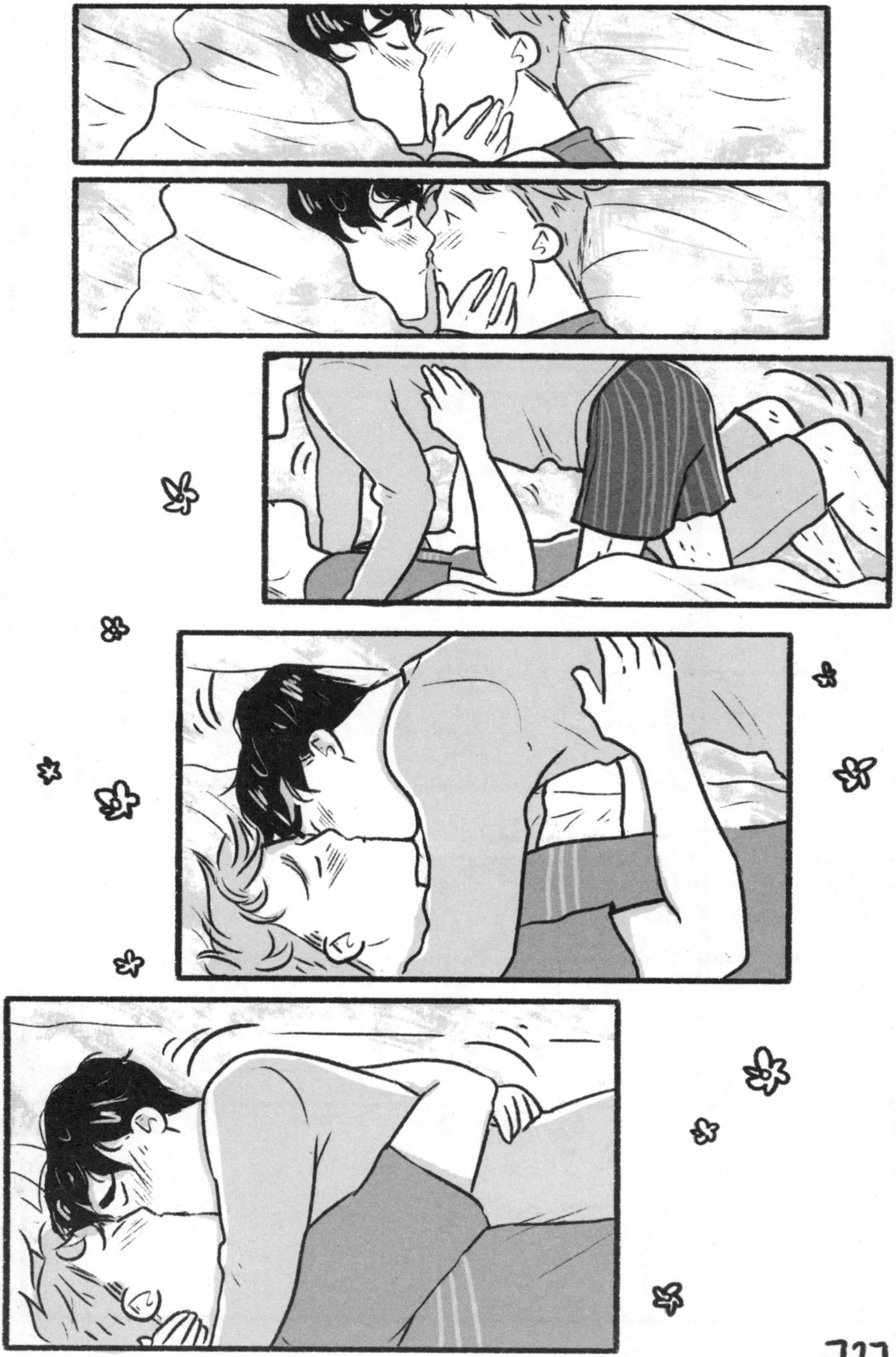

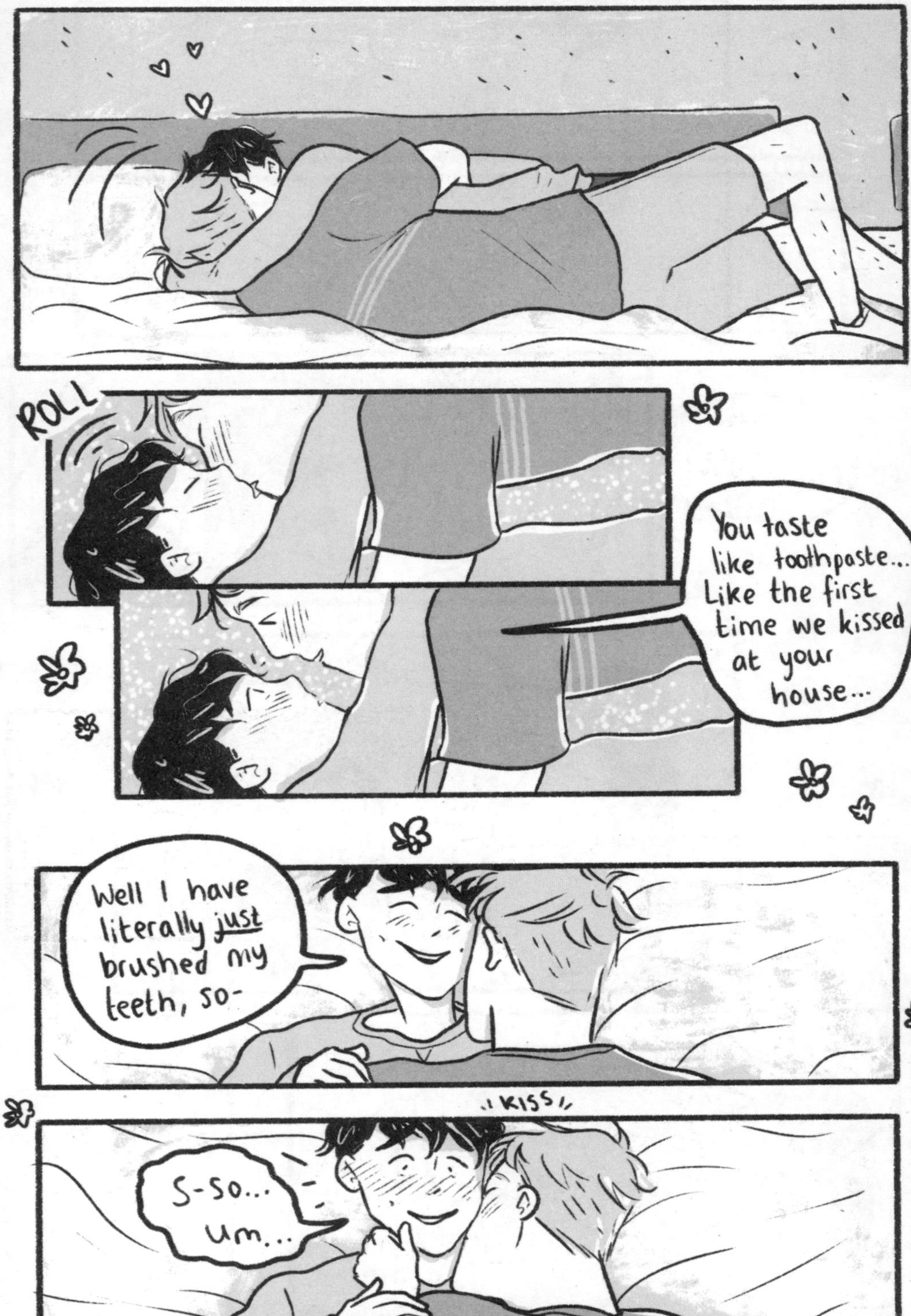
ROLL
You taste like toothpaste... Like the first time we kissed at your house...
Well I have literally just brushed my teeth, so-
KISS
S-so... um...

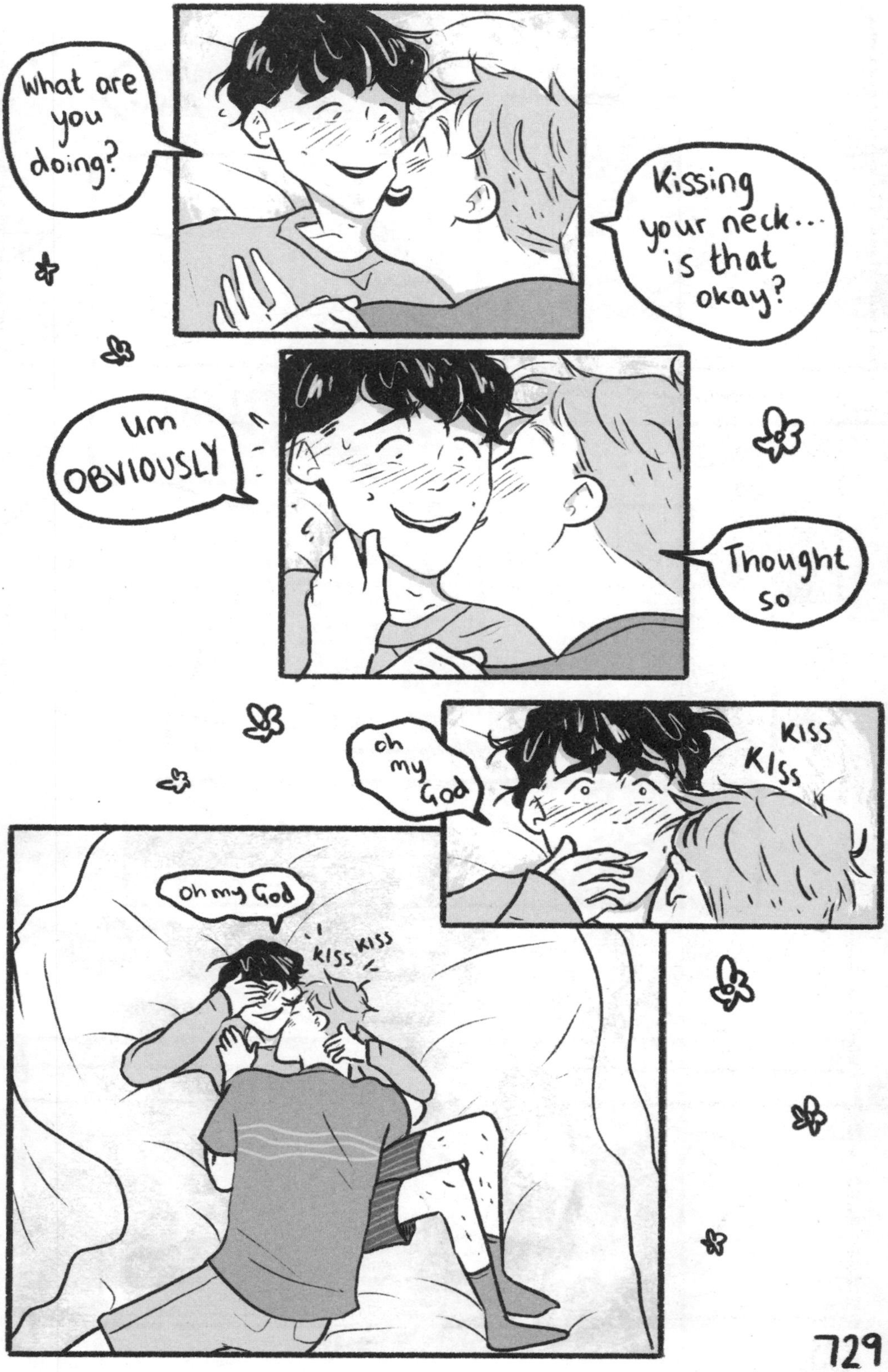
what are you doing?
Kissing your neck... is that okay?
Um OBVIOUSLY
Thought so
oh my God
KISS
KISS
oh my God
KISS KISS

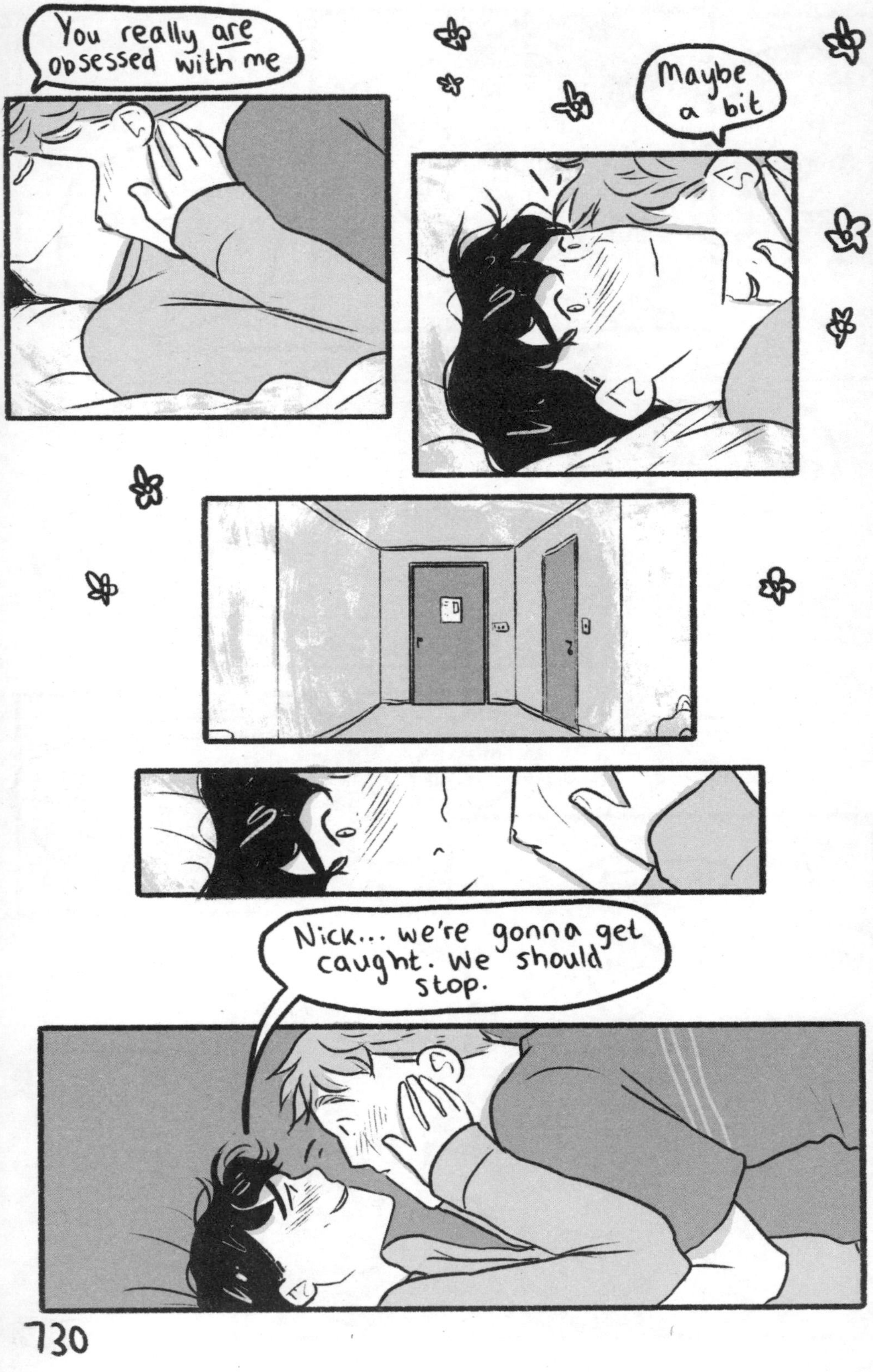
You really are obsessed with me
Maybe a bit
Nick... we're gonna get caught. We should stop.

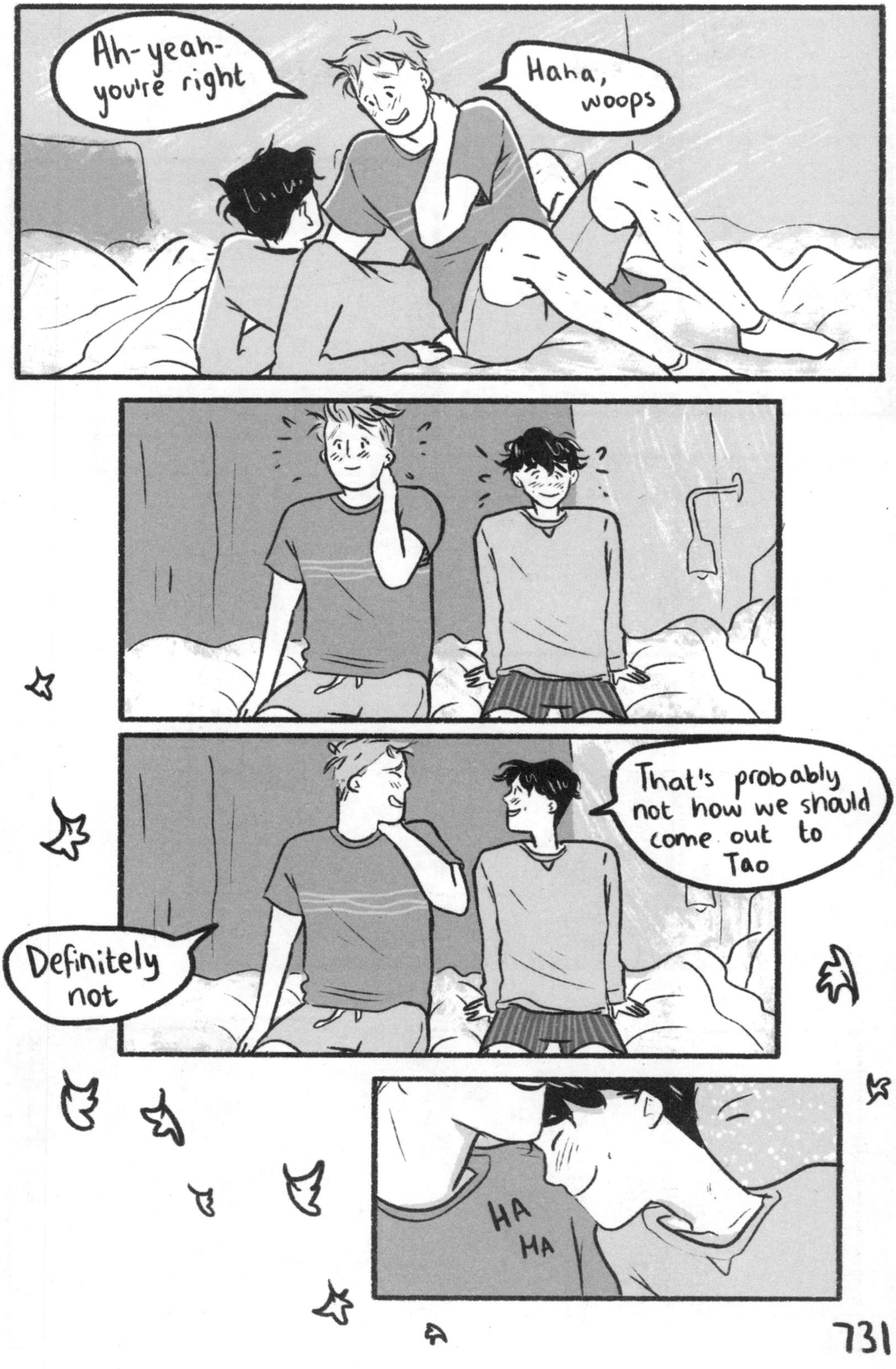
Ah-yeah-
you're right
Haha,
woops
That's probably not how we should come out to Tao
Definitely not
HA HA

Paris - Day 3

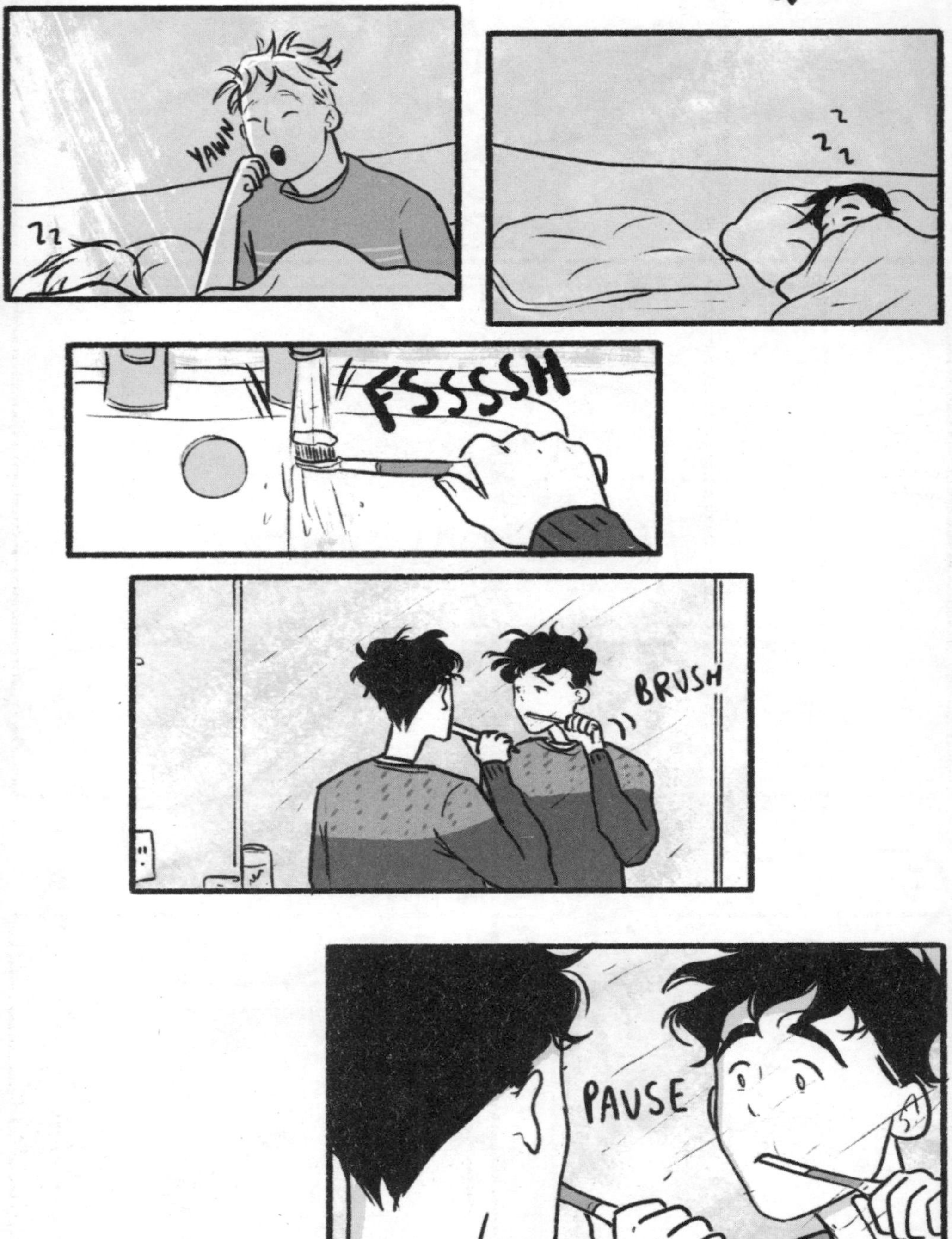
YAWN
ZZ
Z Z Z
FSSSSH
BRUSH
PAUSE

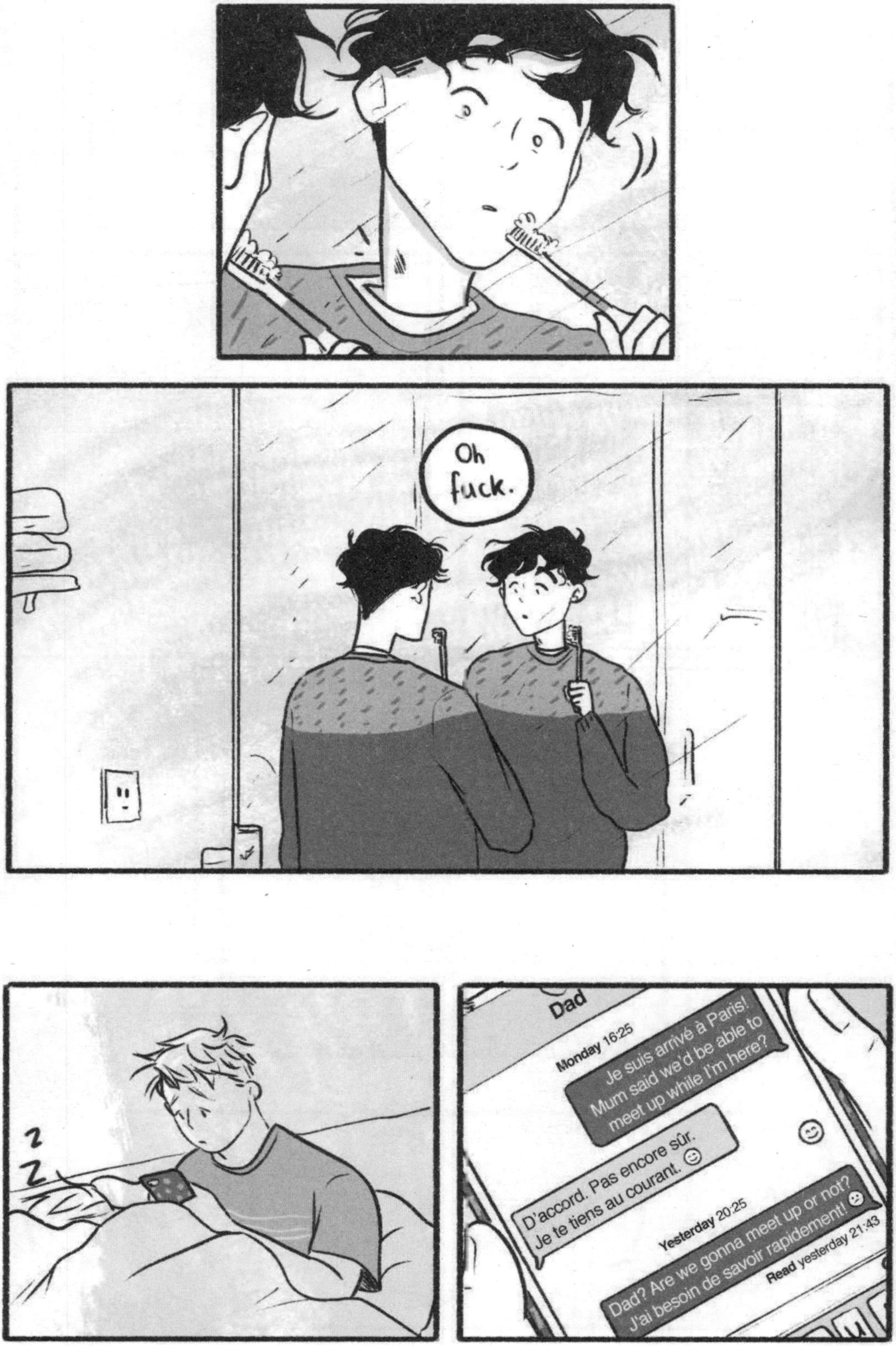

Oh fuck.
z
z
Dad
Monday 16:25
Je suis arrivé à Paris! Mum said we'd be able to meet up while I'm here?
D'accord. Pas encore sûr. Je te tiens au courant.
Yesterday 20:25
Dad? Are we gonna meet up or not? J'ai besoin de savoir rapidement!
Read yesterday 21:43

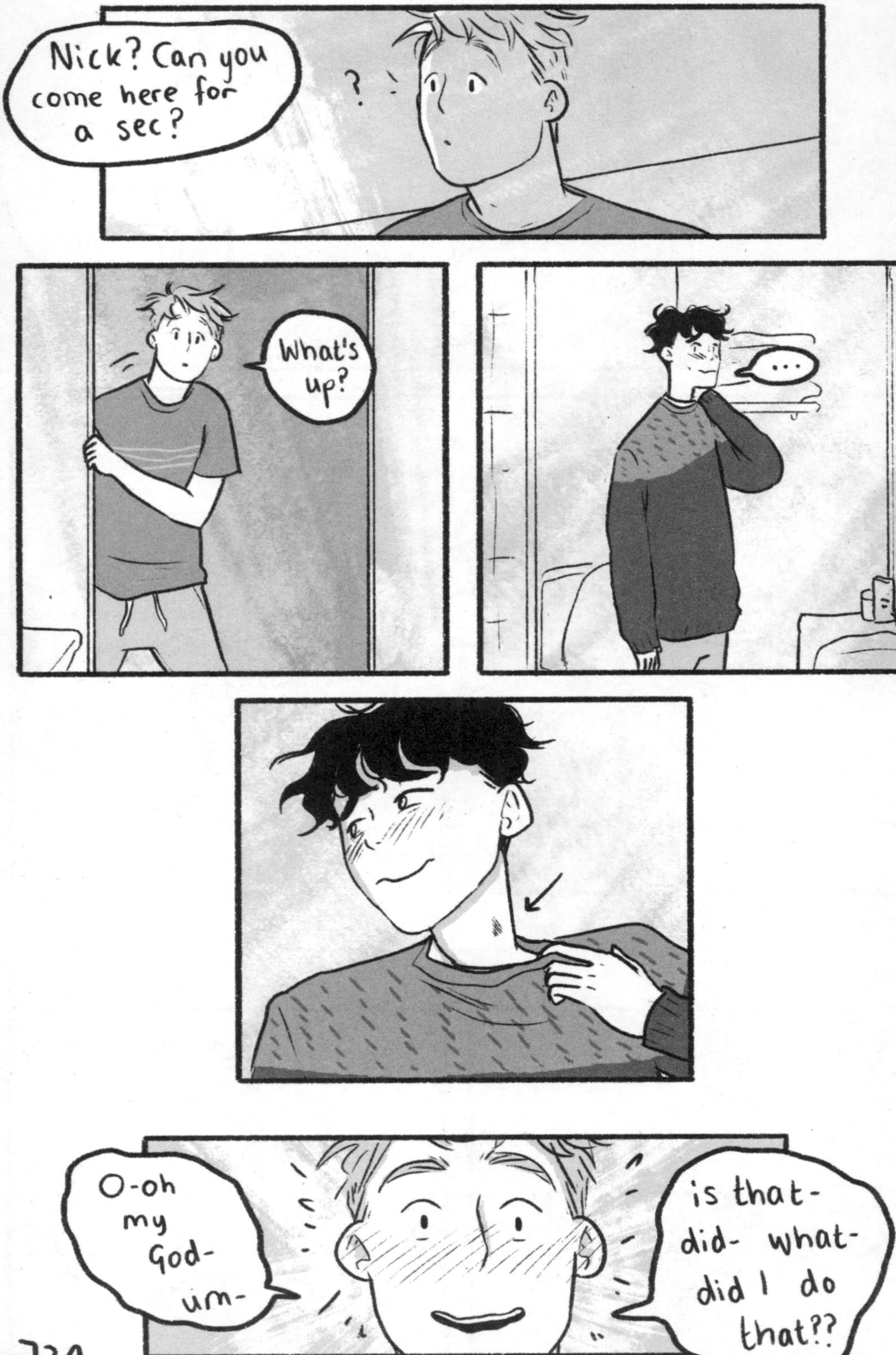
Nick? Can you come here for a sec?
?
What's up?
...
O-oh my God- um-
is that- did- what- did I do that??

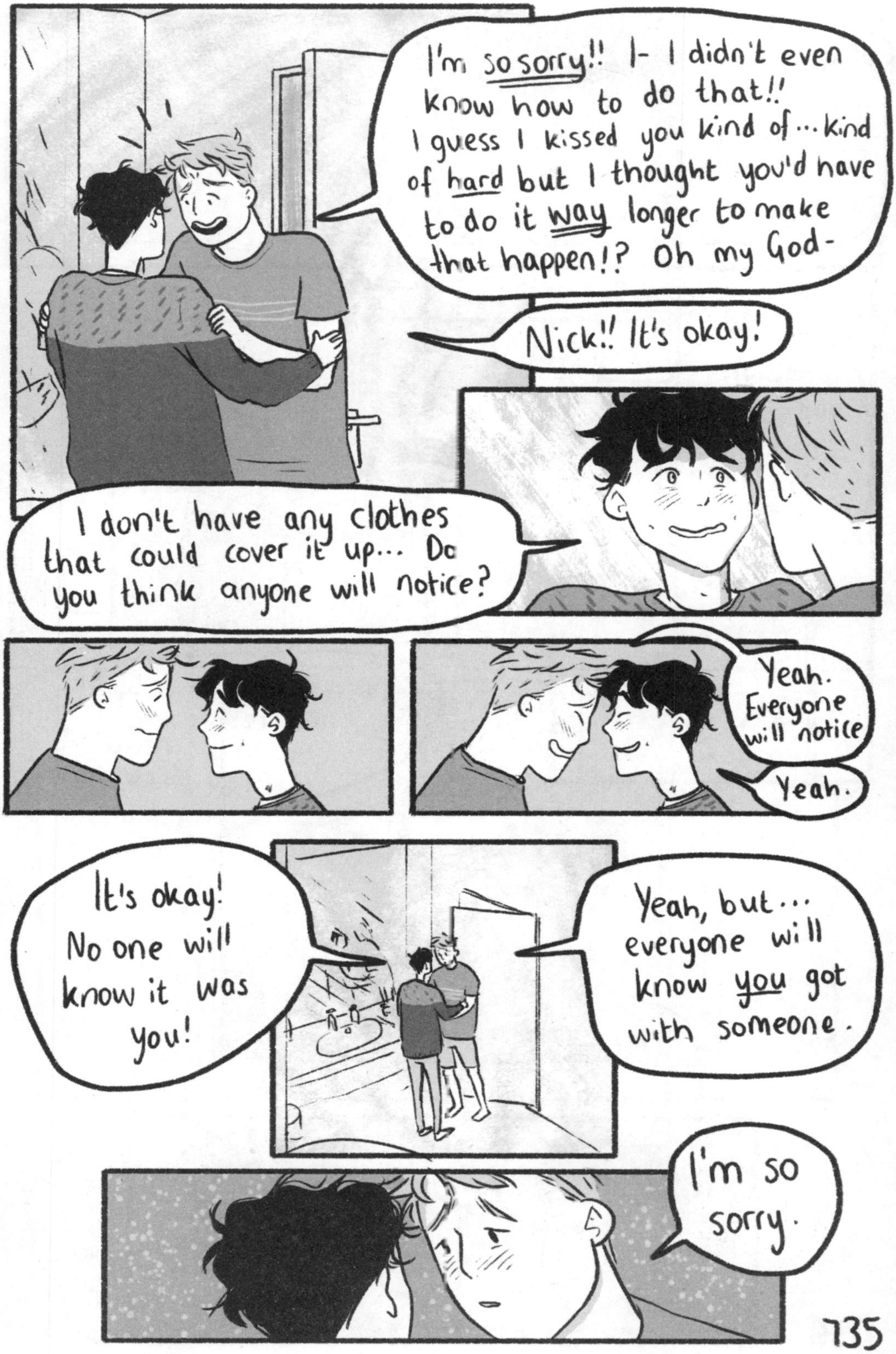
I'm so sorry!! I- I didn't even know how to do that!! I guess I kissed you kind of... kind of hard but I thought you'd have to do it way longer to make that happen!? Oh my God-
Nick!! It's okay!
I don't have any clothes that could cover it up... Do you think anyone will notice?
Yeah. Everyone will notice
Yeah.
It's okay! No one will know it was you!
Yeah, but... everyone will know you got with someone.
I'm so sorry.

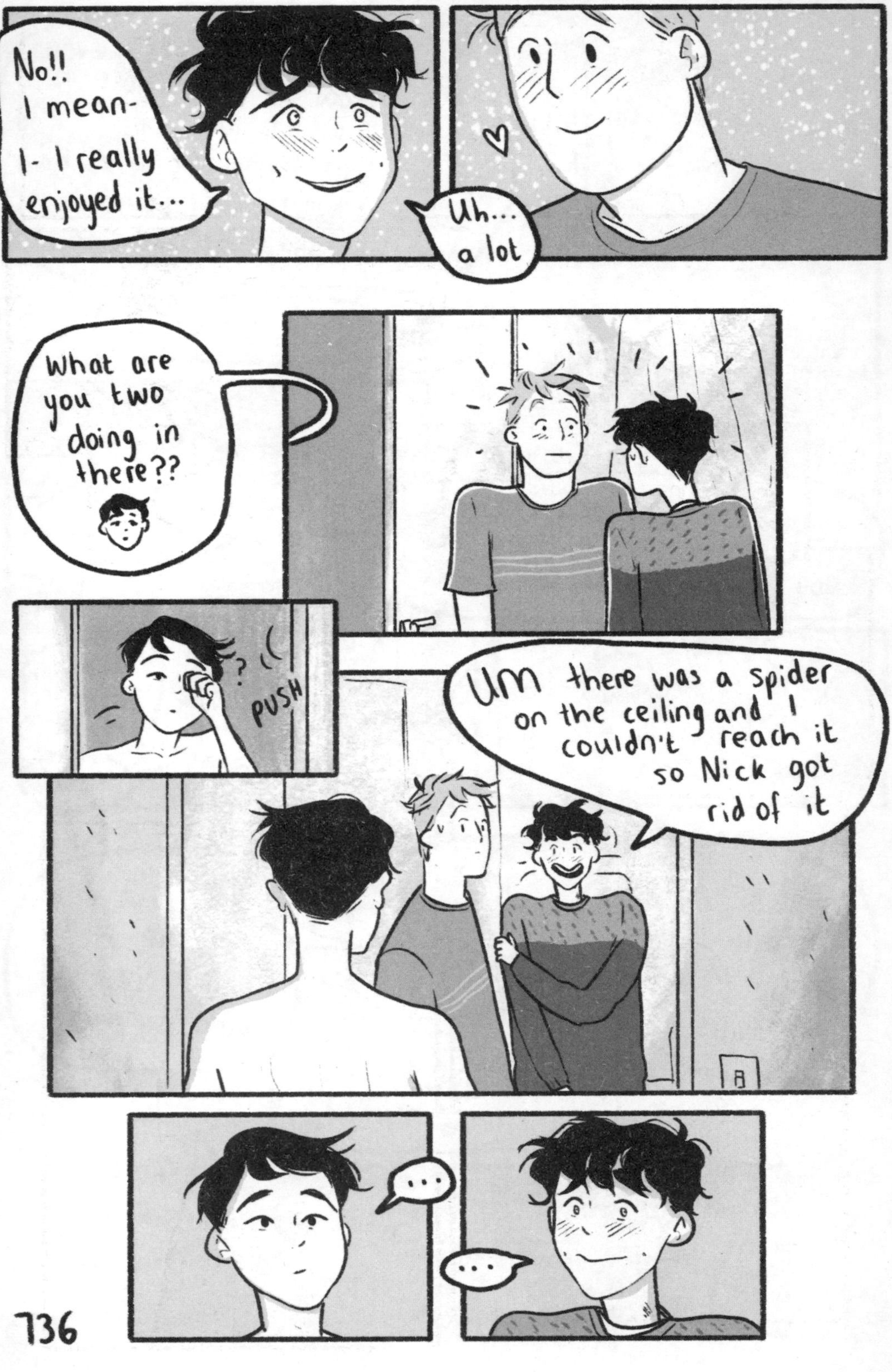
No!! I mean- I- I really enjoyed it...
Uh... a lot
What are you two doing in there??
PUSH
Um there was a spider on the ceiling and I couldn't reach it so Nick got rid of it
...
...

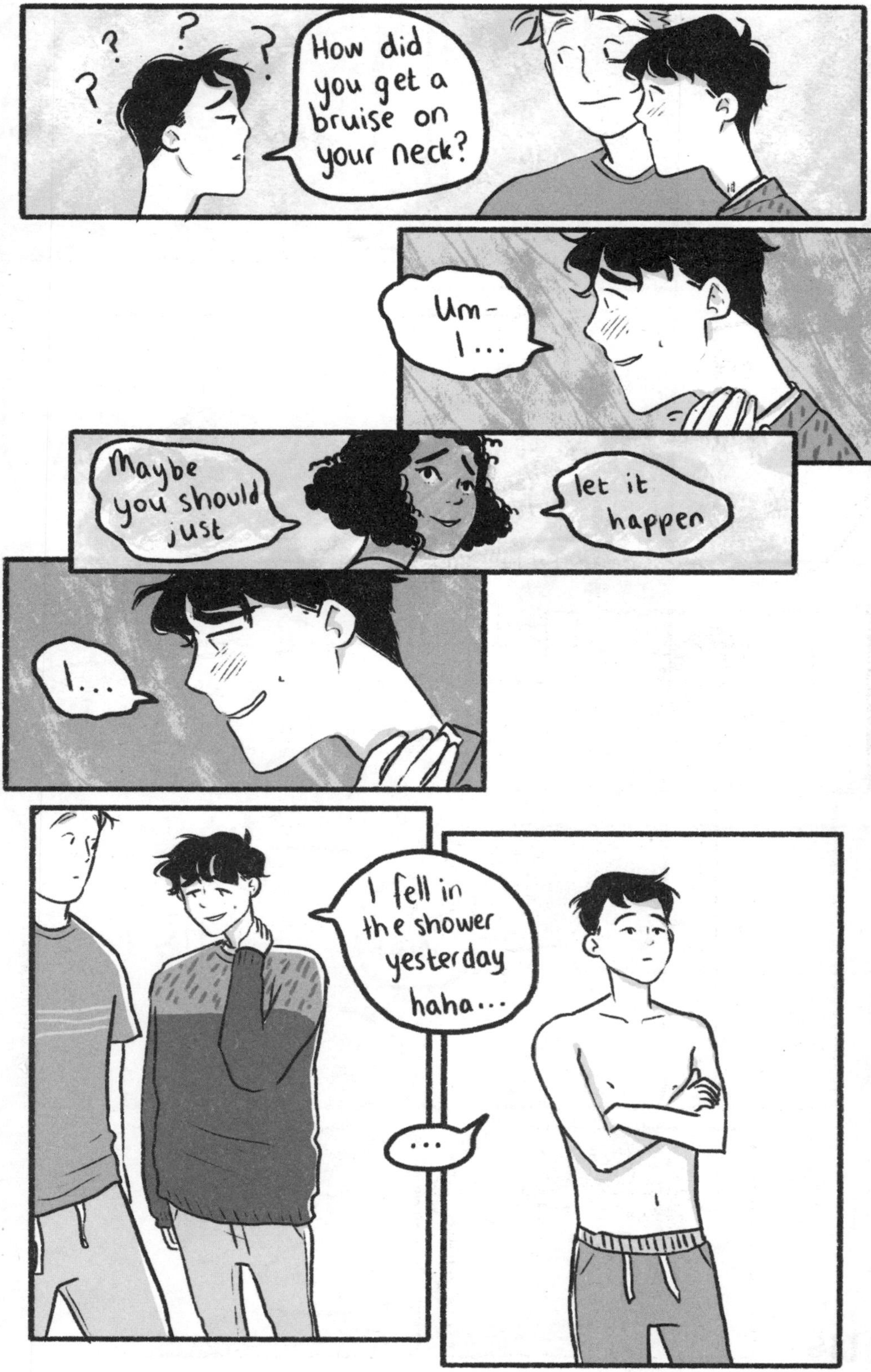
? ? ? ?
How did you get a bruise on your neck?
Um- I...
Maybe you should just
let it happen
I...
I fell in the shower yesterday haha...
...

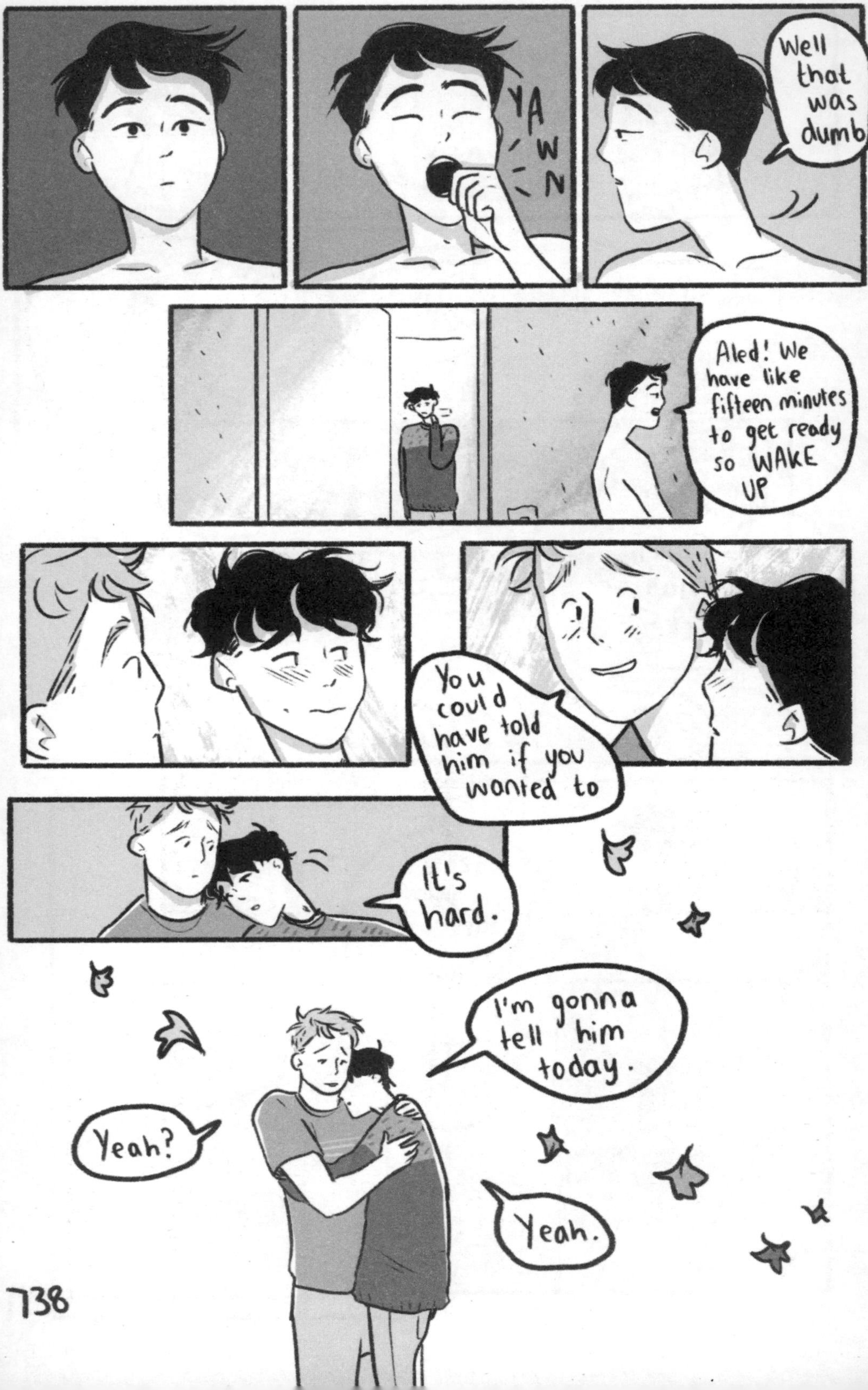
YAWN
Well that was dumb
Aled! We have like fifteen minutes to get ready so WAKE UP
You could have told him if you wanted to
It's hard.
I'm gonna tell him today.
Yeah?
Yeah.

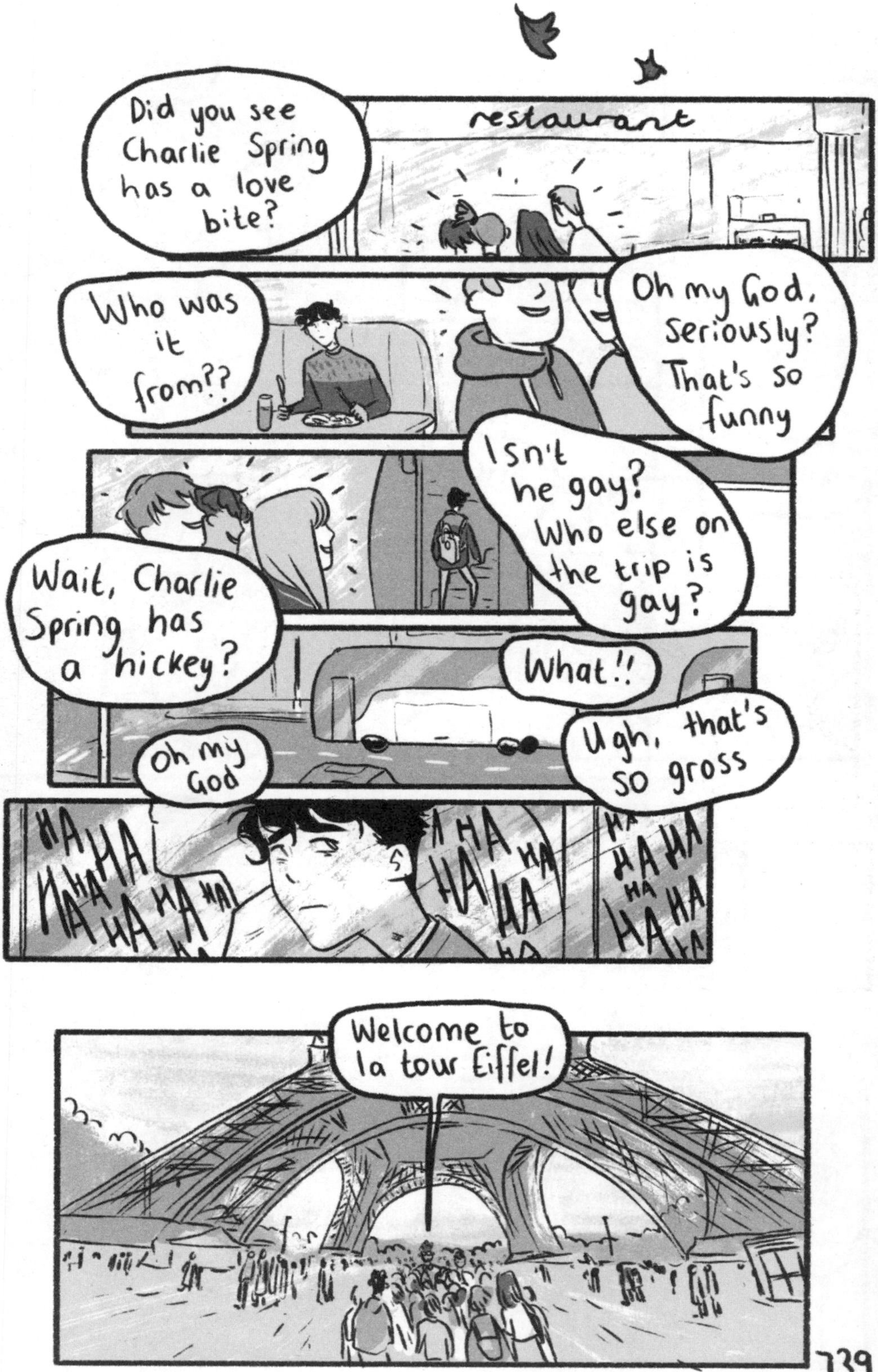
restaurant
Did you see Charlie Spring has a love bite?
Who was it from??
Oh my God, seriously? That's so funny
Isn't he gay? Who else on the trip is gay?
Wait, Charlie Spring has a hickey?
What!!
Ugh, that's so gross
Oh my God
HA HA HA HA HA HA HA HA HA HA HA HA HA HA HA HA HA HA HA HA HA HA
Welcome to la tour Eiffel!

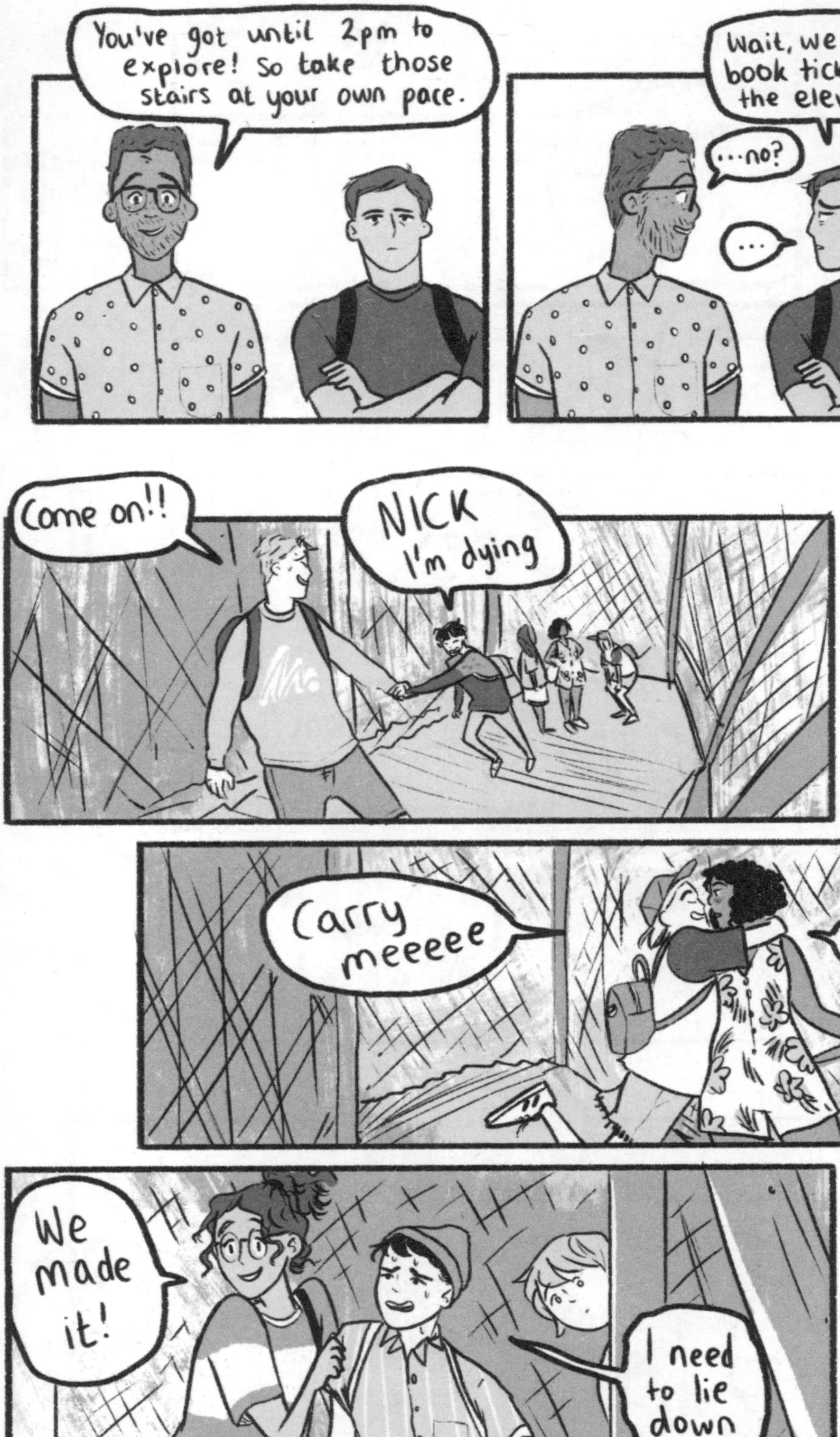
You've got until 2pm to explore! So take those stairs at your own pace.
Wait, we didn't book tickets for the elevator?
...no?
...
Come on!!
NICK I'm dying
Carry meeeee
No
We made it!
I need to lie down

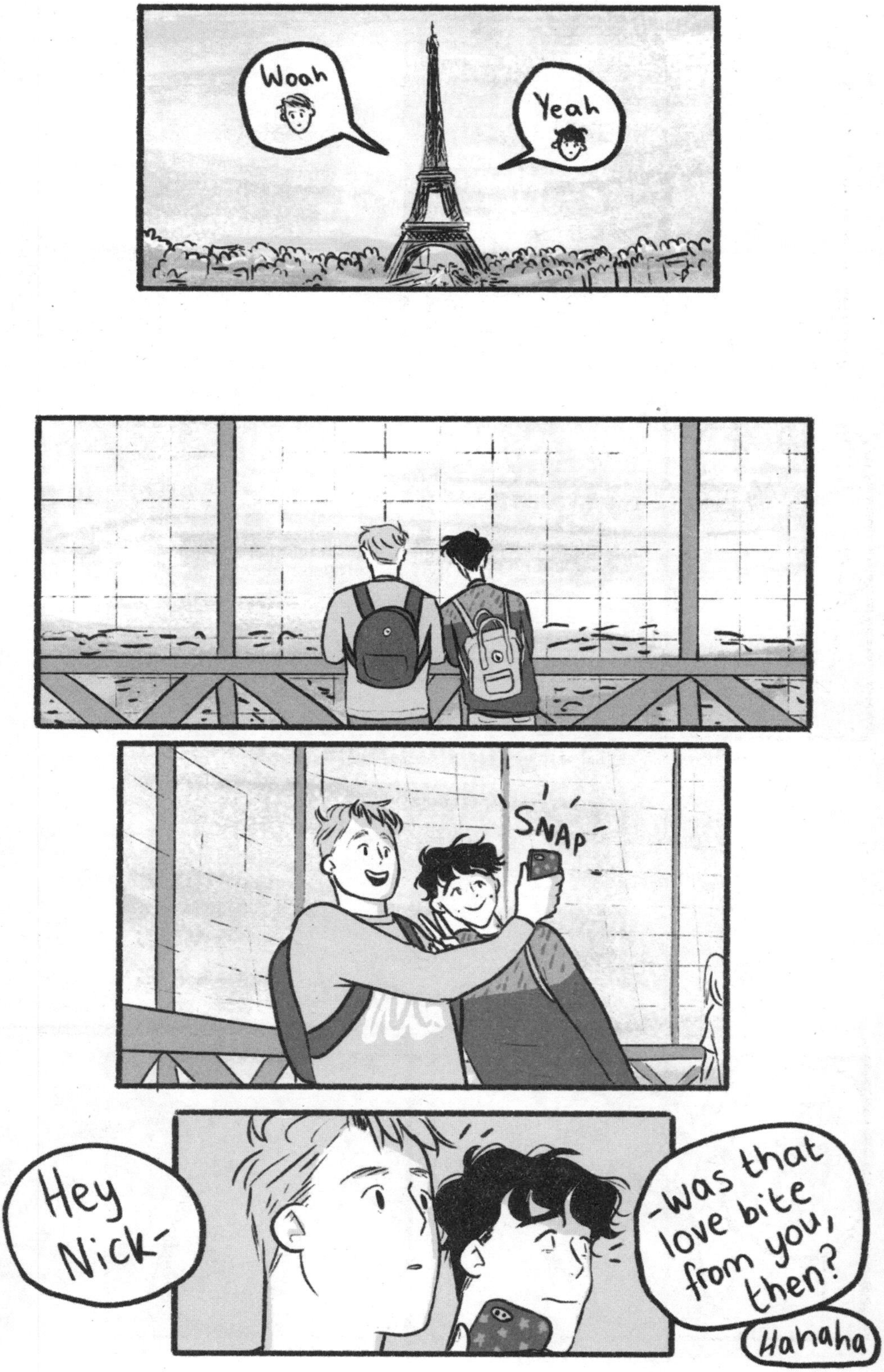
Woah
Yeah
SNAP
Hey Nick-
-was that love bite from you, then?
Hahaha

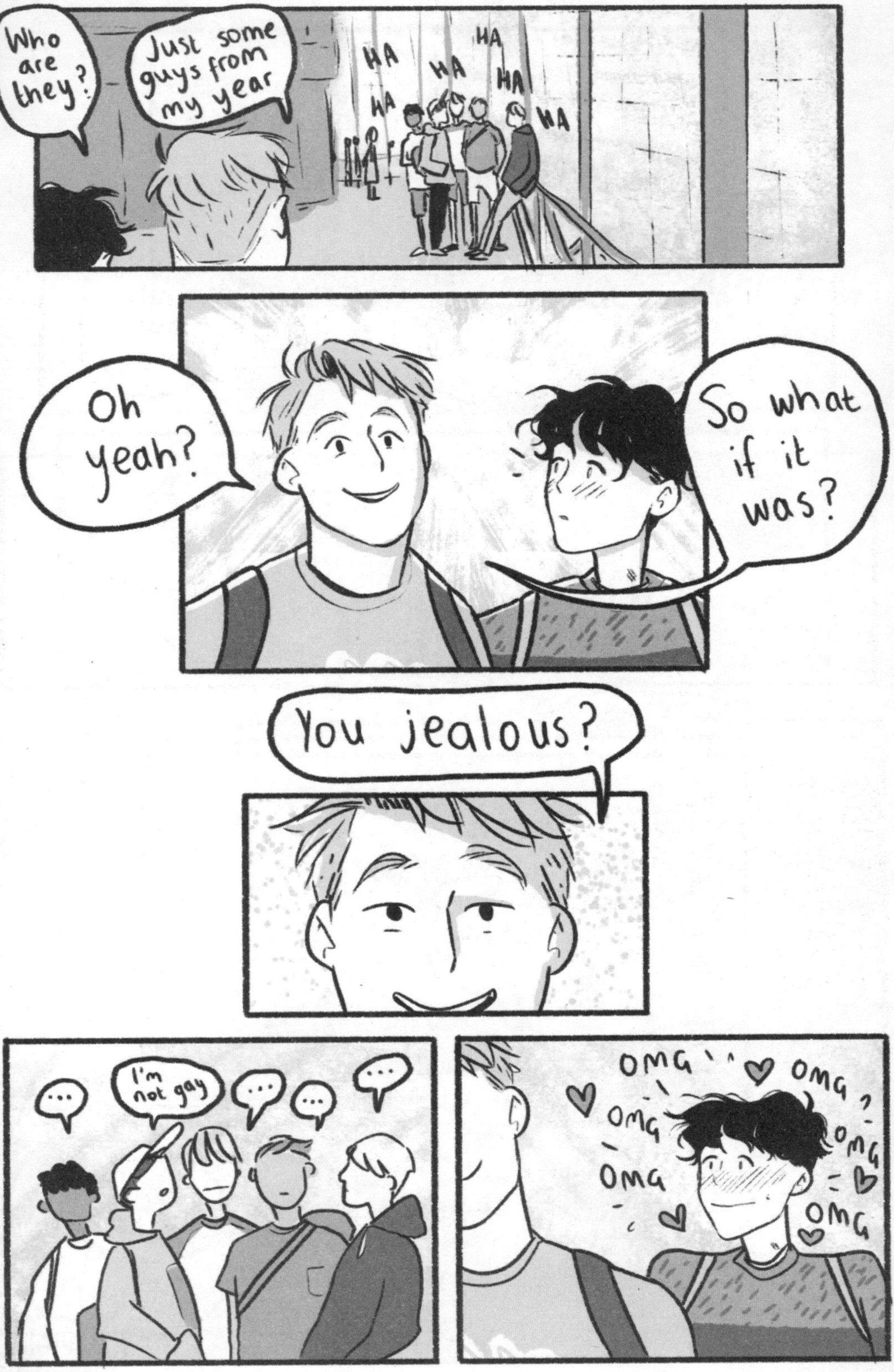
Who are they?
Just some guys from my year
HA
HA
HA
HA
HA
HA
Oh yeah?
So what if it was?
You jealous?
...
I'm not gay
...
...
...
OMG
OMG
OMG
OMG
OMG
OMG

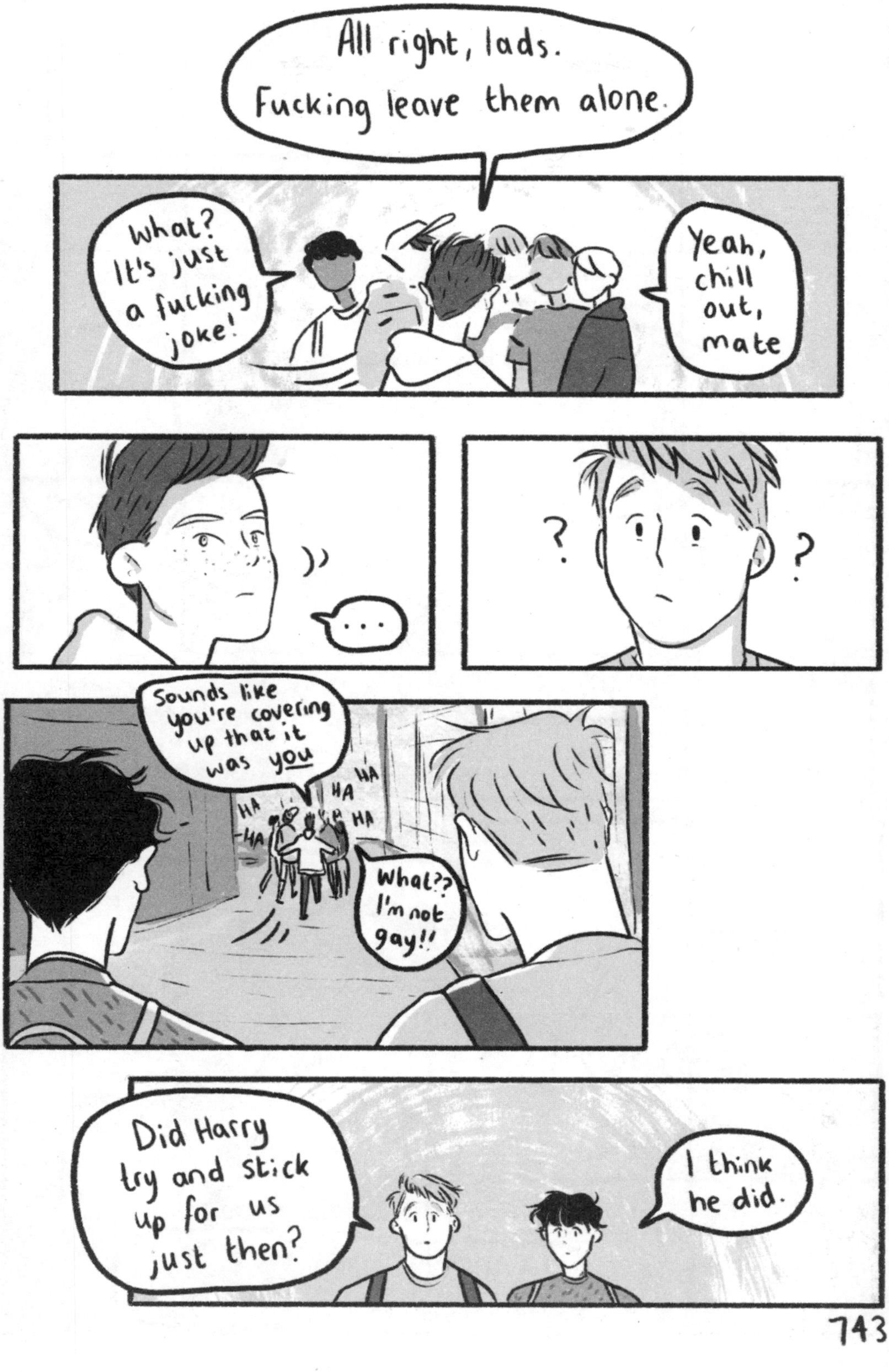
All right, lads. Fucking leave them alone.
What? It's just a fucking joke!
Yeah, chill out, mate
...
? ?
Sounds like you're covering up that it was YOU
HA HA HA HA HA HA
What?? I'm not gay!!
Did Harry try and stick up for us just then?
I think he did.

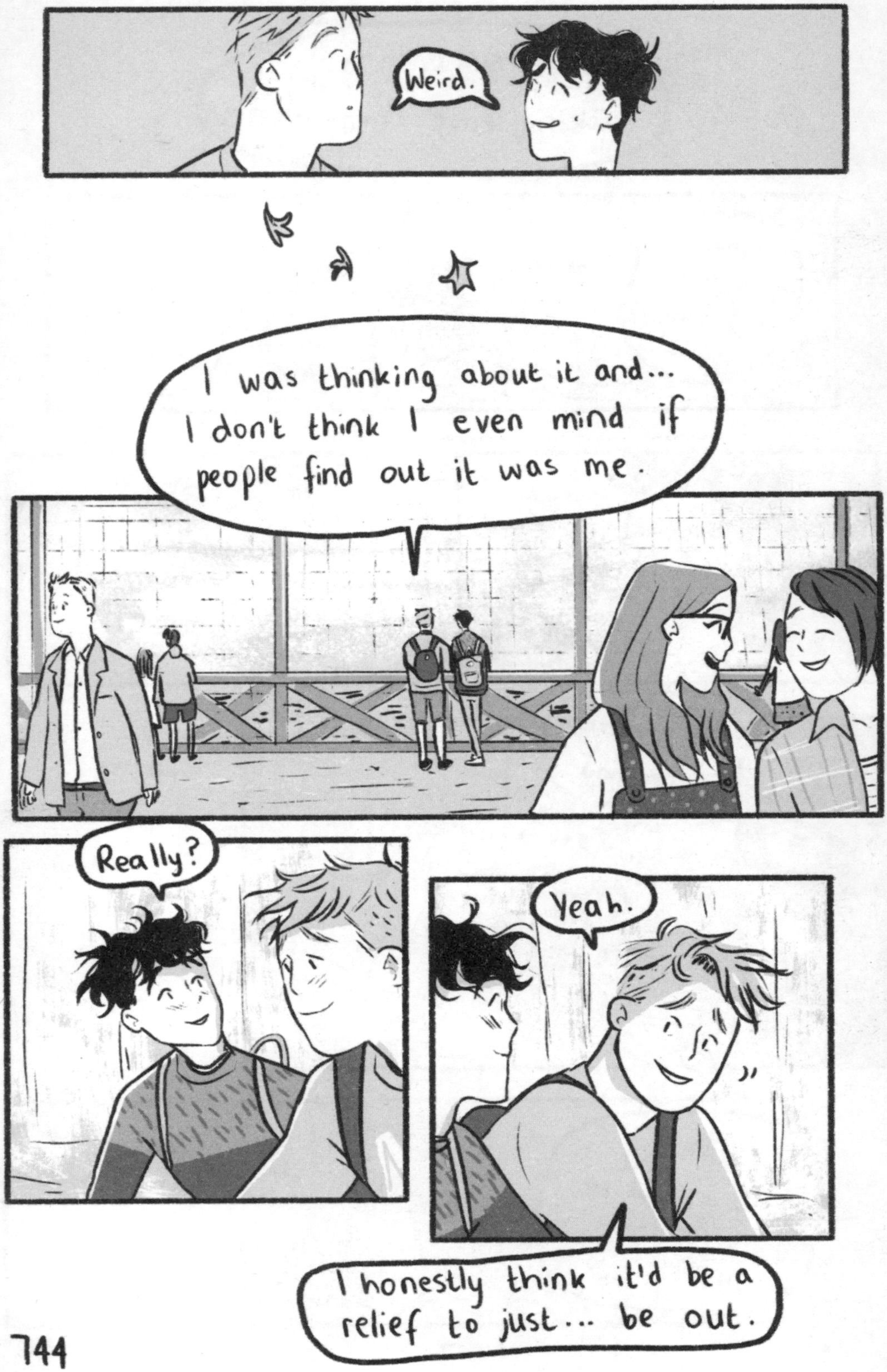
Weird.
I was thinking about it and... I don't think I even mind if people find out it was me.
Really?
Yeah.
I honestly think it'd be a relief to just... be out.

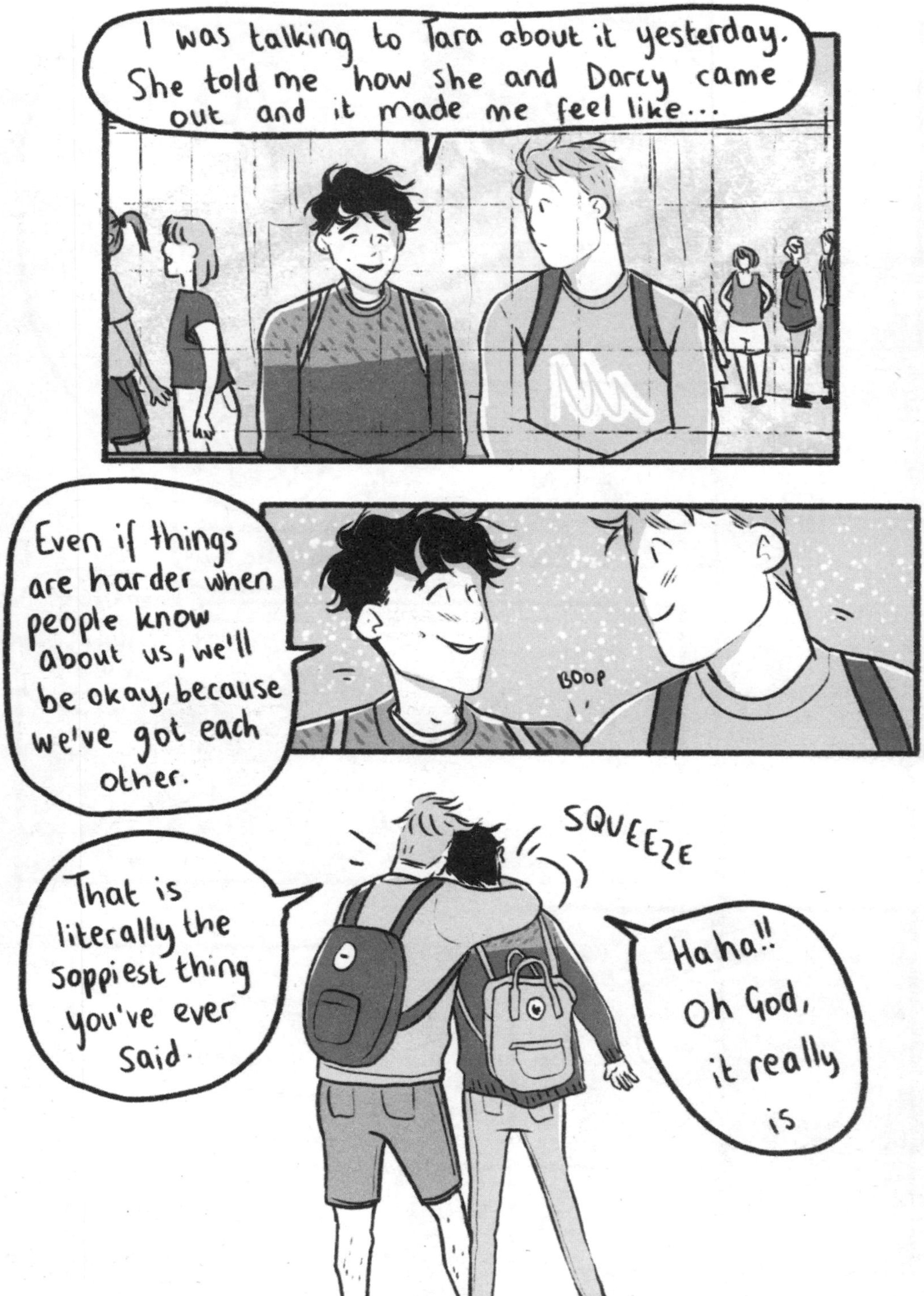
I was talking to Tara about it yesterday. She told me how she and Darcy came out and it made me feel like...
Even if things are harder when people know about us, we'll be okay, because we've got each other.
BOOP
SQUEEZE
That is literally the soppiest thing you've ever said.
Haha!! Oh God, it really is

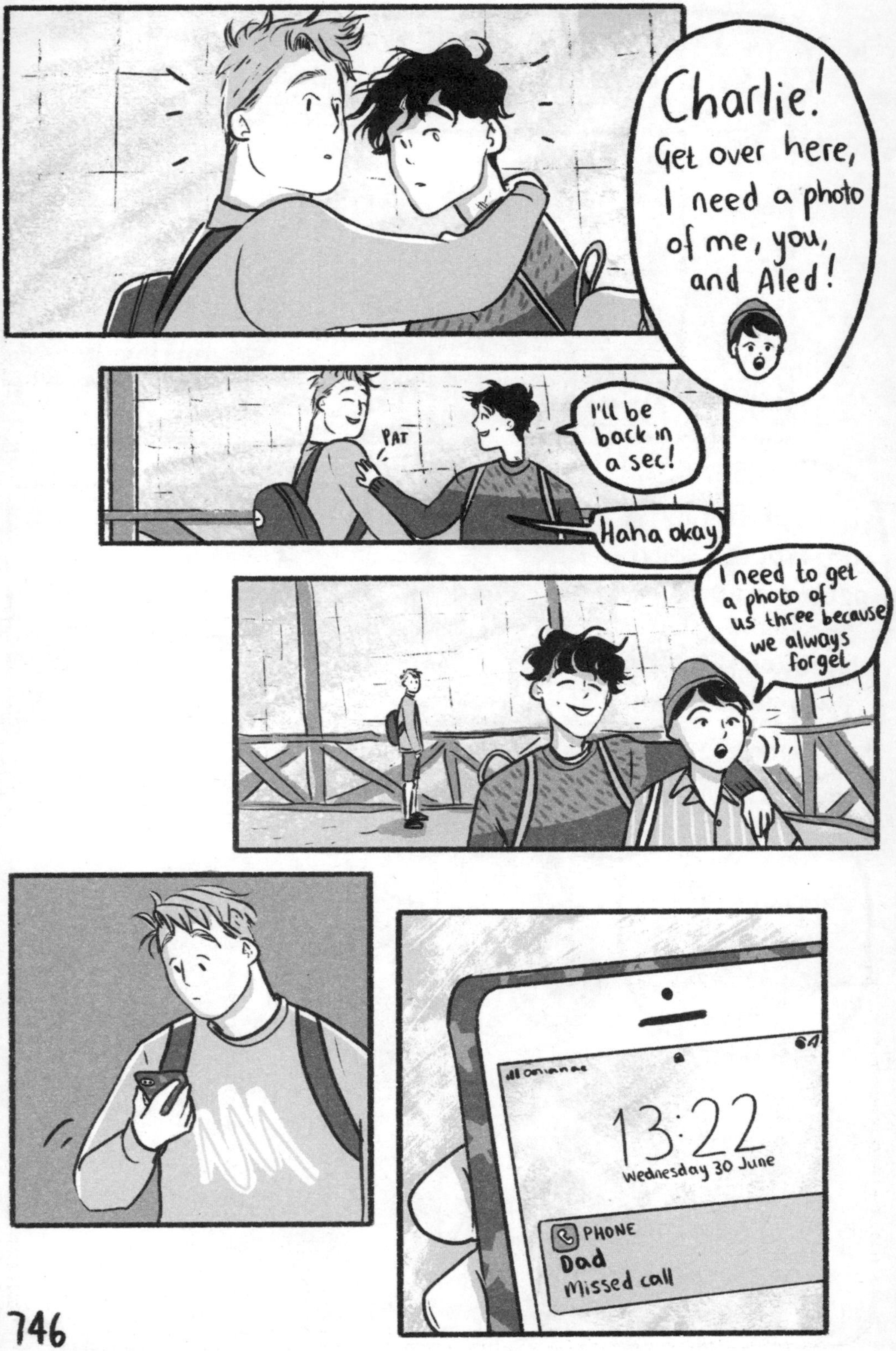

Charlie! Get over here, I need a photo of me, you, and Aled!
PAT
I'll be back in a sec!
Haha okay
I need to get a photo of us three because we always forget
13:22
Wednesday 30 June
PHONE
Dad
Missed call

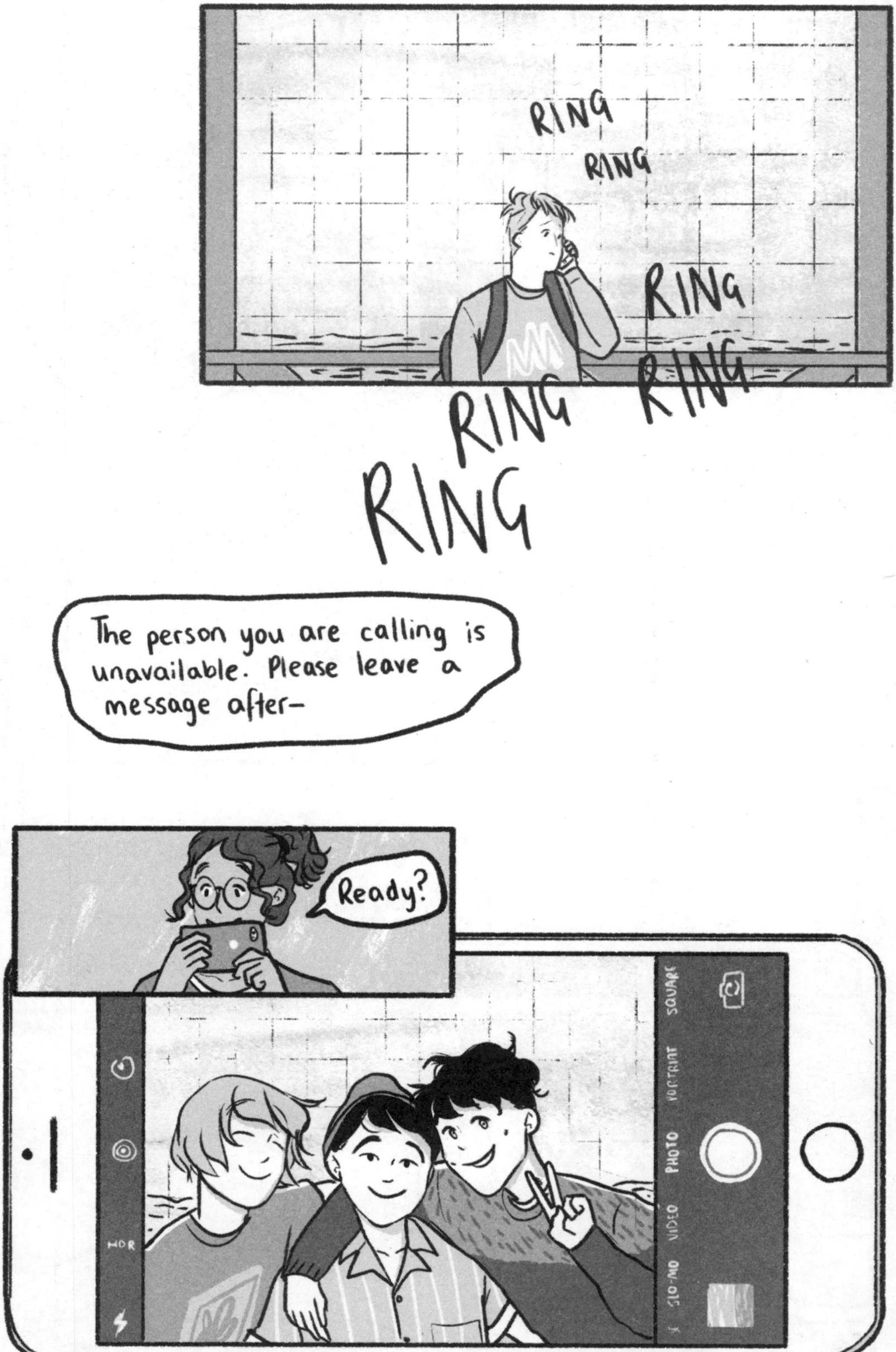
RING
RING
RING
RING
RING
RING
The person you are calling is unavailable. Please leave a message after–
Ready?
SQUARE
PORTRAIT
PHOTO
VIDEO
SLO-MO
HDR

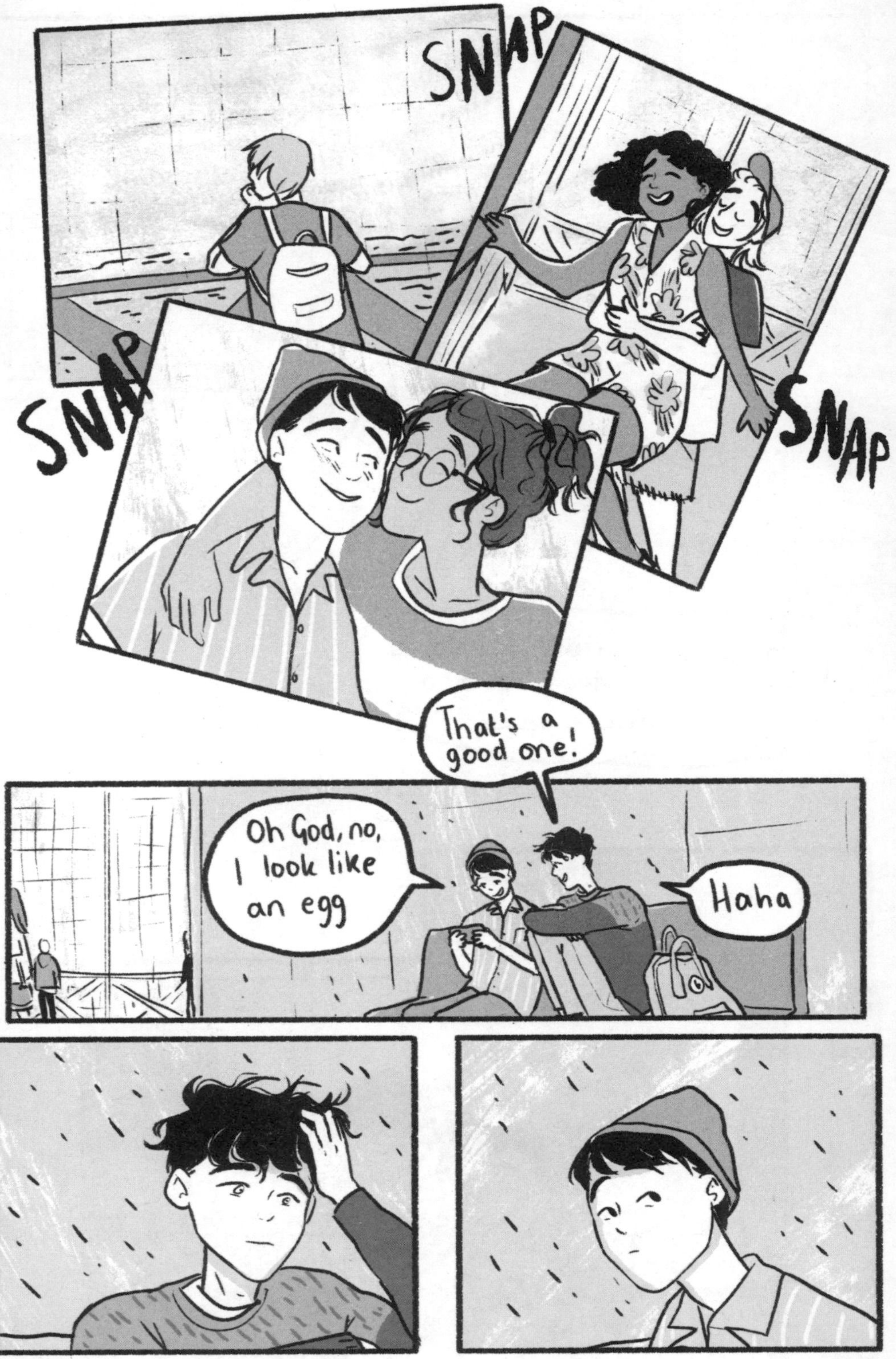
SNAP
SNAP
SNAP
That's a good one!
Oh God, no, I look like an egg
Haha

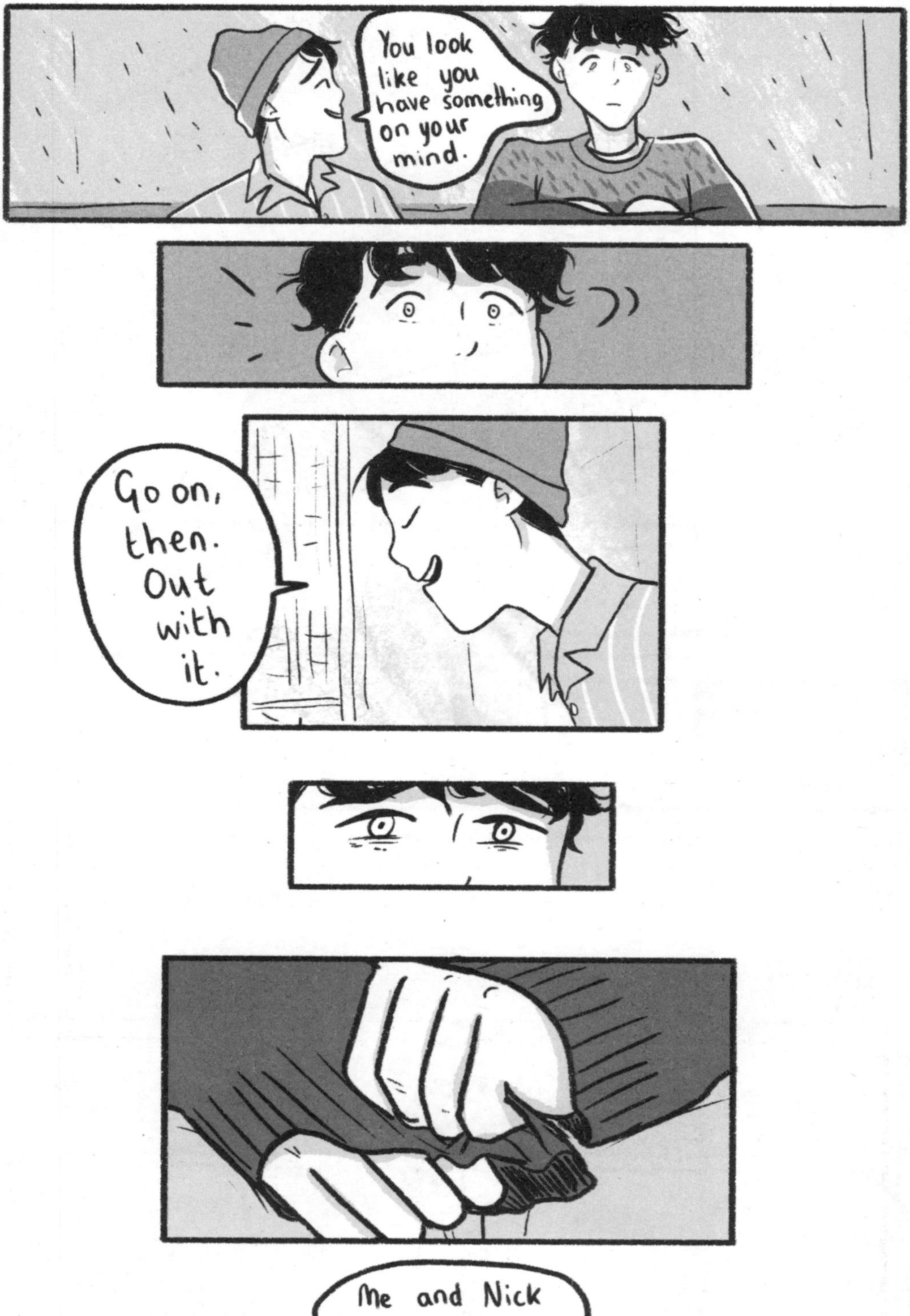
You look like you have something on your mind.
Go on, then. Out with it.
Me and Nick are dating.

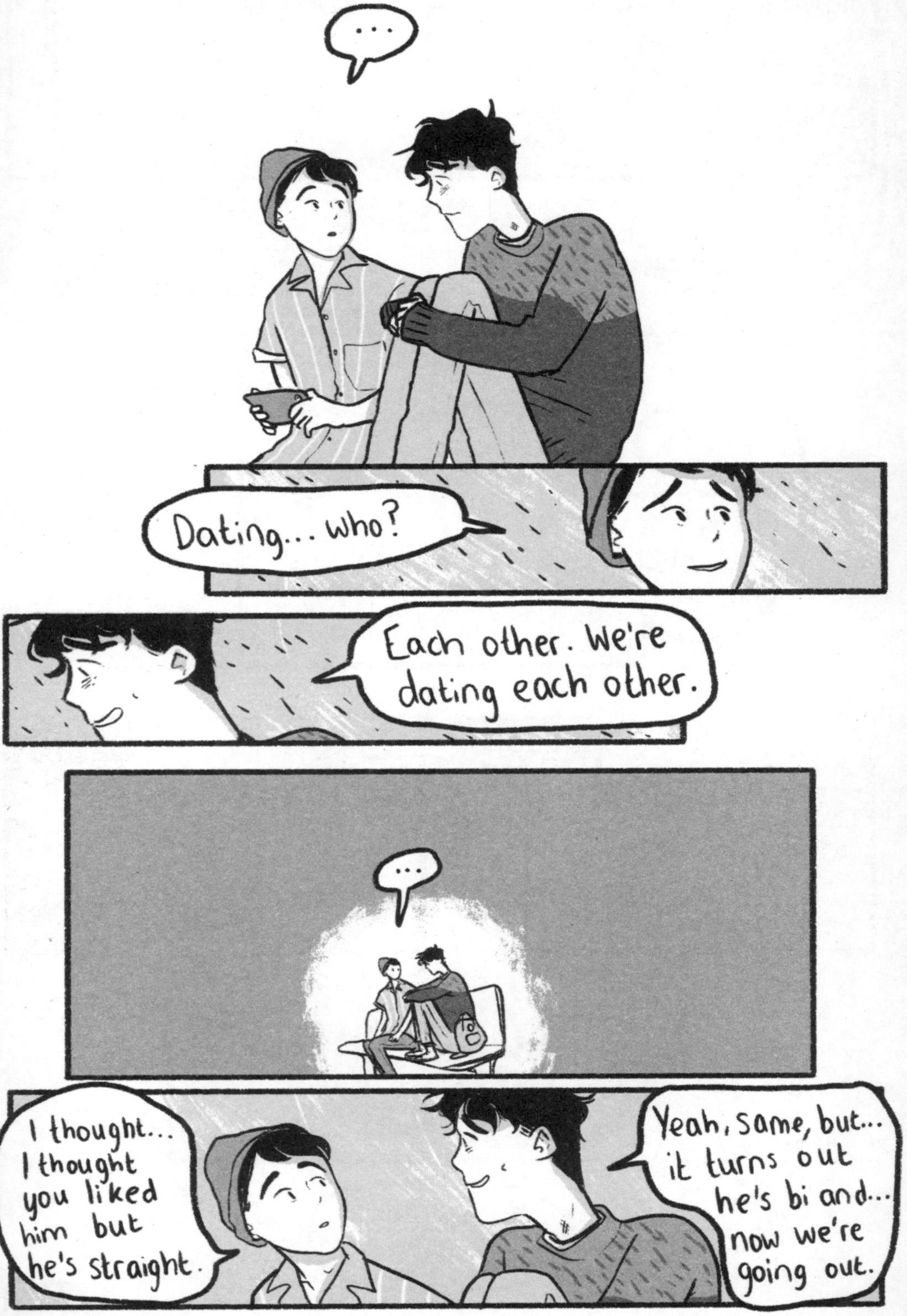
...
Dating... who?
Each other. We're dating each other.
...
I thought... I thought you liked him but he's straight.
Yeah, same, but... it turns out he's bi and... now we're going out.

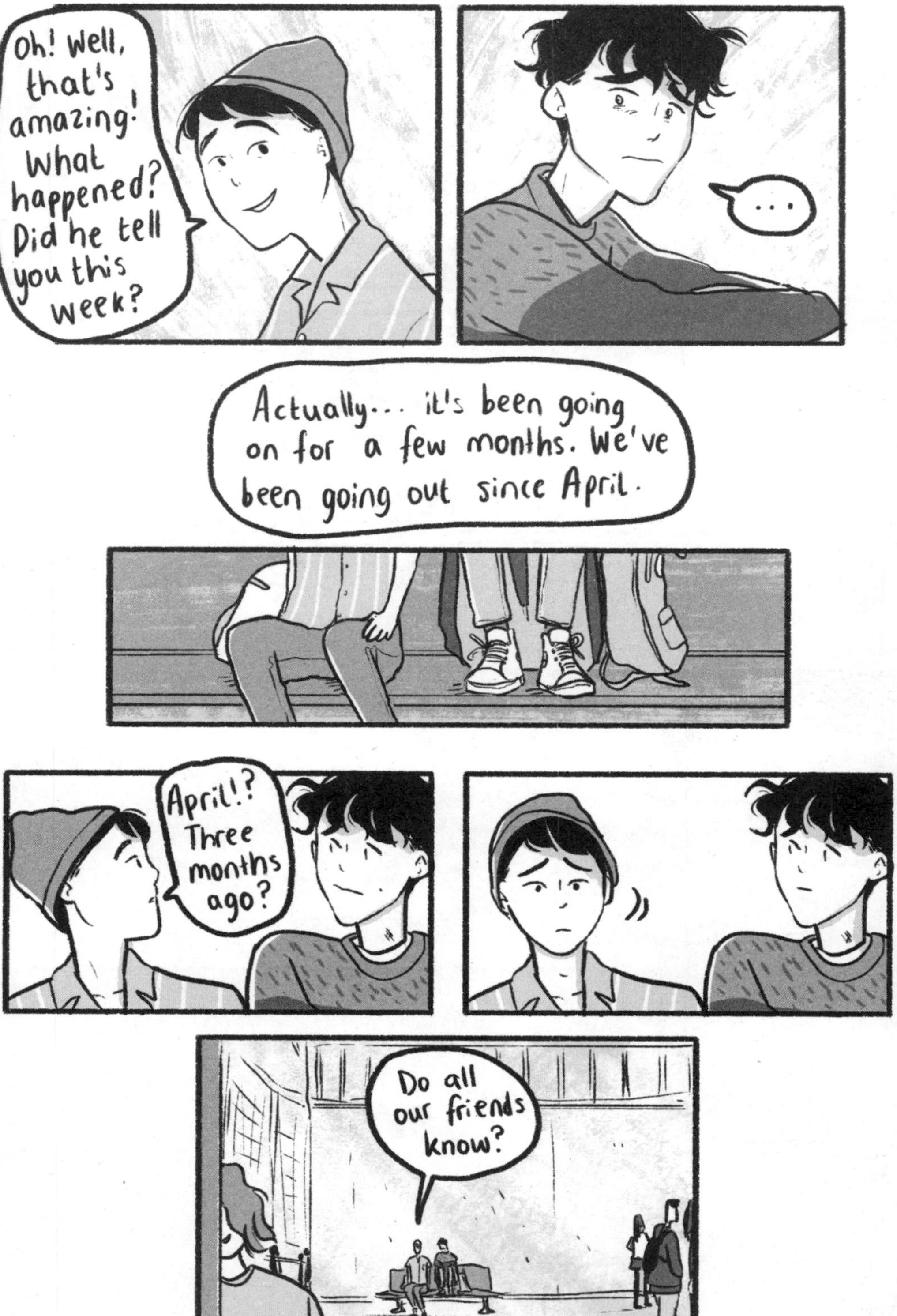
Oh! Well, that's amazing! What happened? Did he tell you this week?
...
Actually... it's been going on for a few months. We've been going out since April.
April!? Three months ago?
Do all our friends know?

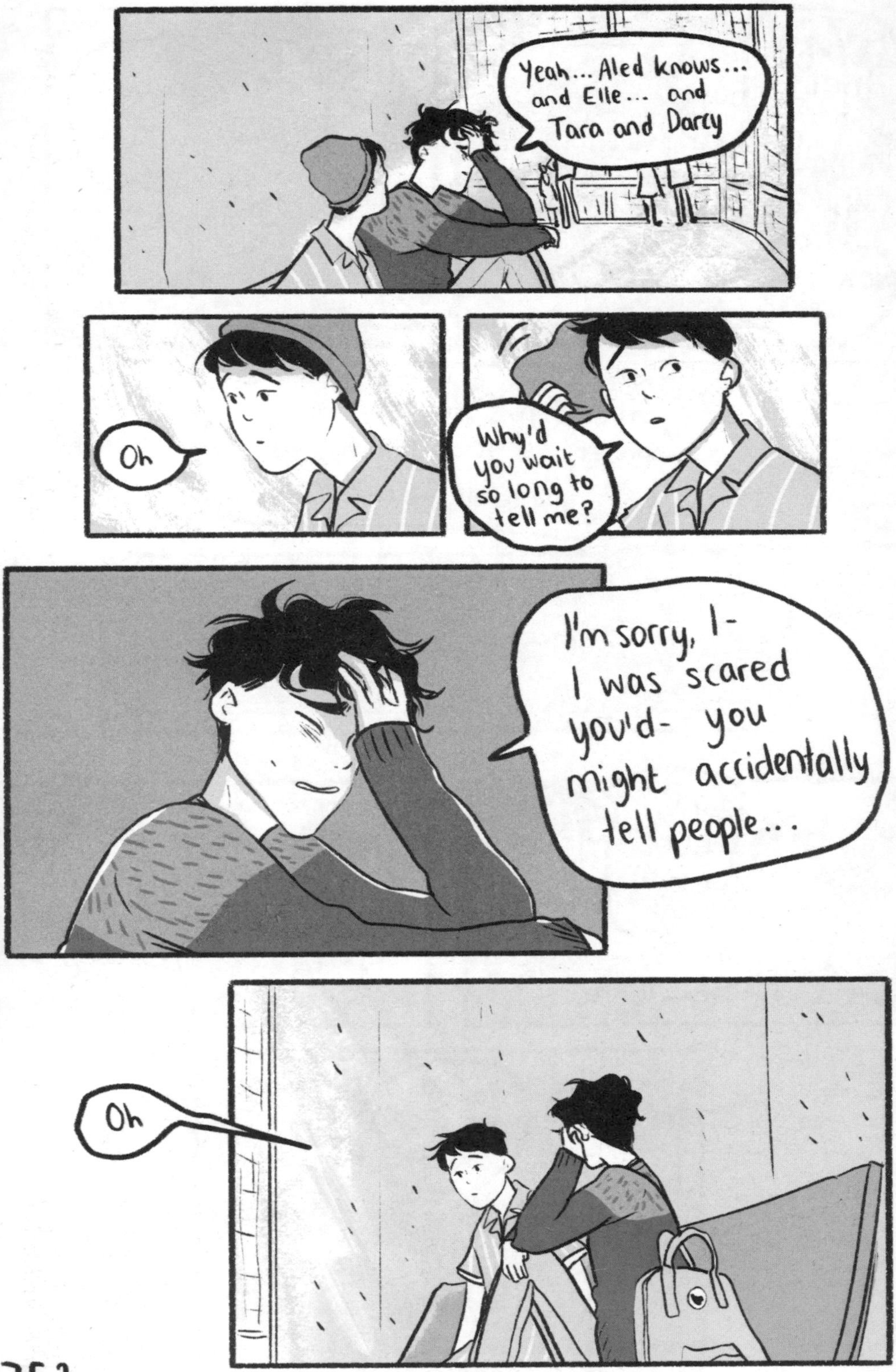
Yeah... Aled knows... and Elle... and Tara and Darcy
Oh
Why'd you wait so long to tell me?
I'm sorry, I- I was scared you'd- you might accidentally tell people...
Oh

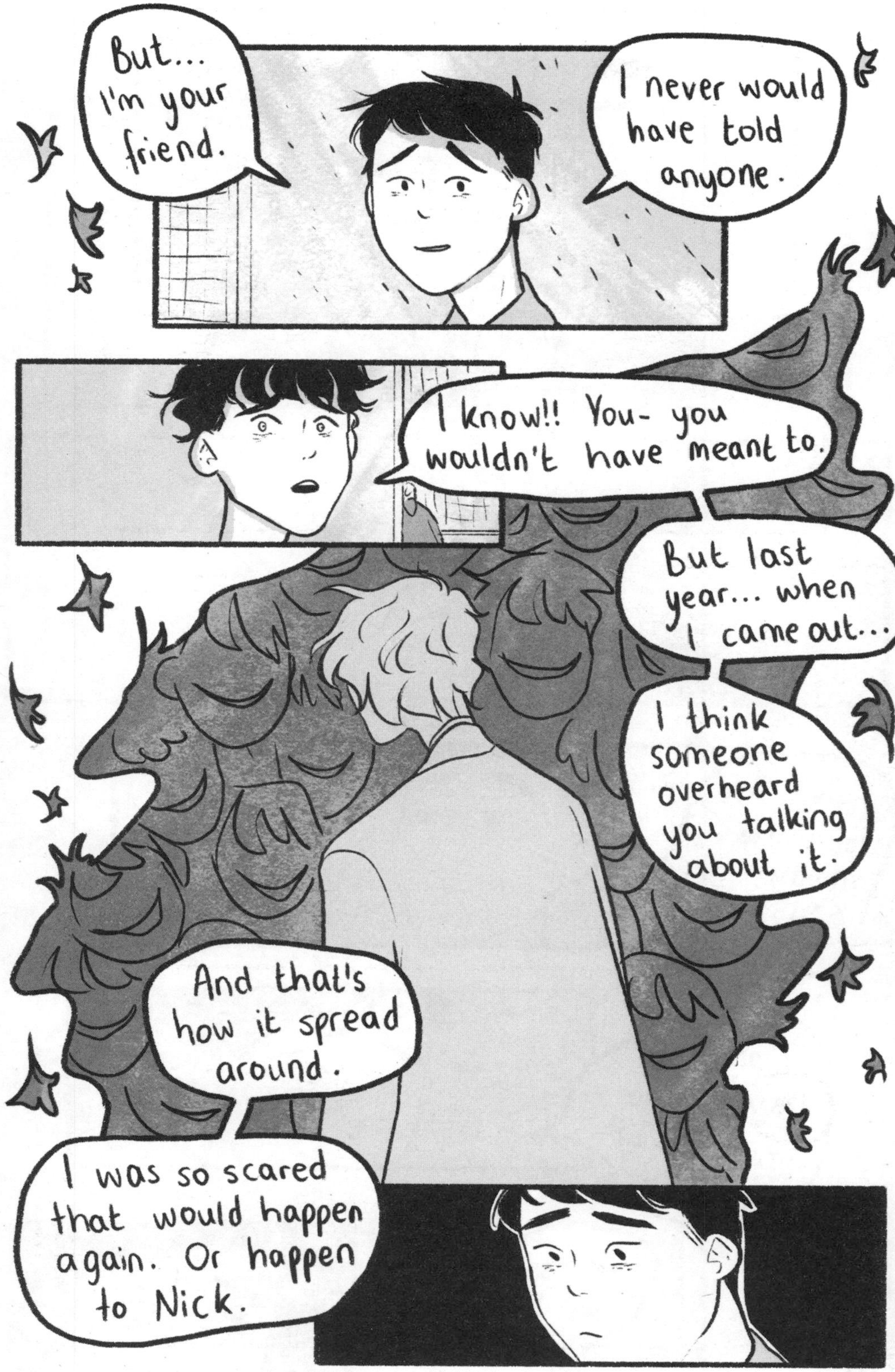
But... I'm your friend.
I never would have told anyone.
I know!! You- you wouldn't have meant to.
But last year... when I came out...
I think someone overheard you talking about it.
And that's how it spread around.
I was so scared that would happen again. Or happen to Nick.

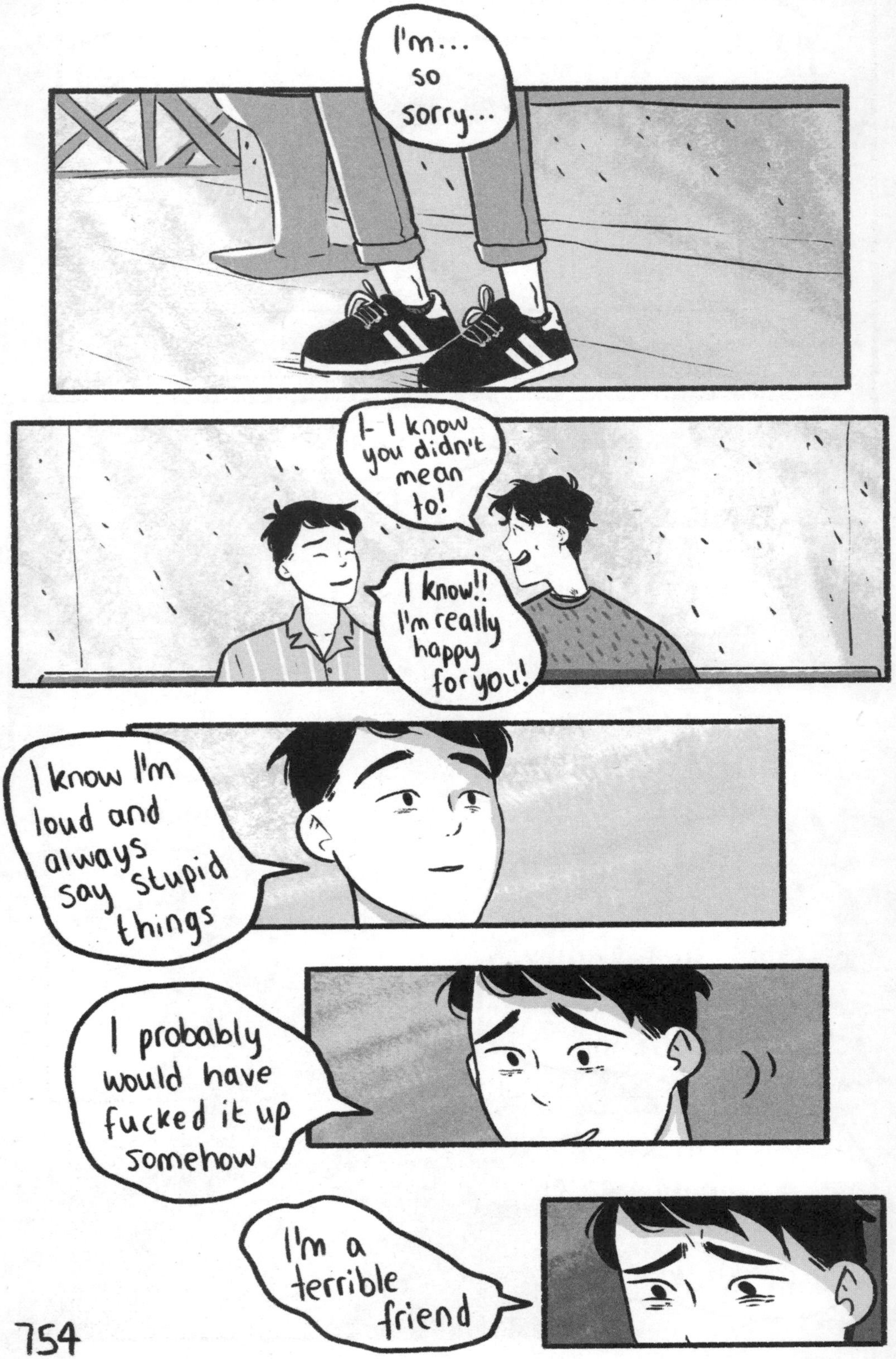
I'm... so sorry...
I- I know you didn't mean to!
I know!! I'm really happy for you!
I know I'm loud and always say stupid things
I probably would have fucked it up somehow
I'm a terrible friend

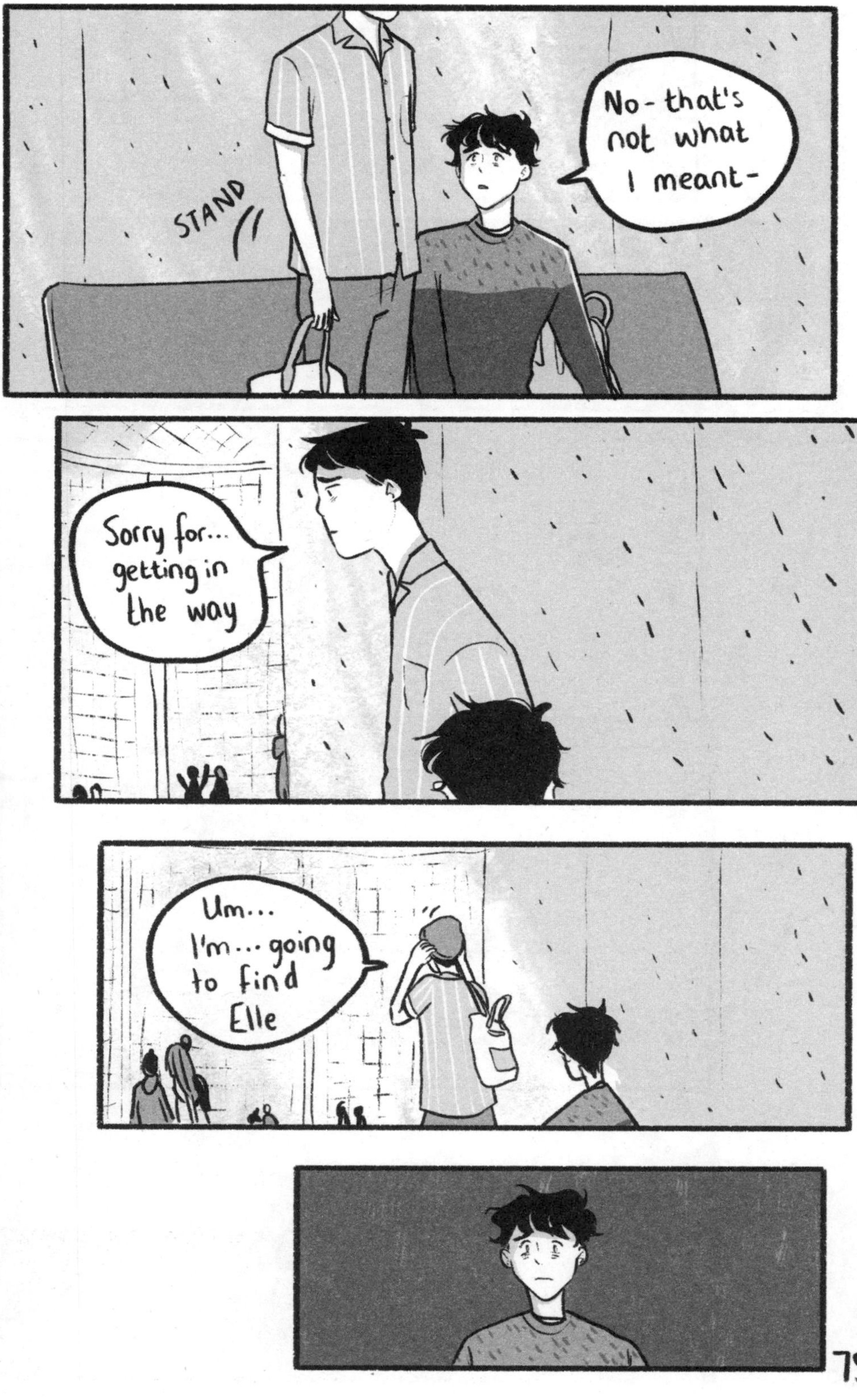
No- that's not what I meant-
STAND
Sorry for... getting in the way
Um... I'm... going to find Elle

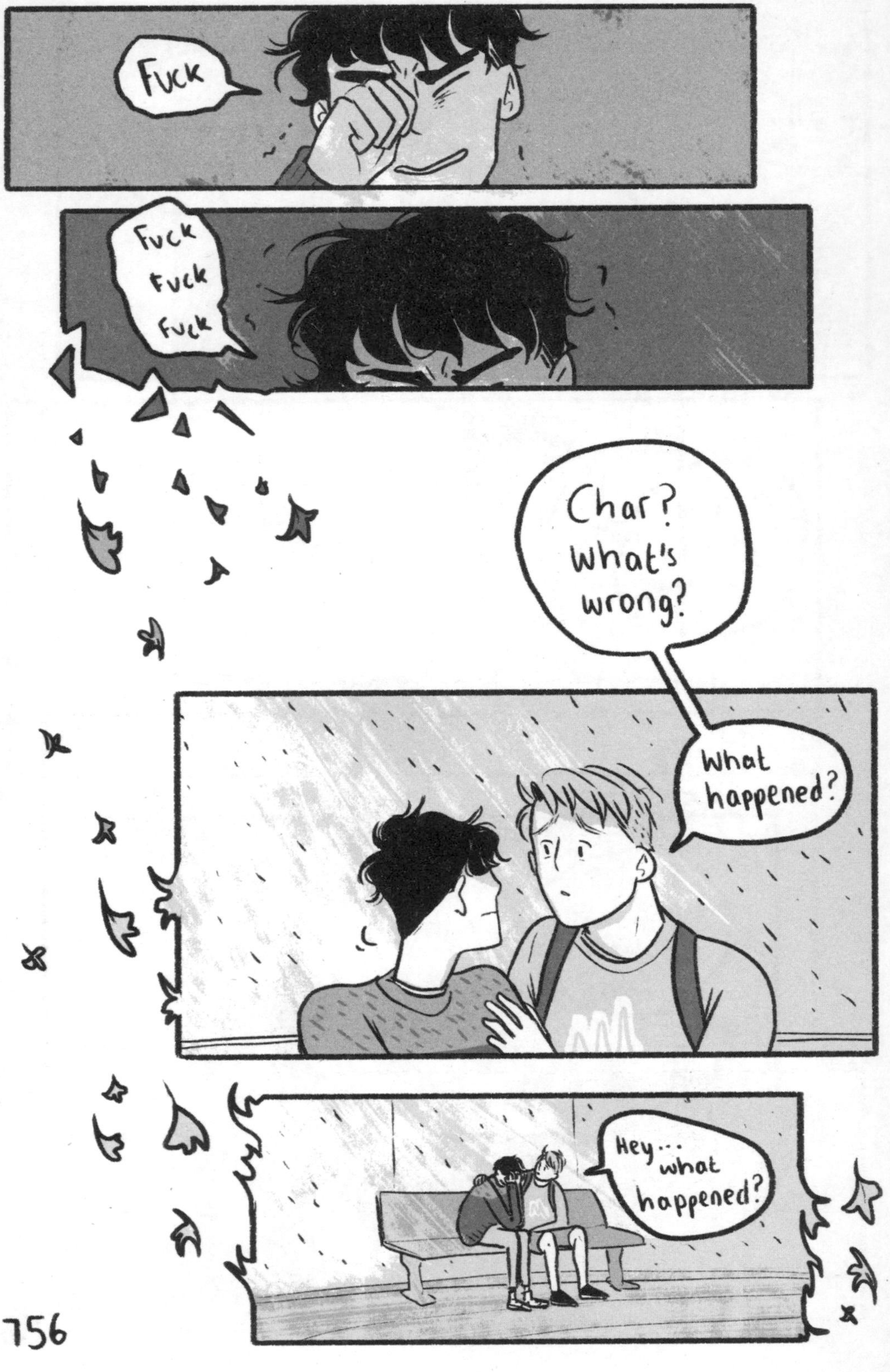
FUCK
FUCK FUCK FUCK
Char? What's wrong?
What happened?
Hey... what happened?

Paris - Day 4

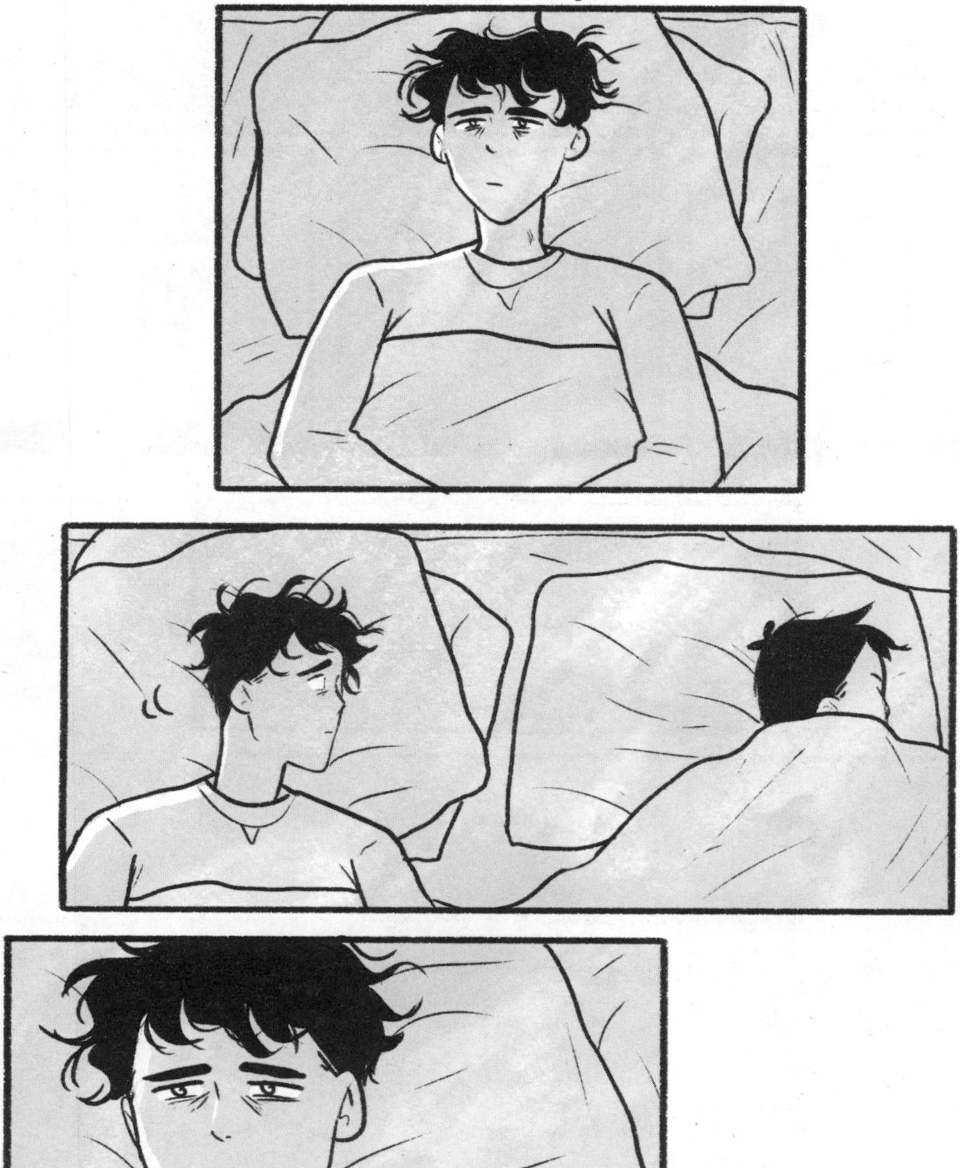

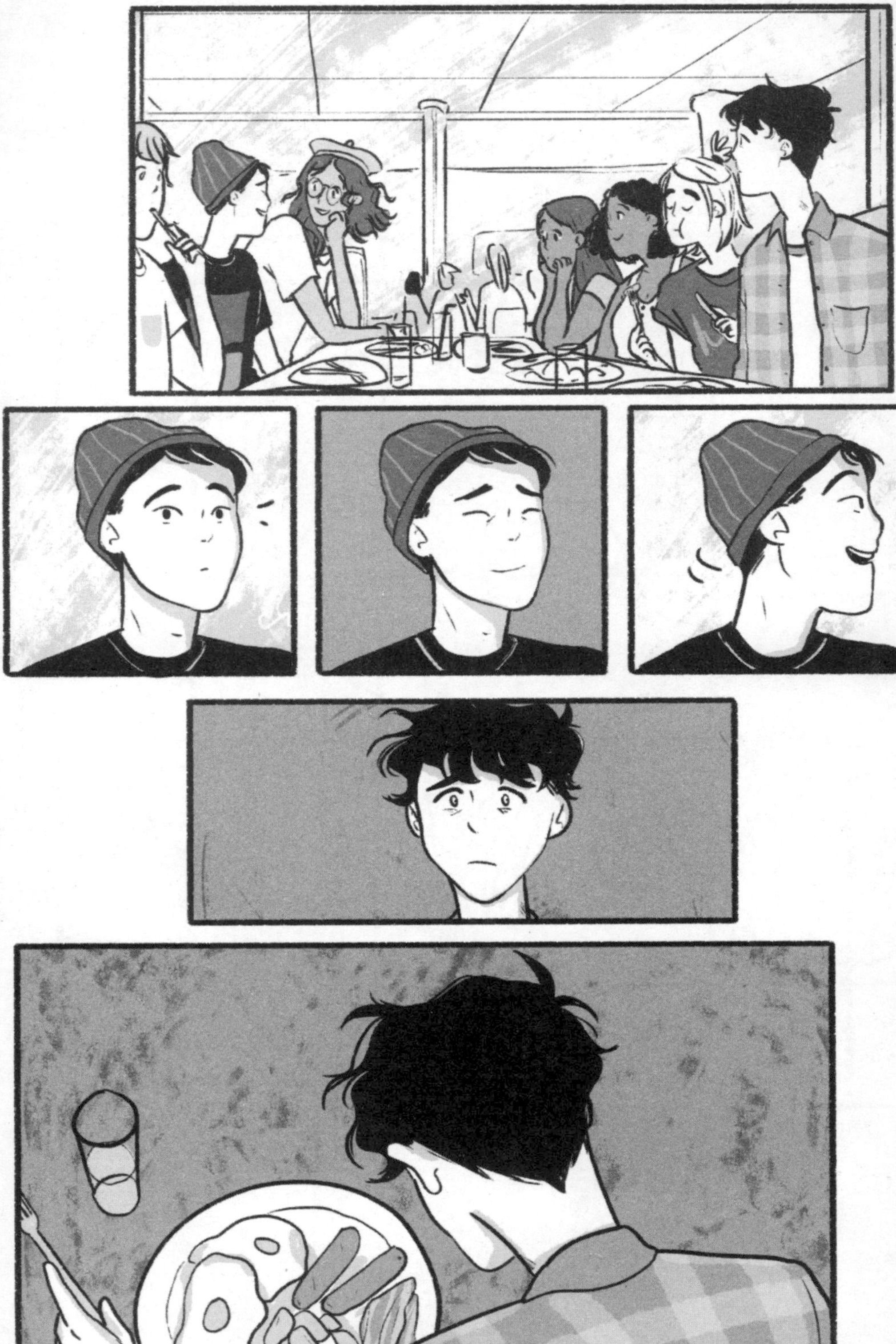

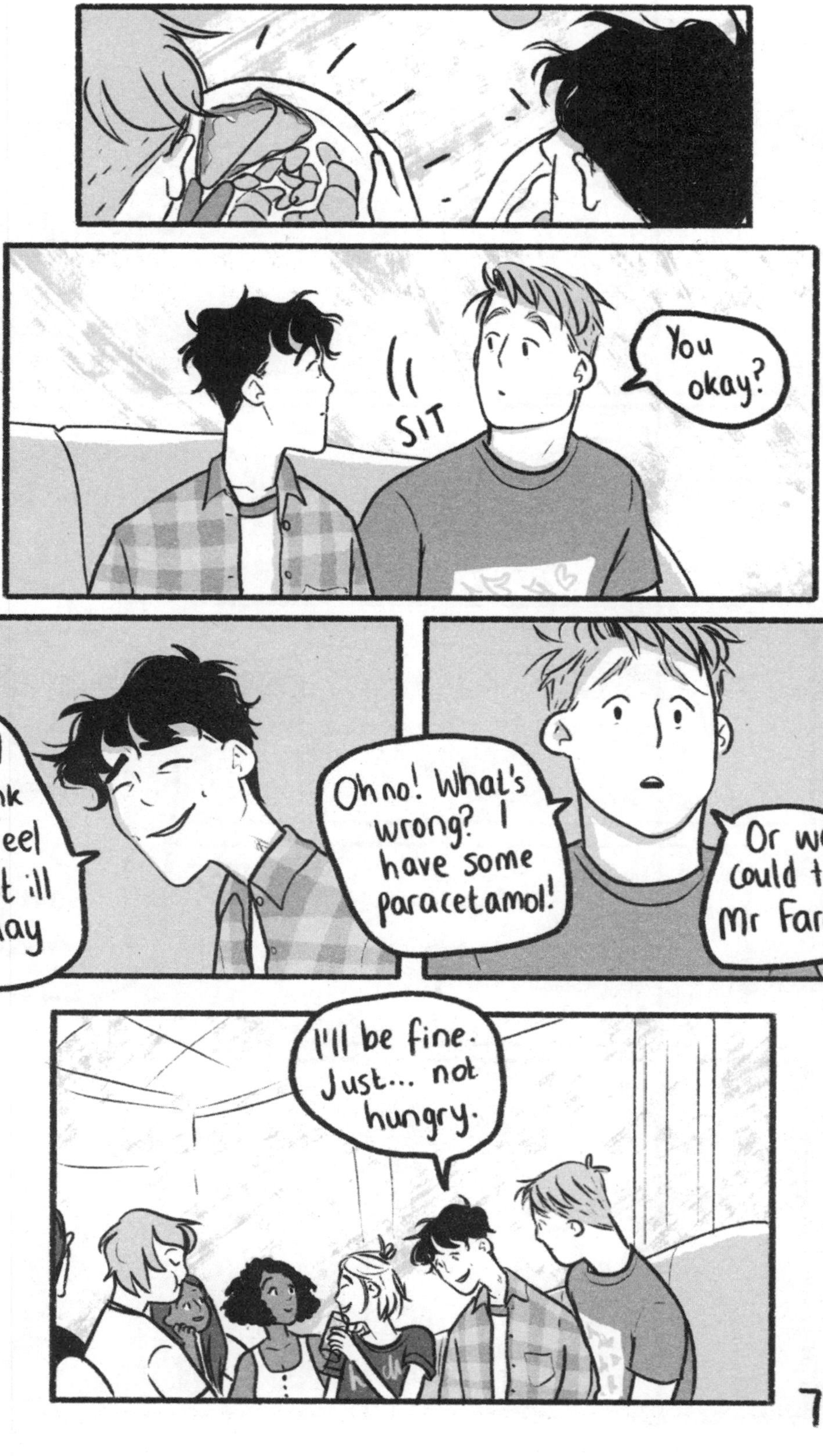

SIT
You okay?
I- I think I feel a bit ill today
Oh no! What's wrong? I have some paracetamol!
Or we could tell Mr Farouk?
I'll be fine. Just... not hungry.

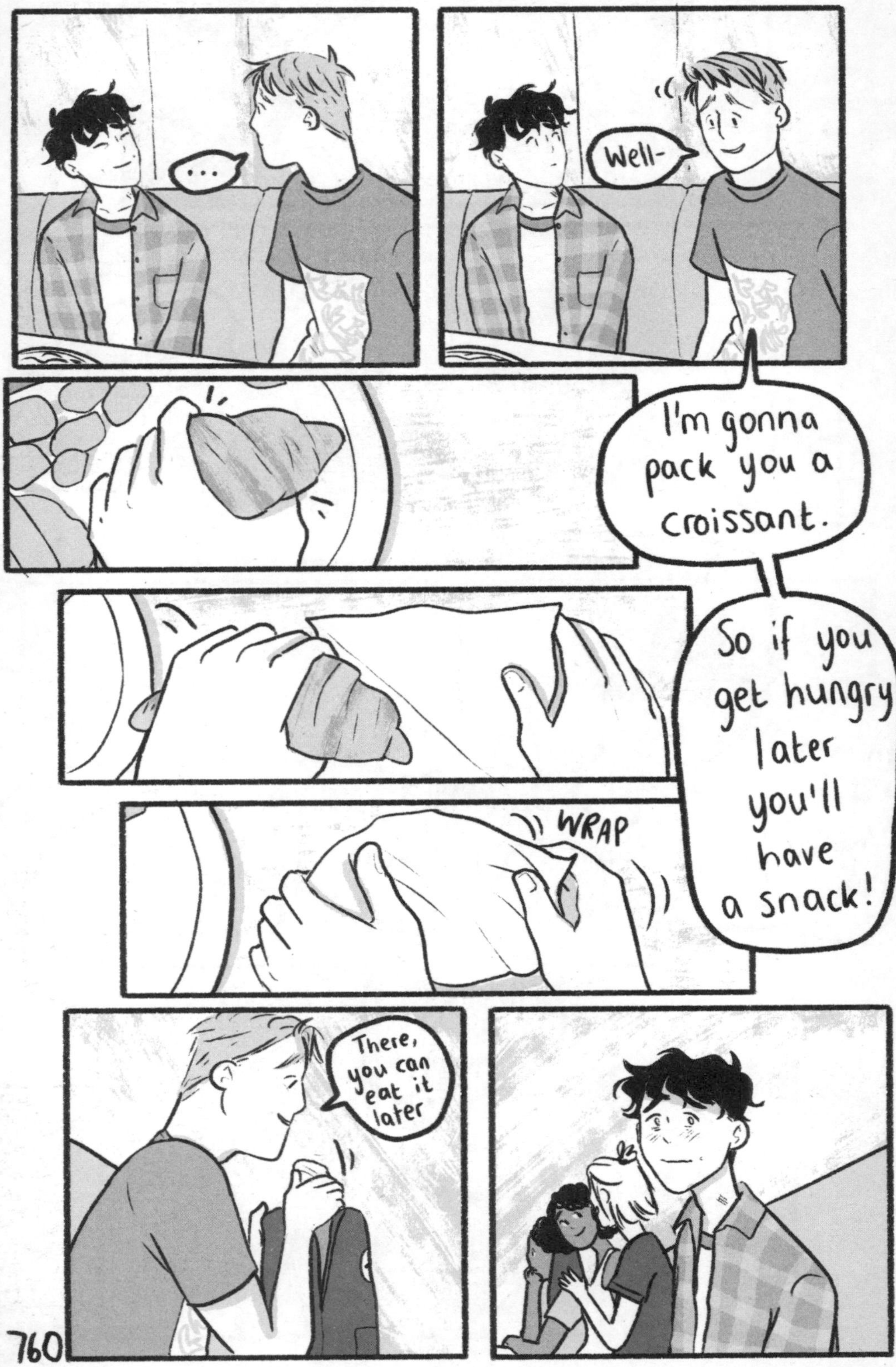
...
Well-
I'm gonna pack you a croissant.
So if you get hungry later you'll have a snack!
WRAP
There, you can eat it later

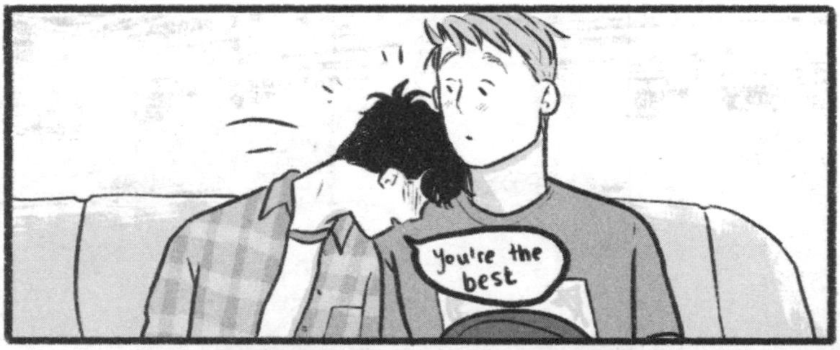
You're the best

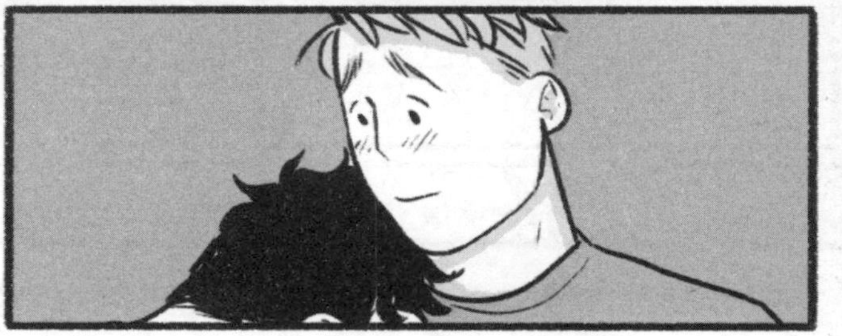

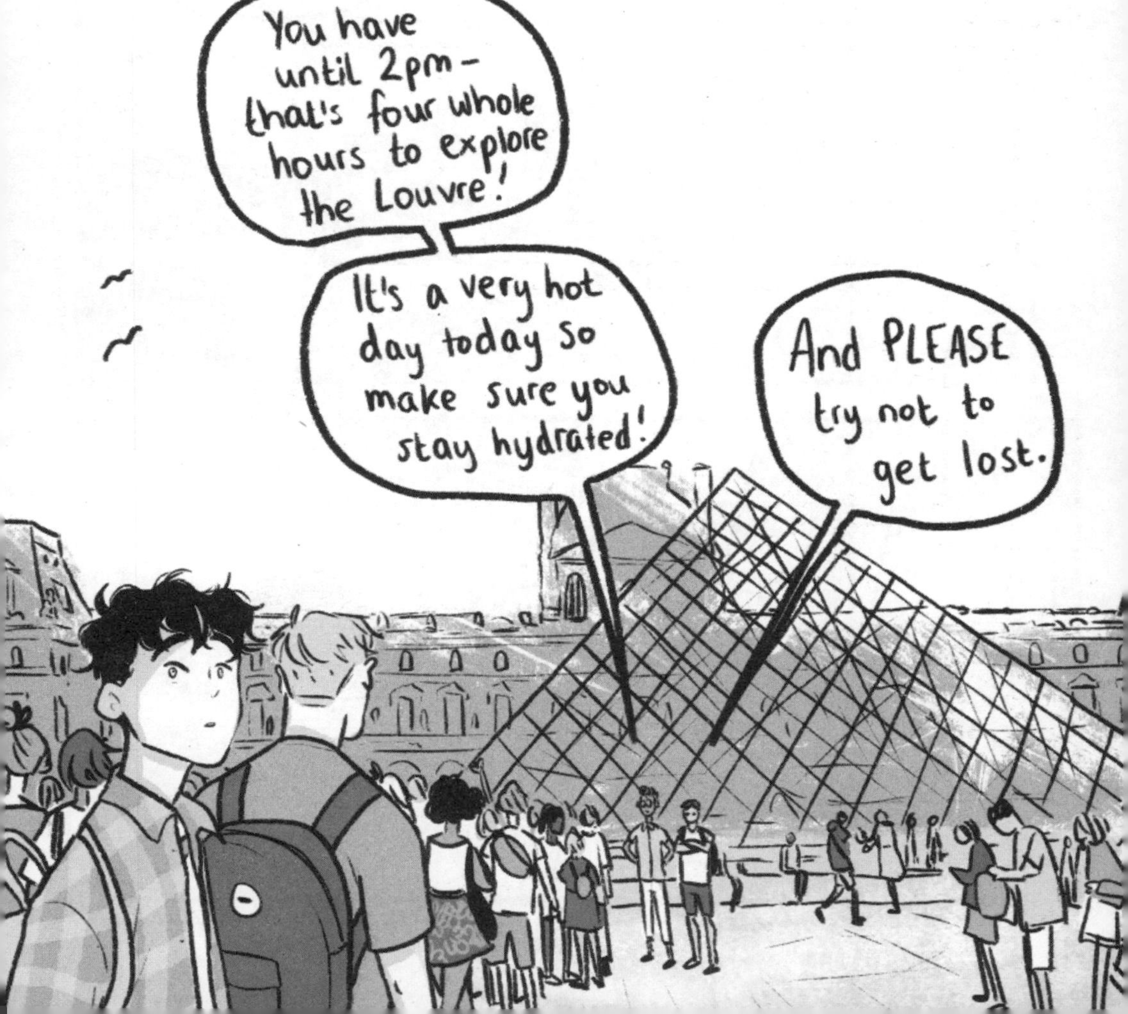
You have until 2pm - that's four whole hours to explore the Louvre!
It's a very hot day today so make sure you stay hydrated!
And PLEASE try not to get lost.

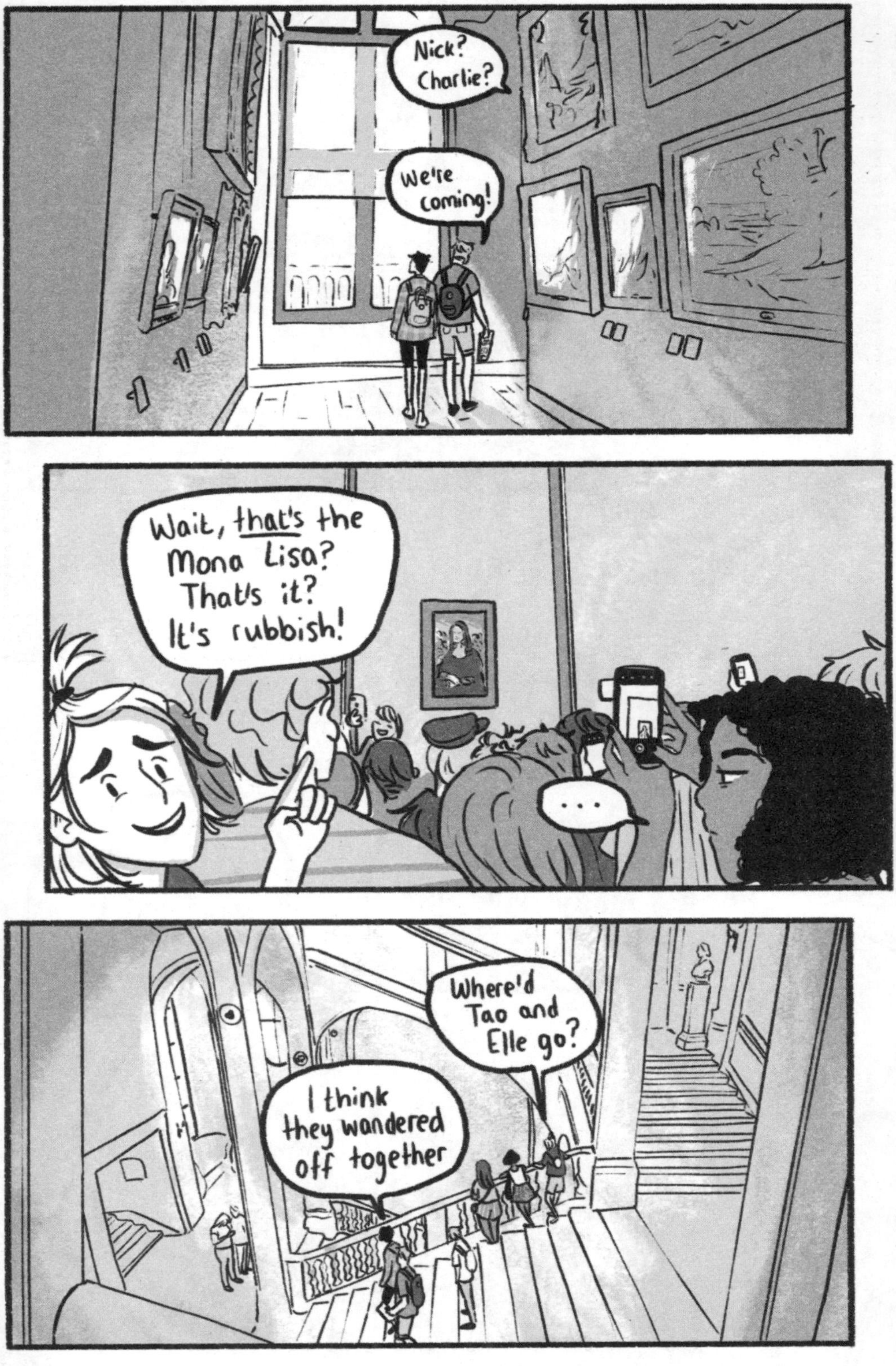
Nick? Charlie?
We're coming!
Wait, that's the Mona Lisa? That's it? It's rubbish!
...
Where'd Tao and Elle go?
I think they wandered off together

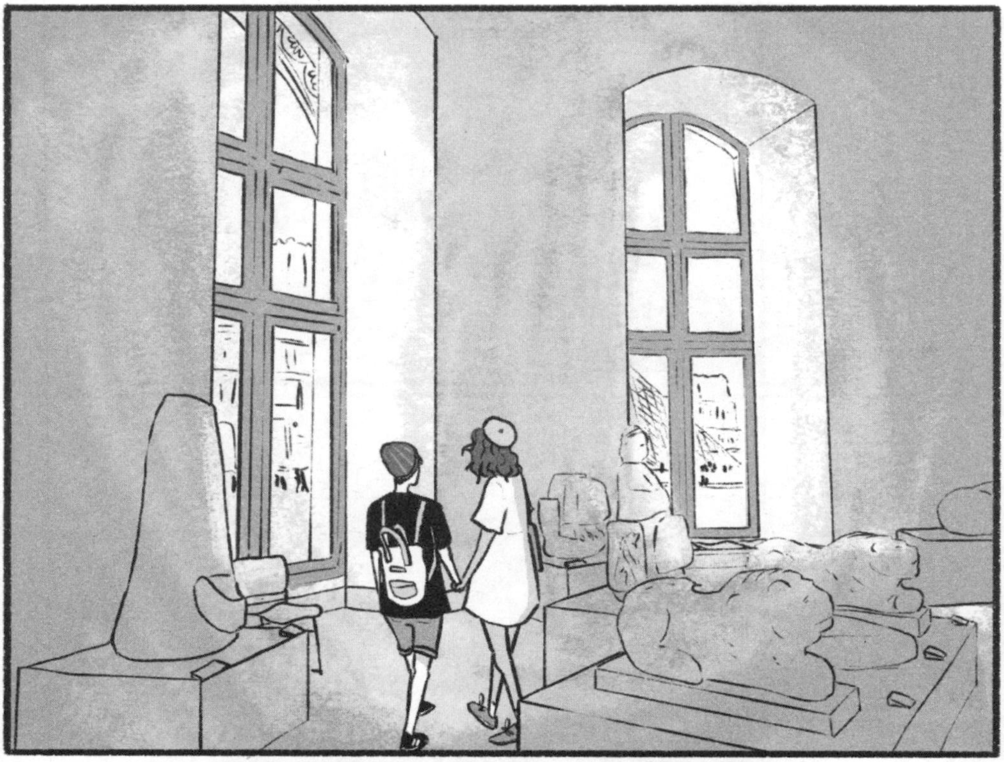

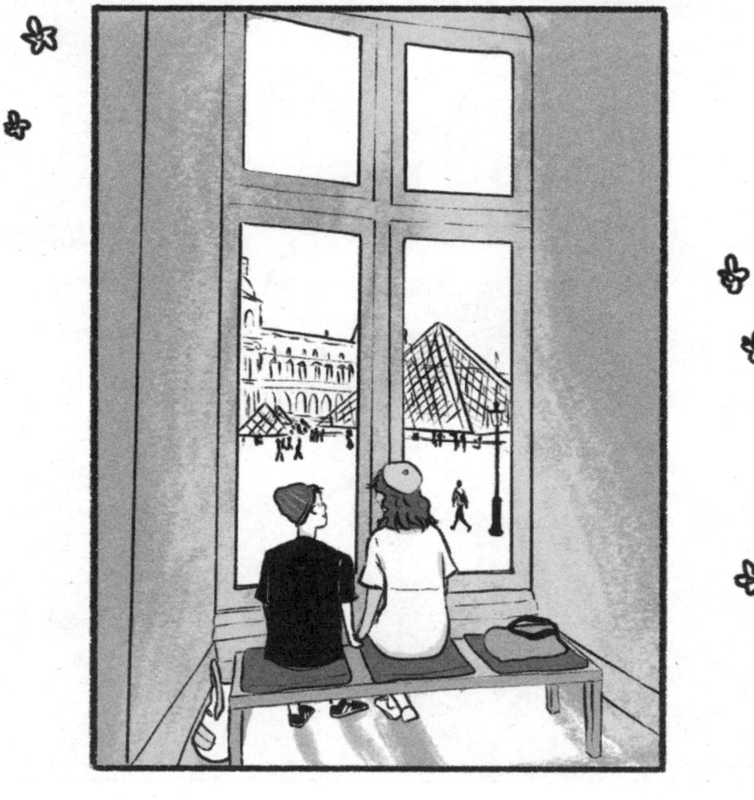

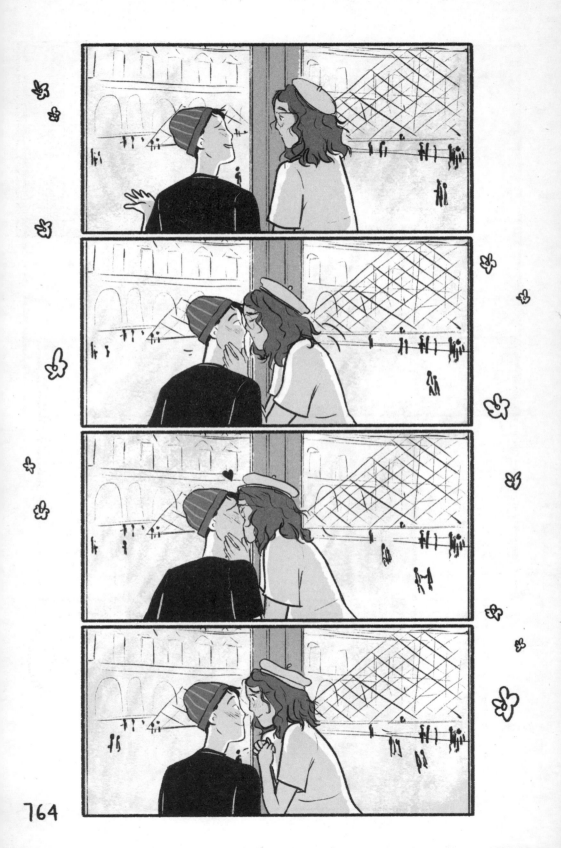

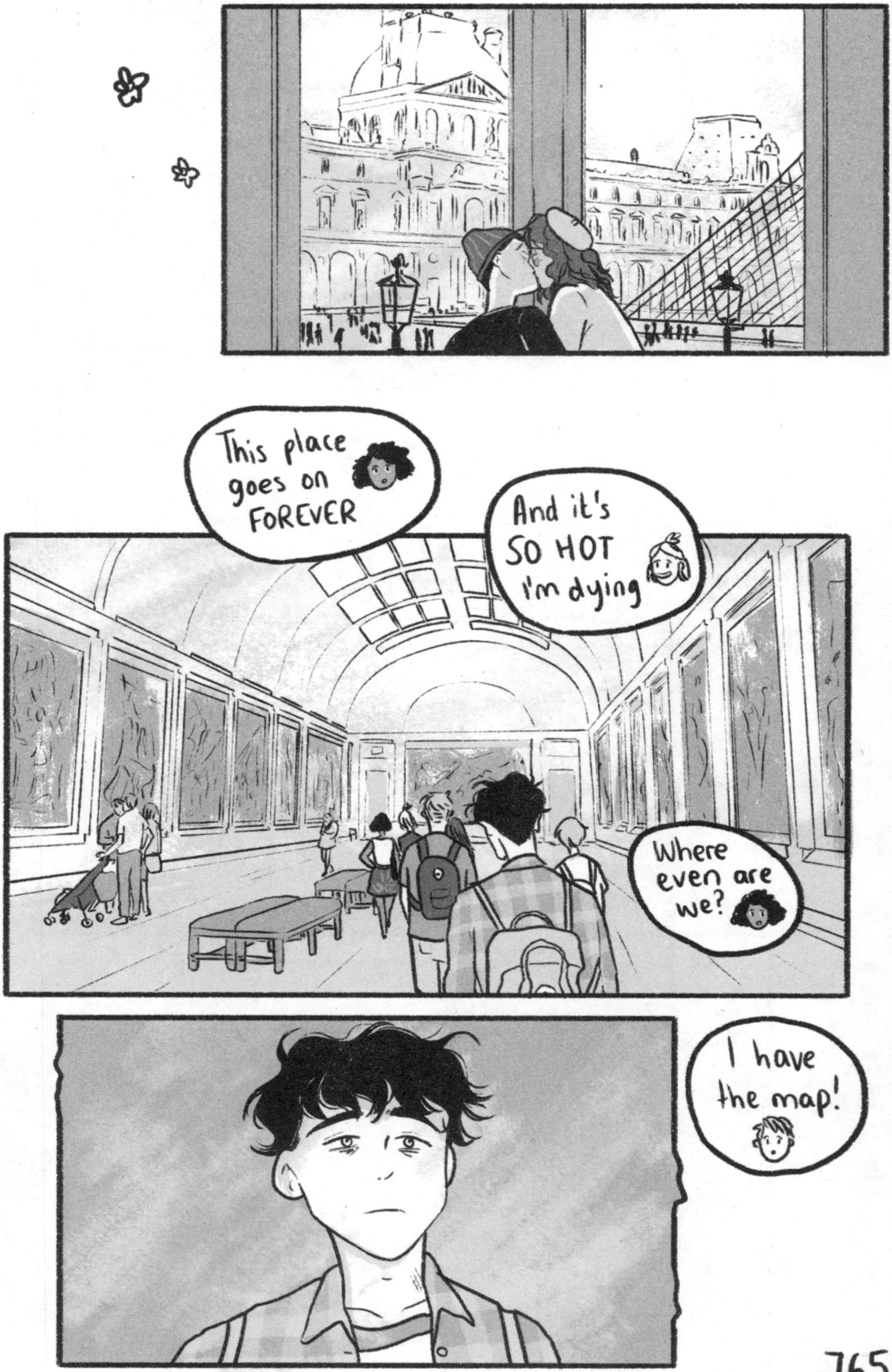
This place goes on FOREVER
And it's SO HOT I'm dying
Where even are we?
I have the map!

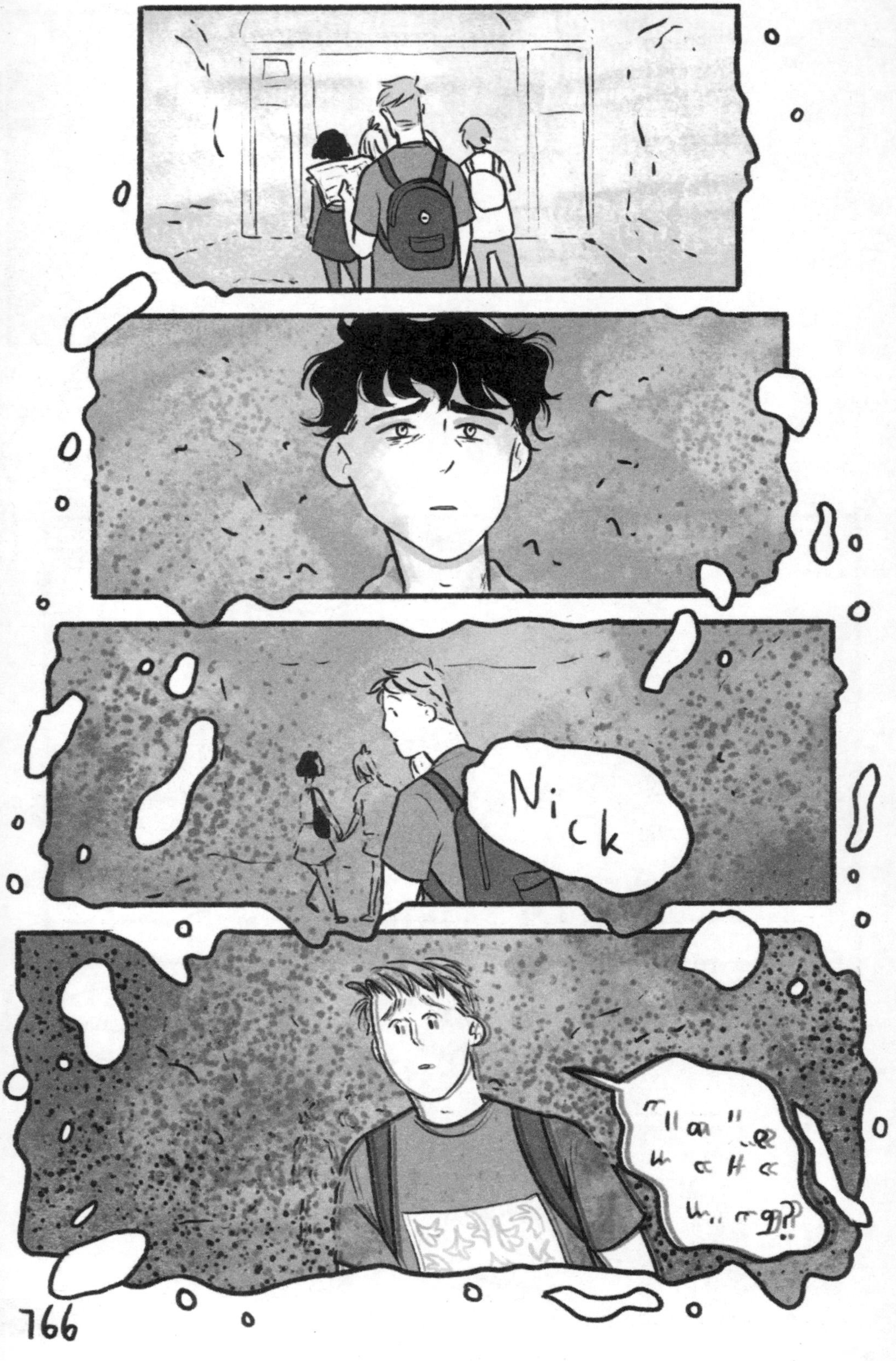
Nick

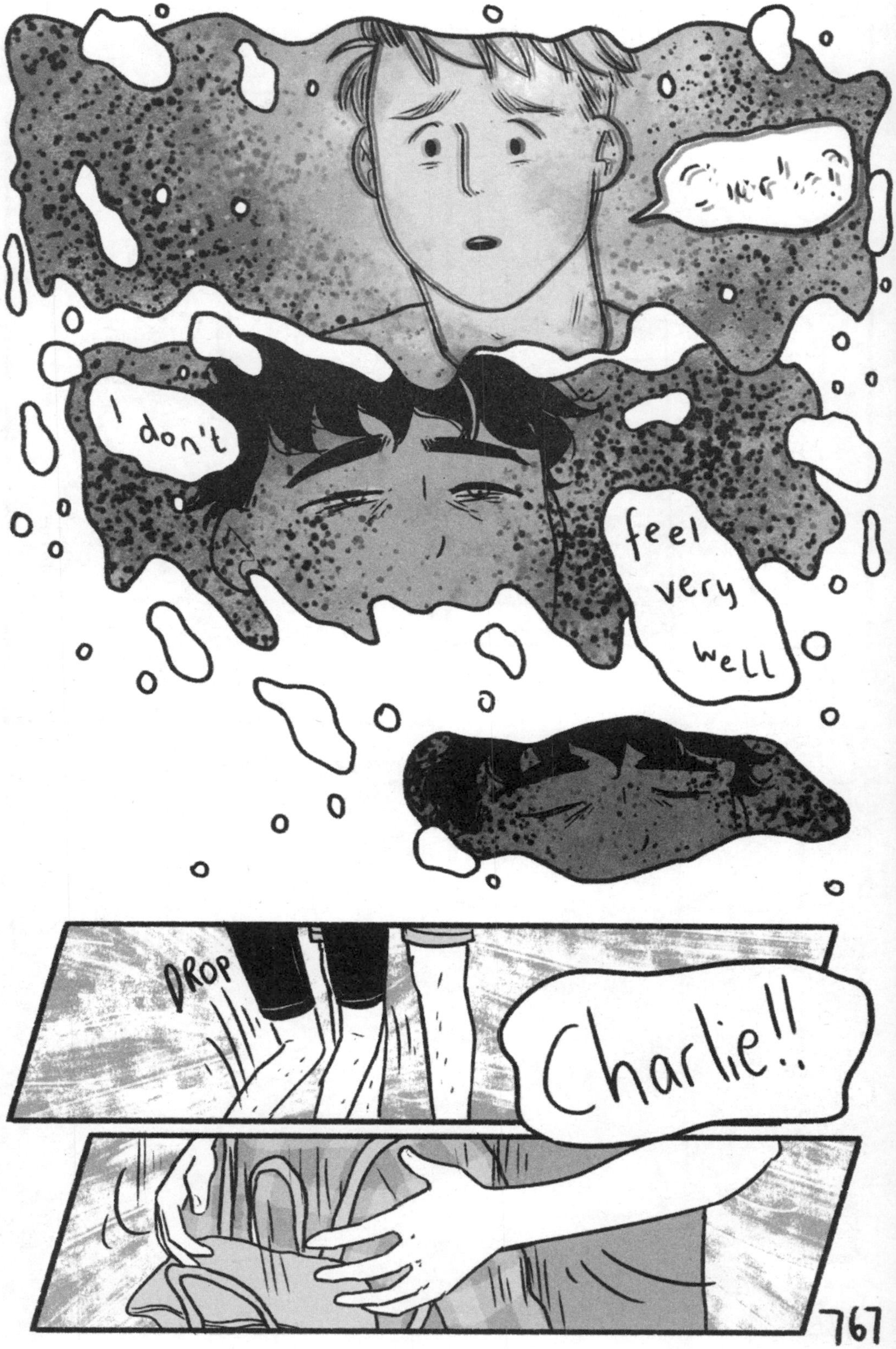
I don't
feel very well
DROP
Charlie!!

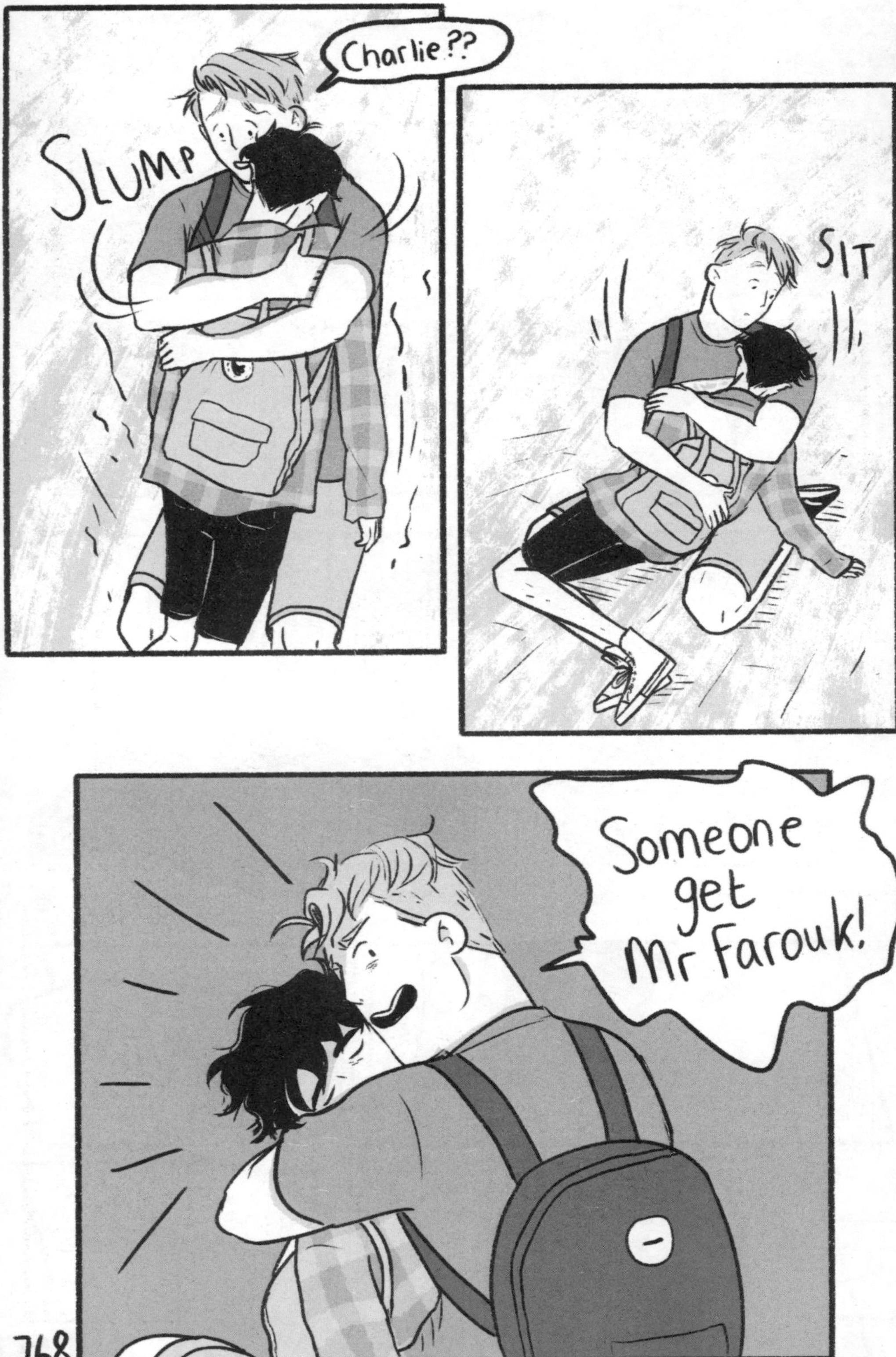
Charlie??
SLUMP
SIT
Someone get Mr Farouk!

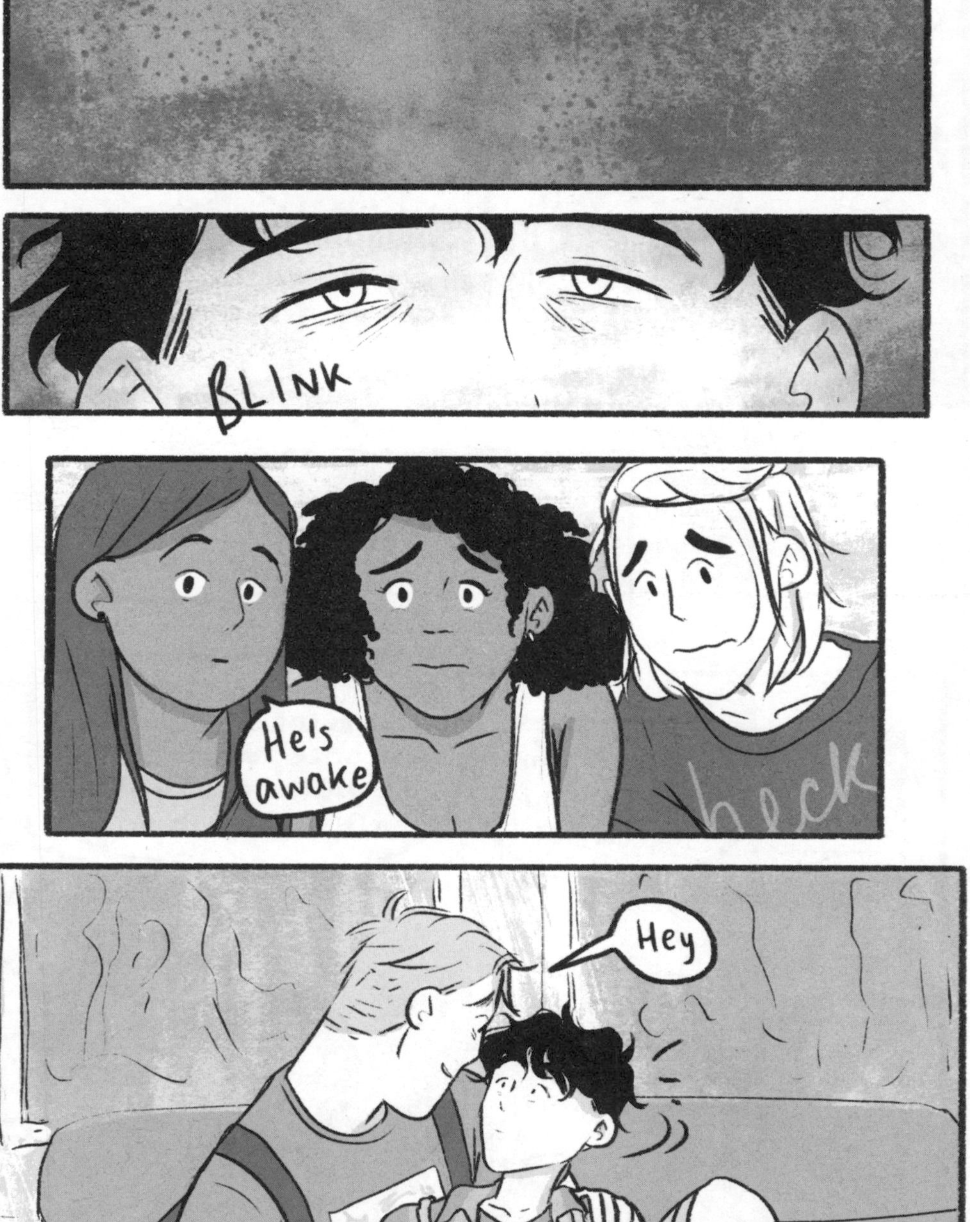
BLINK
He's awake
heck
Hey

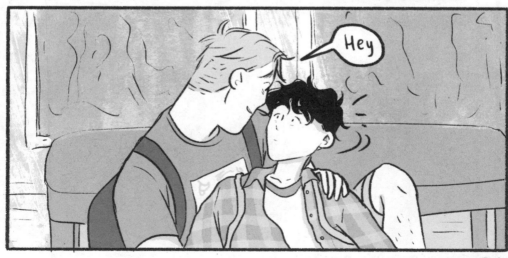

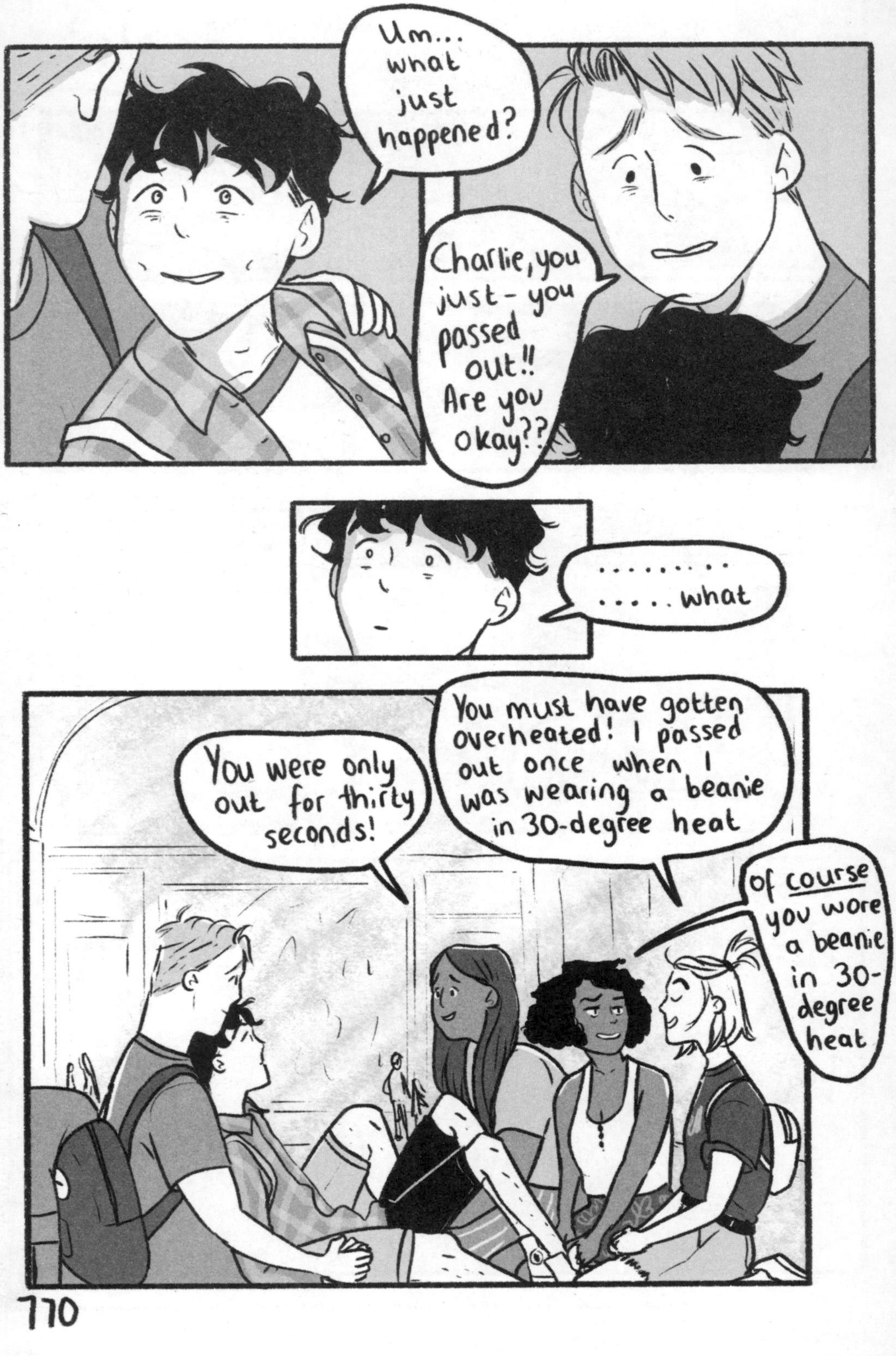
Um... what just happened?
Charlie, you just - you passed out!! Are you okay??
....
.....what
You were only out for thirty seconds!
You must have gotten overheated! I passed out once when I was wearing a beanie in 30-degree heat
of course you wore a beanie in 30-degree heat

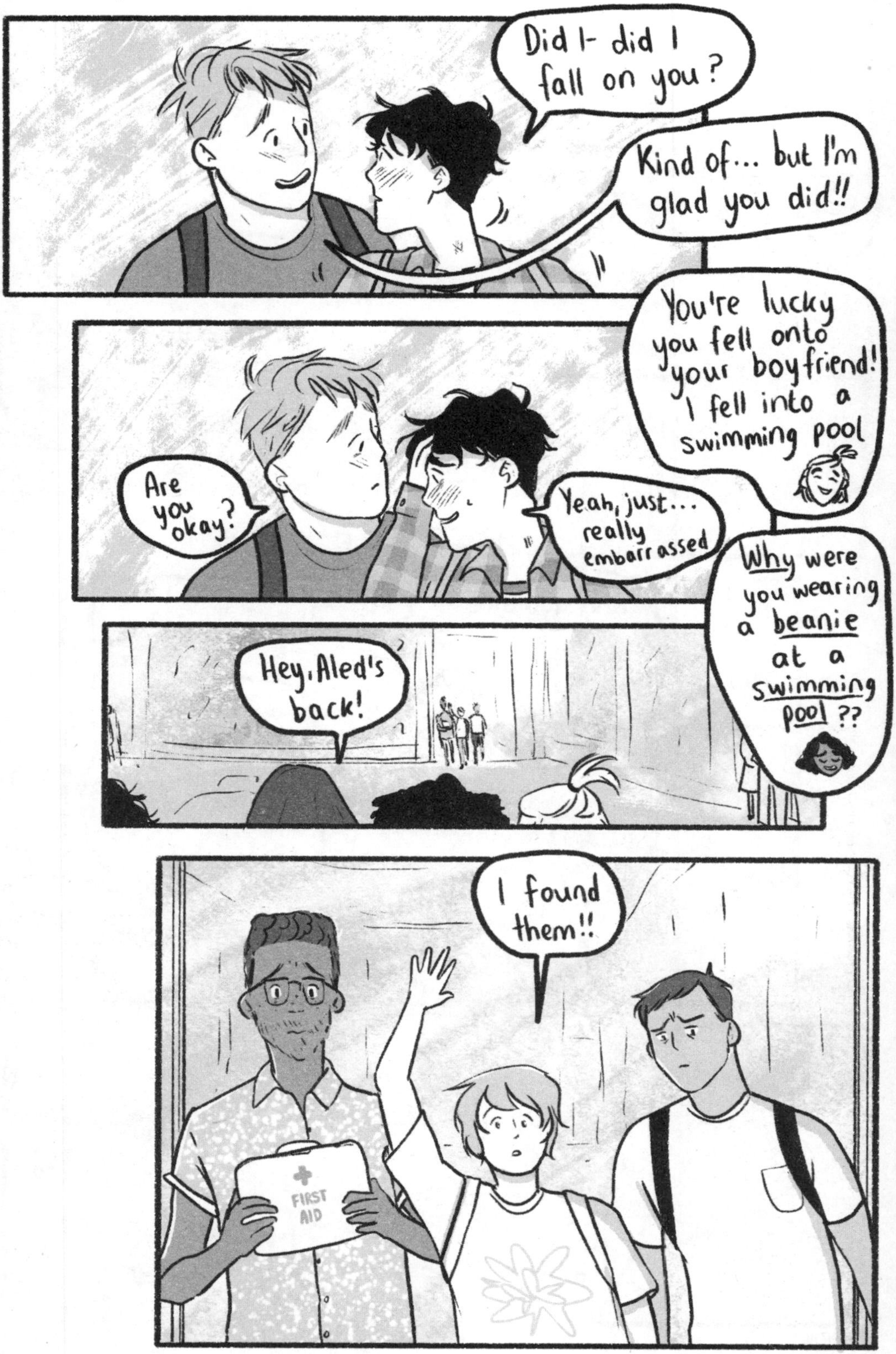
Did I- did I fall on you?
Kind of... but I'm glad you did!!
You're lucky you fell onto your boyfriend! I fell into a swimming pool
Are you okay?
Yeah, just... really embarrassed
Why were you wearing a beanie at a swimming pool??
Hey, Aled's back!
I found them!!
FIRST AID

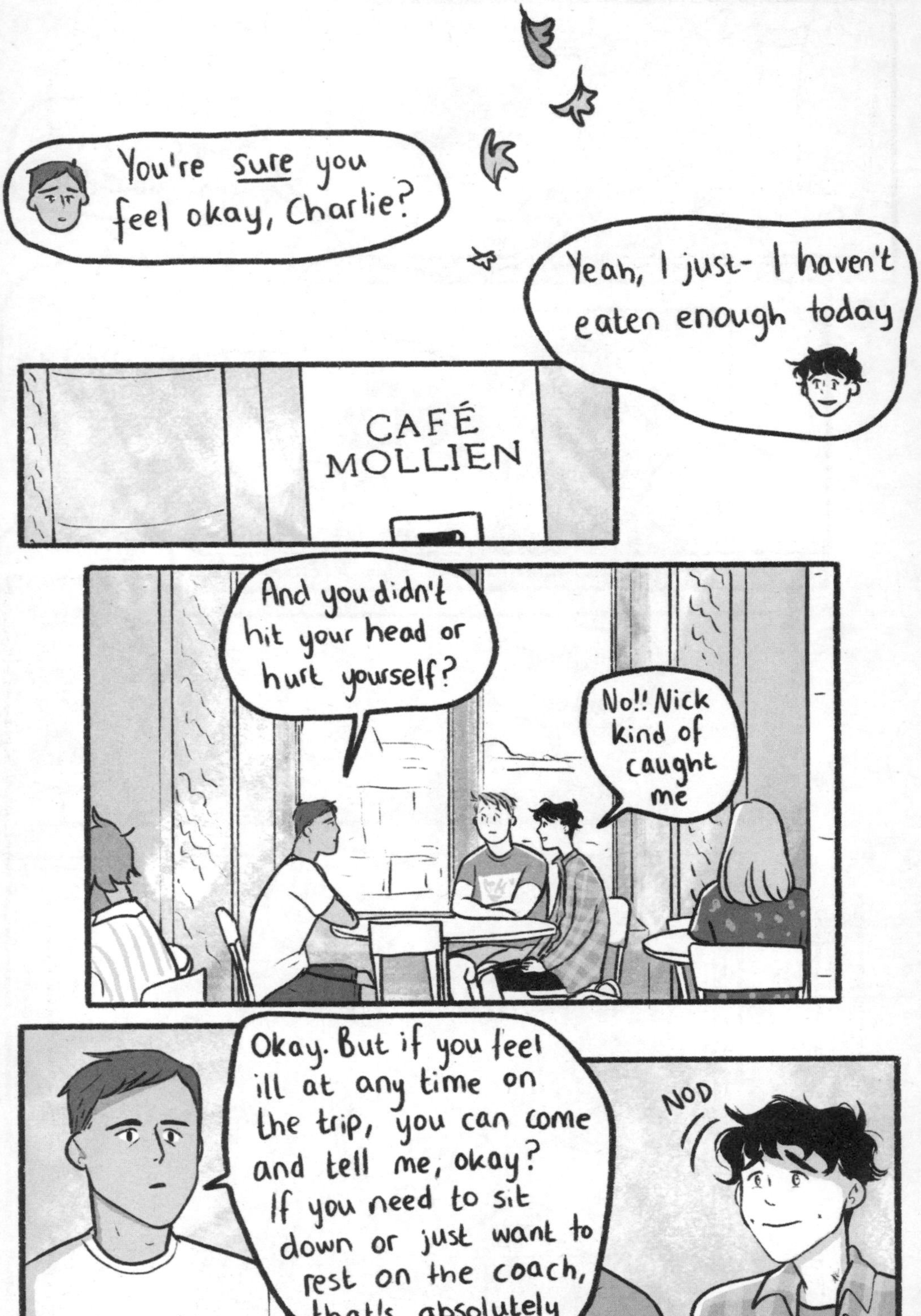

You're sure you feel okay, Charlie?
Yeah, I just- I haven't eaten enough today
CAFÉ MOLLIEN
And you didn't hit your head or hurt yourself?
No!! Nick kind of caught me
Okay. But if you feel ill at any time on the trip, you can come and tell me, okay? If you need to sit down or just want to rest on the coach, that's absolutely fine.
NOD

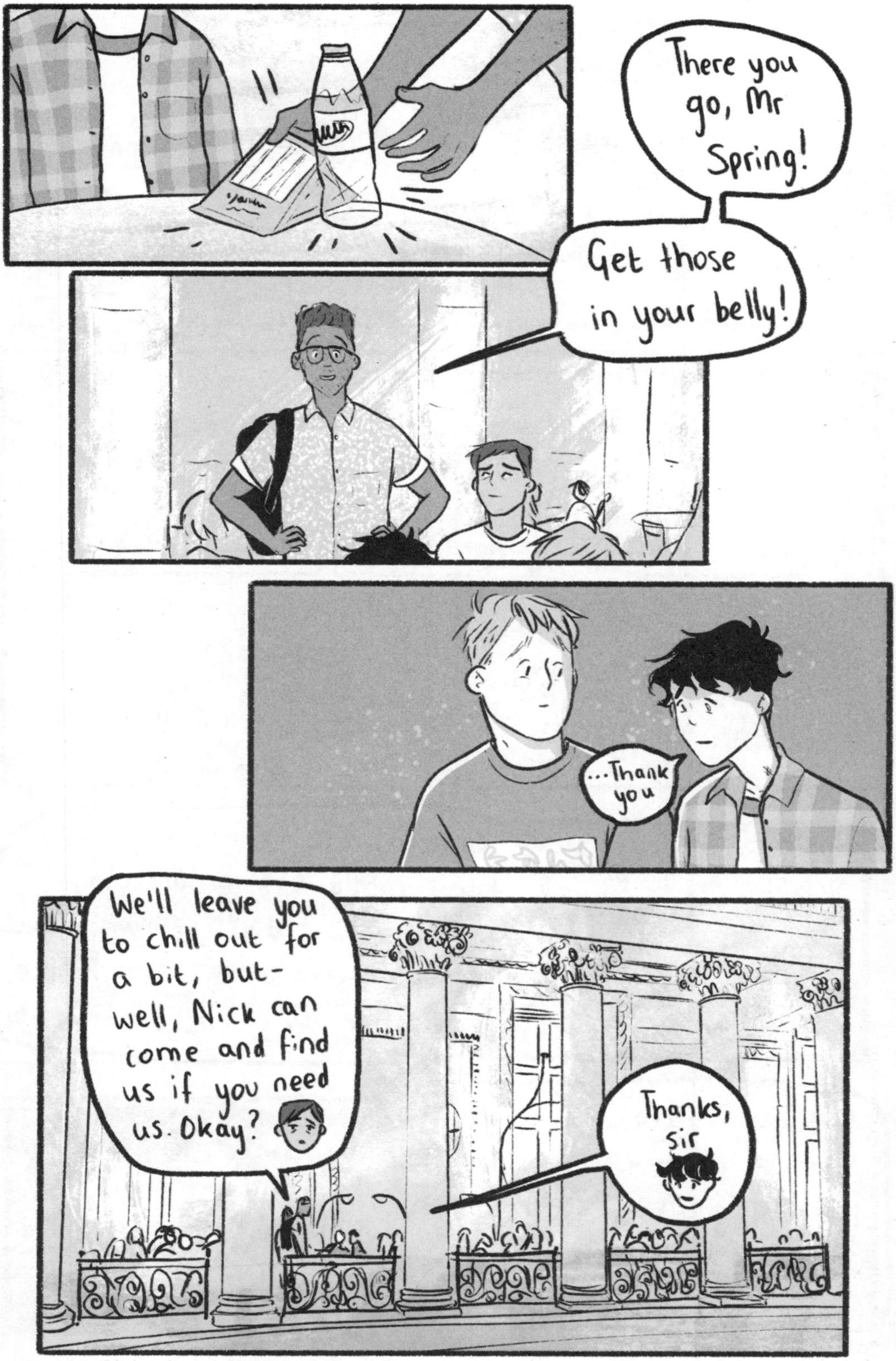
There you go, Mr Spring!
Get those in your belly!
...Thank you
We'll leave you to chill out for a bit, but- well, Nick can come and find us if you need us. Okay?
Thanks, sir

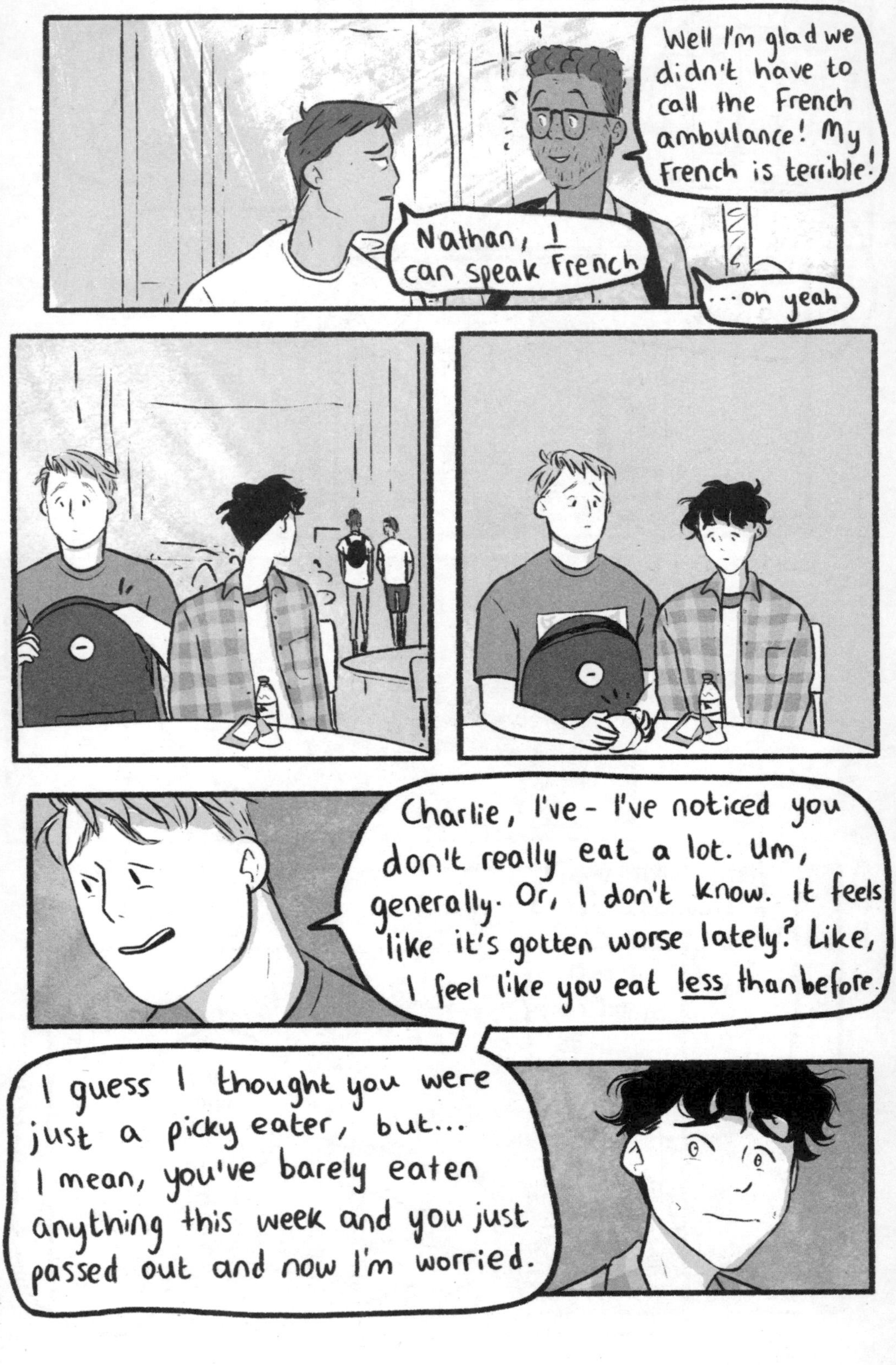
Well I'm glad we didn't have to call the French ambulance! My French is terrible!
Nathan, I can speak French
...oh yeah
Charlie, I've- I've noticed you don't really eat a lot. Um, generally. Or, I don't know. It feels like it's gotten worse lately? Like, I feel like you eat less than before.
I guess I thought you were just a picky eater, but... I mean, you've barely eaten anything this week and you just passed out and now I'm worried.

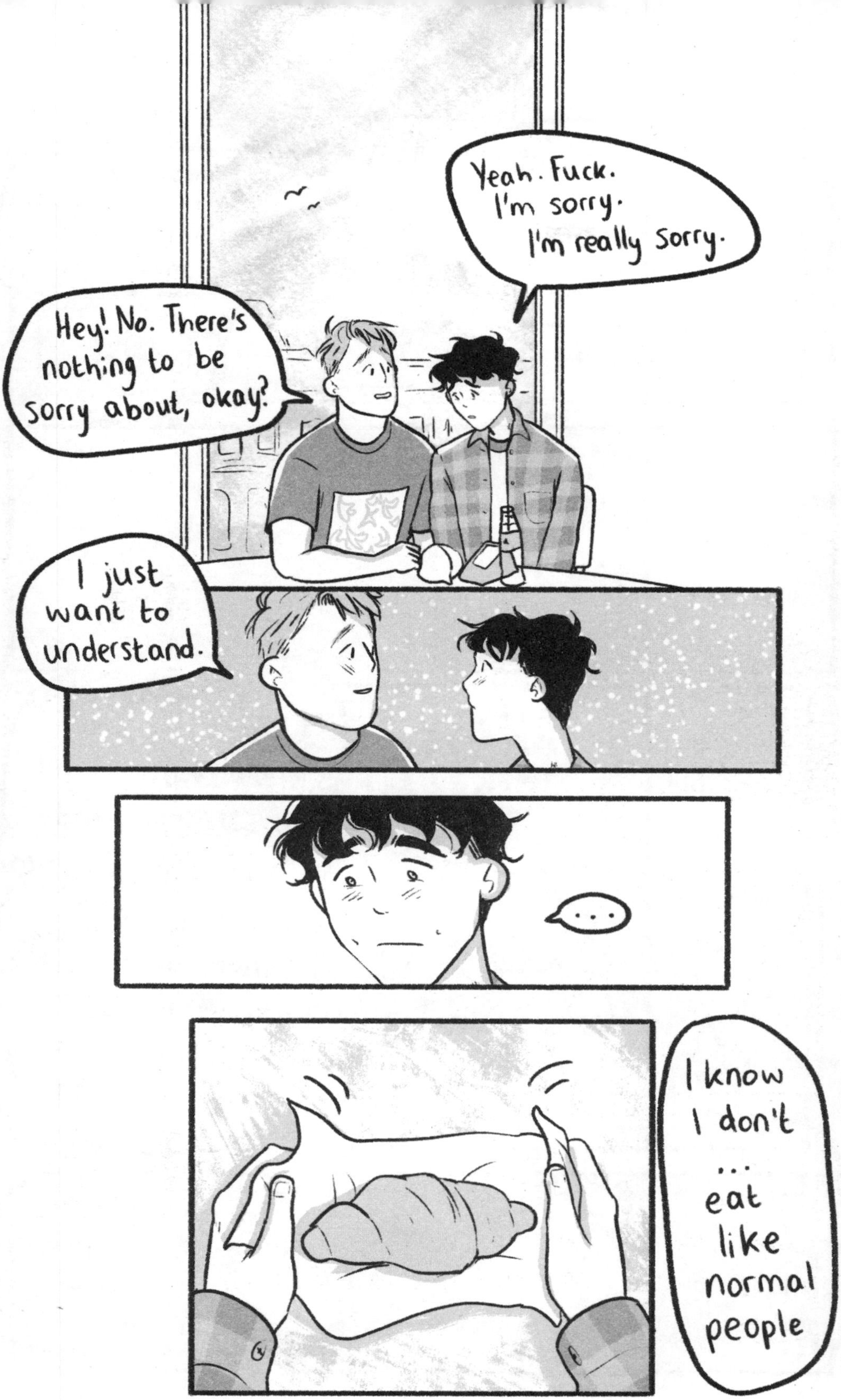
Yeah. Fuck.
I'm sorry.
I'm really sorry.
Hey! No. There's nothing to be sorry about, okay?
I just want to understand.
...
I know I don't ... eat like normal people

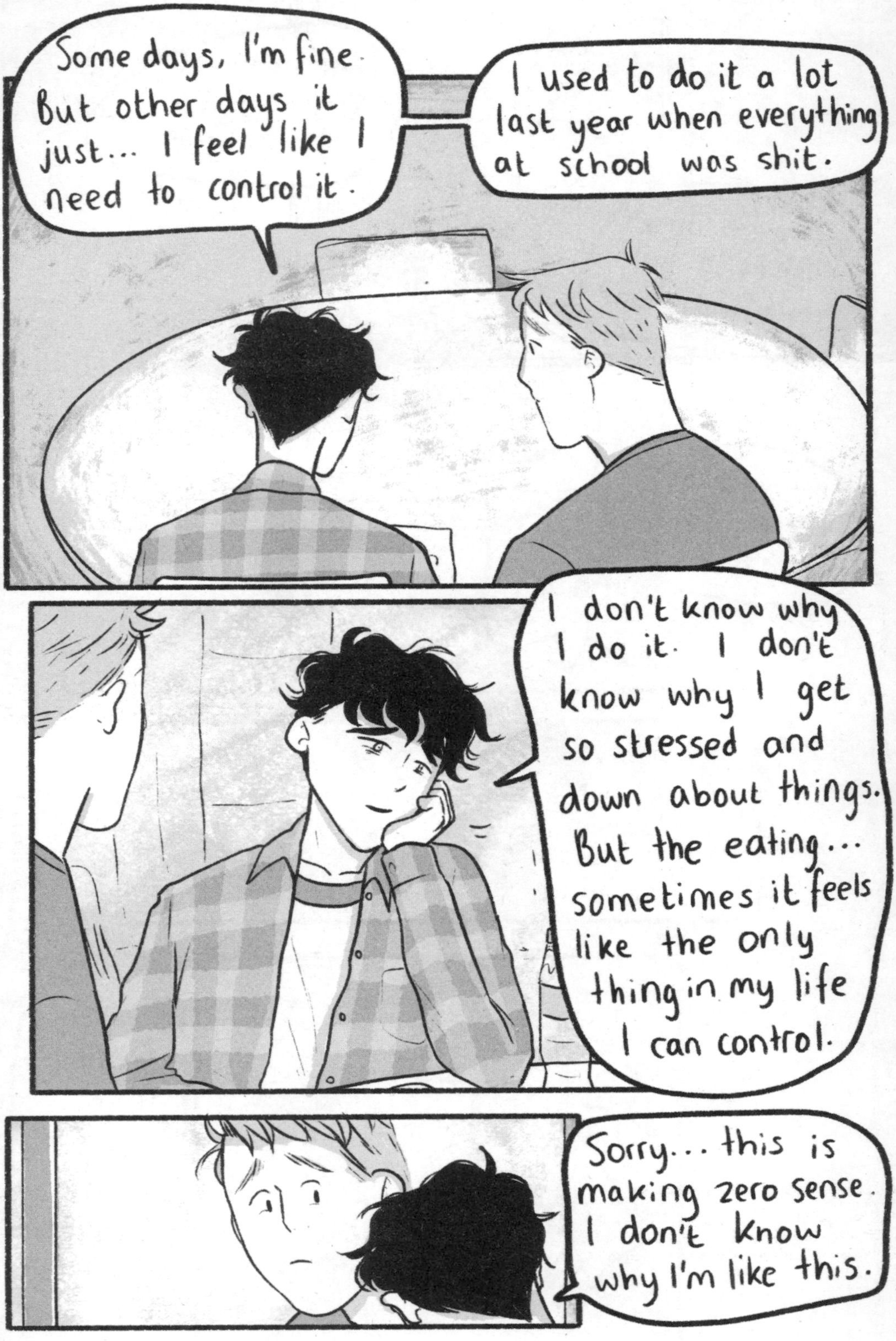
Some days, I'm fine. But other days it just... I feel like I need to control it.
I used to do it a lot last year when everything at school was shit.
I don't know why I do it. I don't know why I get so stressed and down about things. But the eating... sometimes it feels like the only thing in my life I can control.
Sorry... this is making zero sense. I don't know why I'm like this.

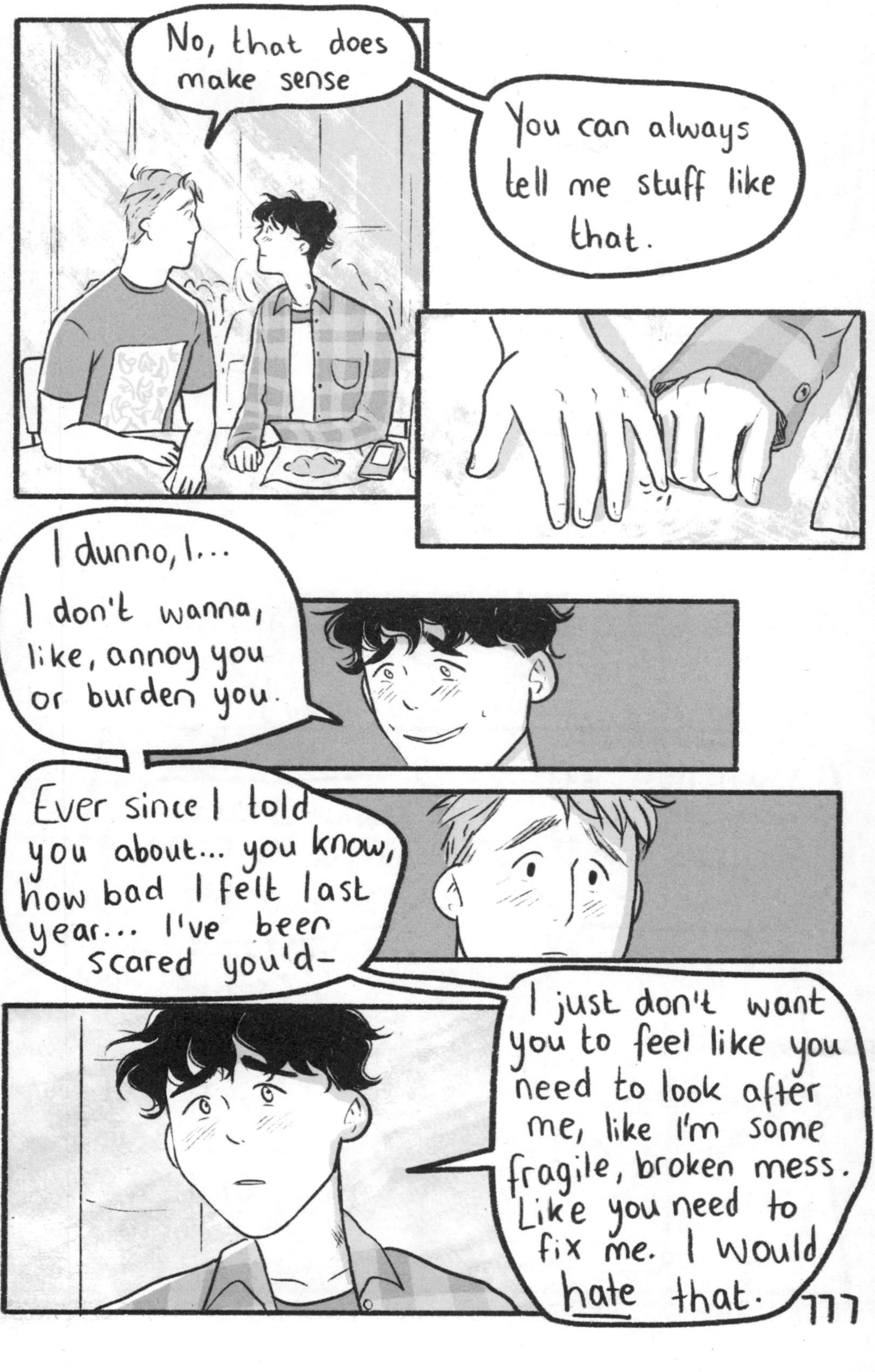
No, that does make sense
You can always tell me stuff like that.
I dunno, I...
I don't wanna, like, annoy you or burden you.
Ever since I told you about... you know, how bad I felt last year... I've been scared you'd-
I just don't want you to feel like you need to look after me, like I'm some fragile, broken mess. Like you need to fix me. I would hate that.

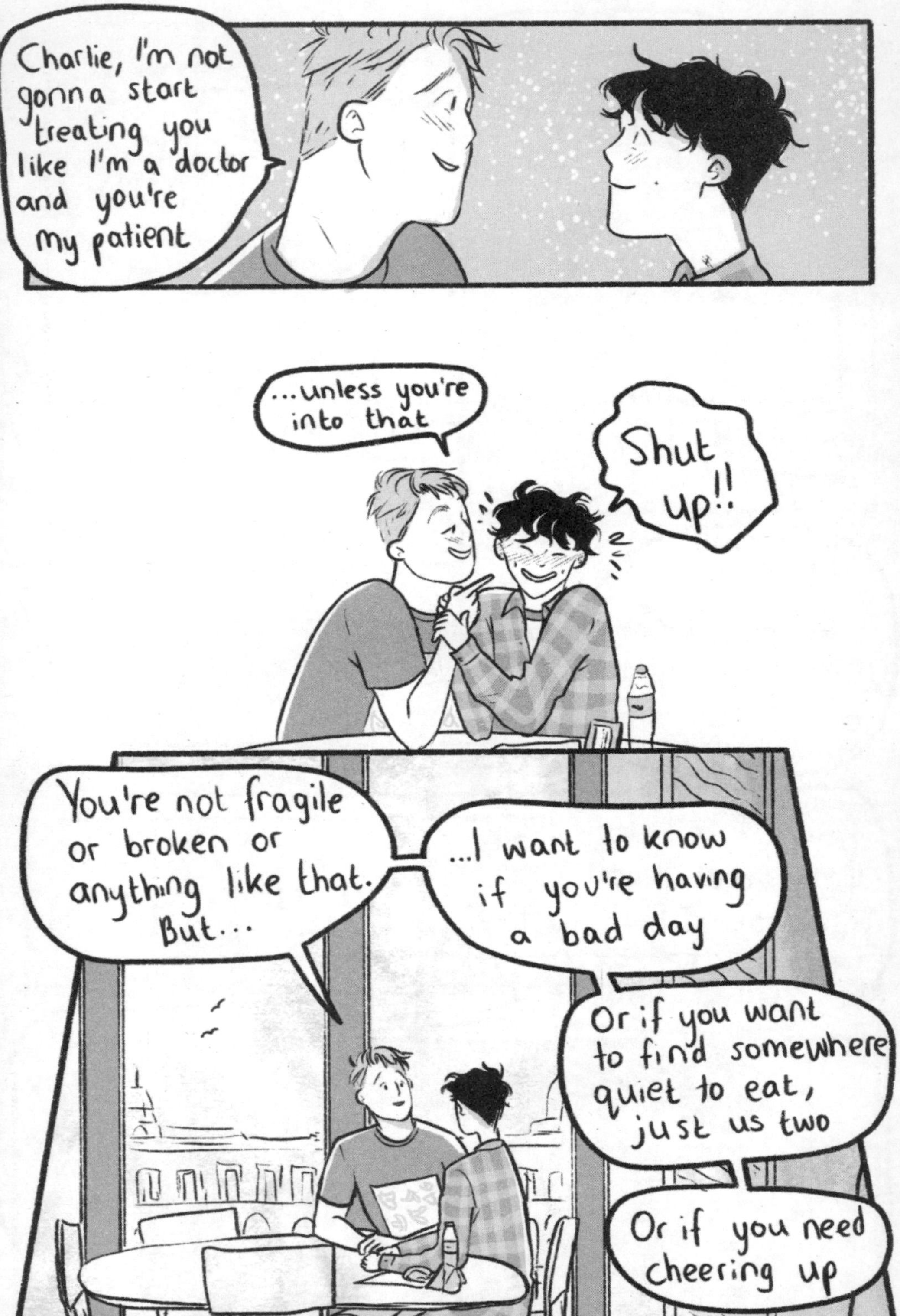
Charlie, I'm not gonna start treating you like I'm a doctor and you're my patient
...unless you're into that
Shut up!!
You're not fragile or broken or anything like that. But...
...I want to know if you're having a bad day
Or if you want to find somewhere quiet to eat, just us two
Or if you need cheering up

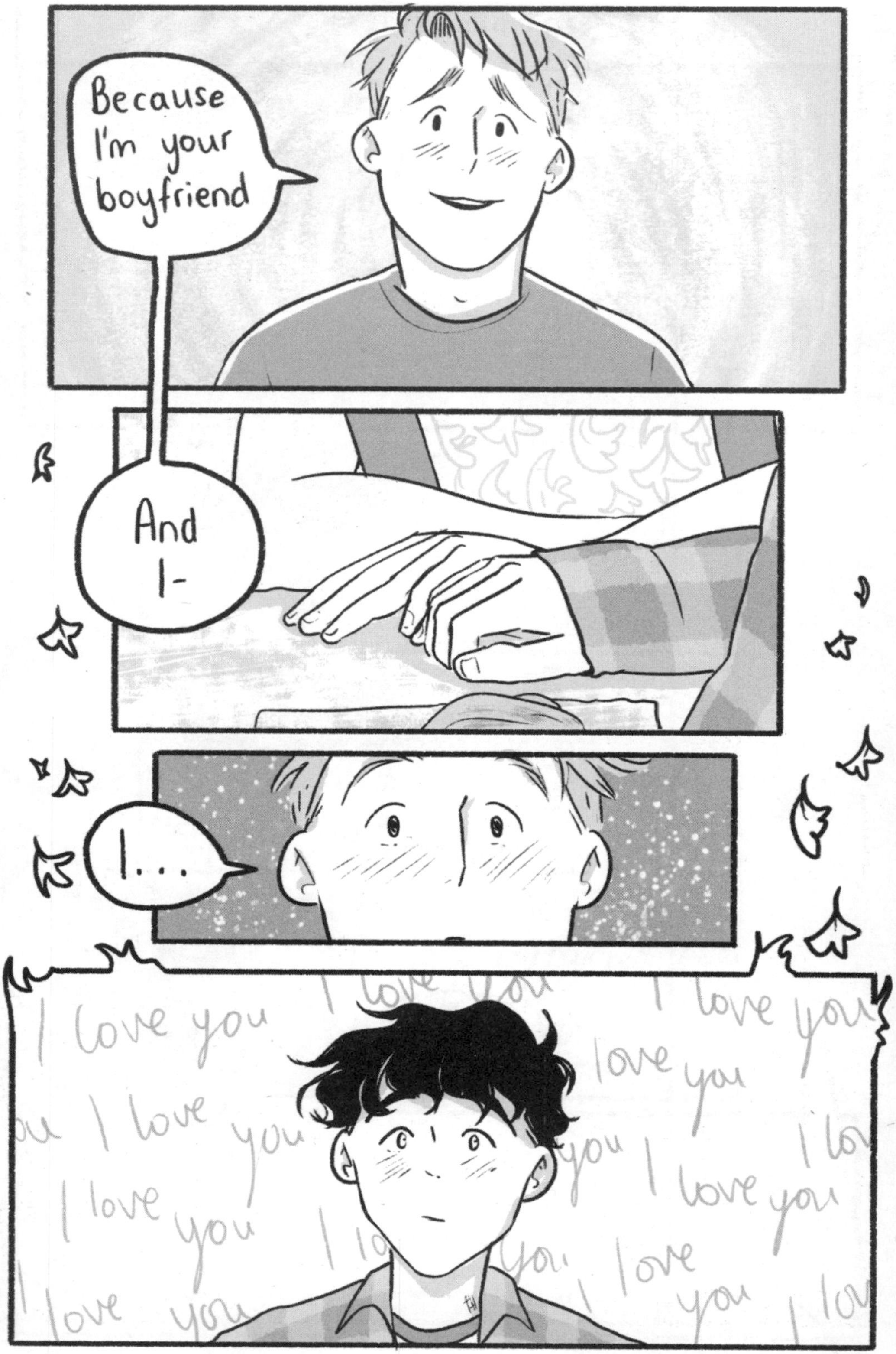
Because I'm your boyfriend
And I-
I...
I love you
I love you
I love you
I love you
I love you
I love you

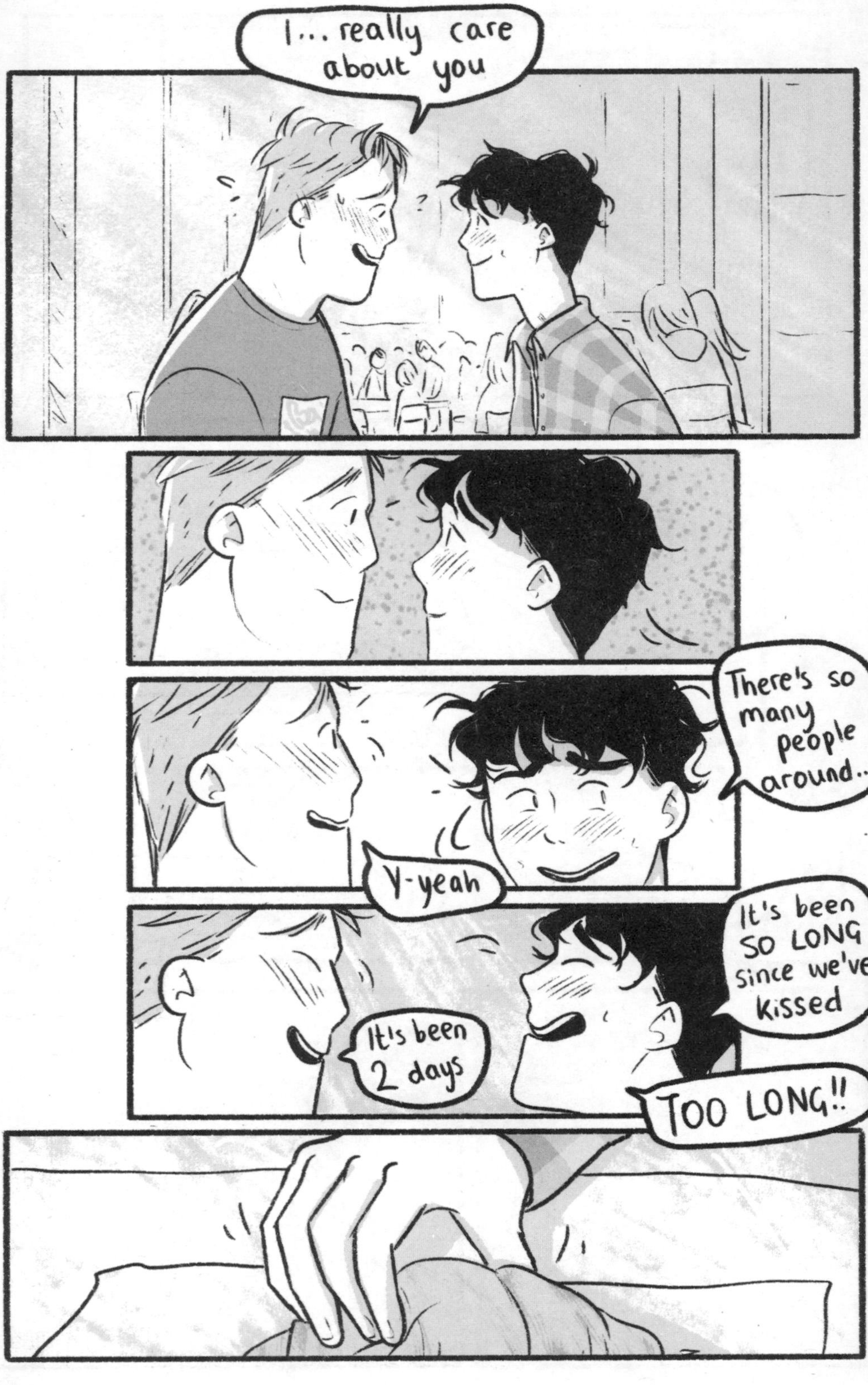
I... really care about you
There's so many people around...
Y-yeah
It's been SO LONG since we've kissed
It's been 2 days
TOO LONG!!

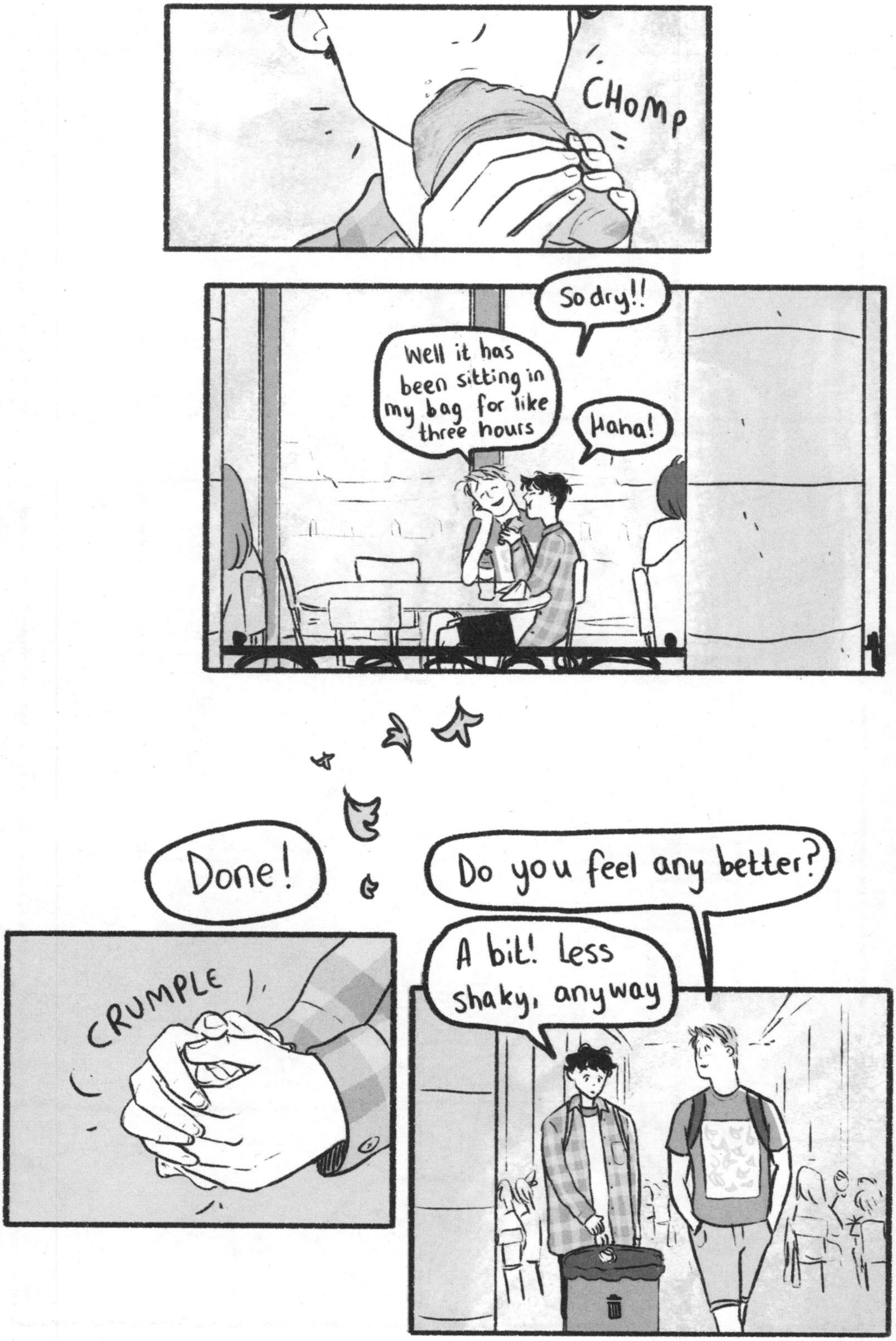
CHOMP
So dry!!
Well it has been sitting in my bag for like three hours
Haha!
Done!
Do you feel any better?
CRUMPLE
A bit! Less shaky, anyway

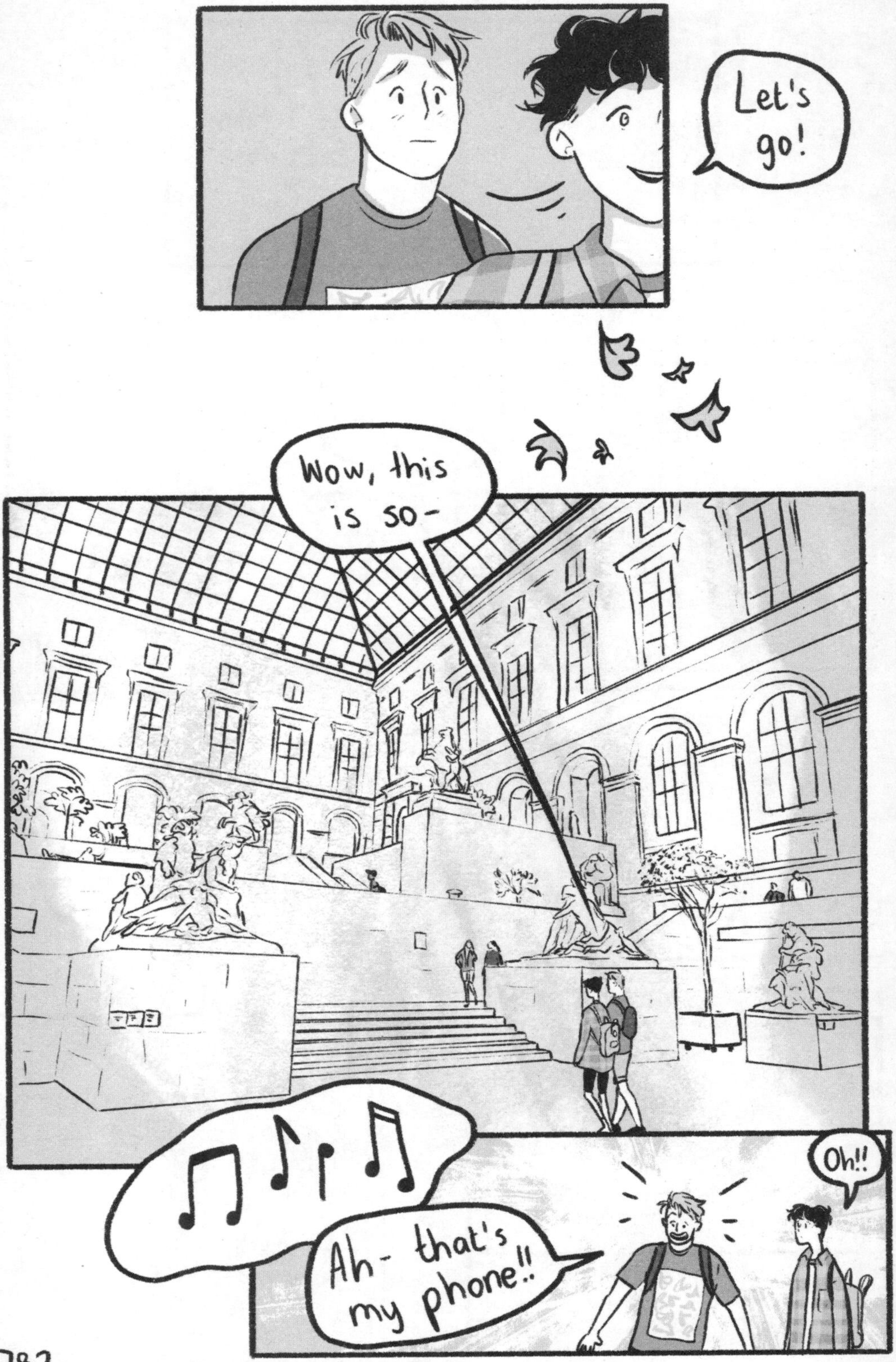

Let's go!
Wow, this is so-
Ah- that's my phone!!
Oh!!

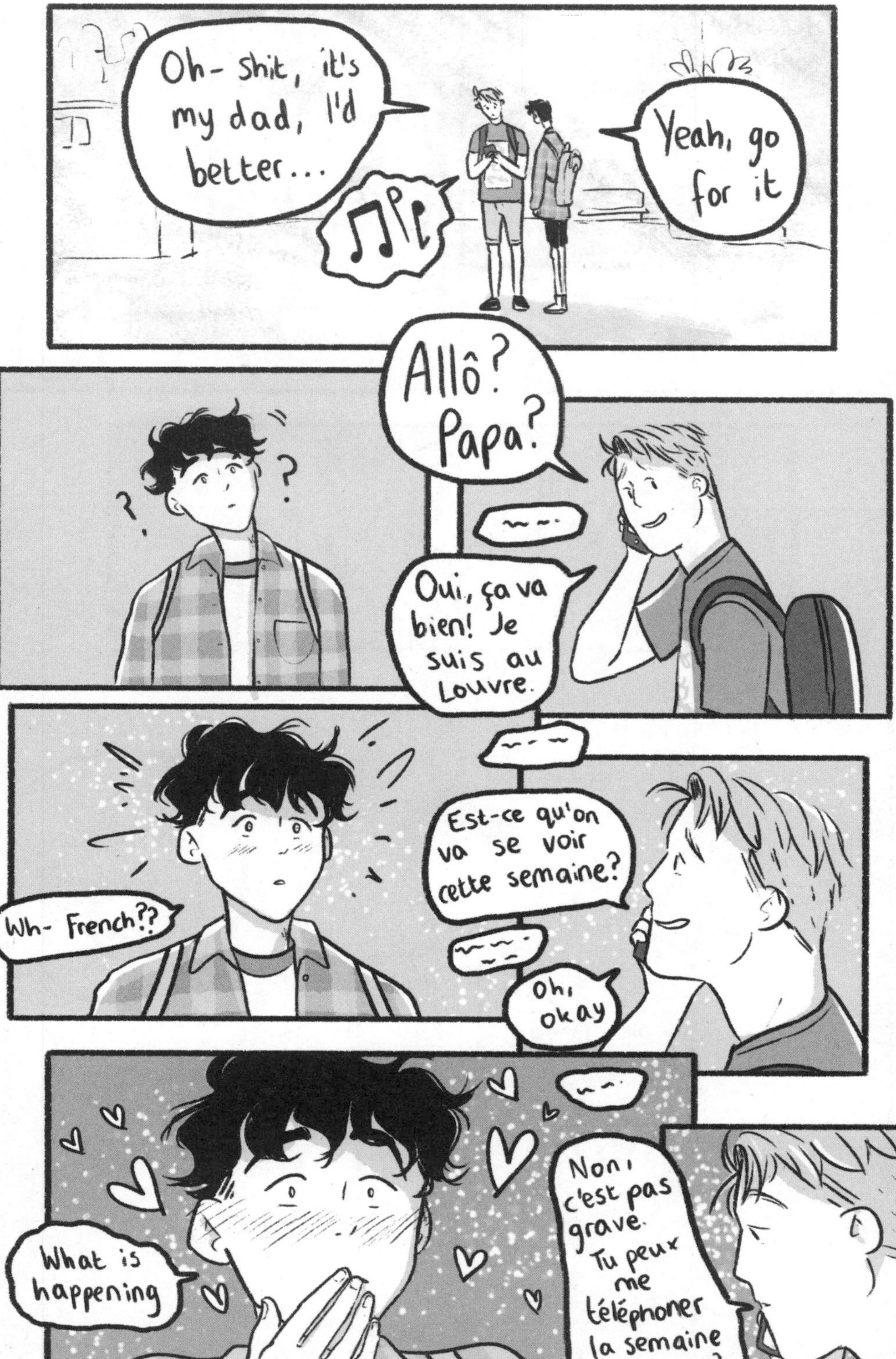
Oh- shit, it's my dad, I'd better...
Yeah, go for it
Allô? Papa?
~~.
Oui, ça va bien! Je suis au Louvre.
~~~
Est-ce qu'on va se voir cette semaine?
Wh- French??
~~~
Oh, okay
~~.
Non, c'est pas grave. Tu peux me téléphoner la semaine prochaine?
What is happening

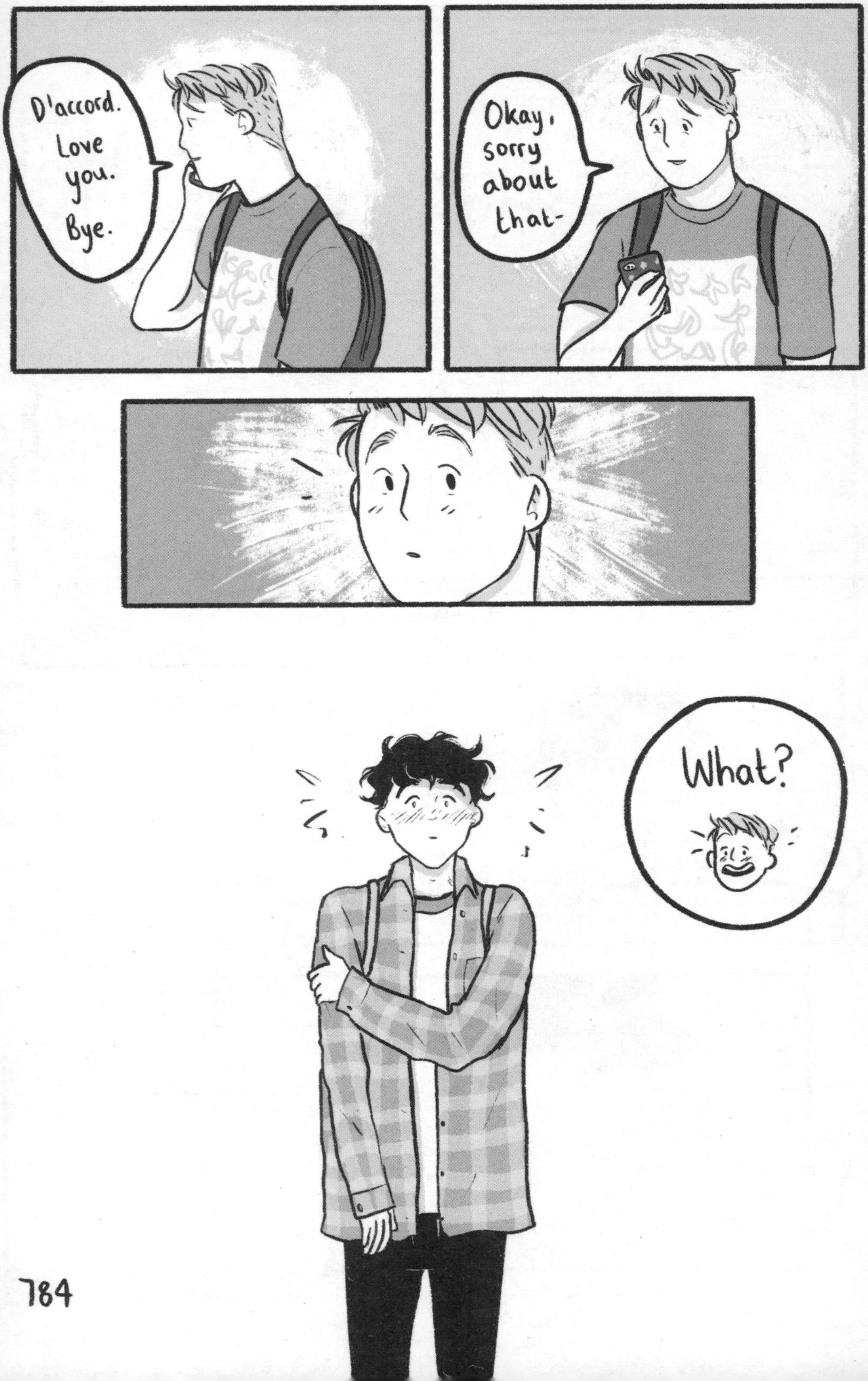
D'accord. Love you. Bye.
Okay, sorry about that-
What?

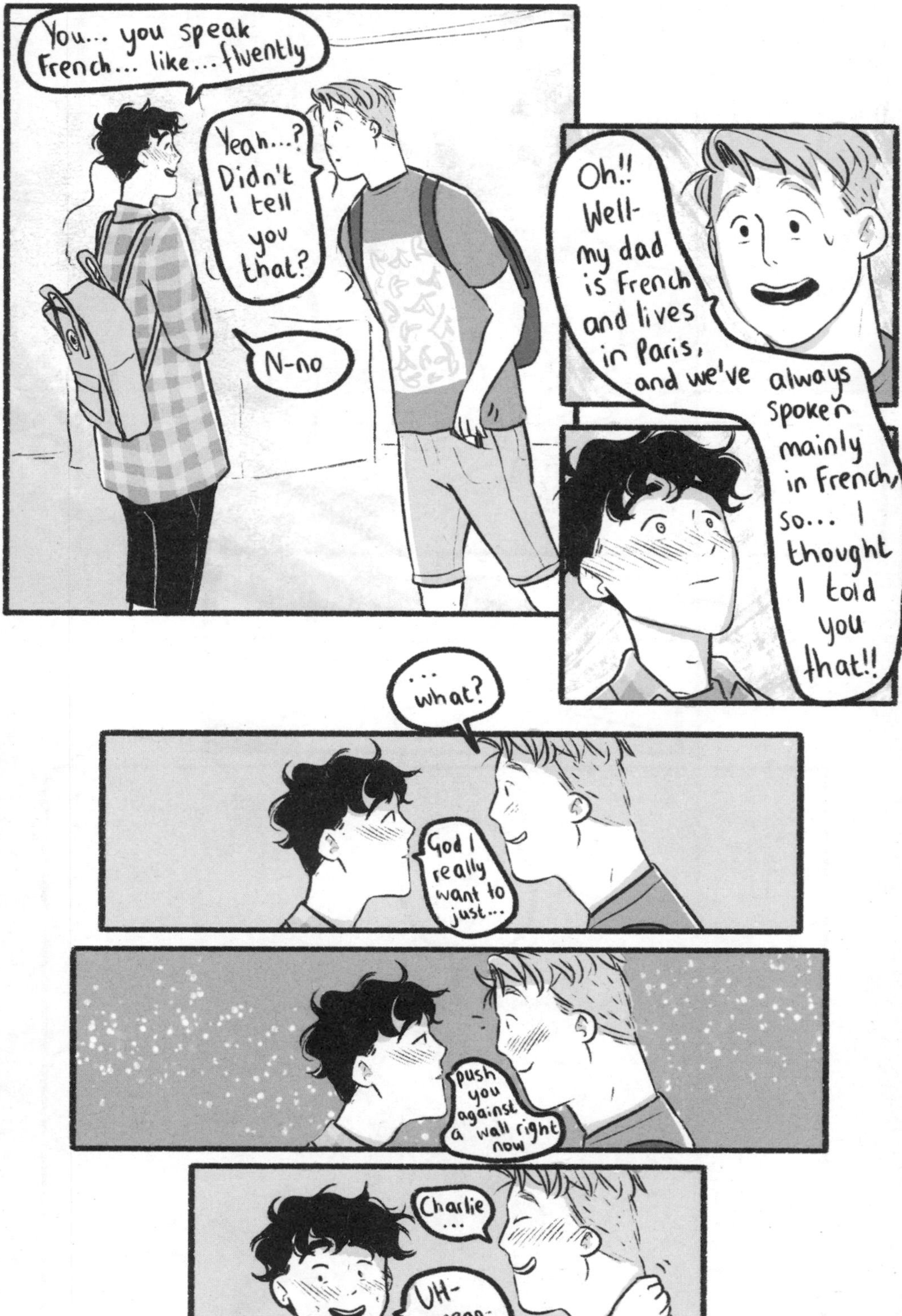
You... you speak French... like... fluently
Yeah...? Didn't I tell you that?
N-no
Oh!! Well- my dad is French and lives in Paris, and we've always spoken mainly in French, so... I thought I told you that!!
... what?
God I really want to just...
push you against a wall right now
Charlie ...
UH- I mean- nothing

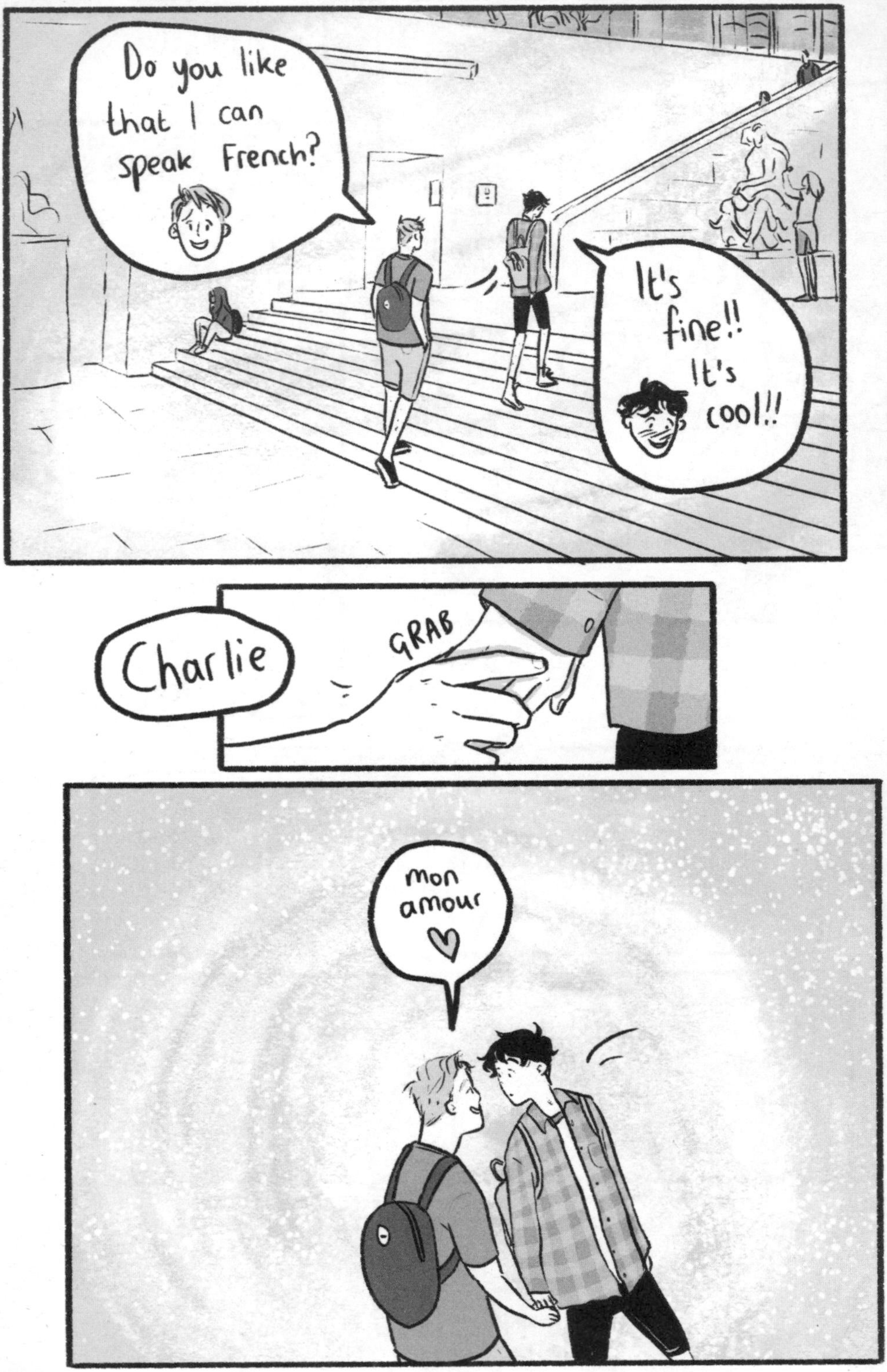
Do you like that I can speak French?
It's fine!! It's cool!!
Charlie
GRAB
mon amour

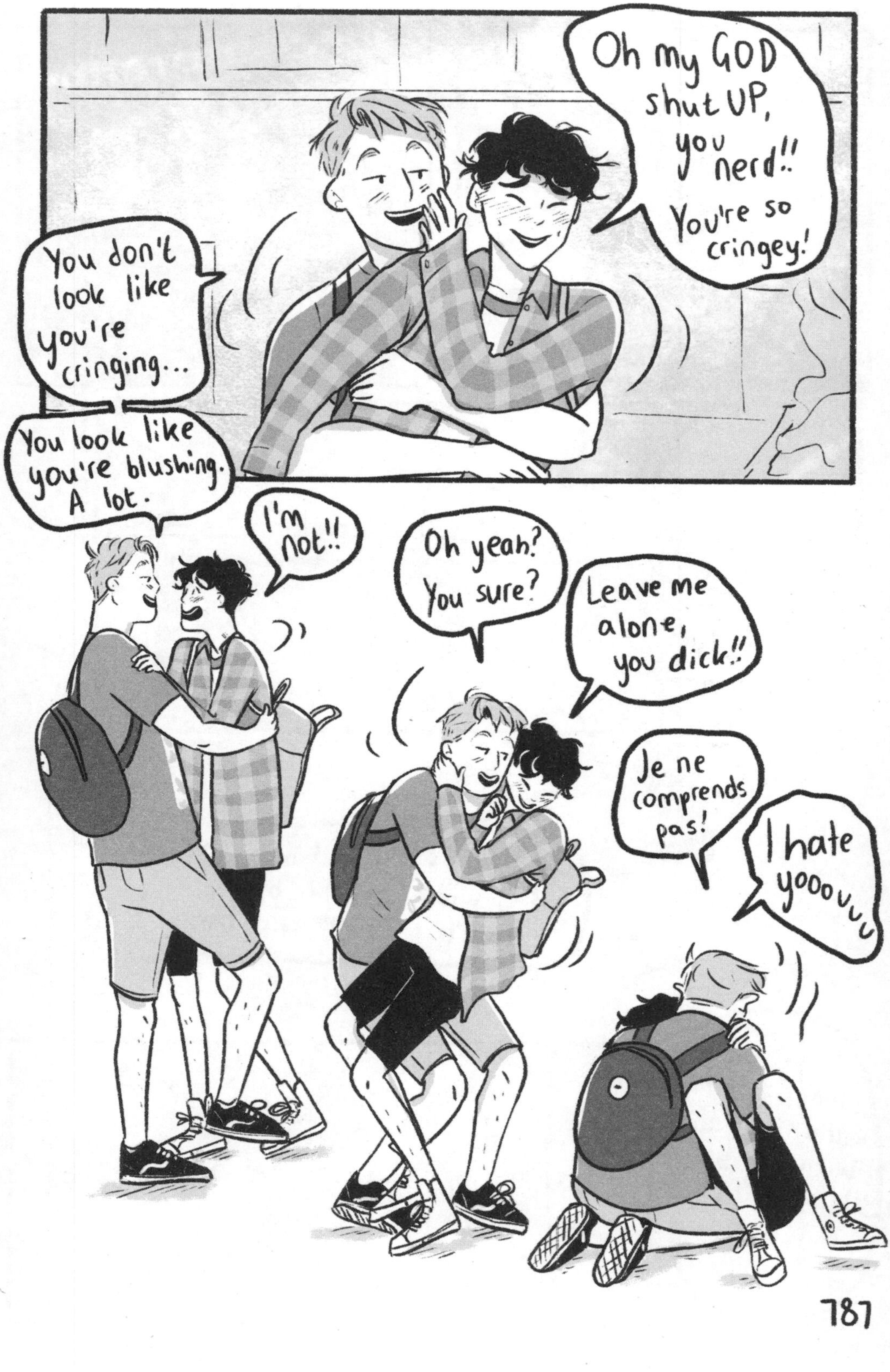
Oh my GOD shut UP, you nerd!! You're so cringey!
You don't look like you're cringing...
You look like you're blushing. A lot.
I'm not!!
Oh yeah? You sure?
Leave me alone, you dick!!
Je ne comprends pas!
I hate yooouuu

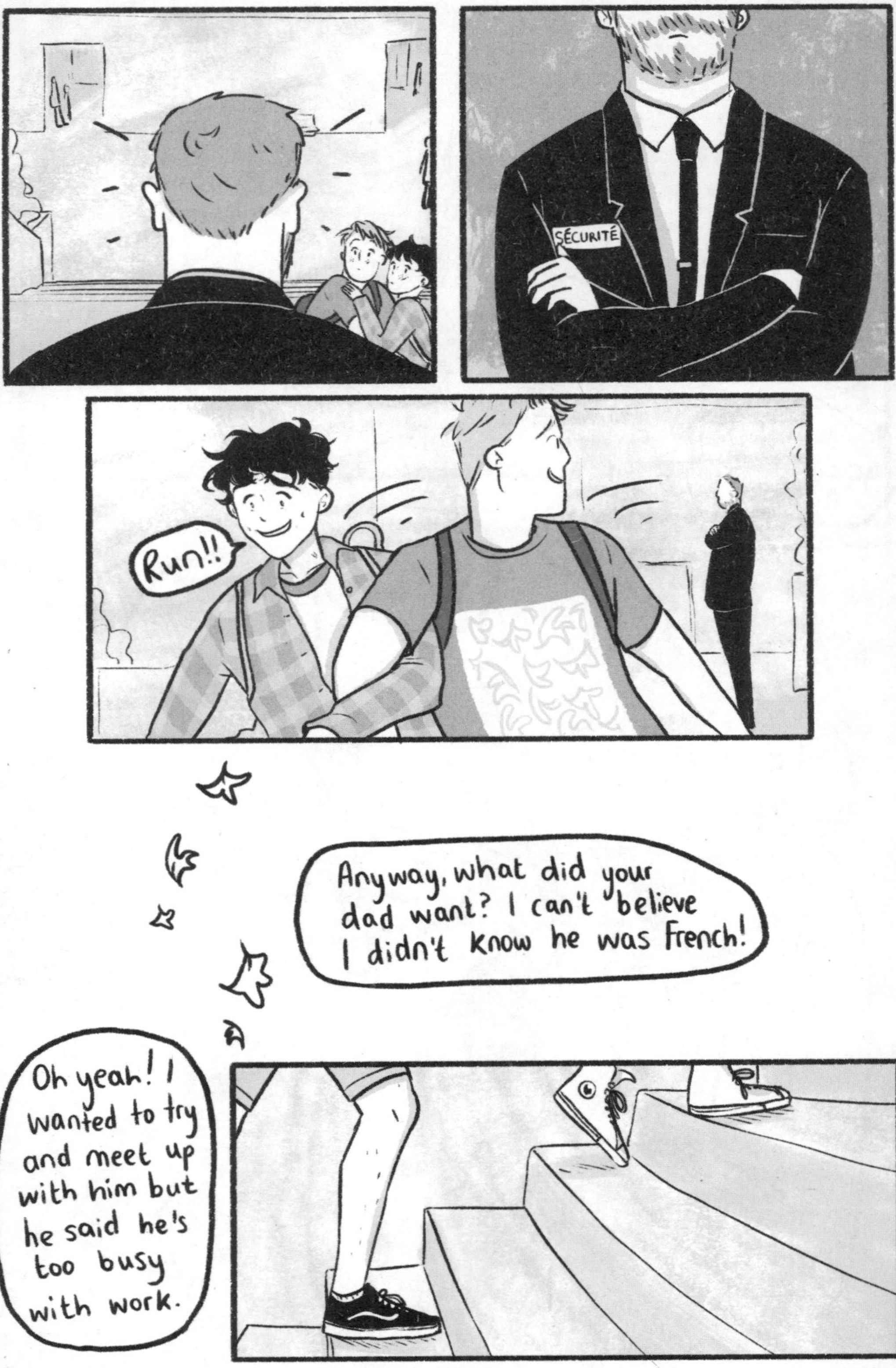
SÉCURITÉ
Run!!
Anyway, what did your dad want? I can't believe I didn't know he was French!
Oh yeah! I wanted to try and meet up with him but he said he's too busy with work.

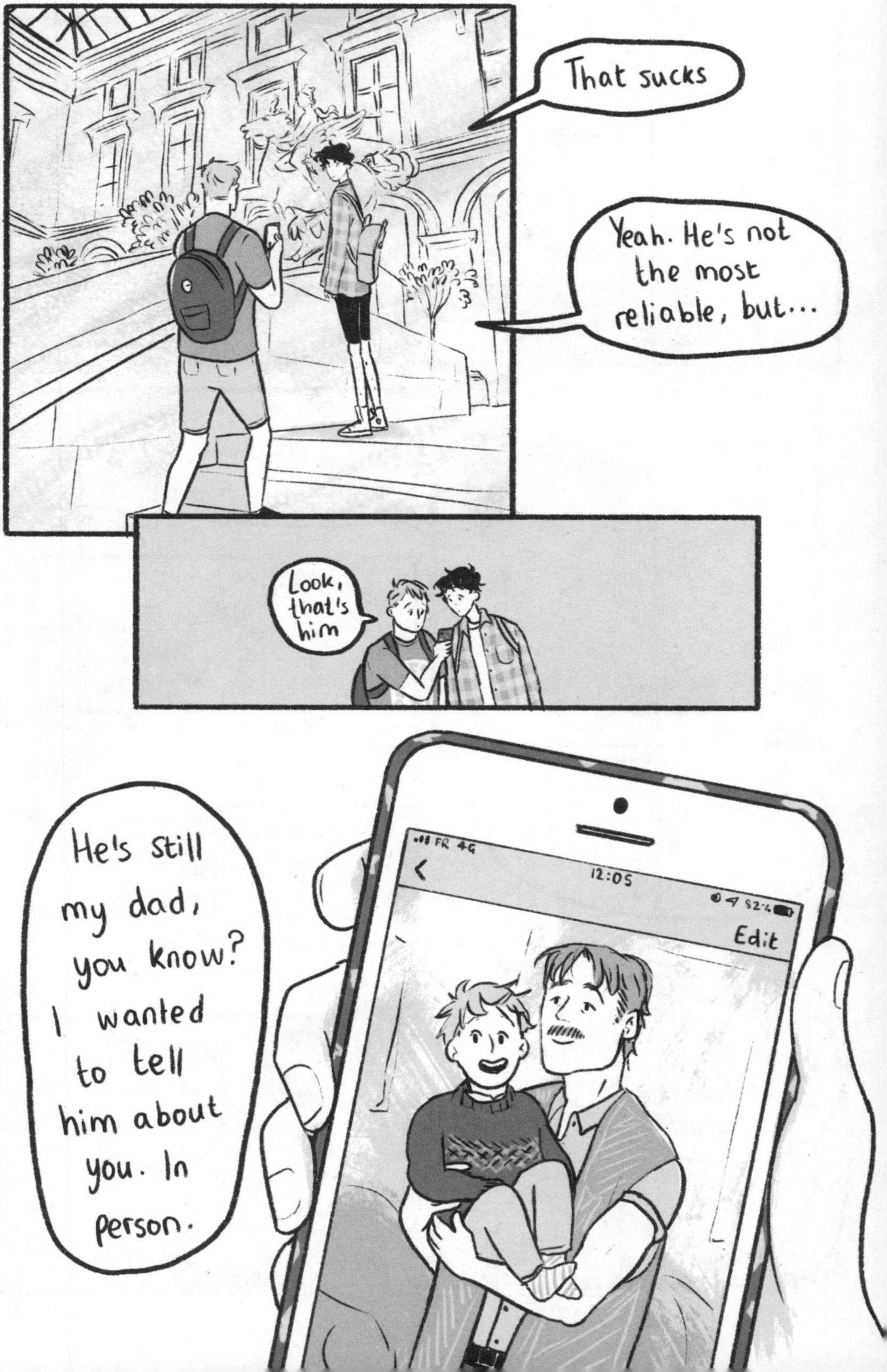
That sucks
Yeah. He's not the most reliable, but...
Look, that's him
12:05
Edit
He's still my dad, you know? I wanted to tell him about you. In person.

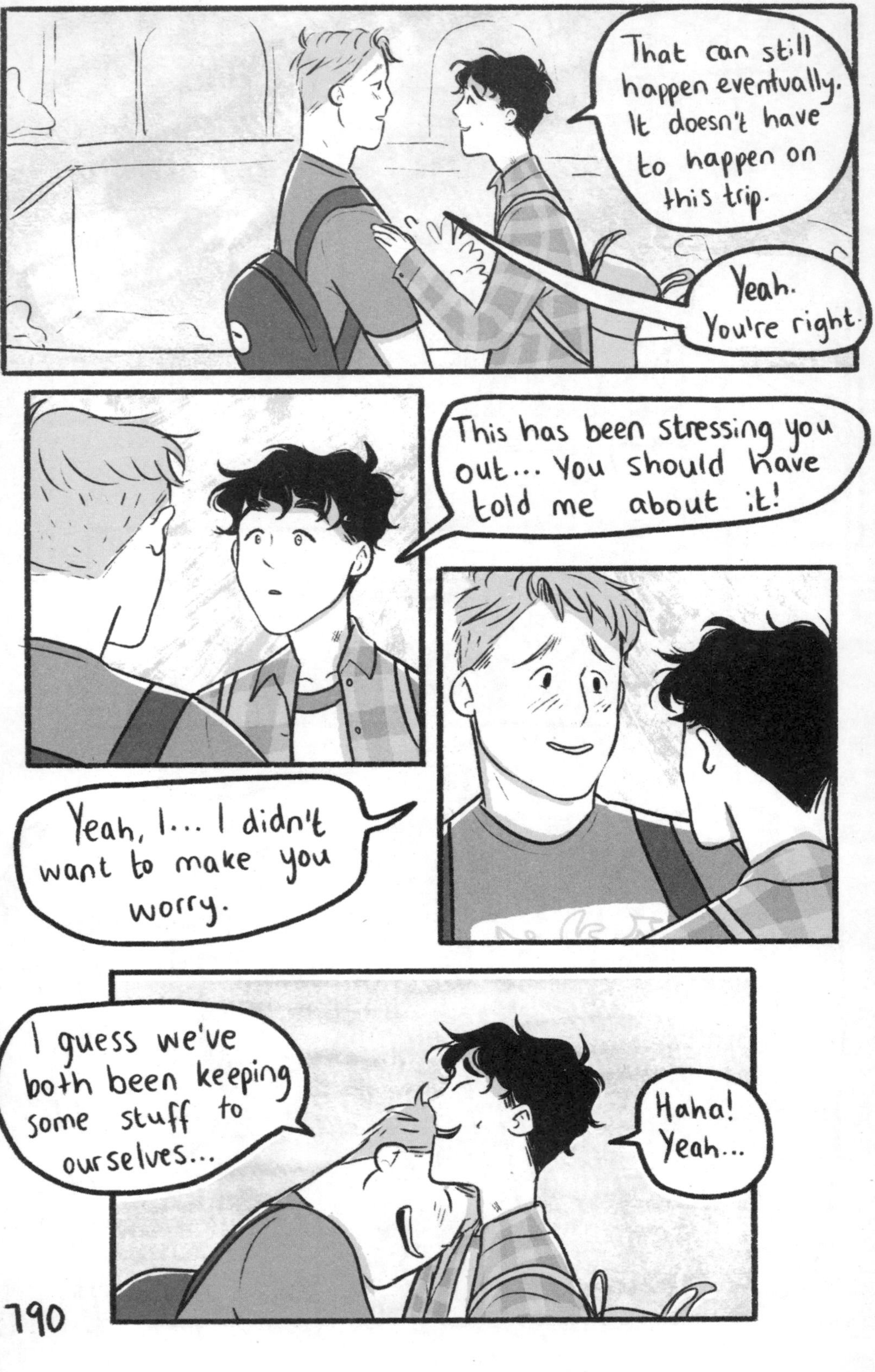
That can still happen eventually. It doesn't have to happen on this trip.
Yeah. You're right.
This has been stressing you out... You should have told me about it!
Yeah, I... I didn't want to make you worry.
I guess we've both been keeping some stuff to ourselves...
Haha! Yeah...

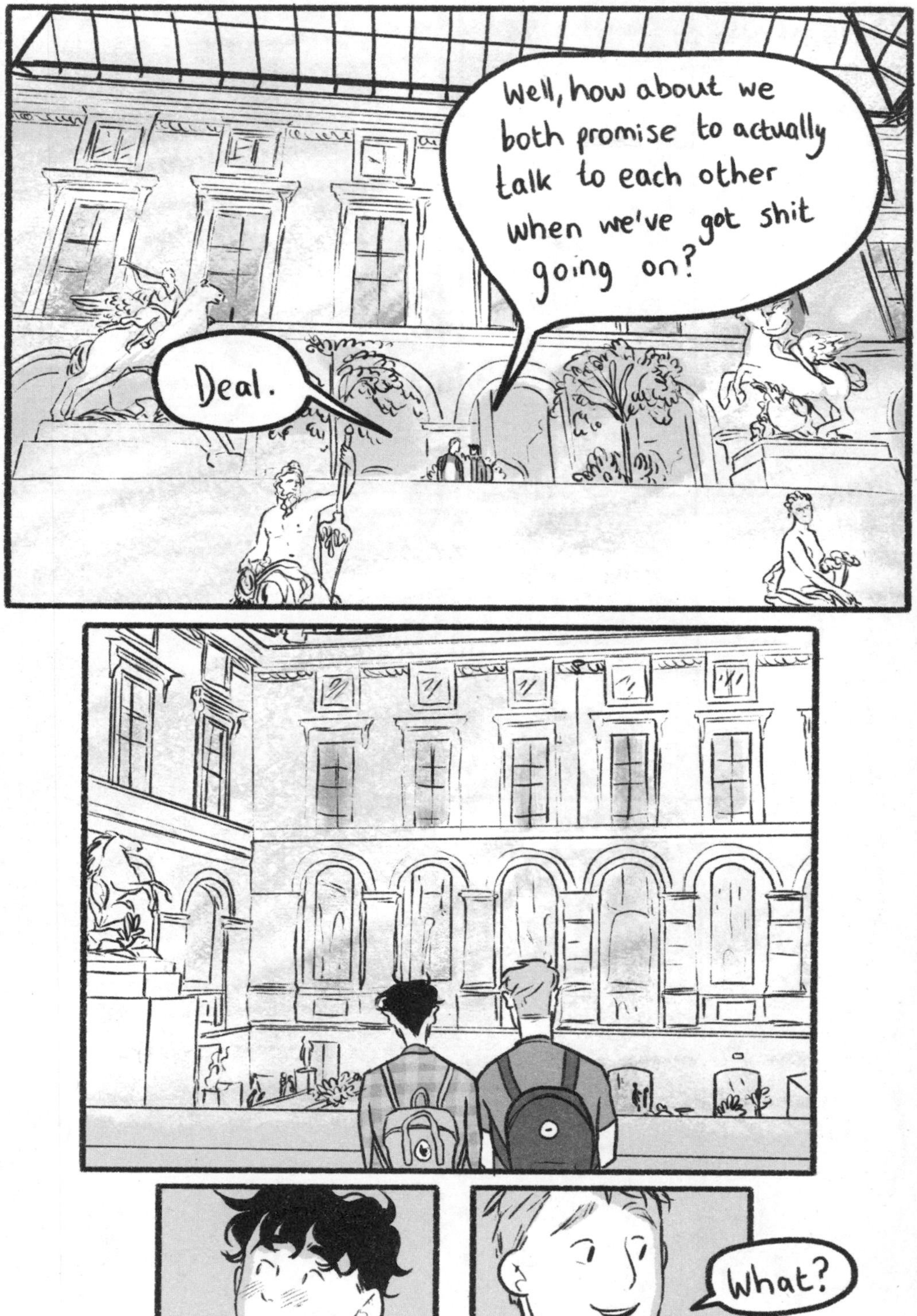
Well, how about we both promise to actually talk to each other when we've got shit going on?
Deal.
What?

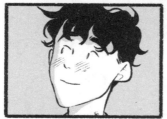

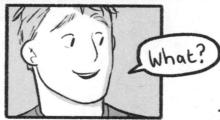

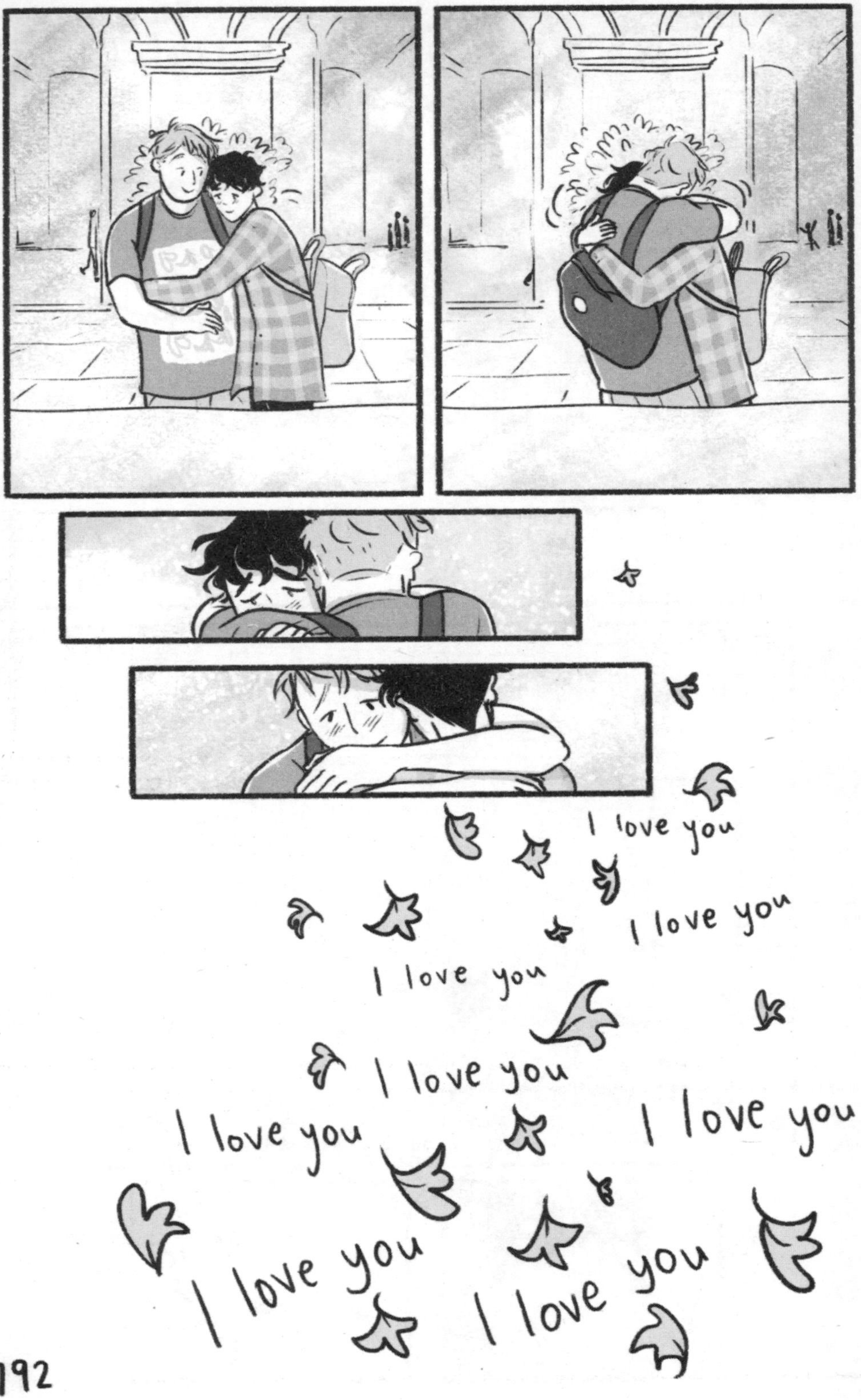
I love you
I love you
I love you
I love you
I love you
I love you
I love you
I love you

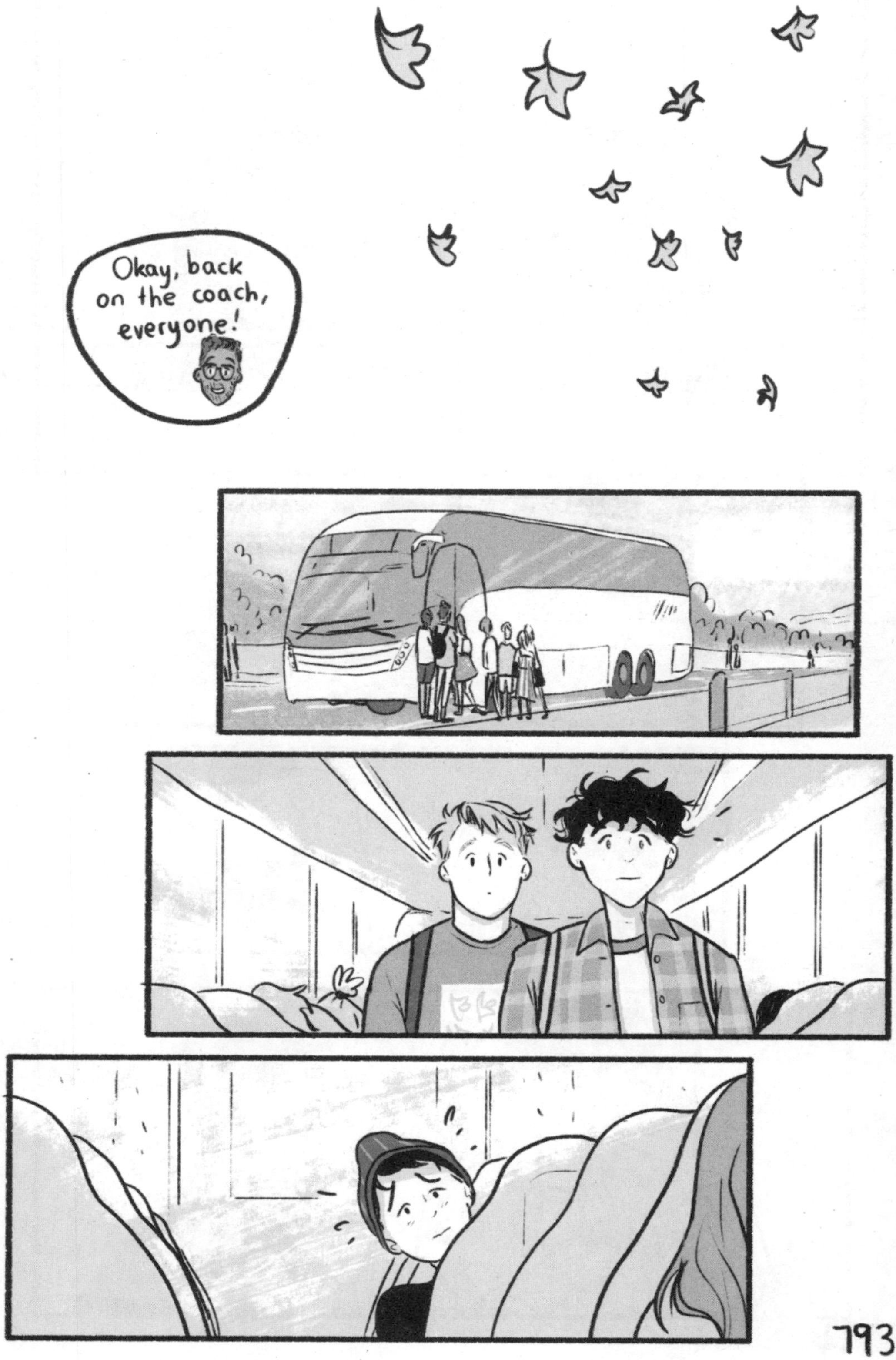
Okay, back on the coach, everyone!

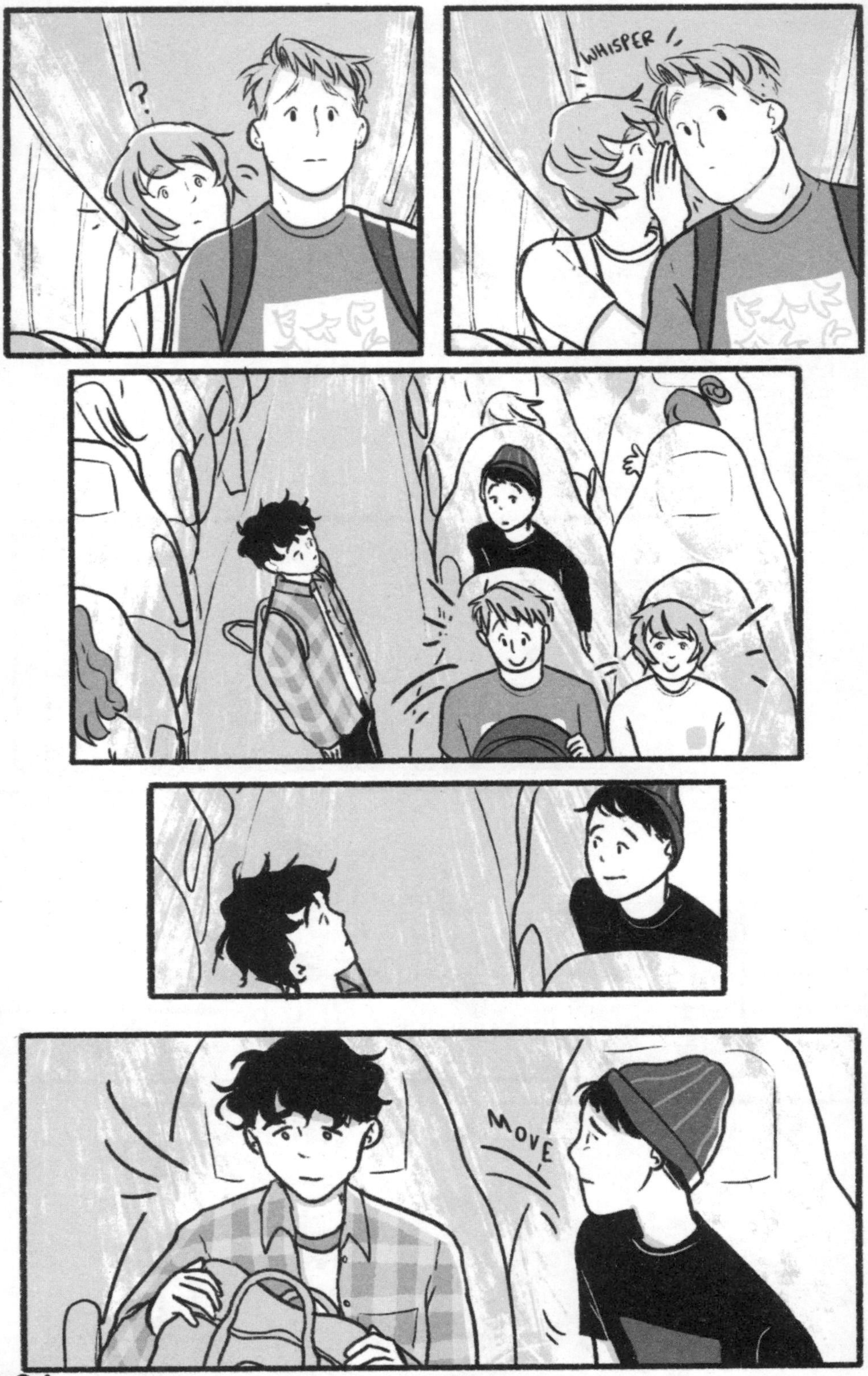
?
WHISPER
MOVE

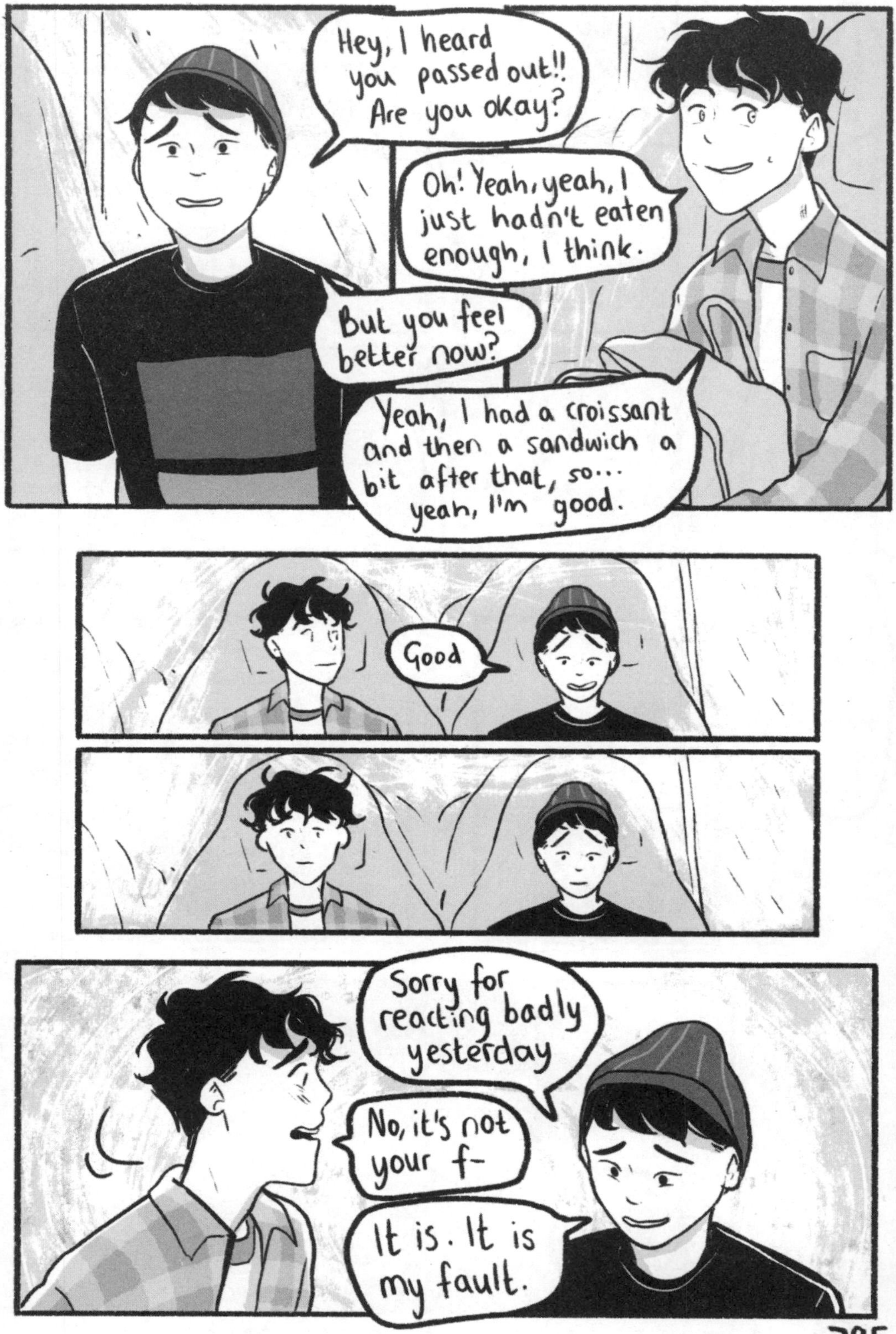
Hey, I heard you passed out!! Are you okay?
Oh! Yeah, yeah, I just hadn't eaten enough, I think.
But you feel better now?
Yeah, I had a croissant and then a sandwich a bit after that, so... yeah, I'm good.
Good
Sorry for reacting badly yesterday
No, it's not your f-
It is. It is my fault.

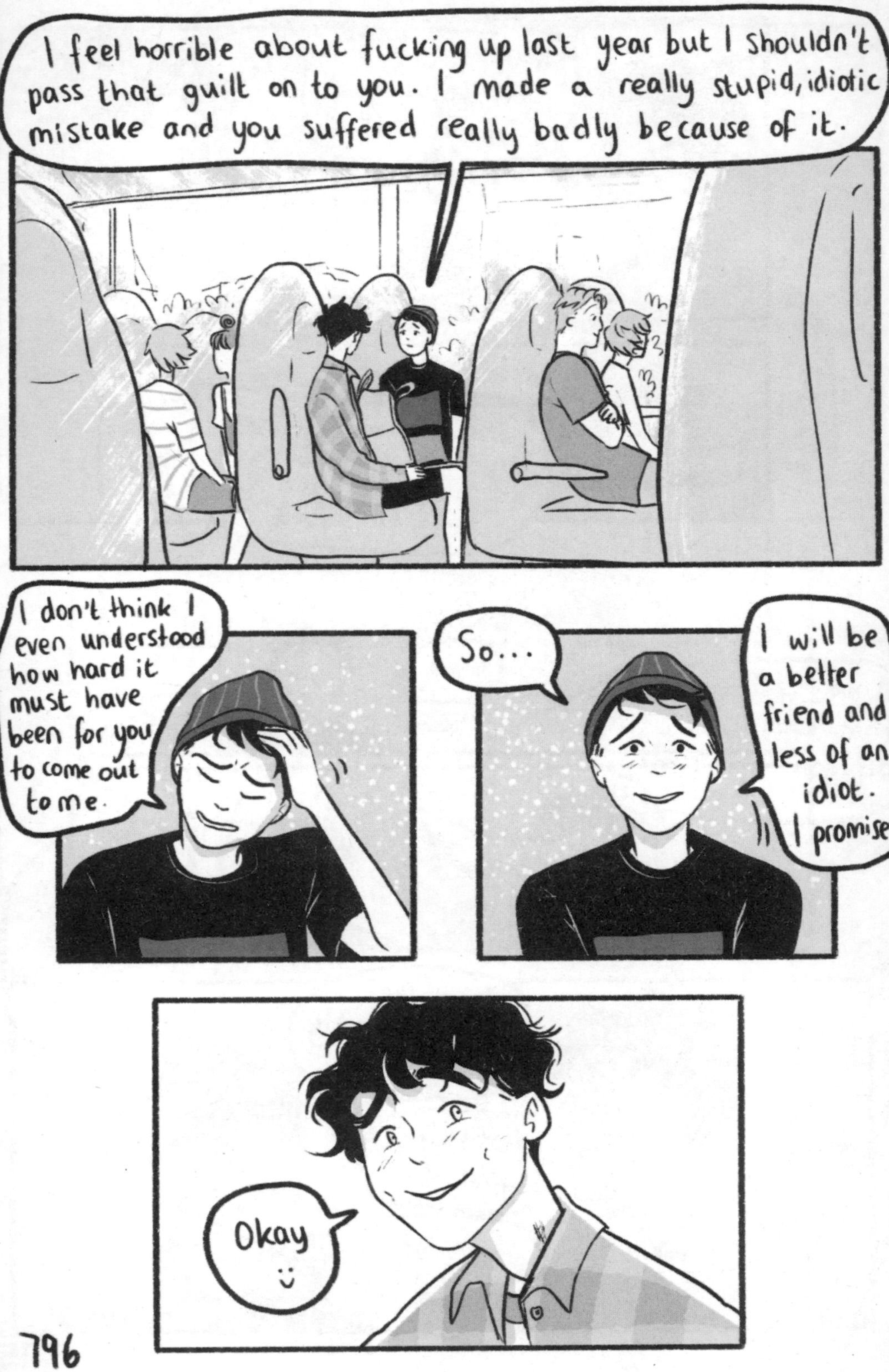
I feel horrible about fucking up last year but I shouldn't pass that guilt on to you. I made a really stupid, idiotic mistake and you suffered really badly because of it.
I don't think I even understood how hard it must have been for you to come out to me.
So...
I will be a better friend and less of an idiot. I promise.
Okay
:)

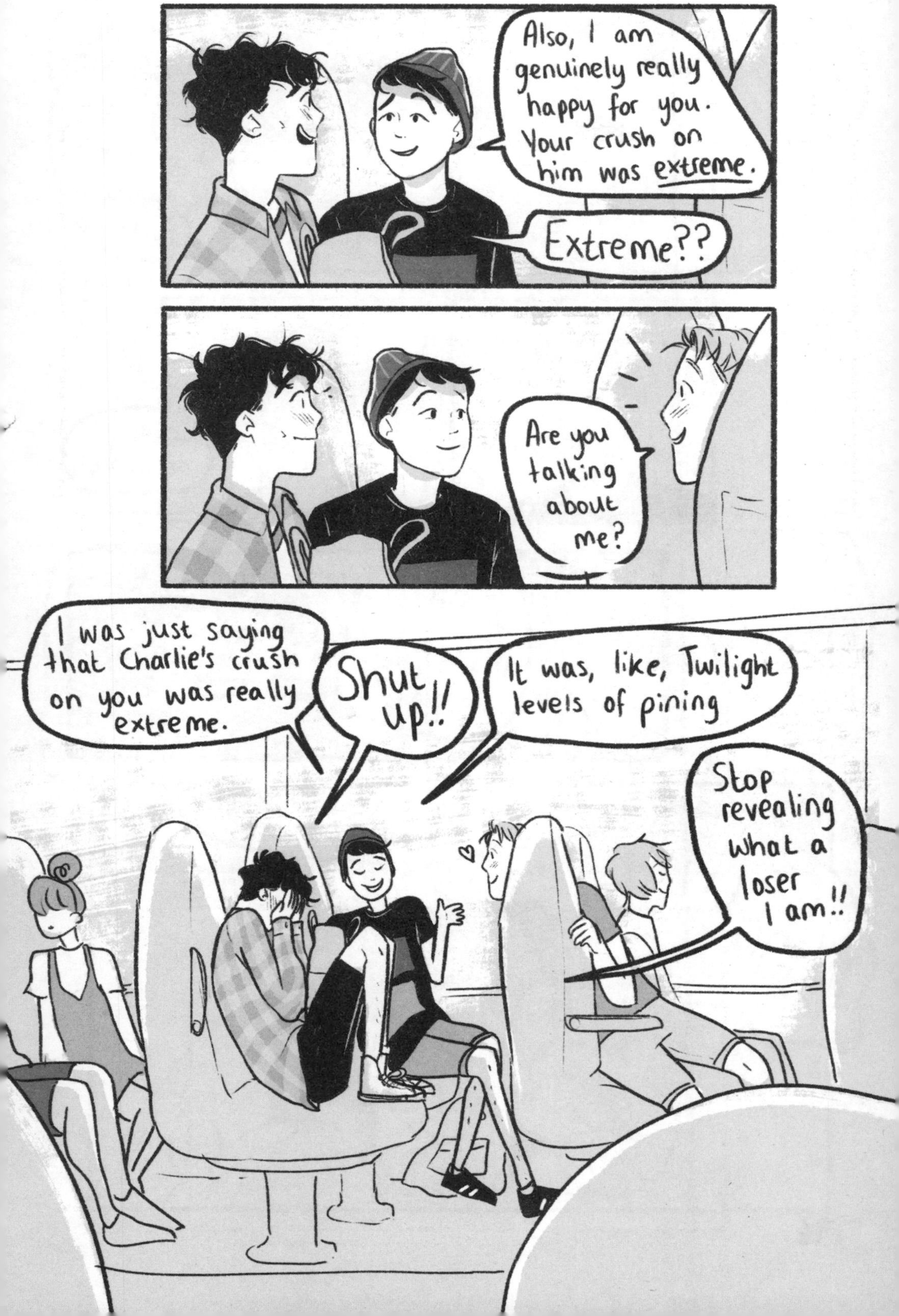
Also, I am genuinely really happy for you. Your crush on him was extreme.
Extreme??
Are you talking about me?
I was just saying that Charlie's crush on you was really extreme.
Shut up!!
It was, like, Twilight levels of pining
Stop revealing what a loser I am!!

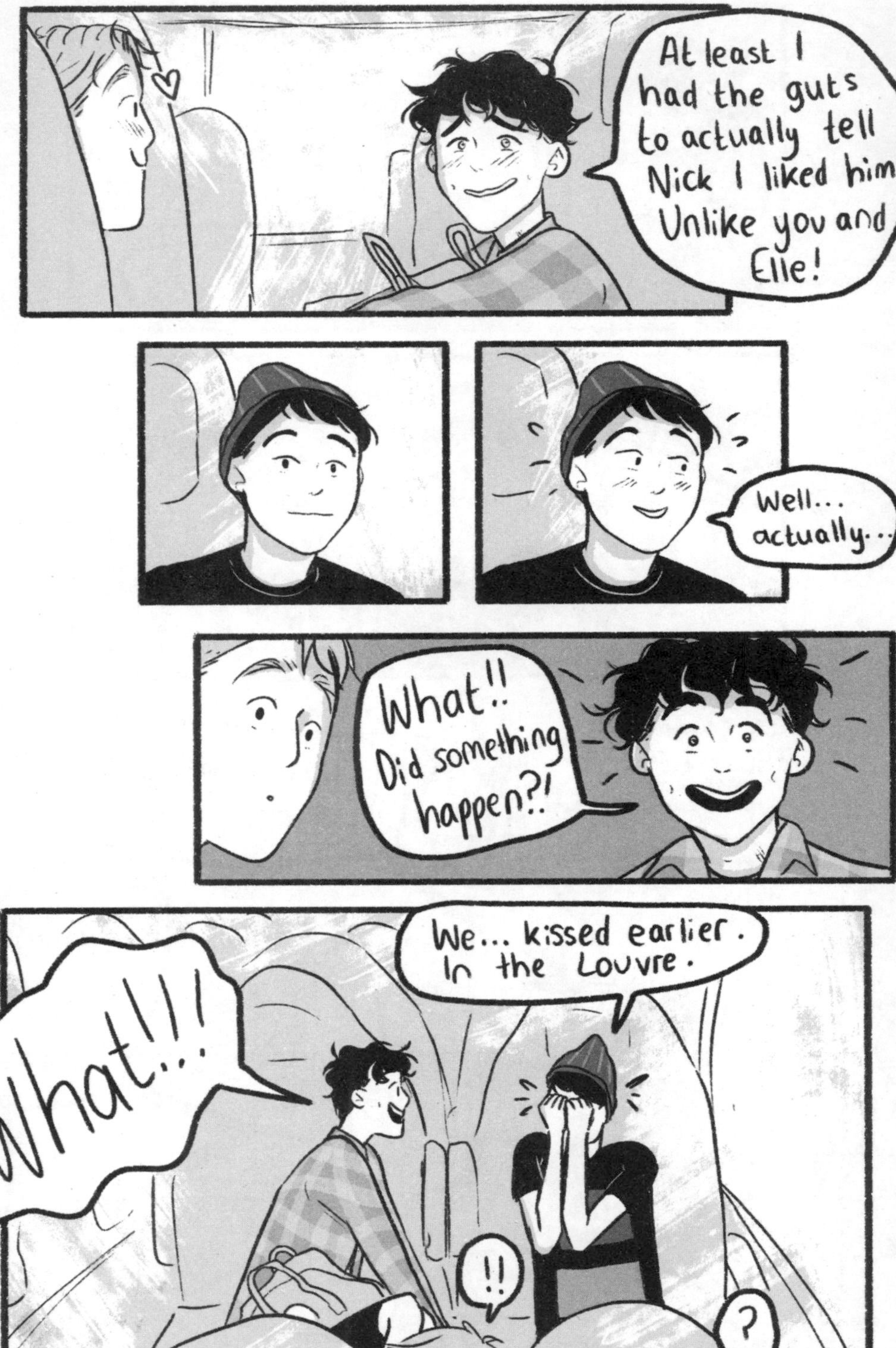
At least I had the guts to actually tell Nick I liked him! Unlike you and Elle!
Well... actually...
What!! Did something happen?!
We... kissed earlier. In the Louvre.
What!!!
!!
?

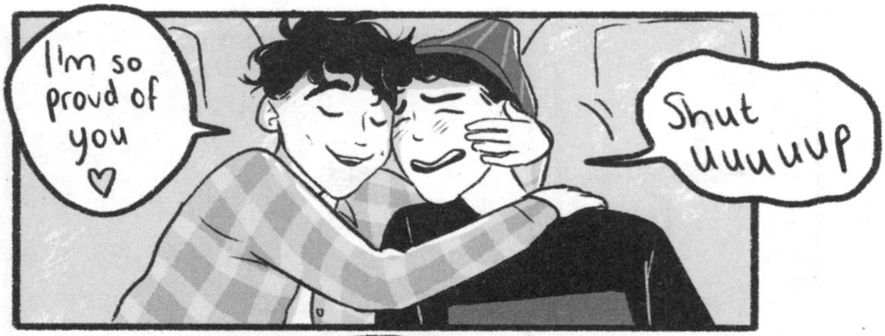
I'm so proud of you ♡
Shut uuuuup

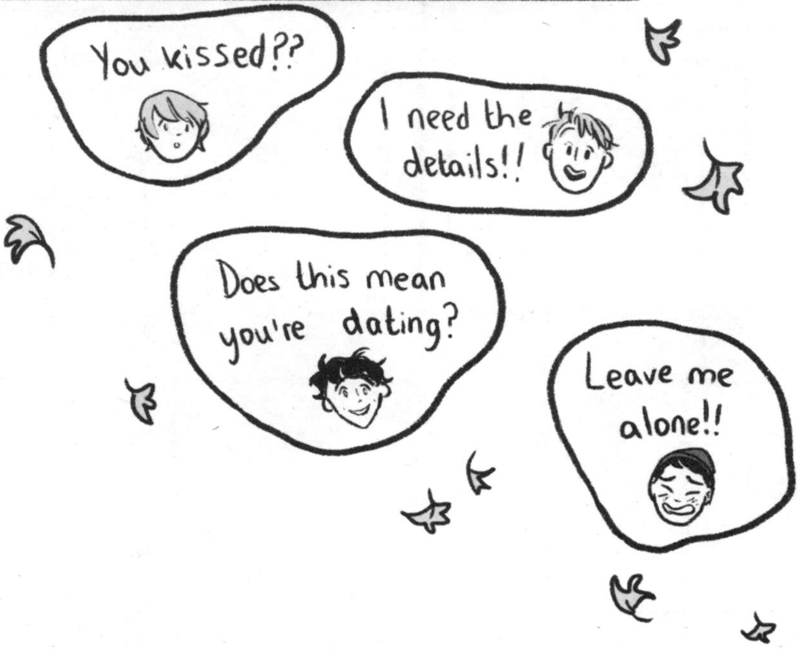
You kissed??
I need the details!!
Does this mean you're dating?
Leave me alone!!

Paris – Day 5

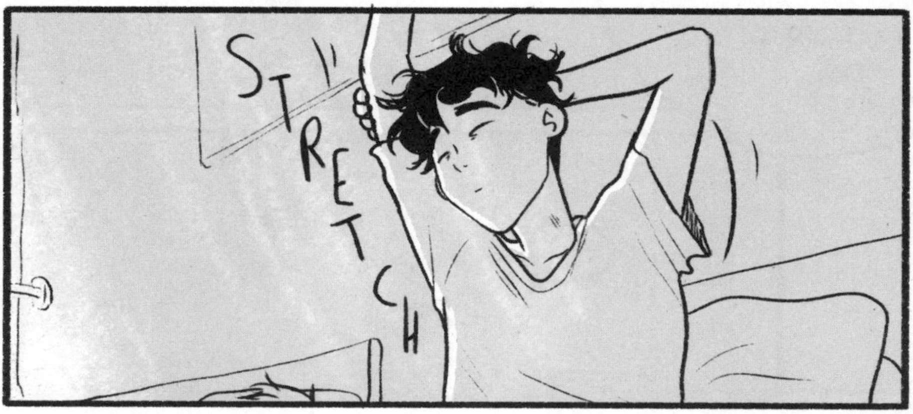
STRETCH

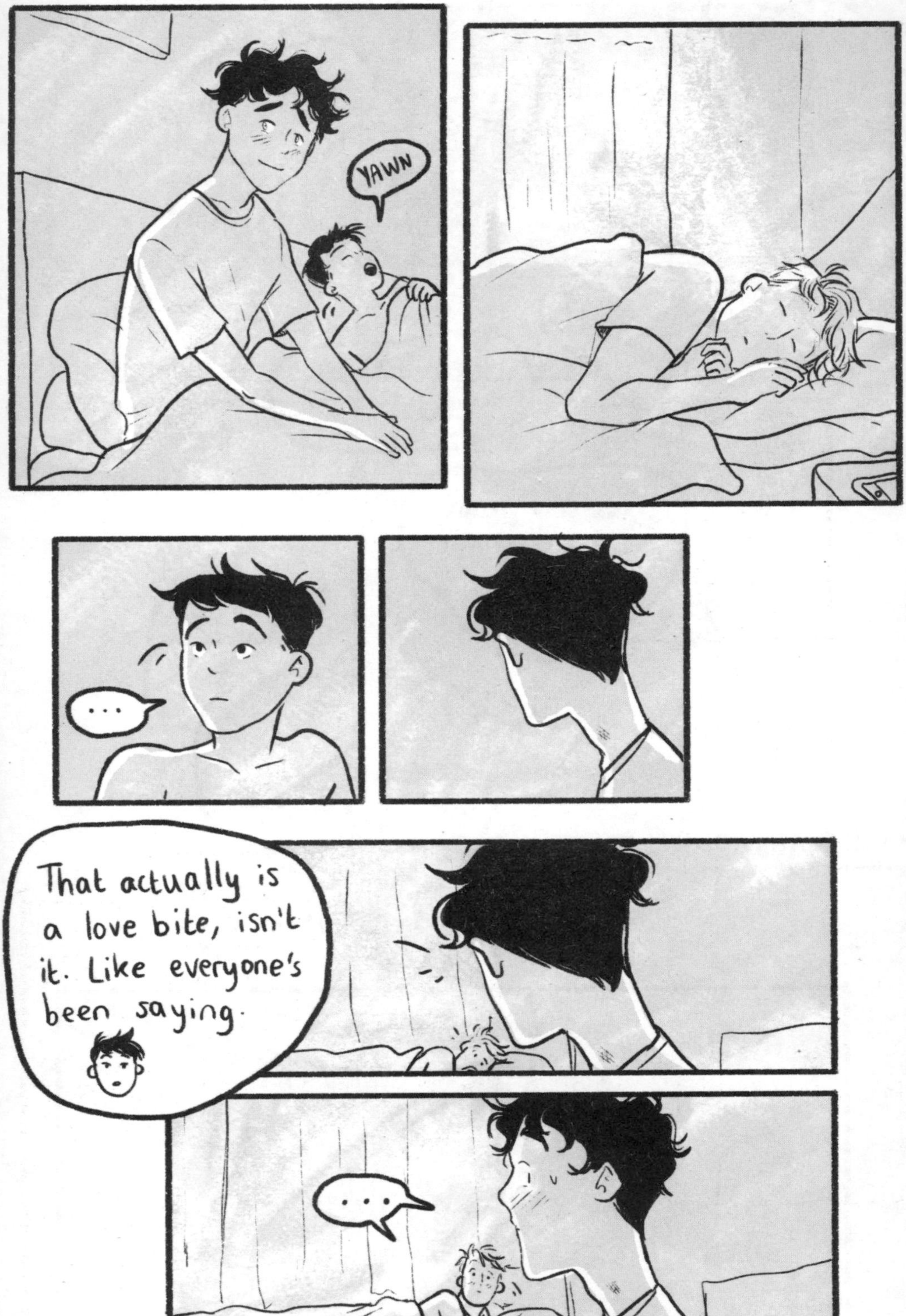
YAWN
...
That actually is a love bite, isn't it. Like everyone's been saying.
...

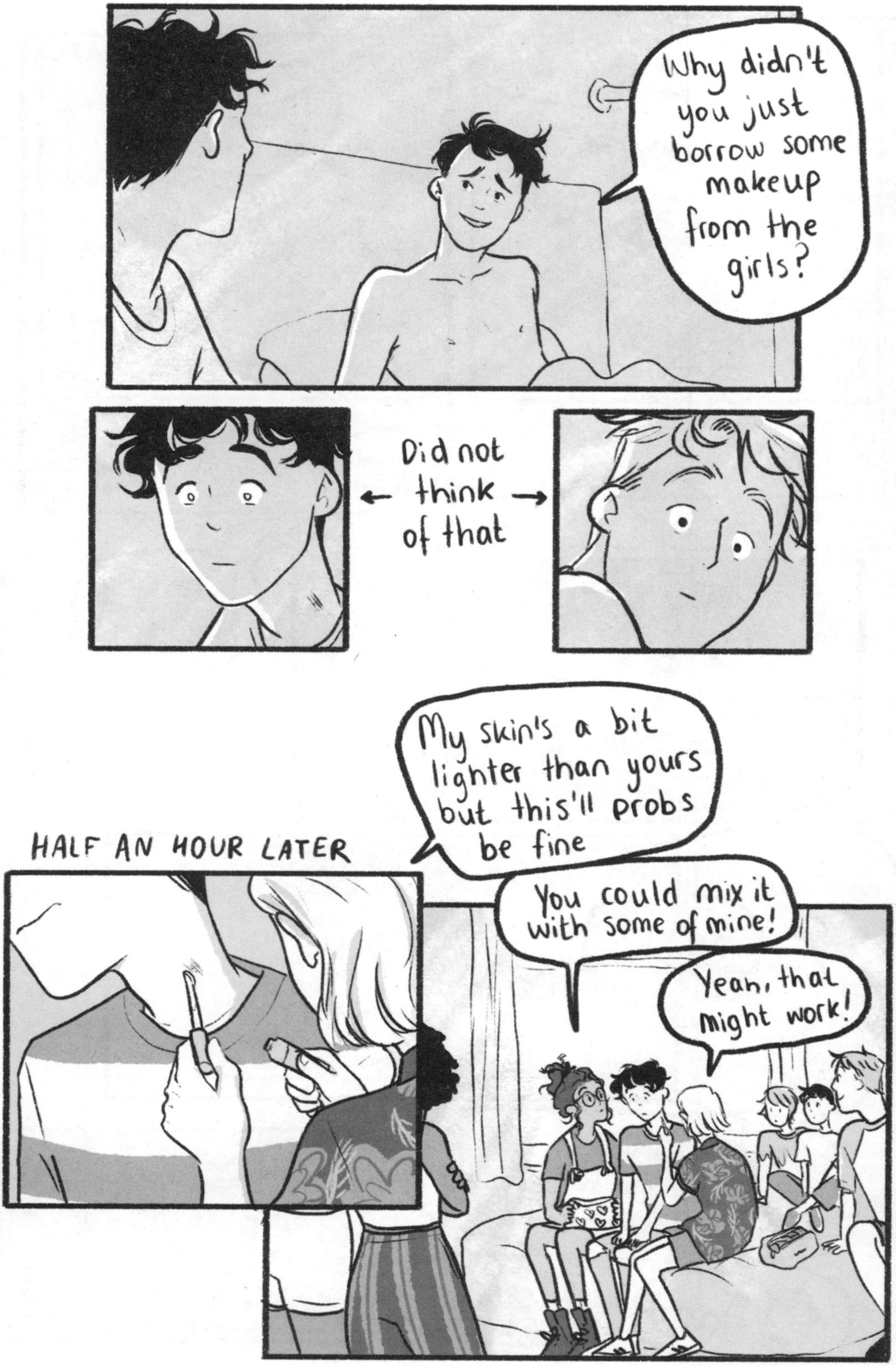

Why didn't you just borrow some makeup from the girls?
Did not think of that
HALF AN HOUR LATER
My skin's a bit lighter than yours but this'll probs be fine
You could mix it with some of mine!
Yeah, that might work!

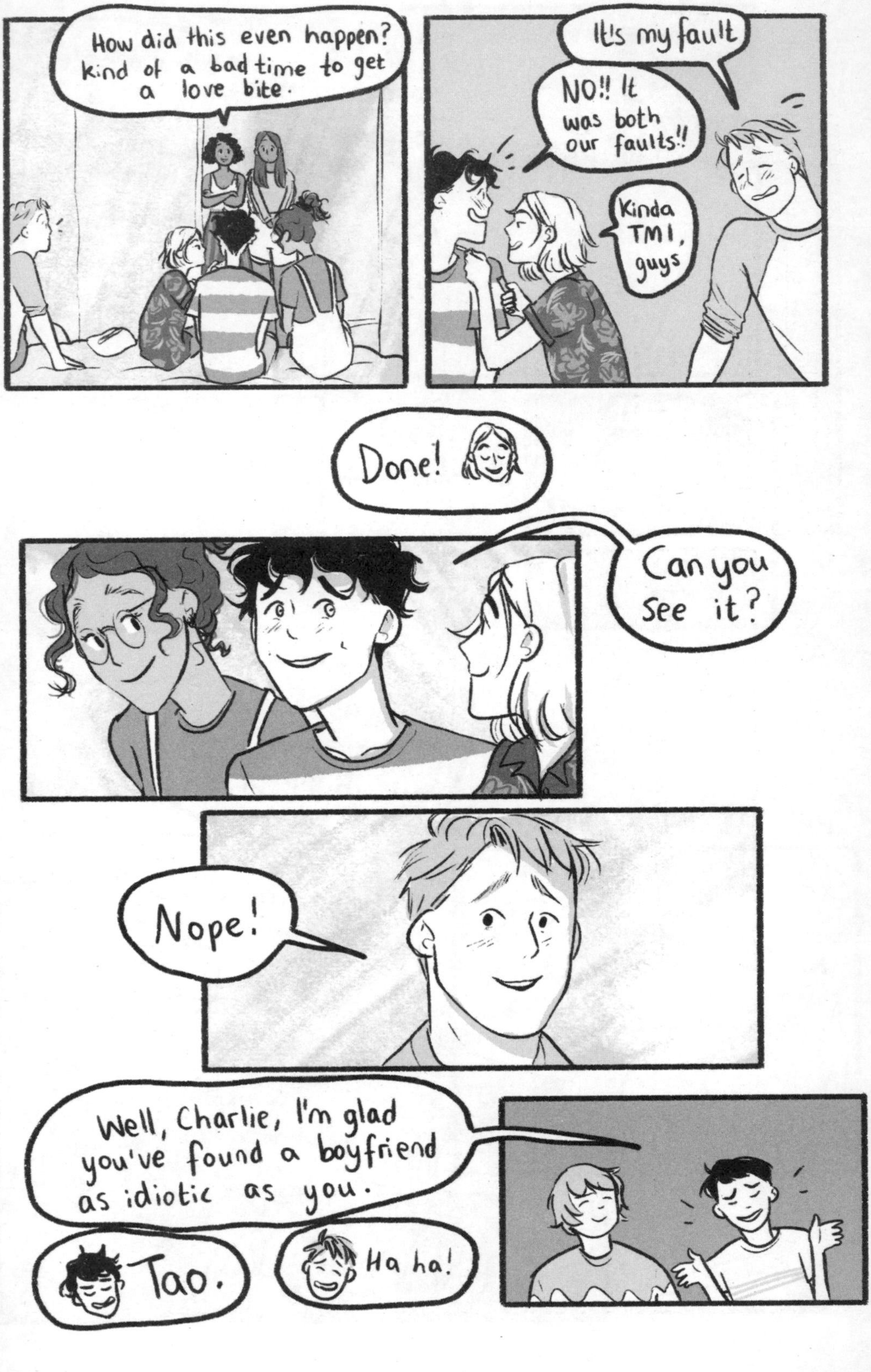
How did this even happen? kind of a bad time to get a love bite.
It's my fault
NO!! It was both our faults!!
Kinda TMI, guys
Done!
Can you see it?
Nope!
Well, Charlie, I'm glad you've found a boyfriend as idiotic as you.
Tao.
Ha ha!

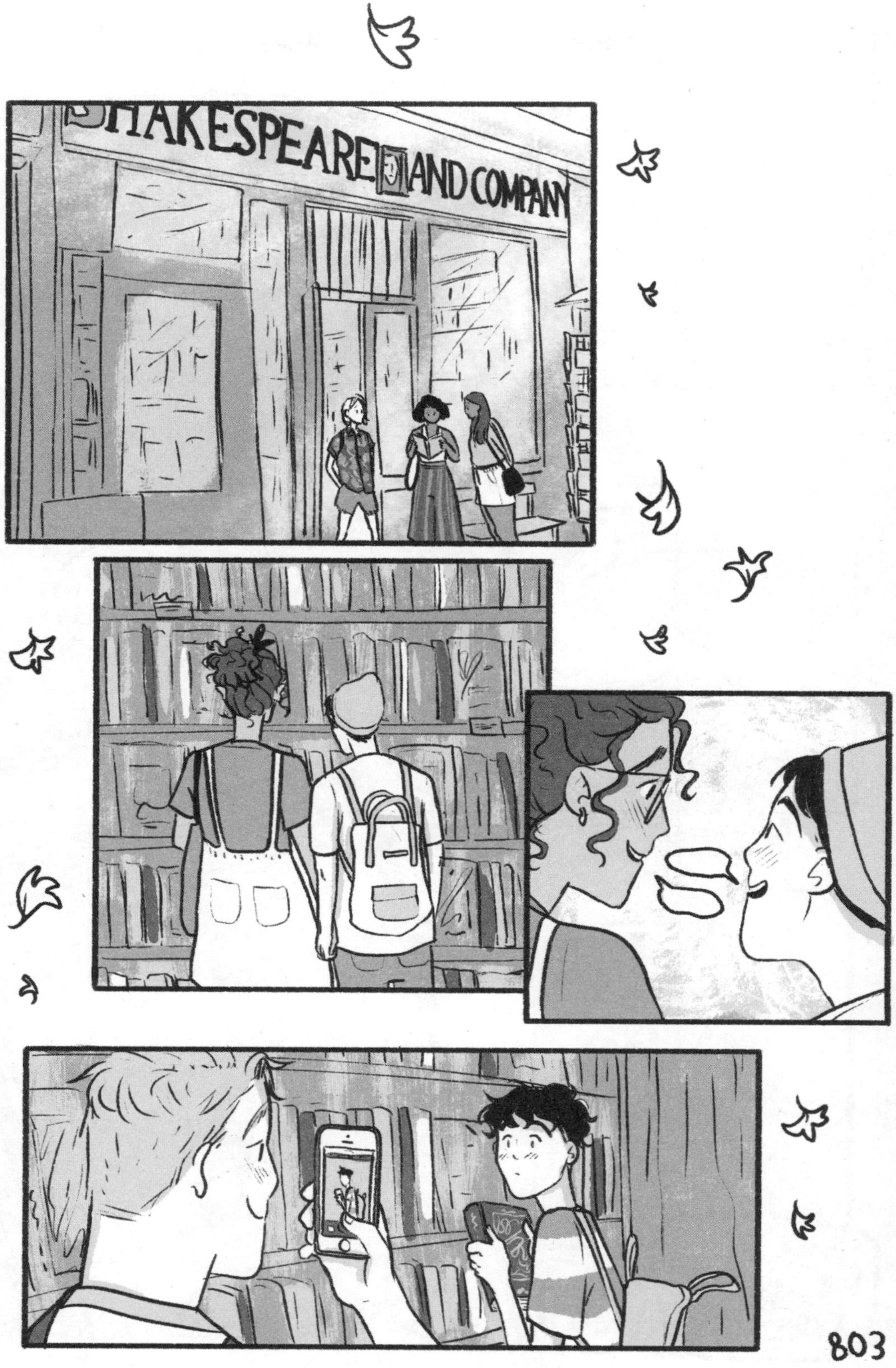
SHAKESPEARE AND COMPANY

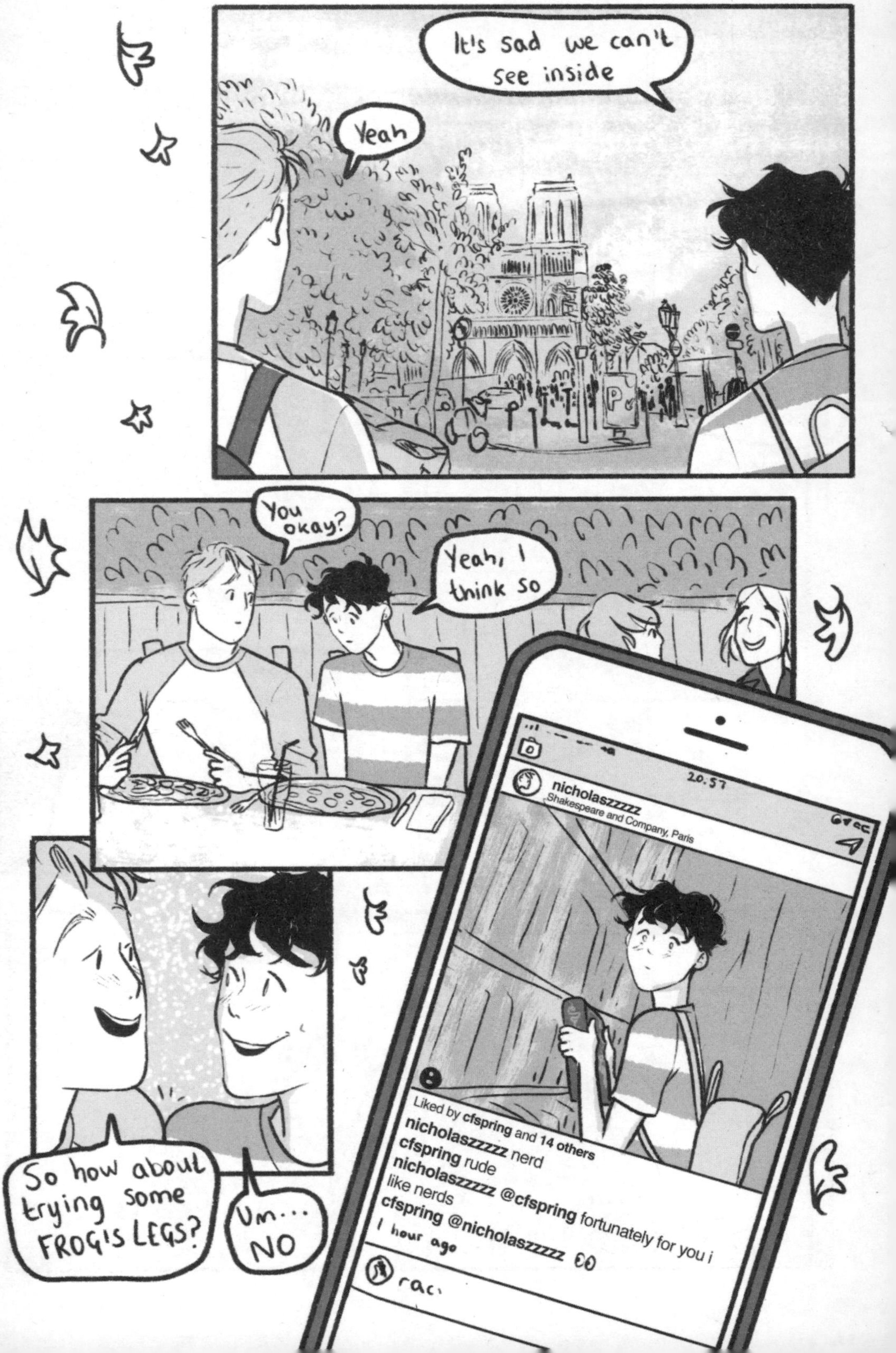
It's sad we can't see inside
Yeah
You okay?
Yeah, I think so
nicholaszzzzz
Shakespeare and Company, Paris
Liked by cfspring and 14 others
nicholaszzzzz nerd
cfspring rude
nicholaszzzzz @cfspring fortunately for you i like nerds
cfspring @nicholaszzzzz
1 hour ago
So how about trying some FROG'S LEGS?
Um... NO

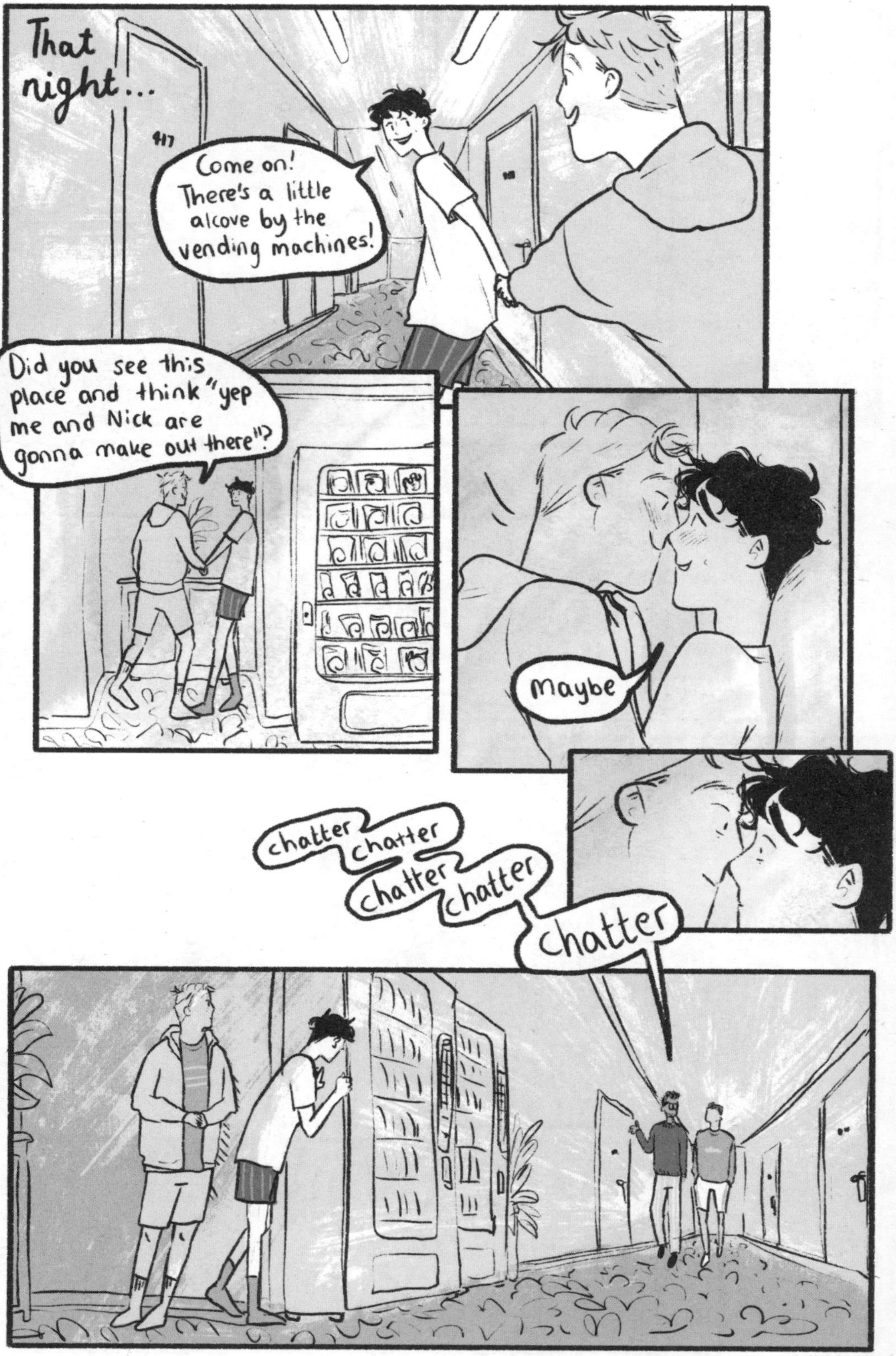
That night...
417
Come on! There's a little alcove by the vending machines!
Did you see this place and think "yep me and Nick are gonna make out there"?
Maybe
chatter chatter
chatter chatter
chatter

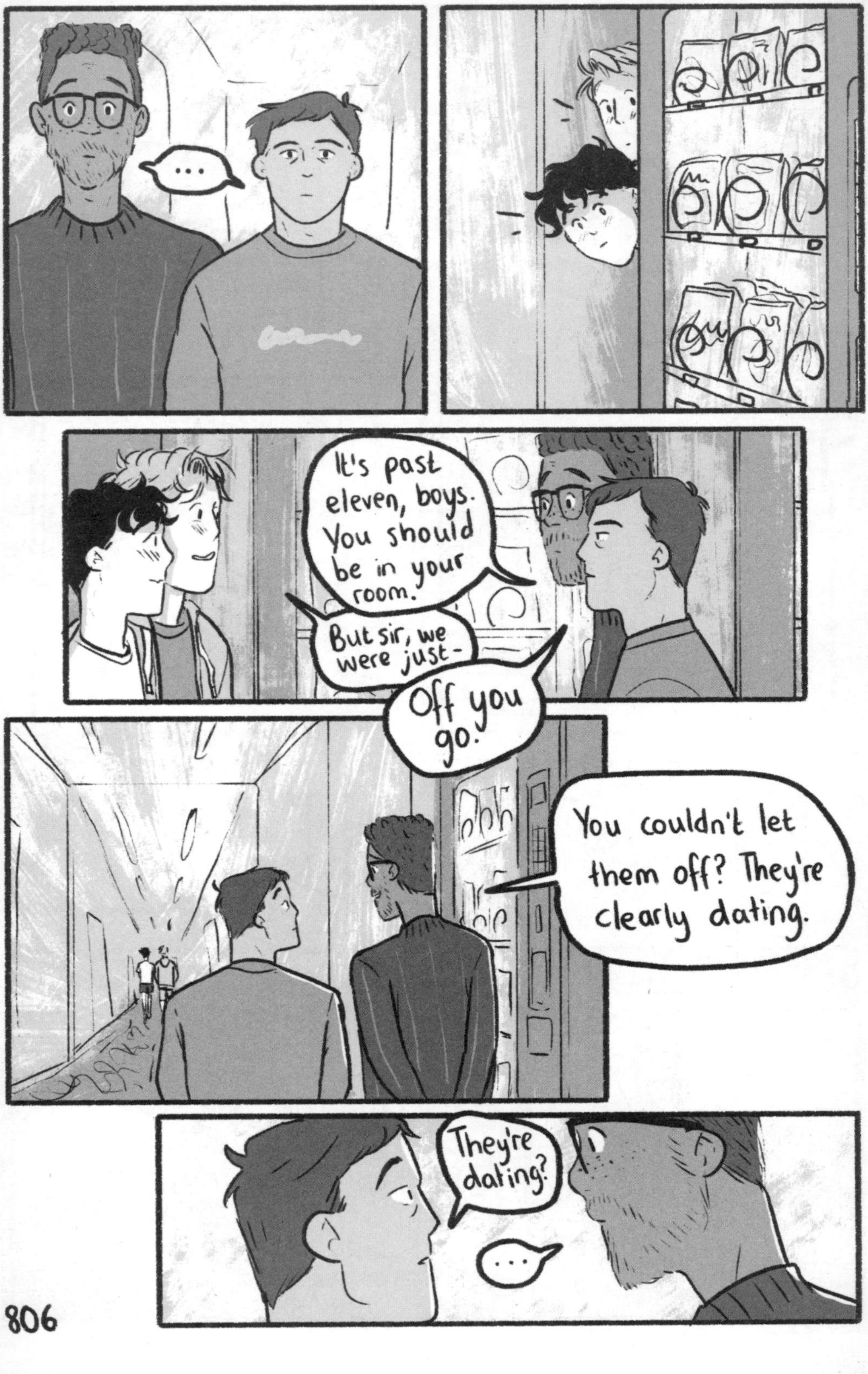
...
It's past eleven, boys. You should be in your room.
But sir, we were just-
Off you go.
You couldn't let them off? They're clearly dating.
They're dating?
...

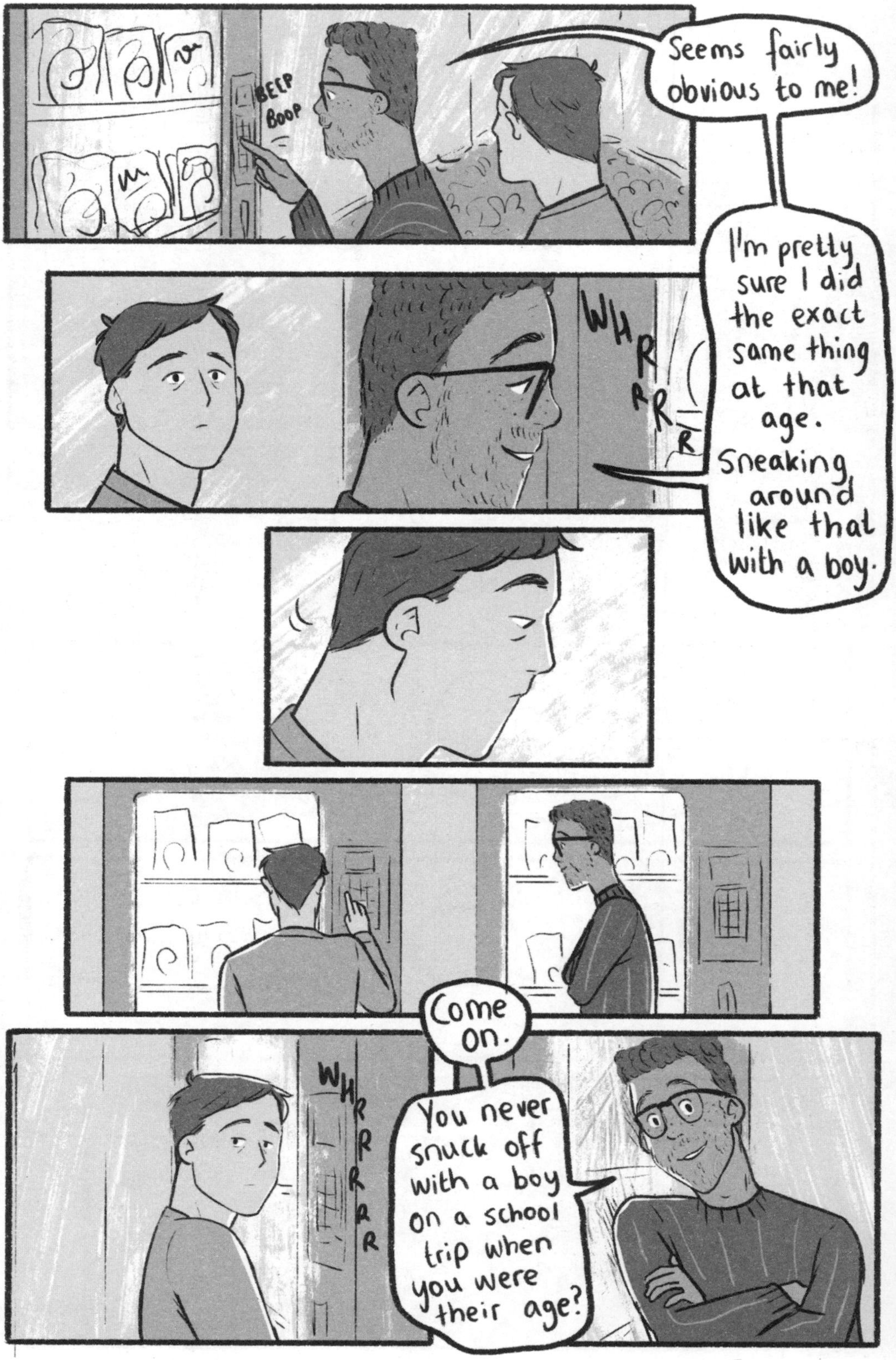
BEEP
BOOP
Seems fairly obvious to me!
I'm pretty sure I did the exact same thing at that age. Sneaking around like that with a boy.
WHRRR
Come on.
You never snuck off with a boy on a school trip when you were their age?
WHRRRRR

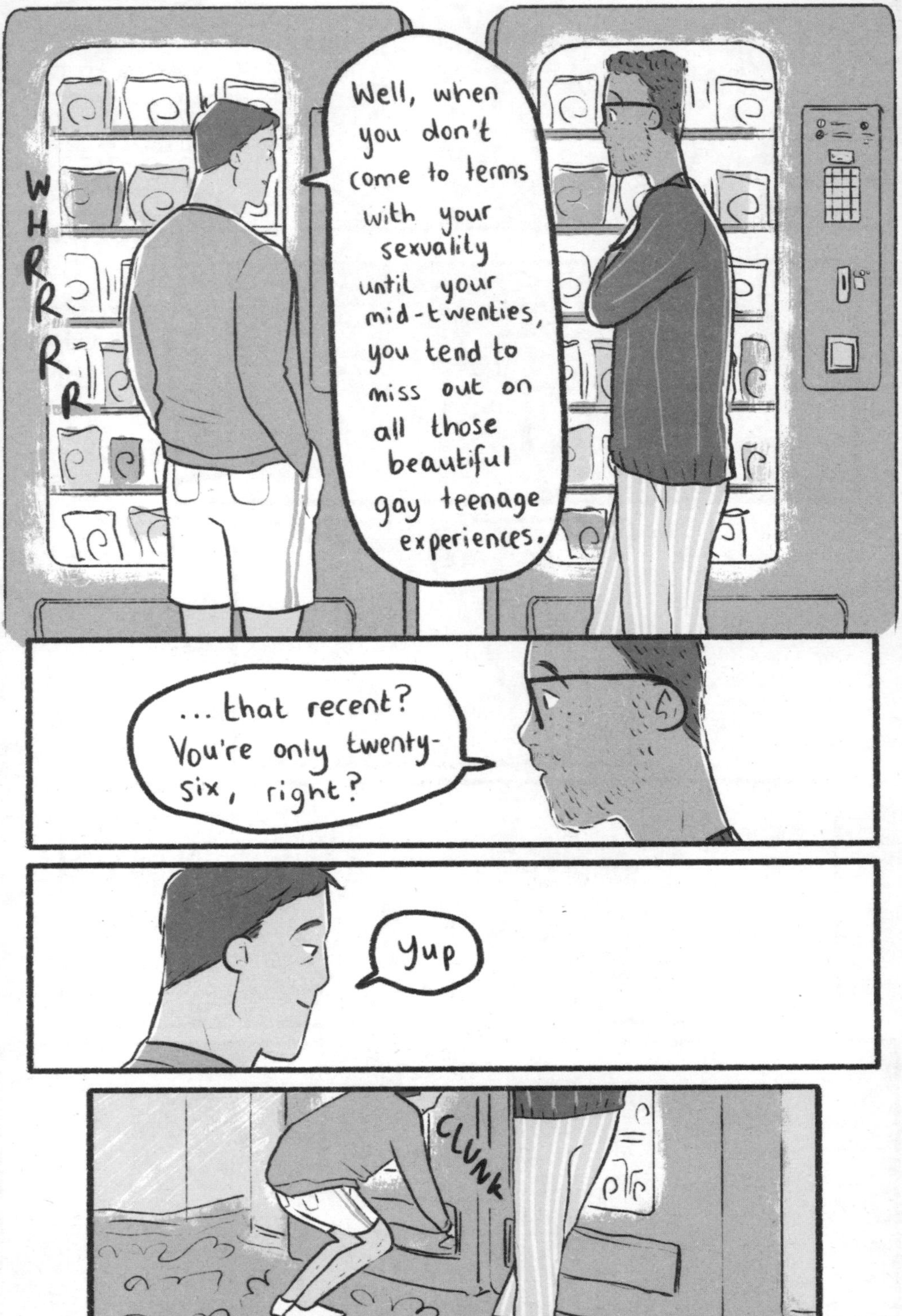
WHRRRR
Well, when you don't come to terms with your sexuality until your mid-twenties, you tend to miss out on all those beautiful gay teenage experiences.
... that recent? You're only twenty-six, right?
Yup
CLUNK

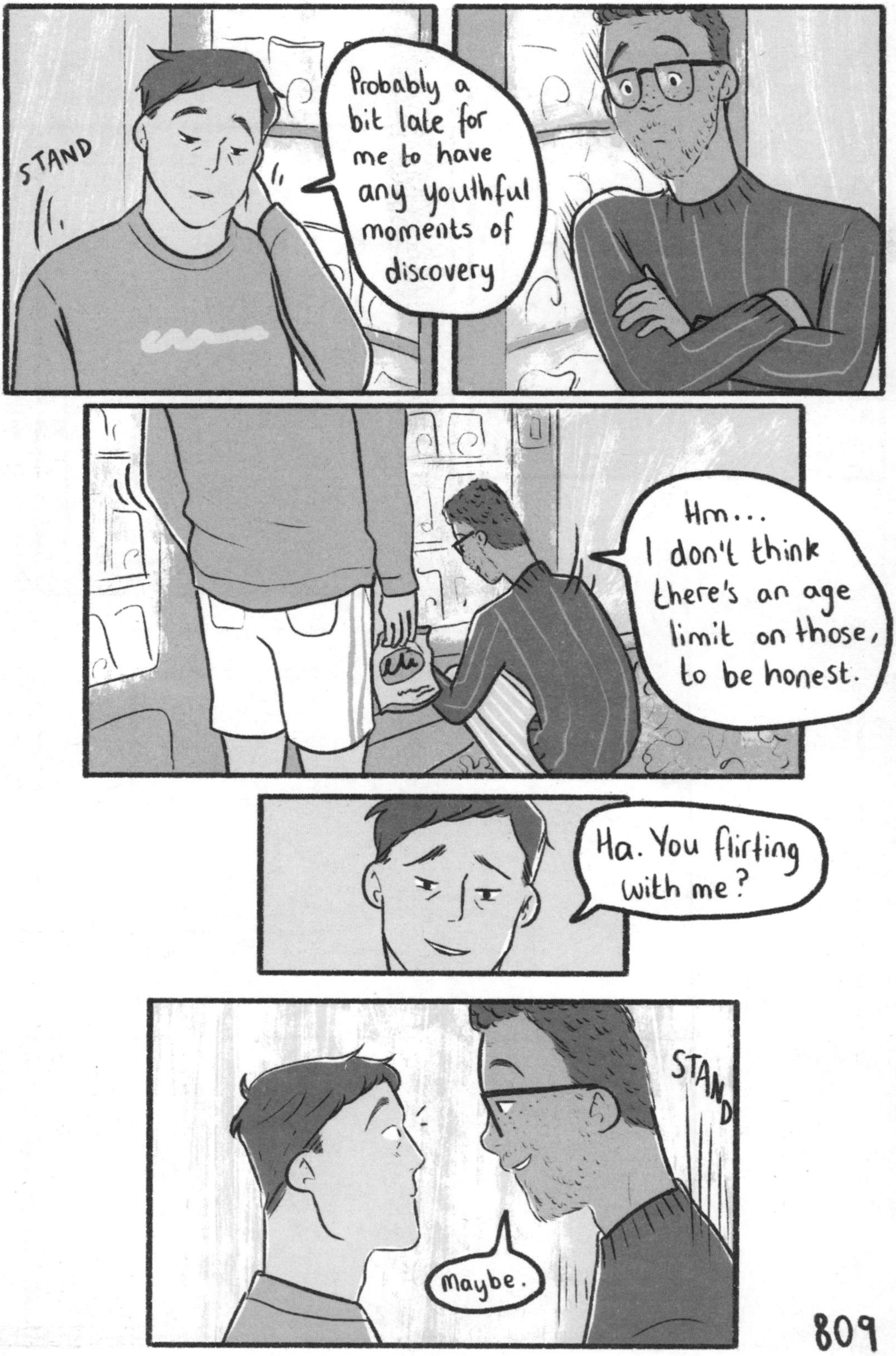
STAND
Probably a bit late for me to have any youthful moments of discovery
Hm... I don't think there's an age limit on those, to be honest.
Ha. You flirting with me?
STAND
Maybe.

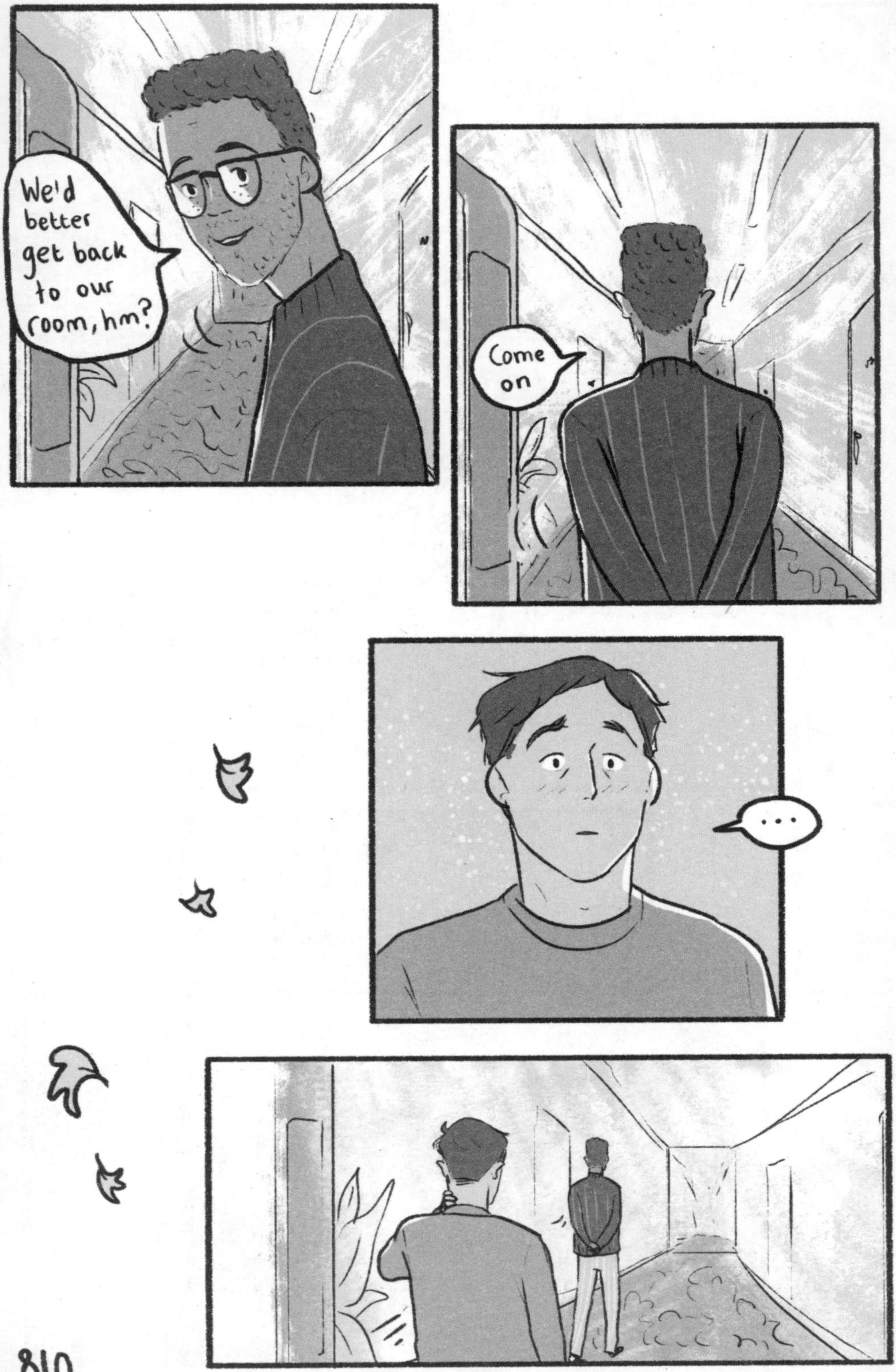
We'd better get back to our room, hm?
Come on
...

Paris - Day 6

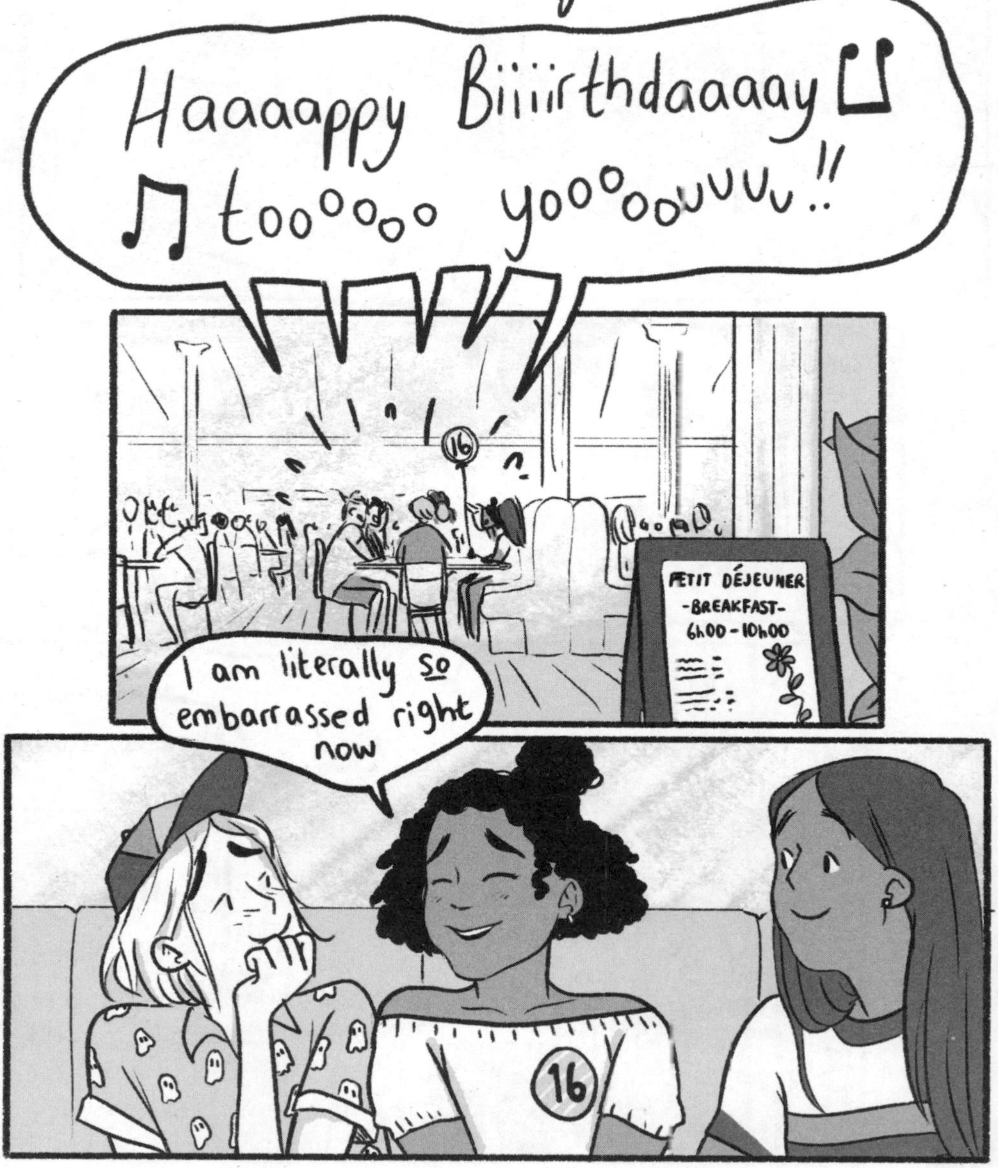
Haaaappy Biiiirthdaaaay
too⁰⁰oo yoo⁰oouuuv!!
PETIT DÉJEUNER
-BREAKFAST-
6h00 - 10h00
I am literally so embarrassed right now

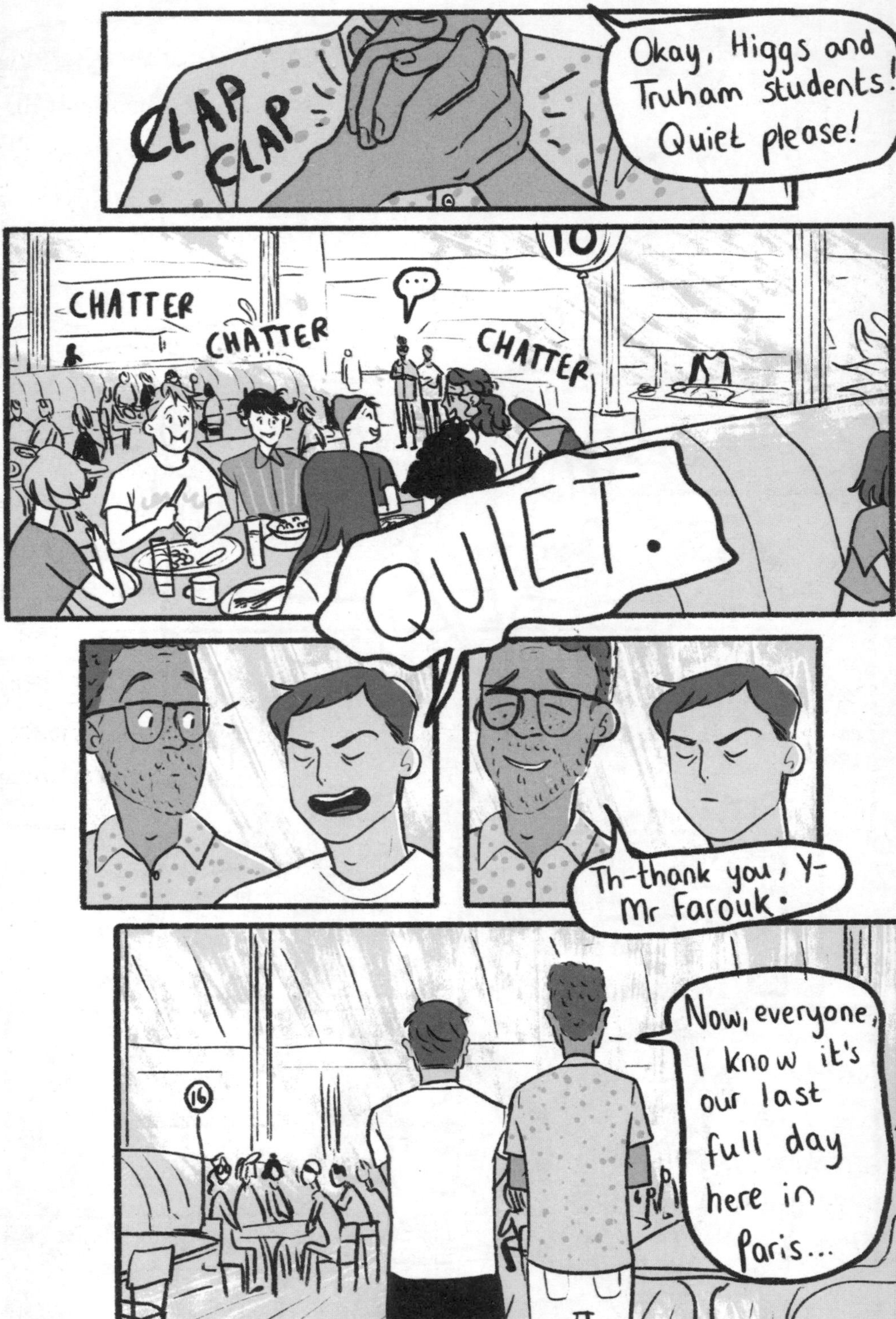
CLAP CLAP
Okay, Higgs and Truham students! Quiet please!
CHATTER
CHATTER
...
CHATTER
QUIET.
Th-thank you, Y- Mr Farouk.
16
16
Now, everyone, I know it's our last full day here in Paris...

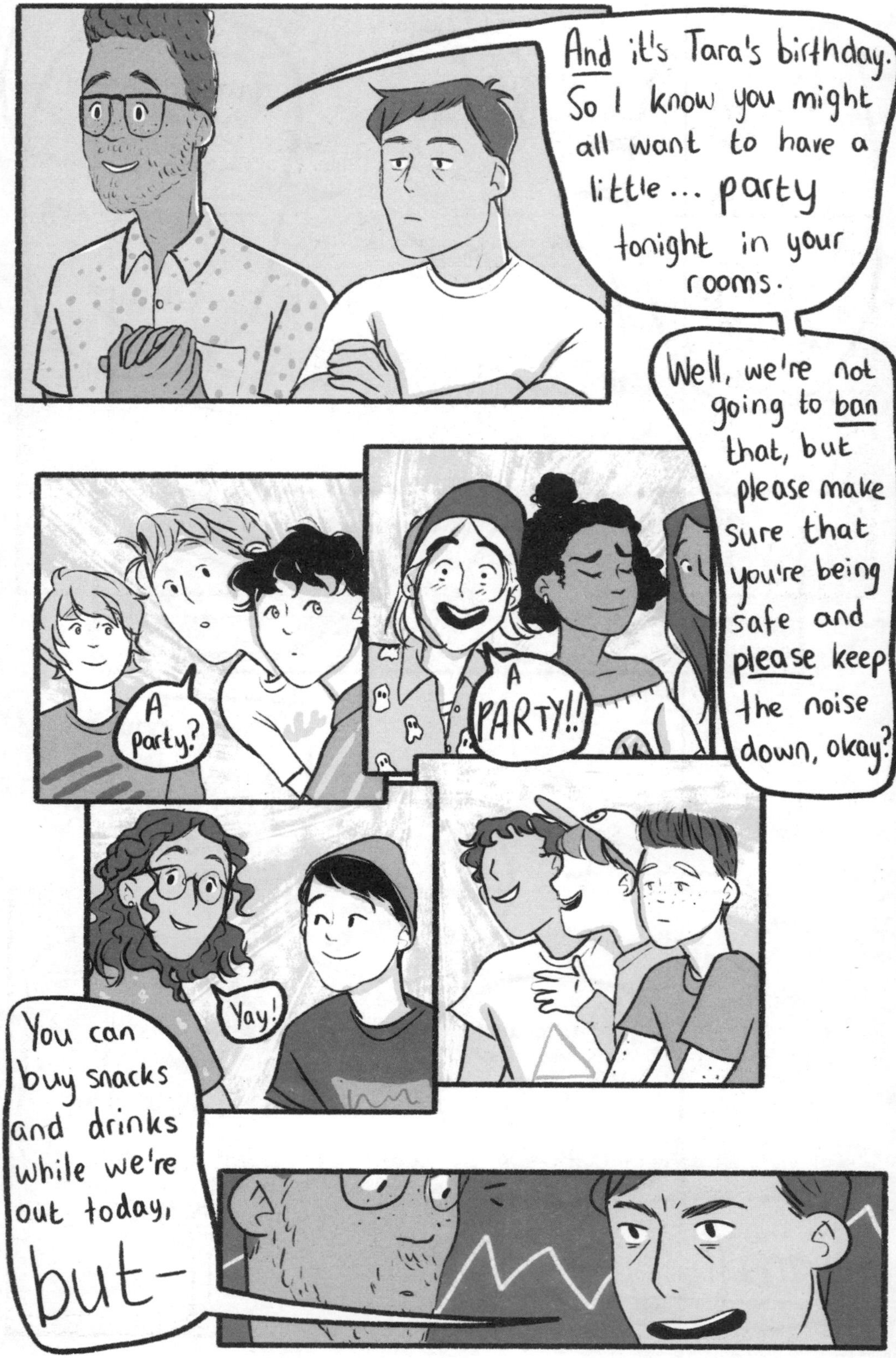

And it's Tara's birthday. So I know you might all want to have a little... party tonight in your rooms.
Well, we're not going to ban that, but please make sure that you're being safe and please keep the noise down, okay?
A party?
A PARTY!!
Yay!
You can buy snacks and drinks while we're out today,
but-

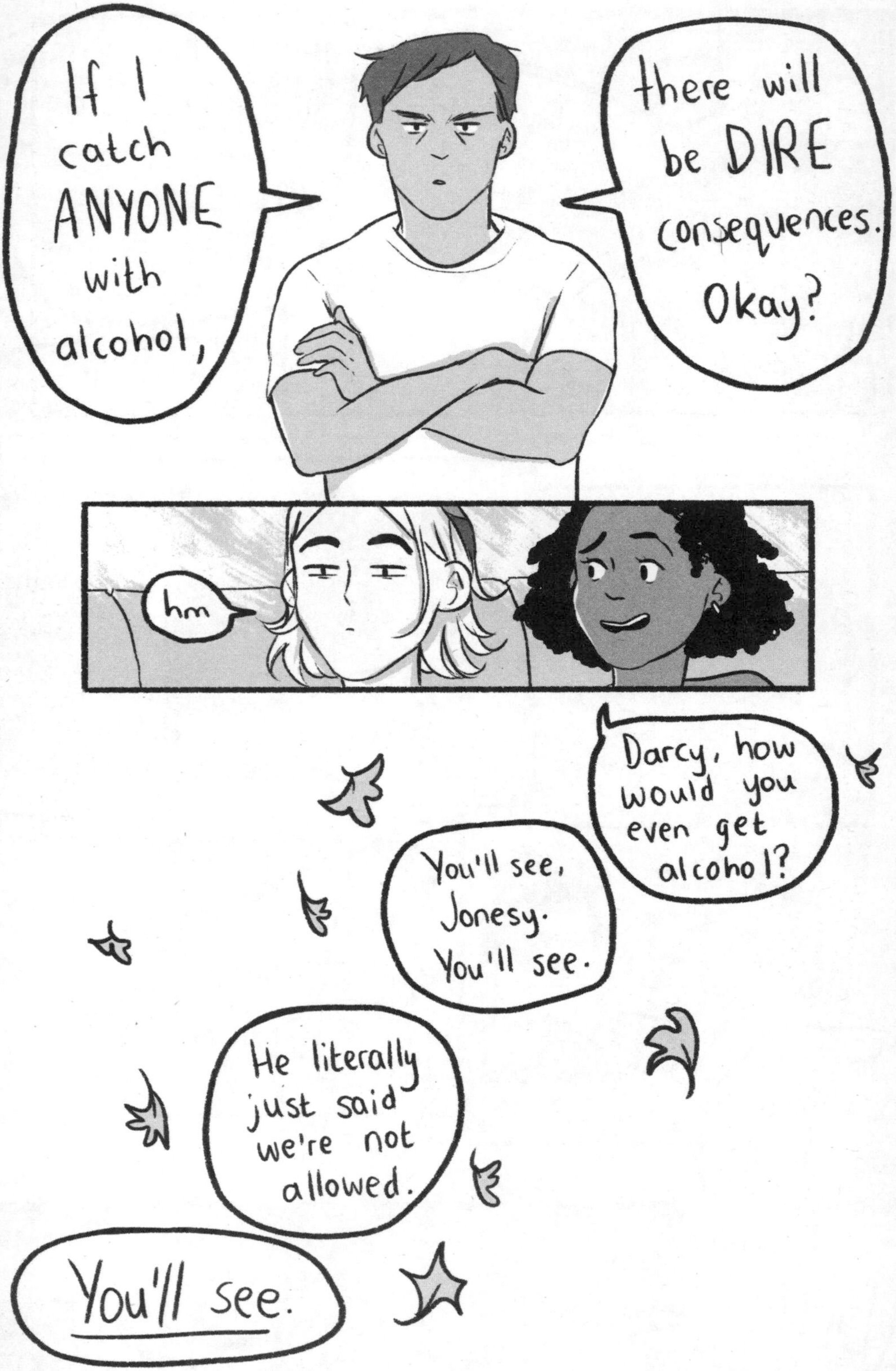
If I catch ANYONE with alcohol,
there will be DIRE consequences. Okay?
hm
Darcy, how would you even get alcohol?
You'll see, Jonesy. You'll see.
He literally just said we're not allowed.
You'll see.

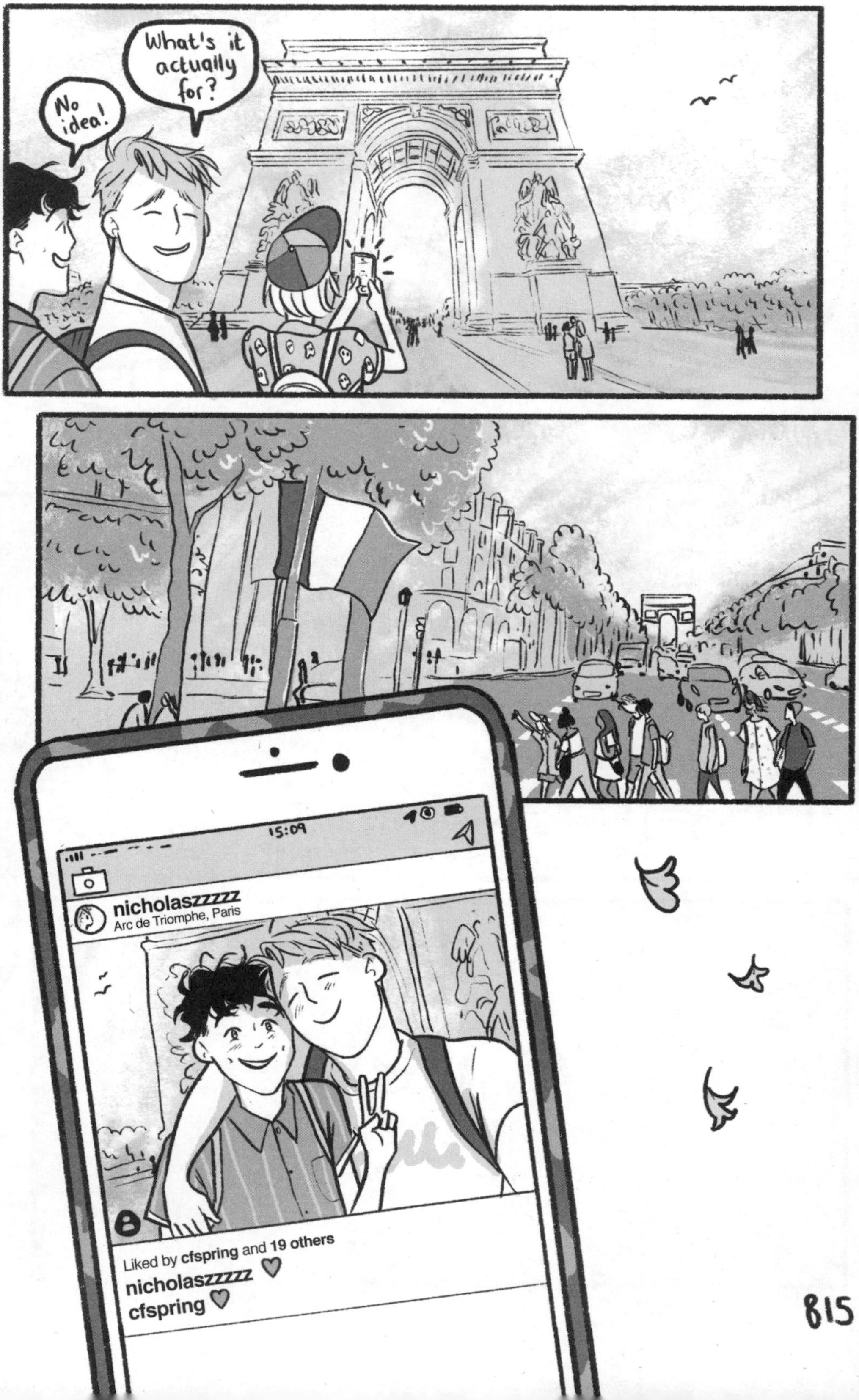
No idea!
What's it actually for?
15:09
nicholaszzzzz
Arc de Triomphe, Paris
Liked by cfspring and 19 others
nicholaszzzzz
cfspring

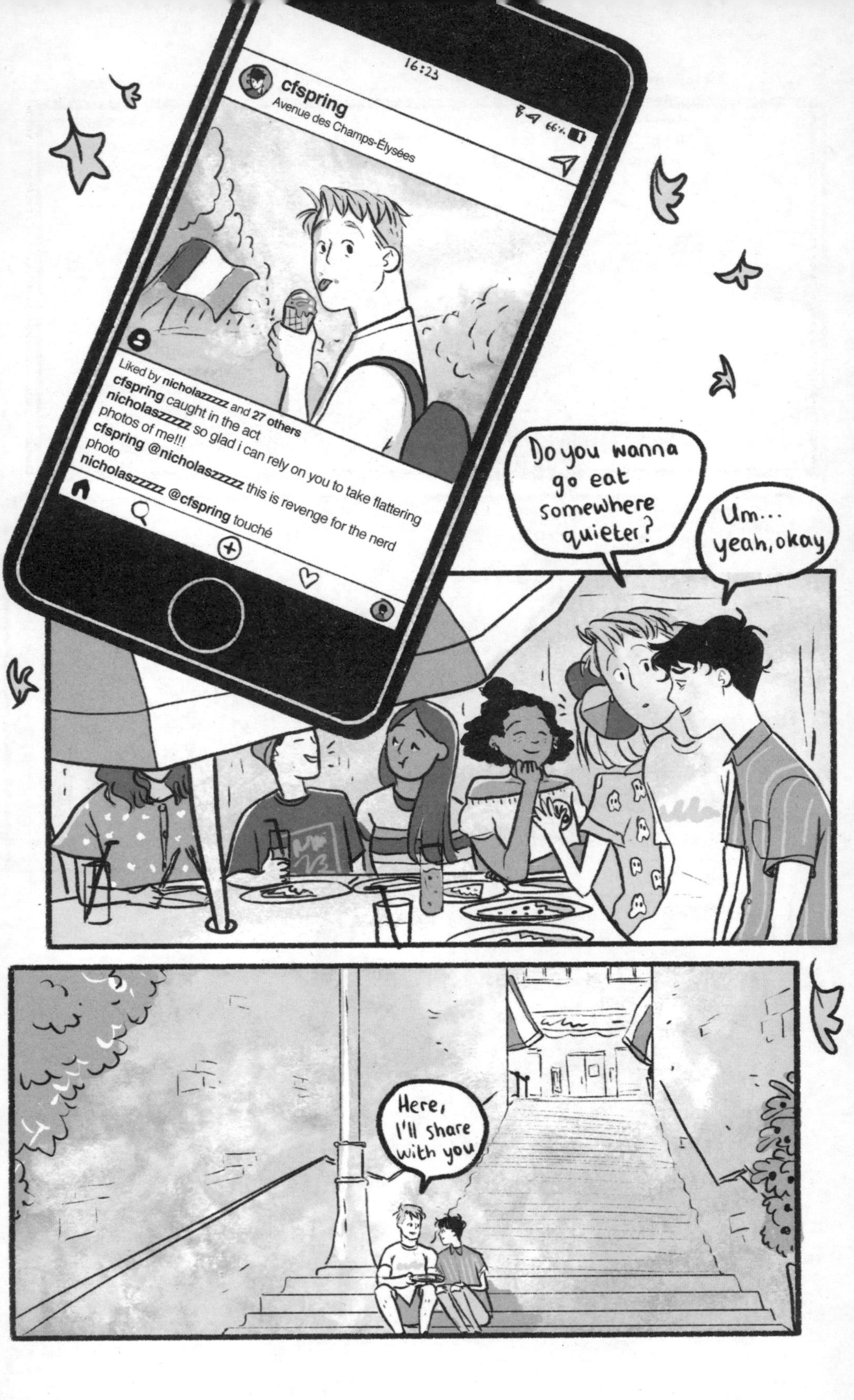
16:23
66%
cfspring
Avenue des Champs-Élysées
Liked by nicholazzzzz and 27 others
cfspring caught in the act
nicholaszzzzz so glad i can rely on you to take flattering photos of me!!!
cfspring @nicholaszzzzz this is revenge for the nerd photo
nicholaszzzzz @cfspring touché
Do you wanna go eat somewhere quieter?
Um... yeah, okay
Here, I'll share with you

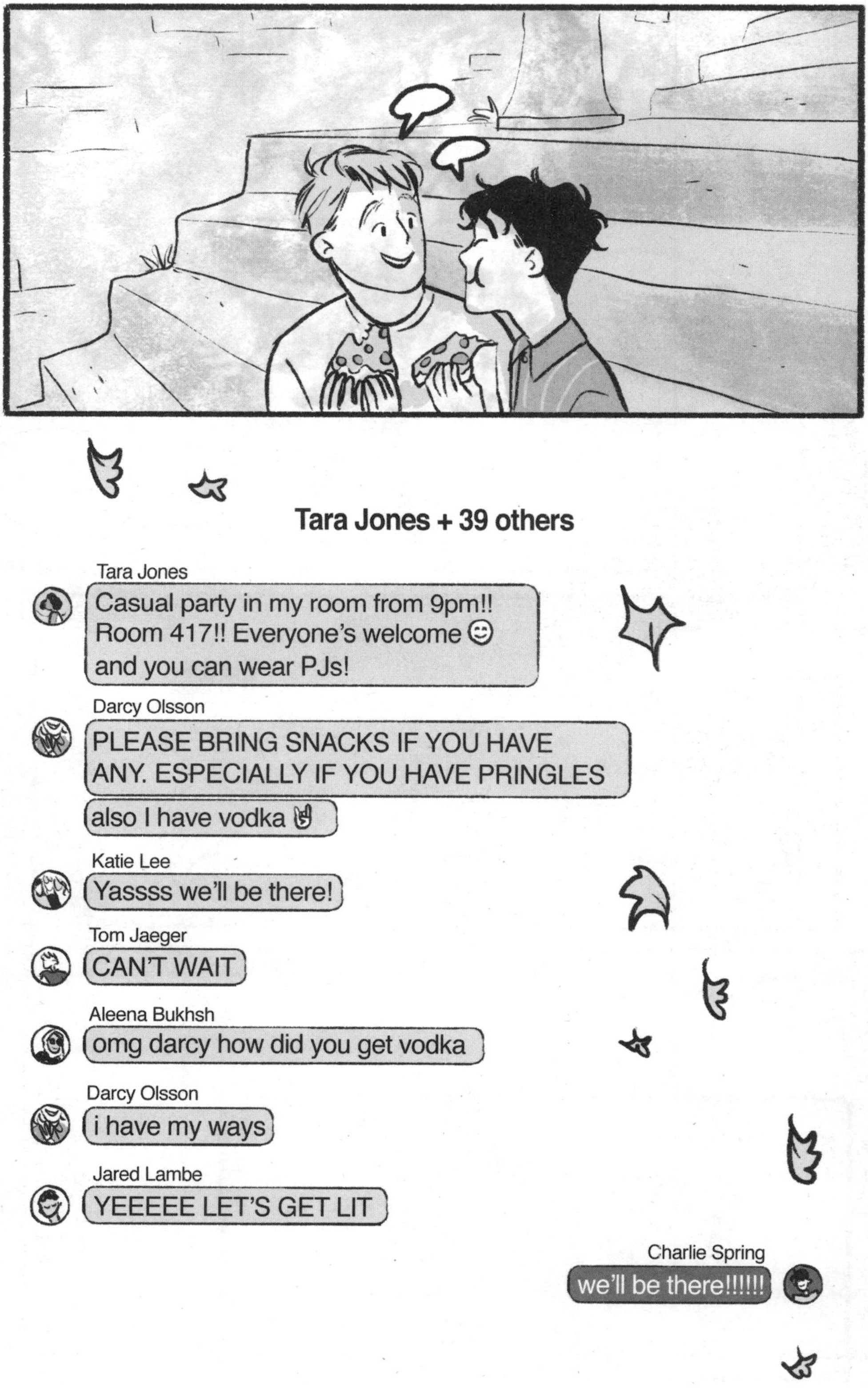
Tara Jones + 39 others
Tara Jones
Casual party in my room from 9pm!! Room 417!! Everyone's welcome 😊 and you can wear PJs!
Darcy Olsson
PLEASE BRING SNACKS IF YOU HAVE ANY. ESPECIALLY IF YOU HAVE PRINGLES
also I have vodka 🤘
Katie Lee
Yassss we'll be there!
Tom Jaeger
CAN'T WAIT
Aleena Bukhsh
omg darcy how did you get vodka
Darcy Olsson
i have my ways
Jared Lambe
YEEEEE LET'S GET LIT
Charlie Spring
we'll be there!!!!!!

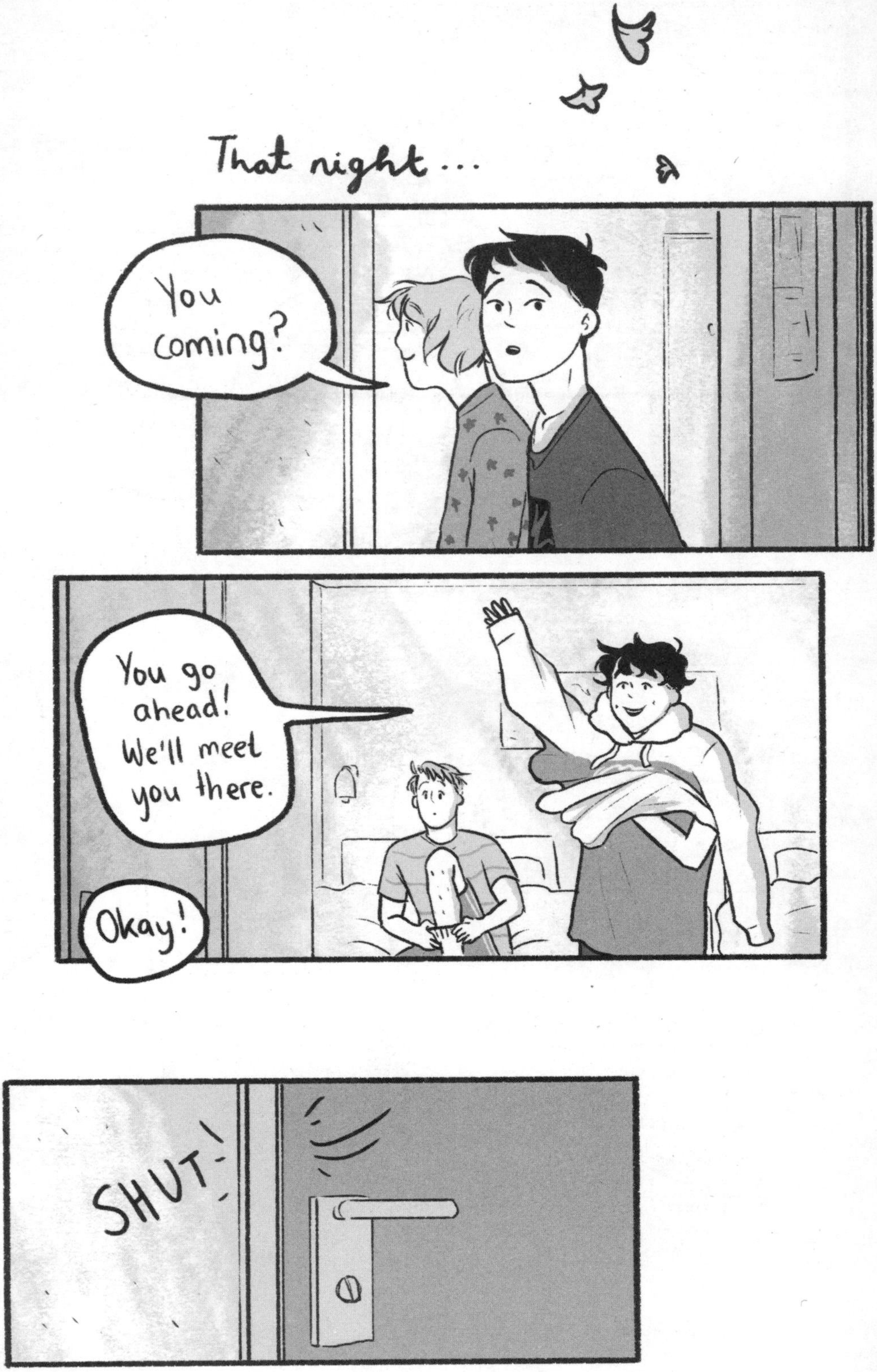
That night...
You coming?
You go ahead! We'll meet you there.
Okay!
SHUT!

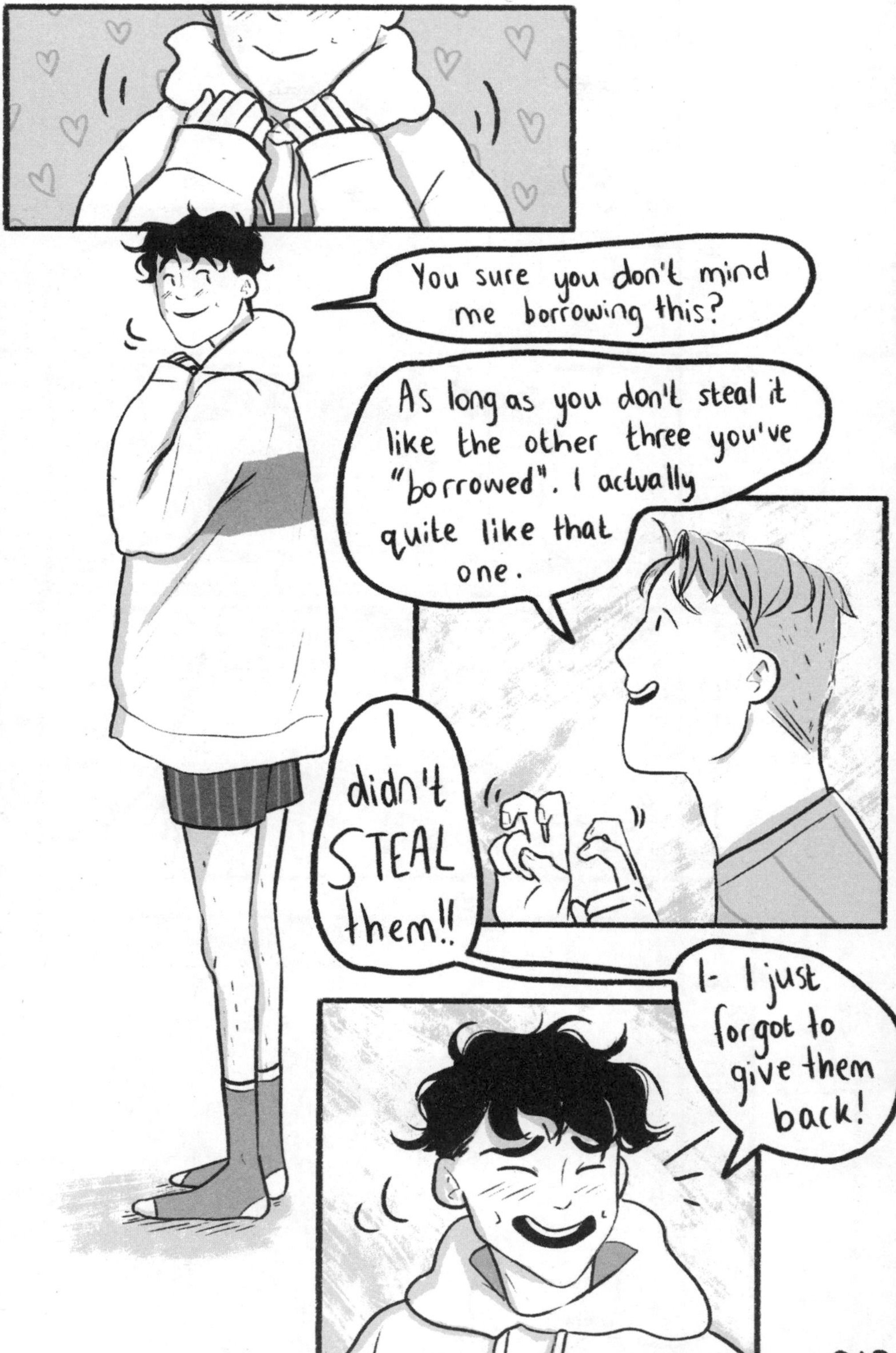
You sure you don't mind me borrowing this?
As long as you don't steal it like the other three you've "borrowed". I actually quite like that one.
I didn't STEAL them!!
I- I just forgot to give them back!

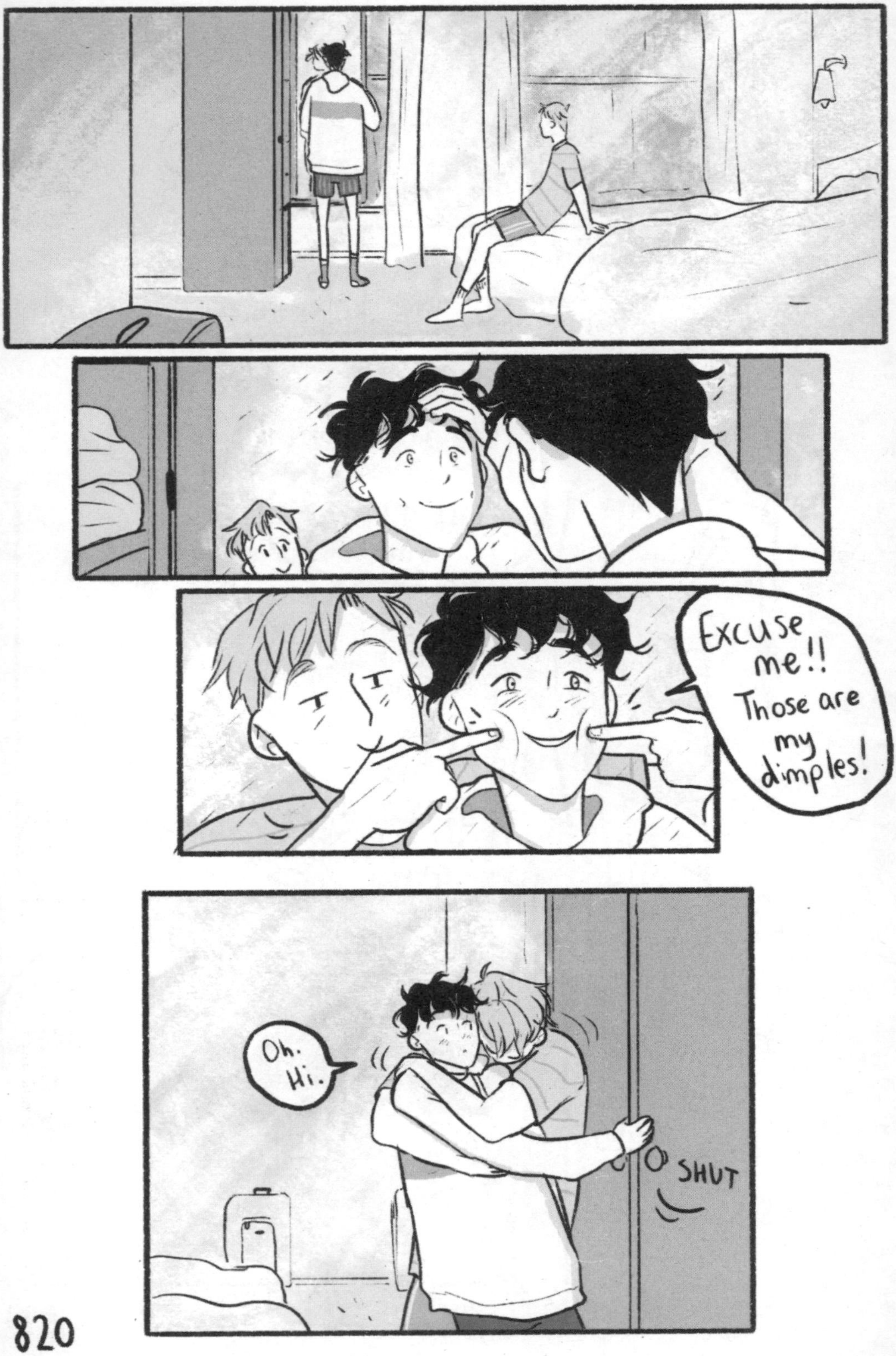
Excuse me!! Those are my dimples!
Oh. Hi.
SHUT

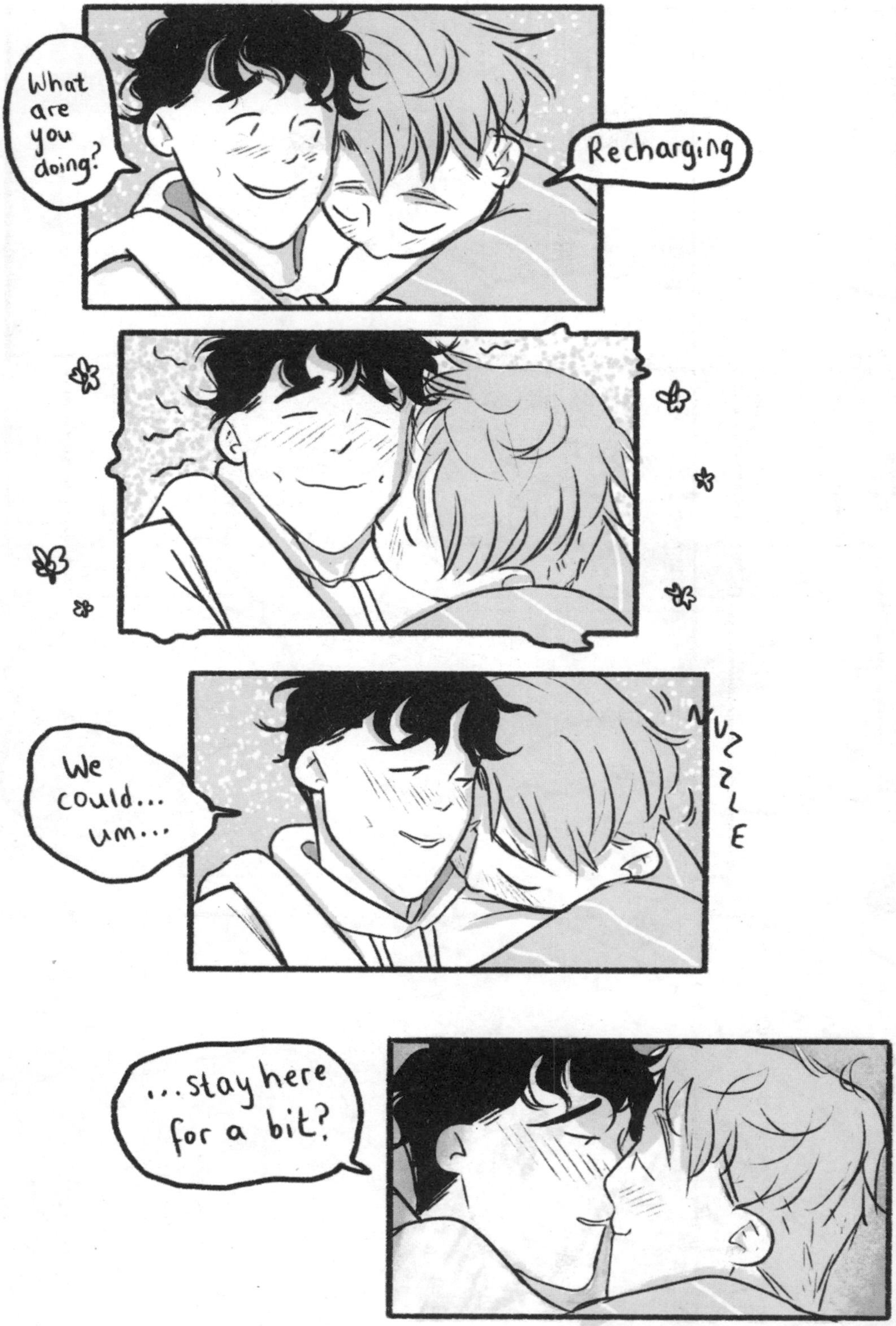
What are you doing?
Recharging
We could... um...
NUZZLE
...stay here for a bit?

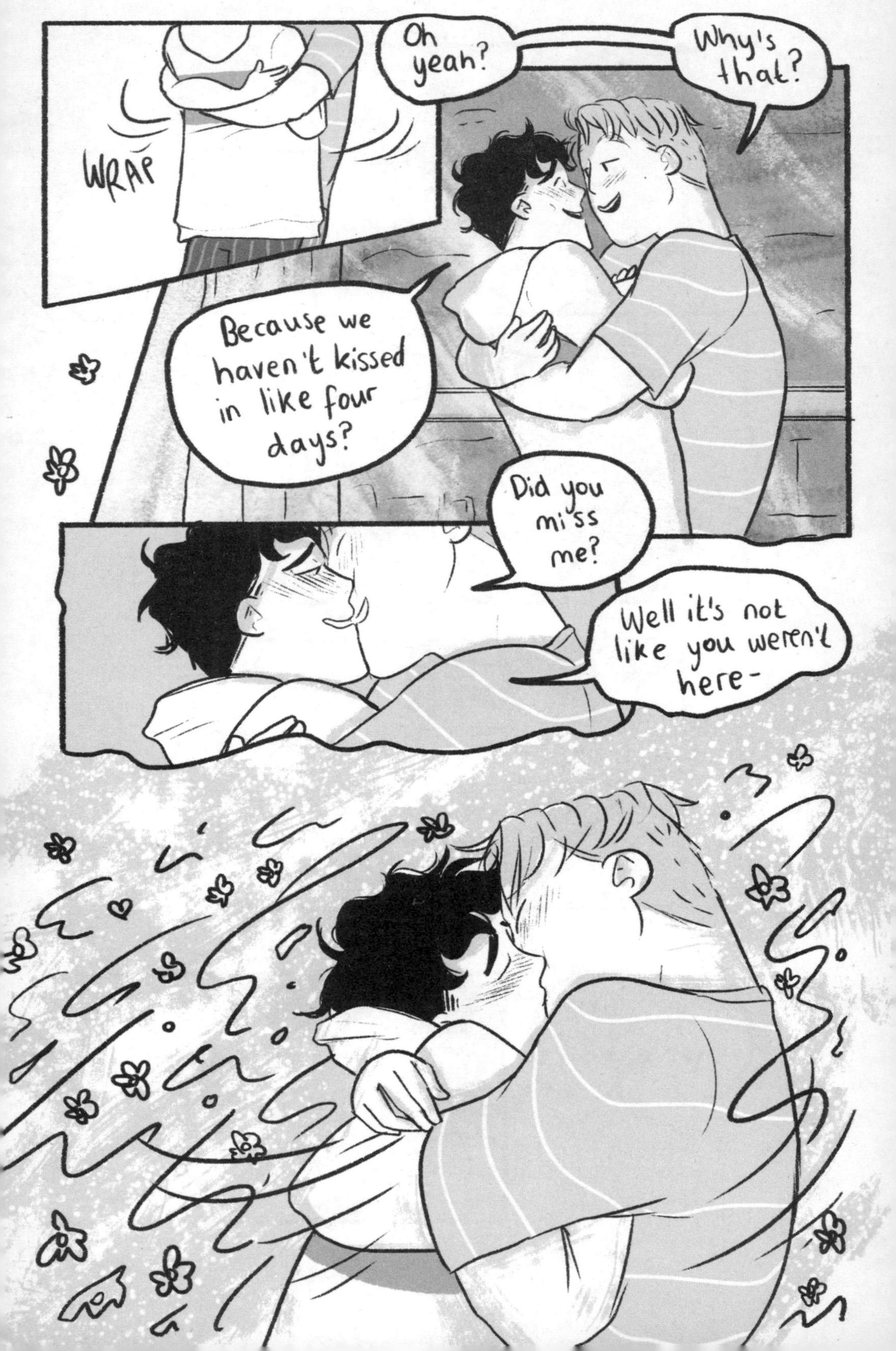
WRAP
Oh yeah?
Why's that?
Because we haven't kissed in like four days?
Did you miss me?
Well it's not like you weren't here-

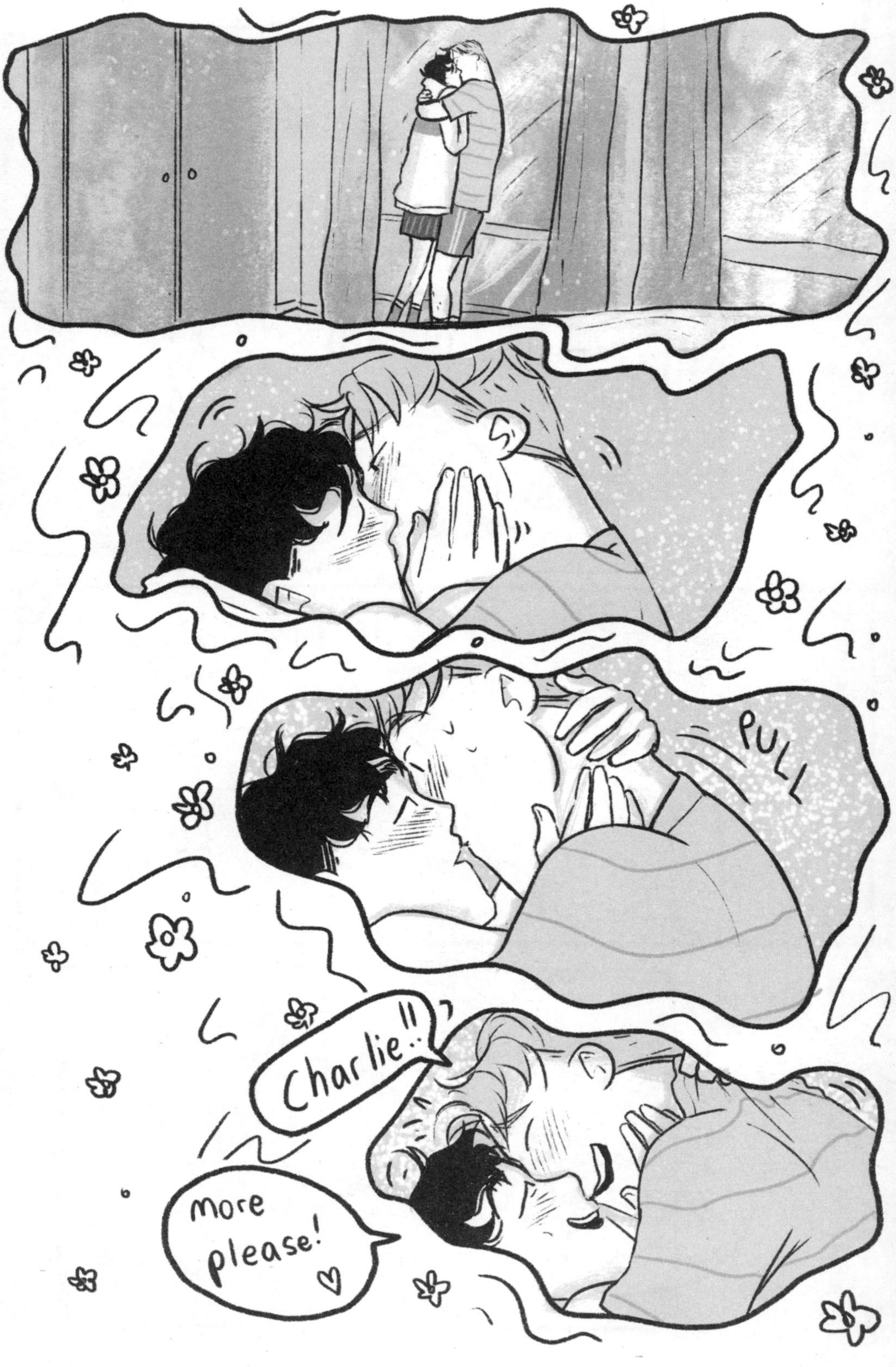
PULL
Charlie!!
more please!

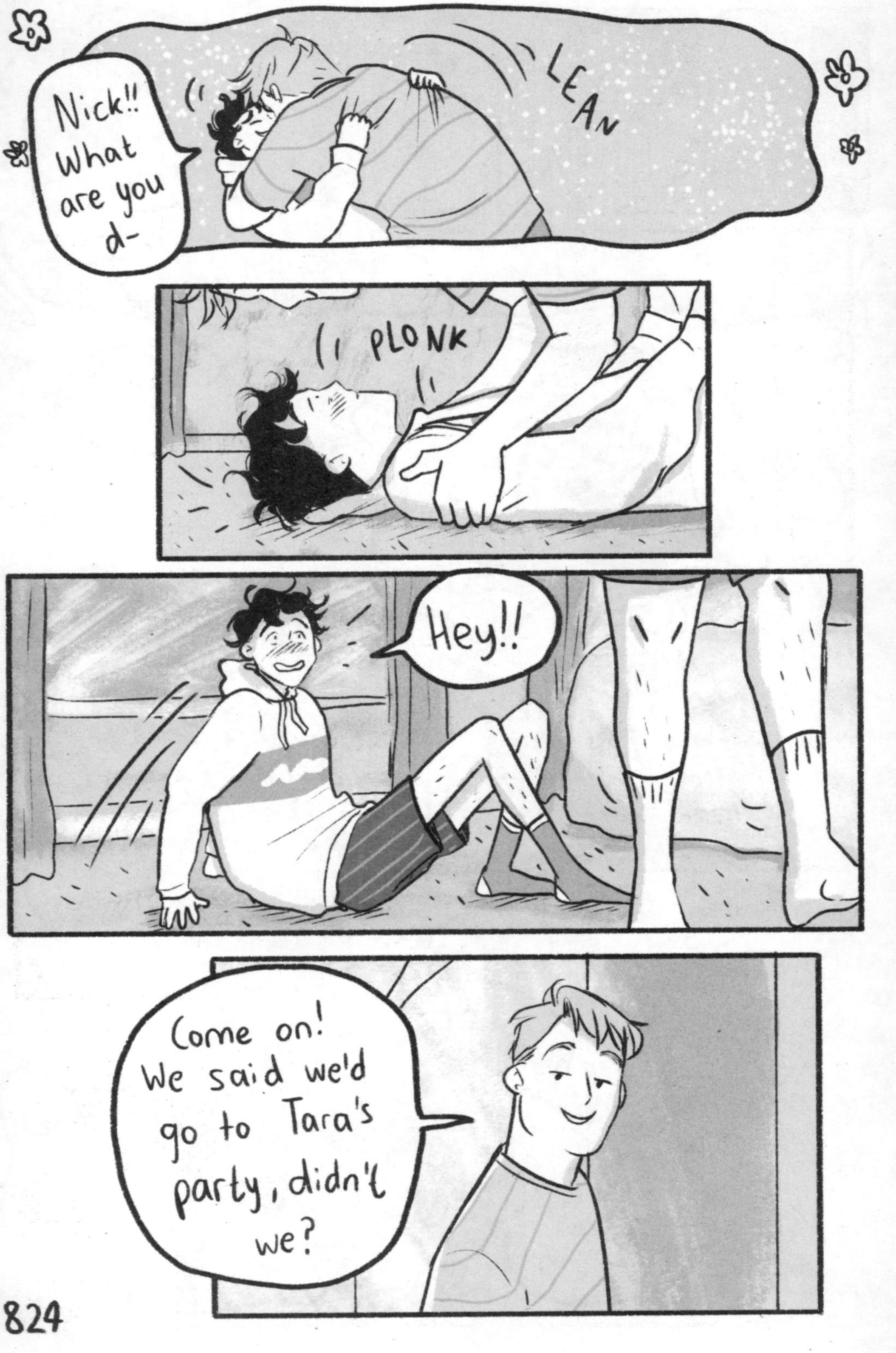
Nick!! What are you d-
LEAN
PLONK
Hey!!
Come on! We said we'd go to Tara's party, didn't we?

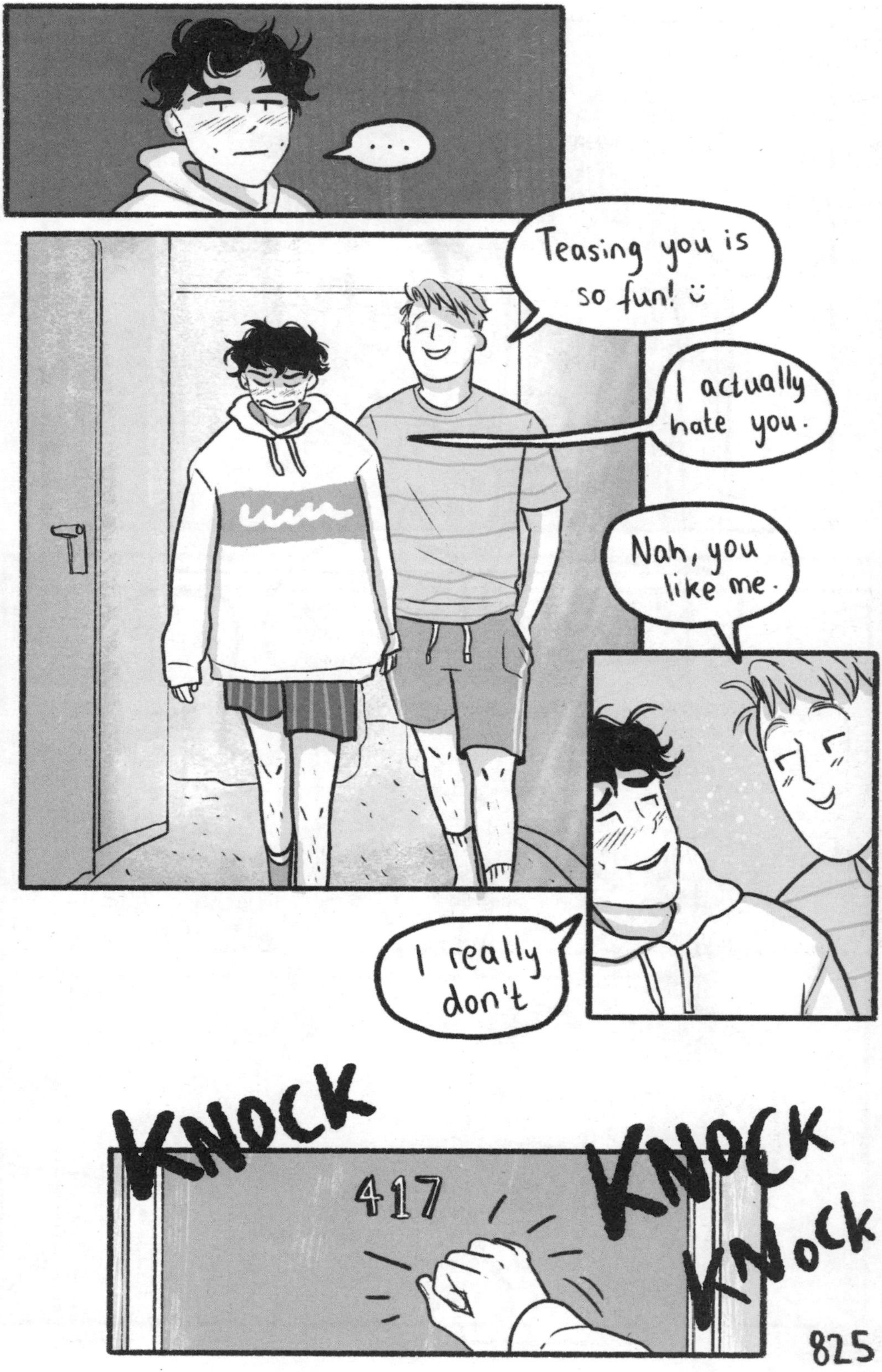
...
Teasing you is so fun! ᵕ
I actually hate you.
Nah, you like me.
I really don't
KNOCK
417
KNOCK
KNOCK

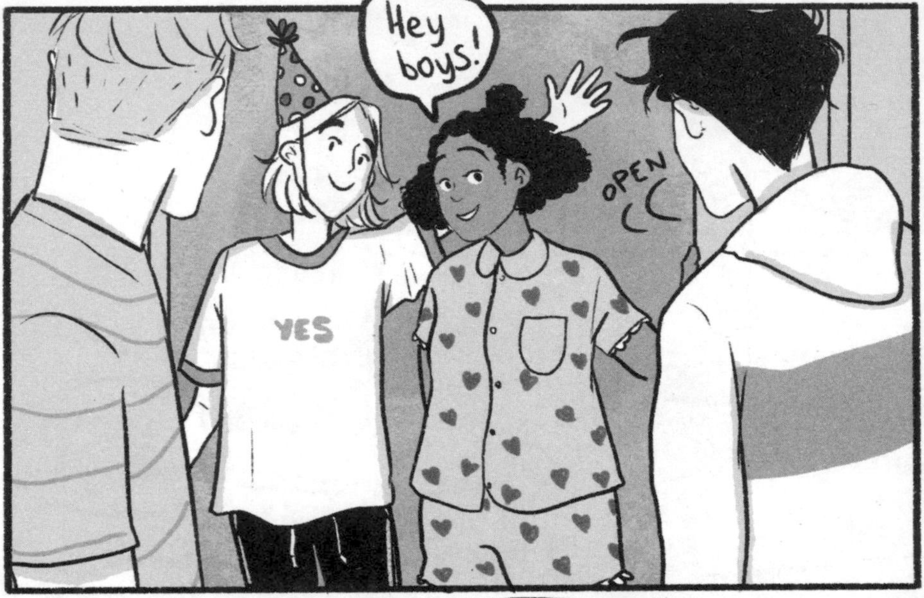
Hey boys!
YES
OPEN

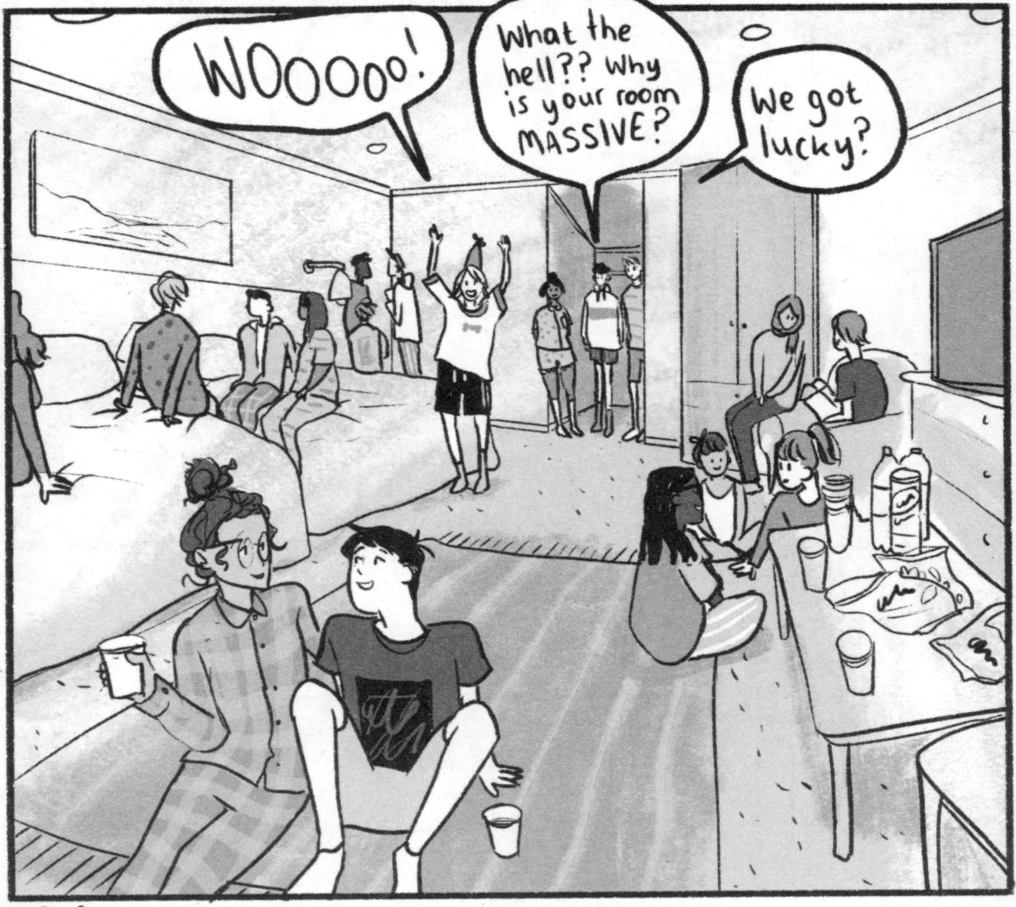
WOOOOo!
What the hell?? Why is your room MASSIVE?
We got lucky?

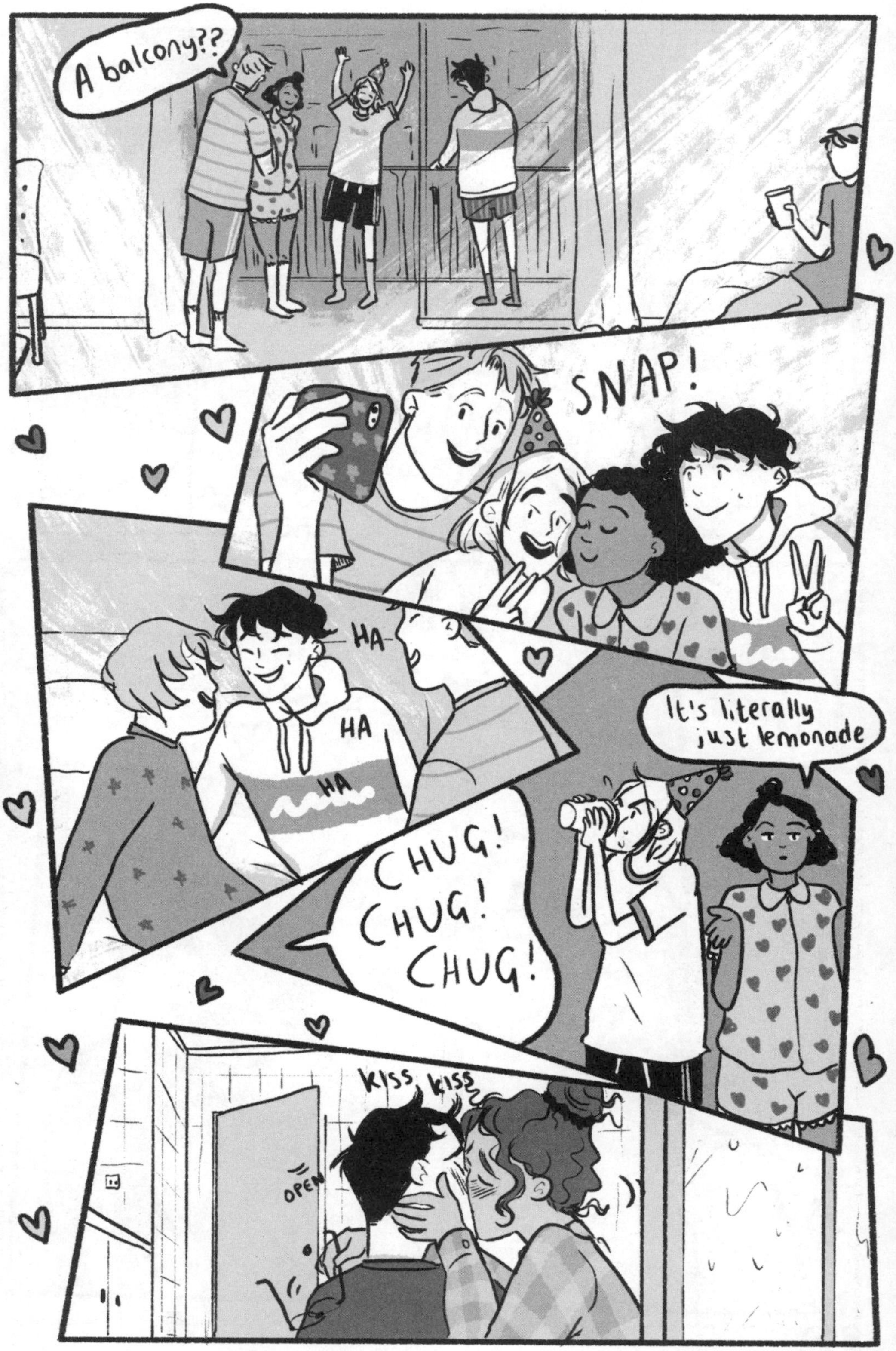
A balcony??
SNAP!
HA
HA
HA
It's literally just lemonade
CHUG! CHUG! CHUG!
KISS KISS
OPEN

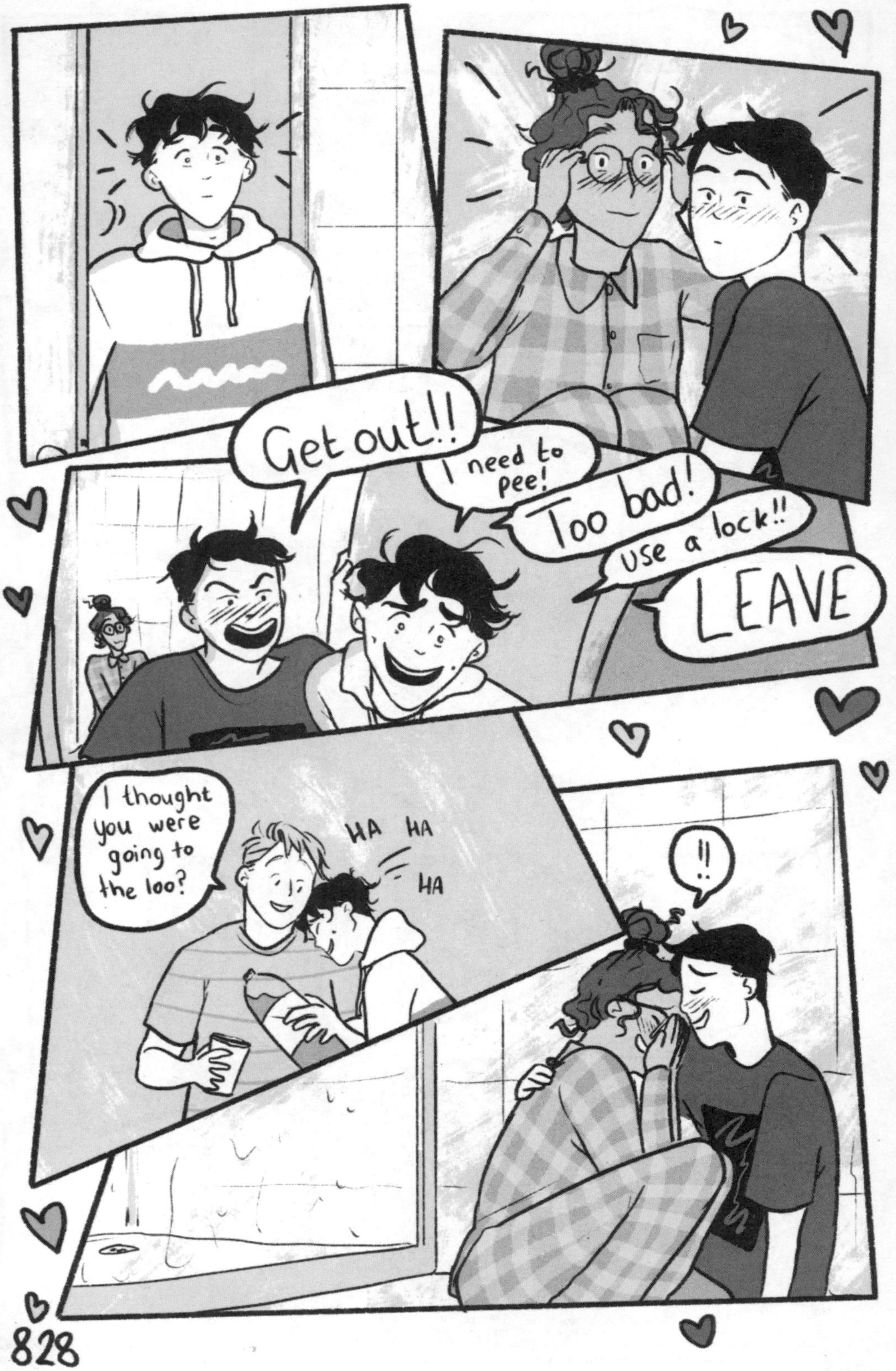
Get out!!
I need to pee!
Too bad!
Use a lock!!
LEAVE
I thought you were going to the loo?
HA HA
HA
!!

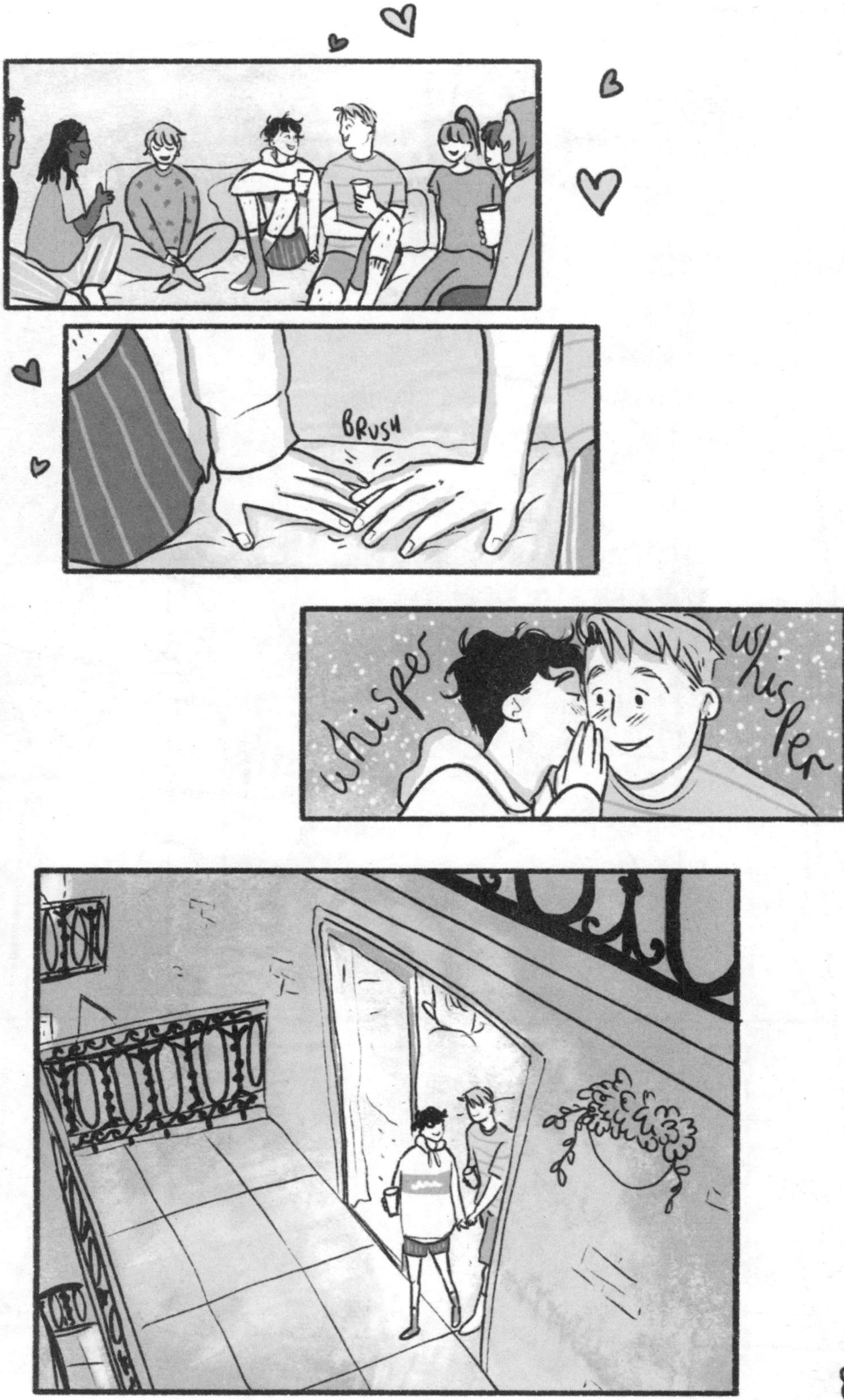
BRUSH
whisper
whisper

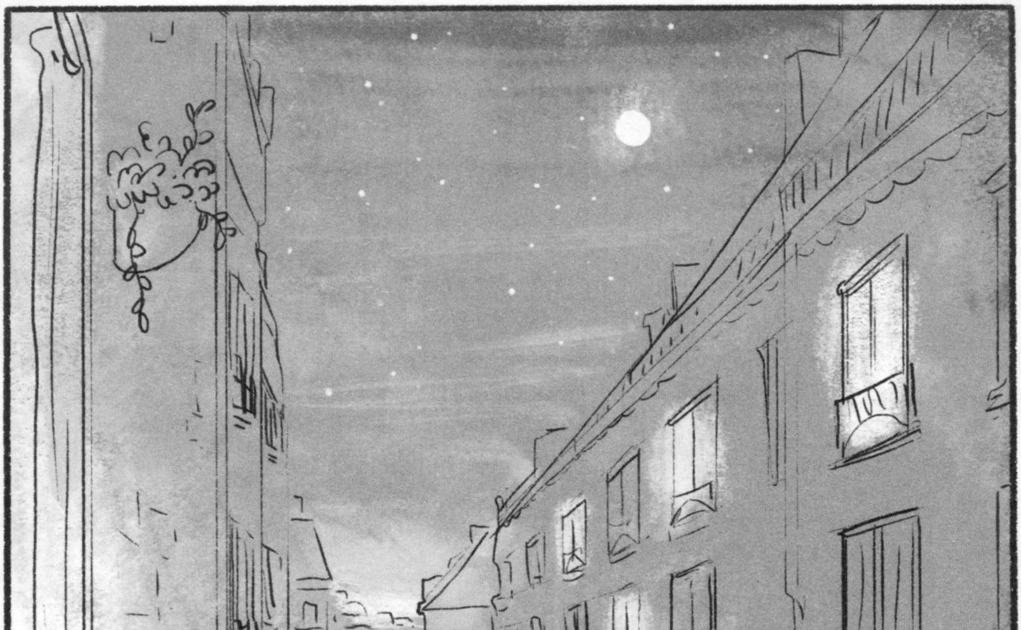

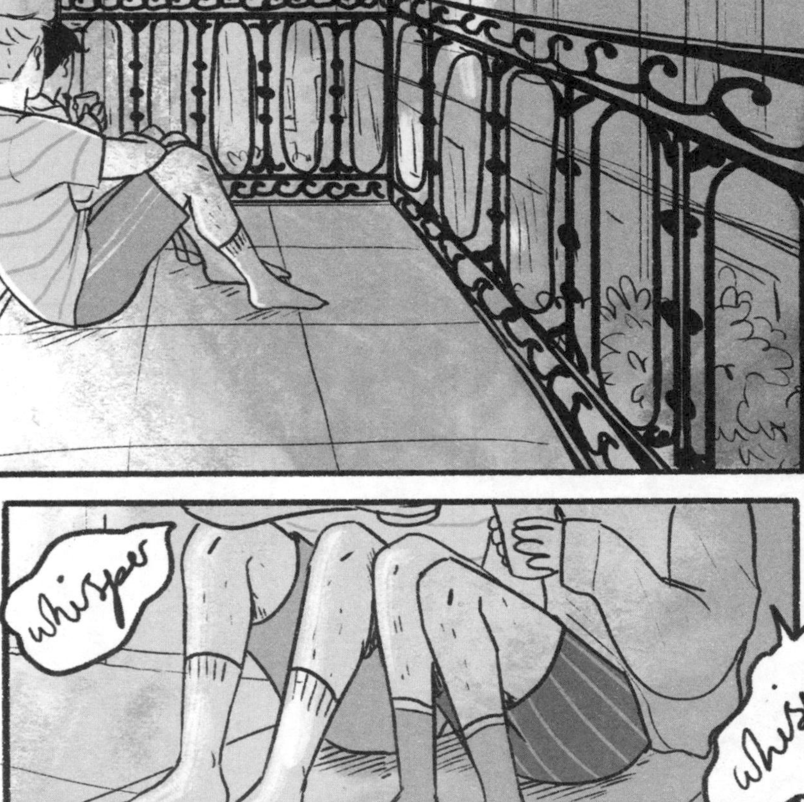
whisper
whisper

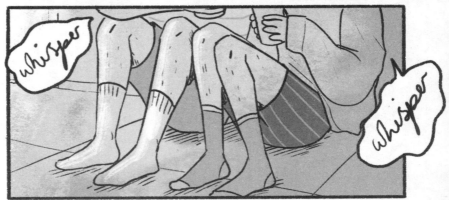

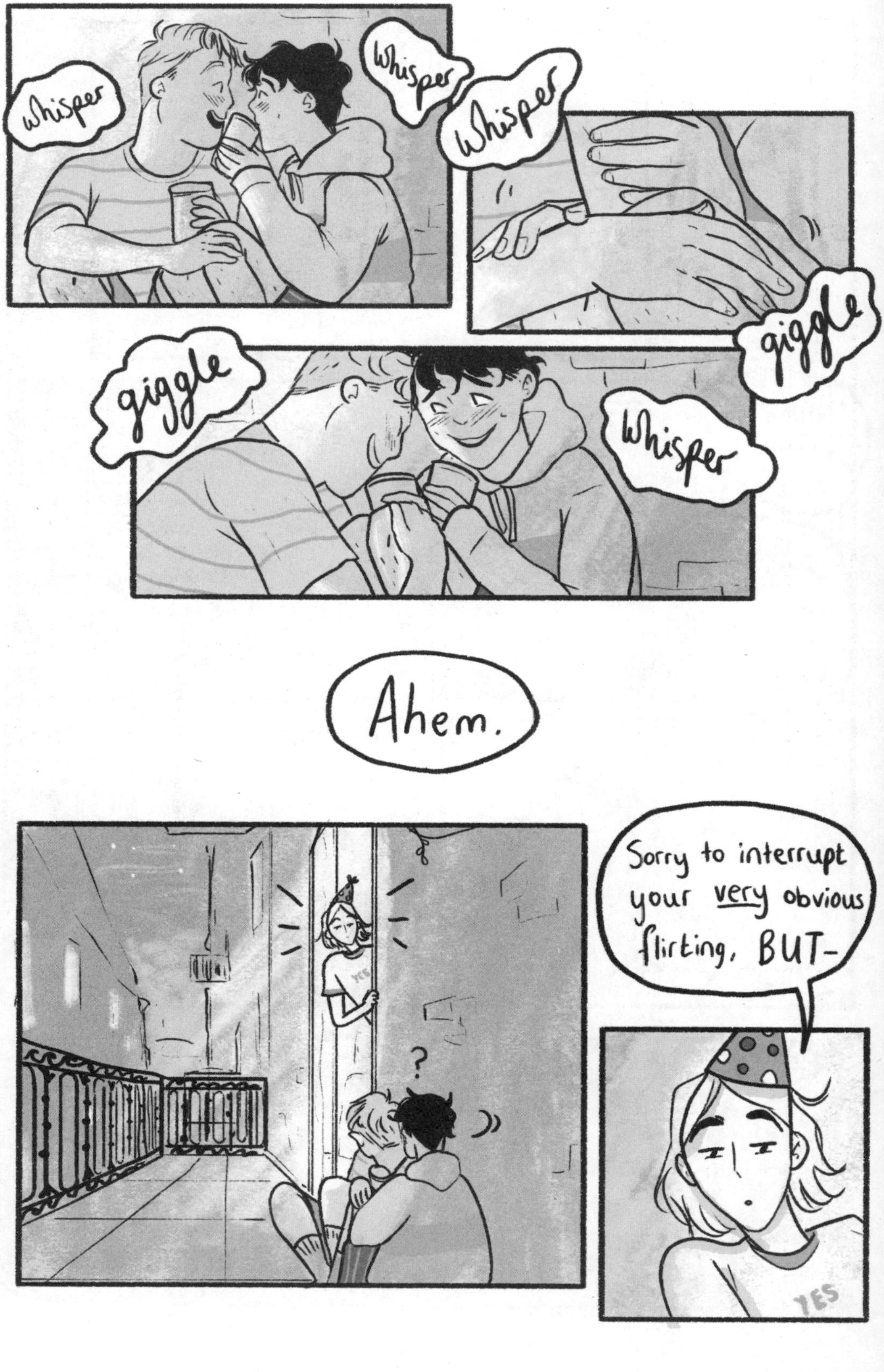
whisper
whisper
whisper
giggle
giggle
whisper
Ahem.
?
Sorry to interrupt your very obvious flirting, BUT-
YES
YES

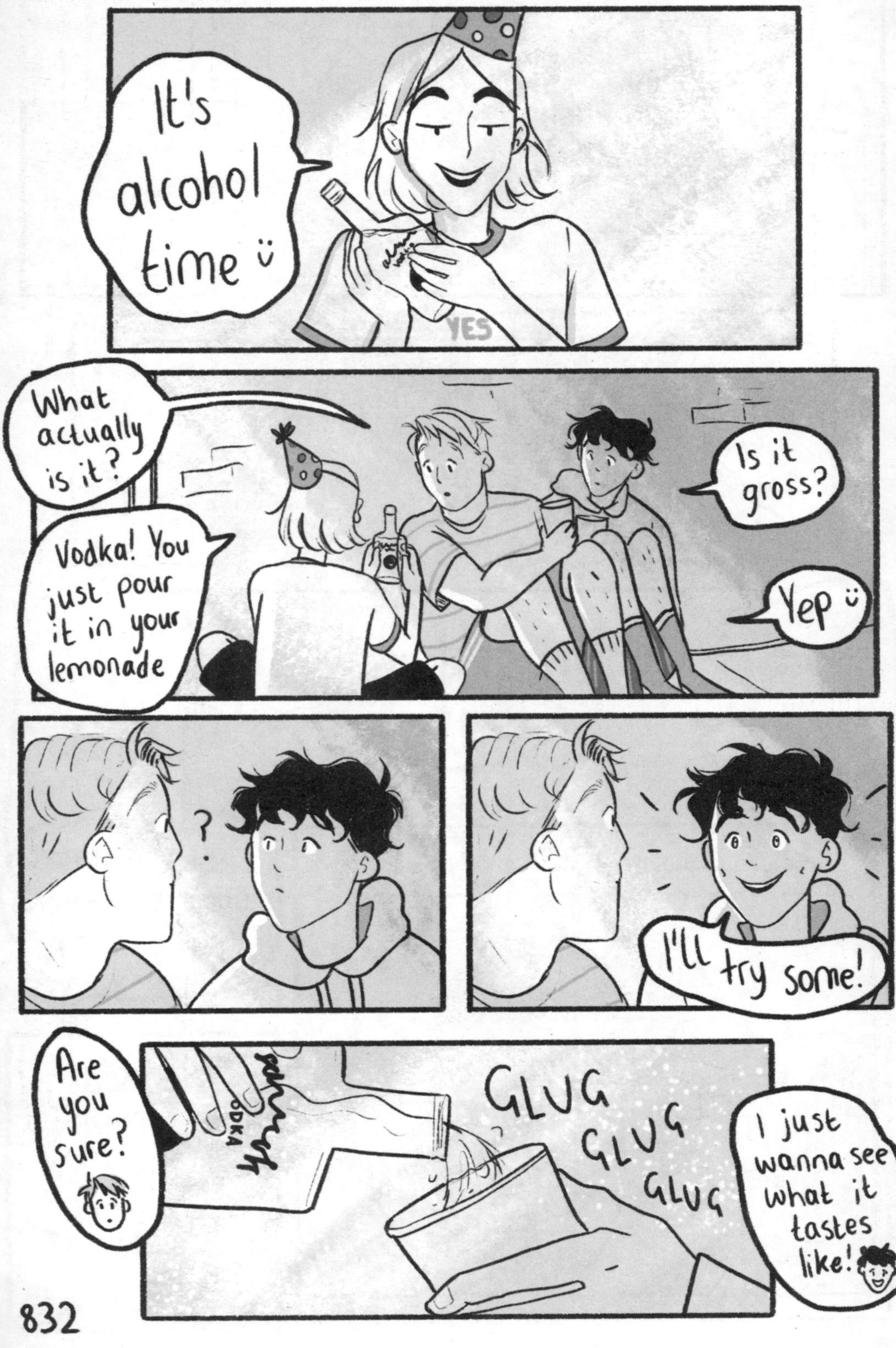
It's alcohol time ü
YES
What actually is it?
Vodka! You just pour it in your lemonade
Is it gross?
Yep ü
?
I'll try some!
Are you sure?
GLUG GLUG GLUG
I just wanna see what it tastes like!

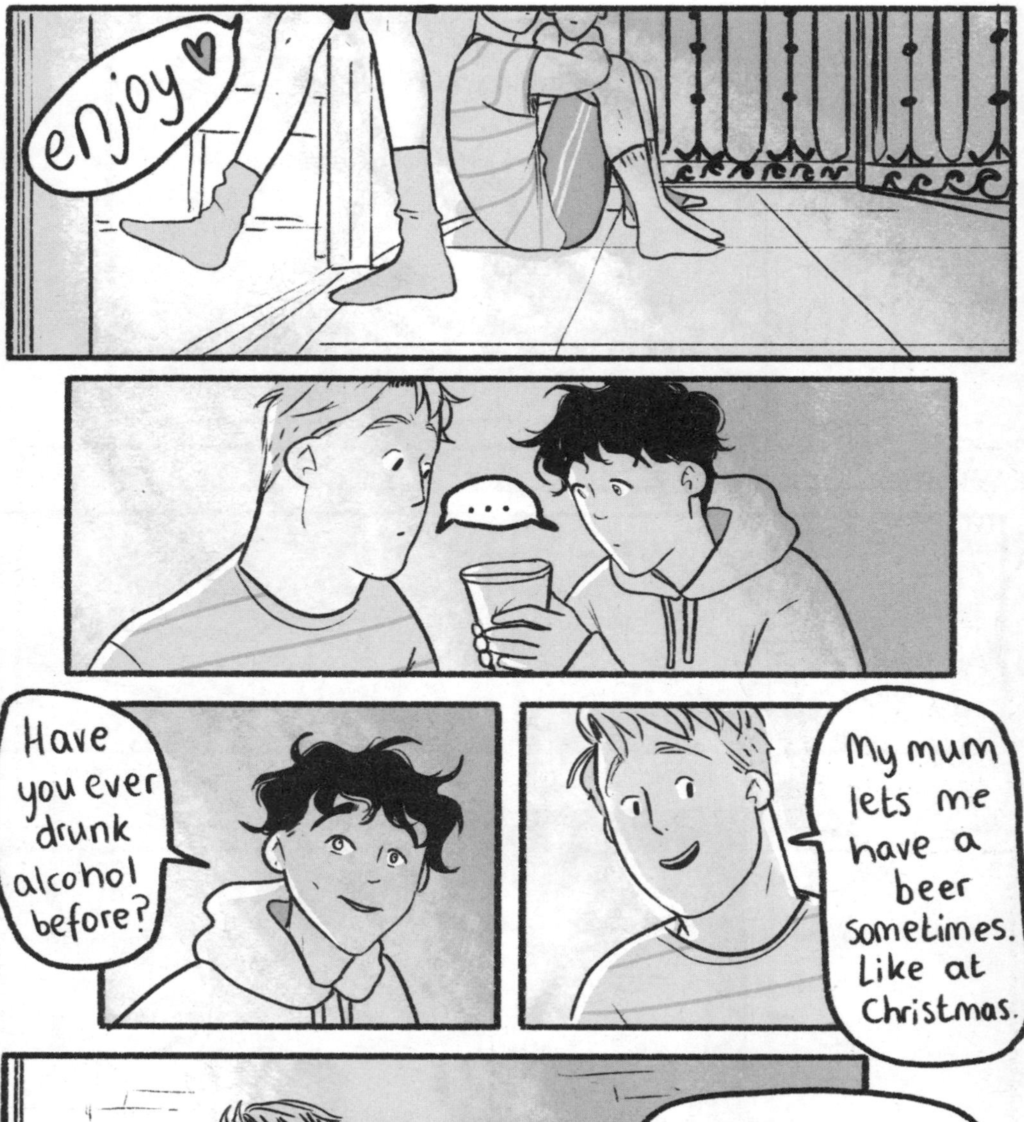
enjoy ♥
...
Have you ever drunk alcohol before?
My mum lets me have a beer sometimes. Like at Christmas.
Lucky. My parents have never let me try it. They're so strict about stuff like that.

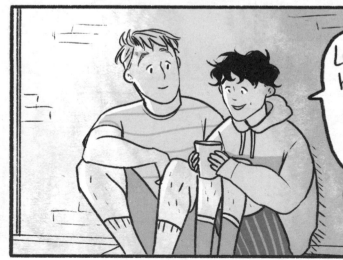

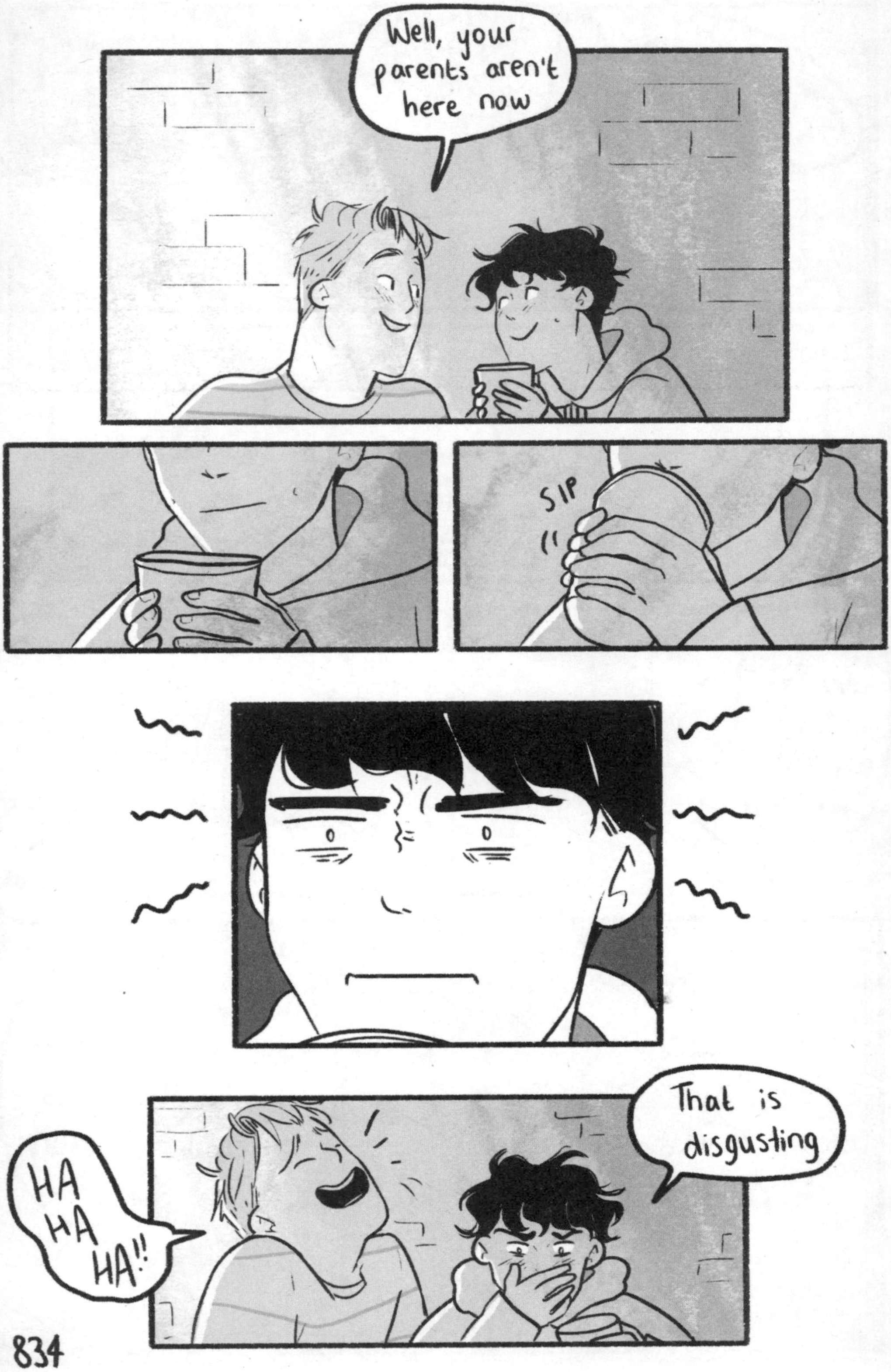
Well, your parents aren't here now
SIP
HA HA HA!!
That is disgusting

Literally why would anyone pay for that
I wanna try!
SIP
It tastes like metal
HA HA HA HA!!

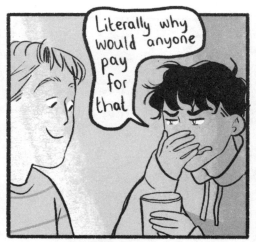

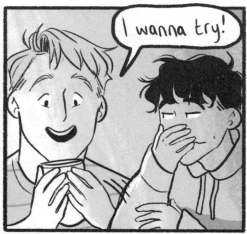

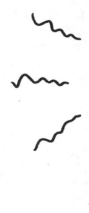

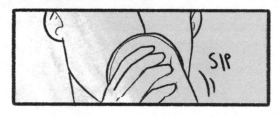

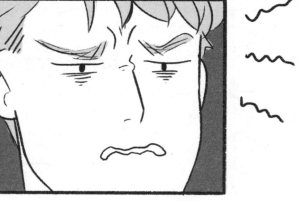

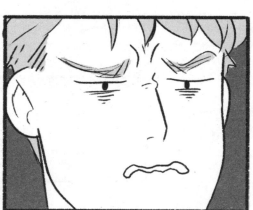

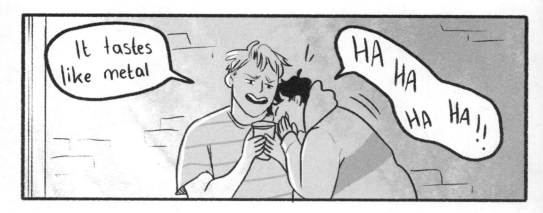

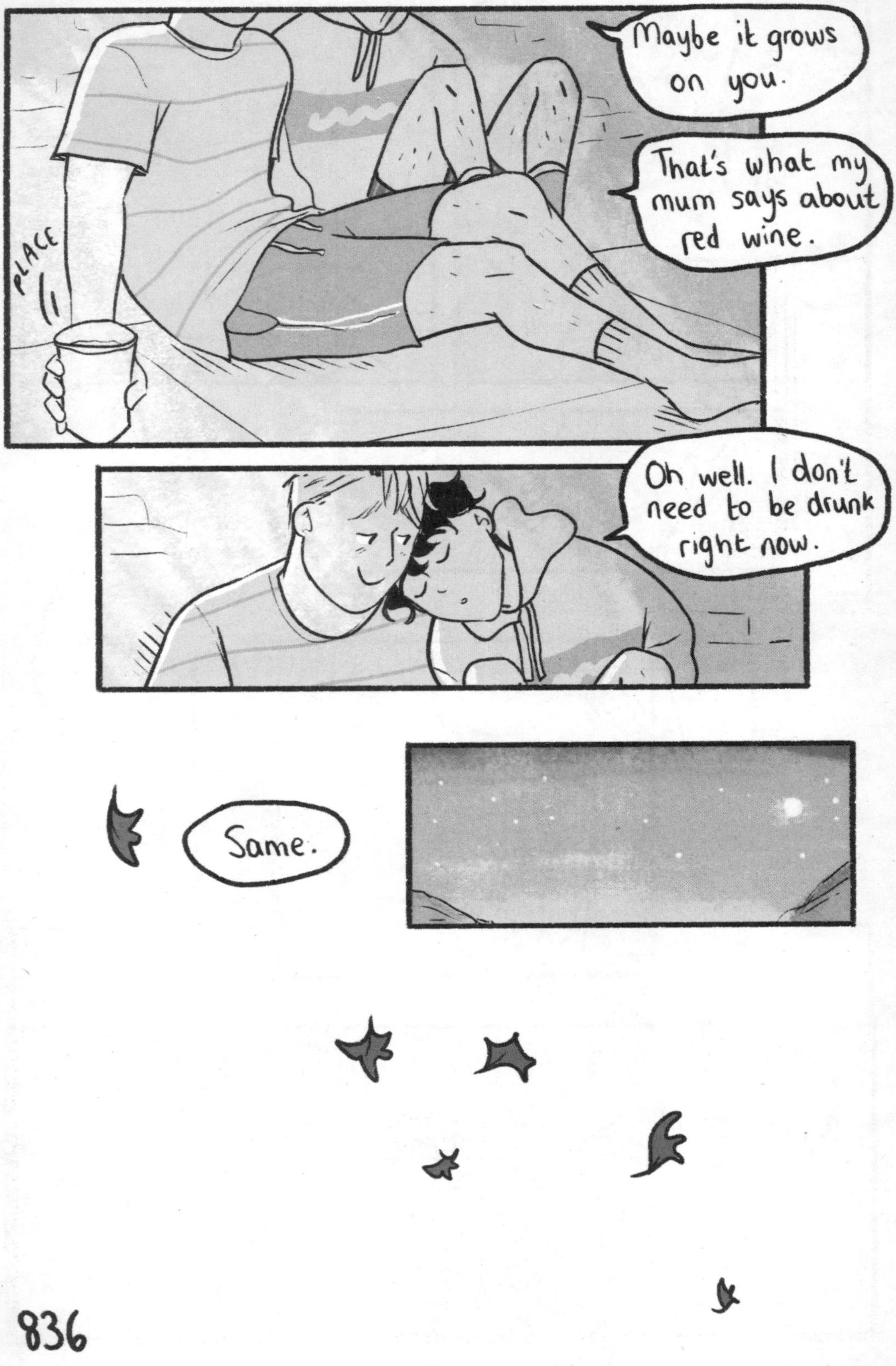
Maybe it grows on you.
That's what my mum says about red wine.
PLACE
Oh well. I don't need to be drunk right now.
Same.

A little while later...

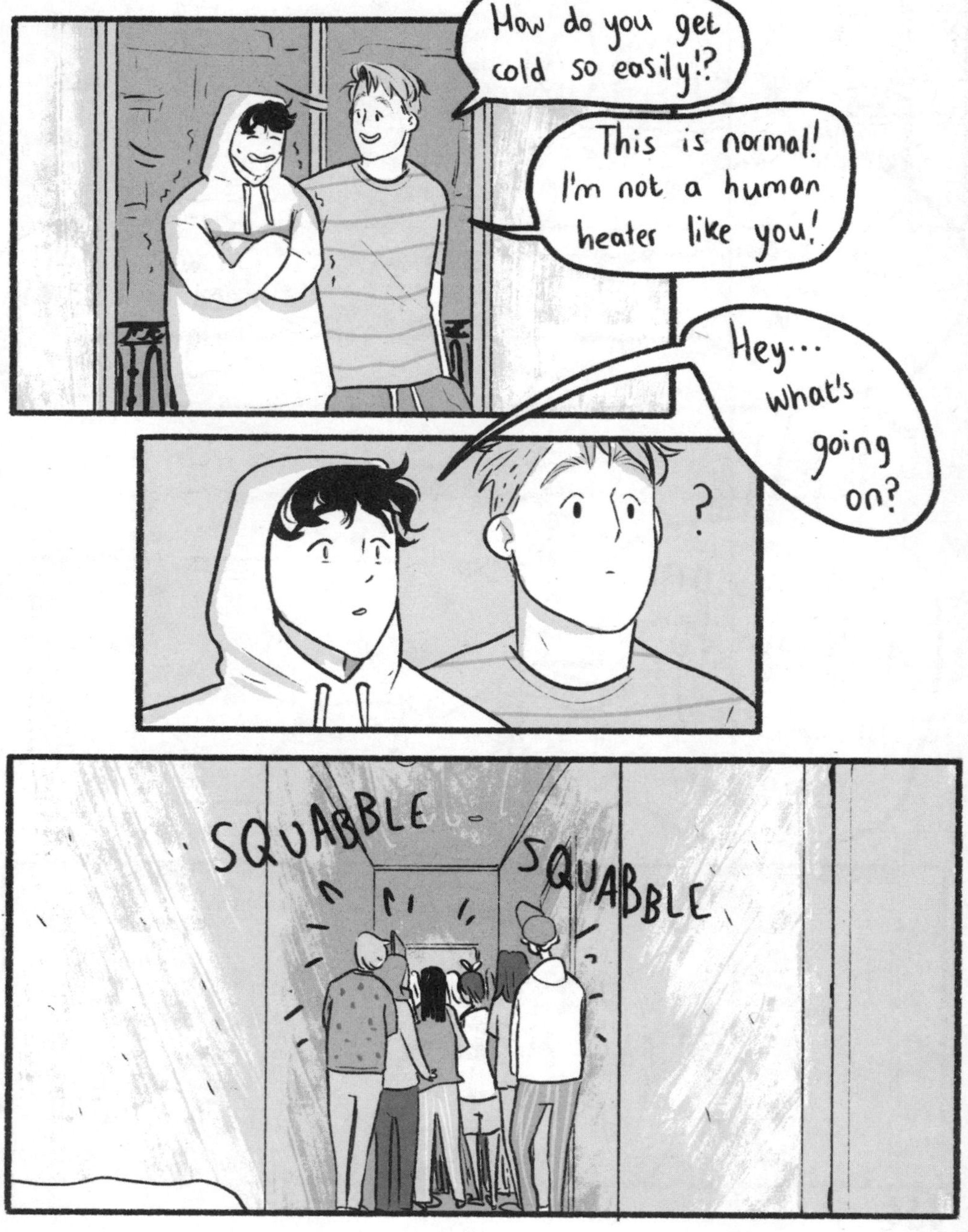
How do you get cold so easily!?
This is normal! I'm not a human heater like you!
Hey... what's going on?
?
SQUABBLE
SQUABBLE

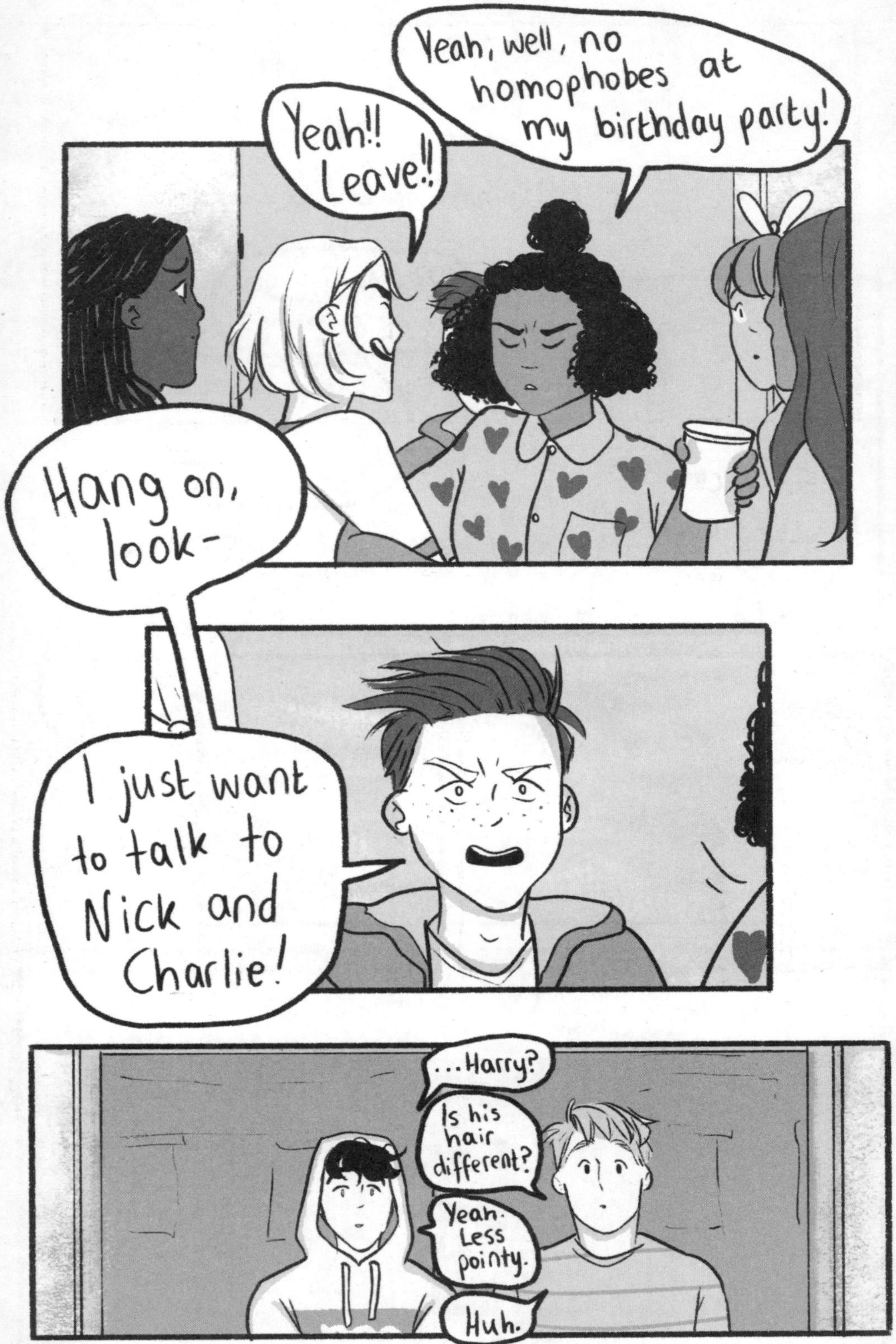
Yeah!! Leave!!
Yeah, well, no homophobes at my birthday party!
Hang on, look-
I just want to talk to Nick and Charlie!
...Harry?
Is his hair different?
Yeah. Less pointy.
Huh.

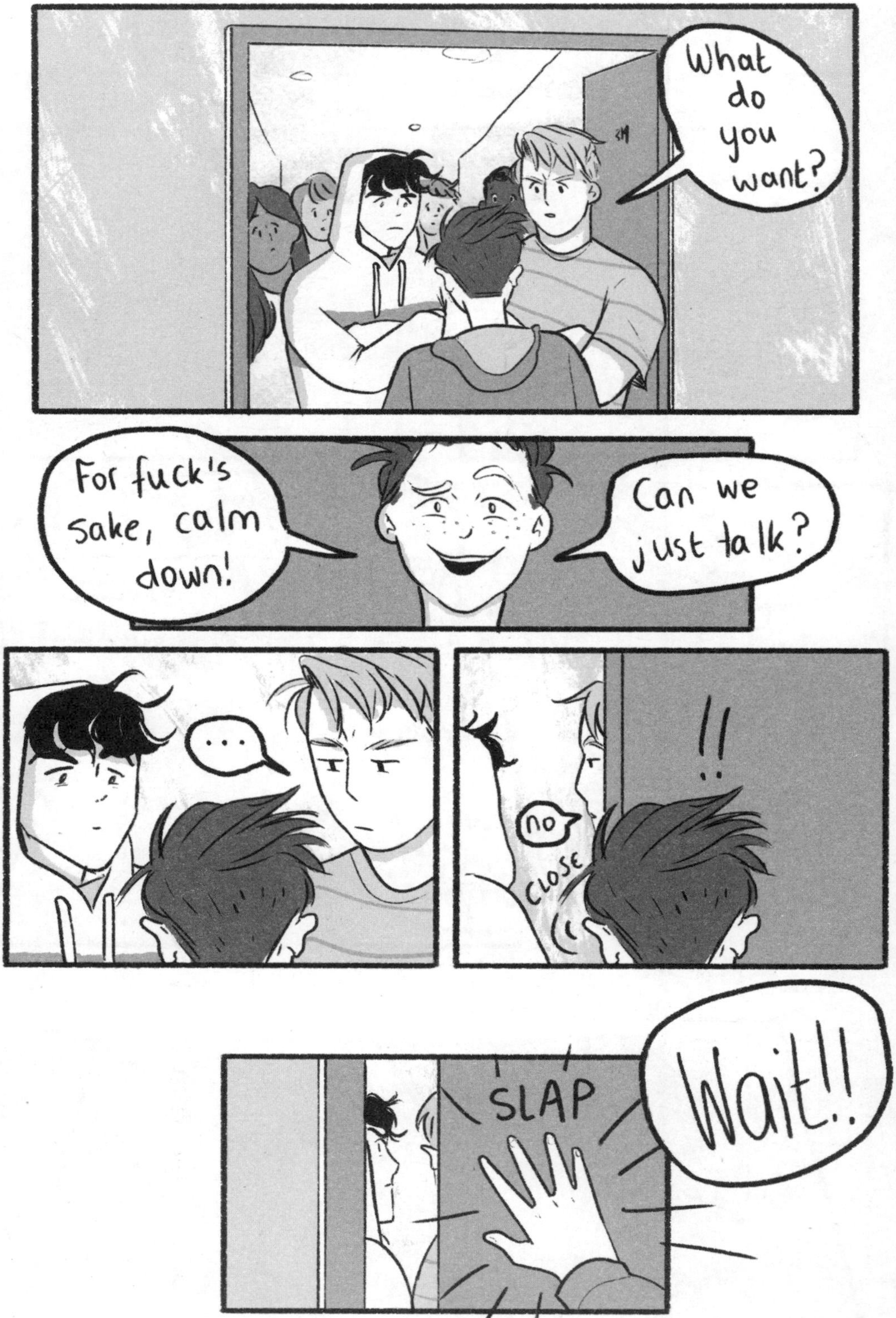
What do you want?
For fuck's sake, calm down!
Can we just talk?
...
!!
no
CLOSE
SLAP
Wait!!

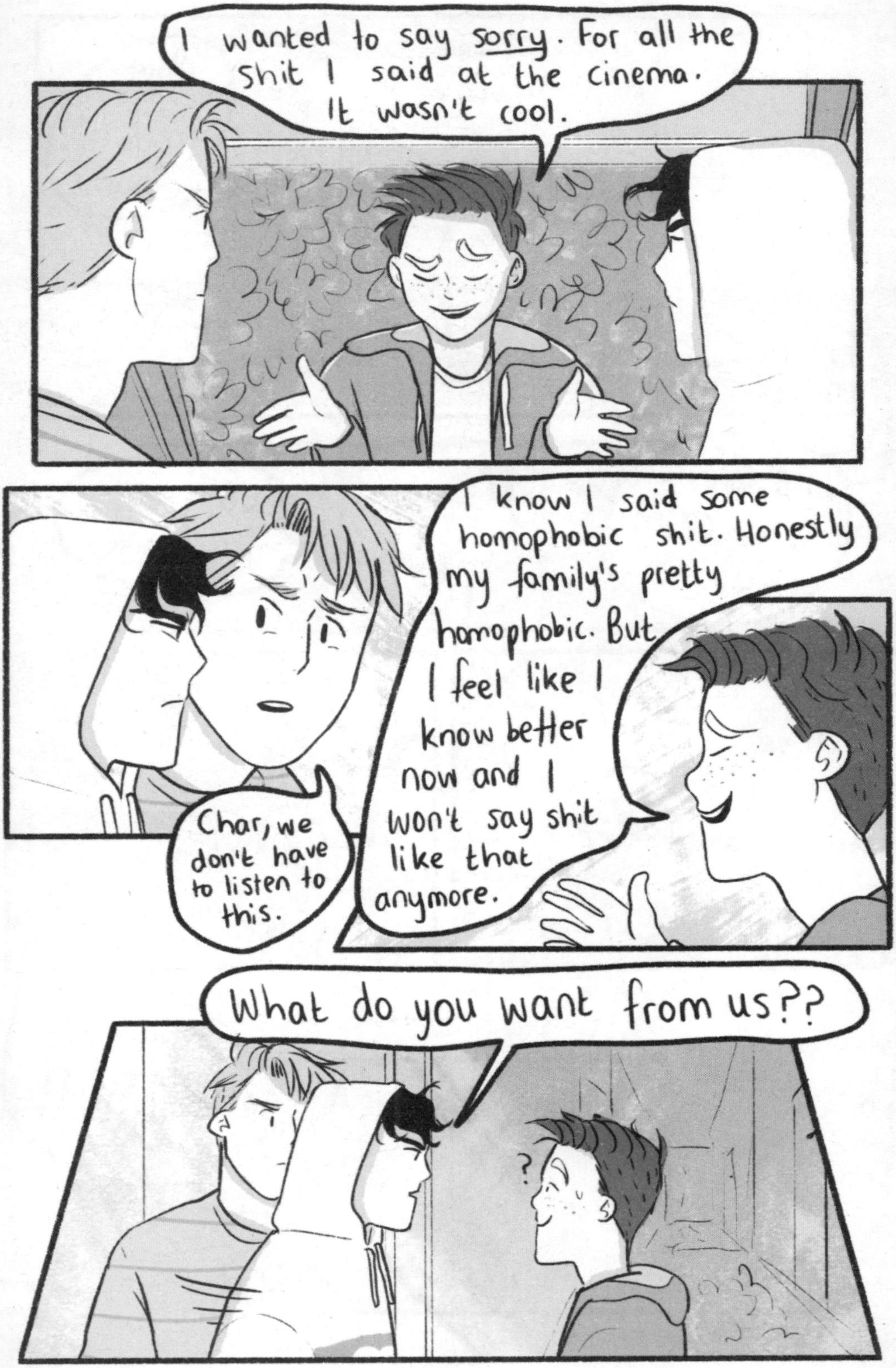
I wanted to say sorry. For all the shit I said at the cinema. It wasn't cool.
I know I said some homophobic shit. Honestly my family's pretty homophobic. But I feel like I know better now and I won't say shit like that anymore.
Char, we don't have to listen to this.
What do you want from us??
?

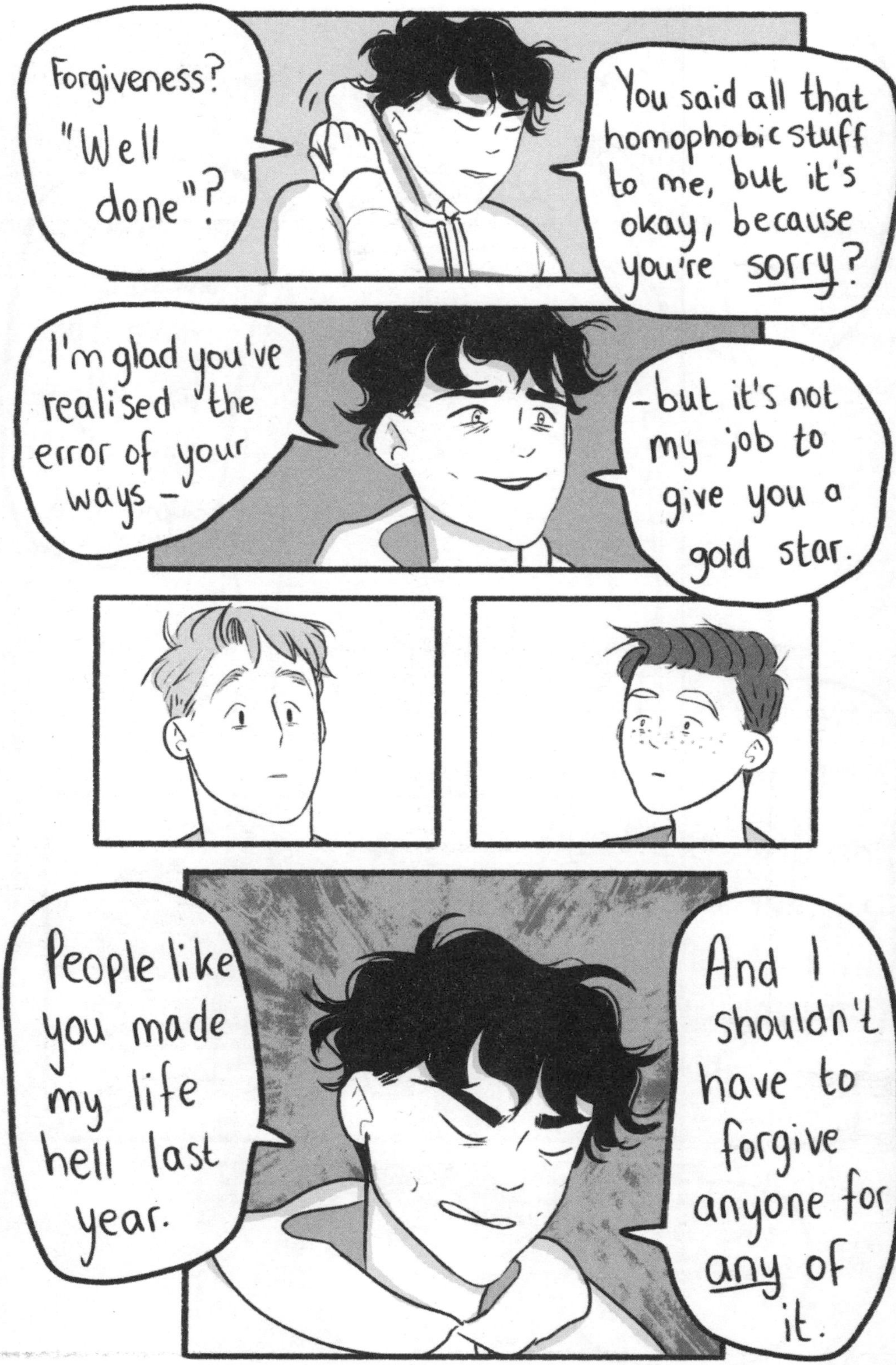
Forgiveness? "Well done"?
You said all that homophobic stuff to me, but it's okay, because you're sorry?
I'm glad you've realised the error of your ways –
– but it's not my job to give you a gold star.
People like you made my life hell last year.
And I shouldn't have to forgive anyone for any of it.

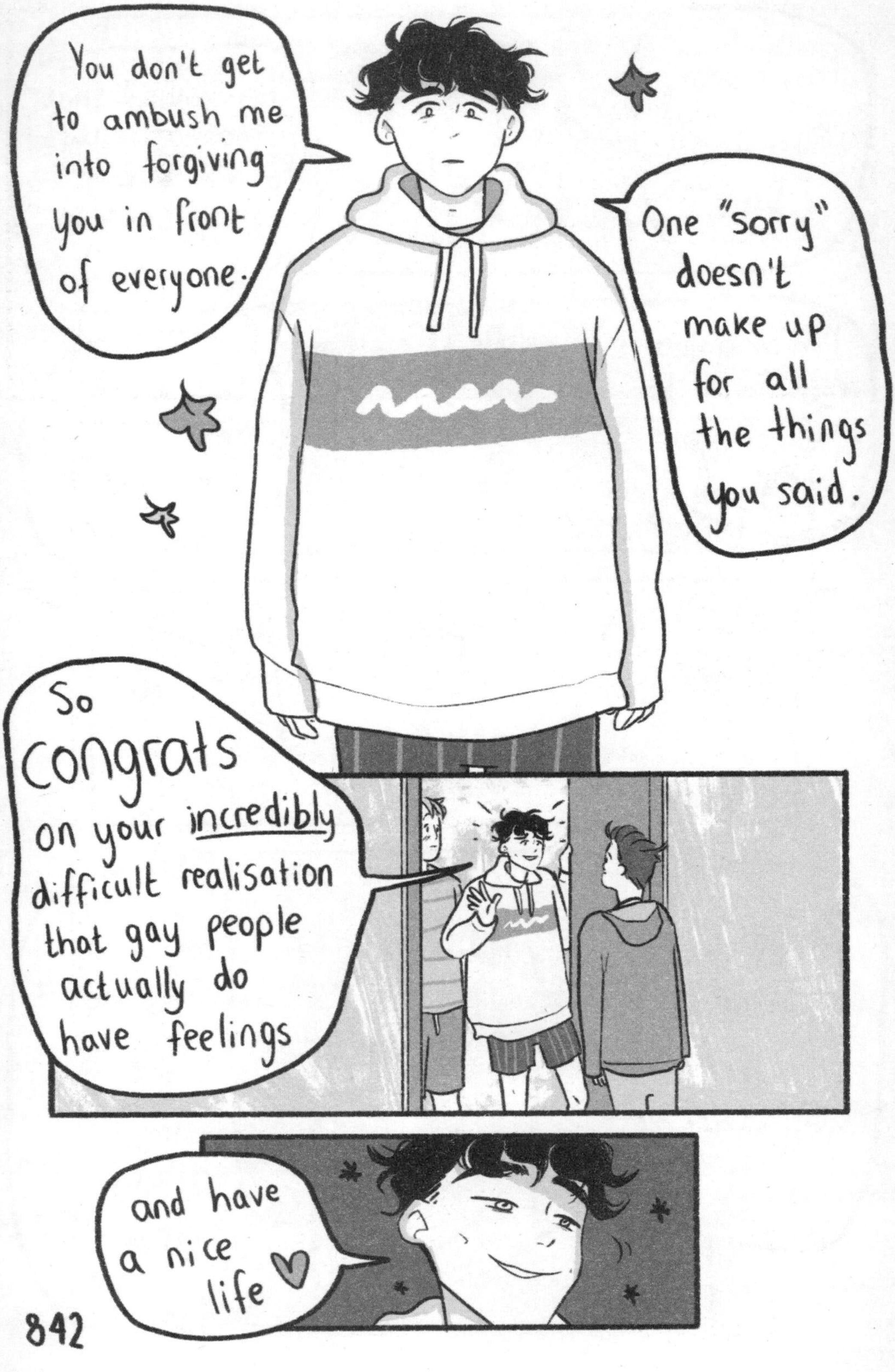
You don't get to ambush me into forgiving you in front of everyone.
One "sorry" doesn't make up for all the things you said.
So congrats on your incredibly difficult realisation that gay people actually do have feelings
and have a nice life

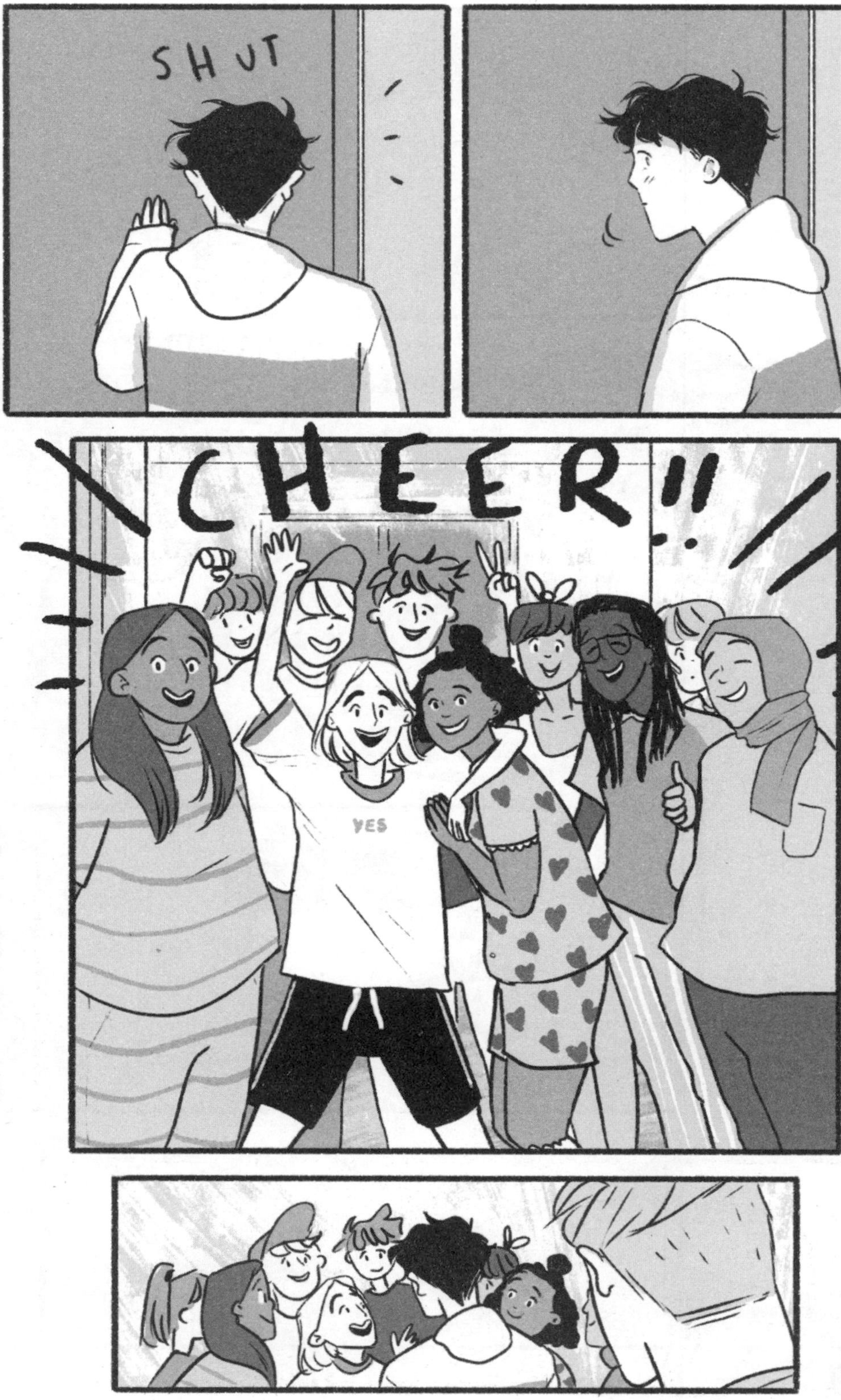
SHUT
CHEER!!
YES

I started to believe what they were saying

It made me really hate myself

...last year when everything at school was shit

TOUCH

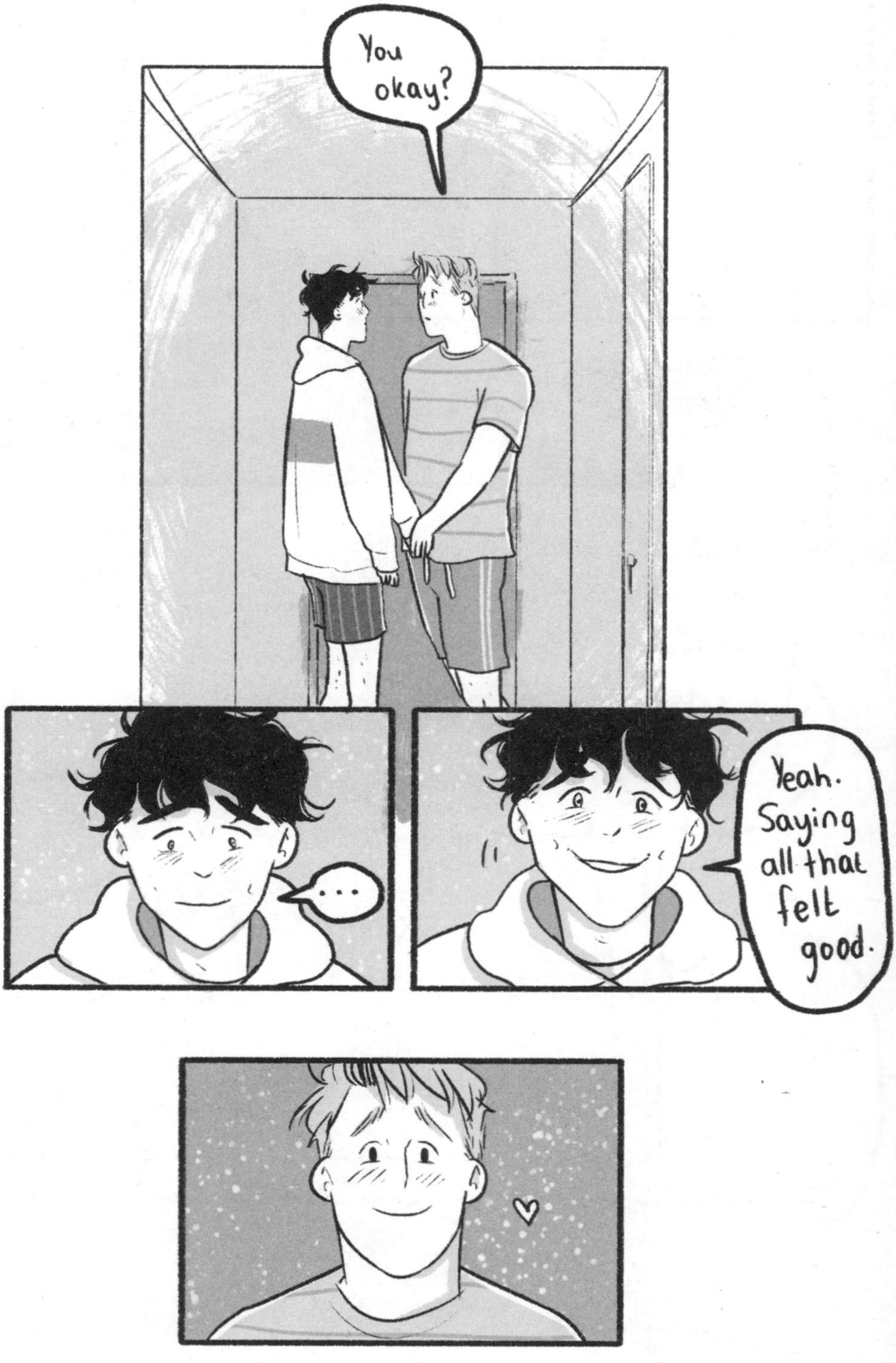
You okay?
...
Yeah. Saying all that felt good.

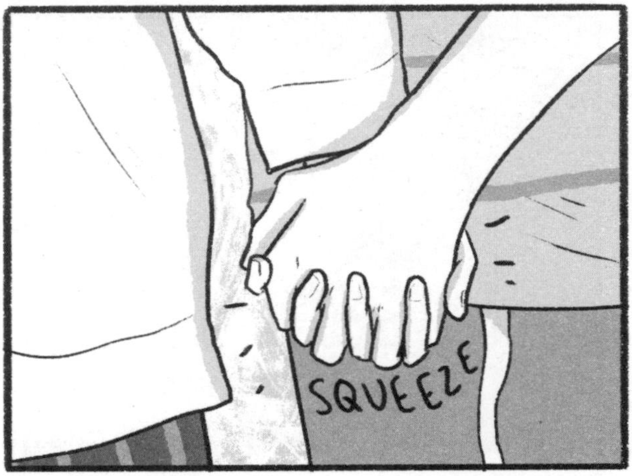
SQUEEZE

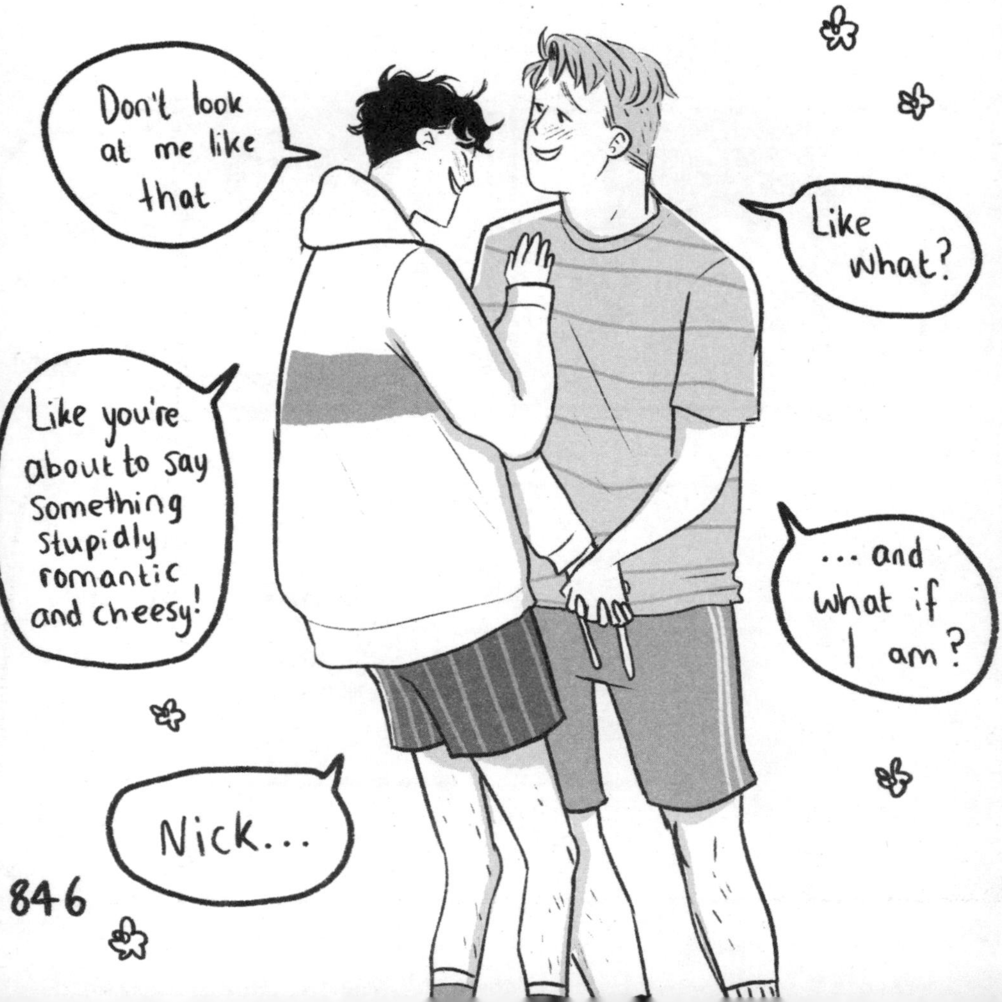
Don't look at me like that
Like what?
Like you're about to say something stupidly romantic and cheesy!
... and what if I am?
Nick...

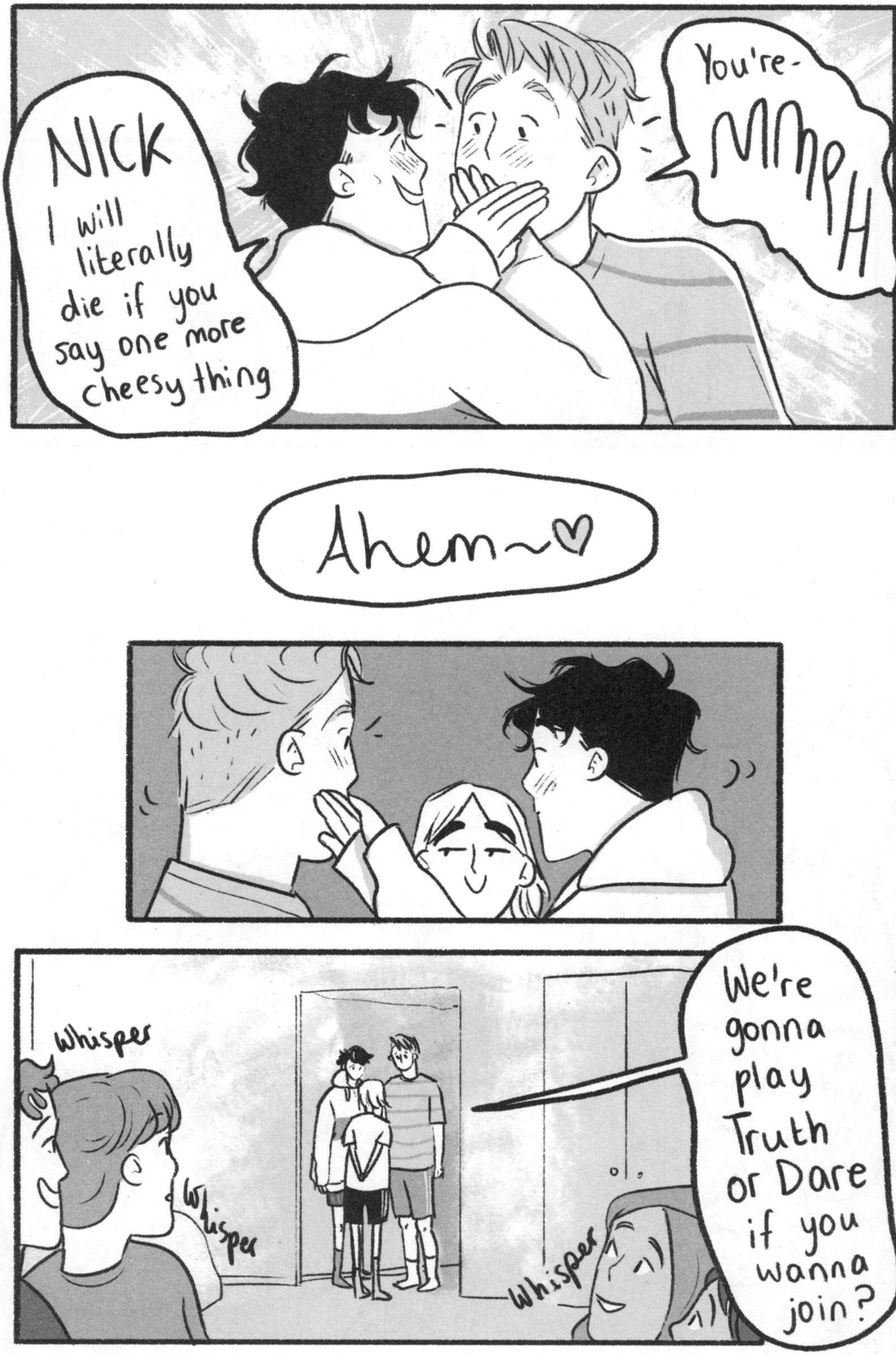
NICK I will literally die if you say one more cheesy thing
You're- MMPH
Ahem~♡
Whisper
Whisper
Whisper
We're gonna play Truth or Dare if you wanna join?

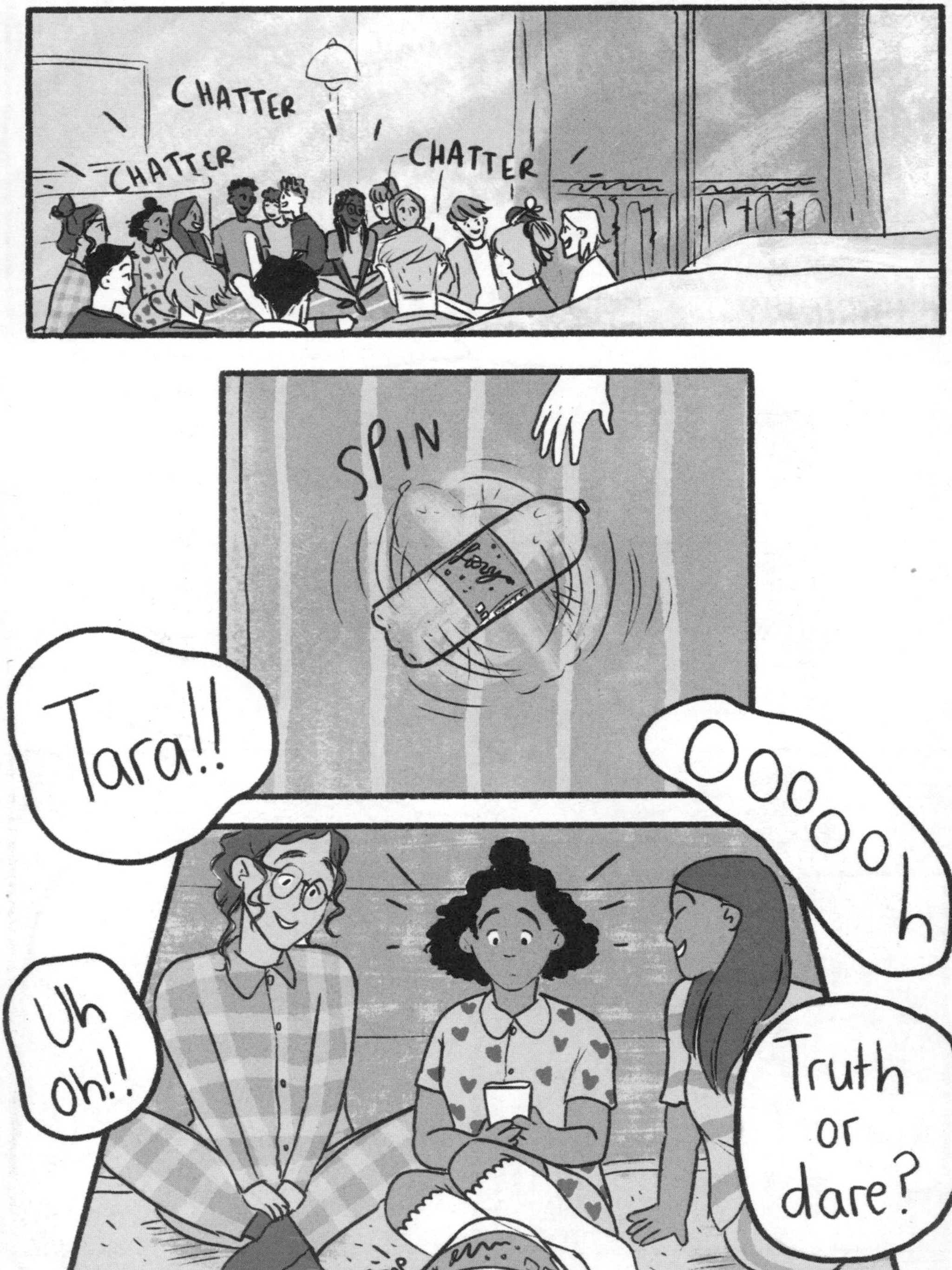
CHATTER
CHATTER
CHATTER
SPIN
Tara!!
Ooooooh
Uh oh!!
Truth or dare?
STOP

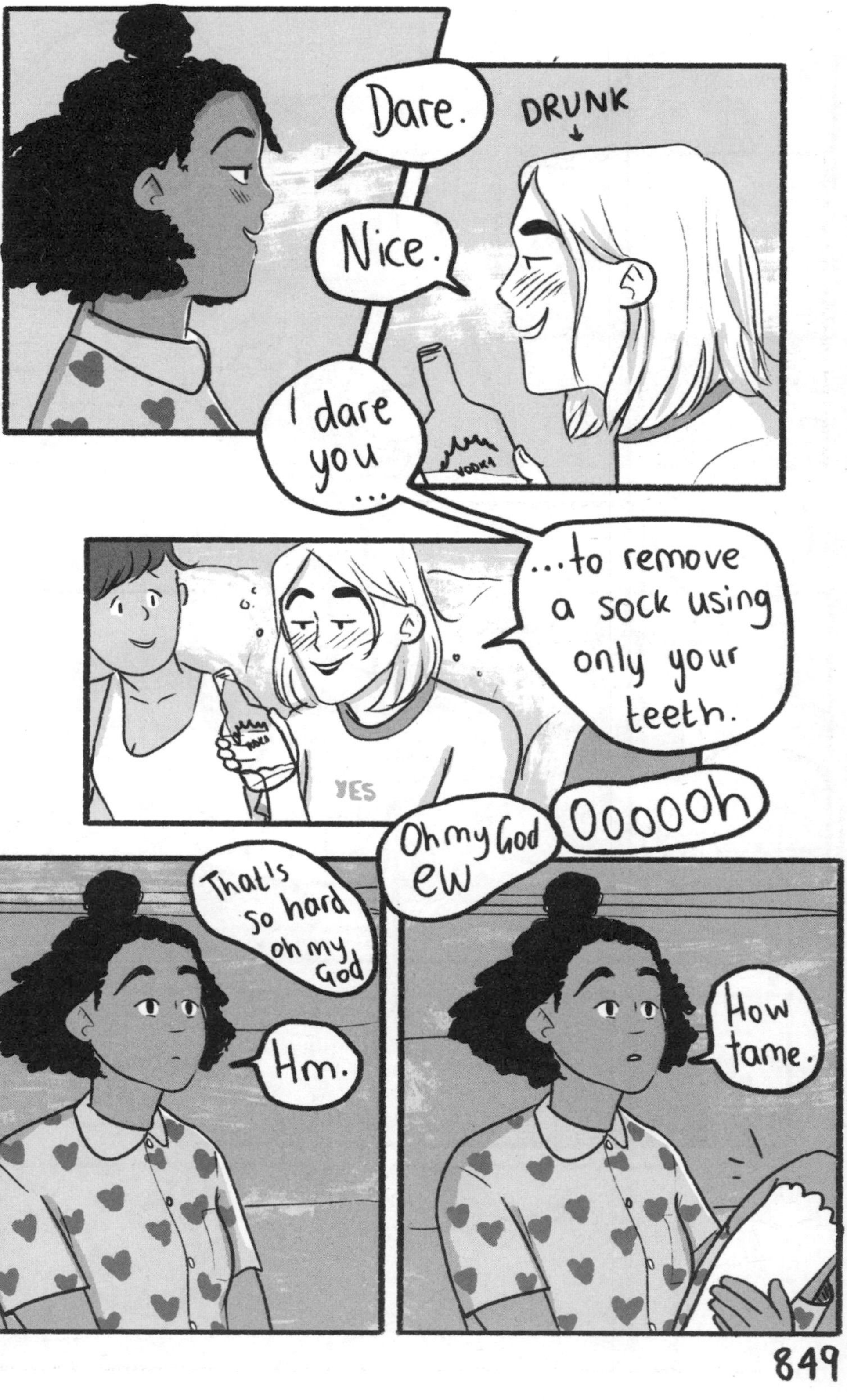
Dare.
DRUNK
Nice.
I dare you ...
...to remove a sock using only your teeth.
VODKA
YES
Ooooooh
Oh my God ew
That's so hard oh my God
Hm.
How tame.

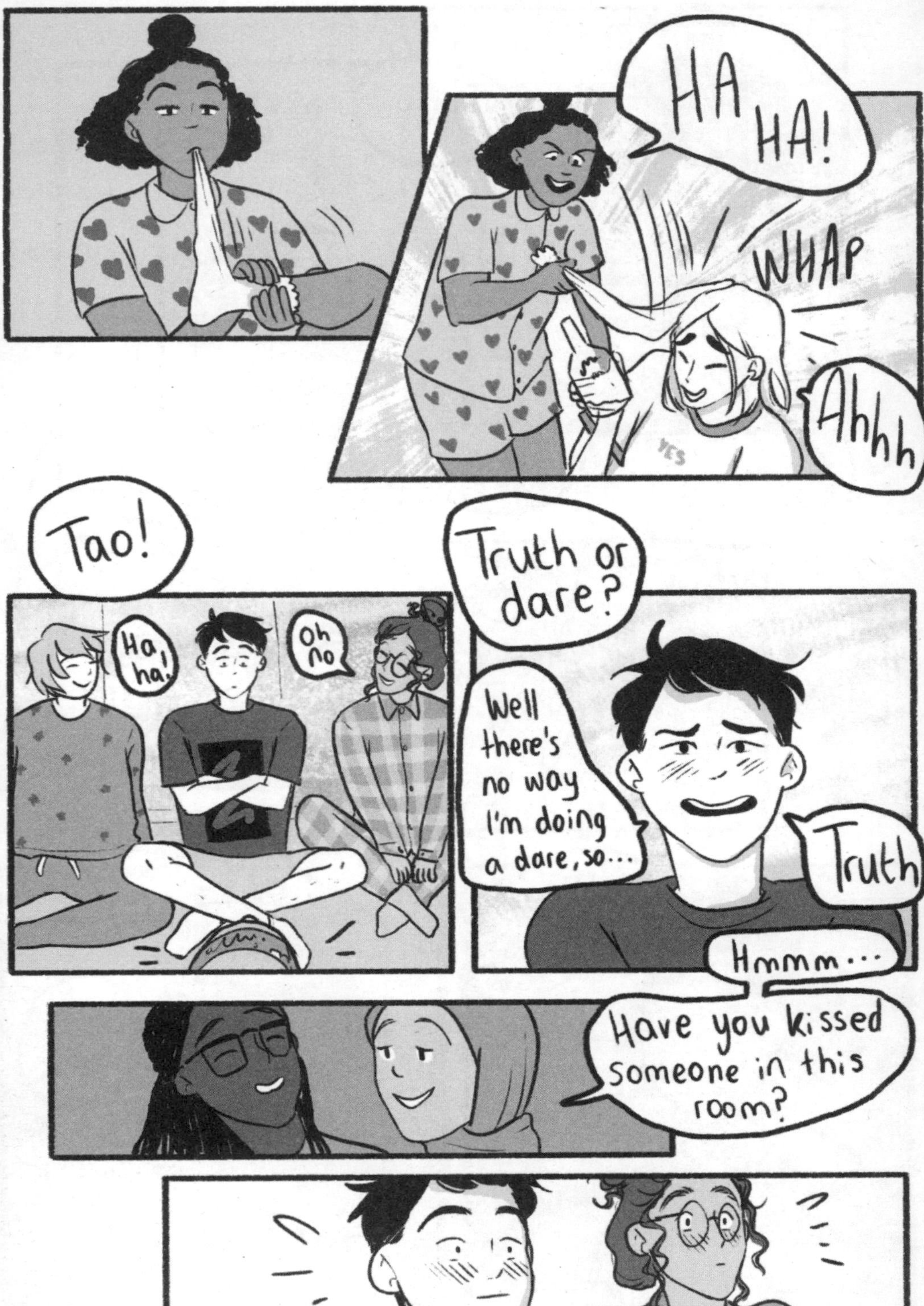
HA HA!
WHAP
Ahhh
Tao!
Ha ha!
Oh no
Truth or dare?
Well there's no way I'm doing a dare, so...
Truth
Hmmm...
Have you kissed someone in this room?

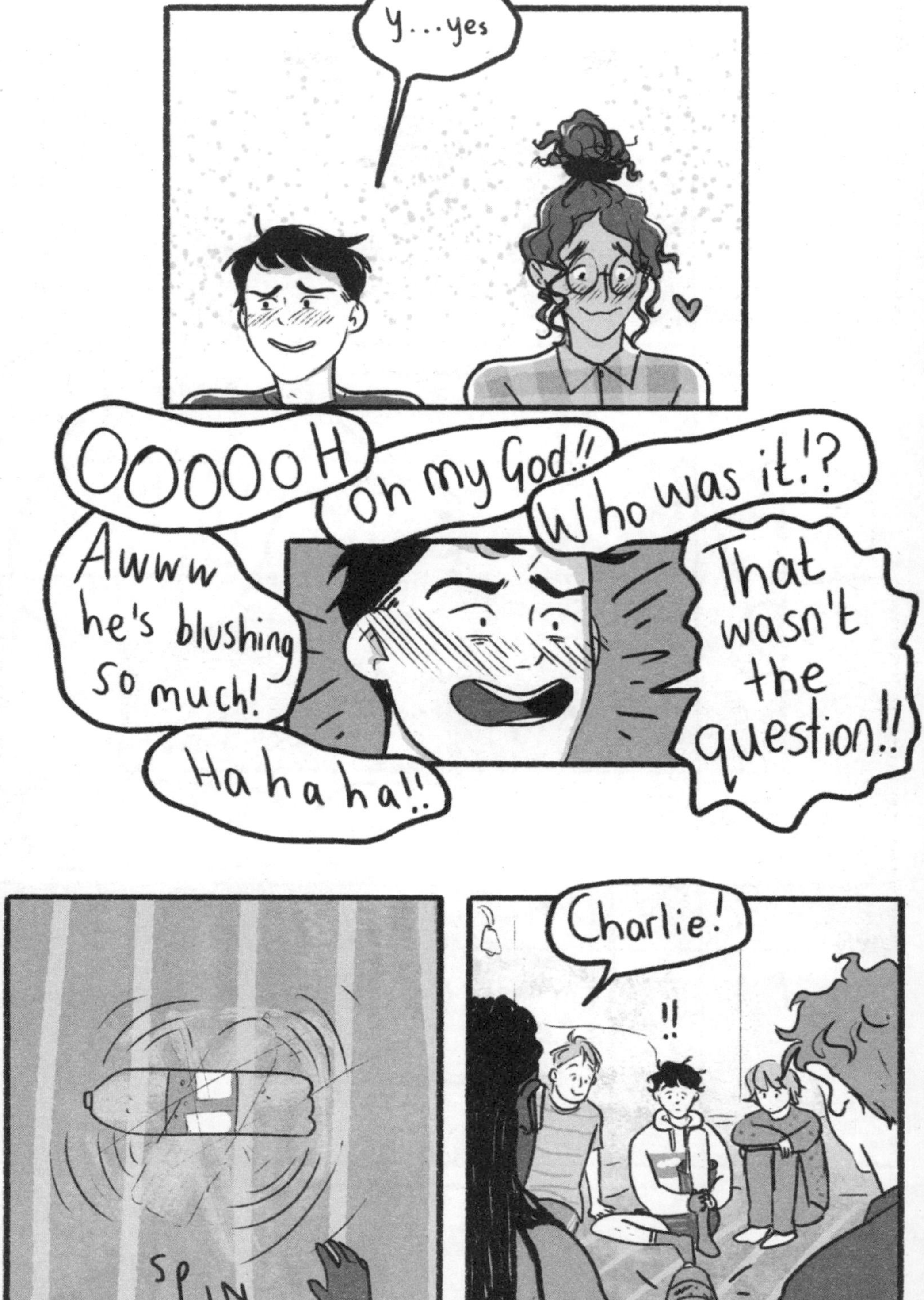
y...yes
OOOOOH
Oh my God!!
Who was it!?
Awww he's blushing so much!
That wasn't the question!!
Ha ha ha ha!!
SPIN
Charlie!
!!

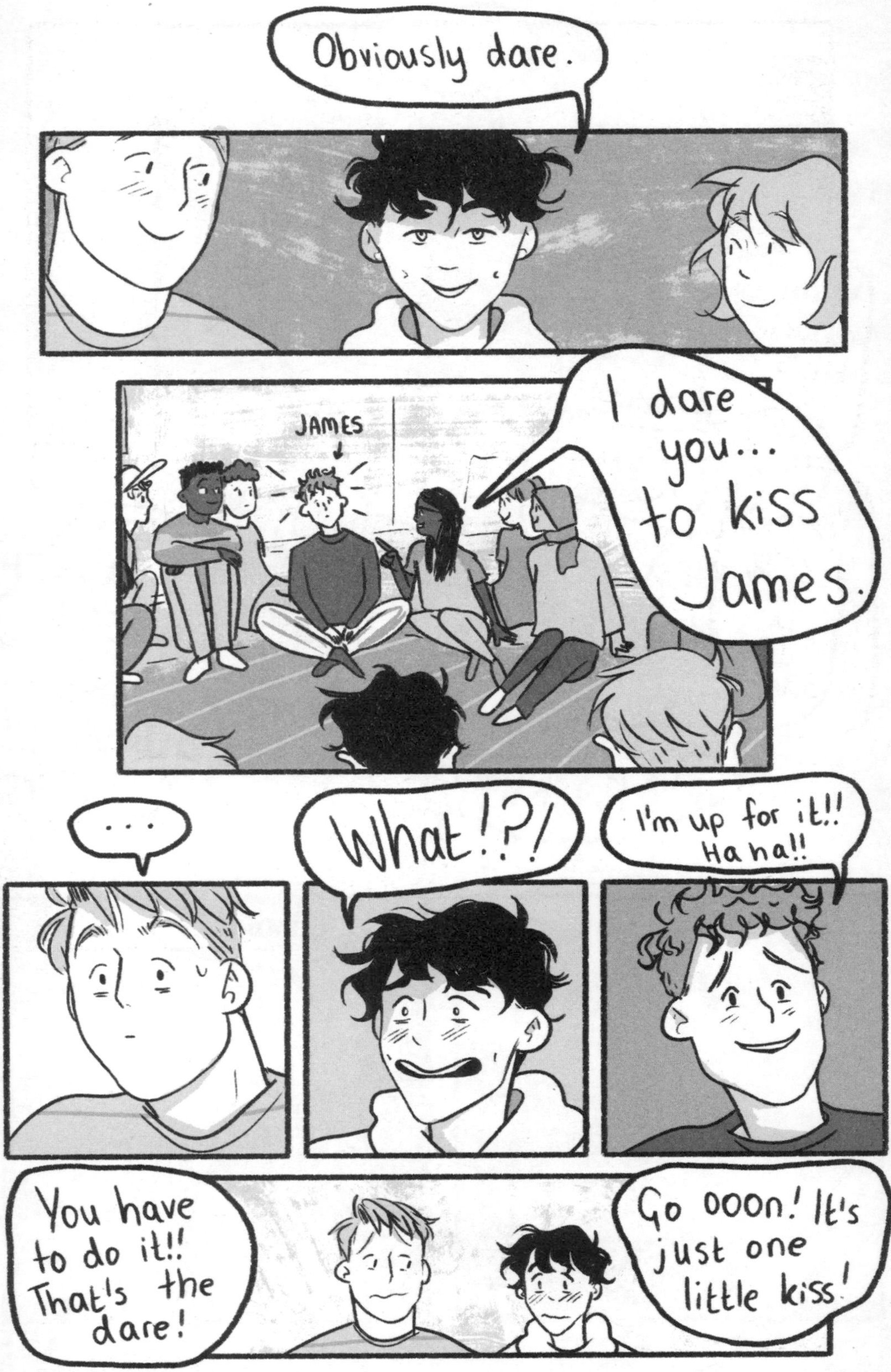
Obviously dare.
JAMES
I dare you... to kiss James.
...
What!?!
I'm up for it!! Ha ha!!
You have to do it!! That's the dare!
Go ooon! It's just one little kiss!

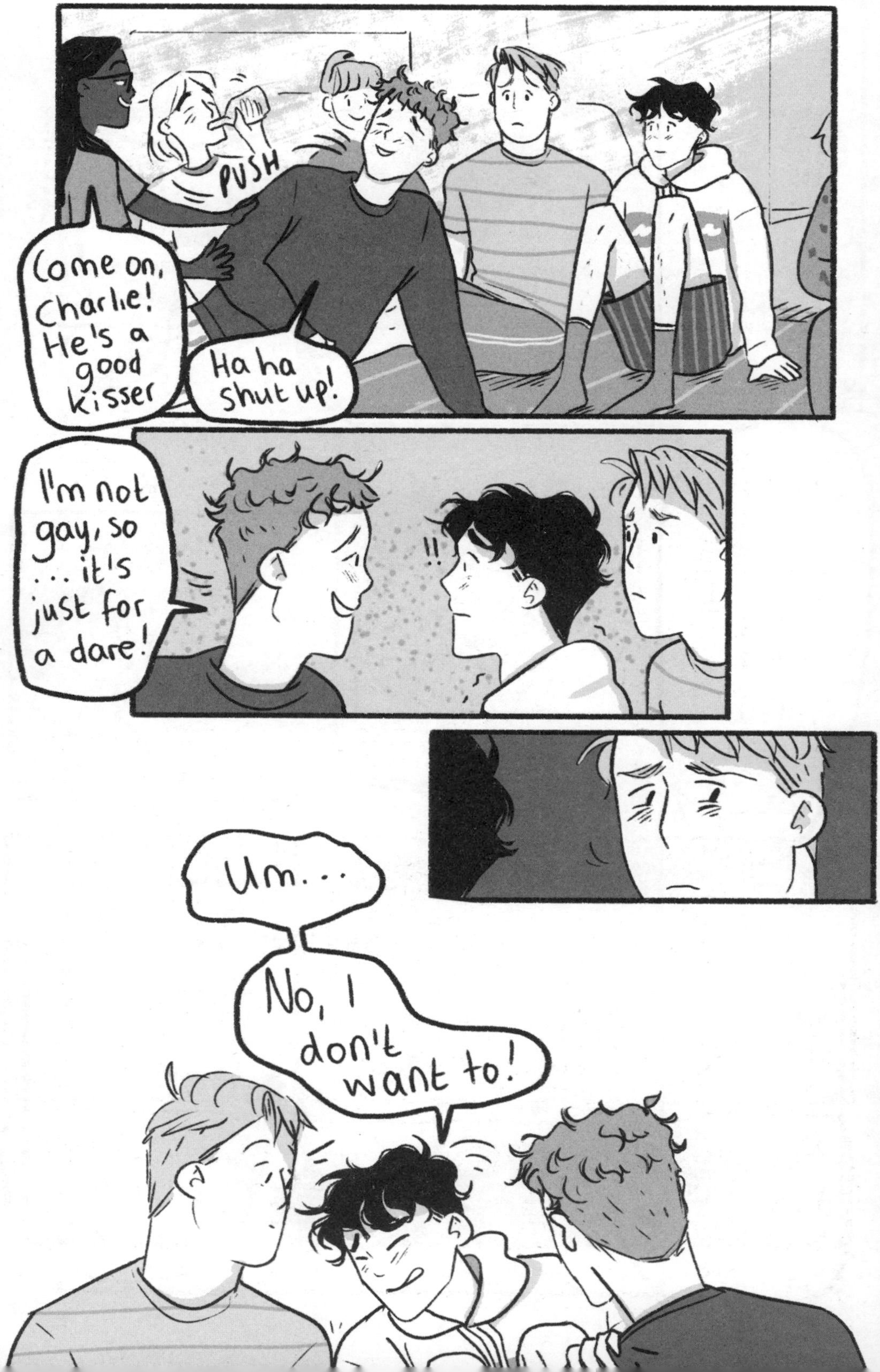
PUSH
Come on, Charlie! He's a good kisser
Ha ha shut up!
I'm not gay, so ... it's just for a dare!
!!
Um...
No, I don't want to!

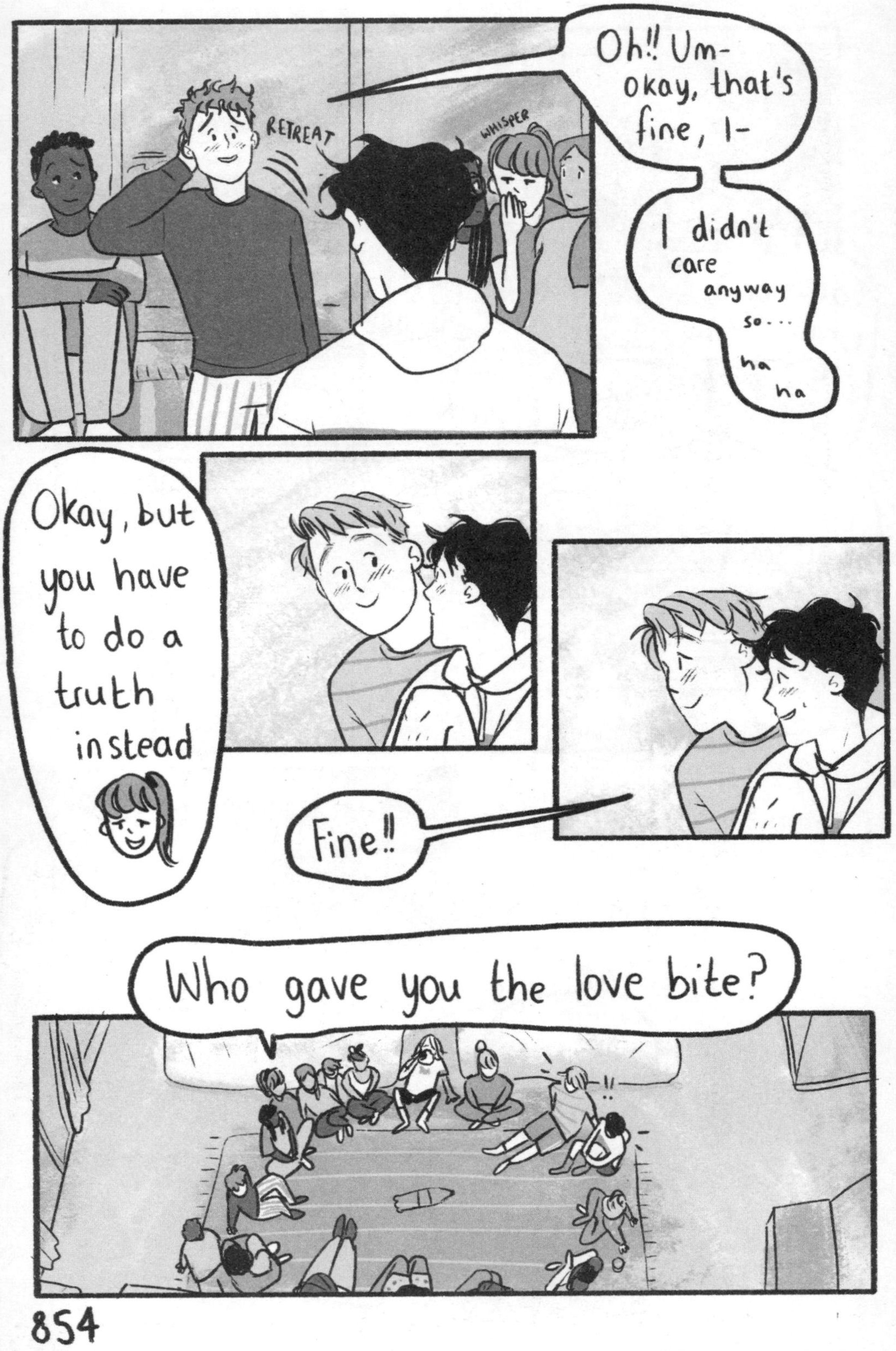
RETREAT
WHISPER
Oh!! Um- okay, that's fine, I-
I didn't care anyway so... ha ha
Okay, but you have to do a truth instead
Fine!!
Who gave you the love bite?
!!

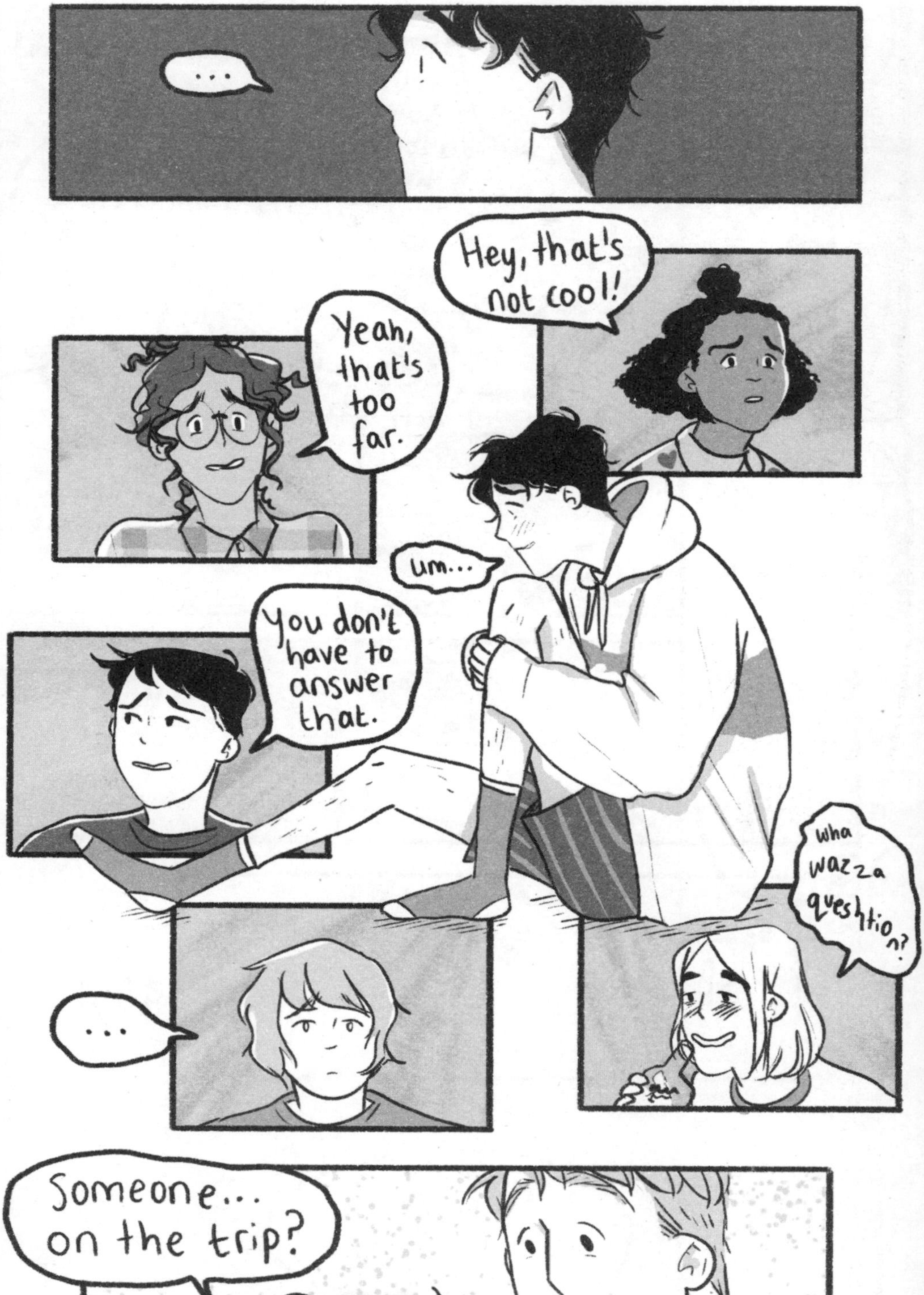
...
Yeah, that's too far.
Hey, that's not cool!
um...
You don't have to answer that.
...
wha wazza queshtion?
Someone... on the trip?

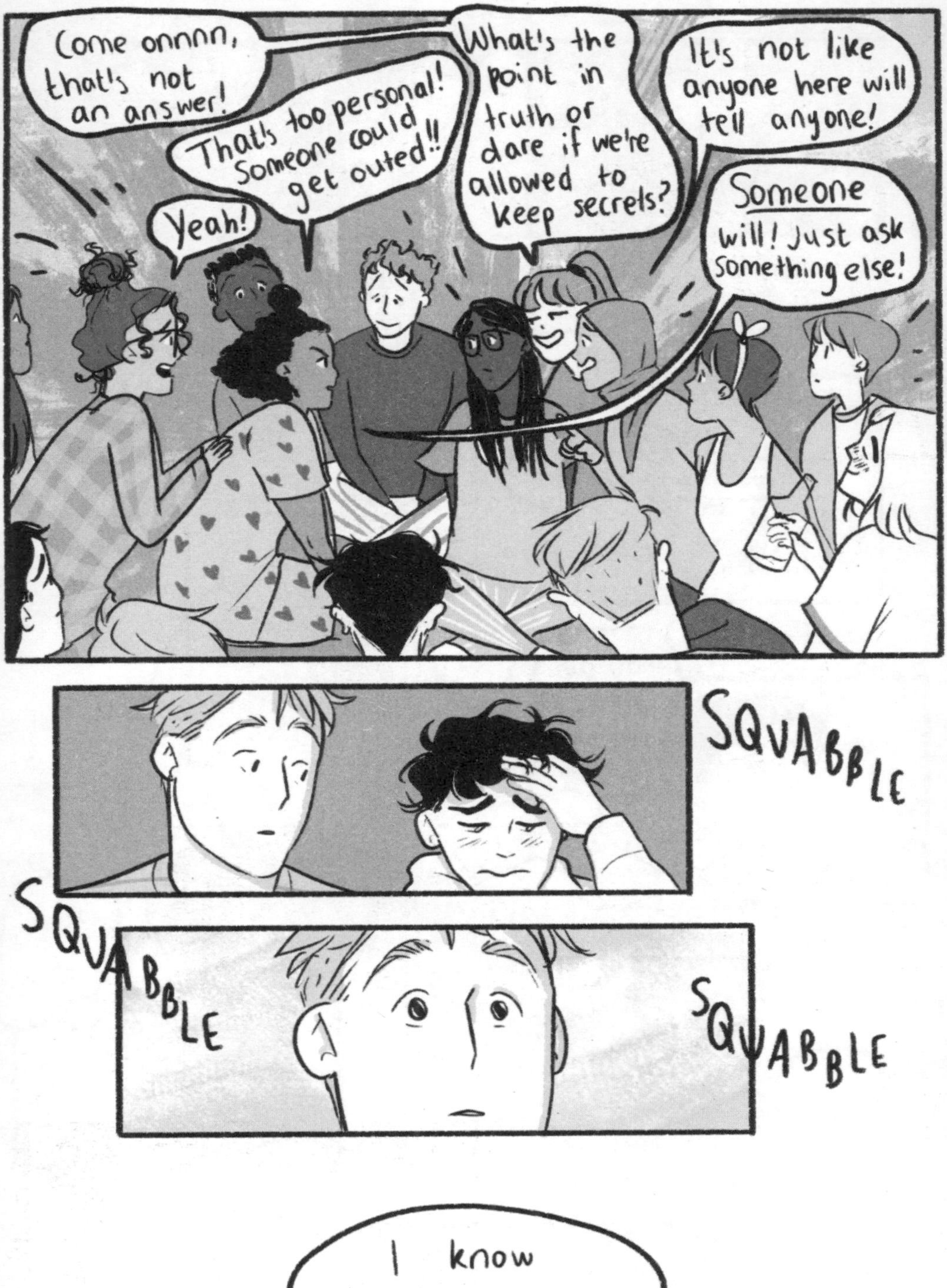

Come onnnn, that's not an answer!
What's the point in truth or dare if we're allowed to keep secrets?
It's not like anyone here will tell anyone!
That's too personal! Someone could get outed!!
Yeah!
Someone will! Just ask something else!
SQUABBLE
SQUABBLE
SQUABBLE
I know who it was.

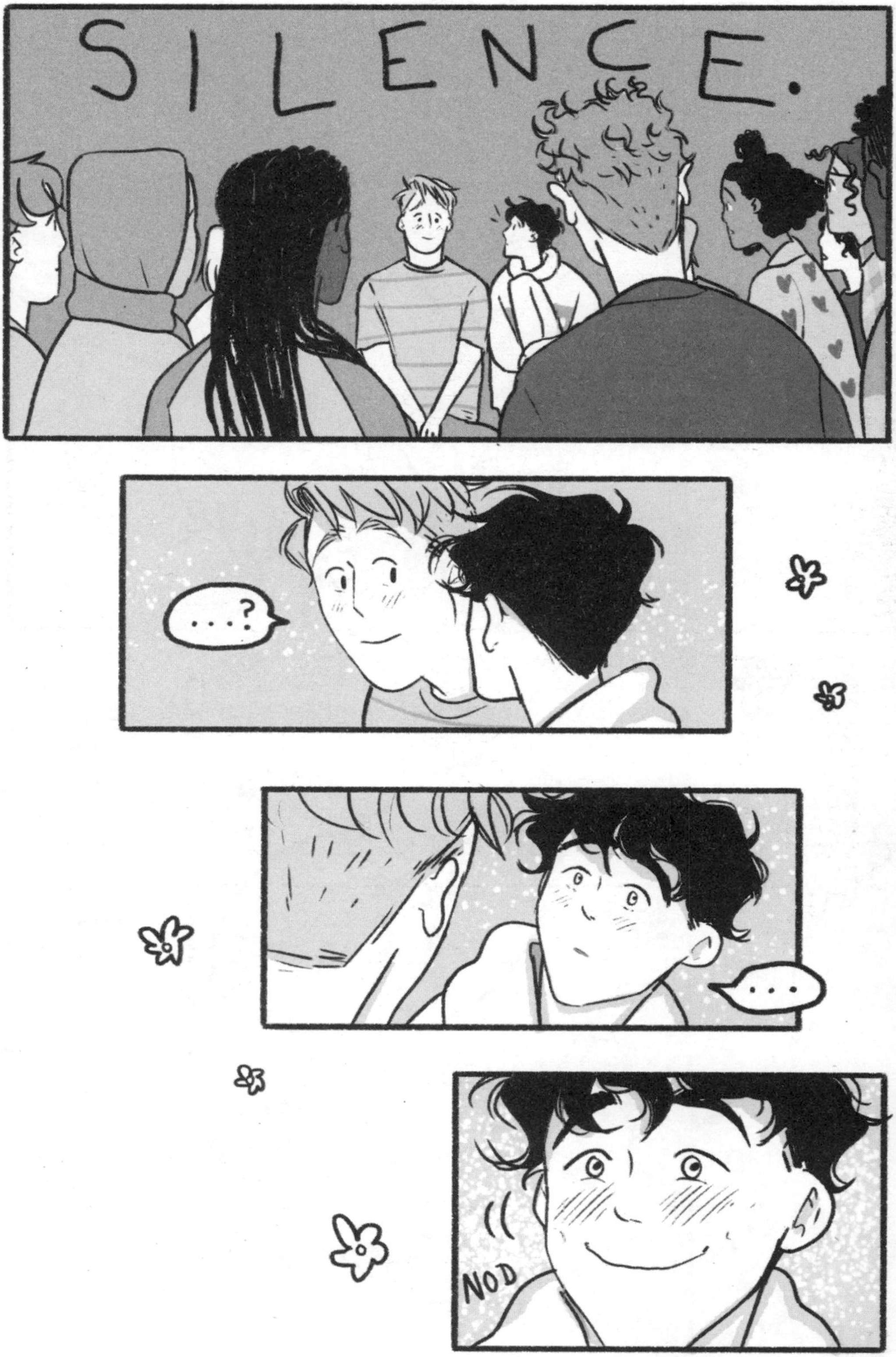
SILENCE.
...?
...
NOD

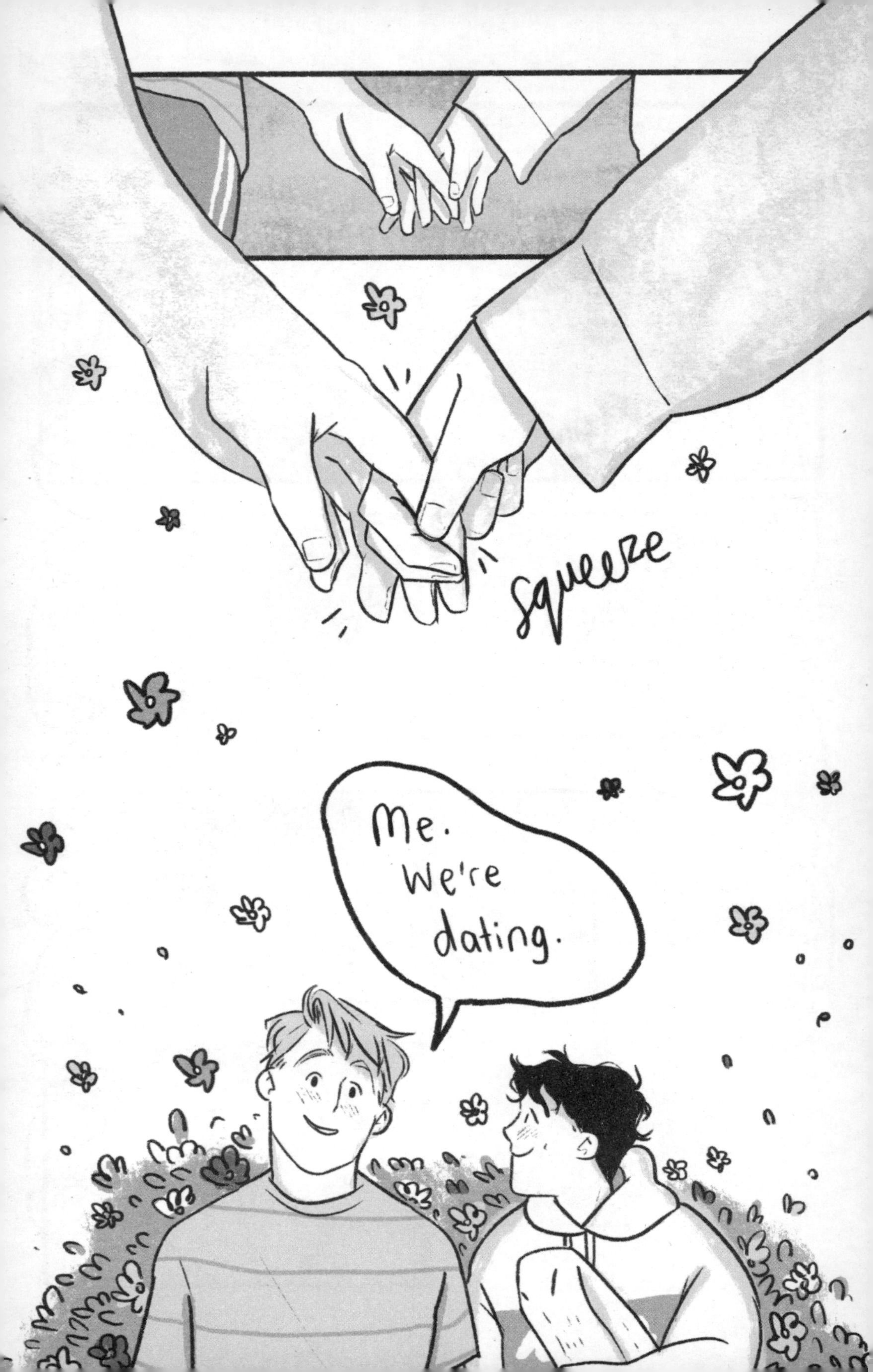
squeeze
Me.
We're
dating.

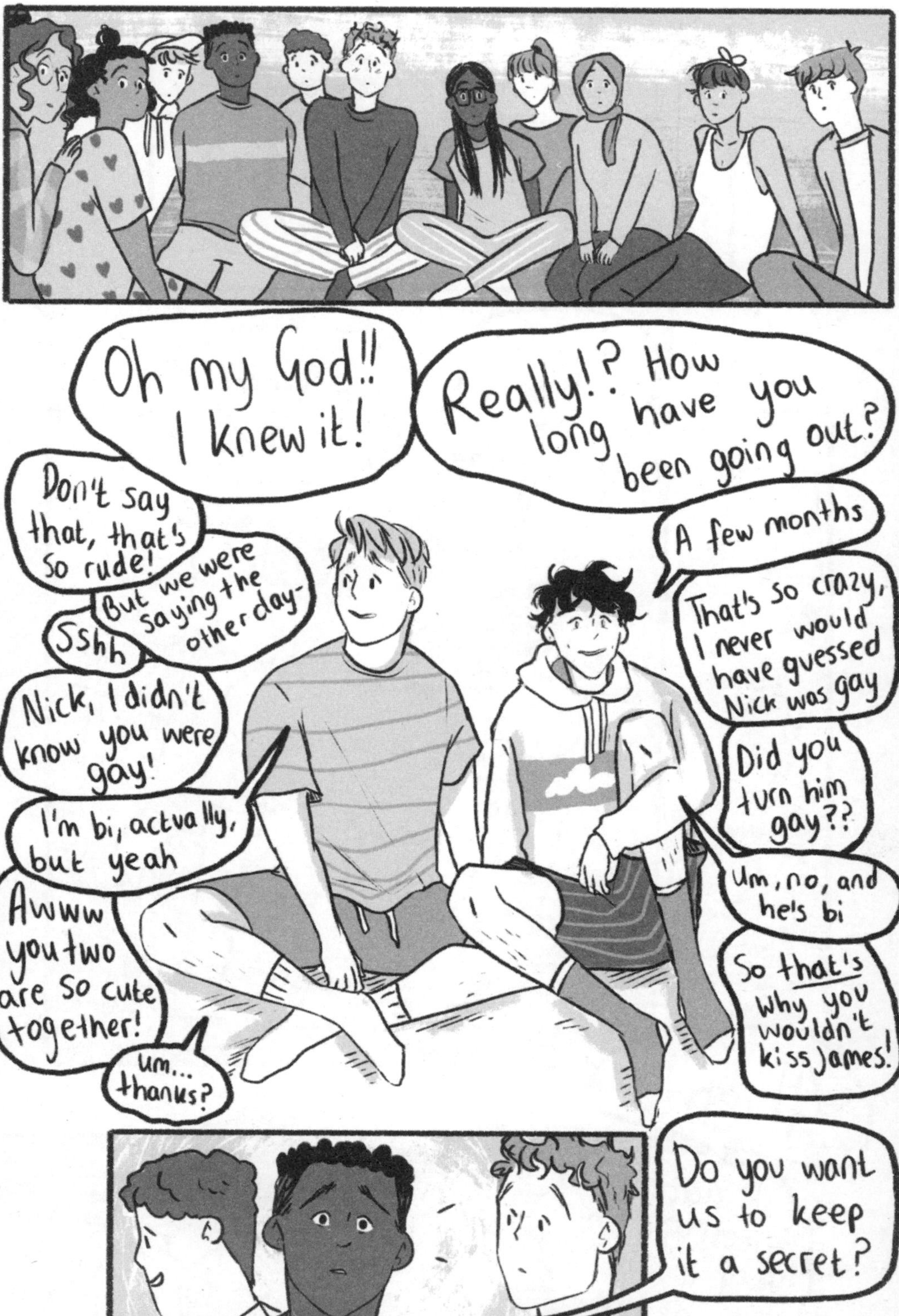
Oh my God!! I knew it!
Really!? How long have you been going out?
Don't say that, that's so rude!
But we were saying the other day-
Sshh
A few months
That's so crazy, I never would have guessed Nick was gay
Nick, I didn't know you were gay!
I'm bi, actually, but yeah
Did you turn him gay??
Um, no, and he's bi
Awww you two are so cute together!
So that's why you wouldn't kiss James!
Um... thanks?
Do you want us to keep it a secret?

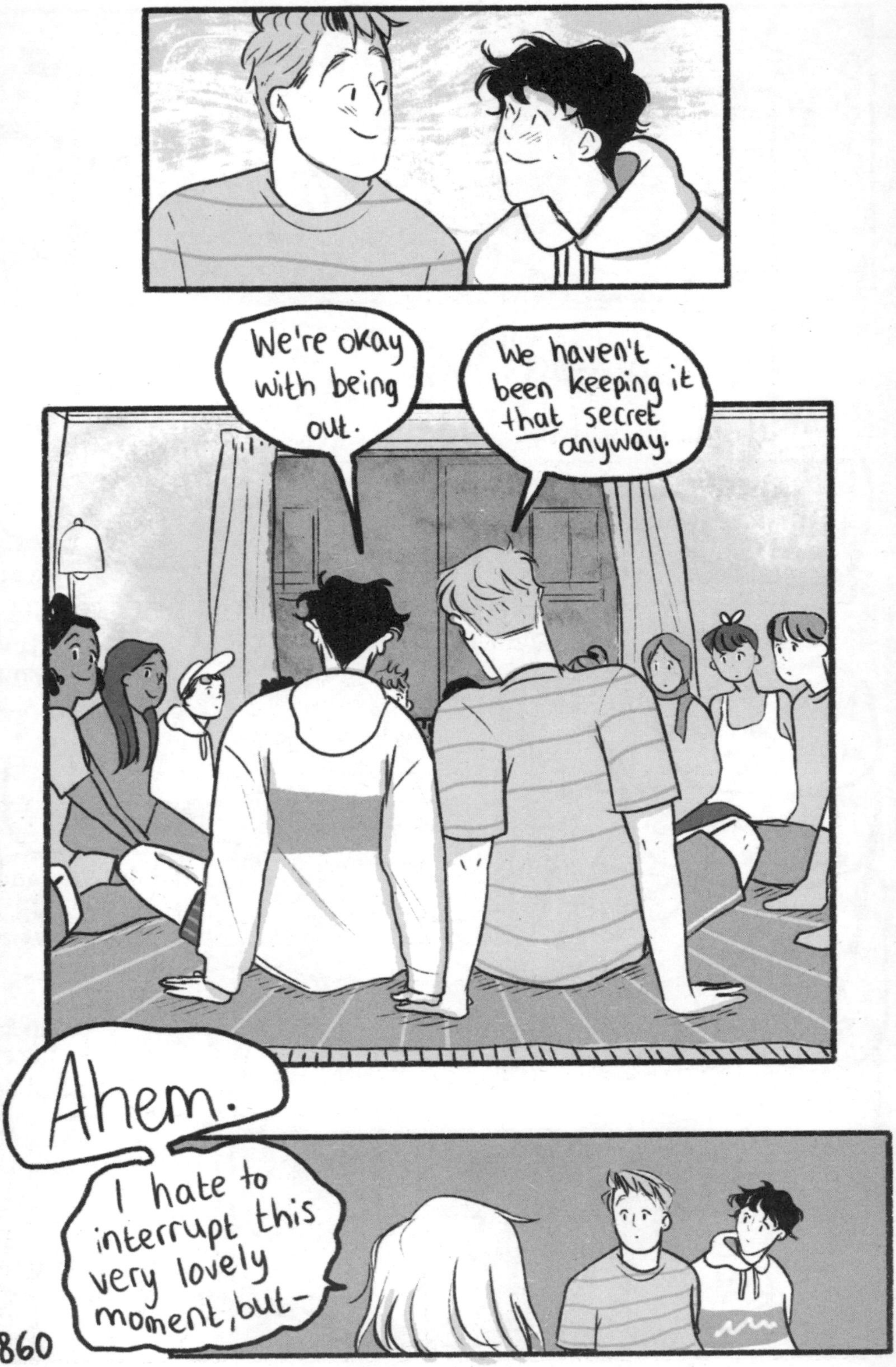
We're okay with being out.
We haven't been keeping it that secret anyway.
Ahem.
I hate to interrupt this very lovely moment, but-

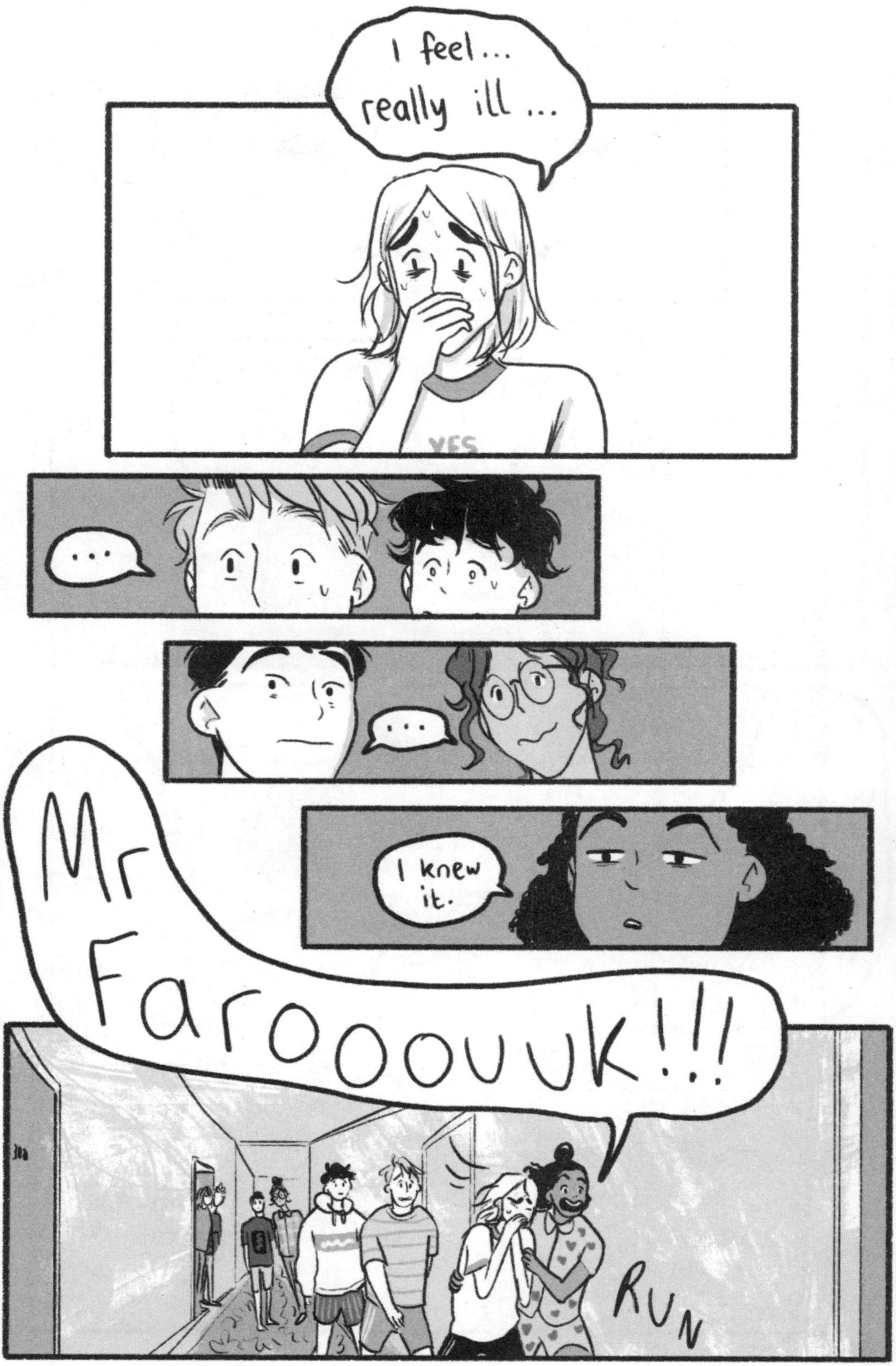
I feel... really ill...
YES
...
...
I knew it.
Mr Faroooouk!!!
RUN

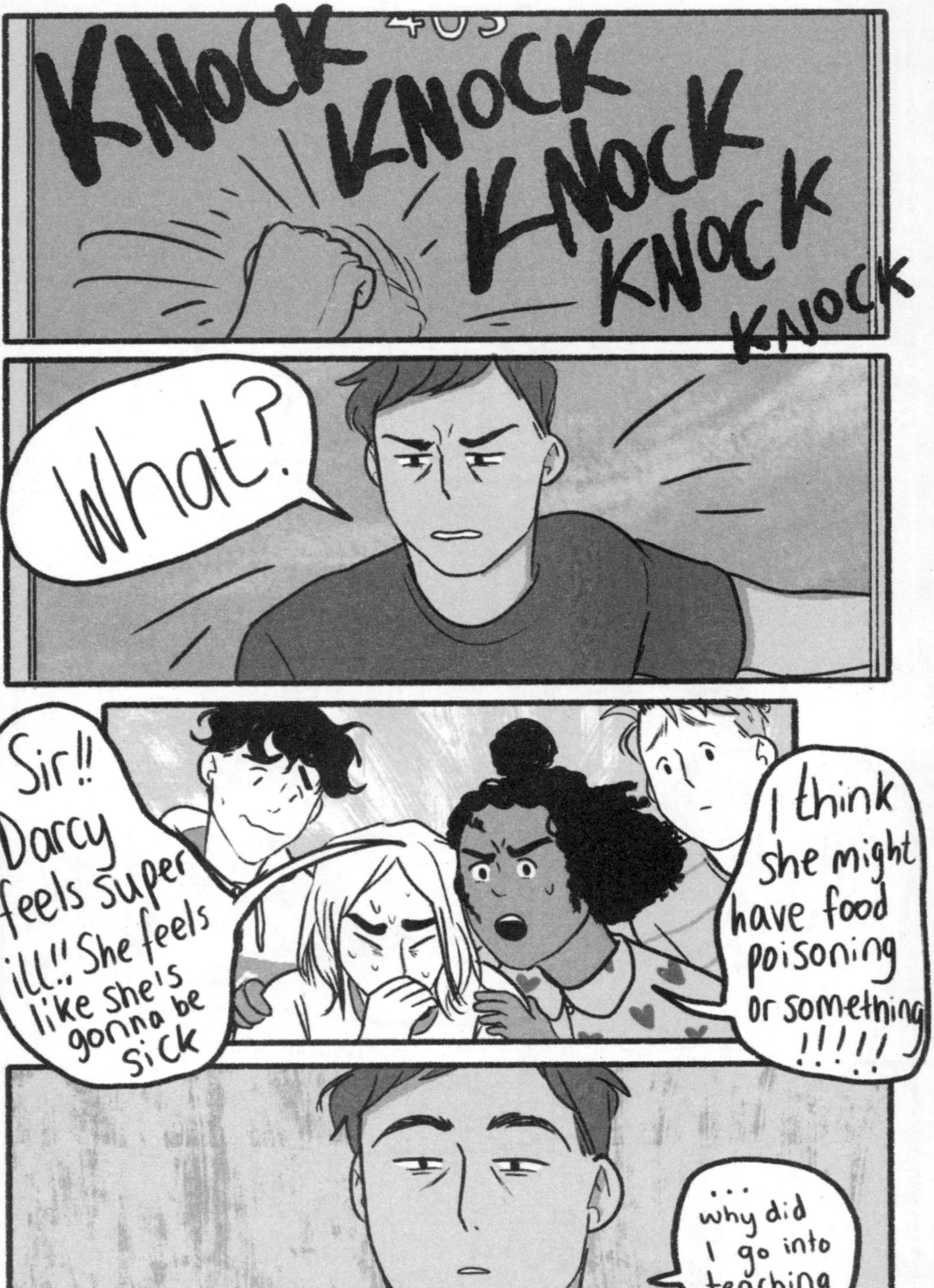
403
KNOCK KNOCK KNOCK KNOCK
KNOCK
What?
Sir!! Darcy feels super feels super ill!! She feels like she's gonna be sick
I think she might have food poisoning or something !!!!!
... why did I go into teaching

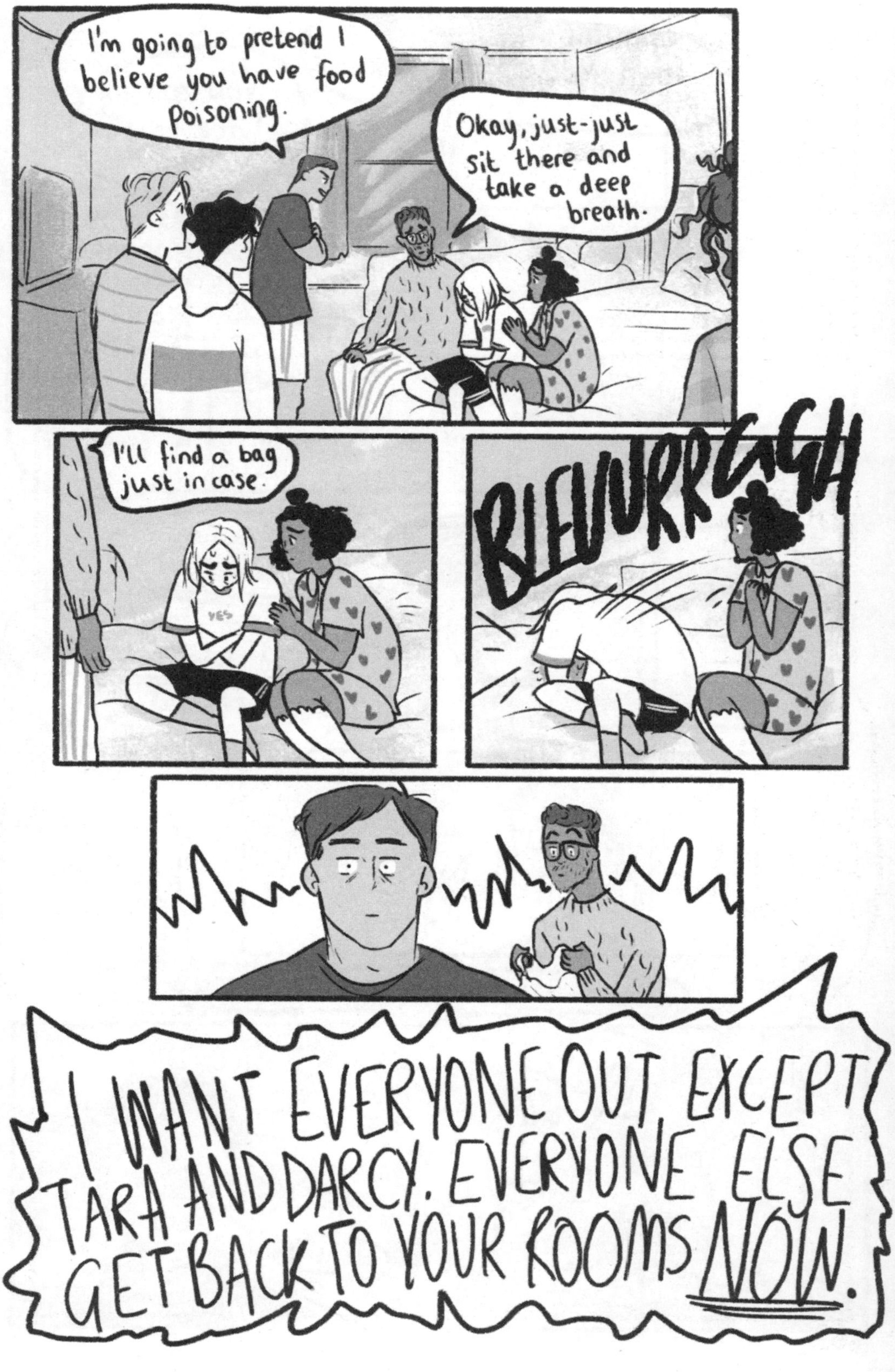
I'm going to pretend I believe you have food poisoning.
Okay, just-just sit there and take a deep breath.
I'll find a bag just in case.
BLEUURRGGH
I WANT EVERYONE OUT EXCEPT TARA AND DARCY. EVERYONE ELSE GET BACK TO YOUR ROOMS NOW.

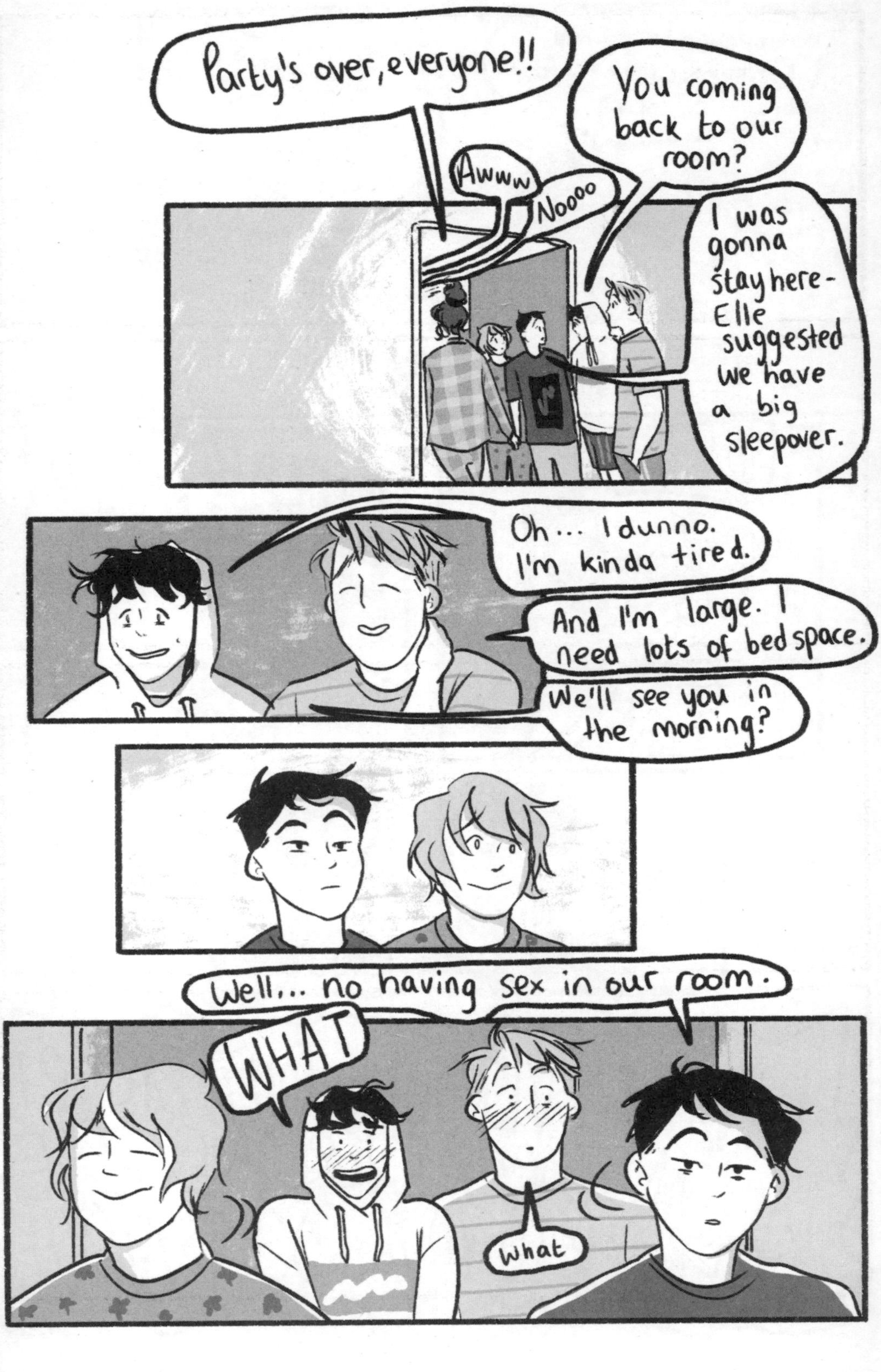
Party's over, everyone!!
Awww
Noooo
You coming back to our room?
I was gonna stay here- Elle suggested we have a big sleepover.
Oh... I dunno. I'm kinda tired.
And I'm large. I need lots of bed space.
We'll see you in the morning?
Well... no having sex in our room.
WHAT
what

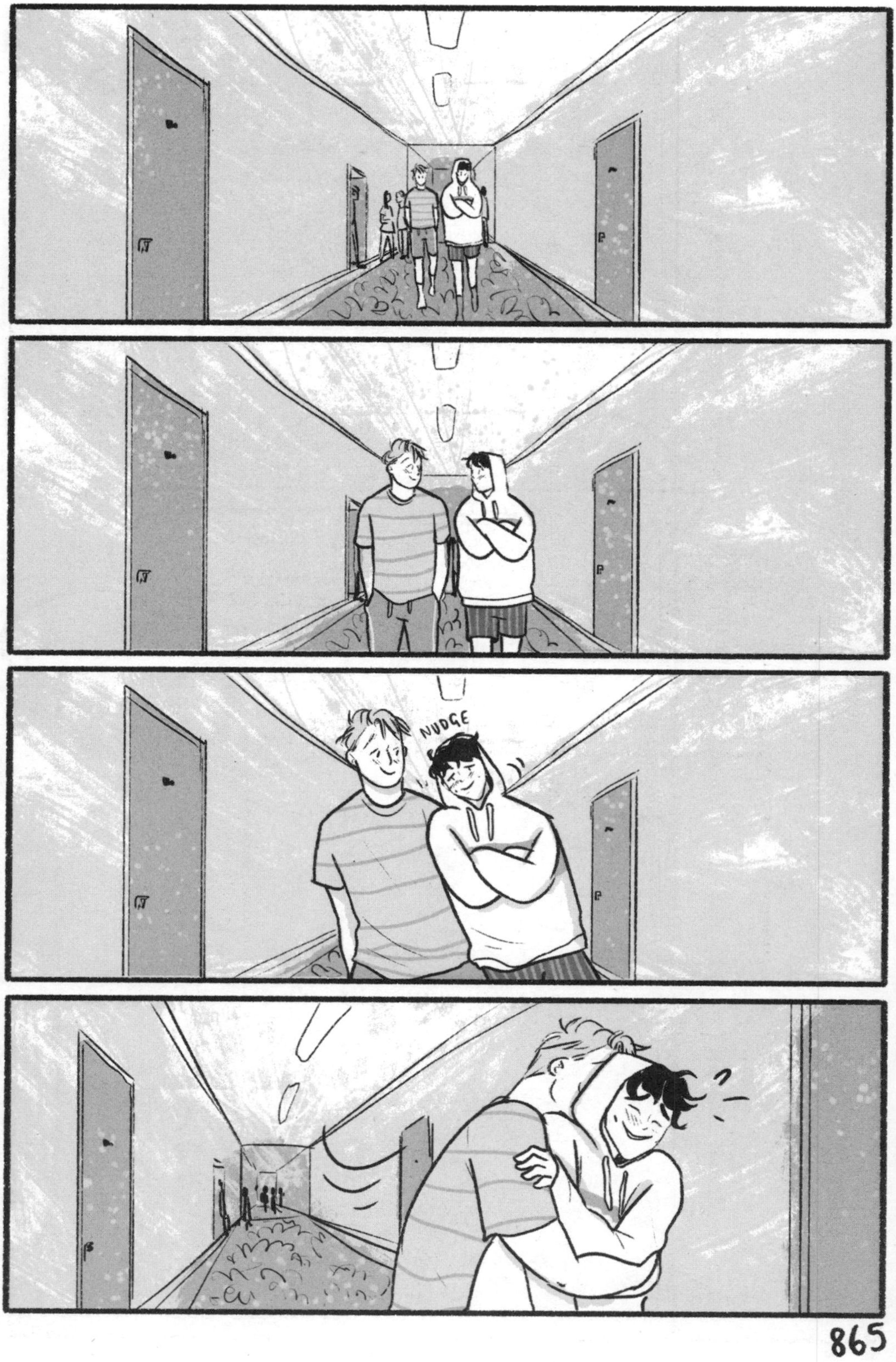
NUDGE

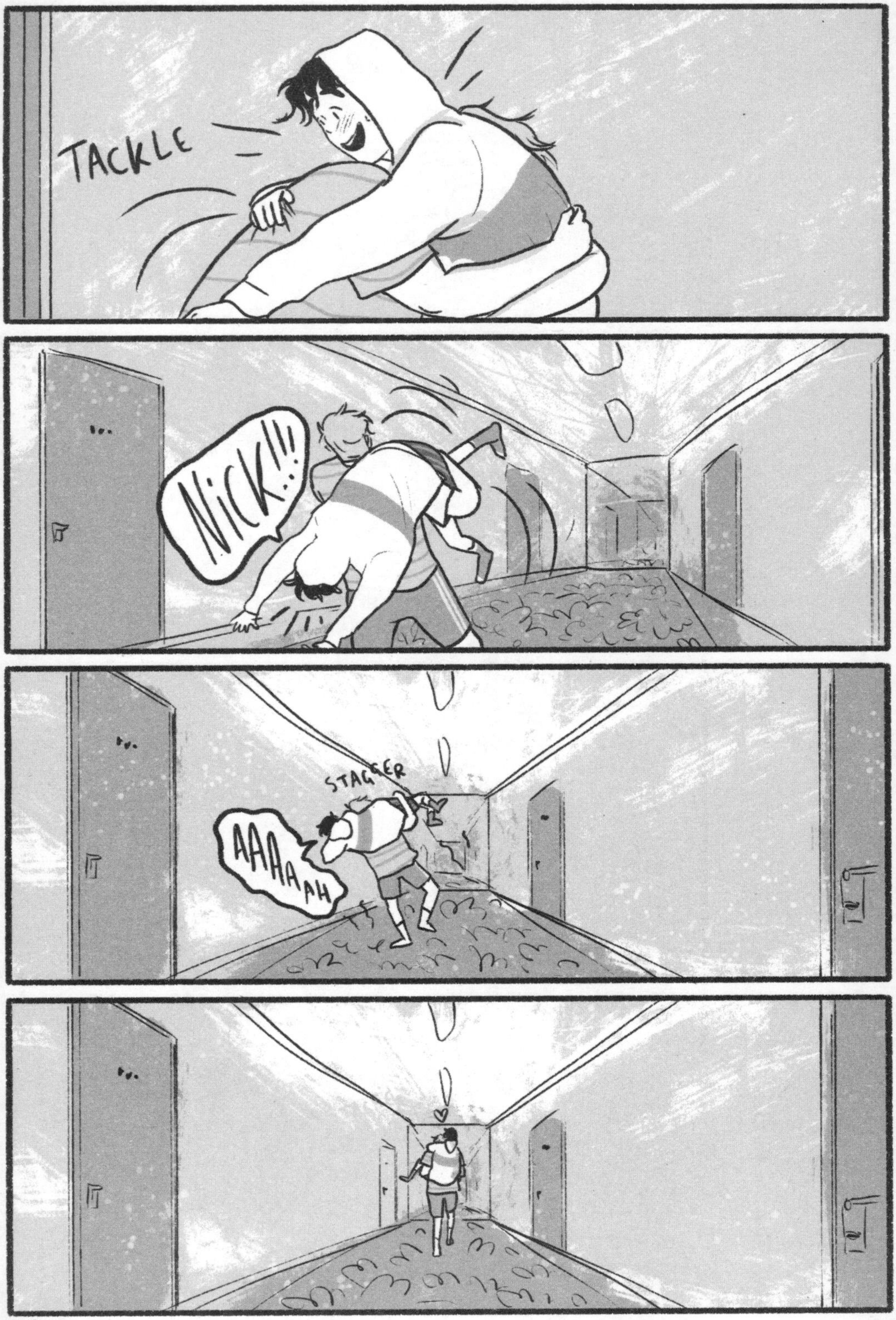
TACKLE
NICK!!!
STAGGER
AAAAAH

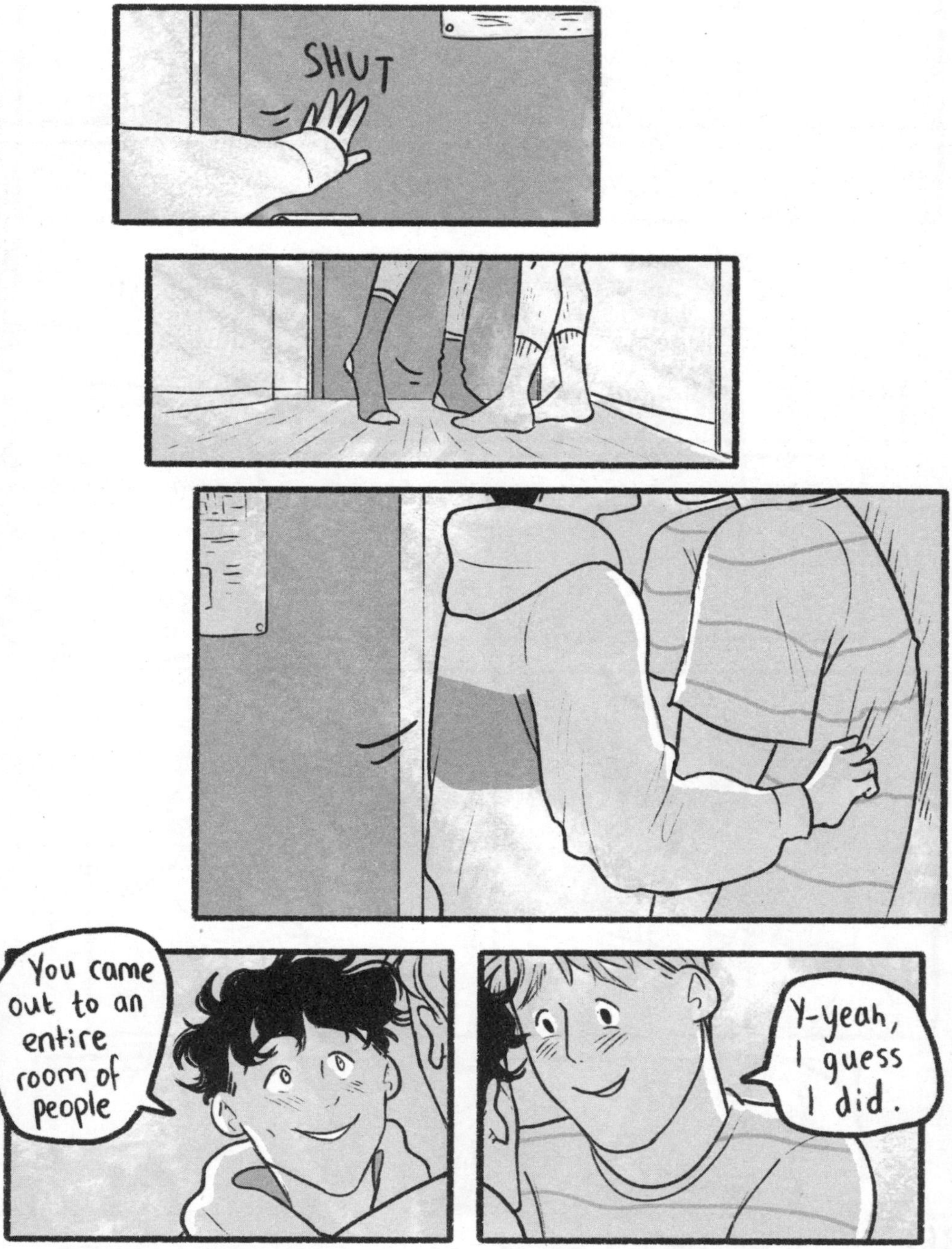
SHUT
You came out to an entire room of people
Y-yeah, I guess I did.

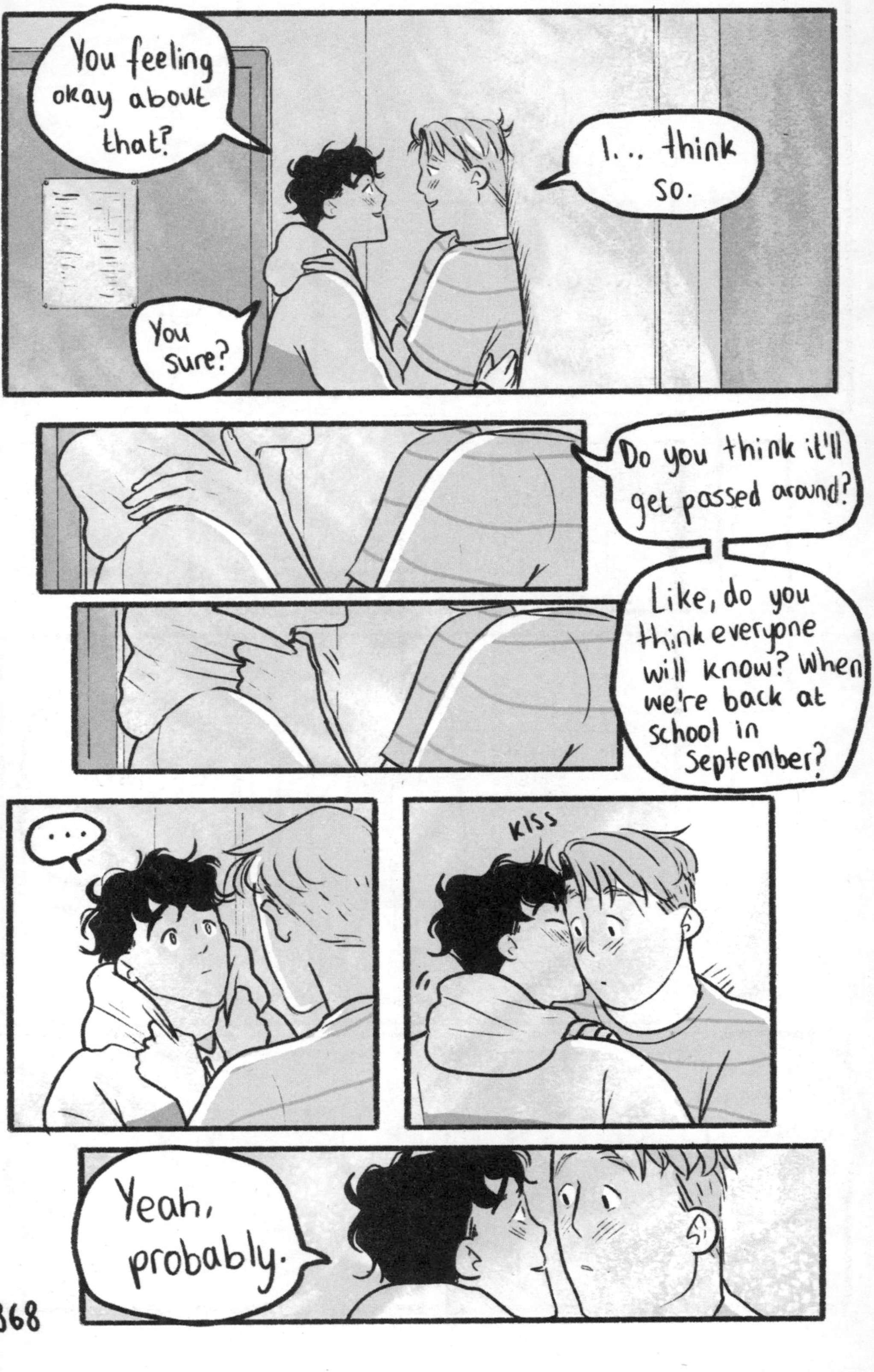
You feeling okay about that?
I... think so.
You sure?
Do you think it'll get passed around?
Like, do you think everyone will know? When we're back at school in September?
...
KISS
Yeah, probably.

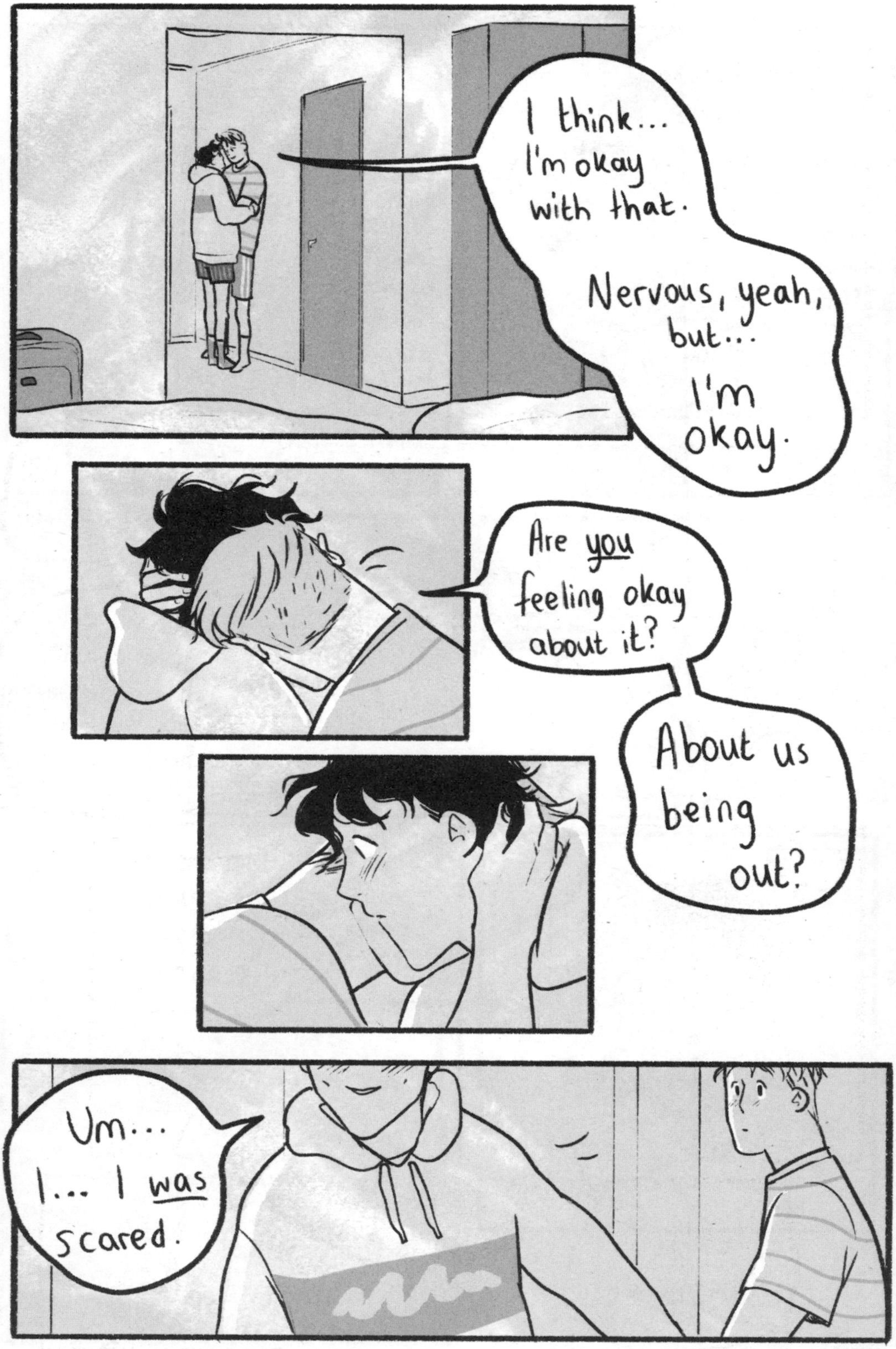
I think... I'm okay with that.
Nervous, yeah, but... I'm okay.
Are you feeling okay about it?
About us being out?
Um... I... I was scared.

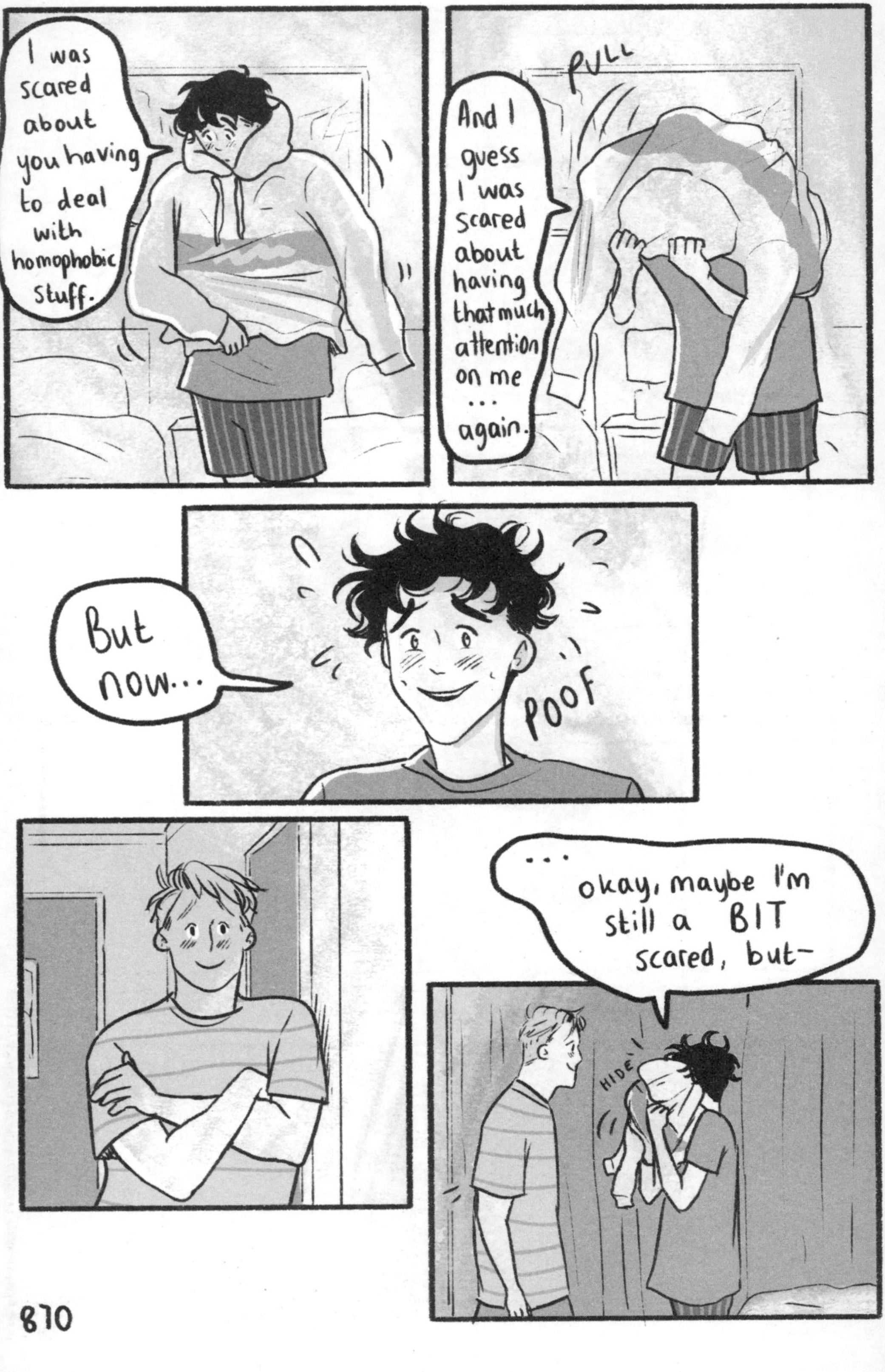
I was scared about you having to deal with homophobic stuff.
PULL
And I guess I was scared about having that much attention on me ... again.
But now...
POOF
... okay, maybe I'm still a BIT scared, but-
HIDE

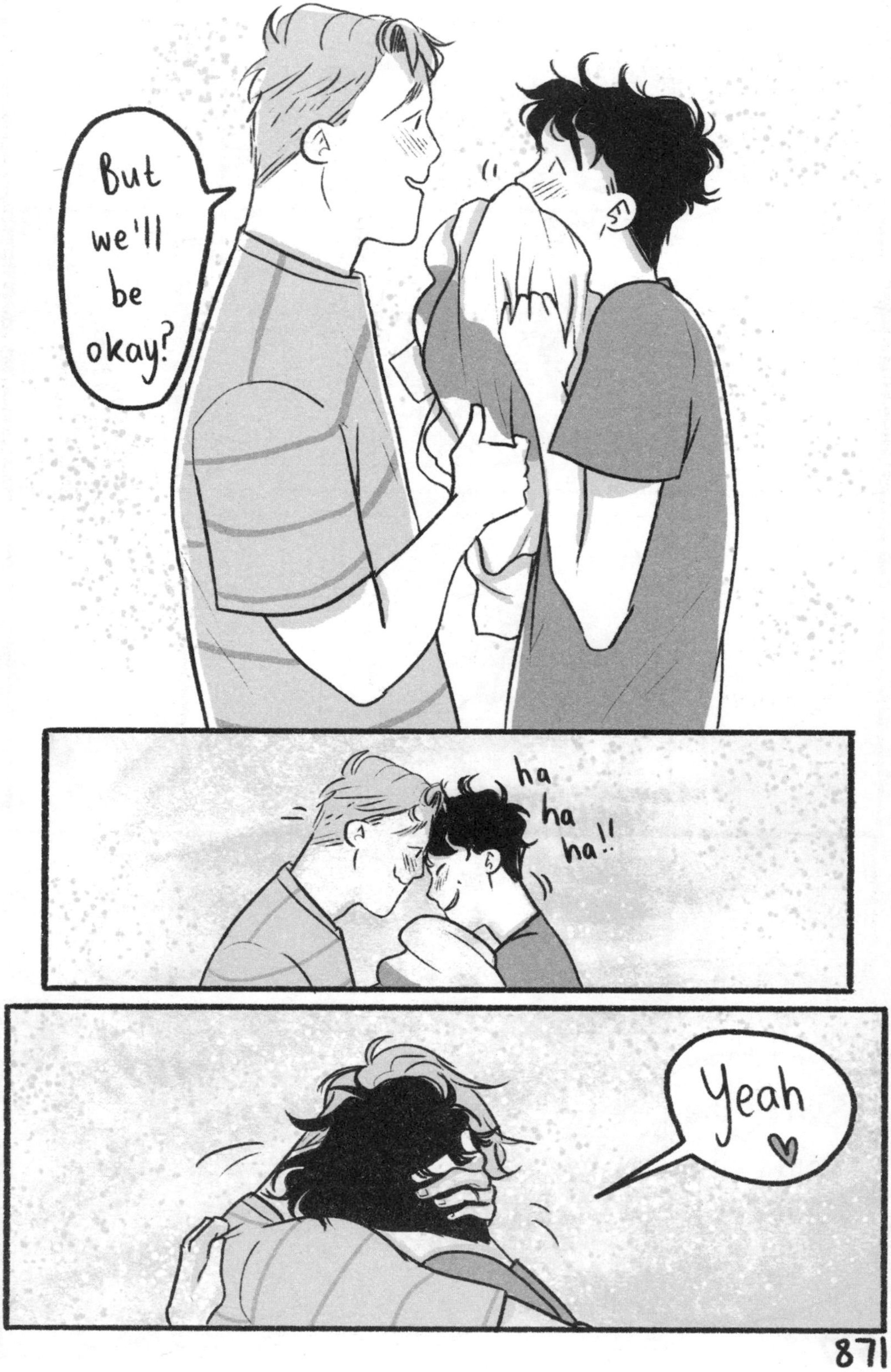
But we'll be okay?
ha ha ha!!
Yeah

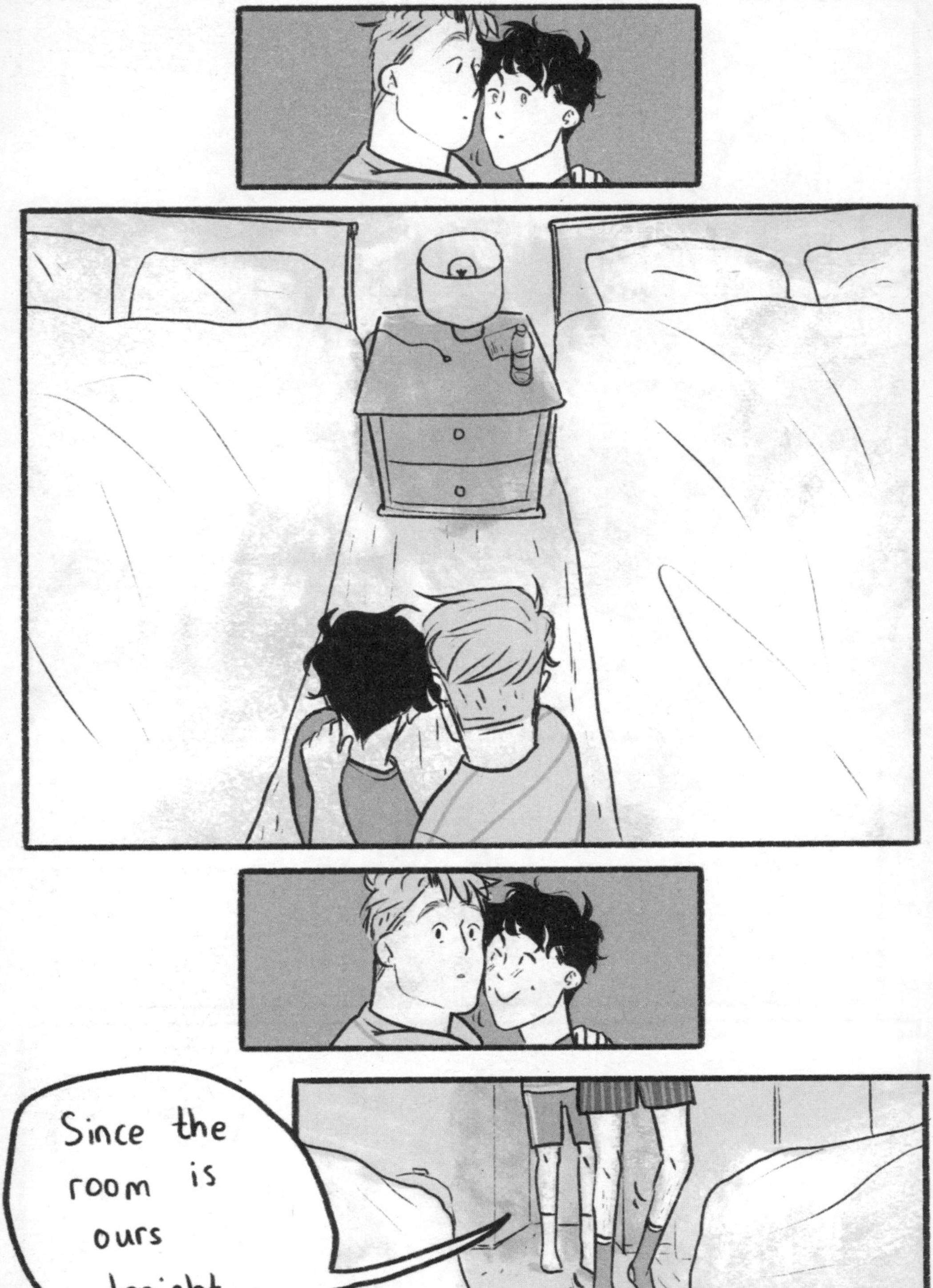
Since the room is ours tonight...

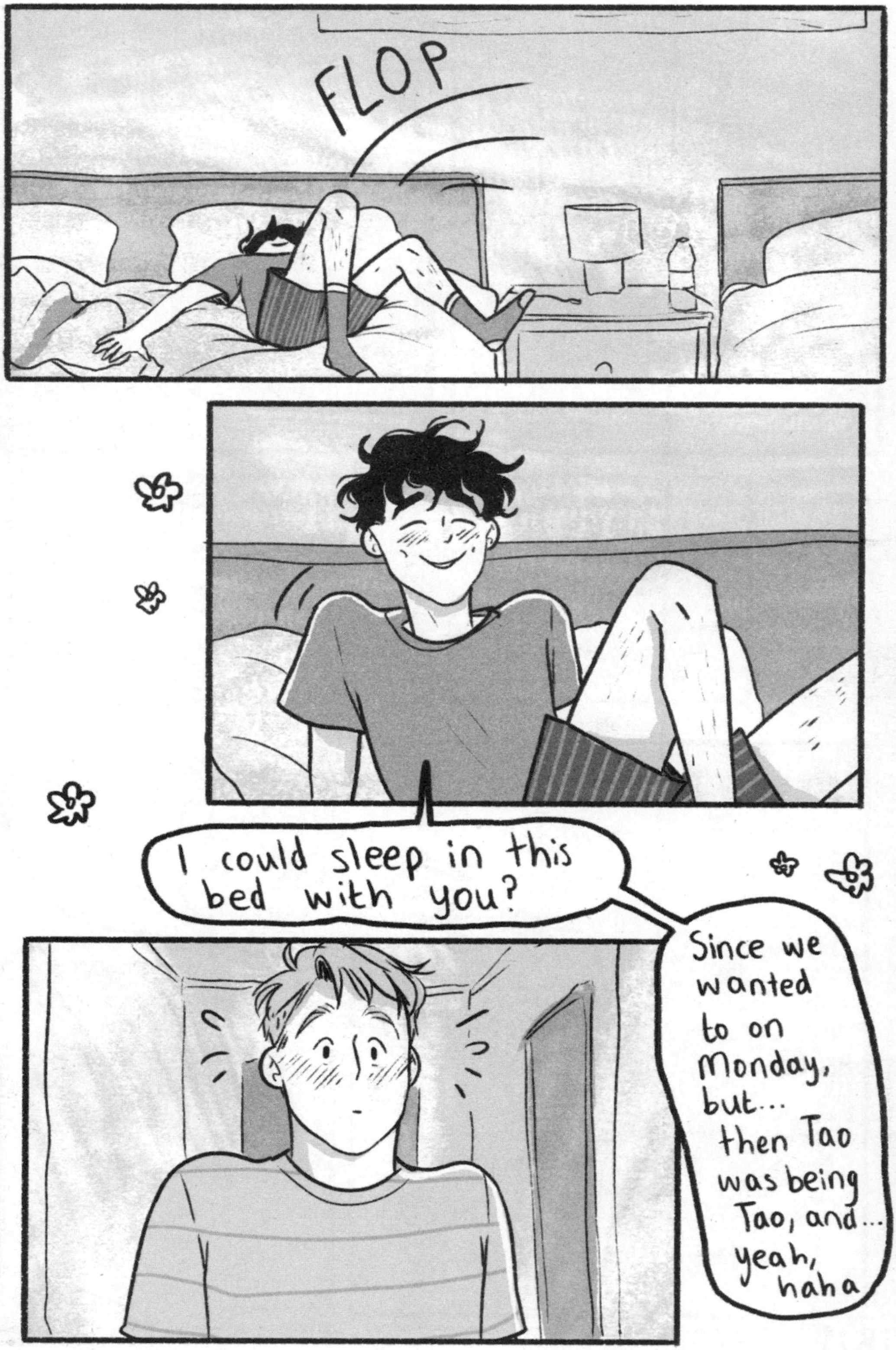
FLOP
I could sleep in this bed with you?
Since we wanted to on Monday, but... then Tao was being Tao, and... yeah, haha

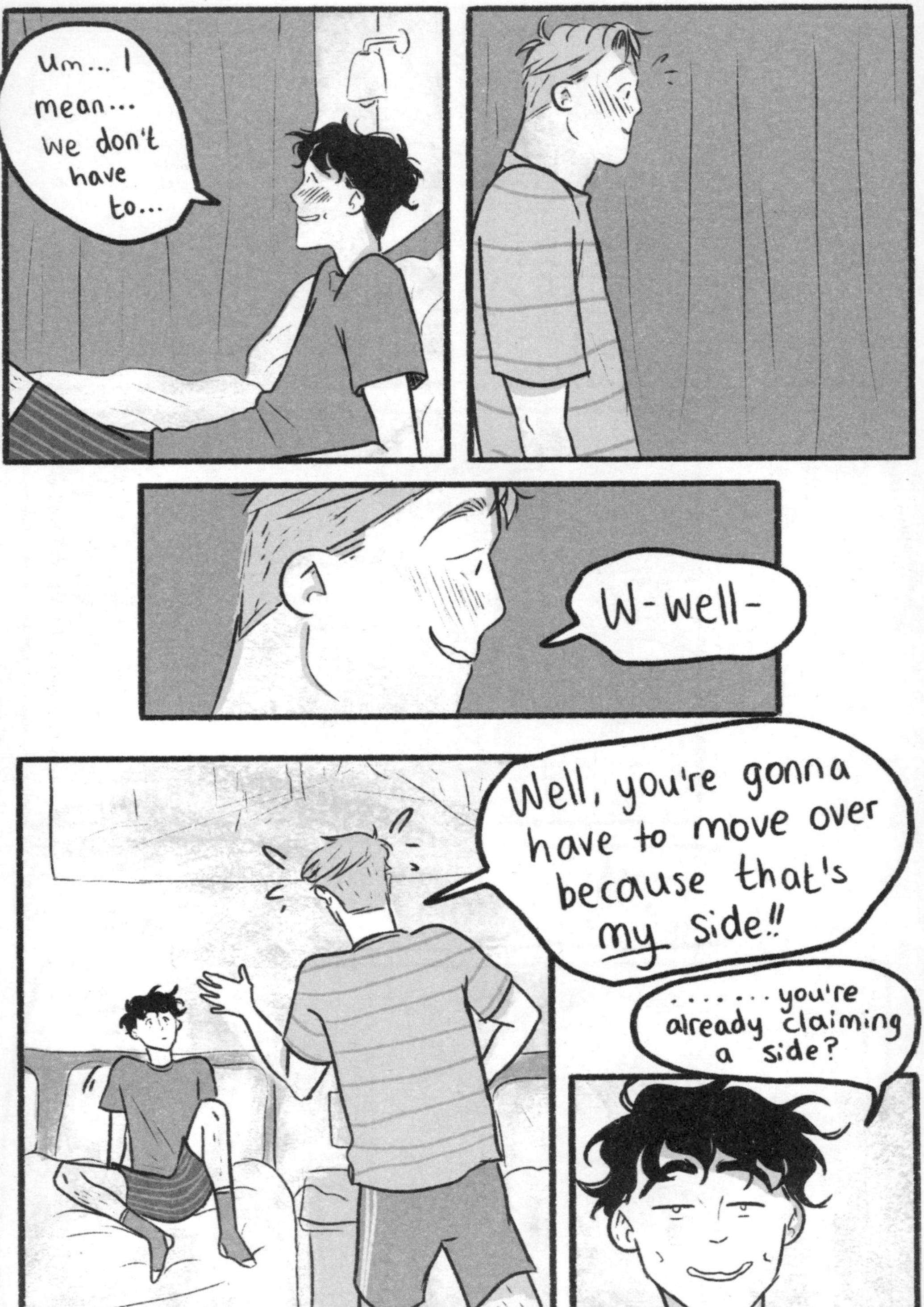
Um... I mean... we don't have to...
W-well-
Well, you're gonna have to move over because that's my side!!
.......you're already claiming a side?

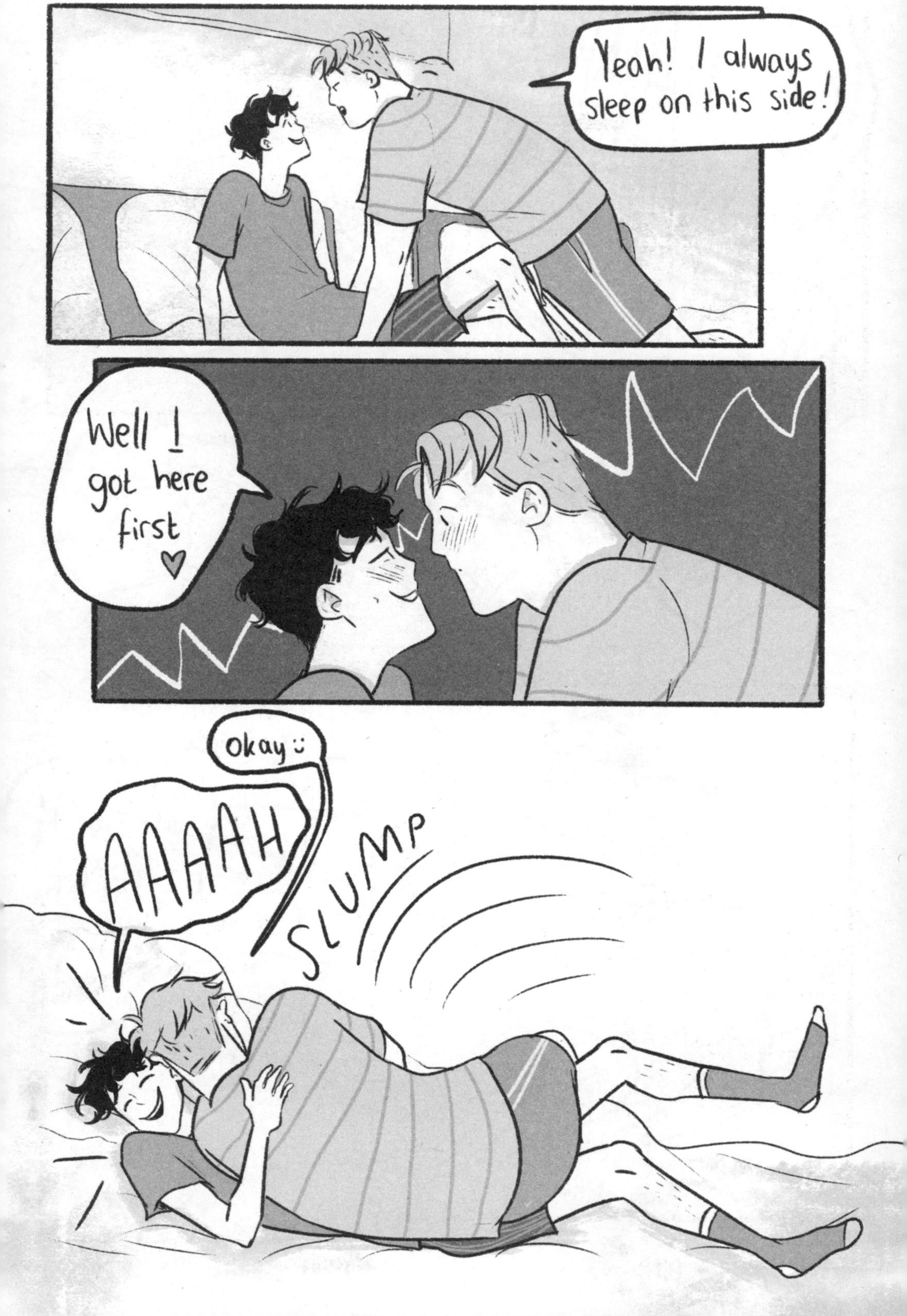
Yeah! I always sleep on this side!
Well I got here first ♥
Okay :)
AAAAH
SLUMP

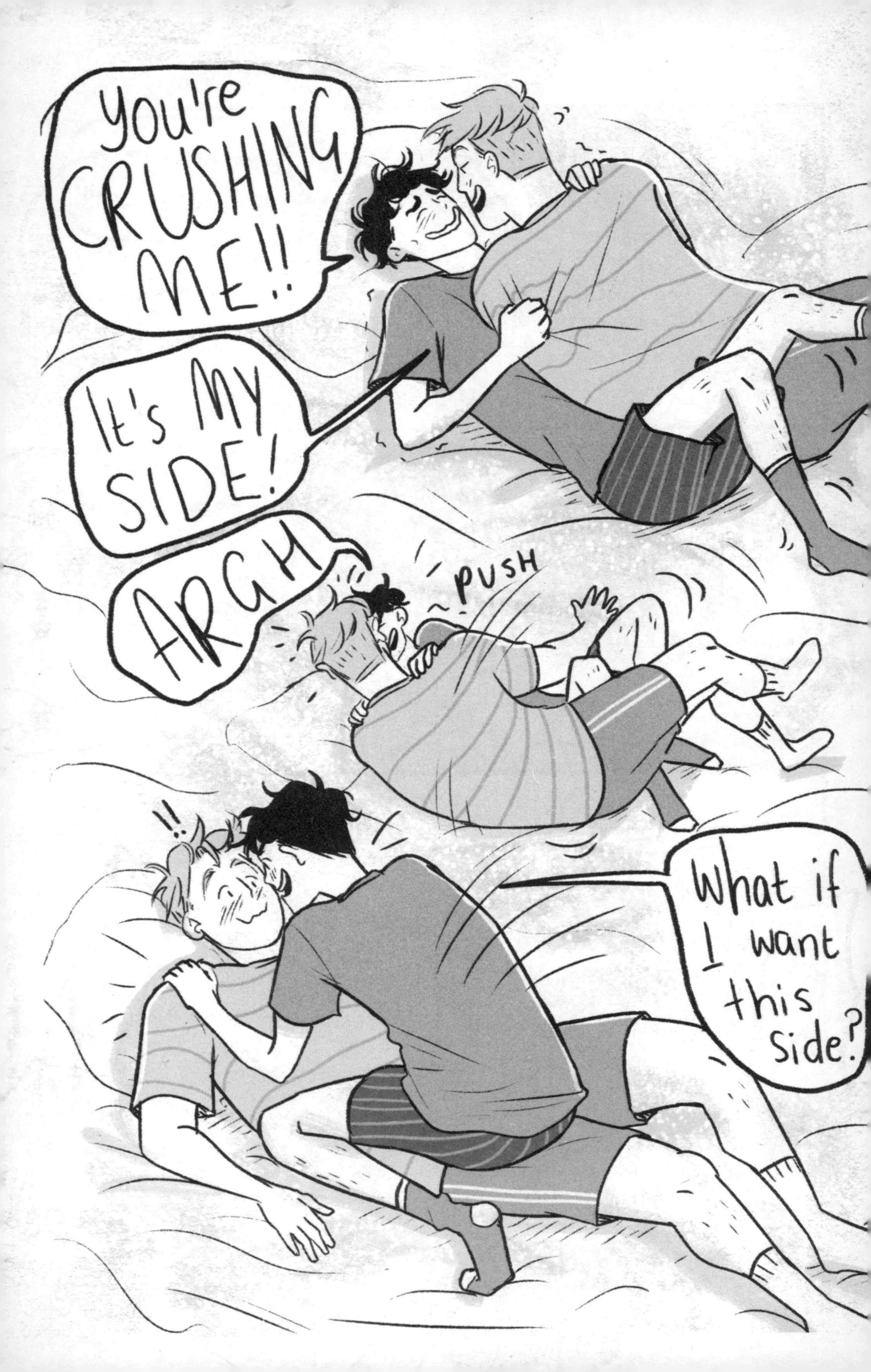
You're CRUSHING ME!!
It's MY SIDE!
ARGH
PUSH
!!
What if I want this side?

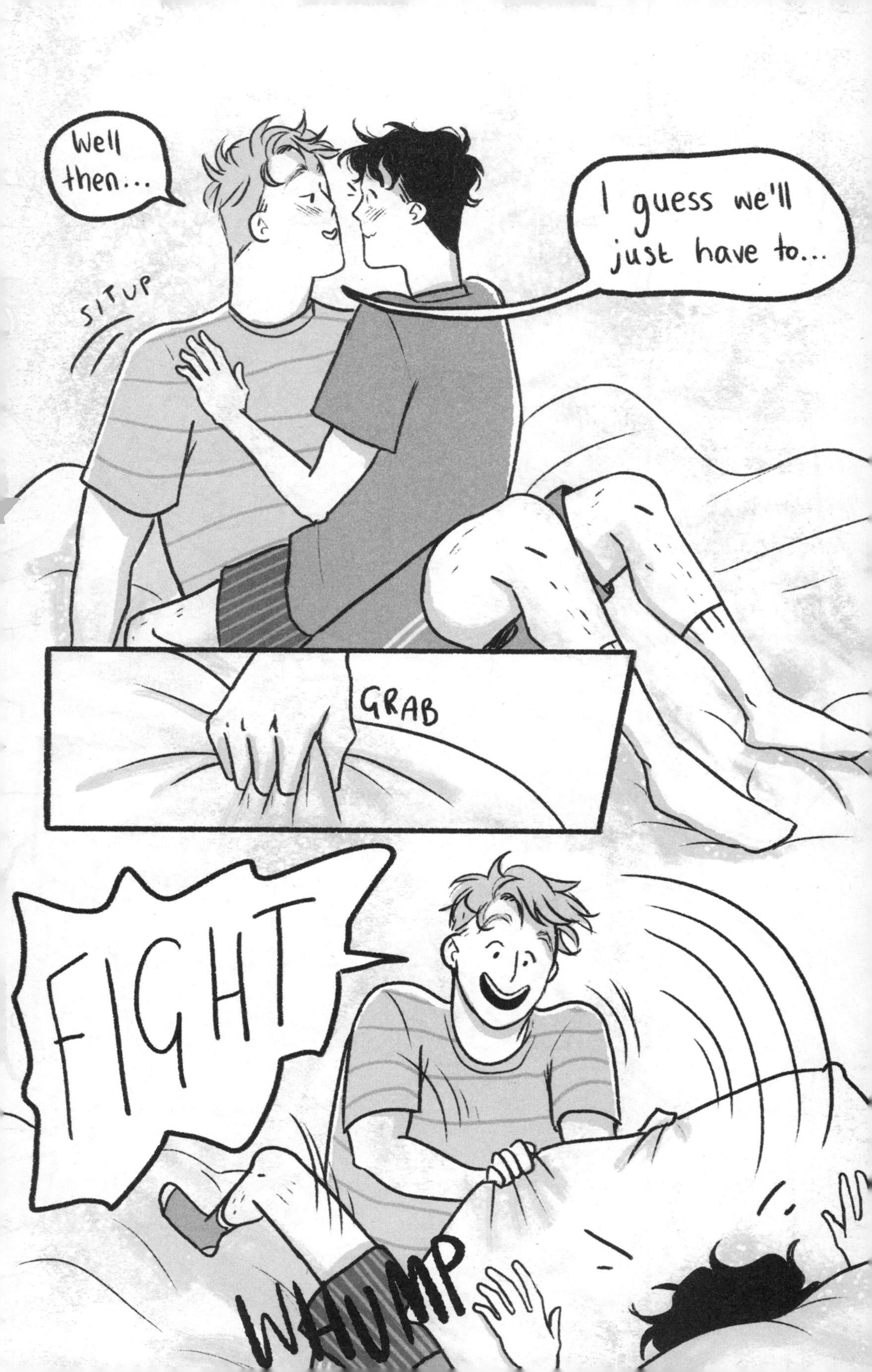
Well then...
SITUP
I guess we'll just have to...
GRAB
FIGHT
WHUMP

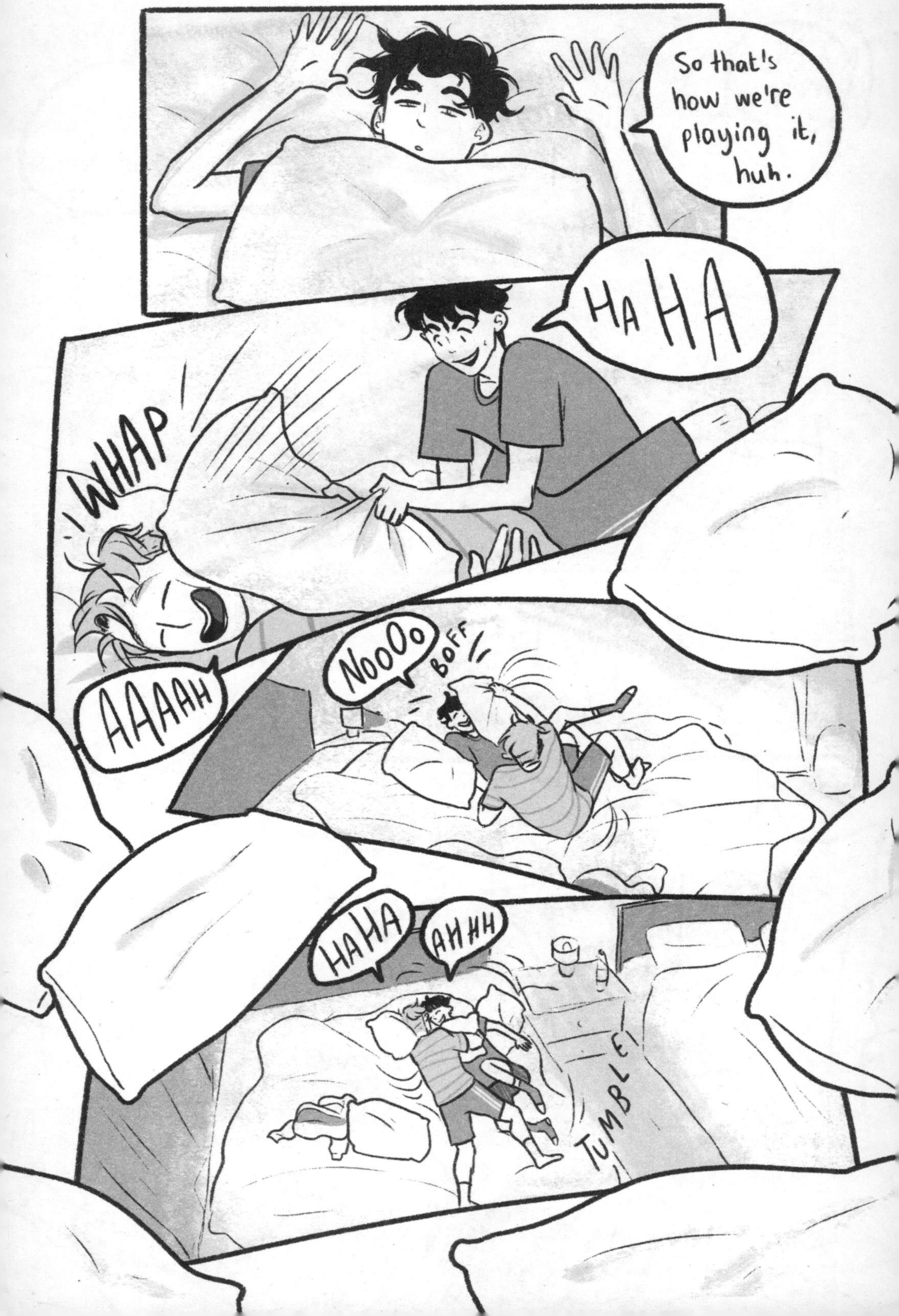
So that's how we're playing it, huh.
HA HA HA
WHAP
AAAAH
NooOo
BOFF
HAHA
AHHH
TUMBLE

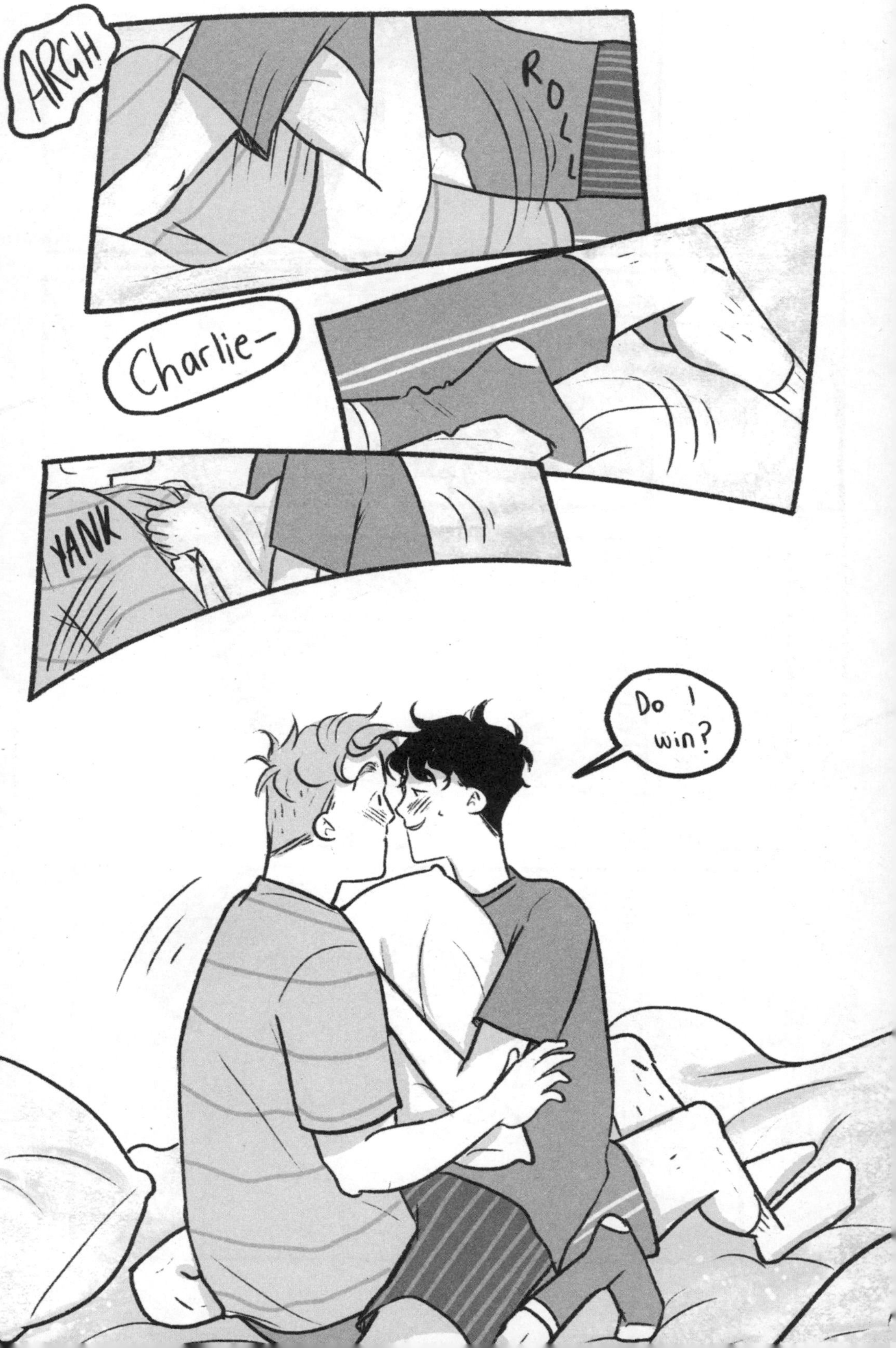
ARGH
ROLL
Charlie-
YANK
Do I win?

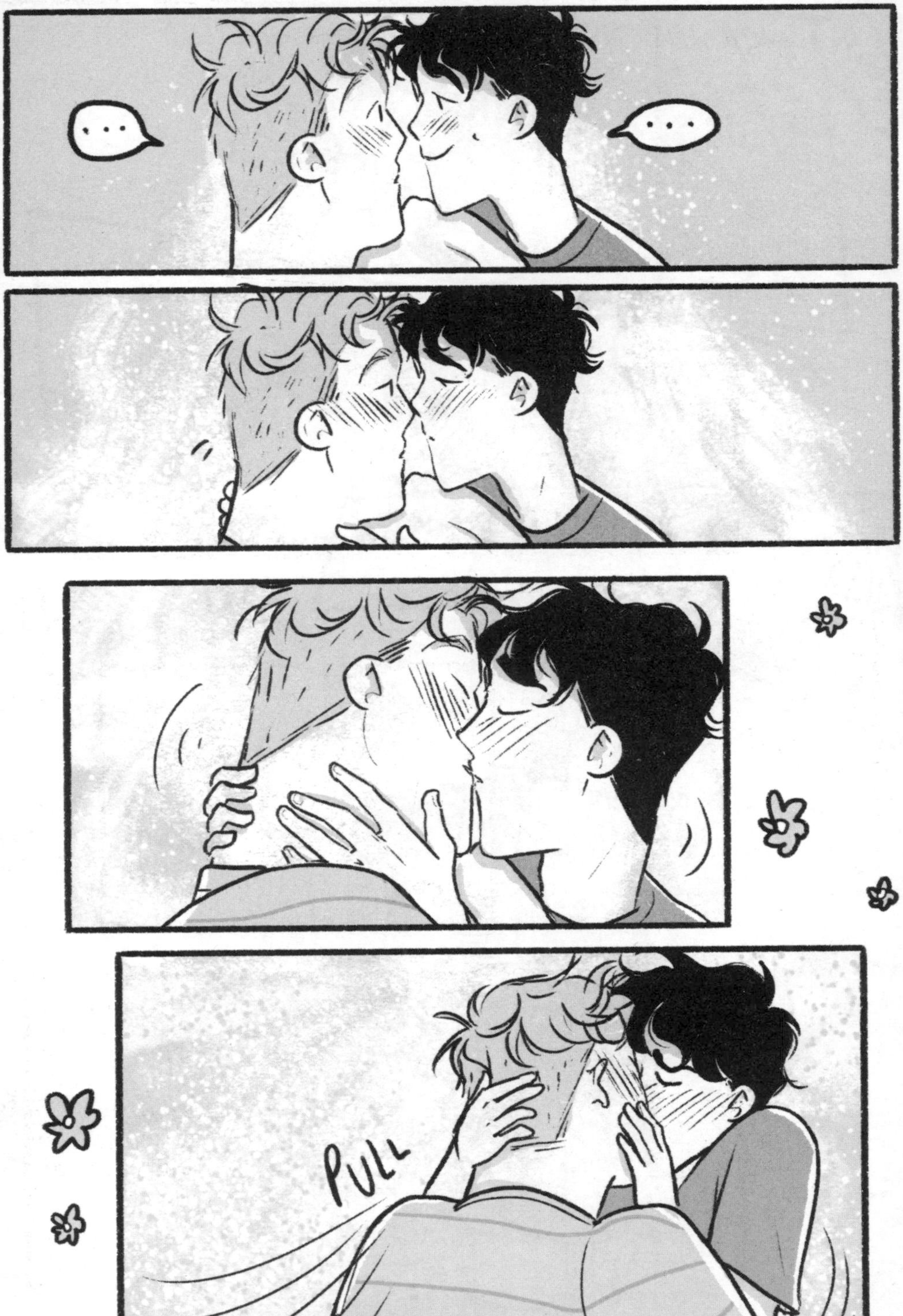
...
...
PULL

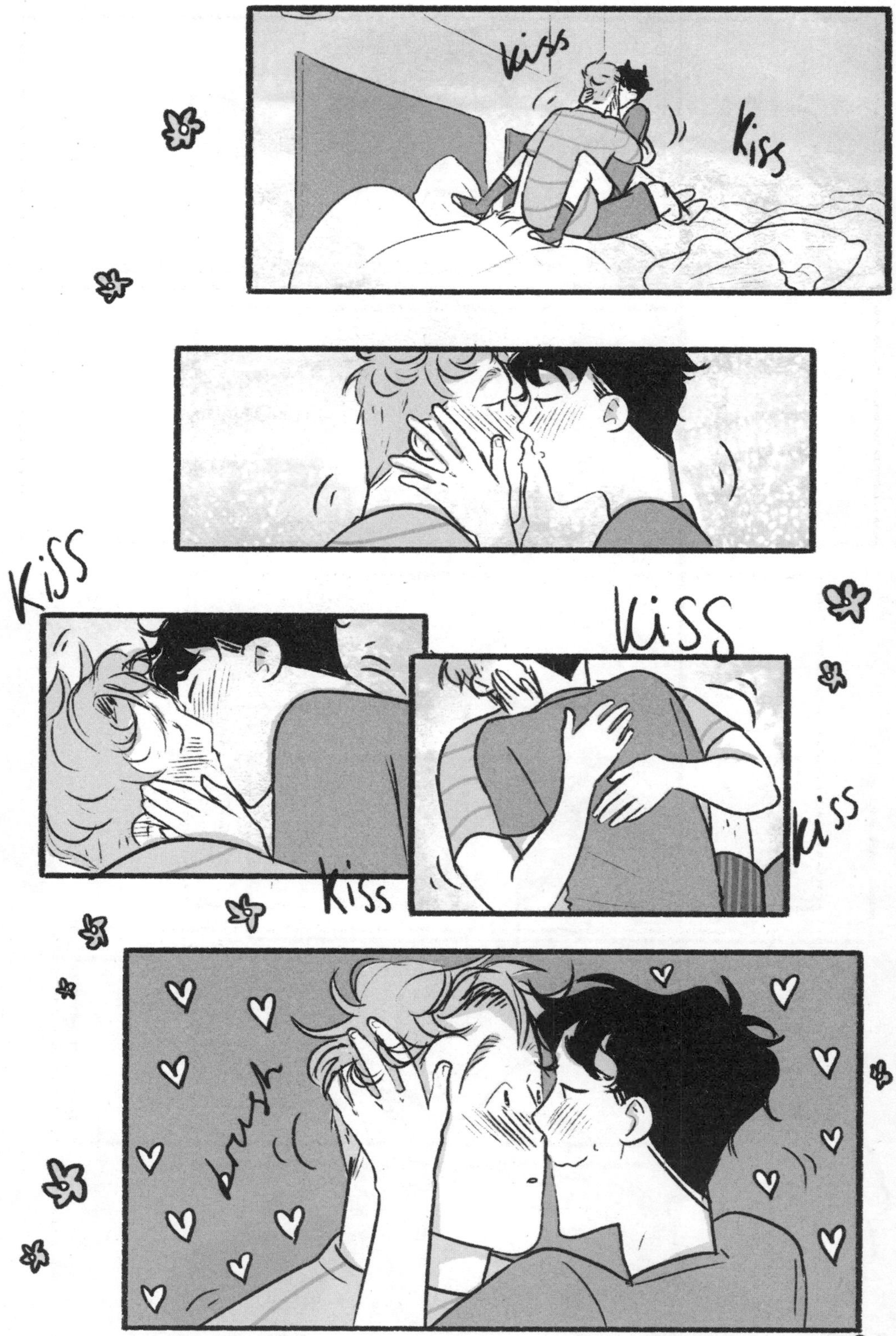
kiss
kiss
kiss
kiss
kiss
kiss
brush

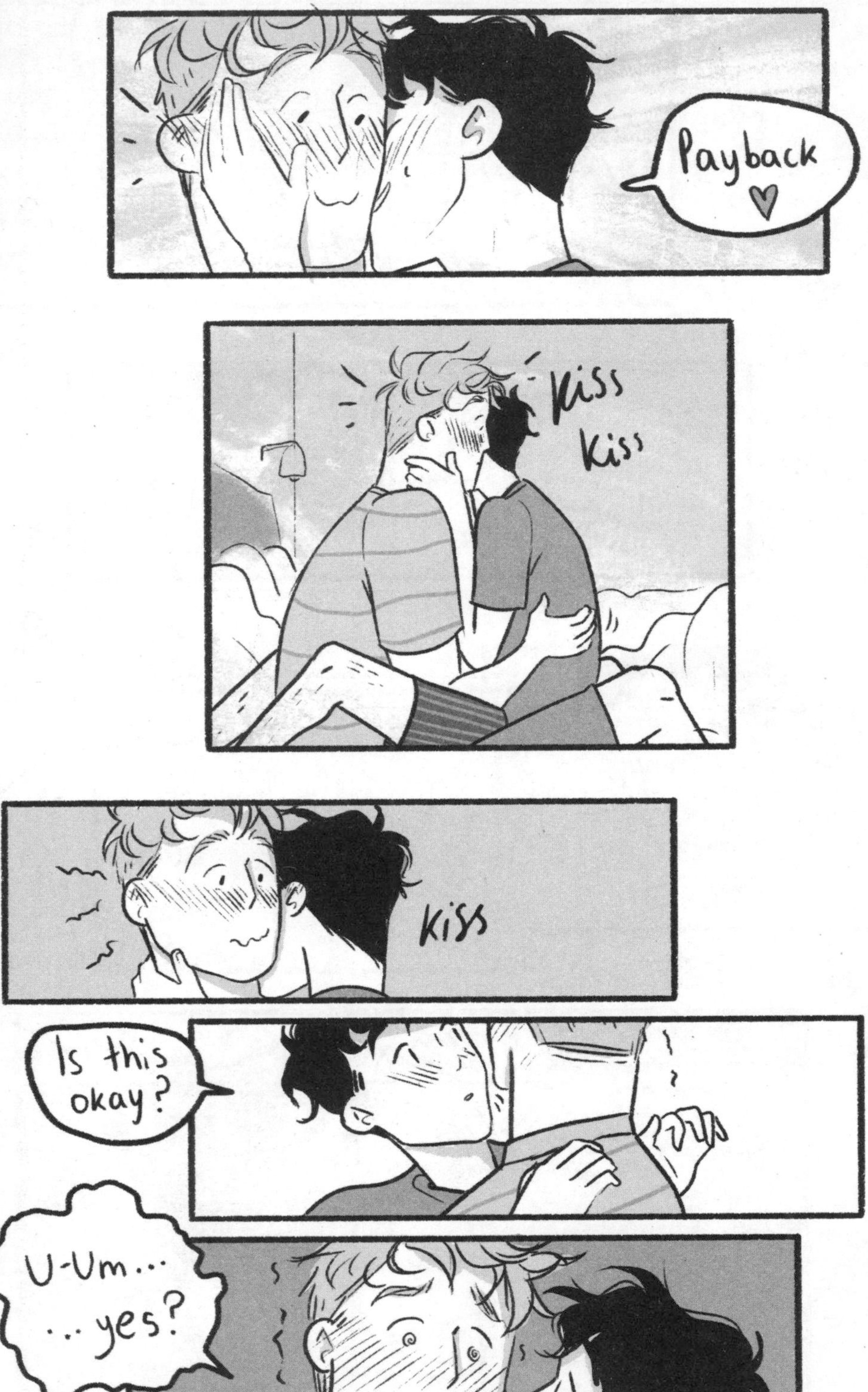
Payback ♥
Kiss
Kiss
Kiss
Is this okay?
U-Um...
...yes?

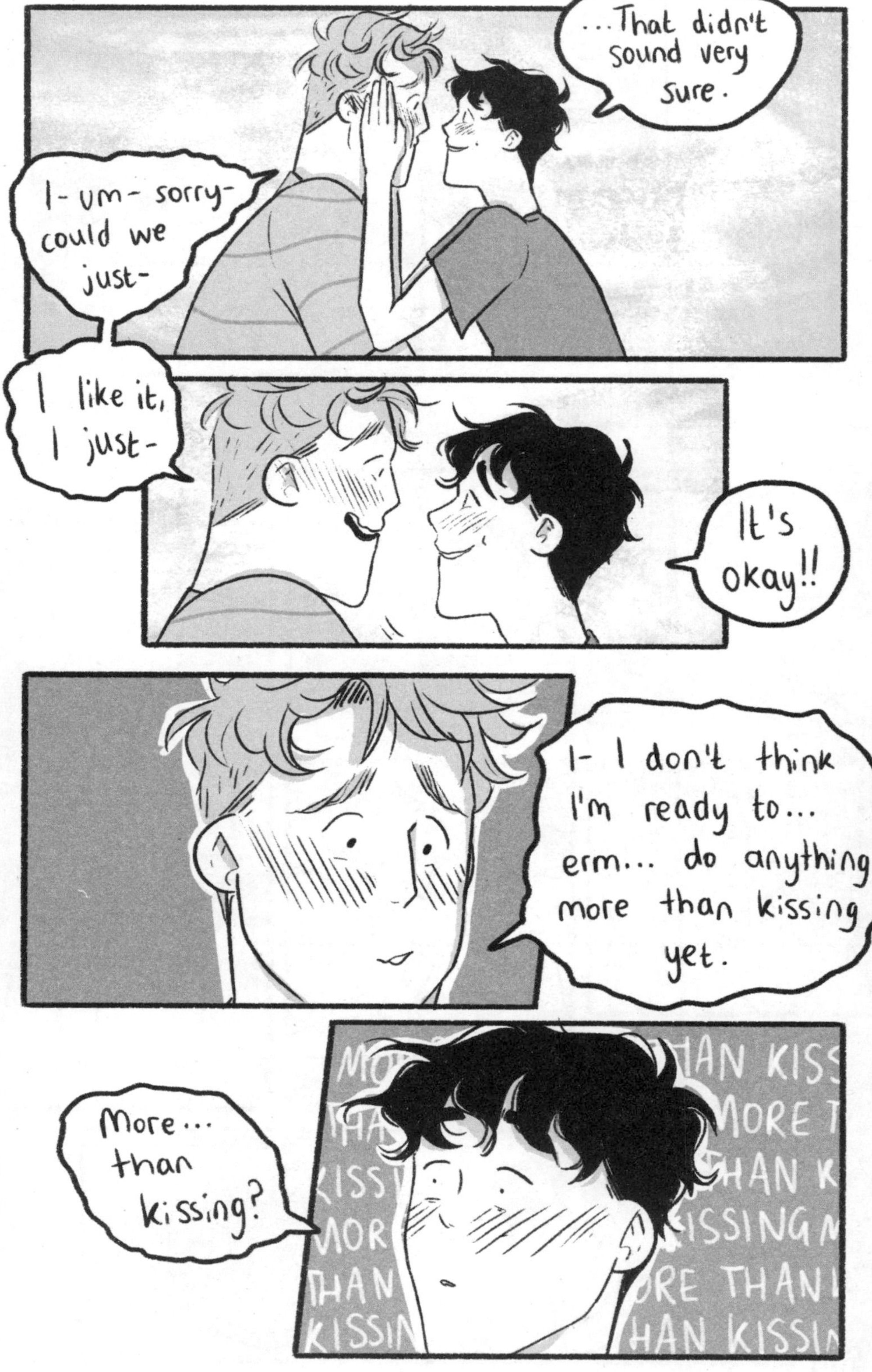
...That didn't sound very sure.
I- um- sorry- could we just-
I like it, I just-
It's okay!!
I- I don't think I'm ready to... erm... do anything more than kissing yet.
More... than kissing?
MORE THAN KISSING

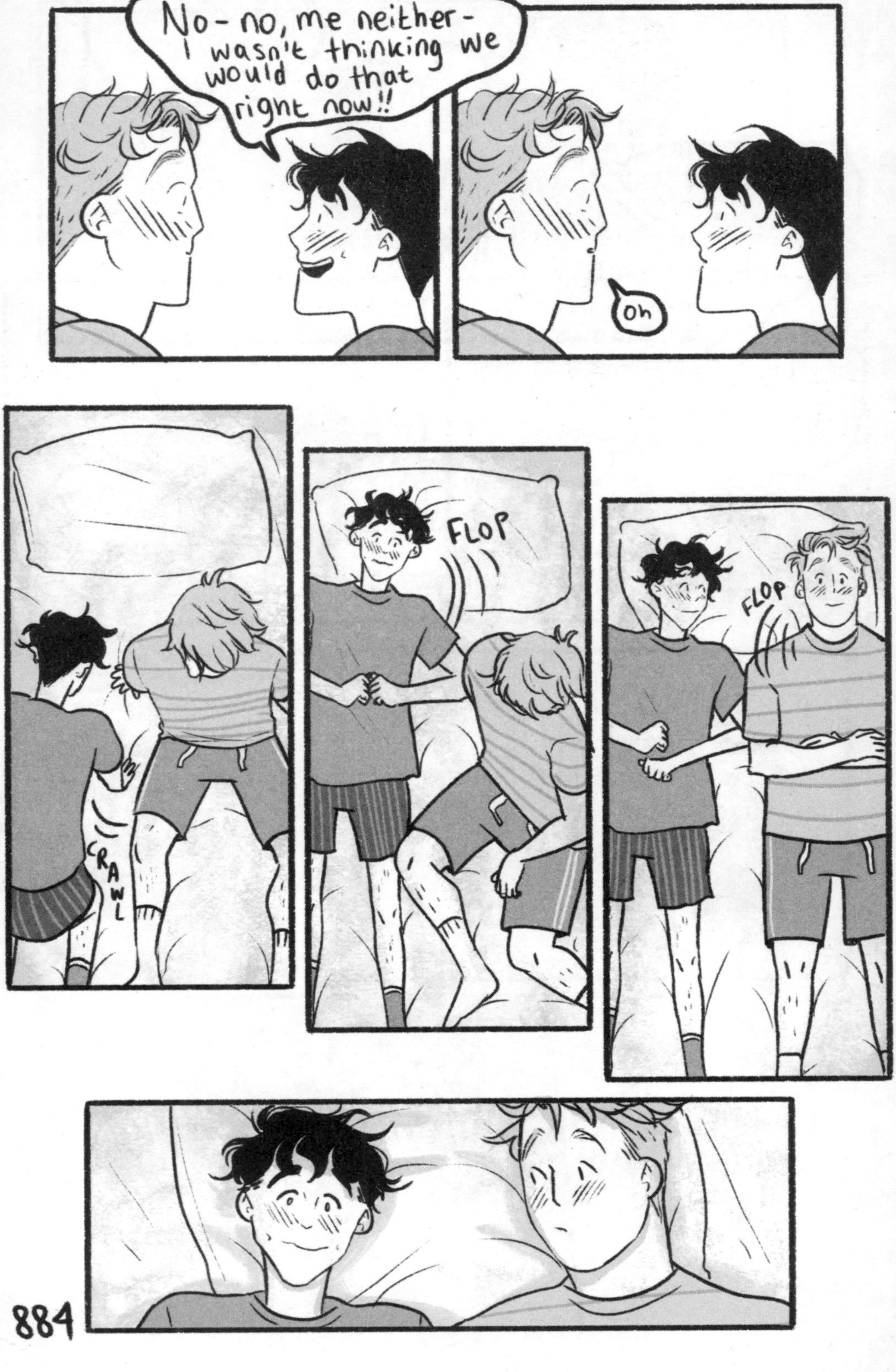
No-no, me neither-
I wasn't thinking we would do that right now!!
Oh
CRAWL
FLOP
FLOP

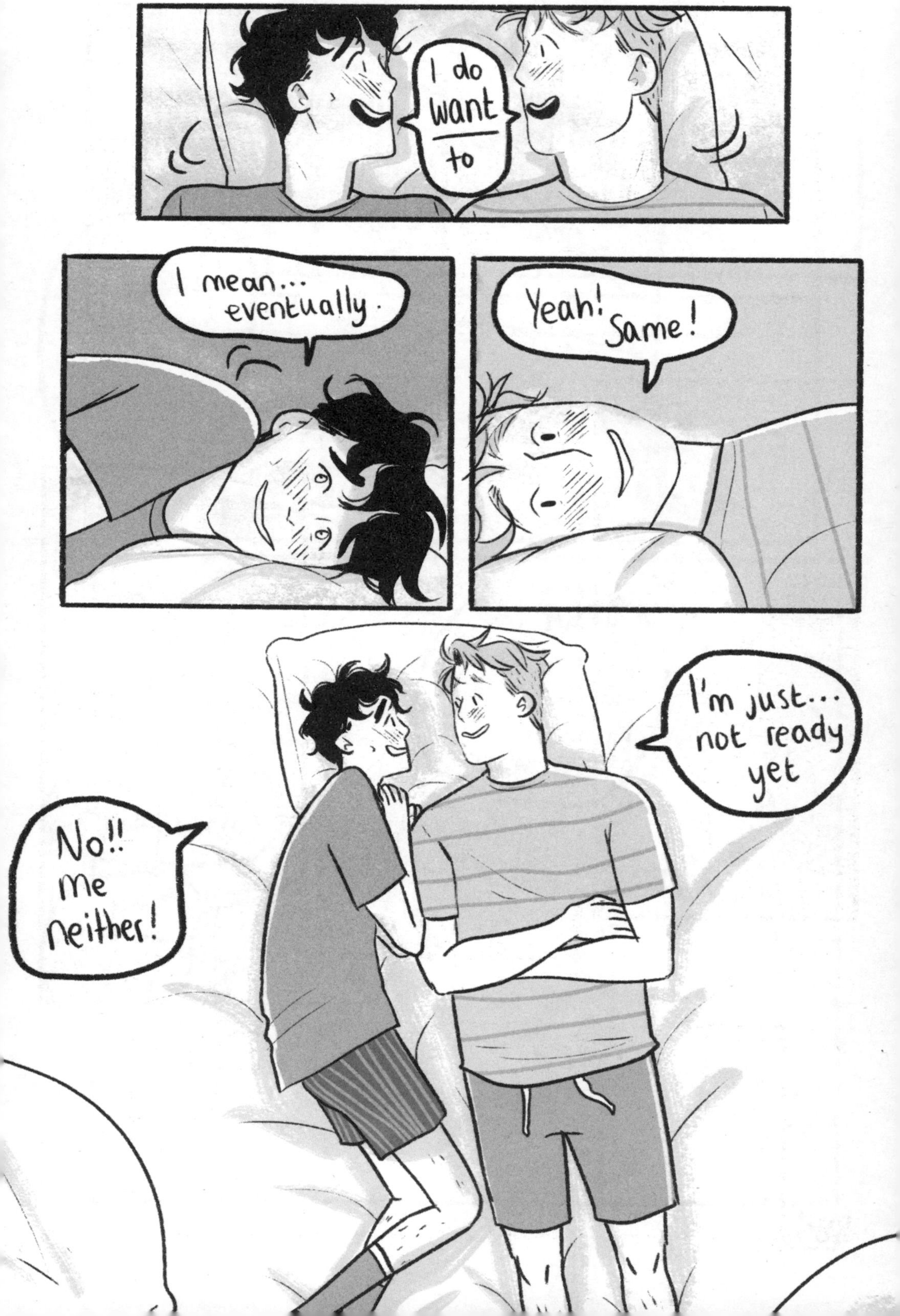
I do want to
I mean... eventually.
Yeah! Same!
I'm just... not ready yet
No!! me neither!

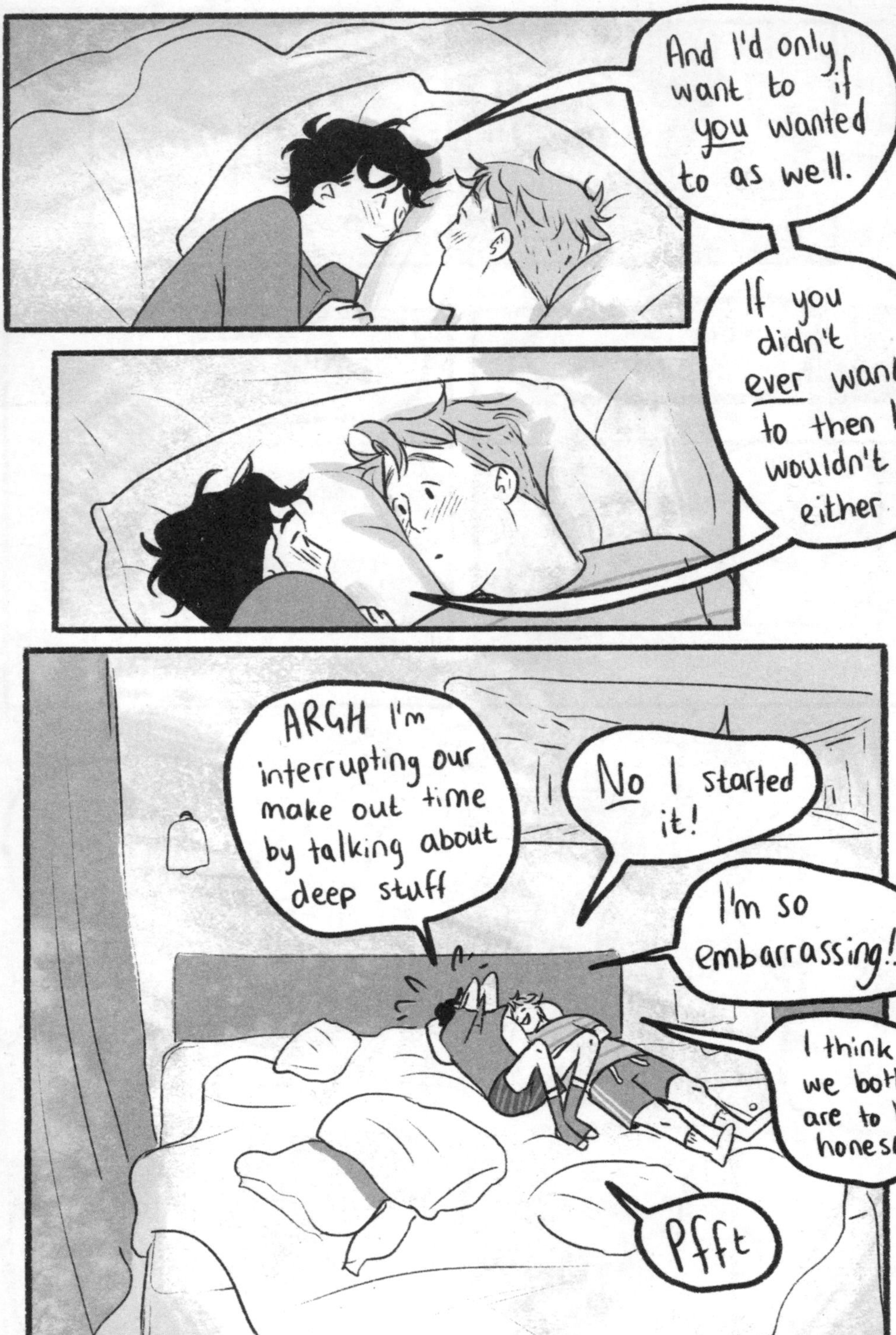
And I'd only want to if you wanted to as well.
If you didn't ever want to then I wouldn't either
ARGH I'm interrupting our make out time by talking about deep stuff
No I started it!
I'm so embarrassing!!
I think we both are to be honest
Pfft

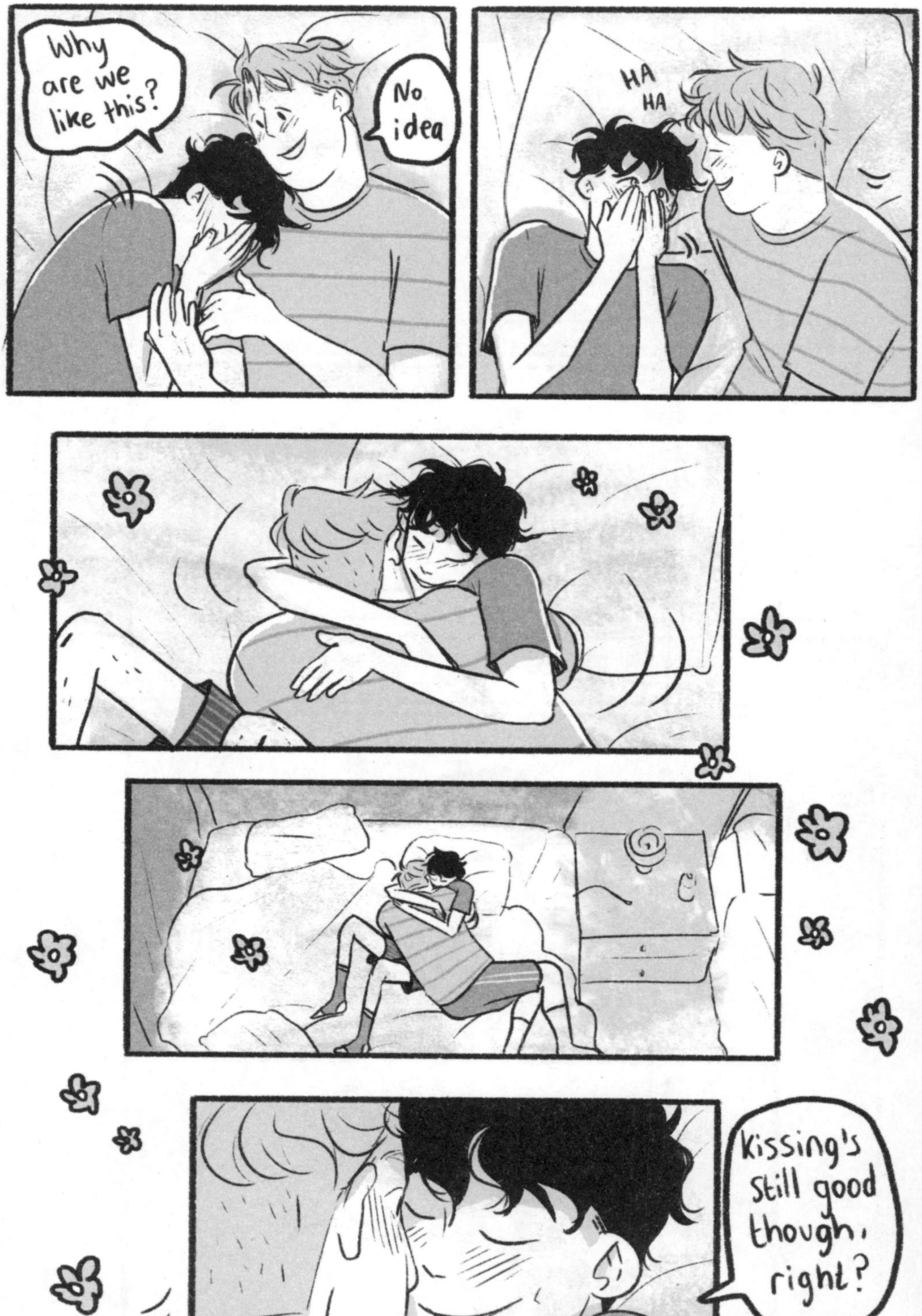
Why are we like this?
No idea
HA HA
Kissing's still good though, right?

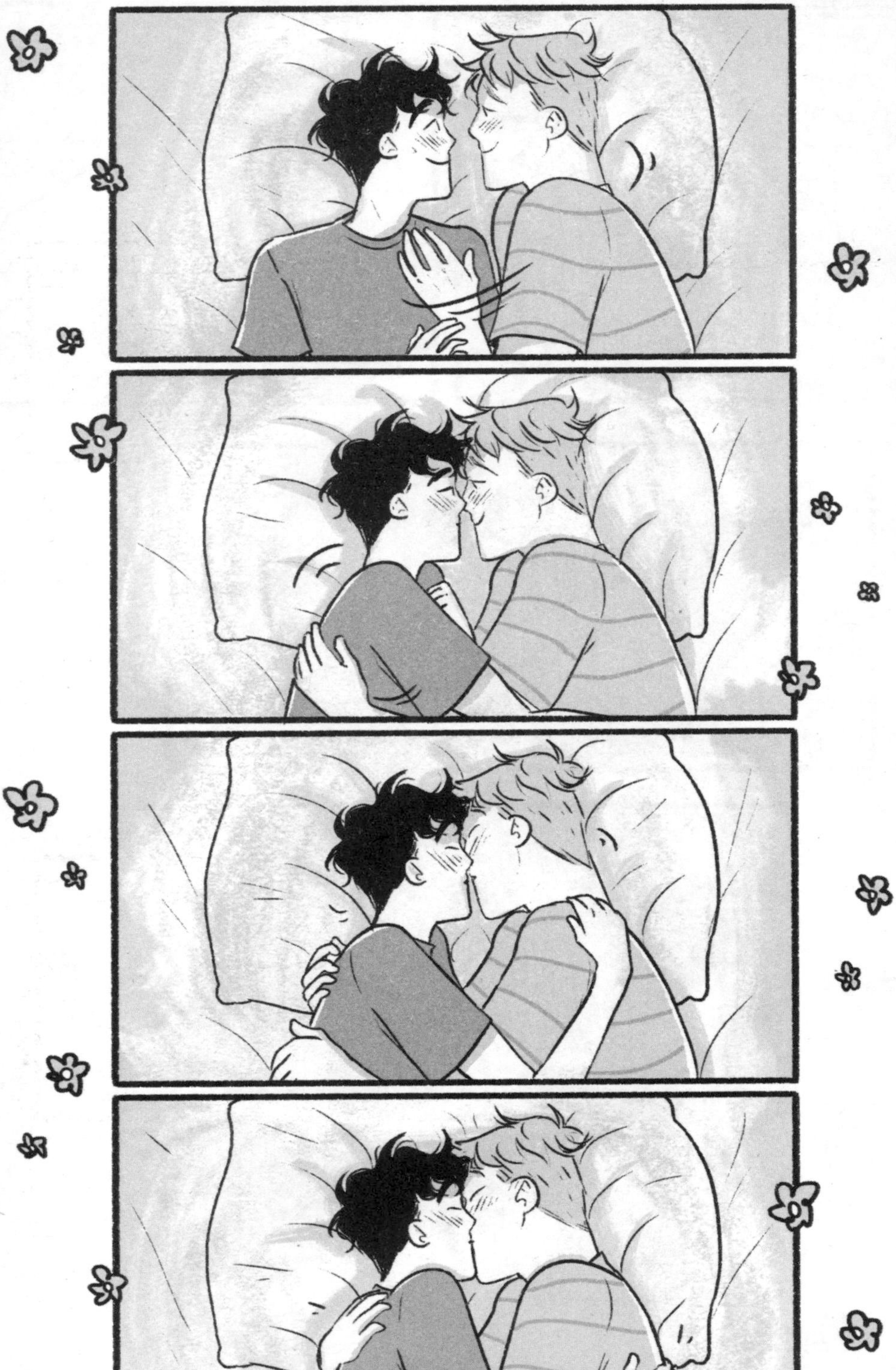

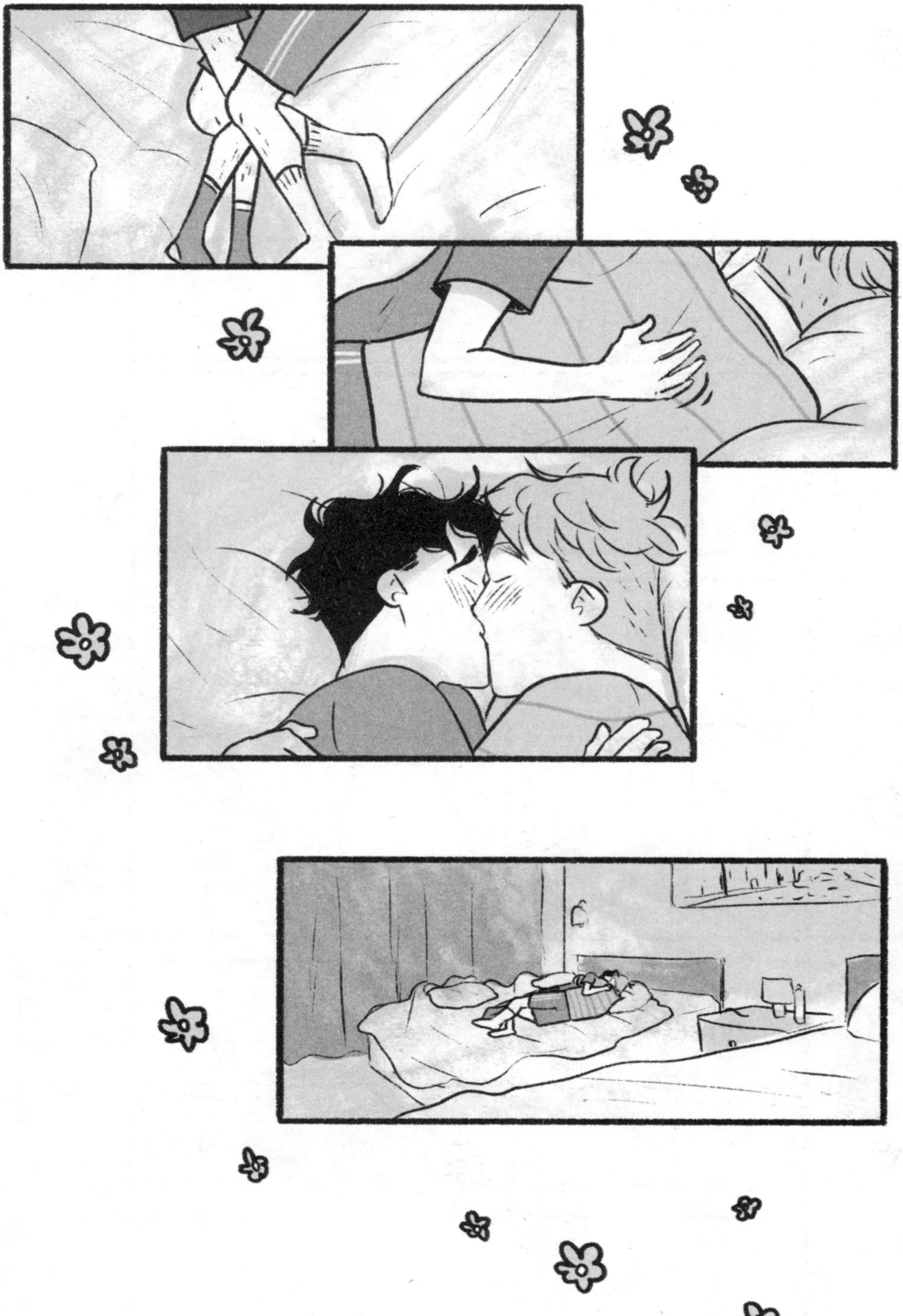

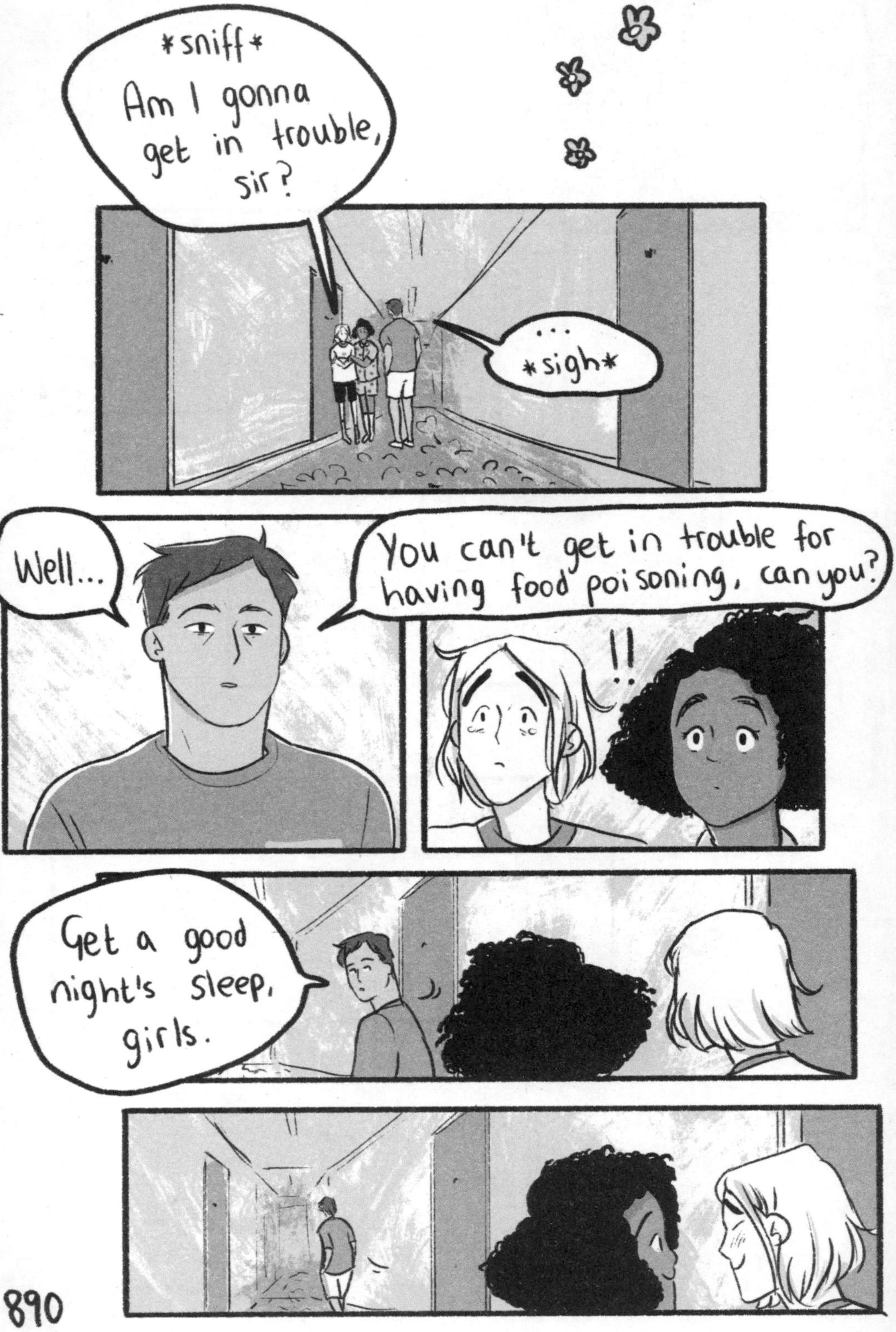
sniff Am I gonna get in trouble, sir?
... *sigh*
Well...
You can't get in trouble for having food poisoning, can you?
!!
Get a good night's sleep, girls.

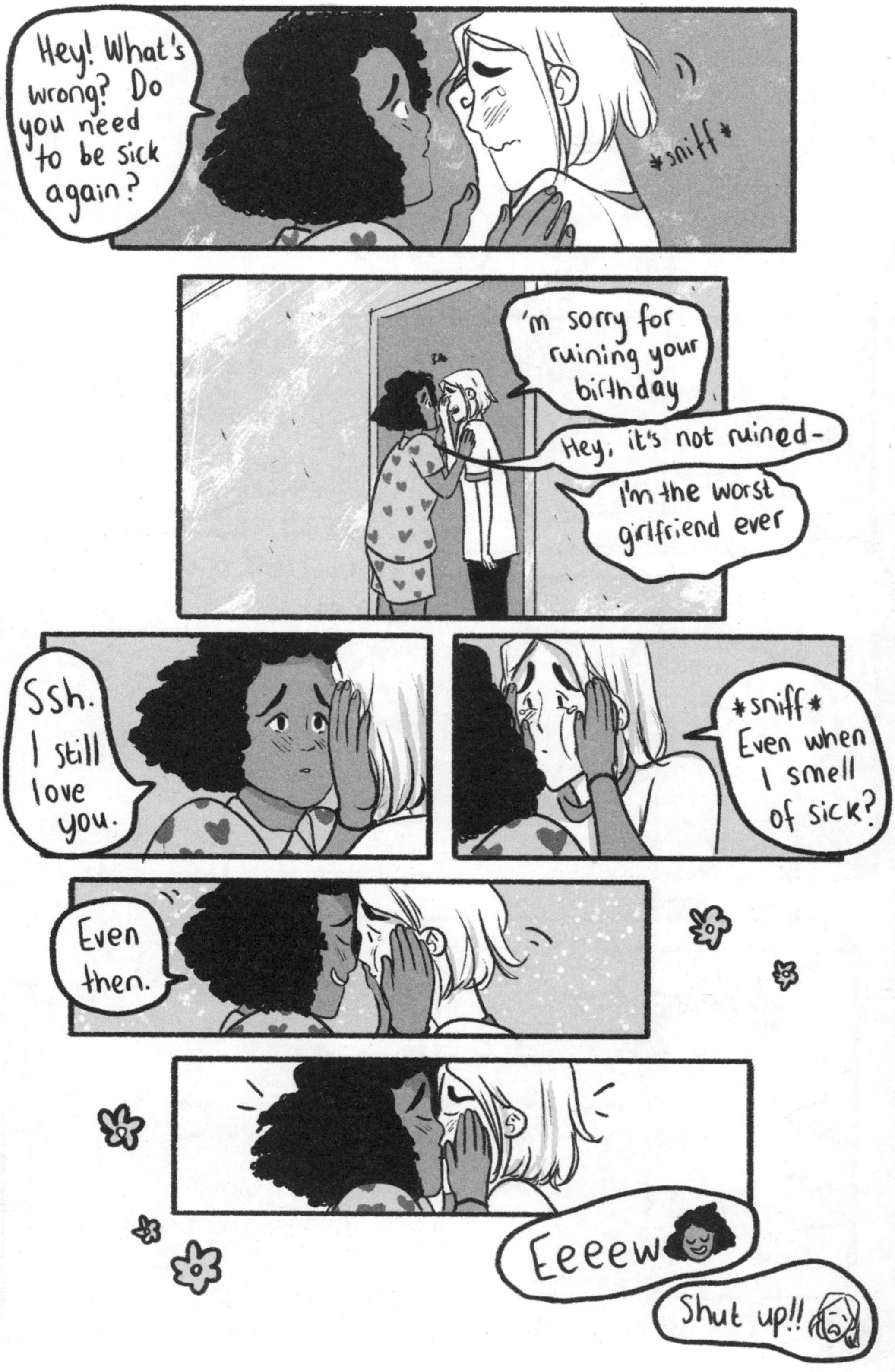

Hey! What's wrong? Do you need to be sick again?
sniff
'm sorry for ruining your birthday
Hey, it's not ruined-
I'm the worst girlfriend ever
Ssh. I still love you.
sniff Even when I smell of sick?
Even then.
Eeeew
Shut up!!

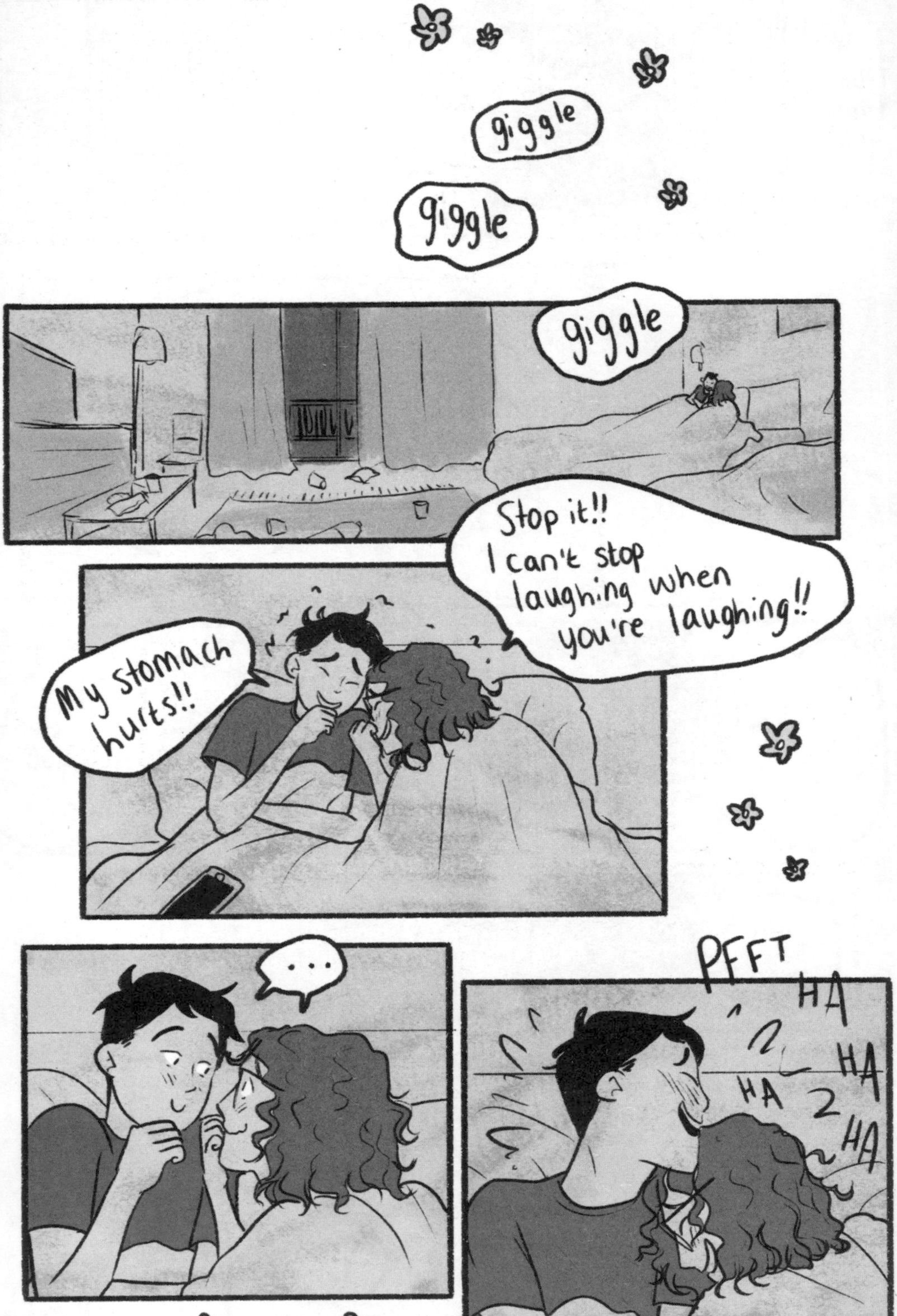
giggle
giggle
giggle
Stop it!! I can't stop laughing when you're laughing!!
My stomach hurts!!
...
PFFT
HA
HA
HA
HA

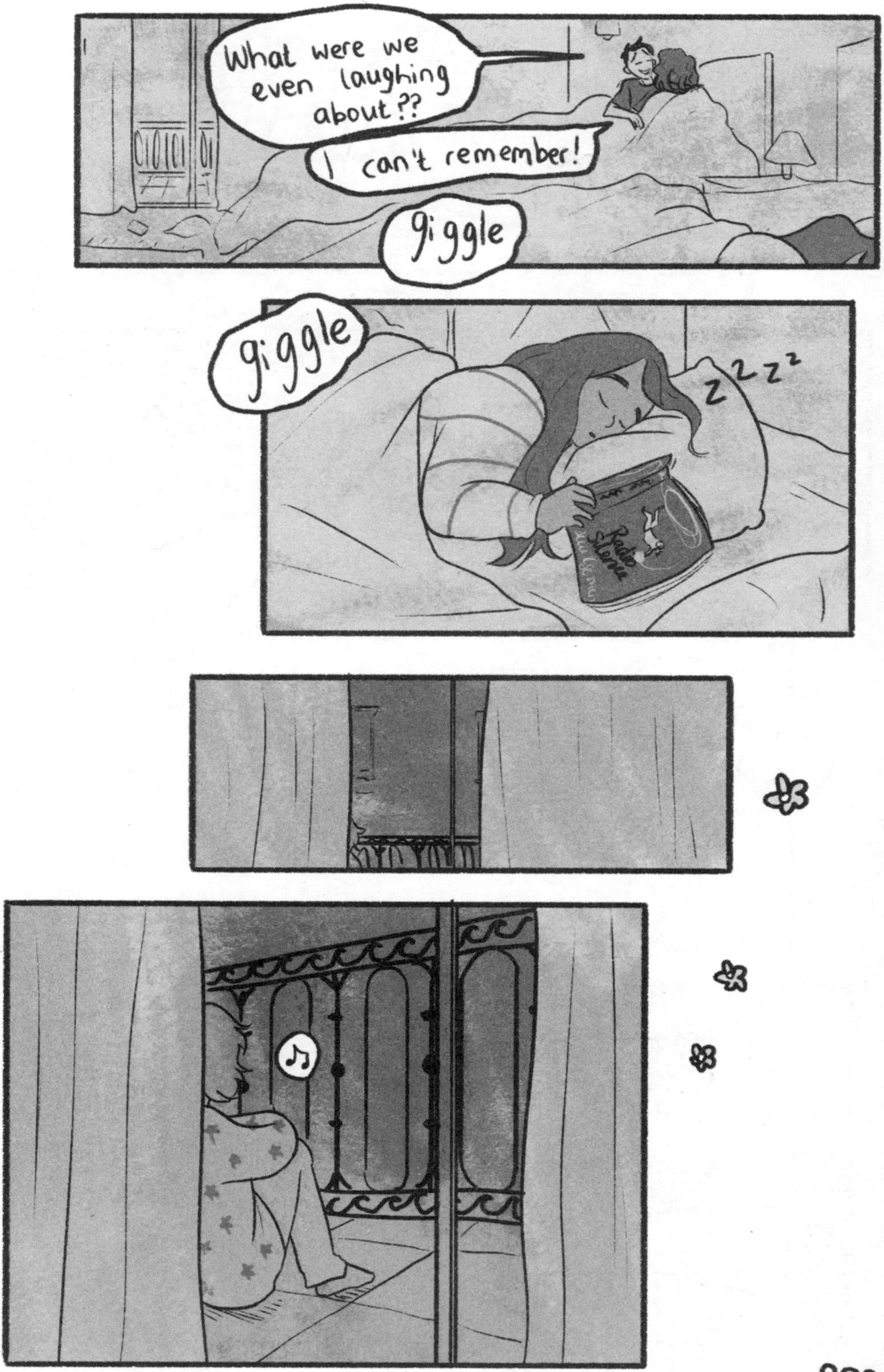
What were we even laughing about??
I can't remember!
giggle
giggle
Z z z z
Radio Silence

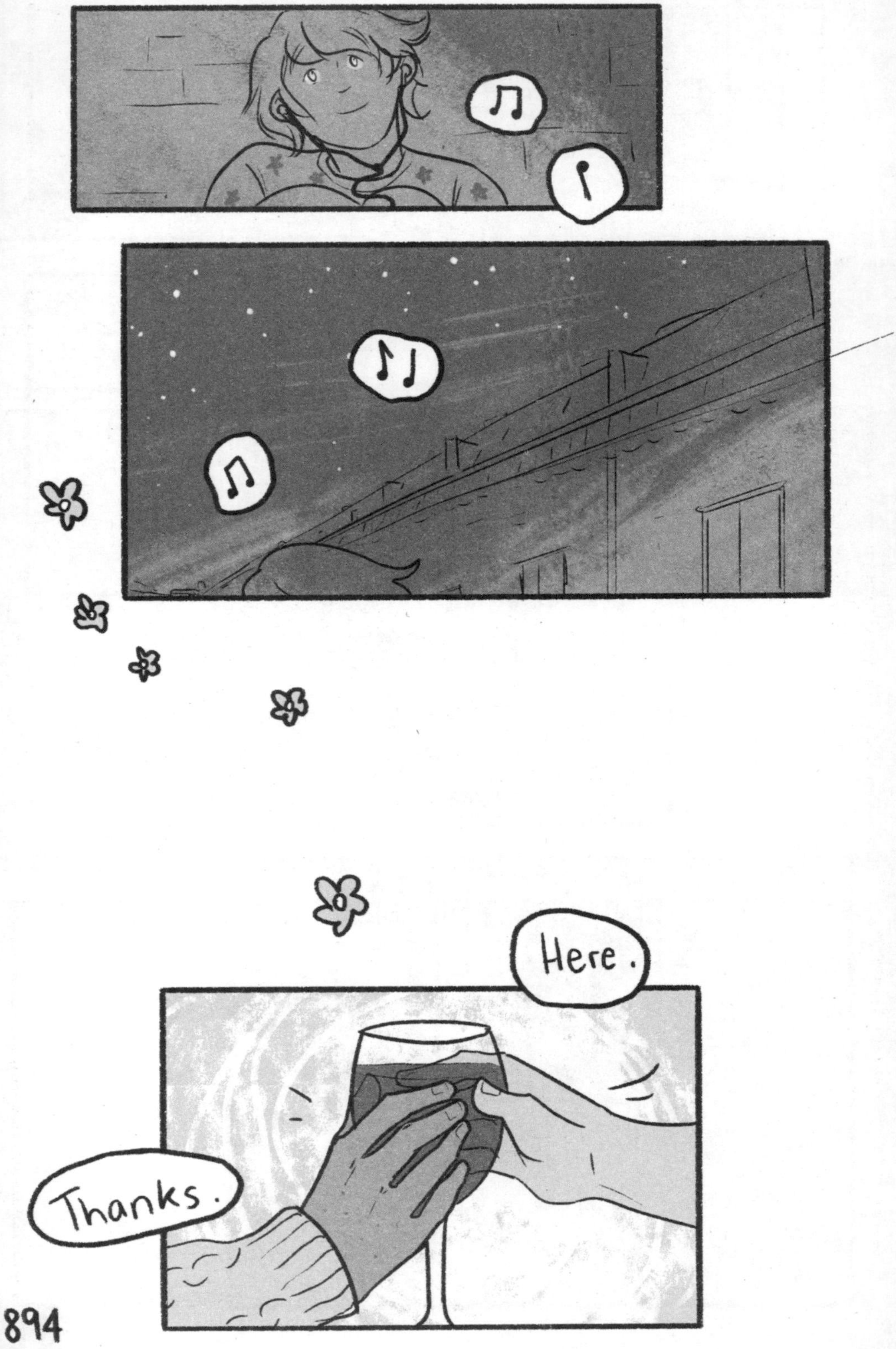
Here.
Thanks.

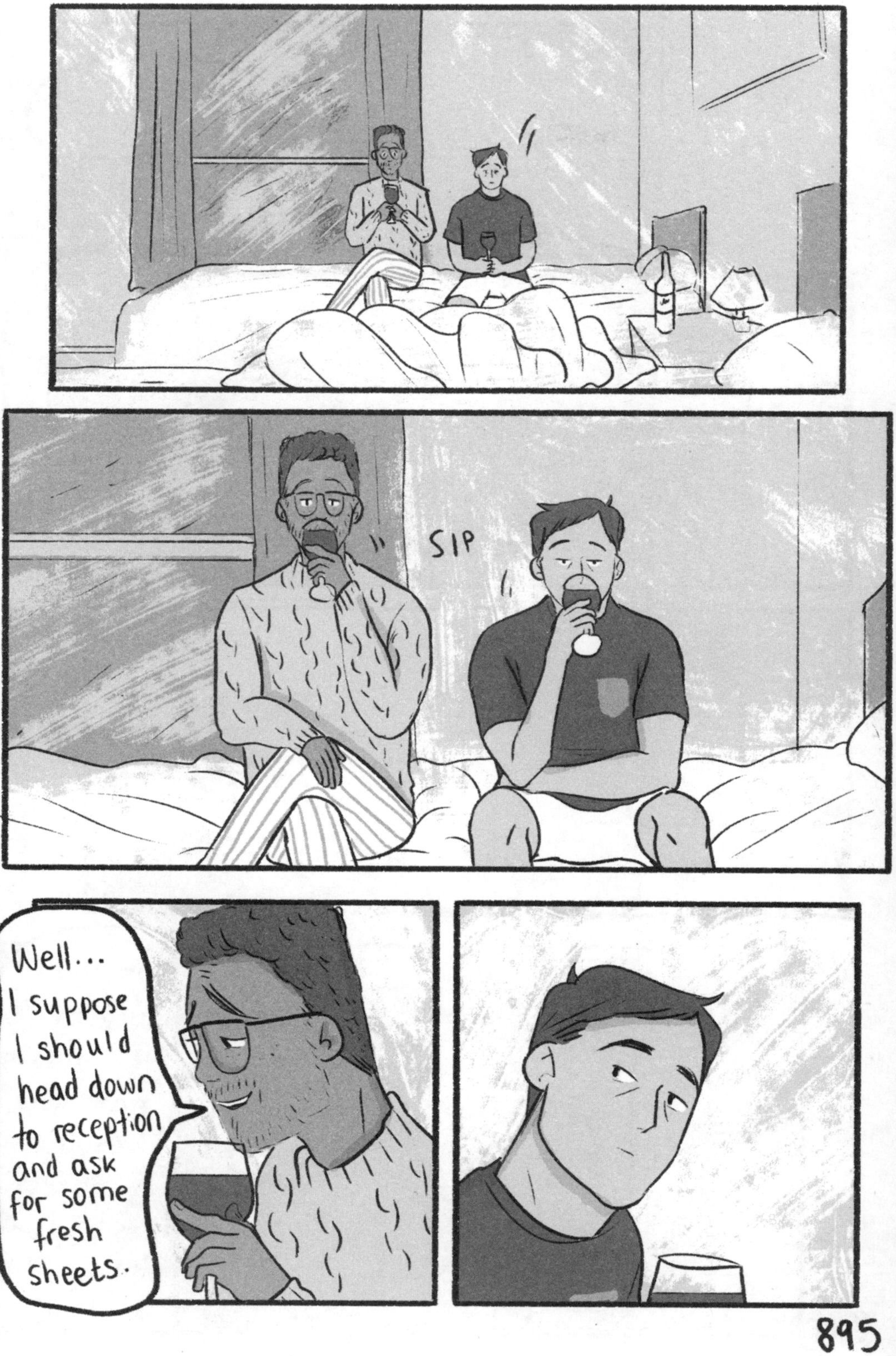
SIP
Well... I suppose I should head down to reception and ask for some fresh sheets.

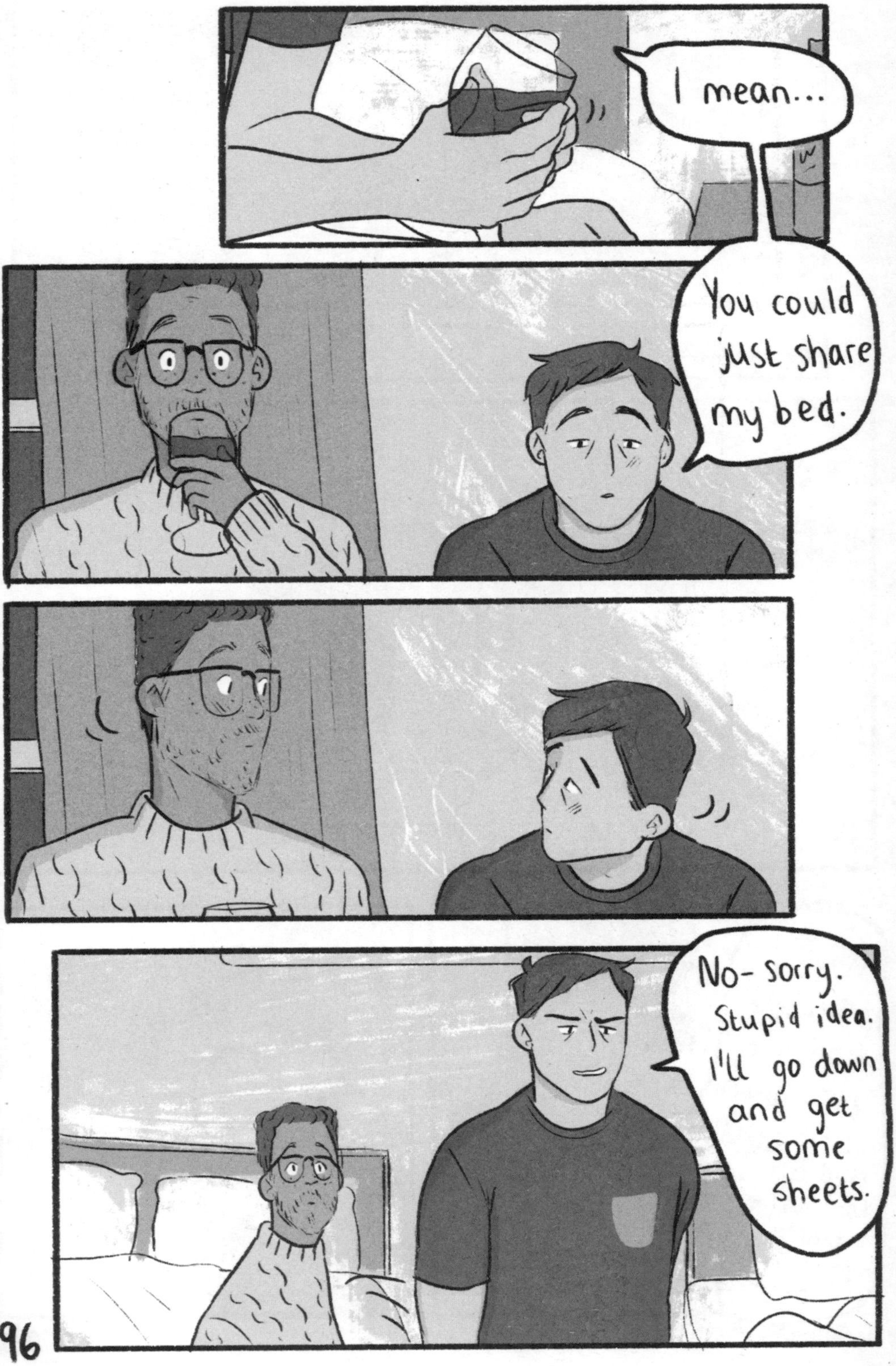
I mean...
You could just share my bed.
No- sorry. Stupid idea. I'll go down and get some sheets.

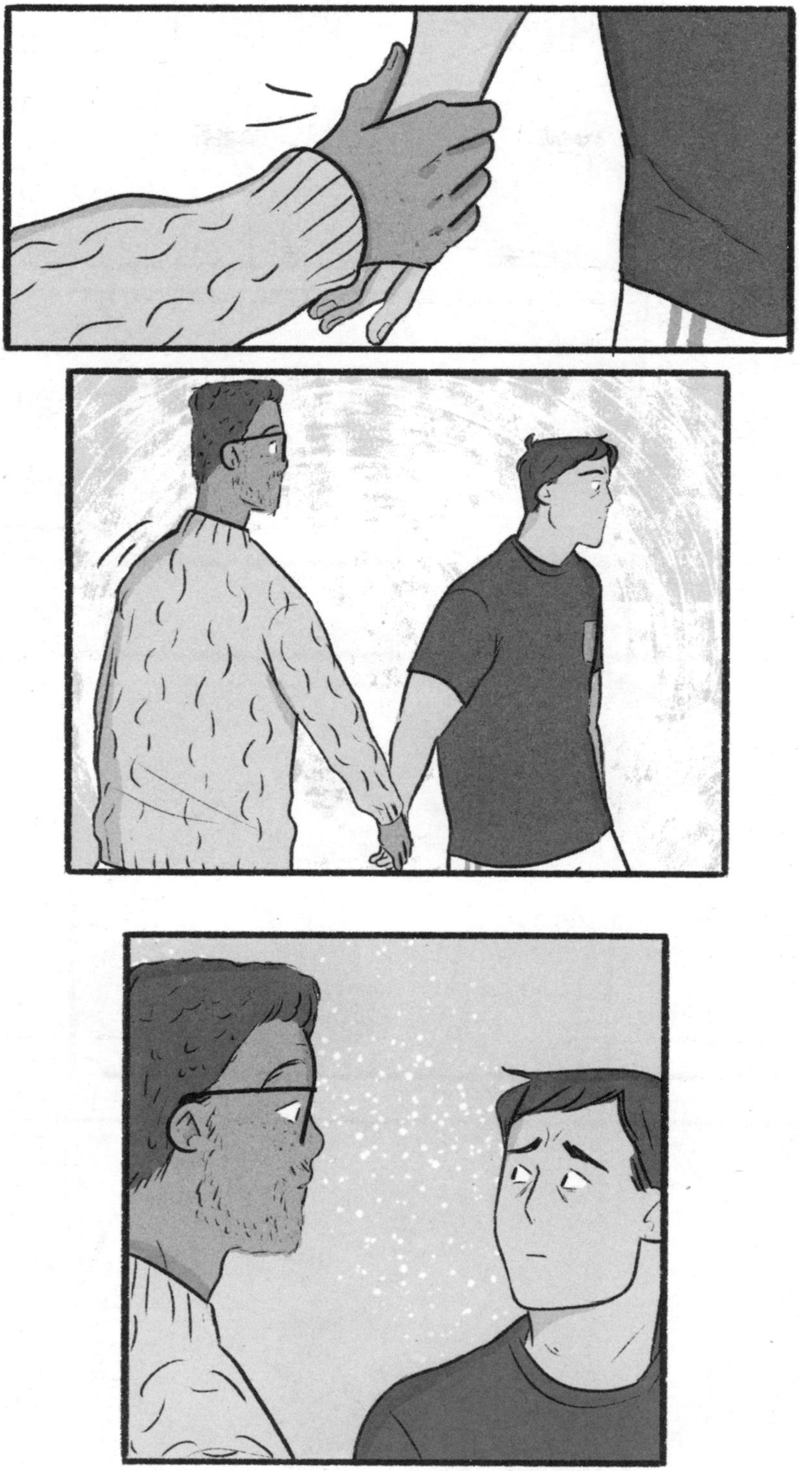

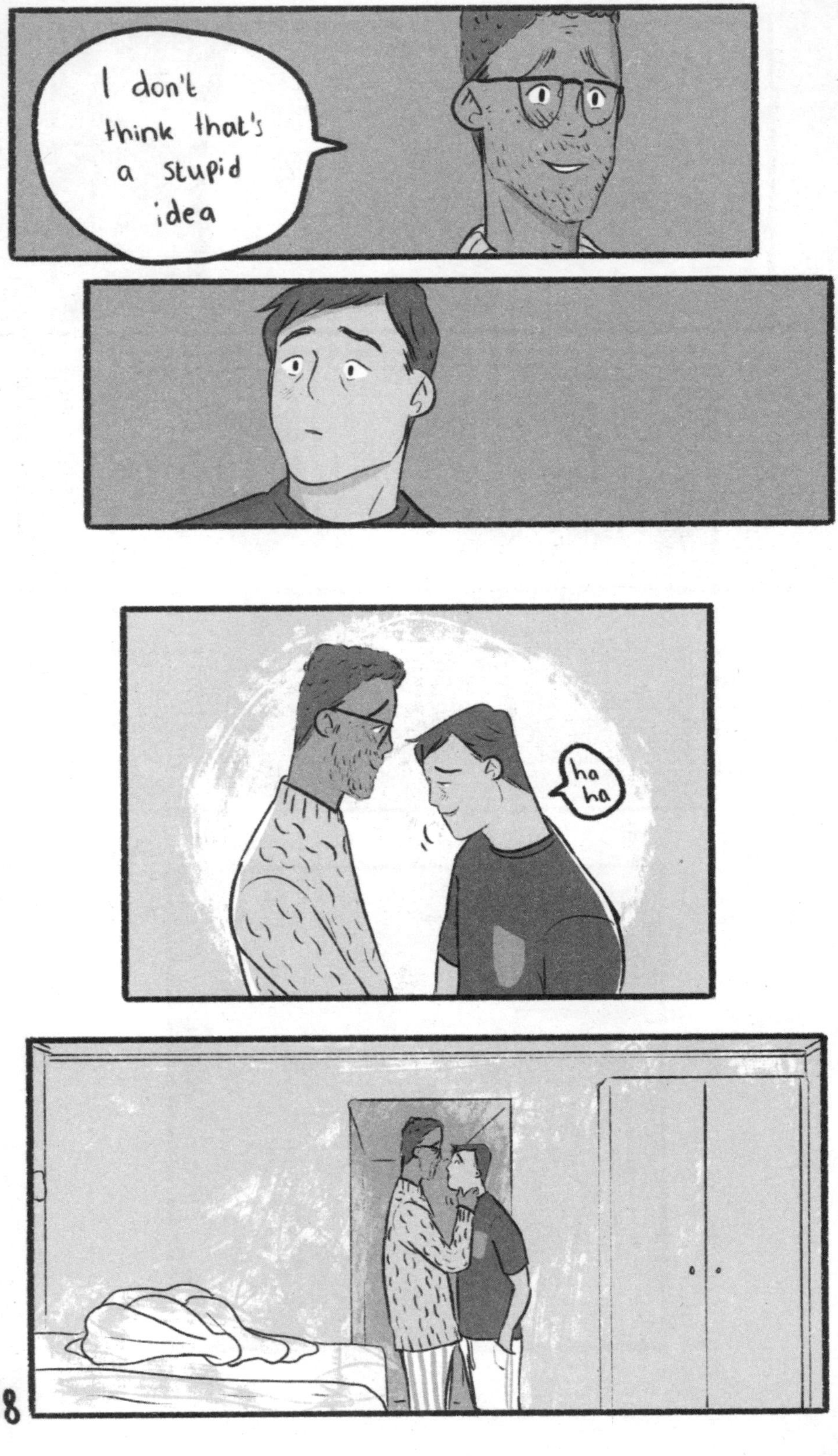
I don't think that's a stupid idea
ha ha

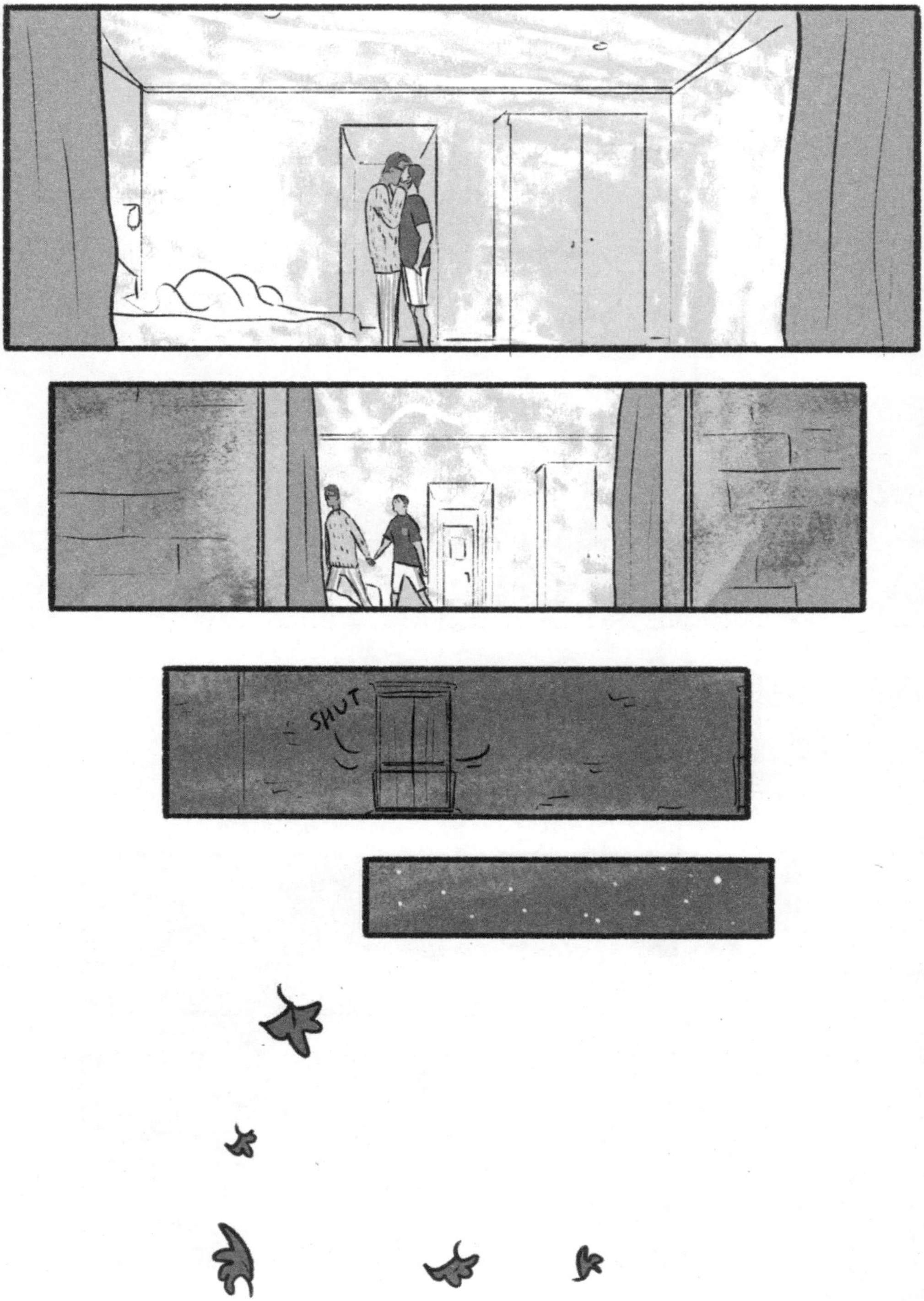
SHUT

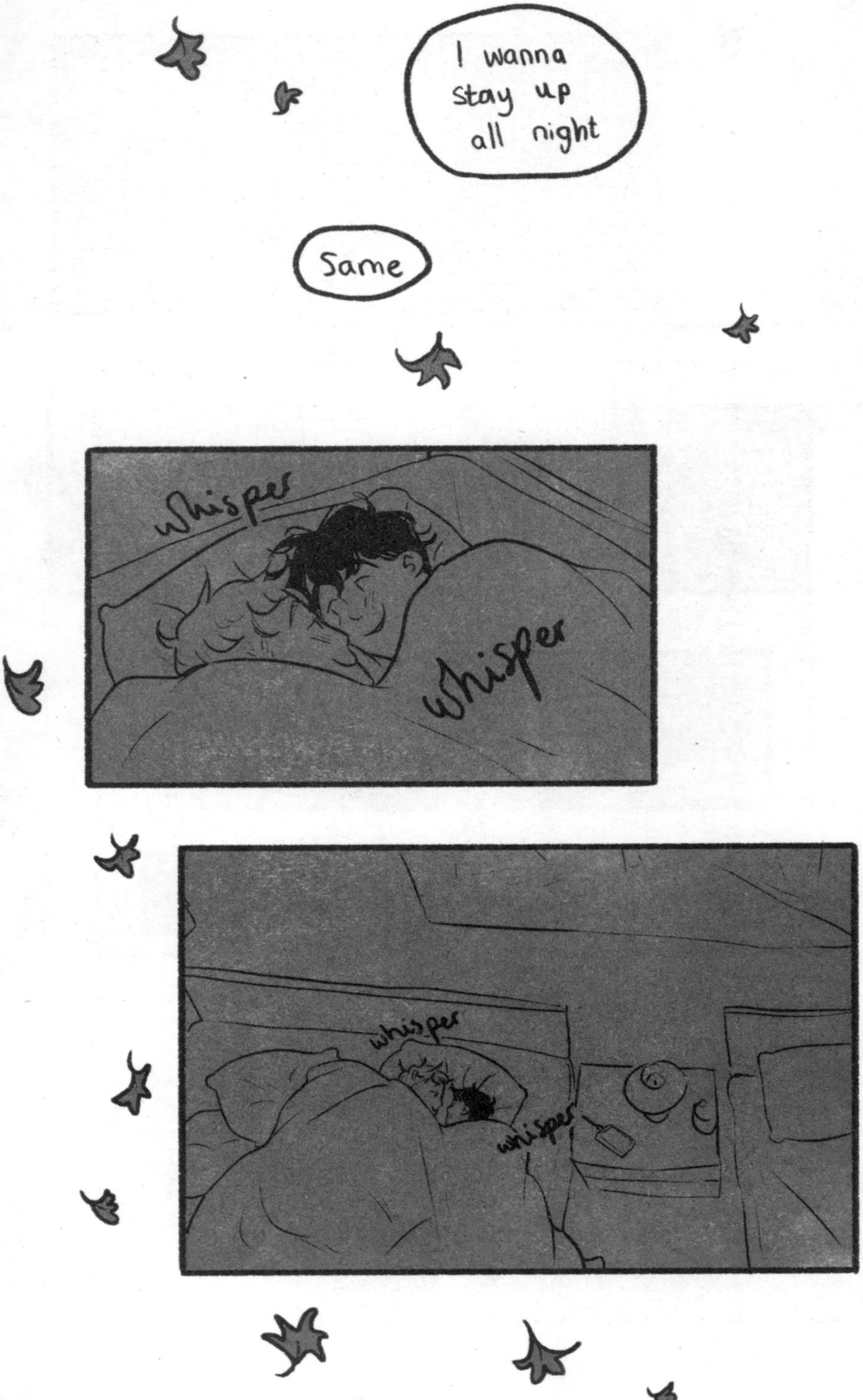
I wanna stay up all night
Same
whisper
whisper
whisper
whisper

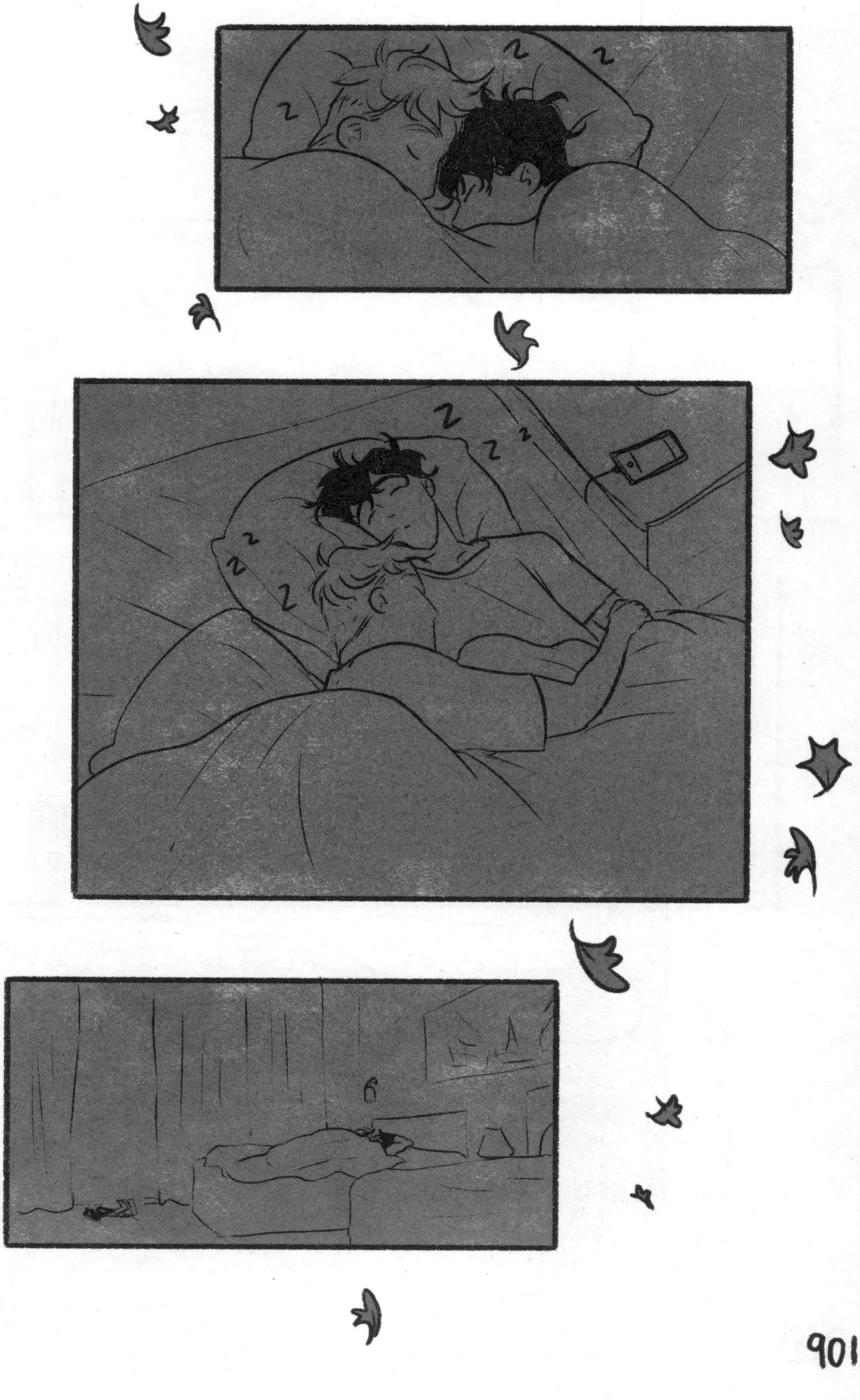

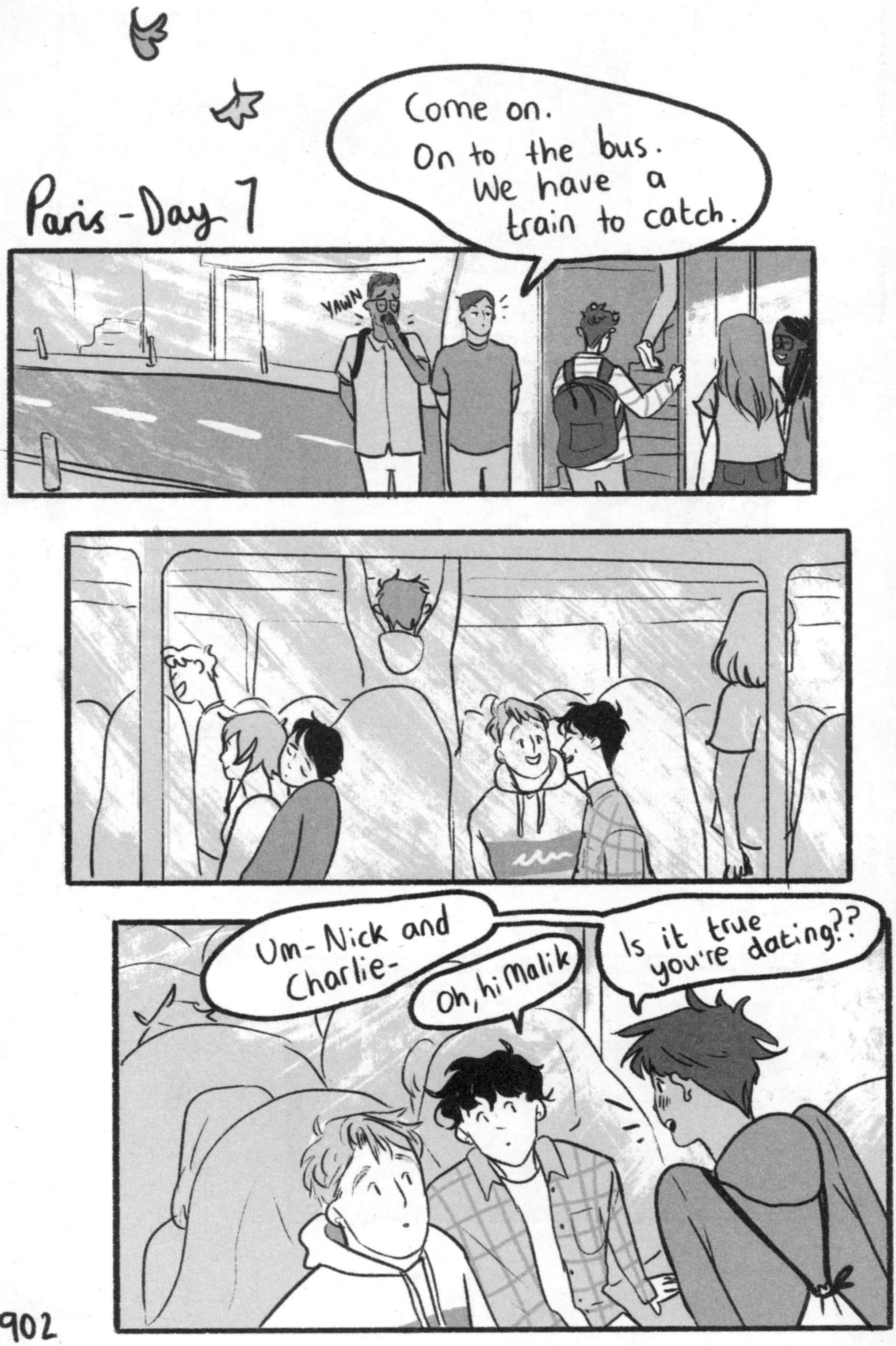
Paris - Day 7
Come on. On to the bus. We have a train to catch.
YAWN
Um- Nick and Charlie-
Oh, hi Malik
Is it true you're dating??

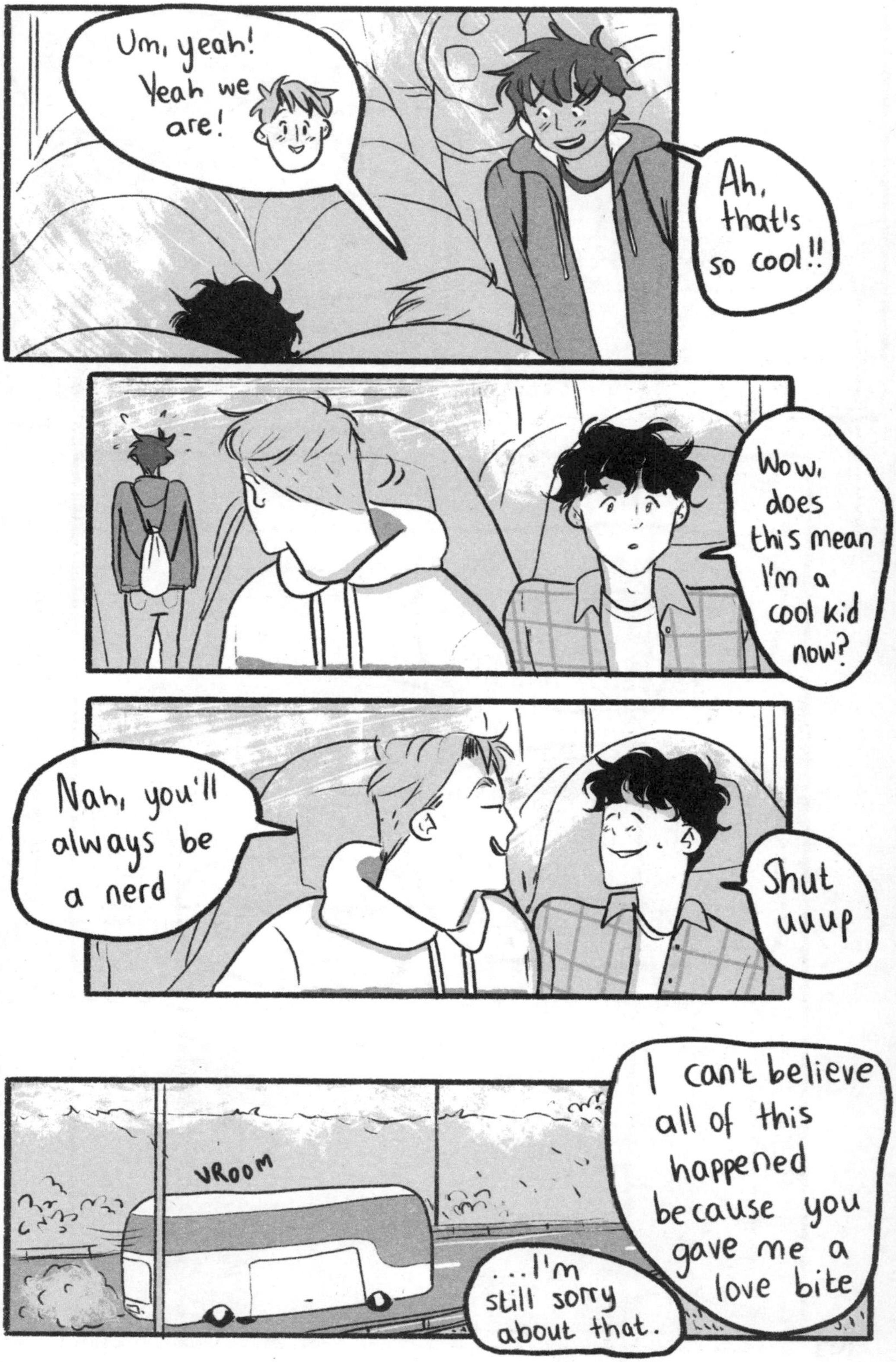
Um, yeah! Yeah we are!
Ah, that's so cool!!
Wow, does this mean I'm a cool kid now?
Nah, you'll always be a nerd
Shut uuup
VROOM
I can't believe all of this happened because you gave me a love bite
...I'm still sorry about that.

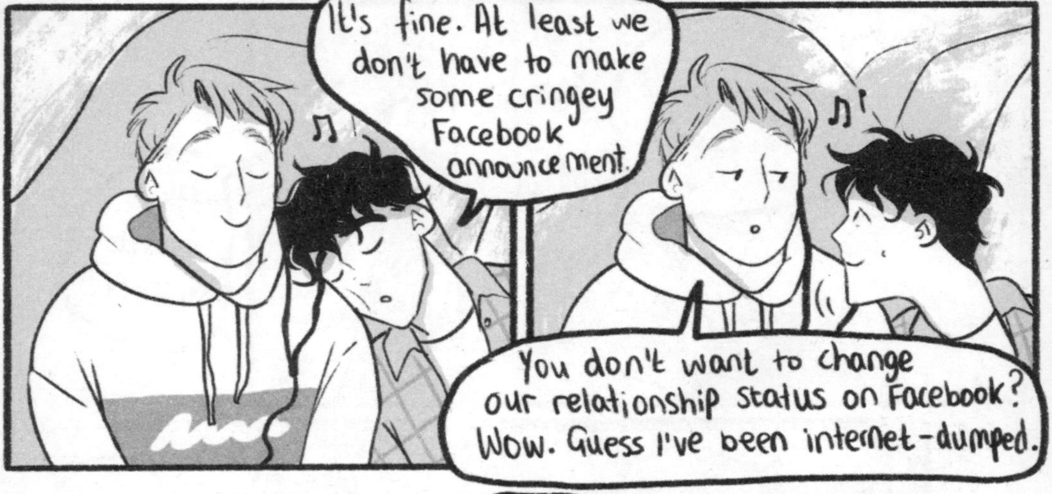
It's fine. At least we don't have to make some cringey Facebook announcement.
You don't want to change our relationship status on Facebook? Wow. Guess I've been internet-dumped.

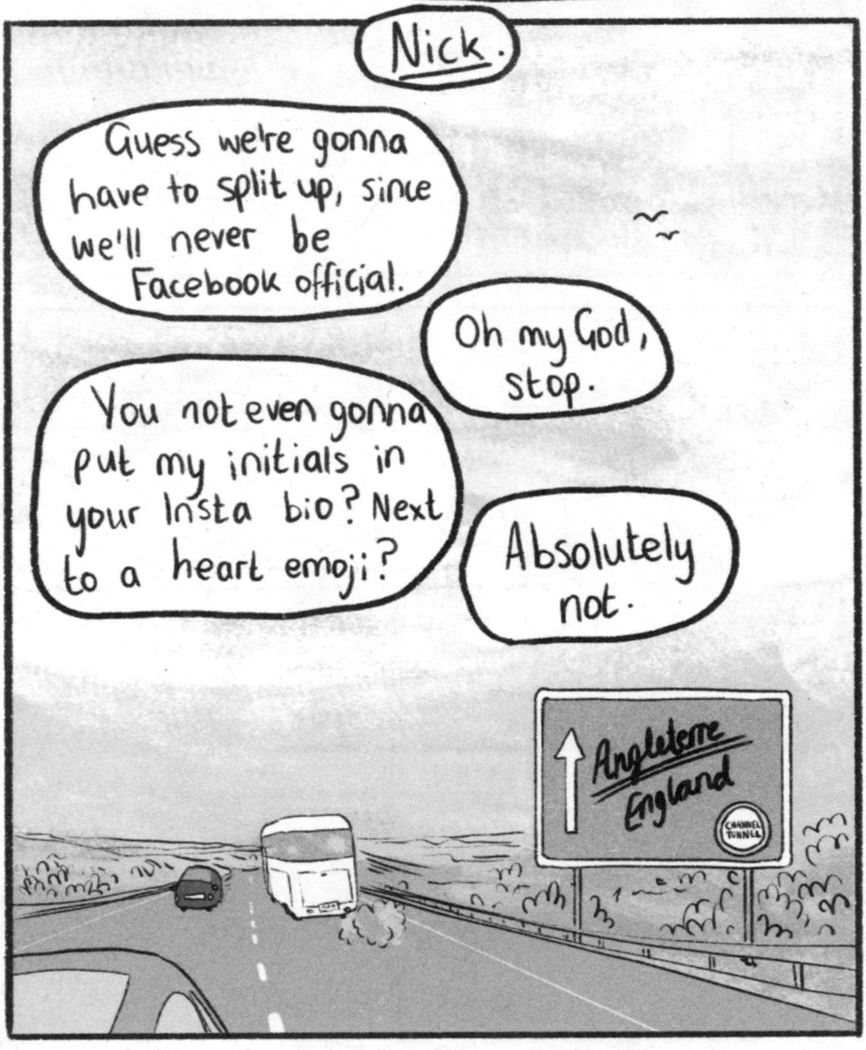
Nick.
Guess we're gonna have to split up, since we'll never be Facebook official.
Oh my God, stop.
You not even gonna put my initials in your Insta bio? Next to a heart emoji?
Absolutely not.
Angleterre
England

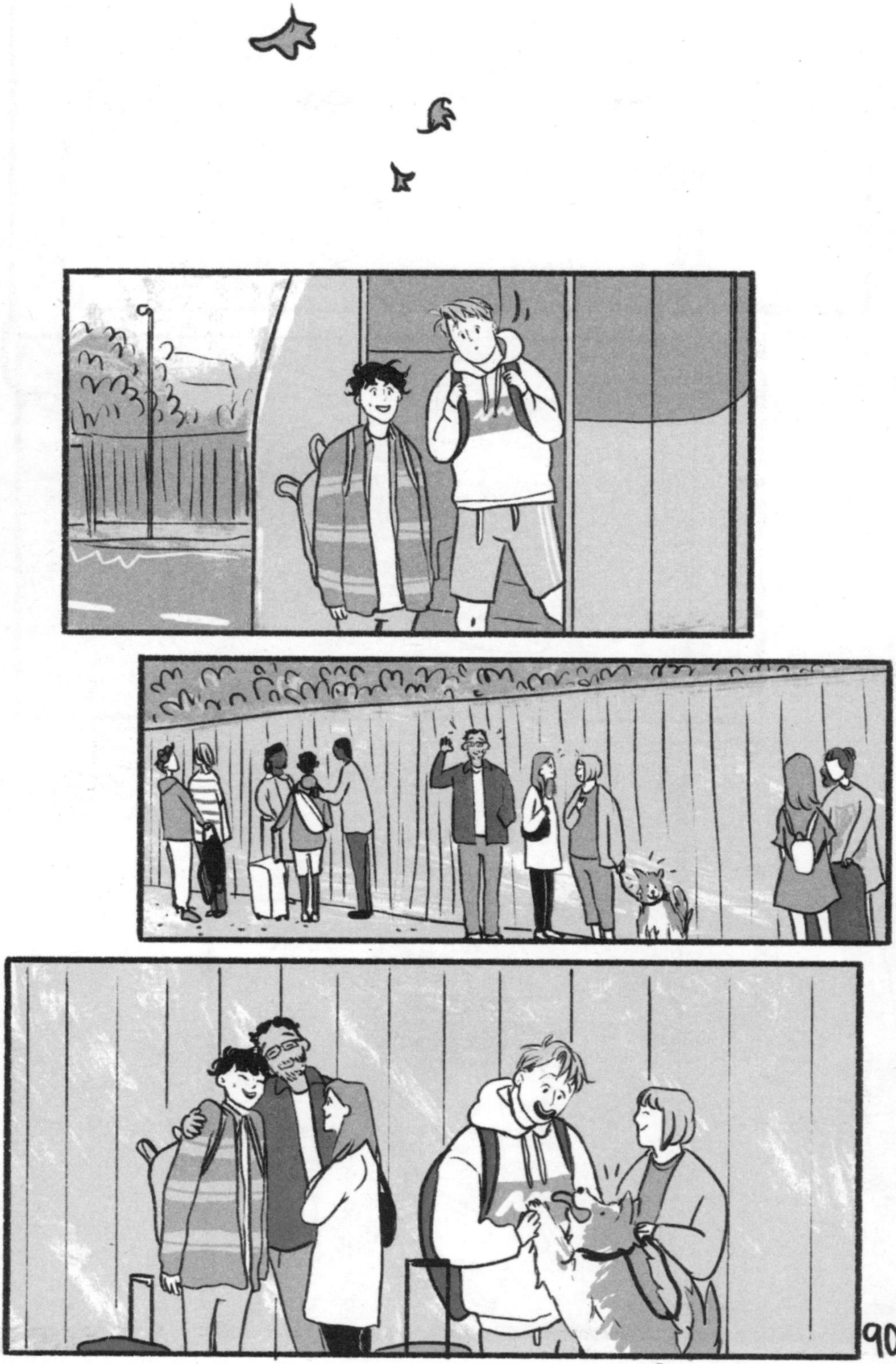

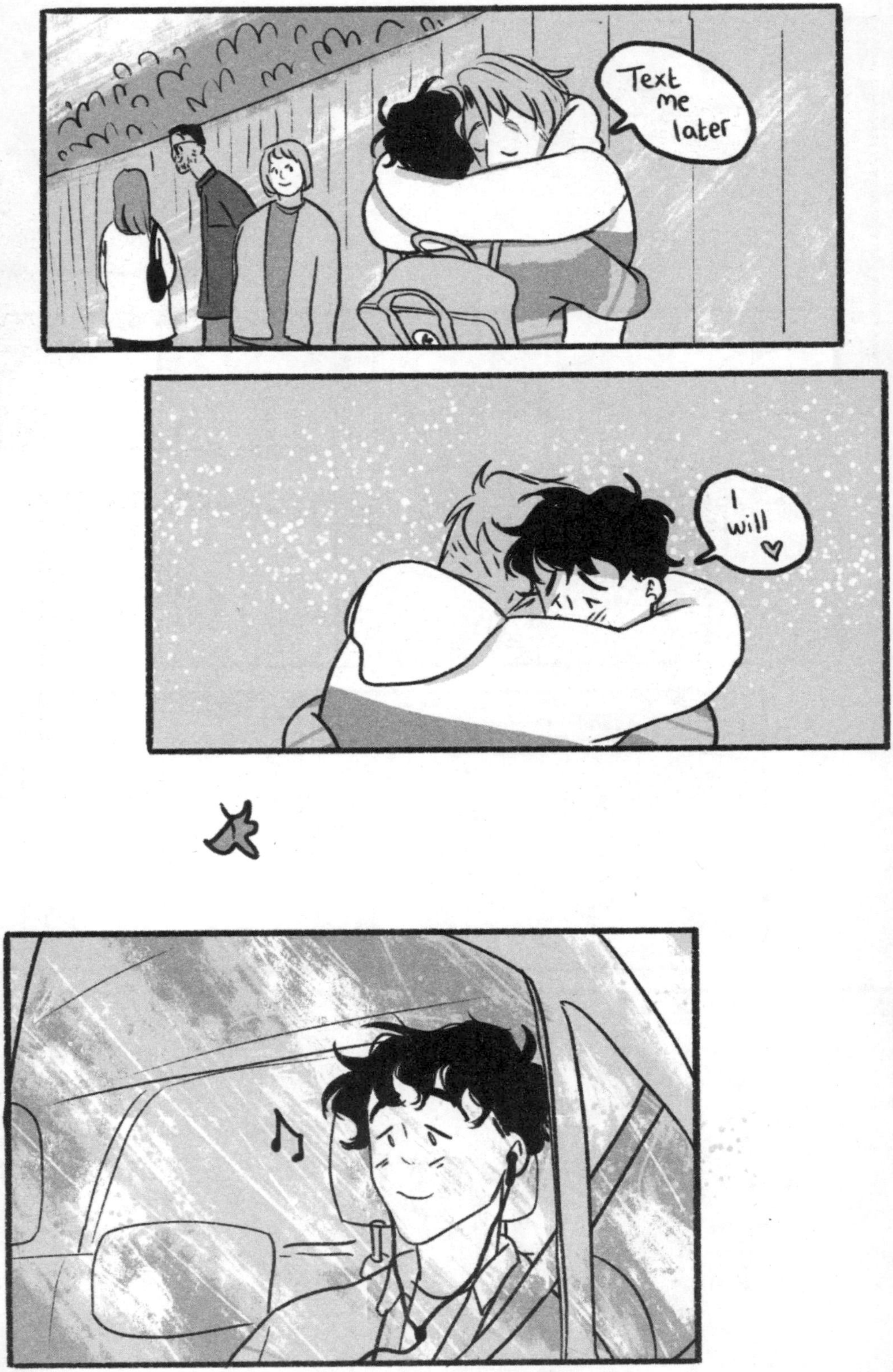
Text me later
I will ♥

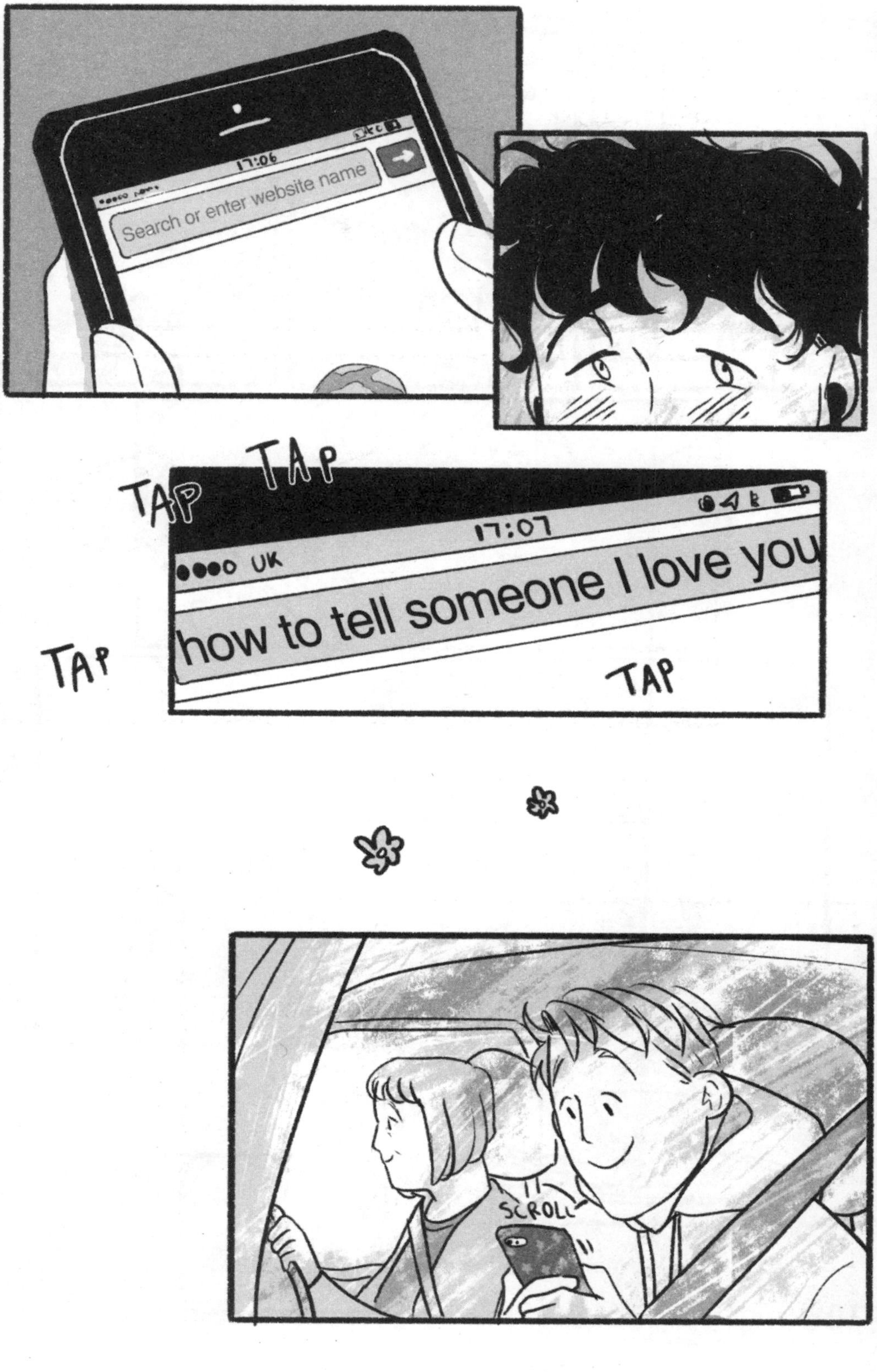
17:06
Search or enter website name
TAP
TAP
17:07
UK
how to tell someone I love you
TAP
TAP
SCROLL

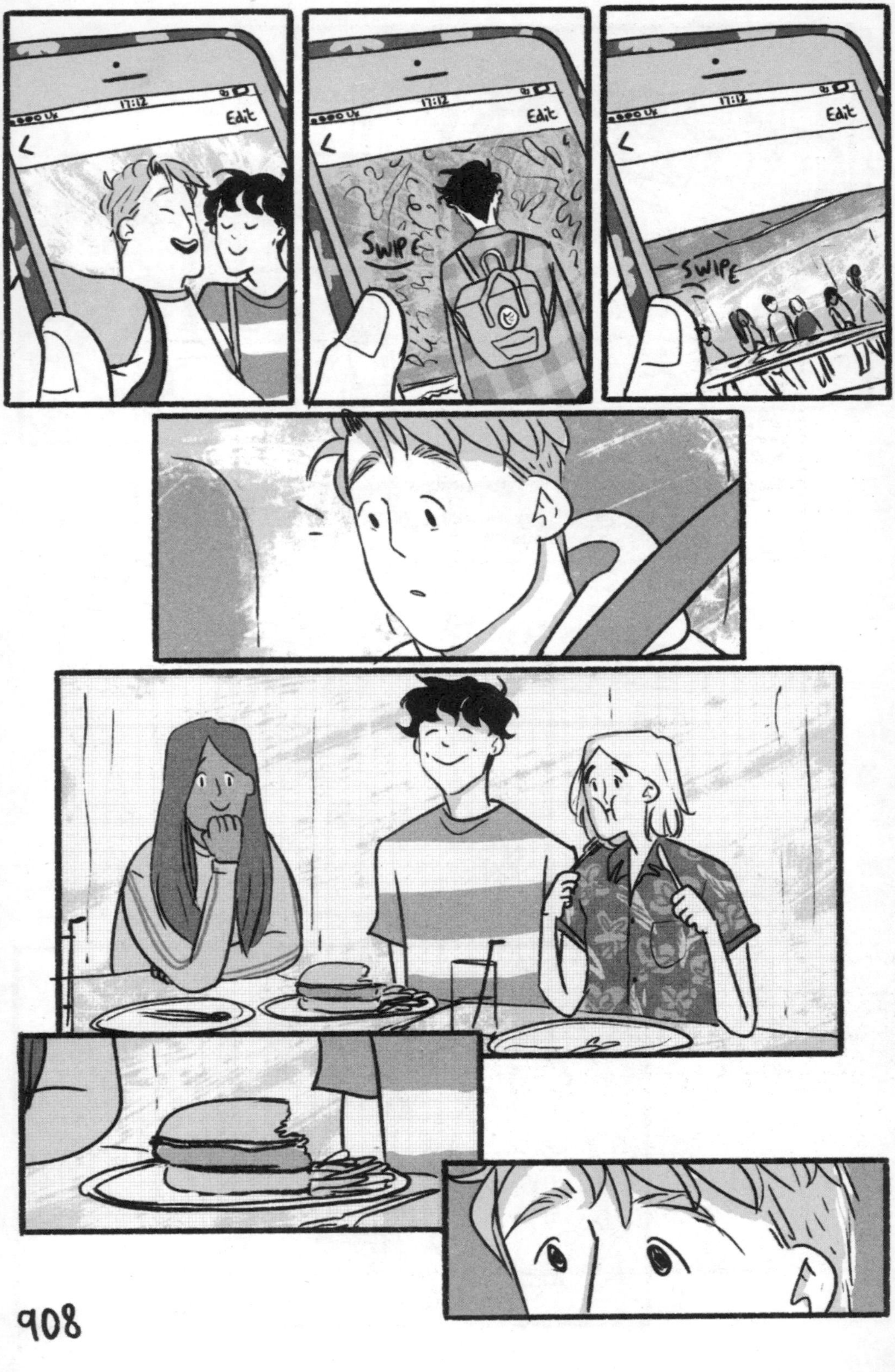
17:12
Edit
17:12
Edit
SWIPE
17:12
Edit
SWIPE

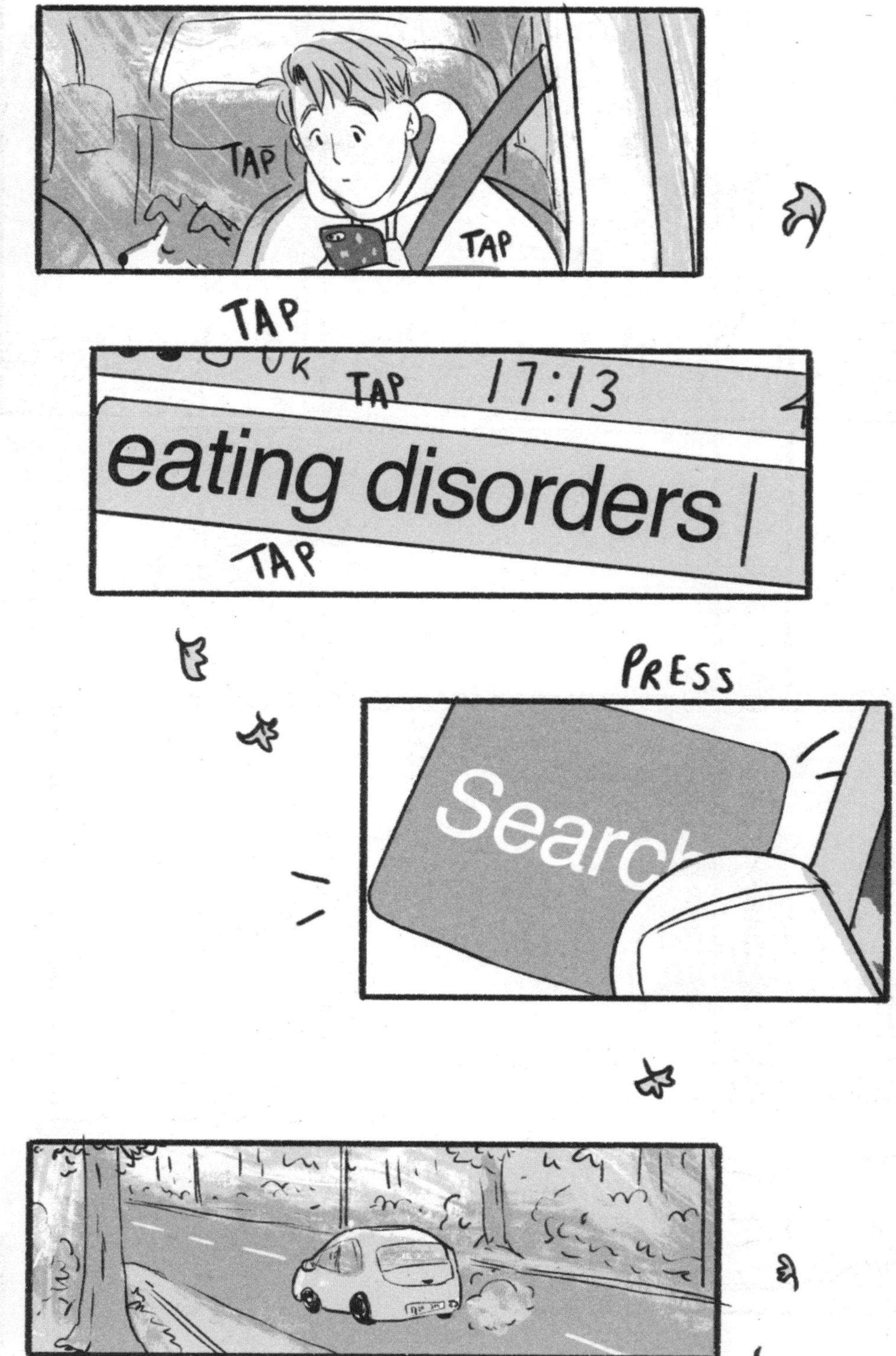
TAP
TAP
TAP
TAP
17:13
eating disorders
TAP
PRESS
Searc

Heartstopper will continue in
Volume 4!

Read more of the comic online:

heartstoppercomic.tumblr.com
tapas.io/series/heartstopper

Sunday 27th June

So tomorrow I'll be going away for a whole week to PARIS.

♡The city of love♡

Okay that's dumb. But I'm very excited!!!

None of my Year 11 friends are going but I'll get to be with Charlie all day every day for a <u>whole week</u>, which is waaaaaaay better than being stuck at home now that my exams are over. And I really like Charlie's friends so I'd like to get to know them better.

I think I'm most looking forward to going up the Eiffel Tower. I always imagined it'd be super romantic to go up the Eiffel Tower with the person you ~~love~~ ~~like~~ love and take cheesy photos :)

very bad drawing of the Eiffel Tower →

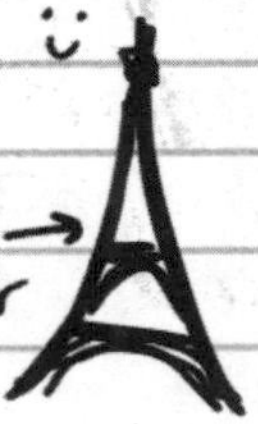

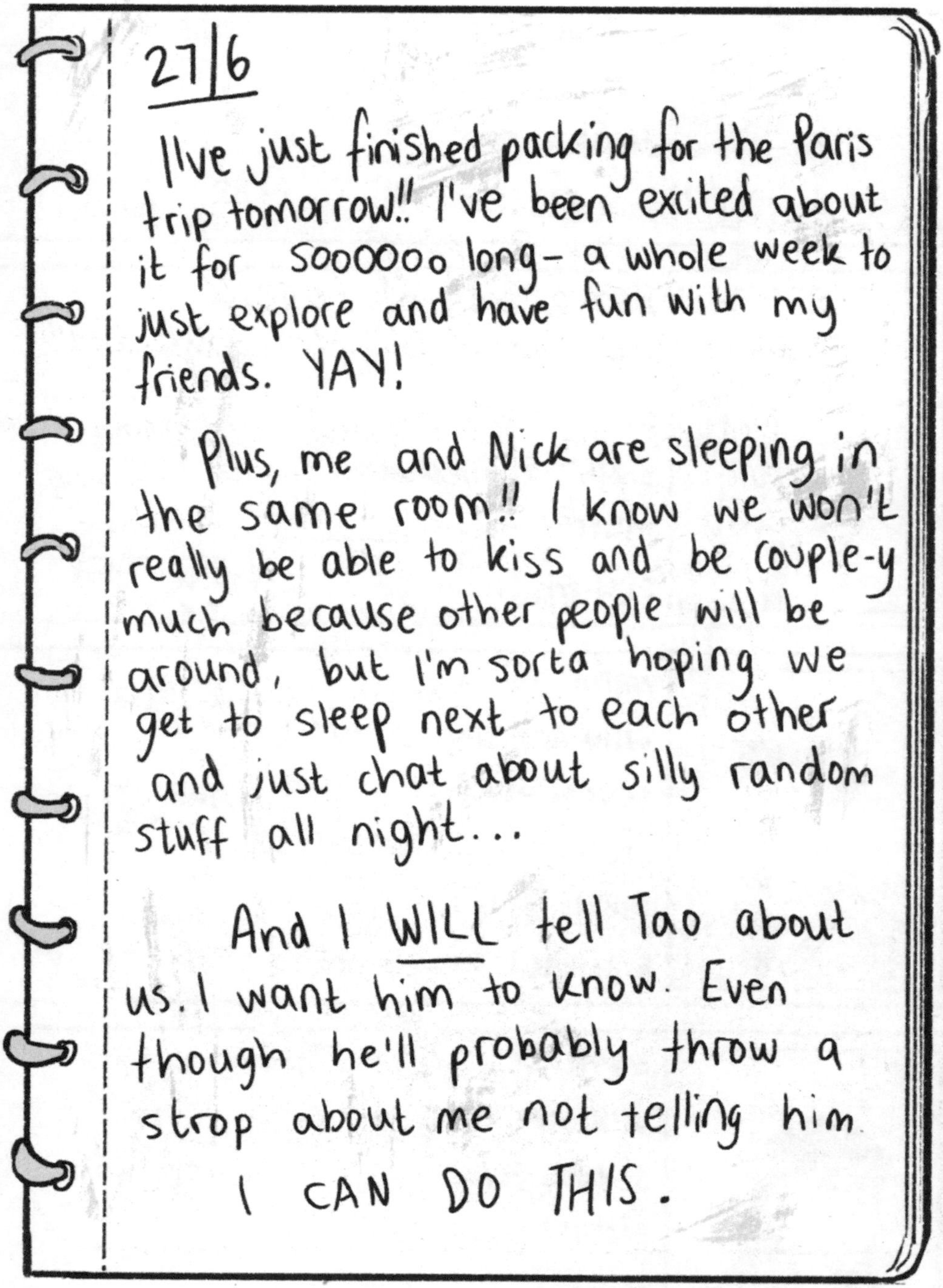
27/6
I've just finished packing for the Paris trip tomorrow!! I've been excited about it for Soooooo long - a whole week to just explore and have fun with my friends. YAY!
Plus, me and Nick are sleeping in the same room!! I know we won't really be able to kiss and be couple-y much because other people will be around, but I'm sorta hoping we get to sleep next to each other and just chat about silly random stuff all night...
And I WILL tell Tao about us. I want him to know. Even though he'll probably throw a strop about me not telling him.
I CAN DO THIS.

NAME: CHARLES "CHARLIE" SPRING

WHO ARE YOU: NICK'S BOYFRIEND

SCHOOL YEAR: YEAR 10   **AGE:** 15

BIRTHDAY: APRIL 27TH

MBTI: ISTP

FUN FACT: I LOVE TO READ!

NAME: Nicholas "Nick" Nelson

WHO ARE YOU: Charlie's boyfriend

SCHOOL YEAR: Year 11   **AGE:** 16

BIRTHDAY: September 4th

MBTI: ESFJ

FUN FACT: I'm great at baking cakes

NAME: Tao Xu

WHO ARE YOU: Charlie's friend

SCHOOL YEAR: Year 10   **AGE:** 15

BIRTHDAY: September 23rd

MBTI: ENFP

FUN FACT: I have a film review blog

NAME: Victoria "Tori" Spring

WHO ARE YOU: Charlie's sister

SCHOOL YEAR: Year 11   **AGE:** 16

BIRTHDAY: April 5th

MBTI: INFJ

FUN FACT: I HATE (ALMOST) EVERYONE

NAME: Elle Argent

WHO ARE YOU: Charlie's friend

SCHOOL YEAR: Year 11   **AGE:** 16

BIRTHDAY: May 4th

MBTI: ENTJ

FUN FACT: I like making clothes ♡

NAME: Tara Jones

WHO ARE YOU: Darcy's girlfriend

SCHOOL YEAR: Year 11   **AGE:** 16

BIRTHDAY: July 3rd

MBTI: INFP

FUN FACT: I love dance! (especially ballet)

NAME: Darcy Olsson

WHO ARE YOU: Tara's girlfriend

SCHOOL YEAR: Year 11   **AGE:** 16

BIRTHDAY: January 9th

MBTI: ESFP

FUN FACT: I once ate a whole jar of mustard for a dare

NAME: Aled Last

WHO ARE YOU: Charlie's friend

SCHOOL YEAR: Year 10   **AGE:** 14

BIRTHDAY: August 15th

MBTI: INFJ

FUN FACT: I want to make a podcast

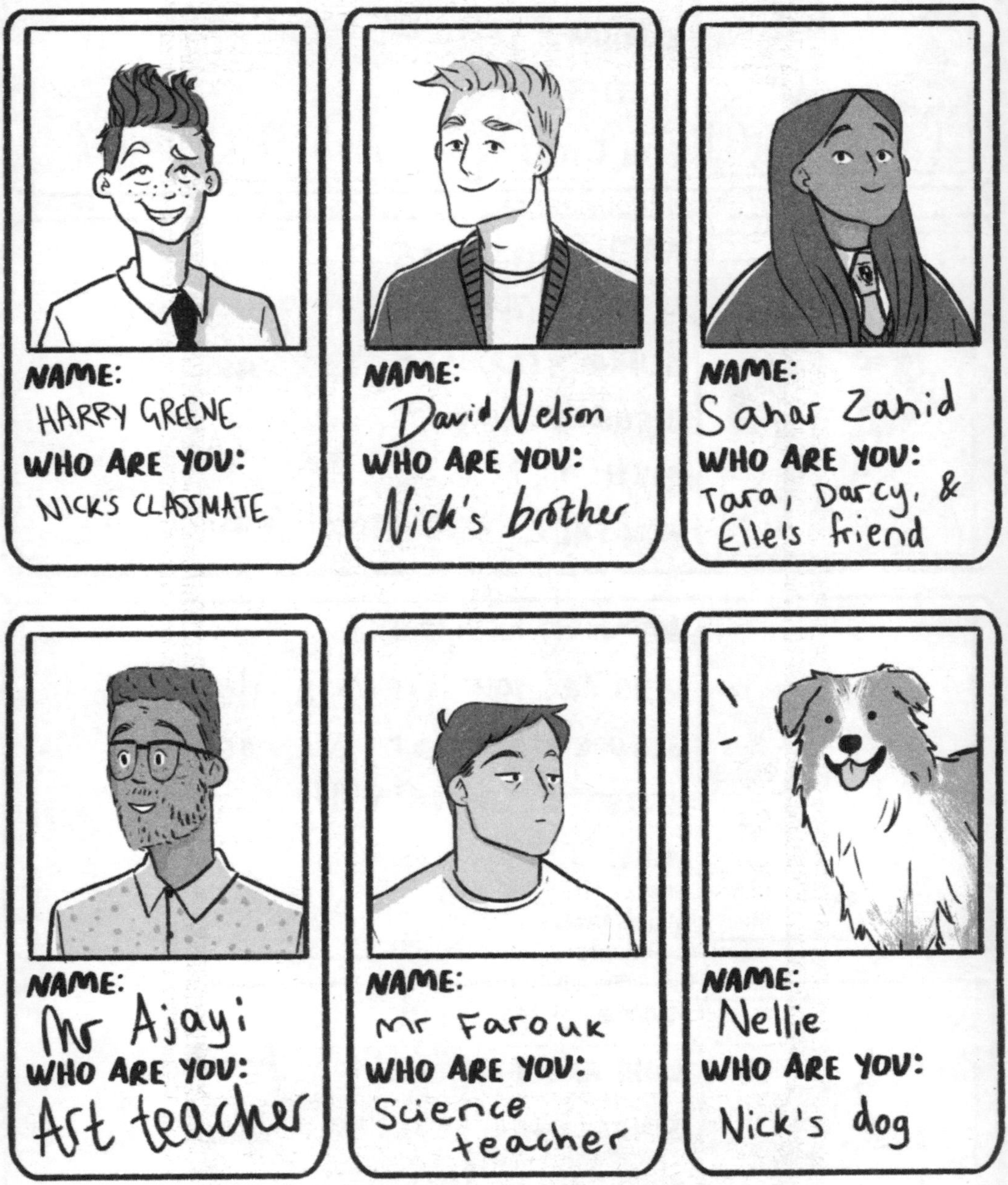
NAME:
HARRY GREENE
WHO ARE YOU:
NICK'S CLASSMATE
NAME:
David Nelson
WHO ARE YOU:
Nick's brother
NAME:
Sahar Zahid
WHO ARE YOU:
Tara, Darcy, & Elle's friend
NAME:
Mr Ajayi
WHO ARE YOU:
Art teacher
NAME:
Mr Farouk
WHO ARE YOU:
Science teacher
NAME:
Nellie
WHO ARE YOU:
Nick's dog

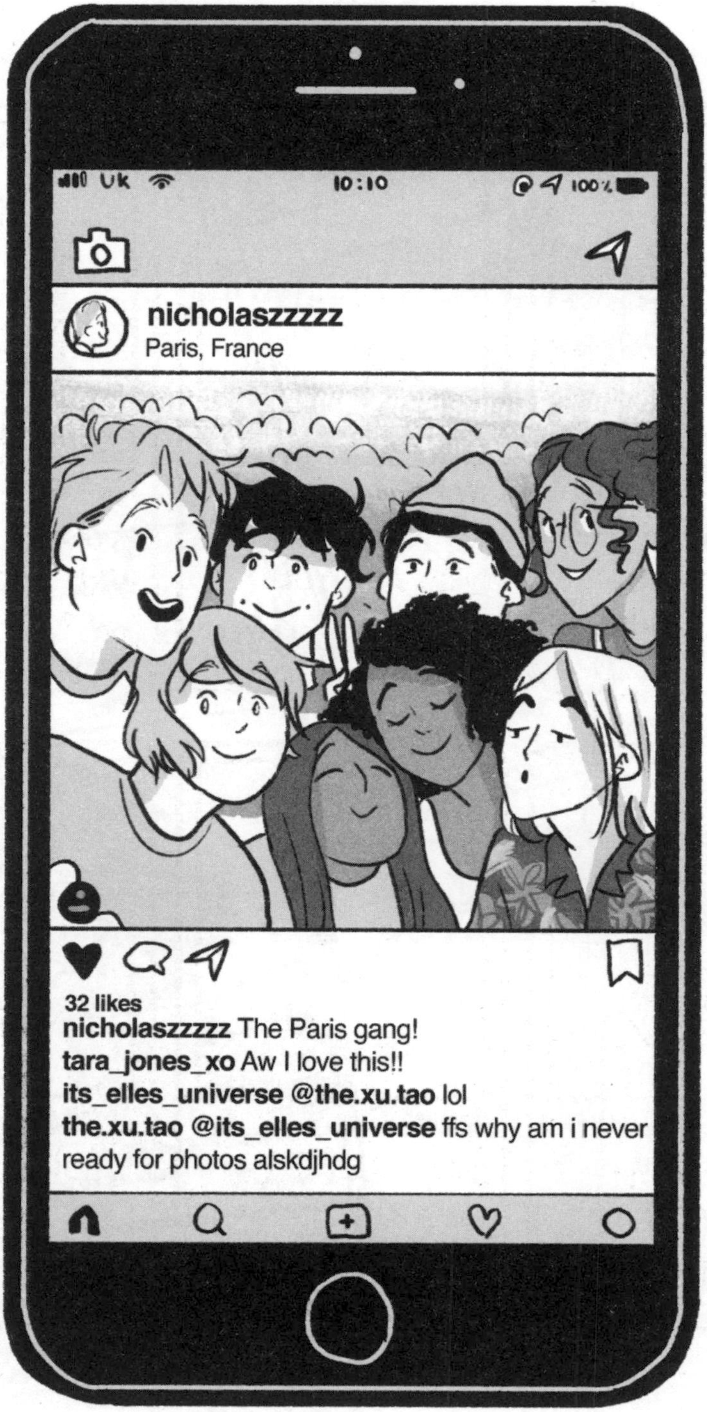
Uk
10:10
100%
nicholaszzzzz
Paris, France
32 likes
nicholaszzzzz The Paris gang!
tara_jones_xo Aw I love this!!
its_elles_universe @the.xu.tao lol
the.xu.tao @its_elles_universe ffs why am i never ready for photos alskdjhdg

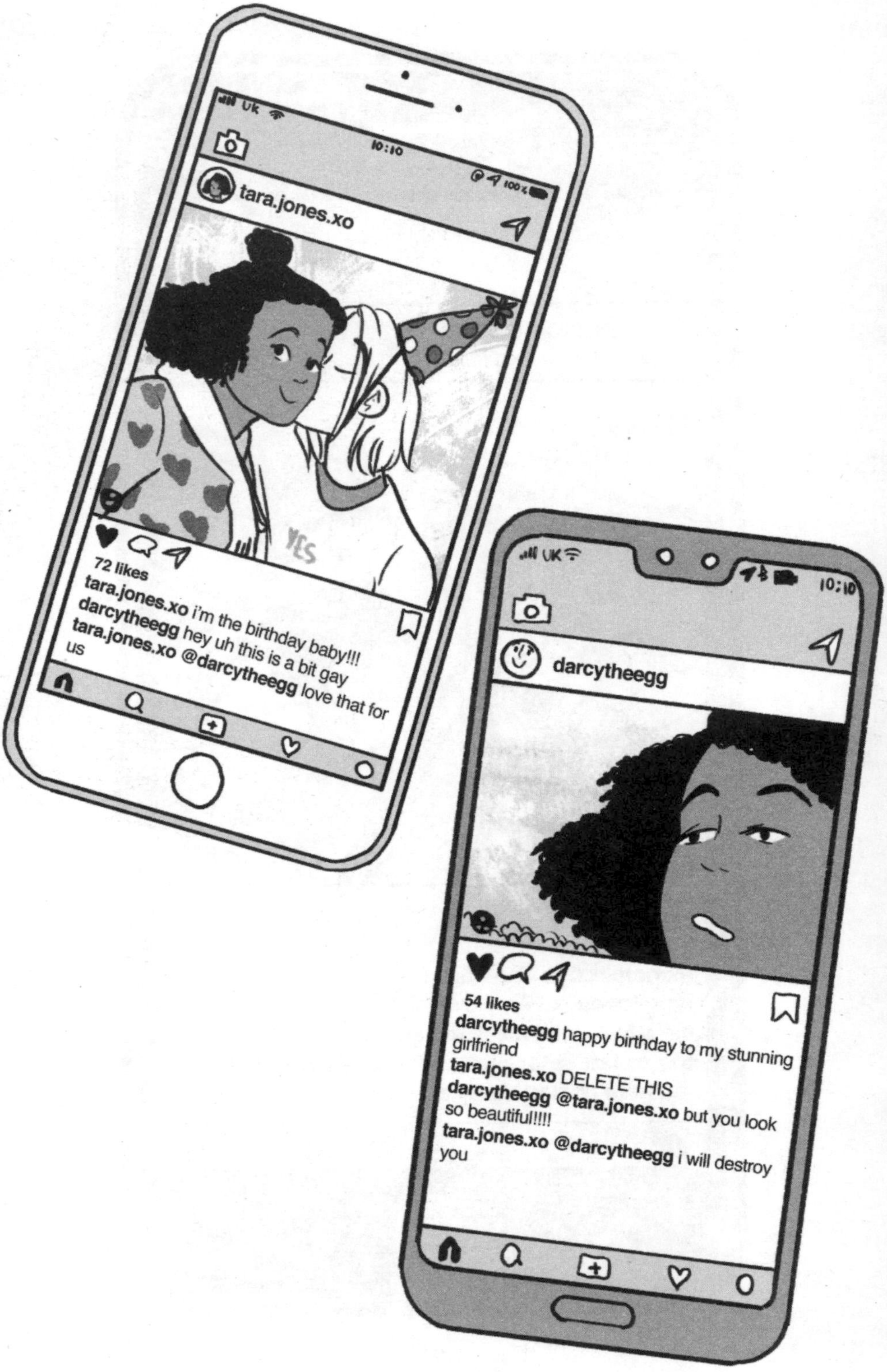
UK
10:10
100%
tara.jones.xo
YES
72 likes
tara.jones.xo i'm the birthday baby!!!
darcytheegg hey uh this is a bit gay
tara.jones.xo @darcytheegg love that for us
UK
10:10
darcytheegg
54 likes
darcytheegg happy birthday to my stunning girlfriend
tara.jones.xo DELETE THIS
darcytheegg @tara.jones.xo but you look so beautiful!!!!
tara.jones.xo @darcytheegg i will destroy you

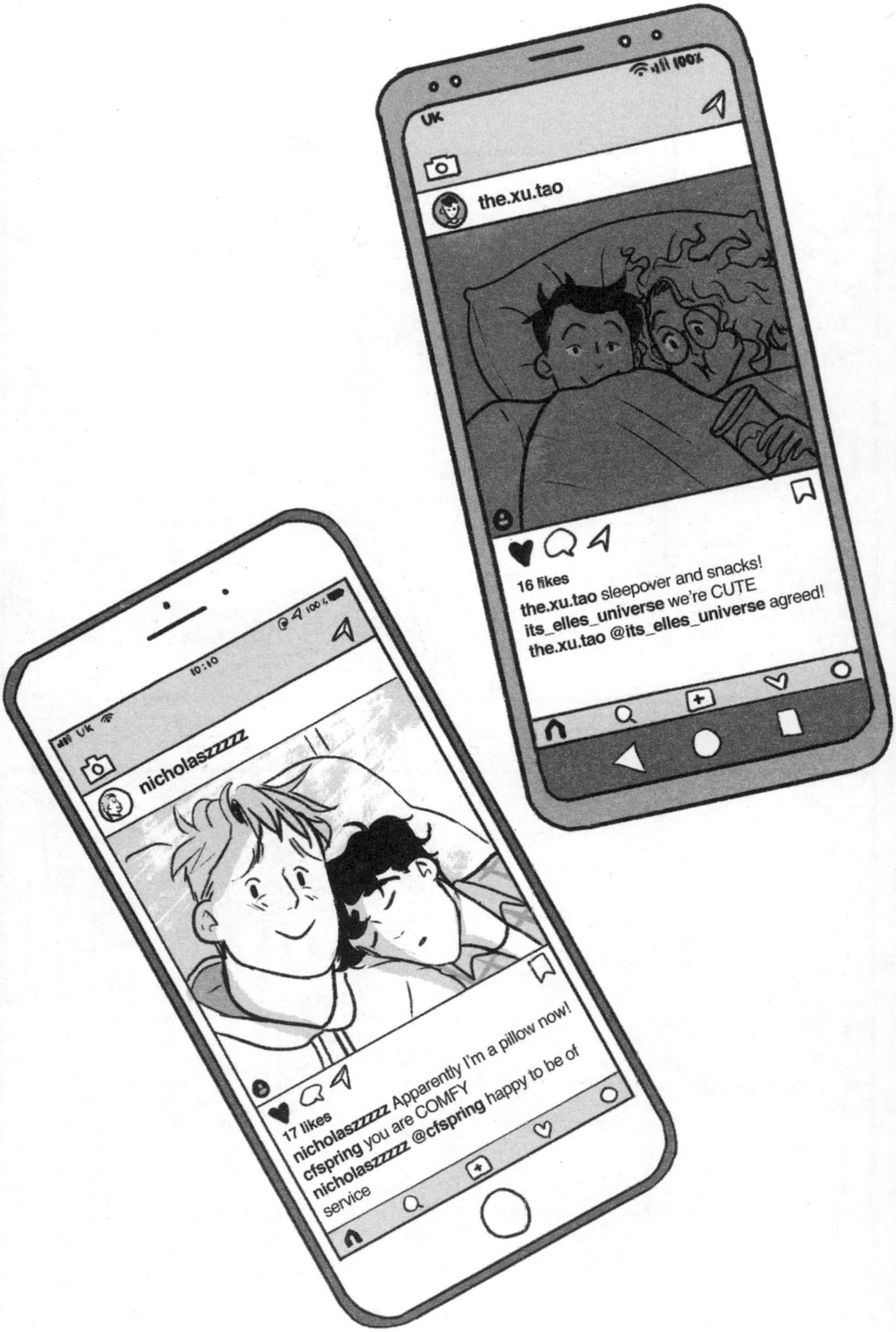

100%
UK
the.xu.tao
16 likes
the.xu.tao sleepover and snacks!
its_elles_universe we're CUTE
the.xu.tao @its_elles_universe agreed!
10:10
UK
nicholaszzzzz
17 likes
nicholaszzzzz Apparently I'm a pillow now!
cfspring you are COMFY
nicholaszzzzz @cfspring happy to be of service

Nick's room

view A

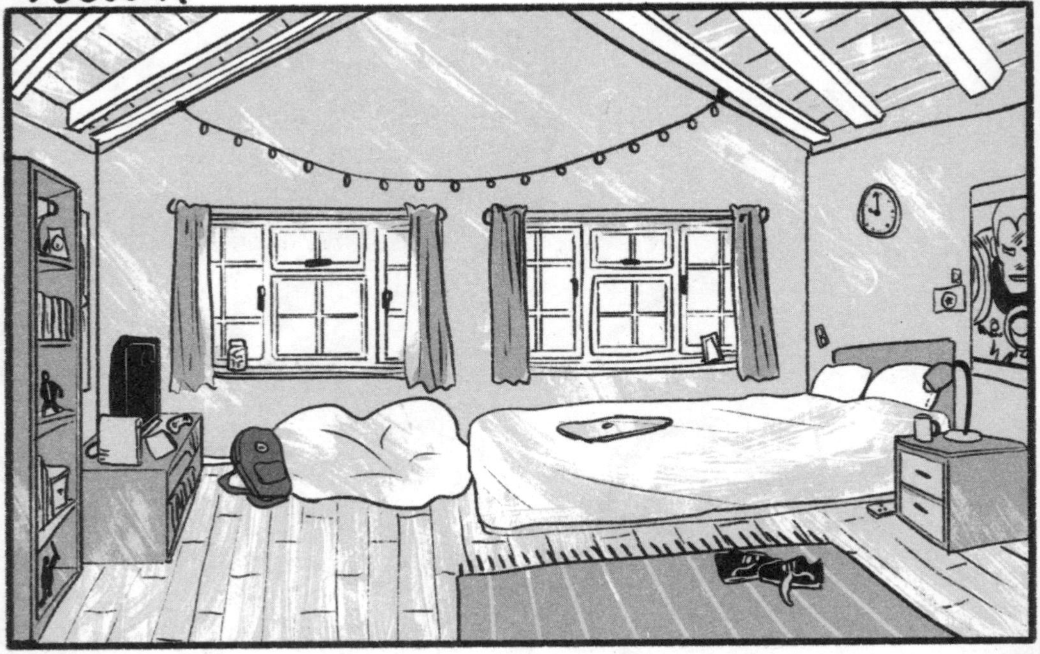

view B

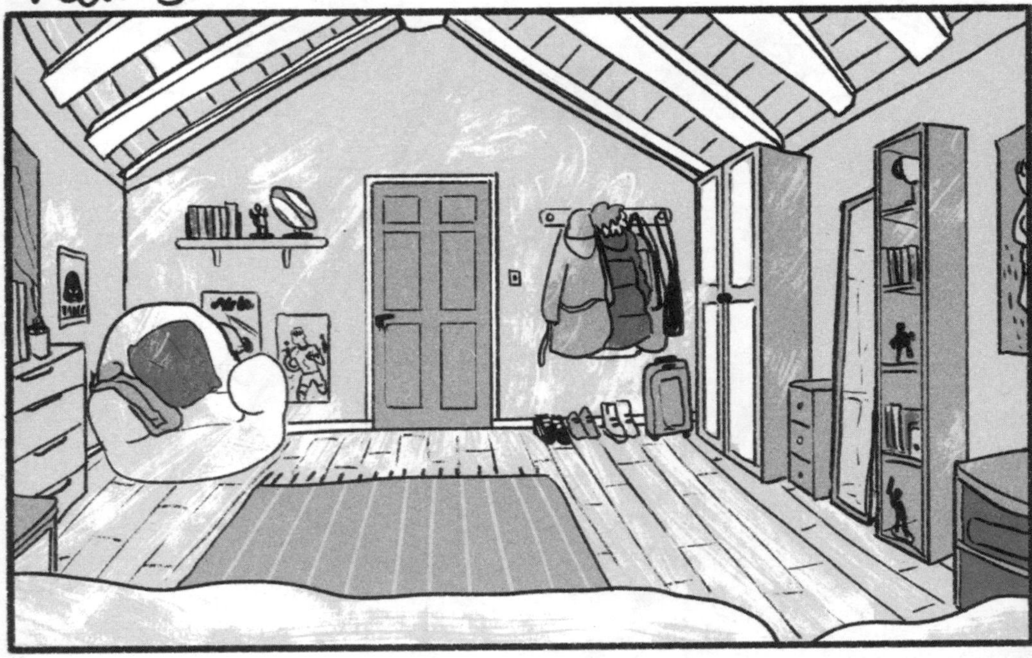

Key features:

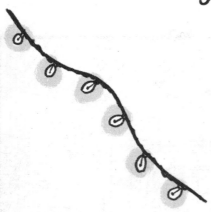

Fairy lights

Nick put up fairy lights in his bedroom one Christmas and forgot to take them down for three months. Eventually he decided he liked having them up all year round!

Bean bag

A comfy, cosy bean bag Nick's had for years. He sits in it sometimes but mostly it's Nellie Nelson's favourite nap spot.

Posters

Along with posters of his favourite movies, Nick has some posters of his two favourite sports: rugby and motor racing.

Charlie's room

View A

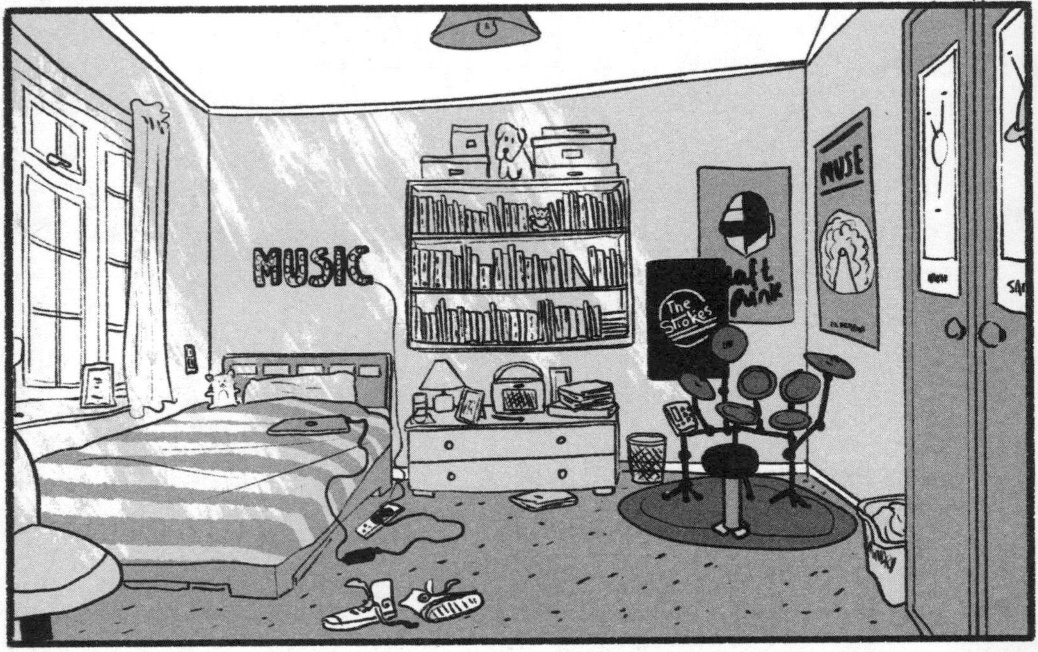
MUSIC
The Strokes
MUSE

View B

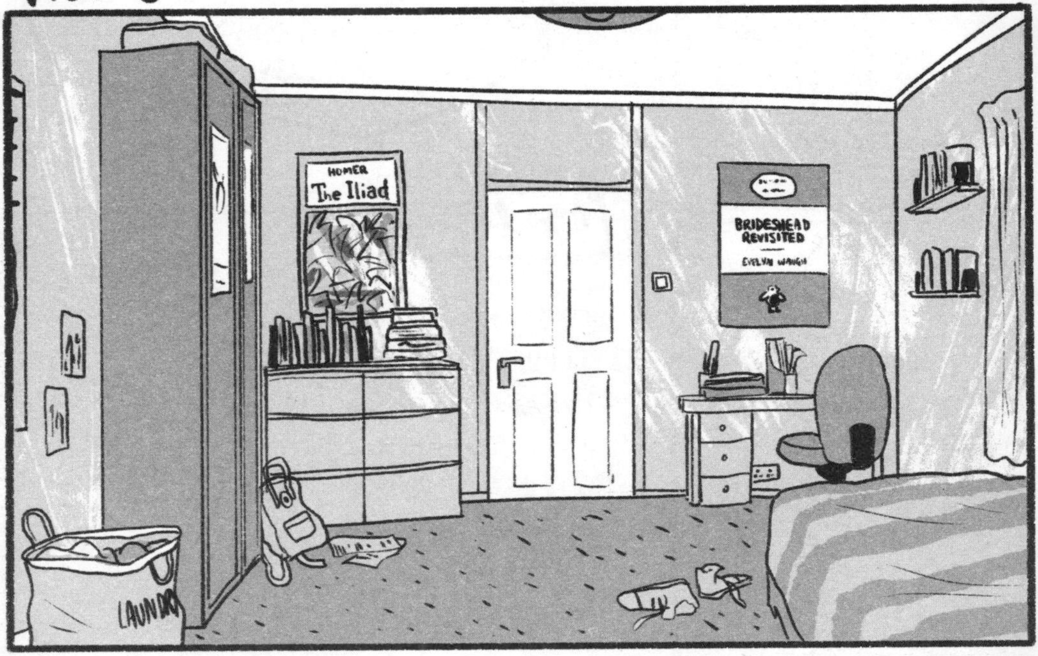
HOMER
The Iliad
BRIDESHEAD REVISITED
EVELYN WAUGH

Key features:

Electronic drum kit

Charlie started learning how to play the drums when he was nine. He doesn't have any particular aspirations to become a musician or be in a band, but he still really loves playing, especially to relieve stress!

The Great Gatsby
F. SCOTT FITZGERALD
Radio Silence
Alice Oseman
I Was Born for This
Alice Oseman
HOMER
THE ILIAD
A Picture of Dorian Gray
ALEX in WONDERLAND
Simon James Green
Malorie Blackman
NOUGHTS & CROSSES
an encyclopedia of SPACE

Bookshelves

Charlie's favourite hobby is reading. He'll read any genre, especially if there are gay characters, but he finds Ancient Greek classical literature the most interesting.

Posters

Along with posters of his favourite bands, Charlie has posters of two of his favourite classic texts: The Iliad by Homer and Brideshead Revisited by Evelyn Waugh.

HOMER
—The Iliad—
BIRD BOOKS
FICTION
BRIDESHEAD REVISITED
FICTION
EVELYN WAUGH

The First Day

a Heartstopper mini-comic

THE PREVIOUS SEPTEMBER...

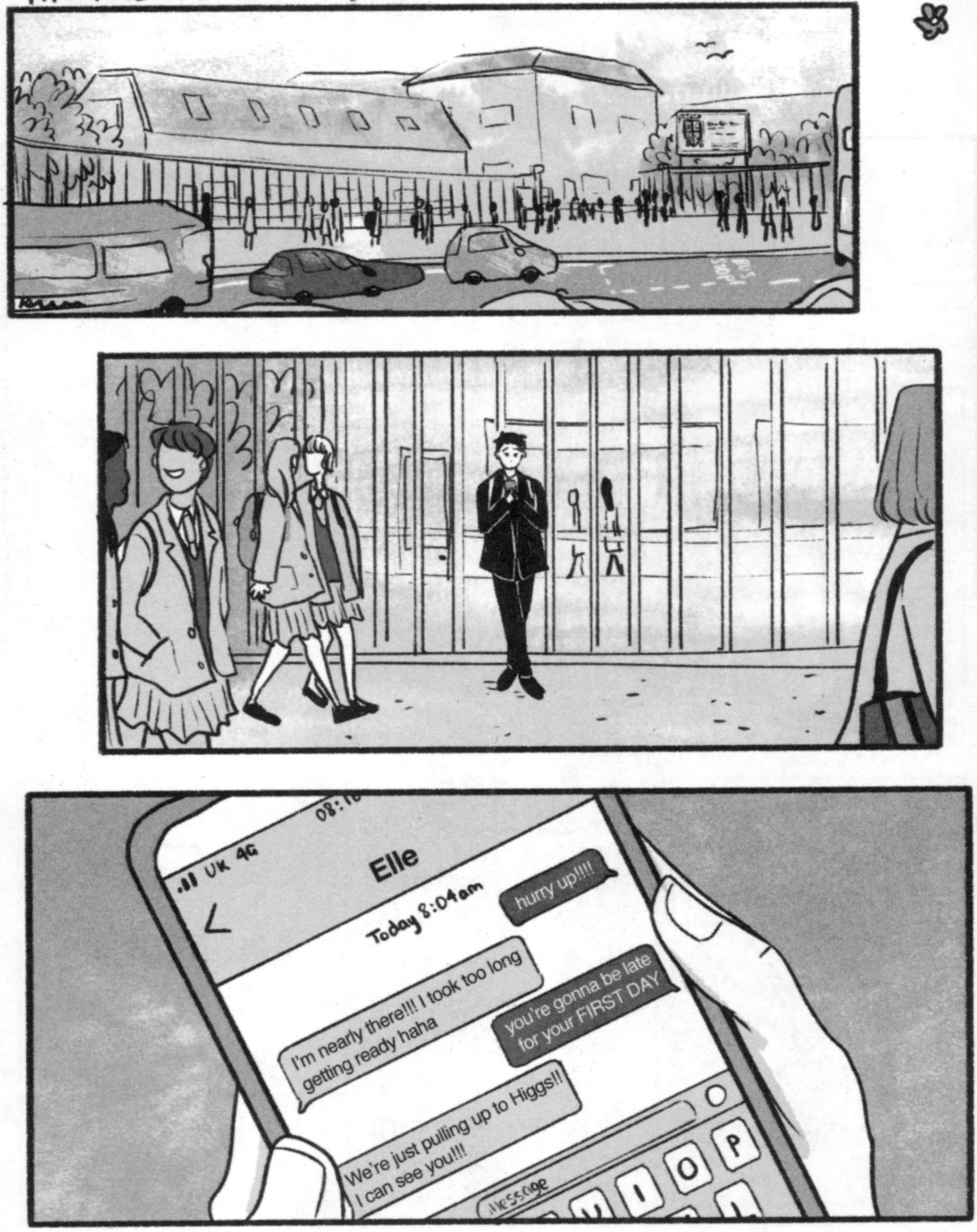

UK 4G
Elle
Today 8:04am
hurry up!!!!
I'm nearly there!!! I took too long getting ready haha
you're gonna be late for your FIRST DAY
We're just pulling up to Higgs!! I can see you!!!
Message

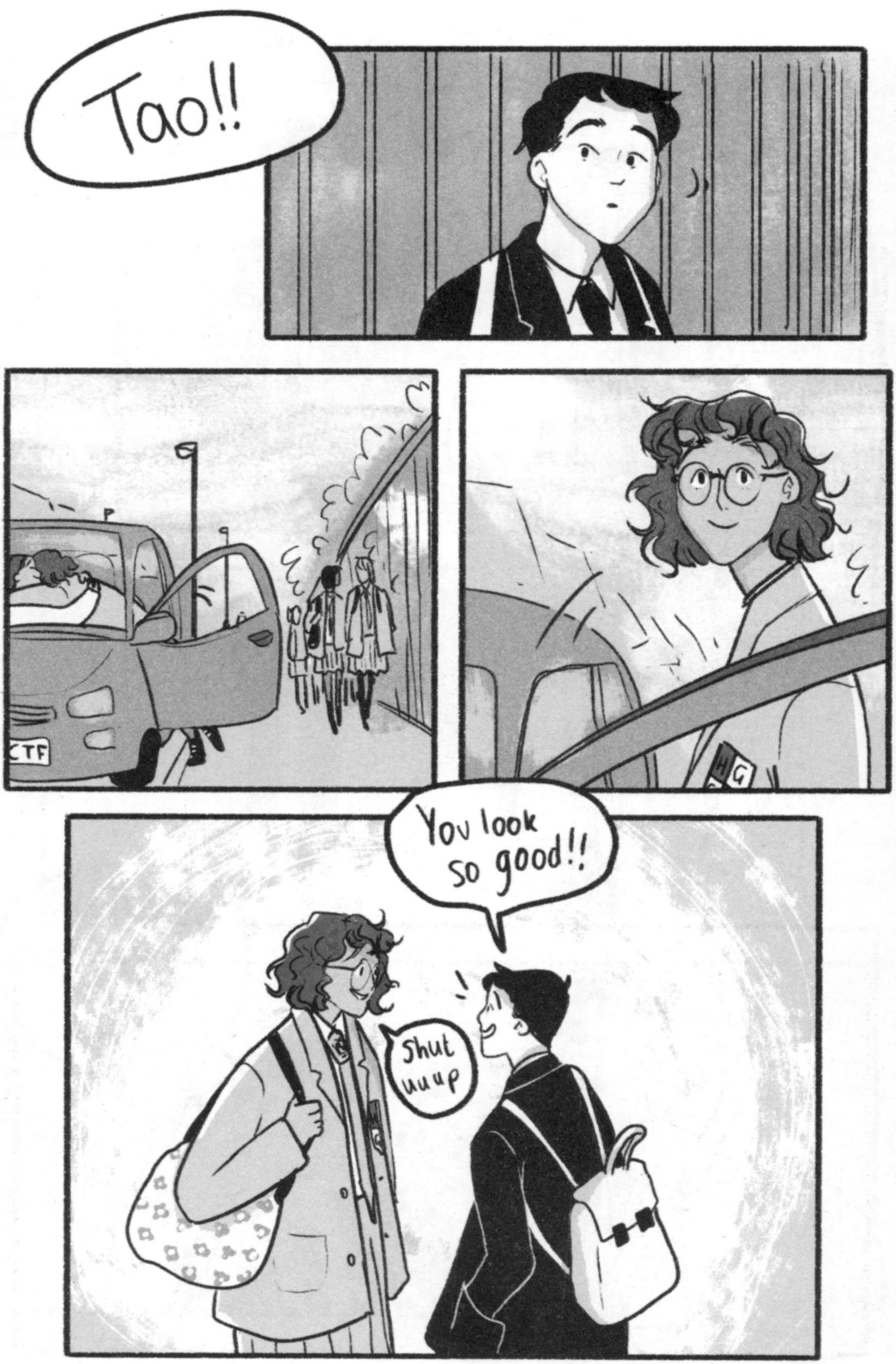
Tao!!
CTF
HG
You look so good!!
Shut uuup

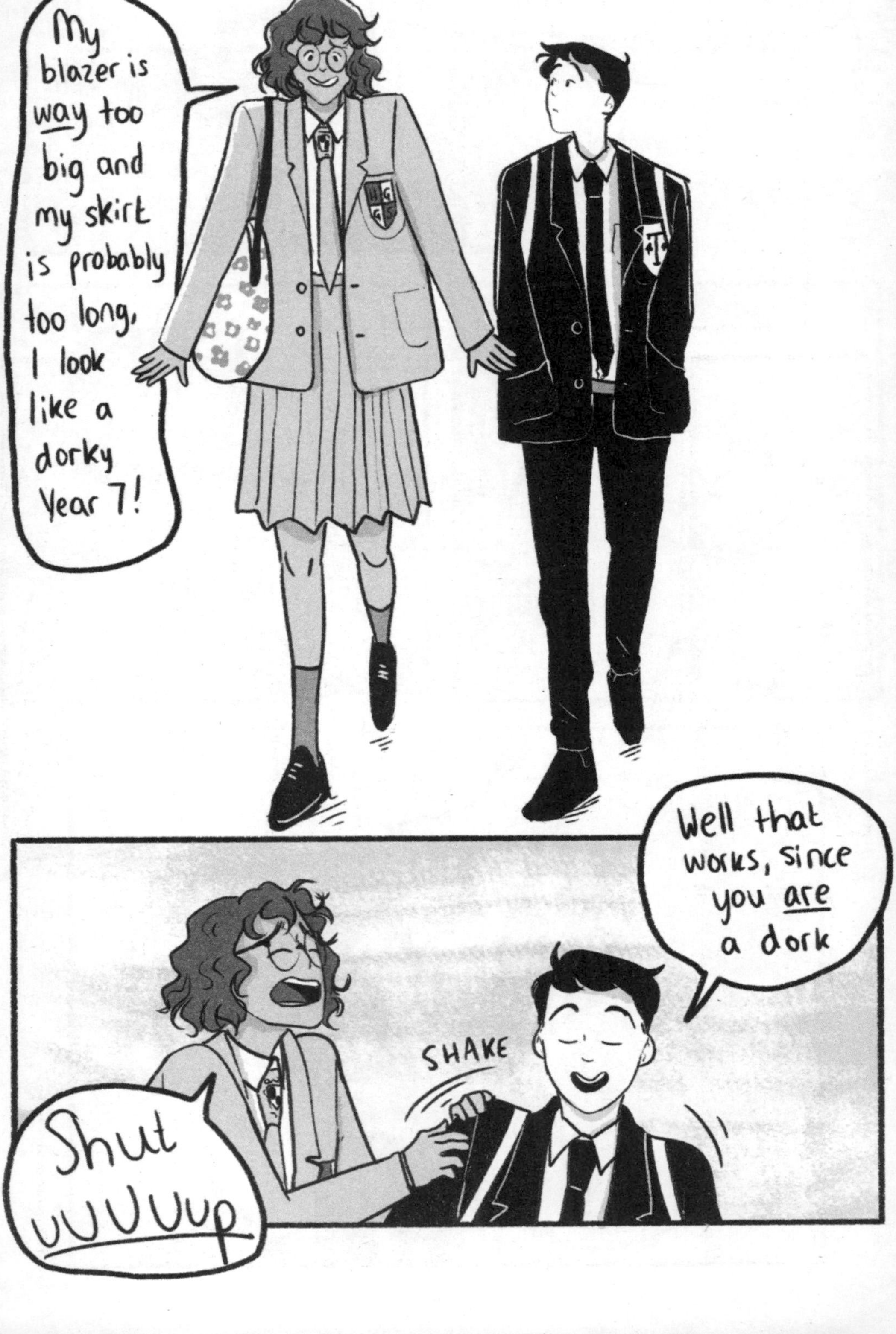
My blazer is way too big and my skirt is probably too long, I look like a dorky Year 7!
Well that works, since you are a dork
SHAKE
Shut uuuuup

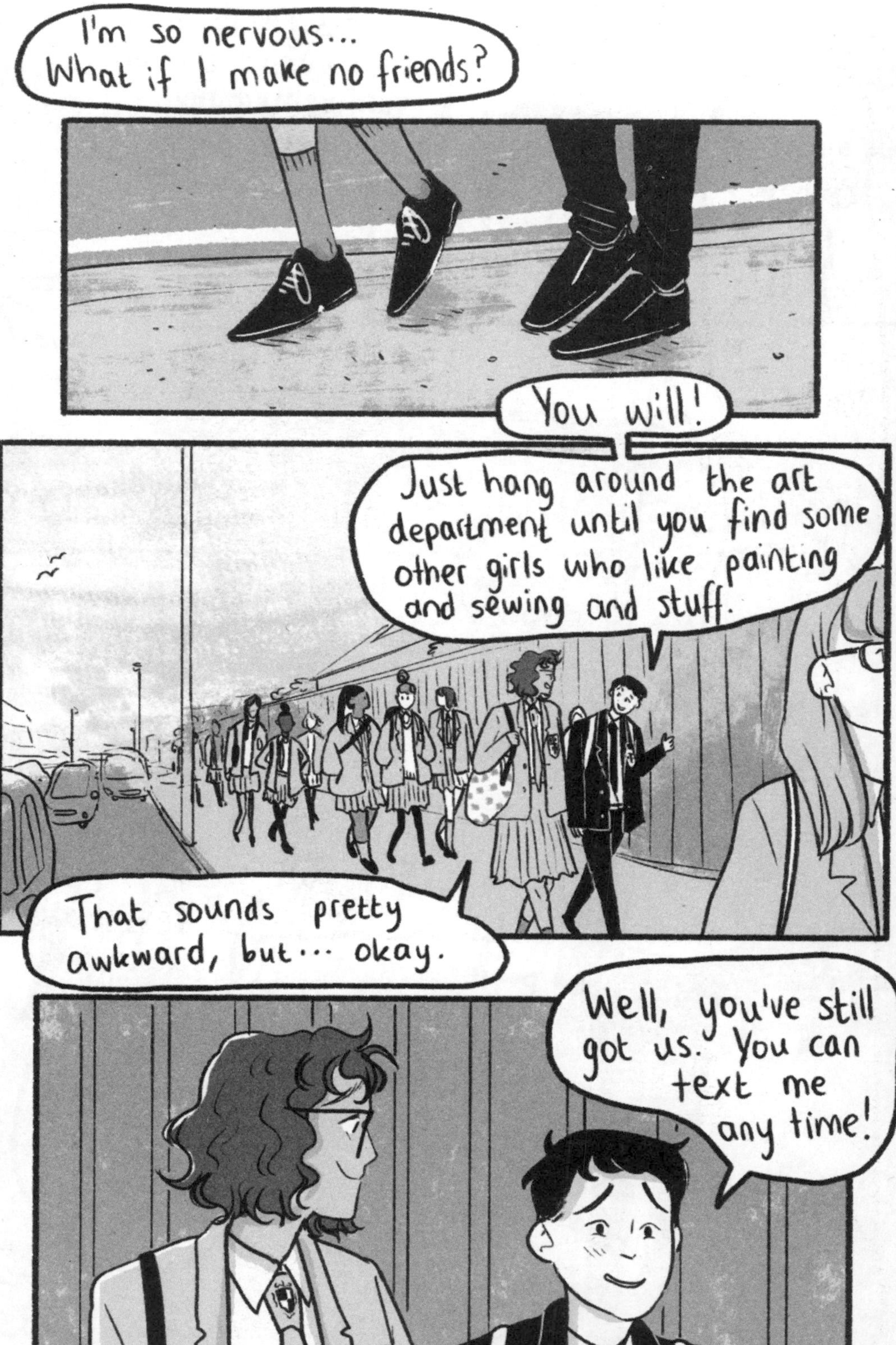
I'm so nervous... What if I make no friends?
You will!
Just hang around the art department until you find some other girls who like painting and sewing and stuff.
That sounds pretty awkward, but... okay.
Well, you've still got us. You can text me any time!

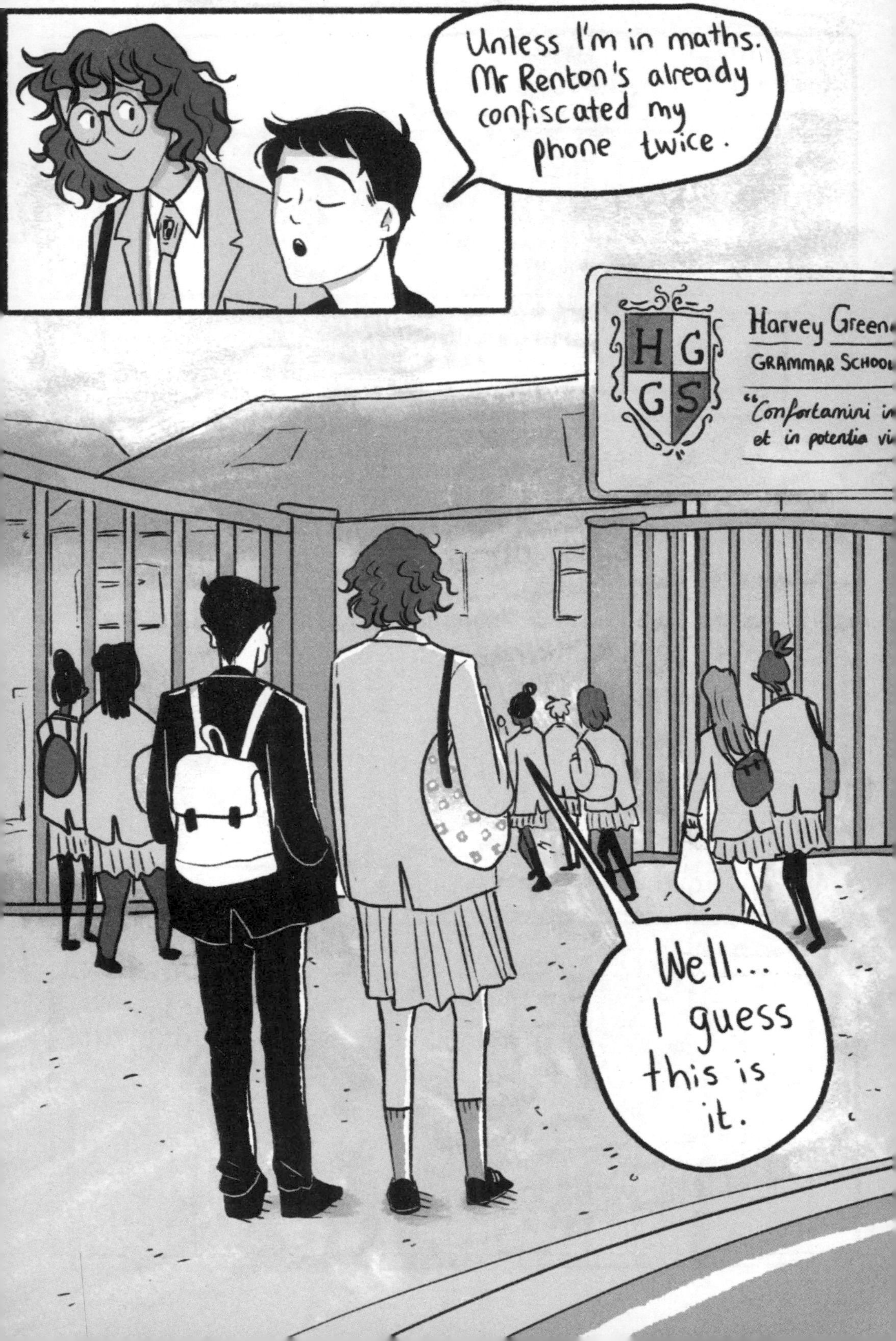
Unless I'm in maths. Mr Renton's already confiscated my phone twice.
HG GS
Well... I guess this is it.

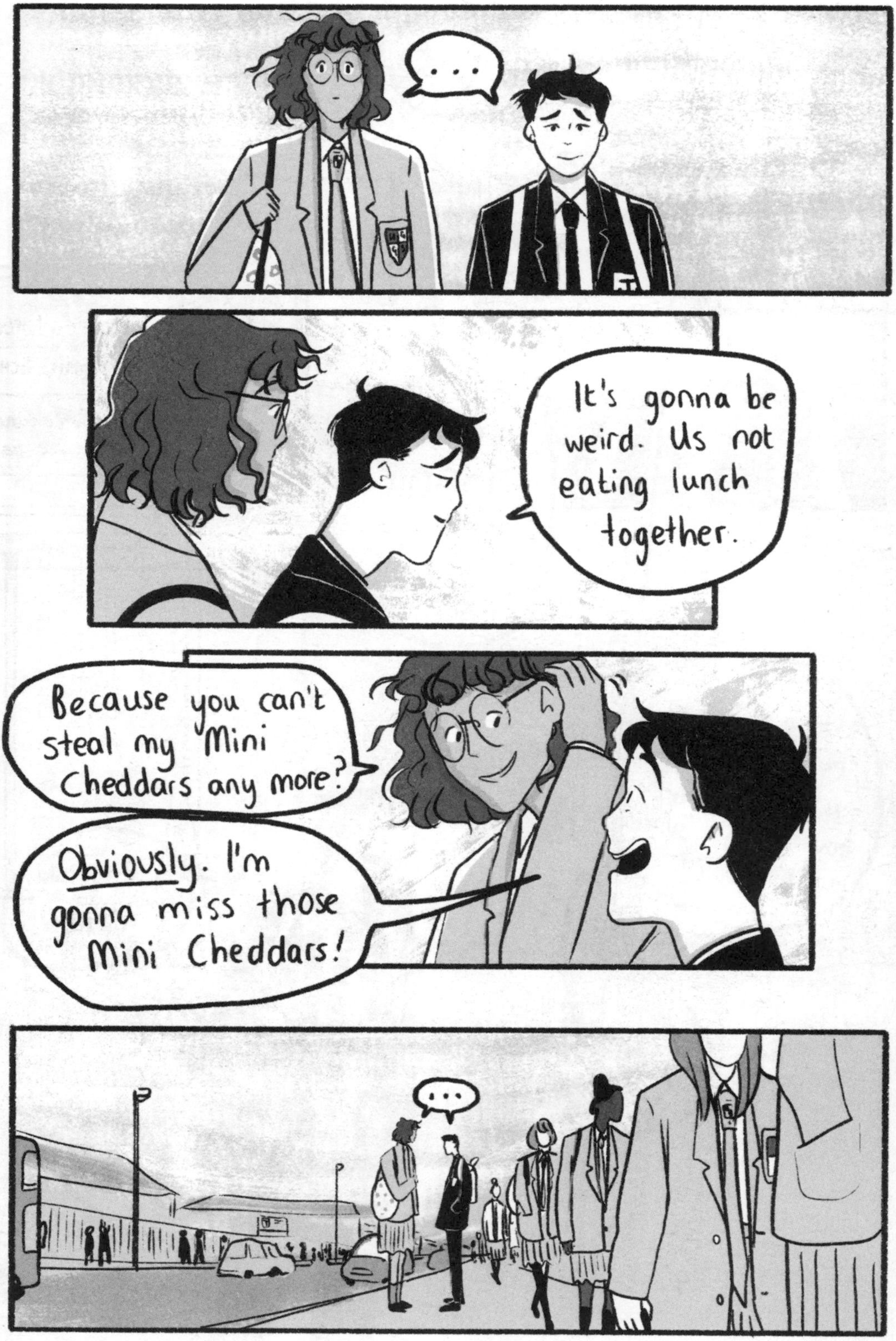
...
It's gonna be weird. Us not eating lunch together.
Because you can't steal my Mini Cheddars any more?
Obviously. I'm gonna miss those Mini Cheddars!
...

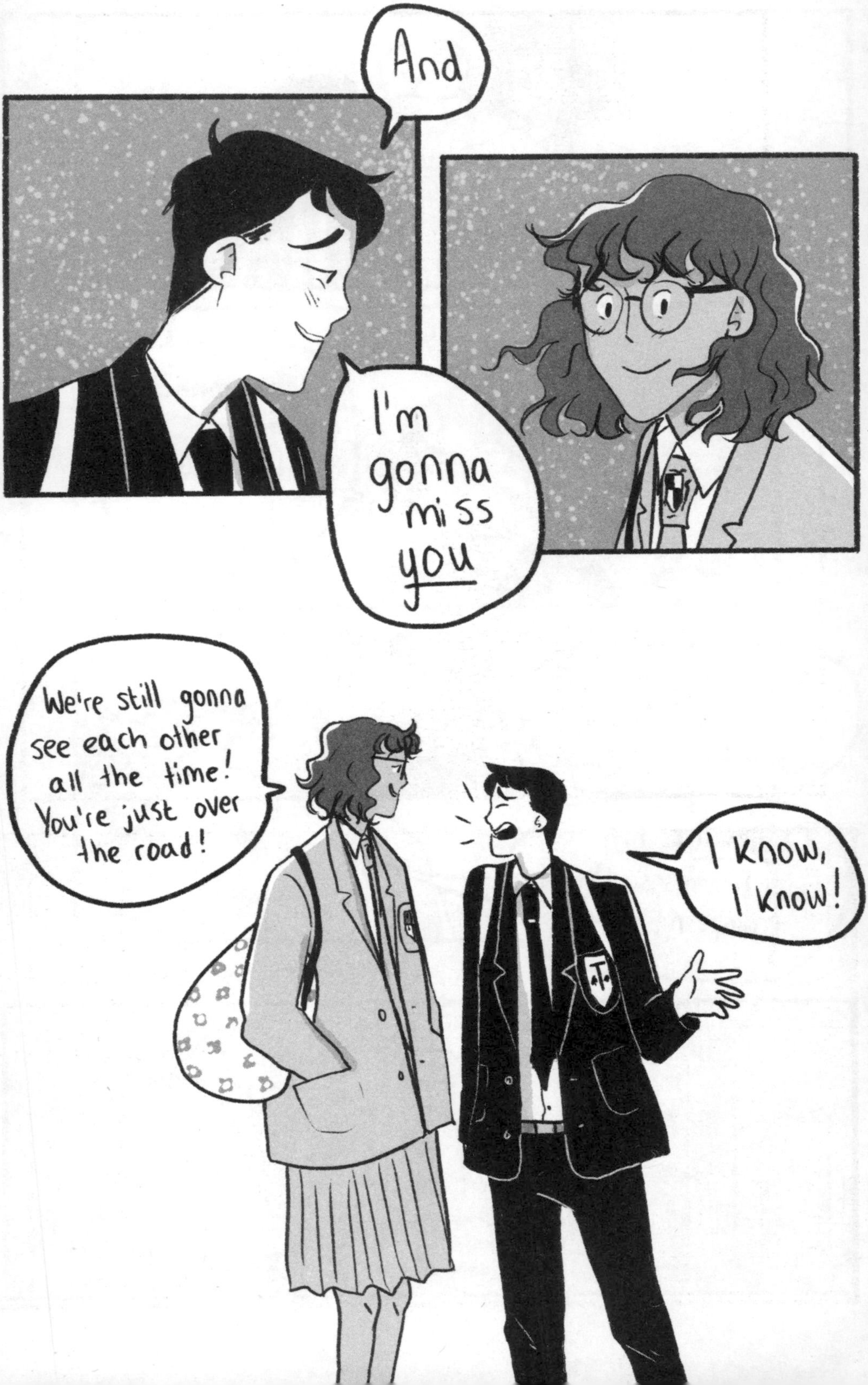
And
I'm gonna miss you
We're still gonna see each other all the time! You're just over the road!
I know, I know!

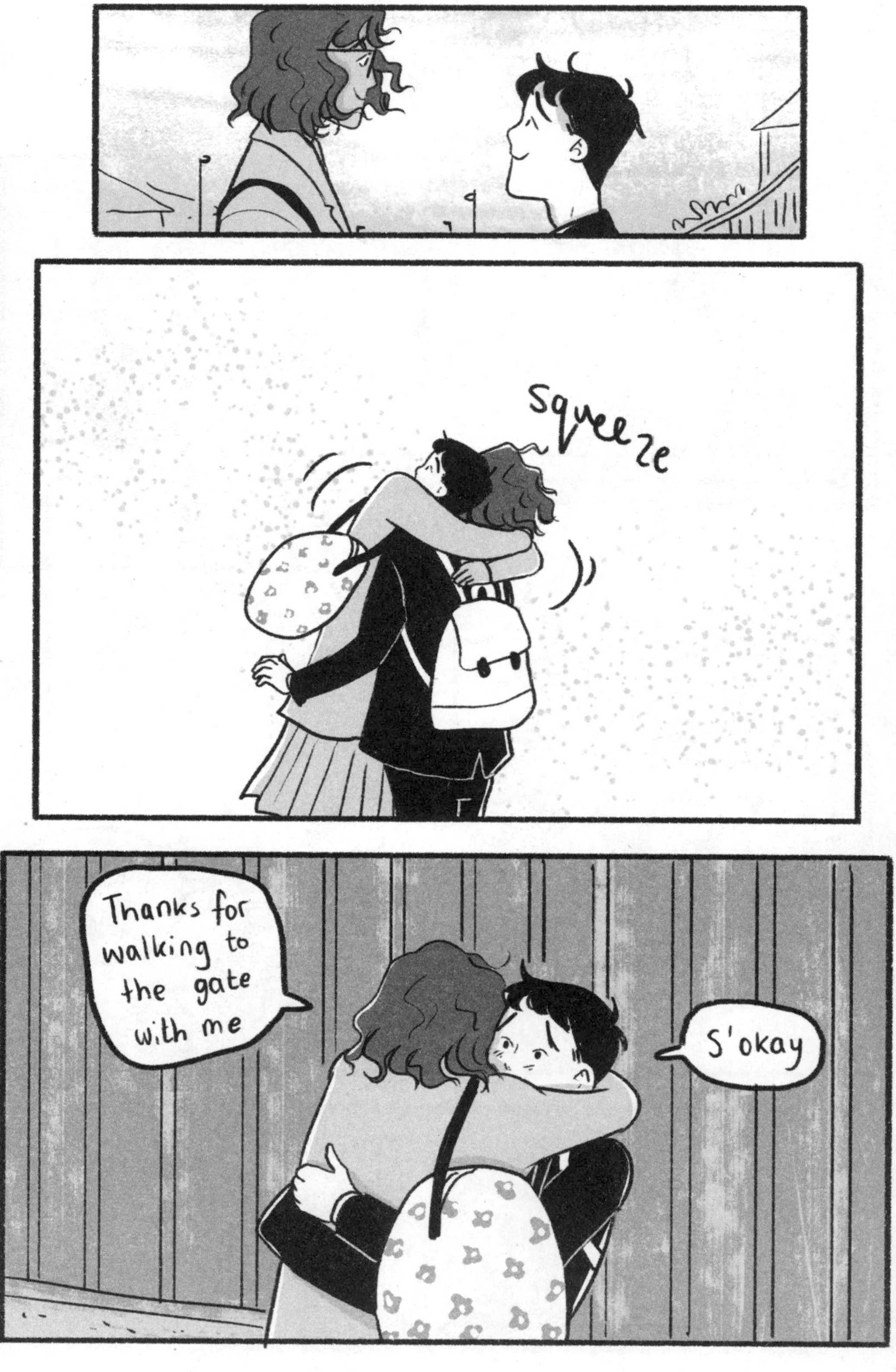
squeeze
Thanks for walking to the gate with me
S'okay

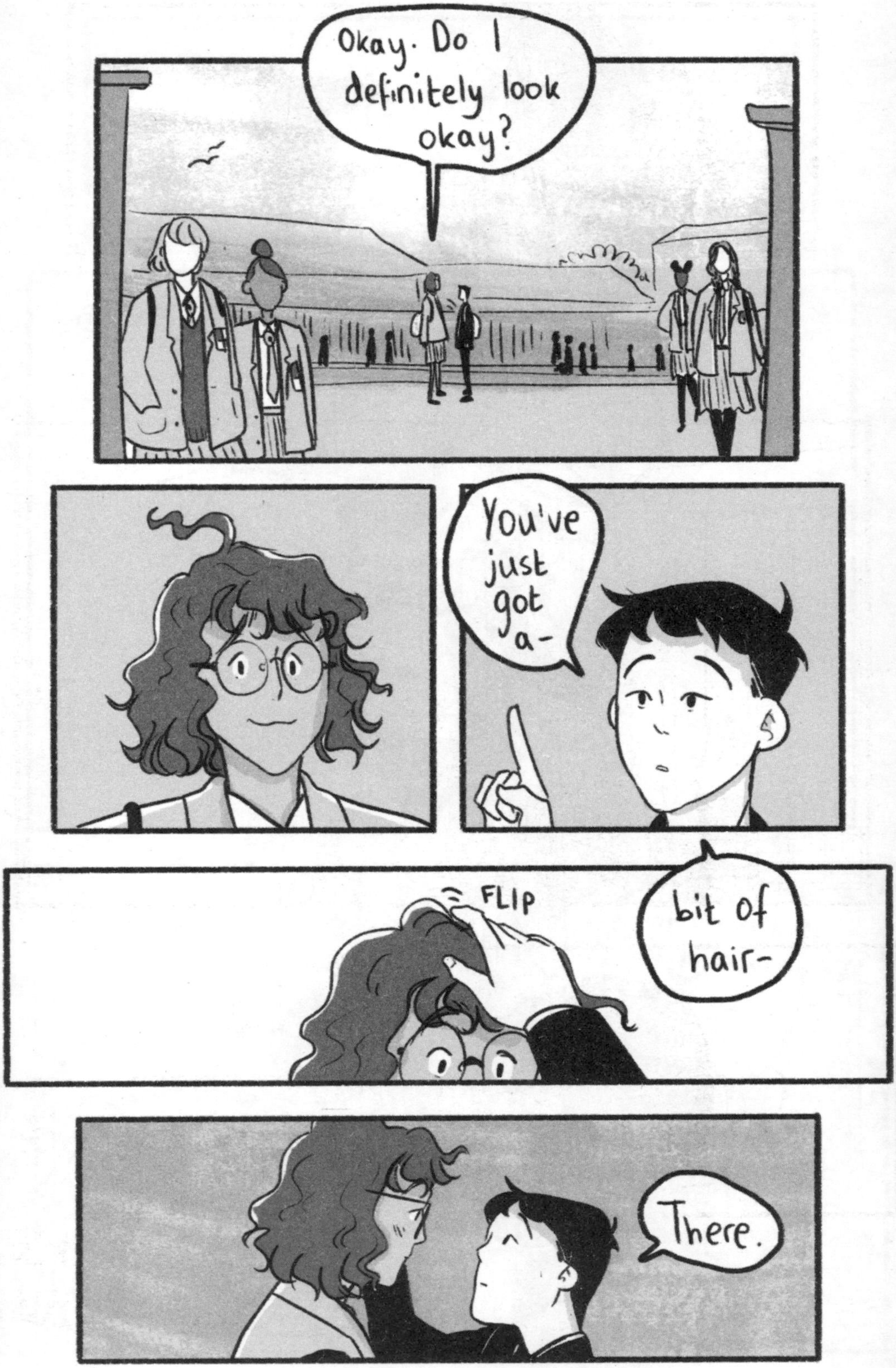
Okay. Do I definitely look okay?
You've just got a-
FLIP
bit of hair-
There.

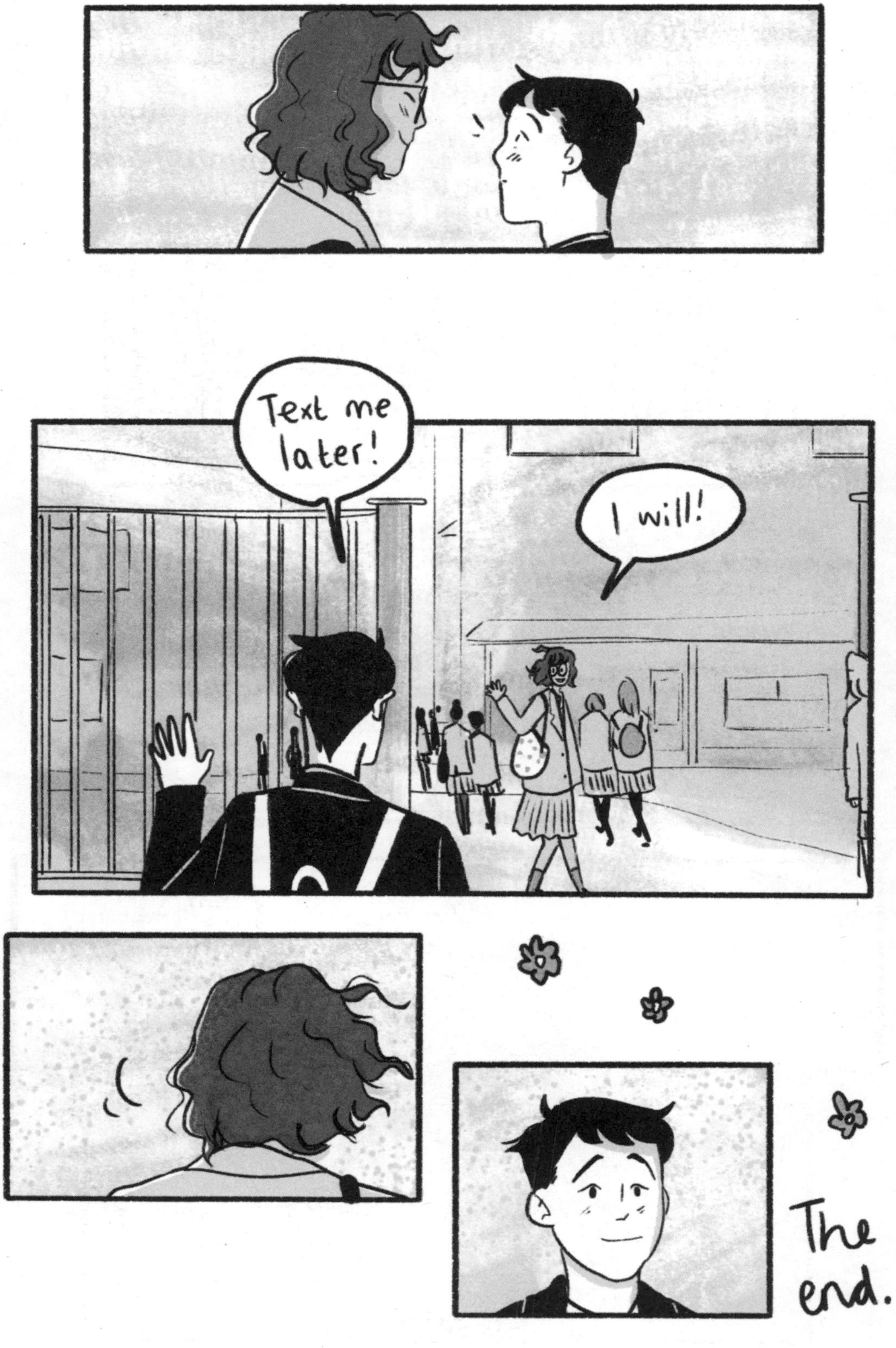
Text me later!
I will!
The end.

Author's note

Here we are in the third volume of Heartstopper! It feels like only yesterday that I had two thousand books stacked in my house, ready to be shipped to my Kickstarter supporters. We've come so far since then!

This volume starts with Nick and Charlie solidly a couple but with a lot to learn about each other. I strongly believe that the 'getting together' part of a romance is just the beginning and there's so much else to explore beyond that, and Nick and Charlie spent much of this volume getting to know each other on a deeper level, which has been such a joy to write. It was also wonderful to get to know some of Heartstopper's side characters in this chapter! Tao, Elle, Tara, Darcy, and even Aled all have a bigger role to play, and I hope we continue to get to know them better in the next volume.

This volume also touched on the more serious topic of mental health; in particular self-harm and eating disorders. Mental health and mental illness are topics that are very close to me and I explore them in all of my works, but here in Heartstopper I want the focus to always be on support, healing, and recovery. If you are struggling with any of the same issues, please do not hesitate to reach out to someone you love, just as Charlie has done, and/or a medical professional. You could also seek help and advice from an online support network, such as:

YoungMinds: https://youngminds.org.uk/
Beat Eating Disorders: https://www.beateatingdisorders.org.uk/
Switchboard LGBT+ Helpline: https://switchboard.lgbt/

Sending so much love and thanks to Heartstopper's online readers, my Patreon patrons, and the Kickstarter supporters! It's thanks to you that the series is able to continue.

To Rachel Wade, Alison Padley, Emily Thomas, Felicity Highet, and everyone else involved in Heartstopper at Hachette - thank you so much for making these books a reality! I'm so grateful to be working with such a passionate and dedicated team.

A huge thanks to my agent, Claire Wilson, who is my guiding light in the world of books!

And thank you, as always, to you, dear reader! I'll see you in the next one.

Alice
x

ALSO BY ALICE OSEMAN:

This is not a love story.
Solitaire
Alice Oseman

SOLITAIRE

Read the novel Nick and Charlie first appeared in!

A pessimistic sixteen-year-old girl, a teenage speed skater with a penchant for solving mysteries, and a series of anonymous pranks at school by an online group who call themselves 'Solitaire'.

Alice's debut novel tells the story of Tori Spring.

Listen to your own voice.
Radio Silence
Alice Oseman

RADIO SILENCE

Everyone thinks seventeen-year-old Frances is destined for a top university - including herself. But, in secret, Frances spends all her free time drawing fan art for a sci-fi podcast, 'Universe City'. And when she discovers that the creator of the podcast lives opposite her, Frances begins to question everything she knew about herself and what she wants from life.

What if everything you set yourself up to be was wrong?

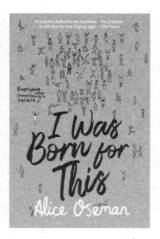

I Was Born for This
Alice Oseman

I WAS BORN FOR THIS

Angel, a massive fangirl of boyband The Ark, is headed to London to see The Ark live for the first time. Jimmy, frontman of The Ark, is struggling to deal with how famous he and his bandmates are becoming.

Over one week in August, Angel and Jimmy's lives begin to intertwine in mysterious ways, and when Angel and Jimmy are unexpectedly thrust together, they will discover just how strange and surprising facing up to reality can be.

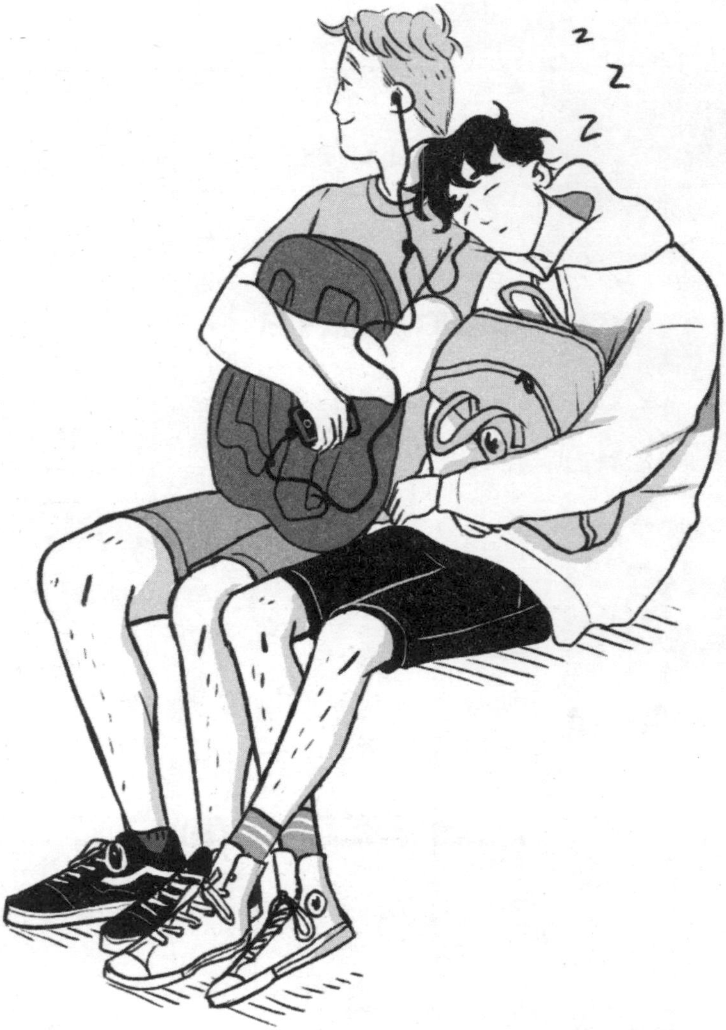
z
z
z